CREATED BY

JOE MADUREIRA

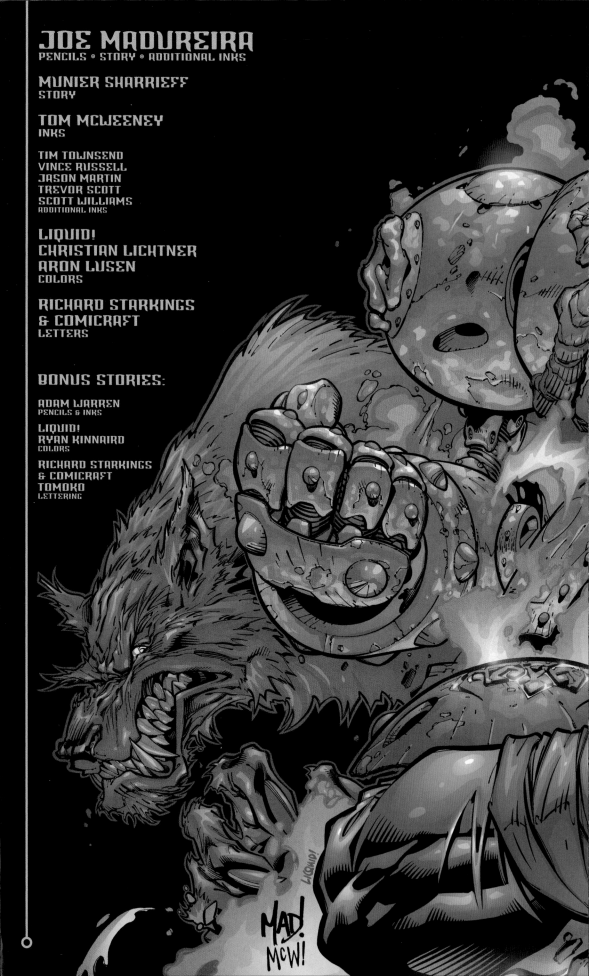

JOE MADUREIRA
PENCILS • STORY • ADDITIONAL INKS

MUNIER SHARRIEFF
STORY

TOM MCWEENEY
INKS

TIM TOWNSEND
VINCE RUSSELL
JASON MARTIN
TREVOR SCOTT
SCOTT WILLIAMS
ADDITIONAL INKS

LIQUID!
CHRISTIAN LICHTNER
ARON LUSEN
COLORS

RICHARD STARKINGS
& COMICRAFT
LETTERS

BONUS STORIES:

ADAM WARREN
PENCILS & INKS

LIQUID!
RYAN KINNAIRD
COLORS

RICHARD STARKINGS
& COMICRAFT
TOMOKO
LETTERING

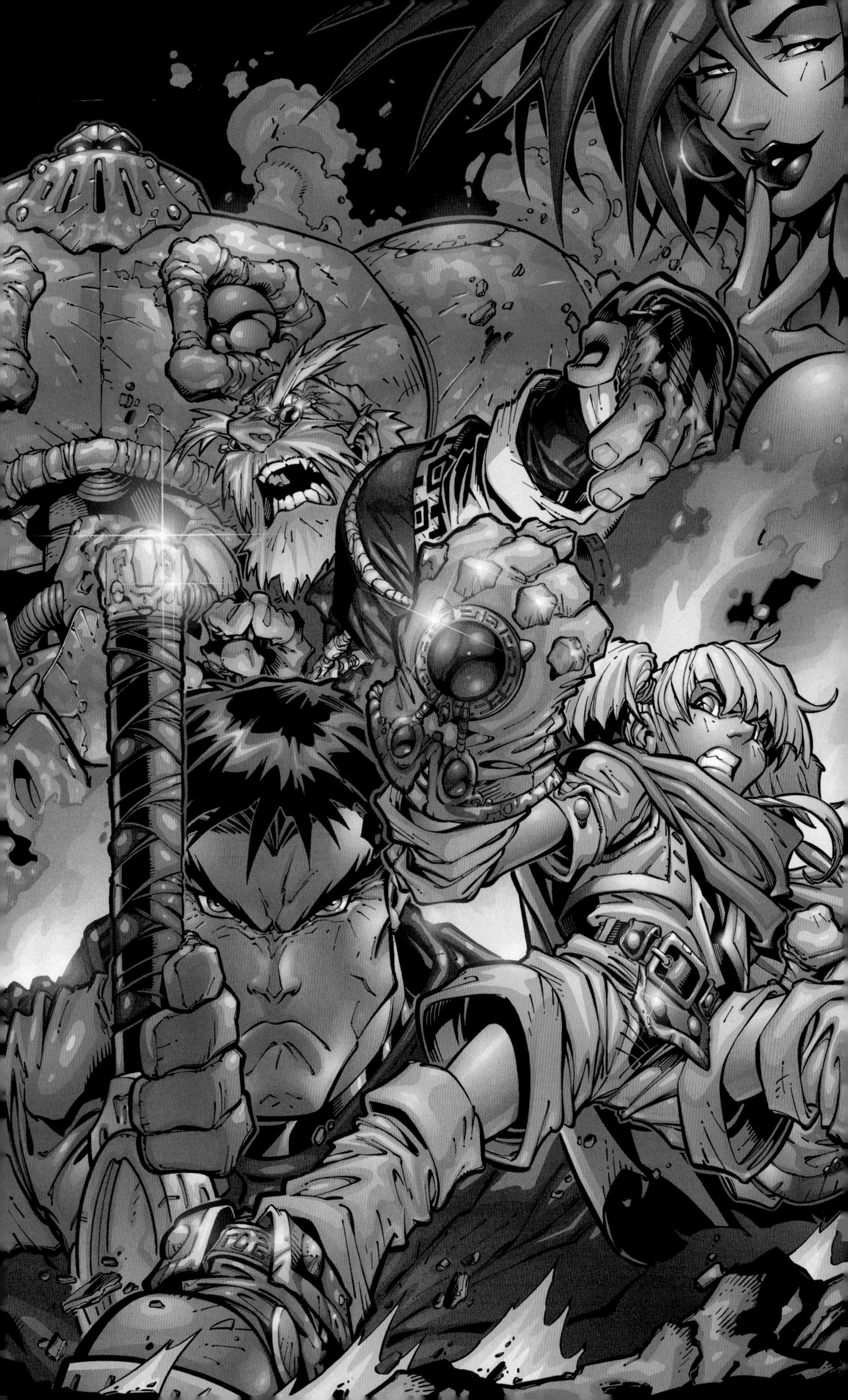

IMAGE COMICS, INC.
Todd McFarlane — President
Jim Valentino — Vice President
Marc Silvestri — Chief Executive Officer
Erik Larsen — Chief Financial Officer
Robert Kirkman — Chief Operating Officer

Eric Stephenson — Publisher / Chief Creative Officer
Shanna Matuszak — Editorial Coordinator
Marla Eizik — Talent Liaison

Nicole Lapalme — Controller
Leanna Caunter — Accounting Analyst
Sue Korpela — Accounting & HR Manager

Jeff Boison — Director of Sales & Publishing Planning
Dirk Wood — Director of International Sales & Licensing
Alex Cox — Director of Direct Market & Specialty Sales
Chloe Ramos-Peterson — Book Market & Library Sales Manager
Emilio Bautista — Digital Sales Coordinator

Kat Salazar — Director of PR & Marketing
Drew Fitzgerald — Marketing Content Associate

Heather Doornink — Production Director
Drew Gill — Art Director
Hilary DiLoreto — Print Manager
Tricia Ramos — Traffic Manager
Erika Schnatz — Senior Production Artist
Ryan Brewer — Production Artist
Deanna Phelps — Production Artist

www.imagecomics.com

BATTLE CHASERS ANTHOLOGY
Second Printing. December 2020.

ISBN: 978-1-5343-1522-8

Published by Image Comics, Inc. Office of publication: 2701 NW Vaughn St., Suite 780, Portland, OR 97210.

PRINTED IN THE USA

A LONG TIME AGO...

...THERE LIVED A VERY YOUNG MAN WITH A NAME THAT FEW COULD PRONOUNCE AND EVEN FEWER COULD SPELL (TO THIS DAY, I STILL CAN'T WITHOUT LOOKING IT UP). HE WAS JUST A KID, A PUNK, WHO DARED TO CHALLENGE THE GREATS WITH HIS SKILLS. MOST LAUGHED AT THE RUNT AS HE WIELDED HIS SOLITARY WEAPON AND TOOK UP ARMS AGAINST THEM ALL.

VICTORY WAS HIS...AT THE SHARP END OF A PENCIL.

THEY CALLED HIM "JOE MAD" FOR SHORT.   SOME OF IT WAS THAT HE HAD TO BE BONKERS TO TRY WHAT HE HAD IN MIND. NO ONE COULD DENY HIS PASSION. IT'S WHAT GOT HIM IN THE DOOR IN THE FIRST PLACE.

JOE STARTED AT MARVEL AT ALL OF 16 YEARS. IT WASN'T LONG BEFORE HIS MAD SKILLS (SORRY!) LANDED HIM THE GOLD STANDARD IN COMICS DRAWING THE UNCANNY X-MEN. LIKE JOHN BRYNE, DAVE COCKRUM, AND JIM LEE BEFORE HIM (TO NAME A FEW), JOE BROUGHT A NEW STYLE TO THE GAME AND MADE THE X-MEN HIS OWN.

BUT IT WASN'T ENOUGH.

DEEP INSIDE, JOE HARBORED A SECRET. HE LOVED COMICS. HE ADORED, IN PARTICULAR, SPIDER-MAN. BUT WHAT TUGGED AT HIS HEART WERE THE ADVENTURES HE'D SPUN AS AN EVEN YOUNGER LAD IN THE GARAGE AT HIS HOUSE GROWING UP.   THE WORLD OF DUNGEONS + DRAGONS. WIZARDS + WARRIORS. SWORDS + SORCERY.   IT WAS ALWAYS THERE, JUST OFF THE EDGE OF THE PAGE HE WAS DRAWING FOR MARVEL. FINALLY, HE WAS NO LONGER ABLE TO CONTAIN IT.

BATTLE CHASERS WAS BORN.

FOR THOSE OF US LUCKY ENOUGH TO READ THE FIRST FEW ISSUES, IT REALLY WAS LIKE NOTHING WE'D SEEN BEFORE. THE FIERCE, YET INNOCENT GULLY. THE MIGHTY AND HUMOROUS CALIBRETTO. THE DANGEROUS, BUT TRAGIC GARRISON. THE, UM...WELL... GRANDEUR OF MONIKA.   EACH PAGE UNCOVERED A NEW EXCITING CHARACTER, A SPECTACULAR ACTION TURN, OR A BOMBASTIC DISPLAY OF ARTISTIC SKILL THAT BROUGHT ABOUT A SMILE.

BATTLE CHASERS HARKENED BACK TO WHEN COMICS WERE FUN. IT'S A STORY THAT GOES AT A BREATHTAKING PACE, PART DISNEY ANIMATION, PART INDIANA JONES, PART SEEING STAR WARS FOR THE FIRST TIME.

AND IT WAS PURE JOE.

THAT'S NOT TO SAY HE DID IT ALL BY HIMSELF. MUNIER SHARRIEFF BROUGHT INCREDIBLE OVER-THE-TOP IDEAS TO THE STORIES. TOM MCWEENEY PROVIDED THE FLAWLESS BLACKS THAT BROUGHT A THUNDEROUS WEIGHT TO HIS PENCILS. RICHARD STARKINGS AND THE COMICRAFTSMEN IMBUED THE WORDS WITH UNIQUE FONTS AND DESIGNS THAT ACTED LIKE THE SCORE TO THE MOVIE. AND MOST GLORIOUS OF ALL, CHRISTIAN LICHTNER AND ARON LUSEN LIT IT ALL UP WITH LUMINESCENT COLOR WORTHY OF THE FINEST CINEMATOGRAPHER.

THEN, AS QUICKLY AS IT HIT US... IT WAS GONE. JOE MAD'S ARTISTIC ENDEAVORS OPENED A NEW DOOR INTO THE VIDEO GAME UNIVERSE AND LIKE THE HEROES HE SO ADMIRED, HE WAS NEEDED ELSEWHERE. CHECK OUT DARKSIDERS (IF YOU HAVEN'T ALREADY) AND YOU'LL SEE WHERE THE MAGIC WENT...

I WAS LUCKY ENOUGH TO GET TO KNOW JOE BACK IN THE X-MEN DAYS. WE REMAINED FRIENDS AND WHEN THE TIME WAS RIGHT, HE RETURNED AND I WAS EVEN LUCKIER TO COLLABORATE WITH HIM ON ULTIMATES 3 AT MARVEL. AFTER THAT, HE ONCE AGAIN VANISHED.

I CAN ONLY HOPE THAT HE'LL STRIKE OUT AGAIN INTO THE VAST REACHES OF THE COMIC BOOK LAND HE ONCE CONQUERED — MAYBE EVEN TO SEE HIM TACKLE THAT WEBHEAD HE LOVES SO MUCH.

UNTIL THEN, WE HAVE THIS AWE-INSPIRING COLLECTION THAT REMINDS US ALL THAT IF WE HAVE A DREAM — CHASE IT!

WITH TREMENDOUS LOVE AND RESPECT,

JEPH LOEB
LOS ANGELES, CA 2011

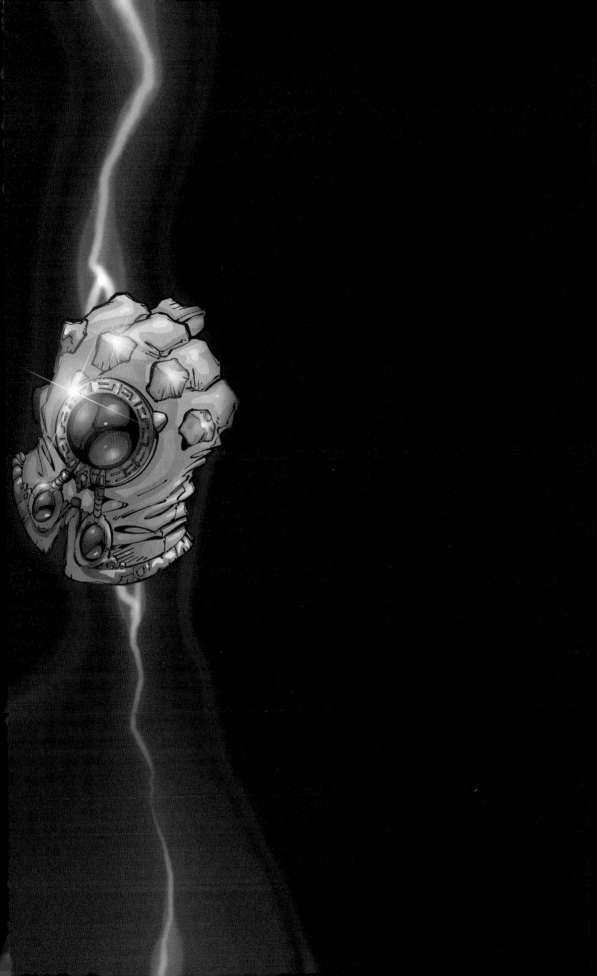

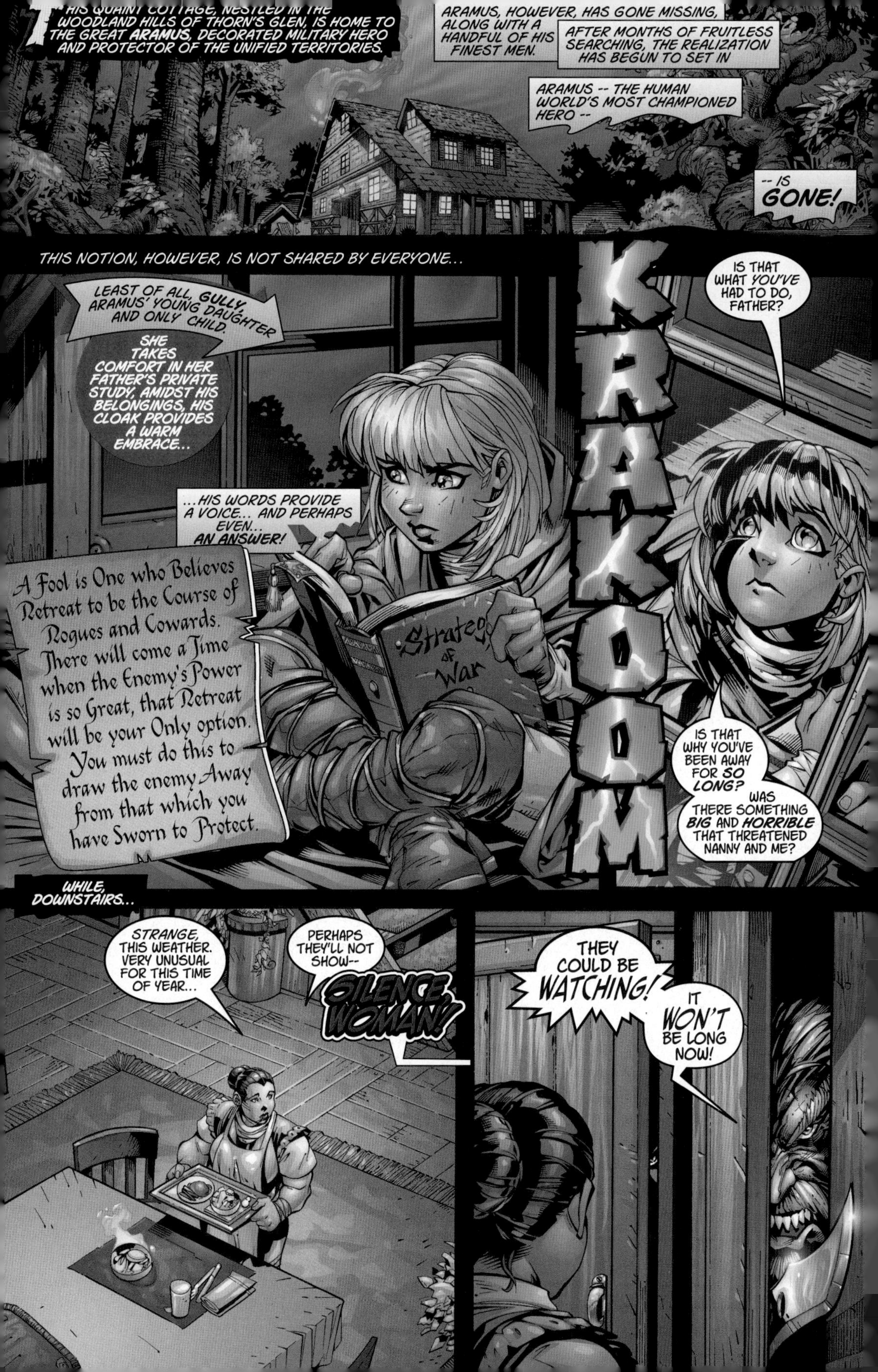
THIS QUAINT COTTAGE, NESTLED IN THE WOODLAND HILLS OF THORN'S GLEN, IS HOME TO THE GREAT ARAMUS, DECORATED MILITARY HERO AND PROTECTOR OF THE UNIFIED TERRITORIES.
ARAMUS, HOWEVER, HAS GONE MISSING, ALONG WITH A HANDFUL OF HIS FINEST MEN.
AFTER MONTHS OF FRUITLESS SEARCHING, THE REALIZATION HAS BEGUN TO SET IN
ARAMUS -- THE HUMAN WORLD'S MOST CHAMPIONED HERO --
-- IS GONE!
THIS NOTION, HOWEVER, IS NOT SHARED BY EVERYONE...
LEAST OF ALL, GULLY, ARAMUS' YOUNG DAUGHTER AND ONLY CHILD.
SHE TAKES COMFORT IN HER FATHER'S PRIVATE STUDY, AMIDST HIS BELONGINGS, HIS CLOAK PROVIDES A WARM EMBRACE...
...HIS WORDS PROVIDE A VOICE... AND PERHAPS EVEN... AN ANSWER!
A Fool is One who Believes Retreat to be the Course of Rogues and Cowards. There will come a Time when the Enemy's Power is so Great, that Retreat will be your Only option. You must do this to draw the enemy Away from that which you have Sworn to Protect.
Strategy of War
KRAKOOM
IS THAT WHAT YOU'VE HAD TO DO, FATHER?
IS THAT WHY YOU'VE BEEN AWAY FOR SO LONG?
WAS THERE SOMETHING BIG AND HORRIBLE THAT THREATENED NANNY AND ME?
WHILE, DOWNSTAIRS...
STRANGE, THIS WEATHER. VERY UNUSUAL FOR THIS TIME OF YEAR...
PERHAPS THEY'LL NOT SHOW--
SILENCE, WOMAN!
THEY COULD BE WATCHING!
IT WON'T BE LONG NOW!

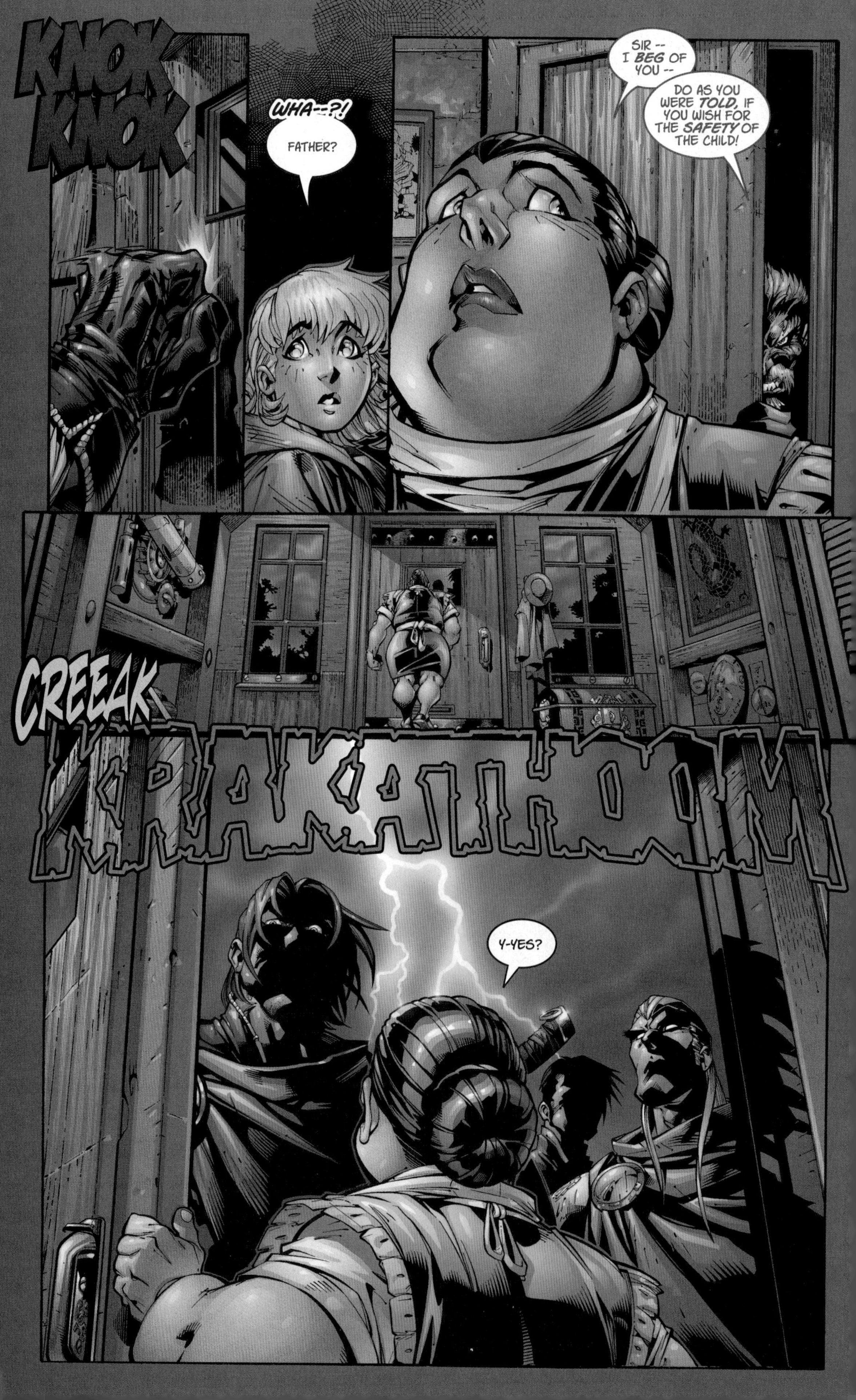
KNOK KNOK
WHA--?!
FATHER?
SIR -- I BEG OF YOU --
DO AS YOU WERE TOLD, IF YOU WISH FOR THE SAFETY OF THE CHILD!
CREEAK
KRAKATHOOM
Y-YES?

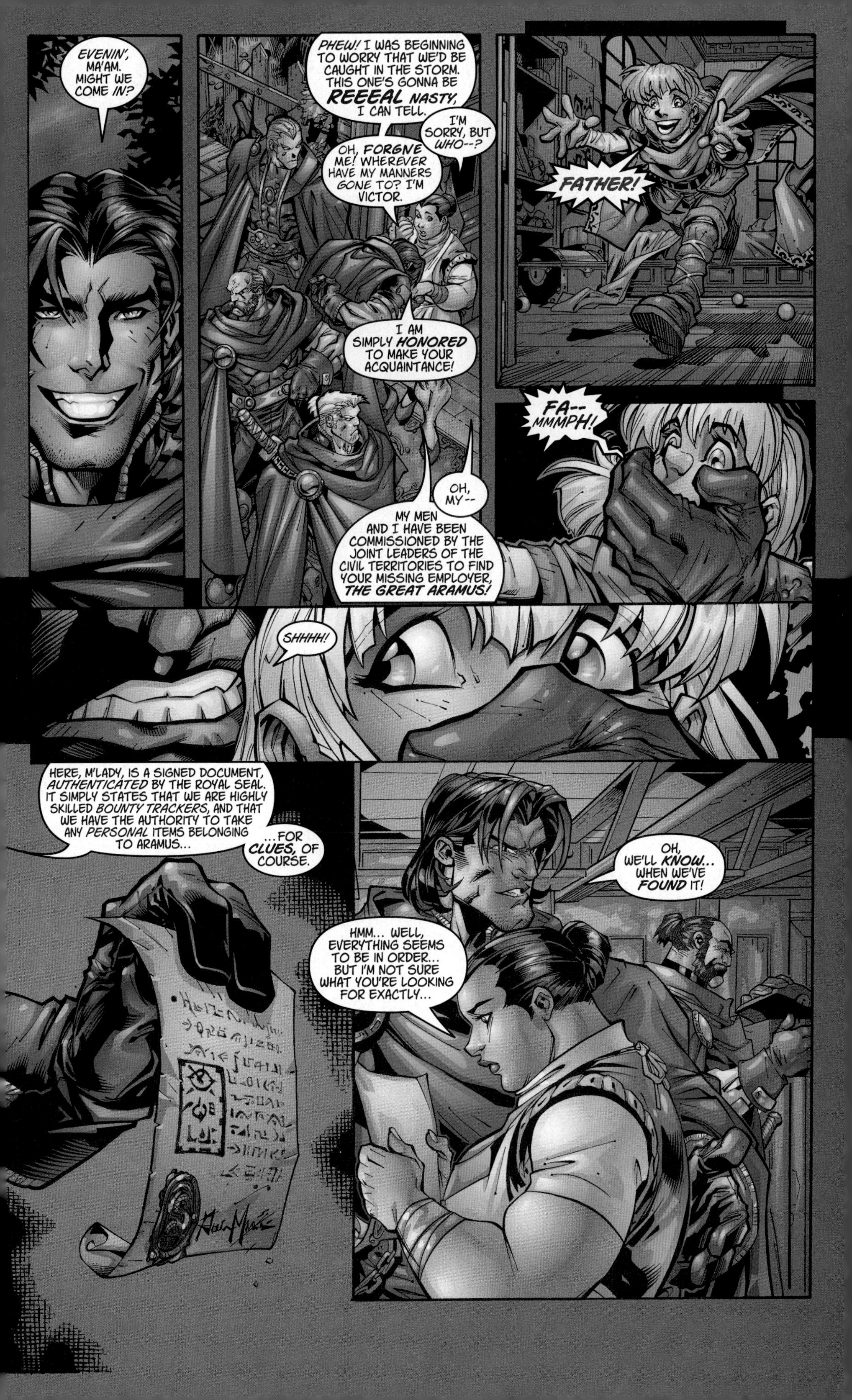
EVENIN', MA'AM. MIGHT WE COME IN?
PHEW! I WAS BEGINNING TO WORRY THAT WE'D BE CAUGHT IN THE STORM. THIS ONE'S GONNA BE REEEAL NASTY, I CAN TELL.
I'M SORRY, BUT WHO--?
OH, FORGIVE ME! WHEREVER HAVE MY MANNERS GONE TO? I'M VICTOR.
I AM SIMPLY HONORED TO MAKE YOUR ACQUAINTANCE!
FATHER!
FA-- MMMPH!
OH, MY --
MY MEN AND I HAVE BEEN COMMISSIONED BY THE JOINT LEADERS OF THE CIVIL TERRITORIES TO FIND YOUR MISSING EMPLOYER, THE GREAT ARAMUS!
SHHHH!
HERE, M'LADY, IS A SIGNED DOCUMENT, AUTHENTICATED BY THE ROYAL SEAL. IT SIMPLY STATES THAT WE ARE HIGHLY SKILLED BOUNTY TRACKERS, AND THAT WE HAVE THE AUTHORITY TO TAKE ANY PERSONAL ITEMS BELONGING TO ARAMUS...
...FOR CLUES, OF COURSE.
HMM... WELL, EVERYTHING SEEMS TO BE IN ORDER... BUT I'M NOT SURE WHAT YOU'RE LOOKING FOR EXACTLY...
OH, WE'LL KNOW... WHEN WE'VE FOUND IT!

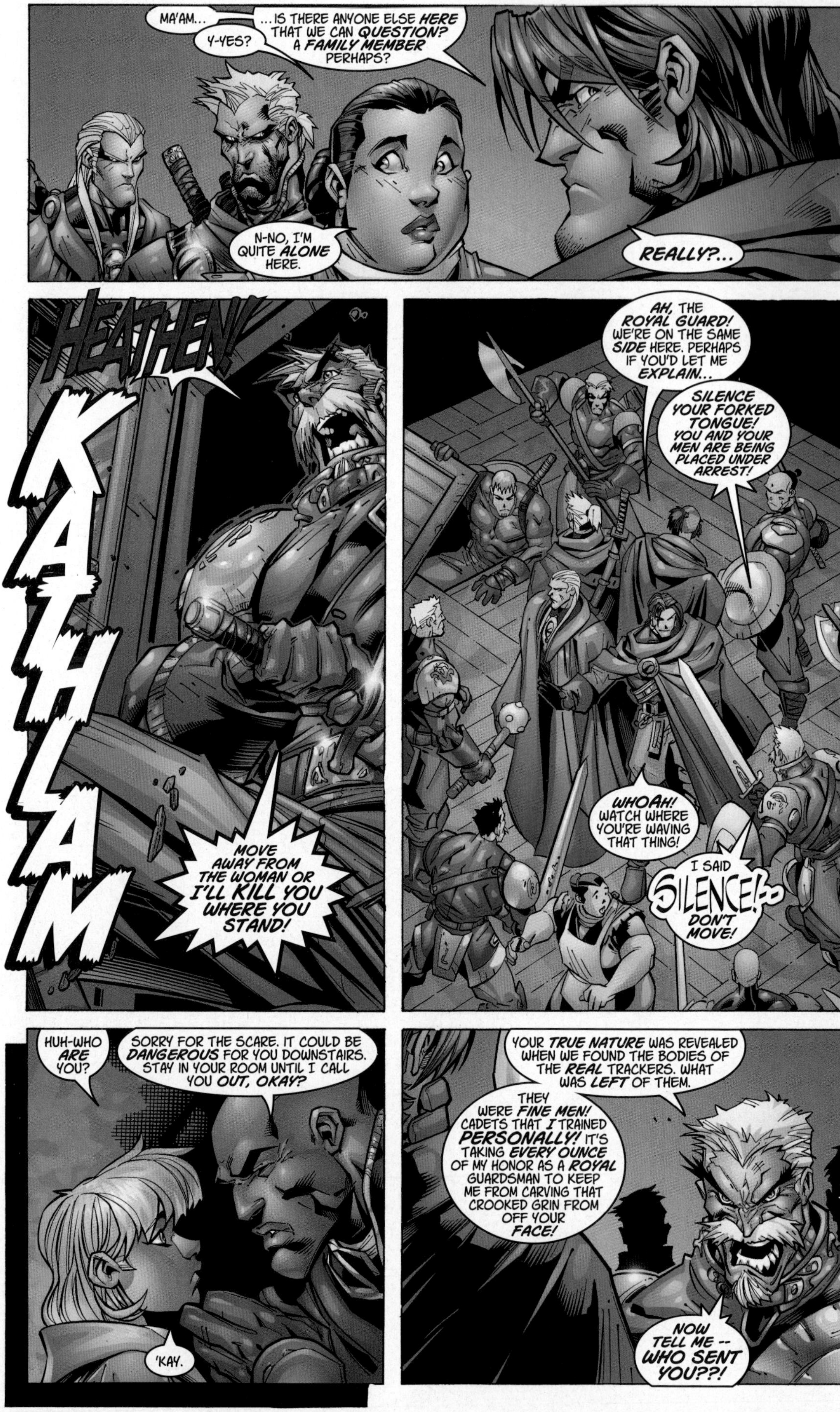
MA'AM...
Y-YES?
...IS THERE ANYONE ELSE HERE THAT WE CAN QUESTION? A FAMILY MEMBER PERHAPS?
N-NO, I'M QUITE ALONE HERE.
REALLY?...
HEATHEN!
KAHLAM
MOVE AWAY FROM THE WOMAN OR I'LL KILL YOU WHERE YOU STAND!
AH, THE ROYAL GUARD! WE'RE ON THE SAME SIDE HERE. PERHAPS IF YOU'D LET ME EXPLAIN...
SILENCE YOUR FORKED TONGUE! YOU AND YOUR MEN ARE BEING PLACED UNDER ARREST!
WHOAH! WATCH WHERE YOU'RE WAVING THAT THING!
I SAID SILENCE!-- DON'T MOVE!
HUH-WHO ARE YOU?
SORRY FOR THE SCARE. IT COULD BE DANGEROUS FOR YOU DOWNSTAIRS. STAY IN YOUR ROOM UNTIL I CALL YOU OUT, OKAY?
'KAY.
YOUR TRUE NATURE WAS REVEALED WHEN WE FOUND THE BODIES OF THE REAL TRACKERS. WHAT WAS LEFT OF THEM.
THEY WERE FINE MEN! CADETS THAT I TRAINED PERSONALLY! IT'S TAKING EVERY OUNCE OF MY HONOR AS A ROYAL GUARDSMAN TO KEEP ME FROM CARVING THAT CROOKED GRIN FROM OFF YOUR FACE!
NOW TELL ME -- WHO SENT YOU??!

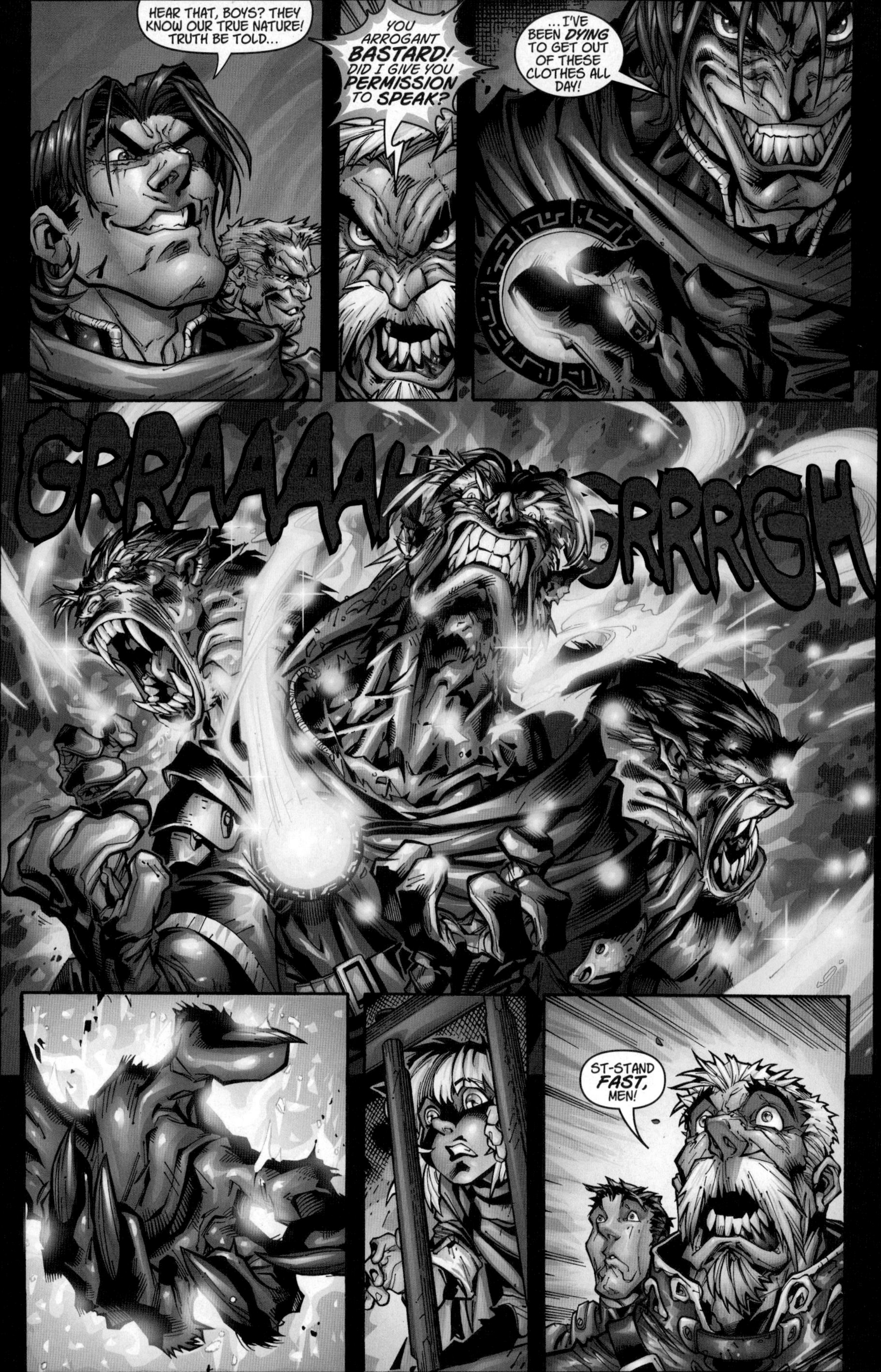
HEAR THAT, BOYS? THEY KNOW OUR TRUE NATURE! TRUTH BE TOLD...
YOU ARROGANT BASTARD! DID I GIVE YOU PERMISSION TO SPEAK?
...I'VE BEEN DYING TO GET OUT OF THESE CLOTHES ALL DAY!
GRRAAAAH
GRRRGH
ST-STAND FAST, MEN!

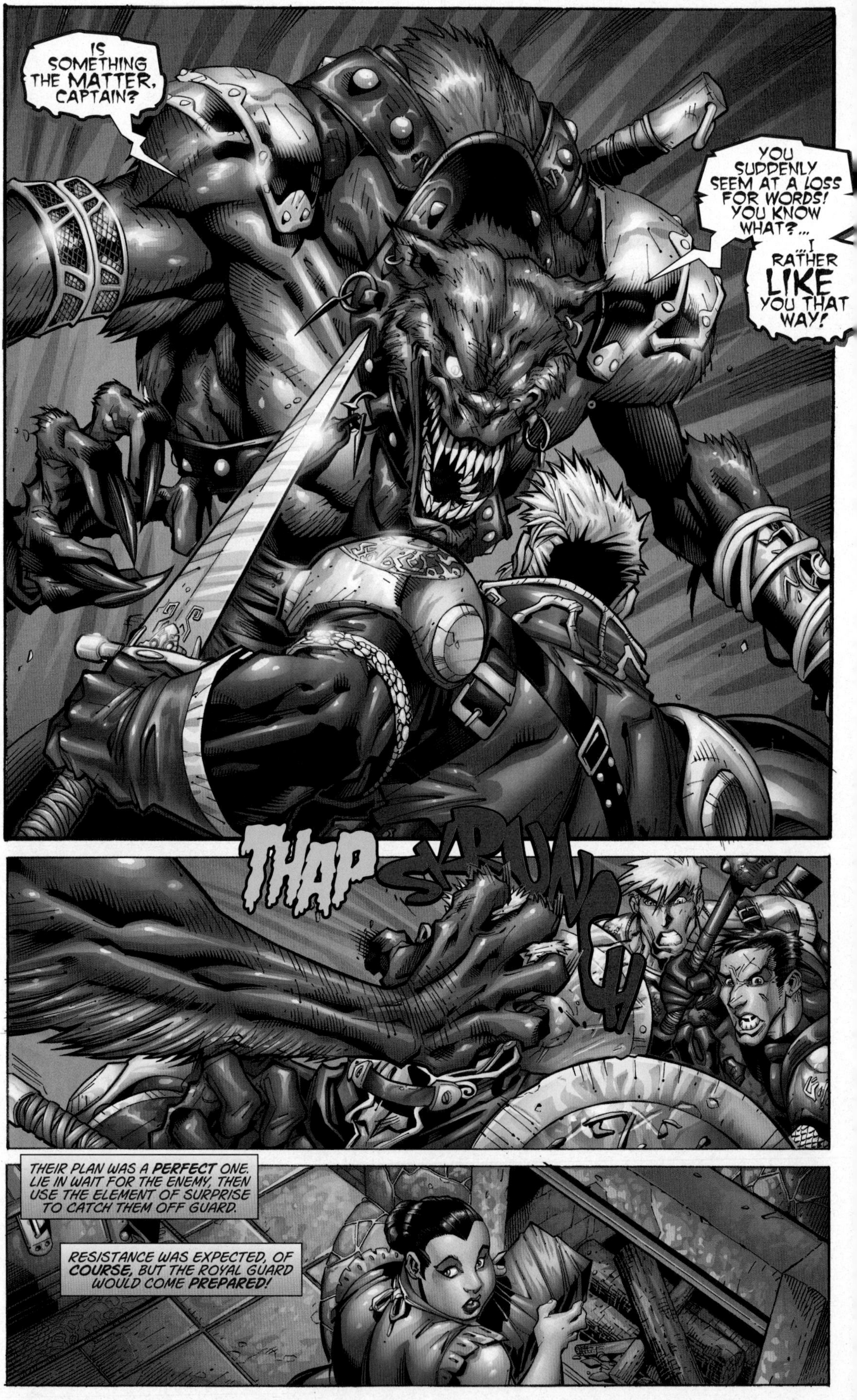
IS SOMETHING THE MATTER, CAPTAIN?
YOU SUDDENLY SEEM AT A LOSS FOR WORDS! YOU KNOW WHAT?...
I RATHER LIKE YOU THAT WAY!
THAP
THEIR PLAN WAS A PERFECT ONE. LIE IN WAIT FOR THE ENEMY, THEN USE THE ELEMENT OF SURPRISE TO CATCH THEM OFF GUARD.
RESISTANCE WAS EXPECTED, OF COURSE, BUT THE ROYAL GUARD WOULD COME PREPARED!

TO FACE **NORMAL** MEN, PERHAPS...

...NOT **NIGHTMARES!**

THE WOMAN'S **HASTENED** ESCAPE DOES NOT GO **UNDETECTED** BY THE PACK LEADER'S **ACUTE** SENSE OF **HEARING.**

HUFF HUFF HUFF

OH **PLEASE** DEAR GOD!

HE HAD **SUSPECTED** THAT **SHE** WOULD BE THE ONE TO LEAD THEM TO WHAT THEY WERE **TRULY** AFTER.

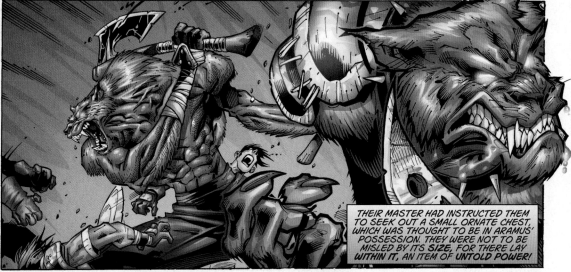

THEIR MASTER HAD INSTRUCTED THEM TO SEEK OUT A SMALL ORNATE CHEST, WHICH WAS THOUGHT TO BE IN ARAMUS' POSSESSION. THEY WERE NOT TO BE MISLED BY ITS **SIZE,** FOR THERE LAY WITHIN IT, AN ITEM OF **UNTOLD POWER!**

AND THEY WERE TO OBTAIN IT **AT ANY PRICE!**

GULLY! **HURRY** CHILD, THERE ISN'T MUCH TIME!

...

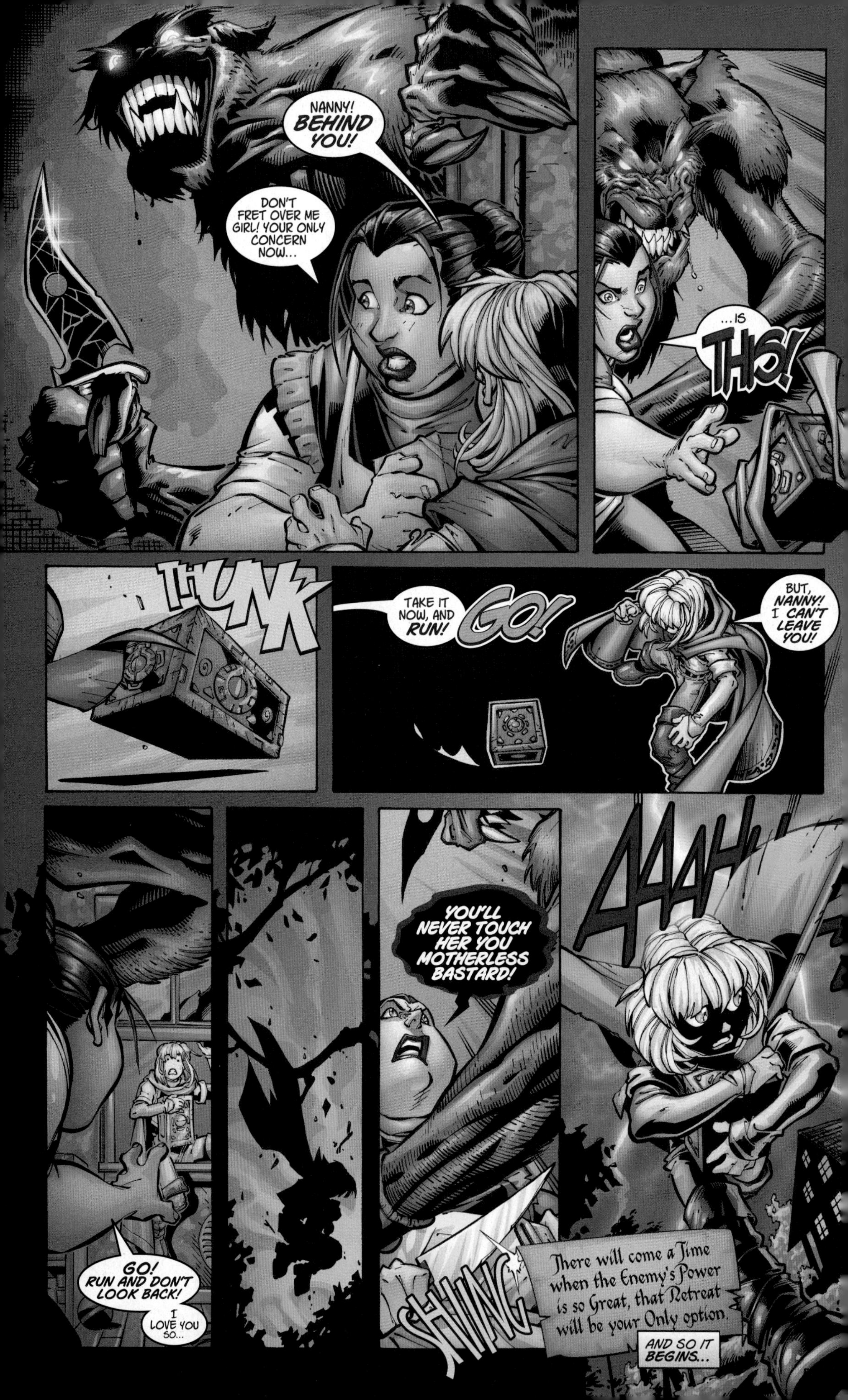
NANNY! BEHIND YOU!
DON'T FRET OVER ME GIRL! YOUR ONLY CONCERN NOW...
...IS THIS!
THUNK
TAKE IT NOW, AND RUN!
GO!
BUT, NANNY! I CAN'T LEAVE YOU!
GO! RUN AND DON'T LOOK BACK!
I LOVE YOU SO...
YOU'LL NEVER TOUCH HER YOU MOTHERLESS BASTARD!
SHING
AAAH
There will come a Time when the Enemy's Power is so Great, that Retreat will be your Only option.
AND SO IT BEGINS...

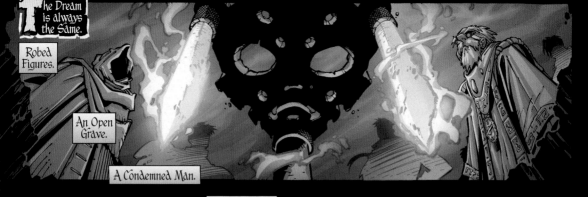

The Dream is always the Same.

Robed Figures.

An Open Grave.

A Condemned Man.

Mystic Armor.

Searing Heat.

Always the Same...
Except the Screams.
They get **Louder** every time.

HUH!!

STRANGE... EVERY TIME I'VE HAD THE DREAM BEFORE, THE OTHERS... THEIR FACES WERE *CLEAR* TO ME. BUT NOW... HMMM...

CALIBRETTO... YOU HERE?! WE NEED MORE WOOD FOR THE FIRE.

AGH! WHERE DID HE RUN OFF TO *NOW..?!*

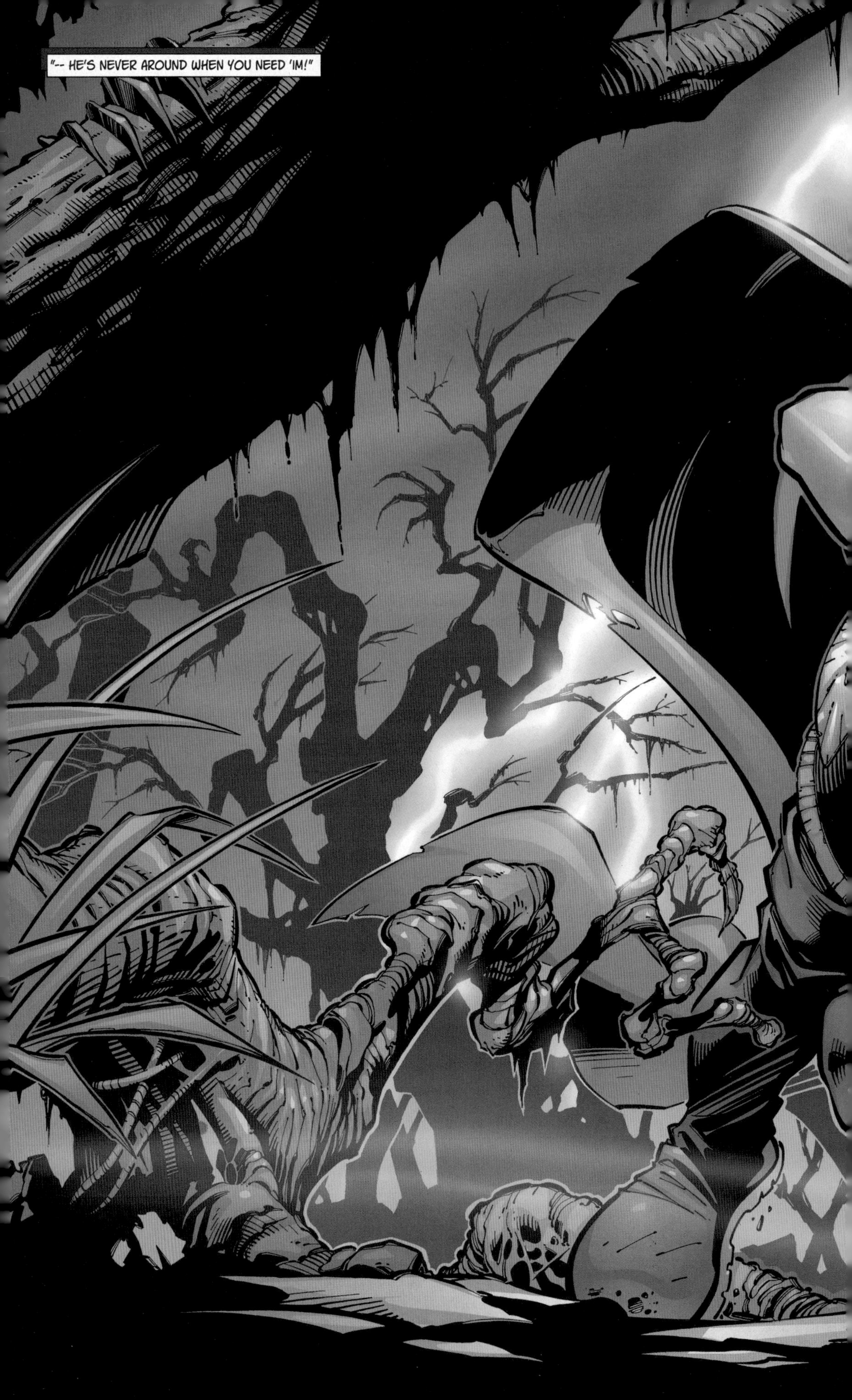
"-- HE'S NEVER AROUND WHEN YOU NEED 'IM!"

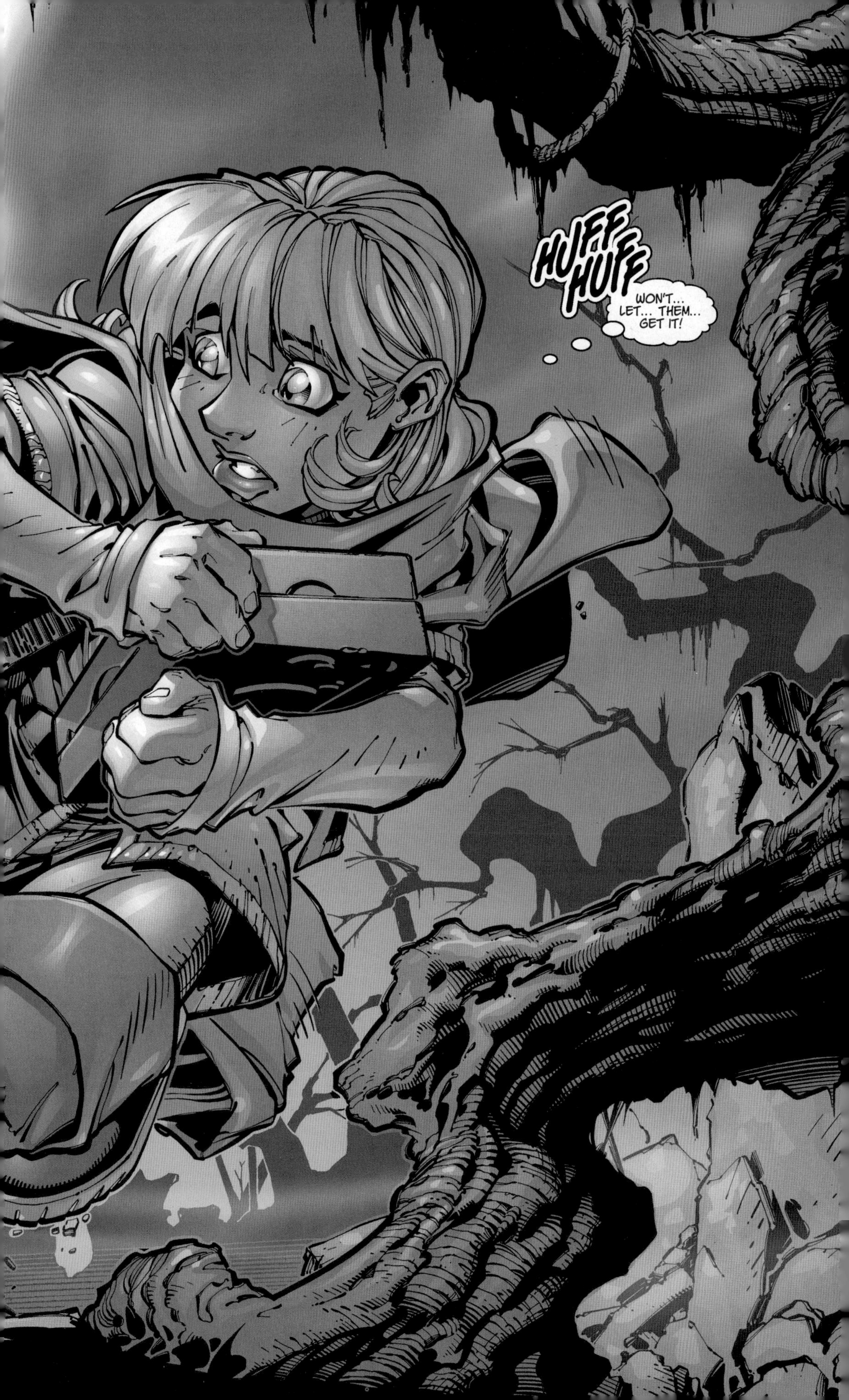
HUFF HUFF
WON'T... LET... THEM... GET IT!

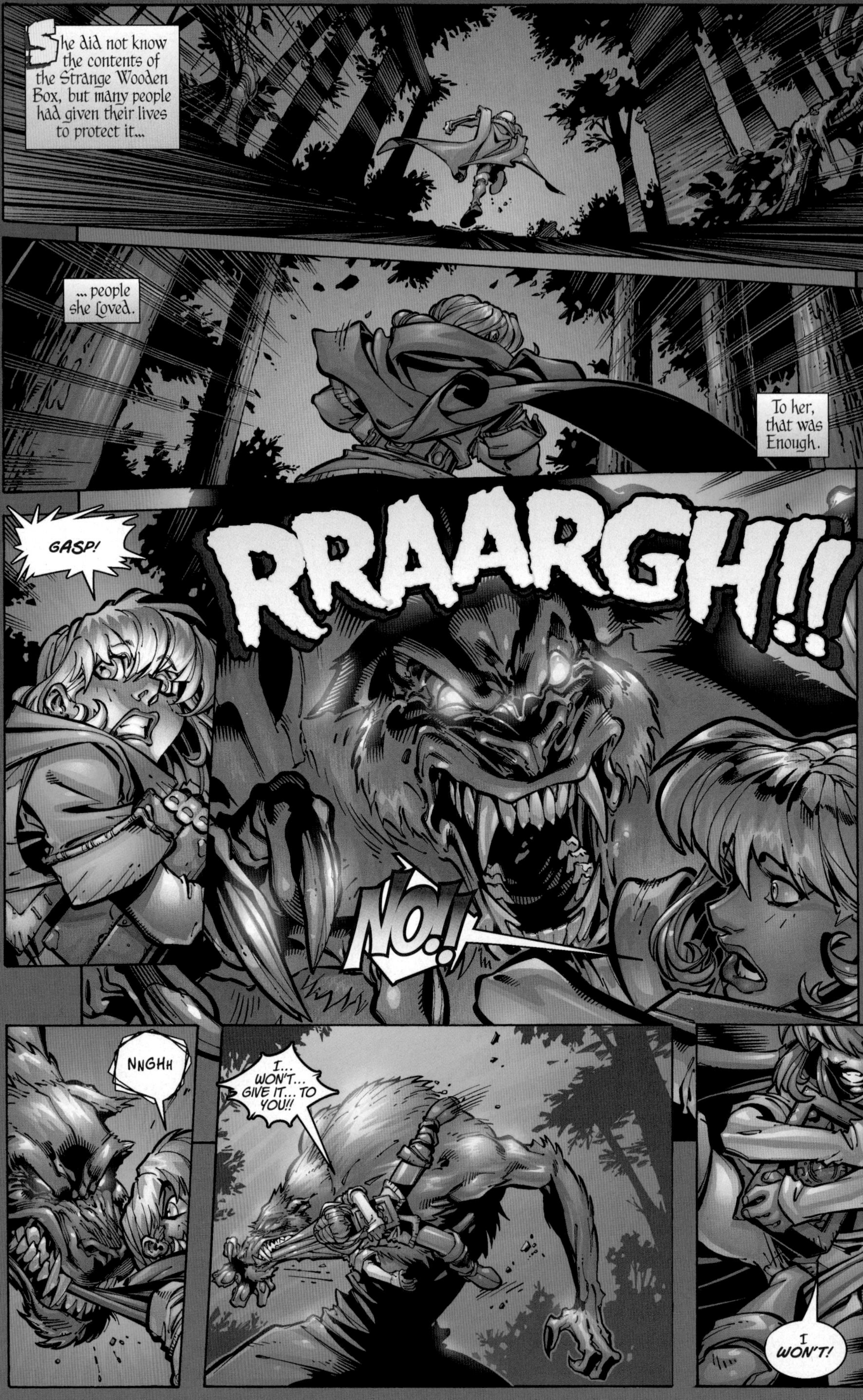
She did not know the contents of the Strange Wooden Box, but many people had given their lives to protect it...
... people she Loved.
To her, that was Enough.
GASP!
RRAARGH!!!
NO!
NNGHH
I... WON'T... GIVE IT... TO YOU!!
I WON'T!

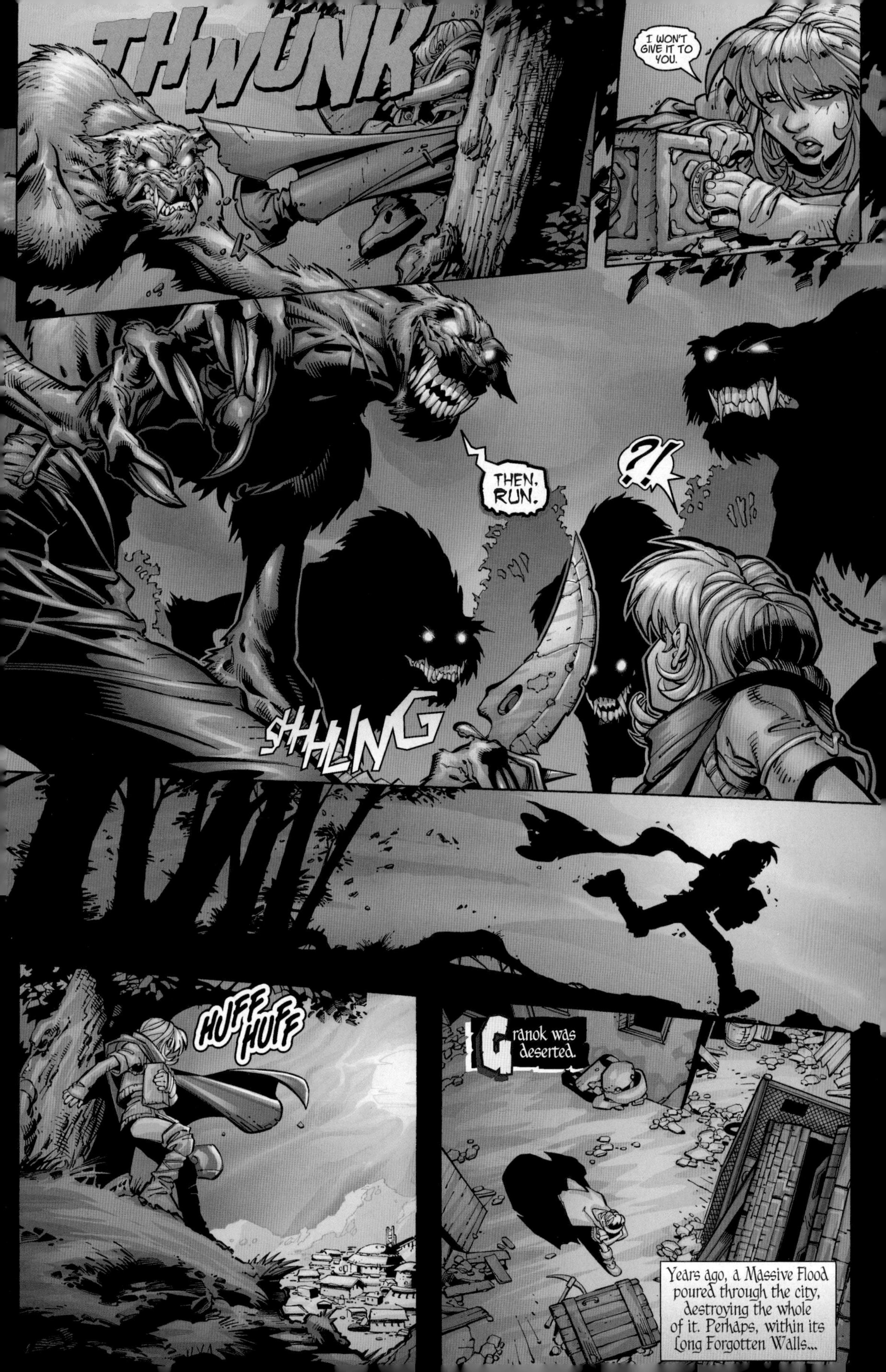
THWUNK
I WON'T GIVE IT TO YOU.
THEN, RUN.
?!
SHHLING
HUFF HUFF
Granok was deserted.
Years ago, a Massive Flood poured through the city, destroying the whole of it. Perhaps, within its Long Forgotten Walls...

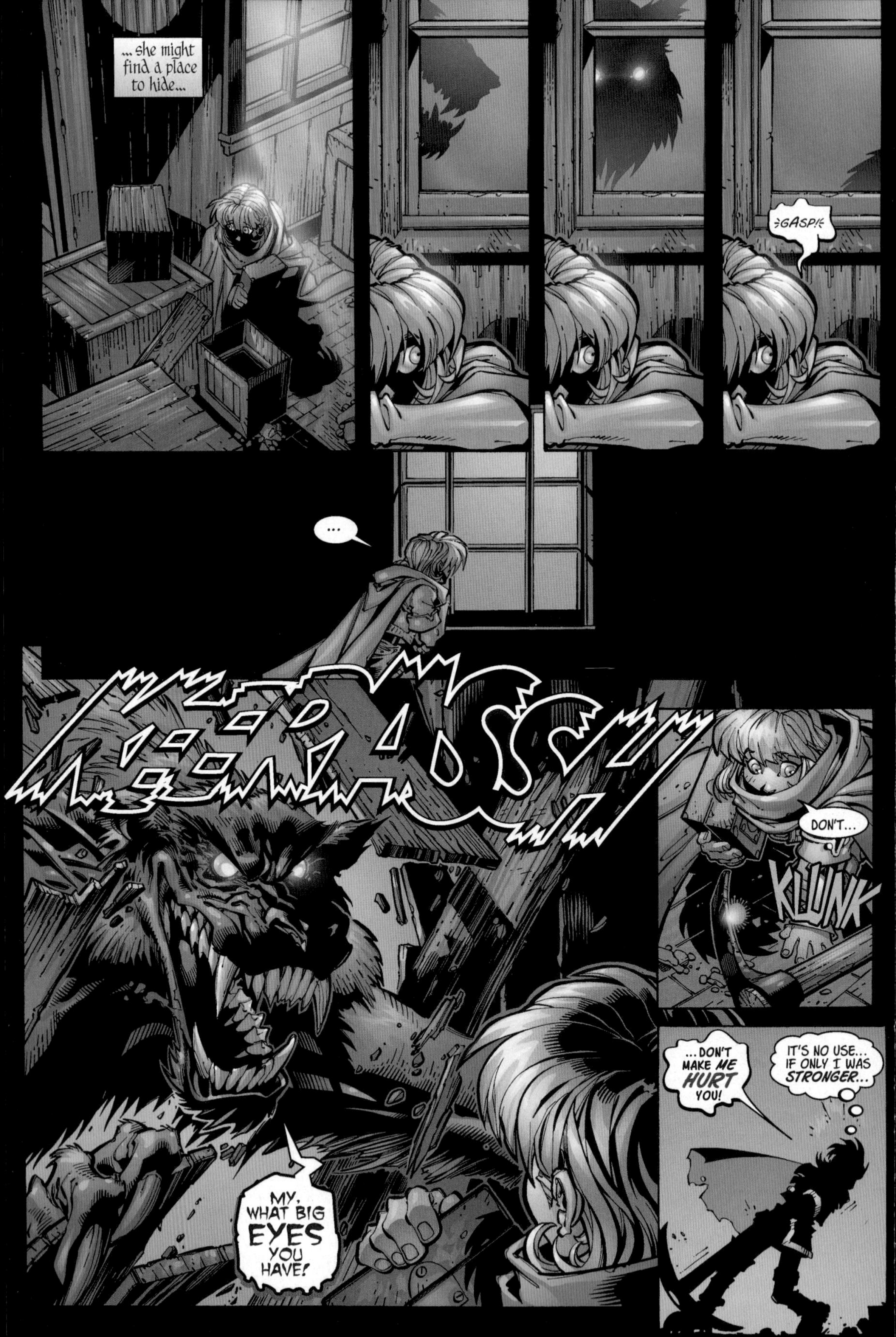
...she might find a place to hide...
GASP!
...
DON'T...
KLUNK
MY, WHAT BIG EYES YOU HAVE!
...DON'T MAKE ME HURT YOU!
IT'S NO USE... IF ONLY I WAS STRONGER...

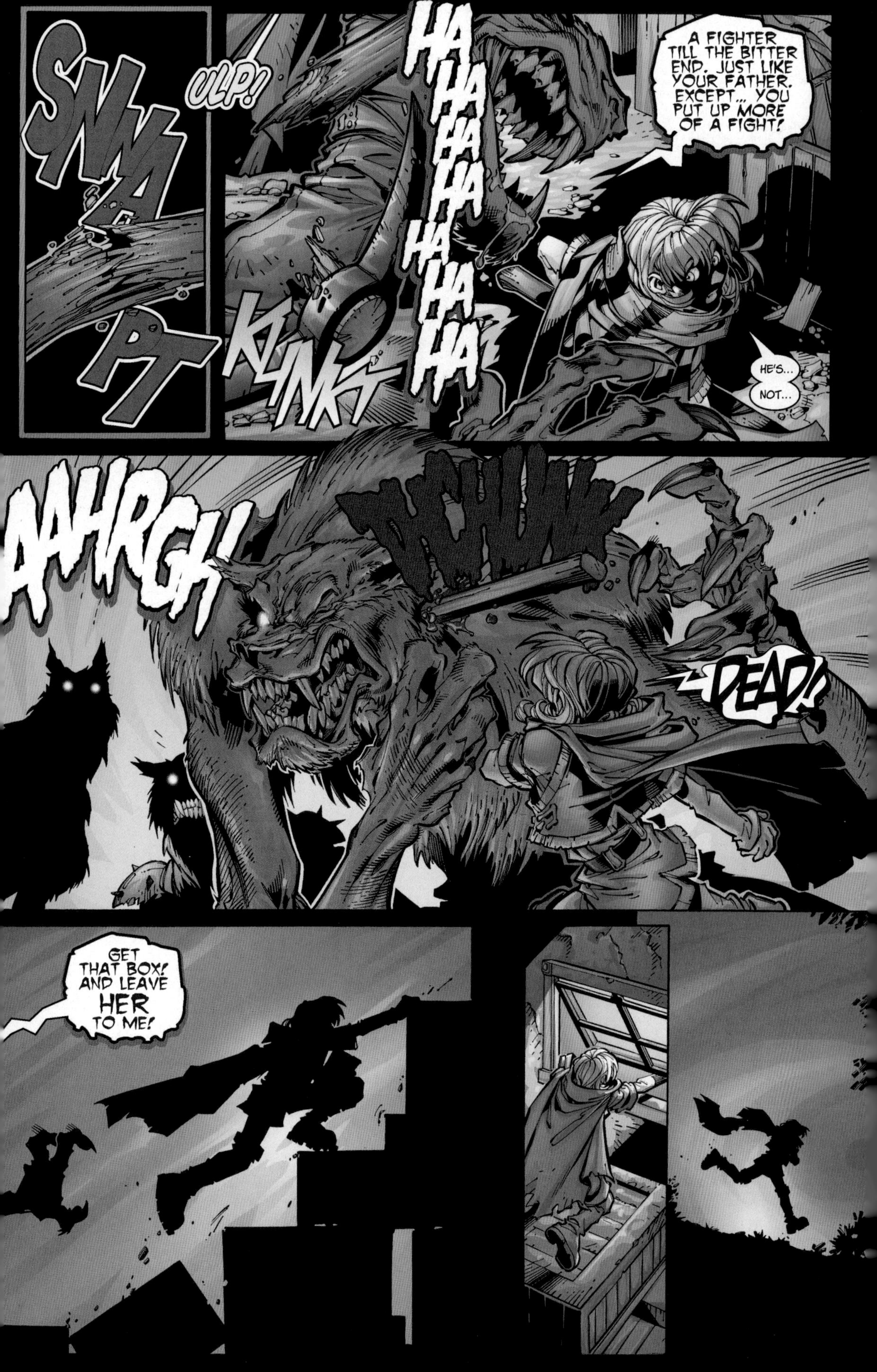
SNNAPT
ULP!
HA HA HA HA HA HA HA HA HA HA
A FIGHTER TILL THE BITTER END. JUST LIKE YOUR FATHER. EXCEPT... YOU PUT UP MORE OF A FIGHT!
KLUNKT
HE'S...
NOT...
AAHRGH
TCHUNK
DEAD!
GET THAT BOX! AND LEAVE HER TO ME!

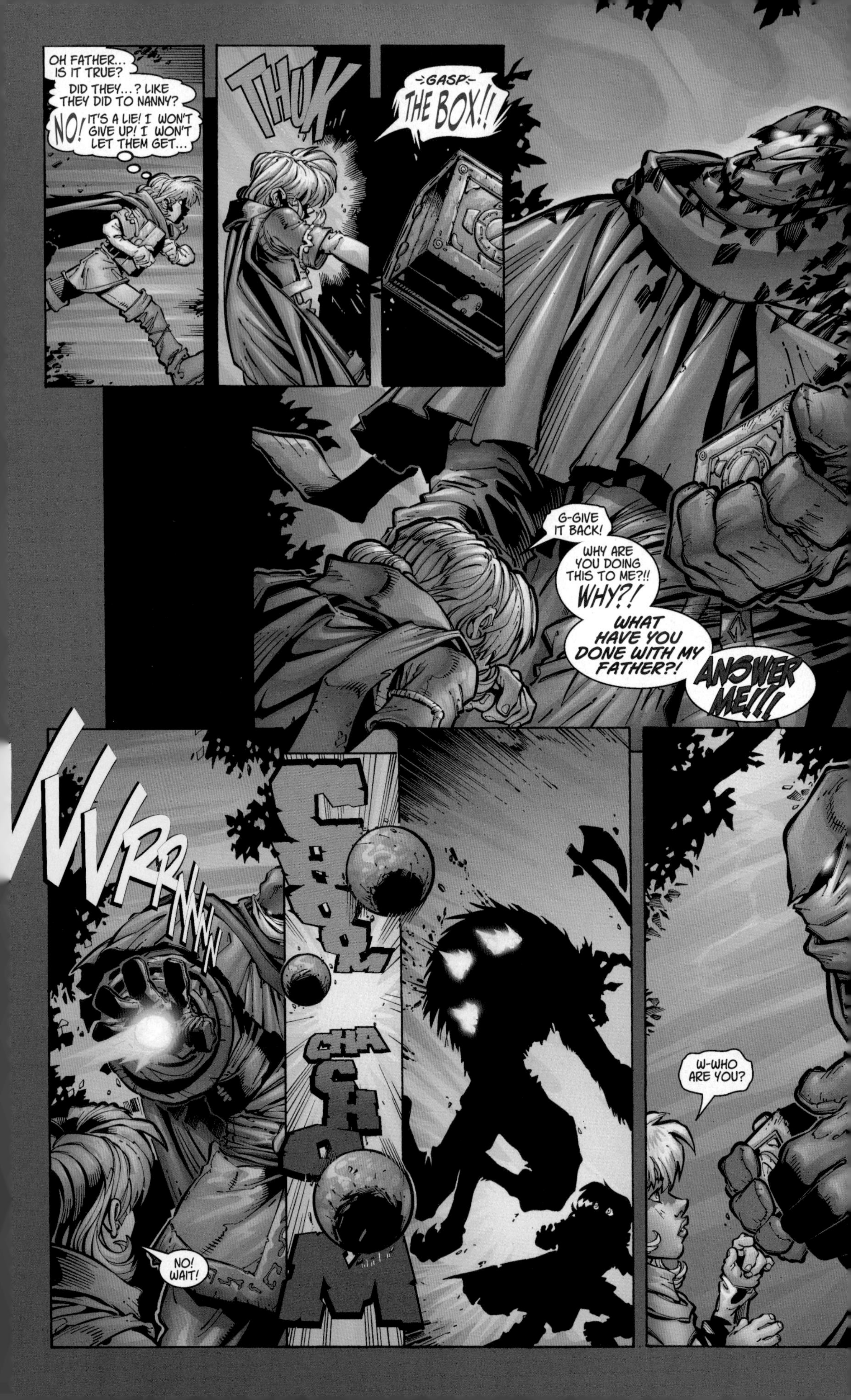
OH FATHER... IS IT TRUE?
DID THEY...? LIKE THEY DID TO NANNY?
NO! IT'S A LIE! I WON'T GIVE UP! I WON'T LET THEM GET...
THUK
-GASP- THE BOX!!
G-GIVE IT BACK!
WHY ARE YOU DOING THIS TO ME?!! WHY?!
WHAT HAVE YOU DONE WITH MY FATHER?!
ANSWER ME!!!
VVVRRNNNN
NO! WAIT!
CHA CHOM
W-WHO ARE YOU?

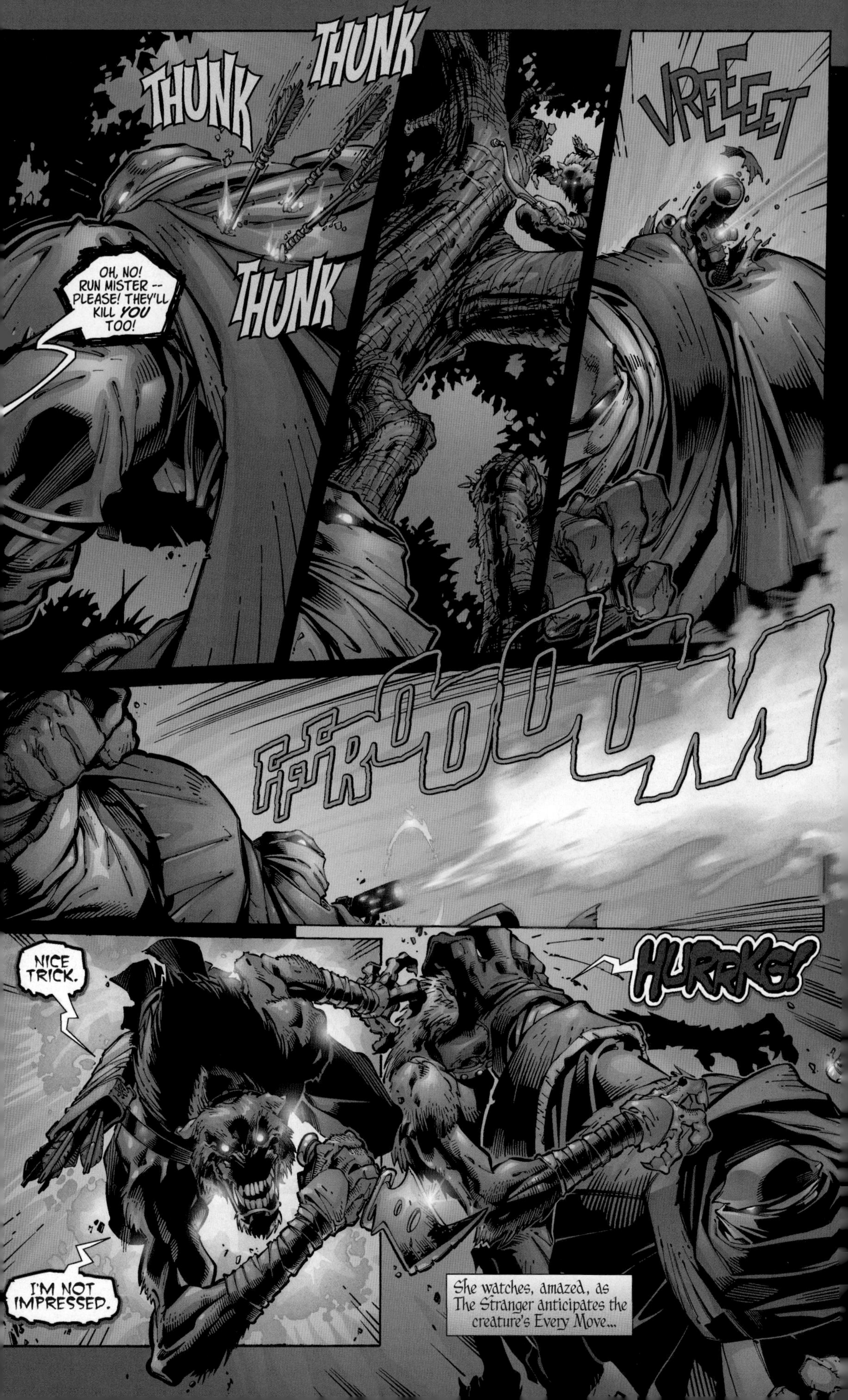
THUNK
THUNK
OH, NO! RUN MISTER -- PLEASE! THEY'LL KILL YOU TOO!
THUNK
VREEEEET
FFFROOOOM
NICE TRICK.
HURRKG!
I'M NOT IMPRESSED.
She watches, amazed, as The Stranger anticipates the creature's Every Move...

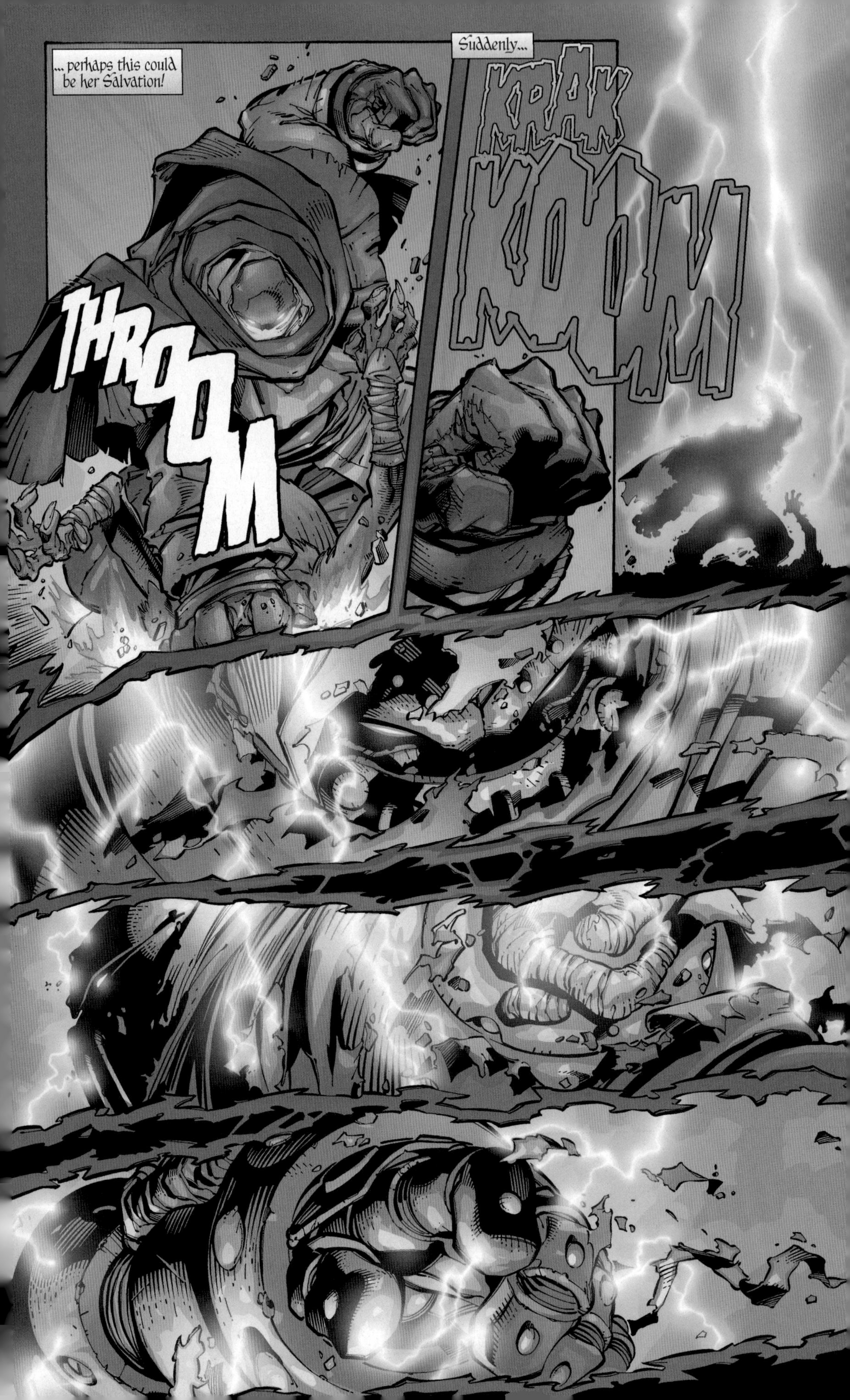
...perhaps this could be her Salvation!
THROOOM
Suddenly...
KRAK
KOOOM

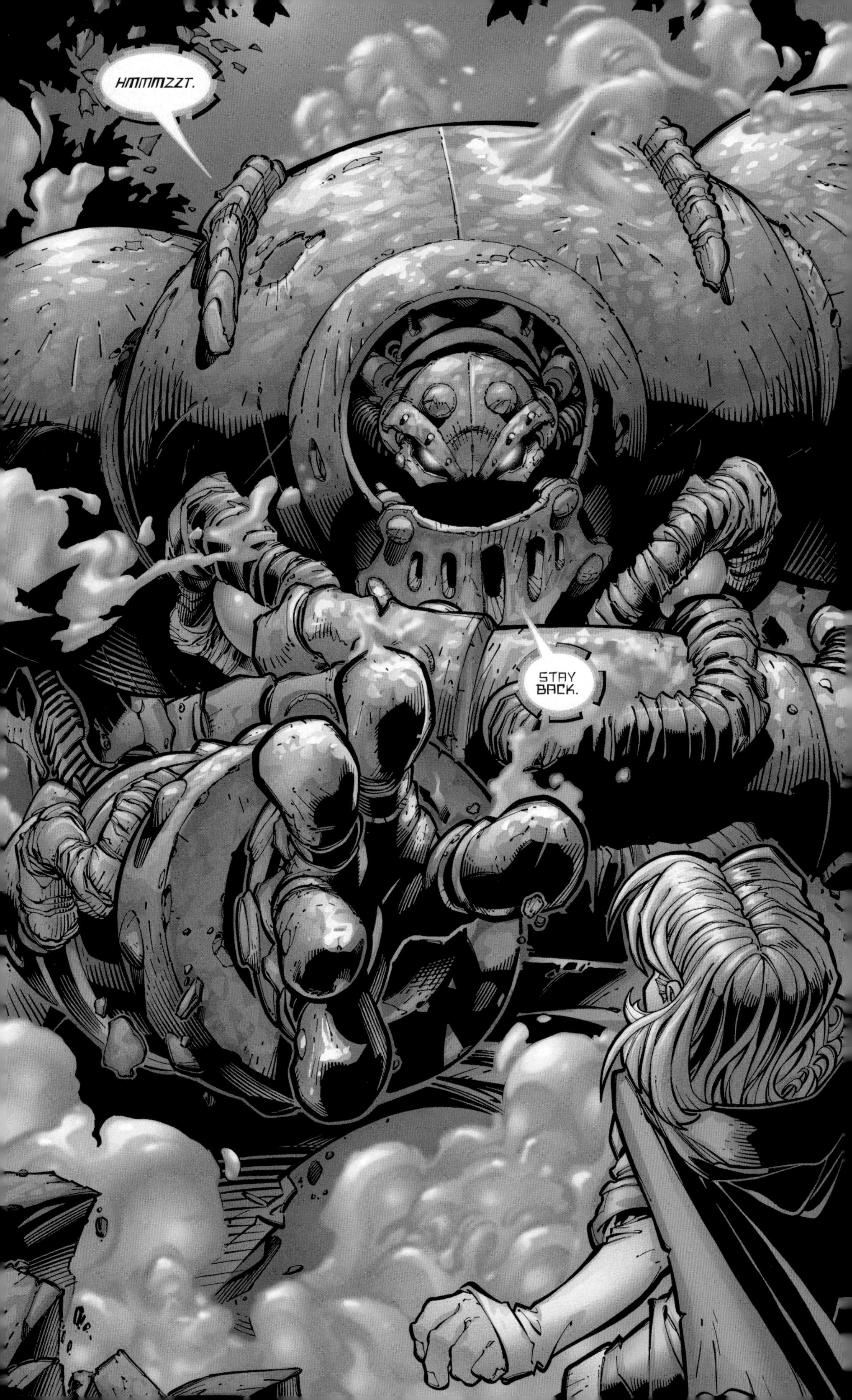
HMMMZZT.
STAY BACK.

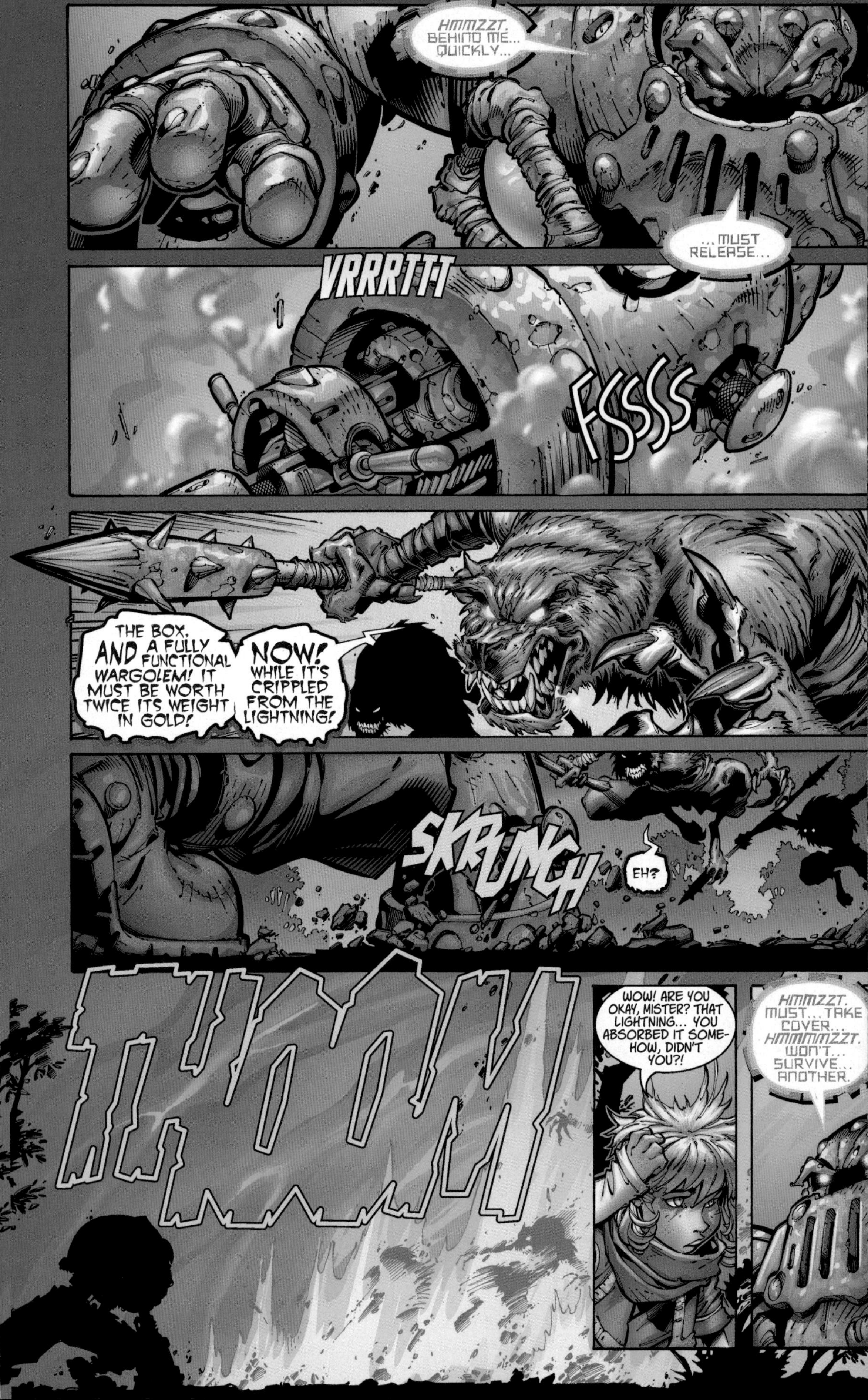
HMMZZT. BEHIND ME... QUICKLY...
...MUST RELEASE...
VRRRTTT
FSSSS
THE BOX. AND A FULLY FUNCTIONAL WARGOLEM! IT MUST BE WORTH TWICE ITS WEIGHT IN GOLD!
NOW! WHILE IT'S CRIPPLED FROM THE LIGHTNING!
SKRUNCH
EH?
WOW! ARE YOU OKAY, MISTER? THAT LIGHTNING... YOU ABSORBED IT SOME-HOW, DIDN'T YOU?!
HMMZZT. MUST... TAKE COVER... HMMMMZZT. WON'T... SURVIVE... ANOTHER.

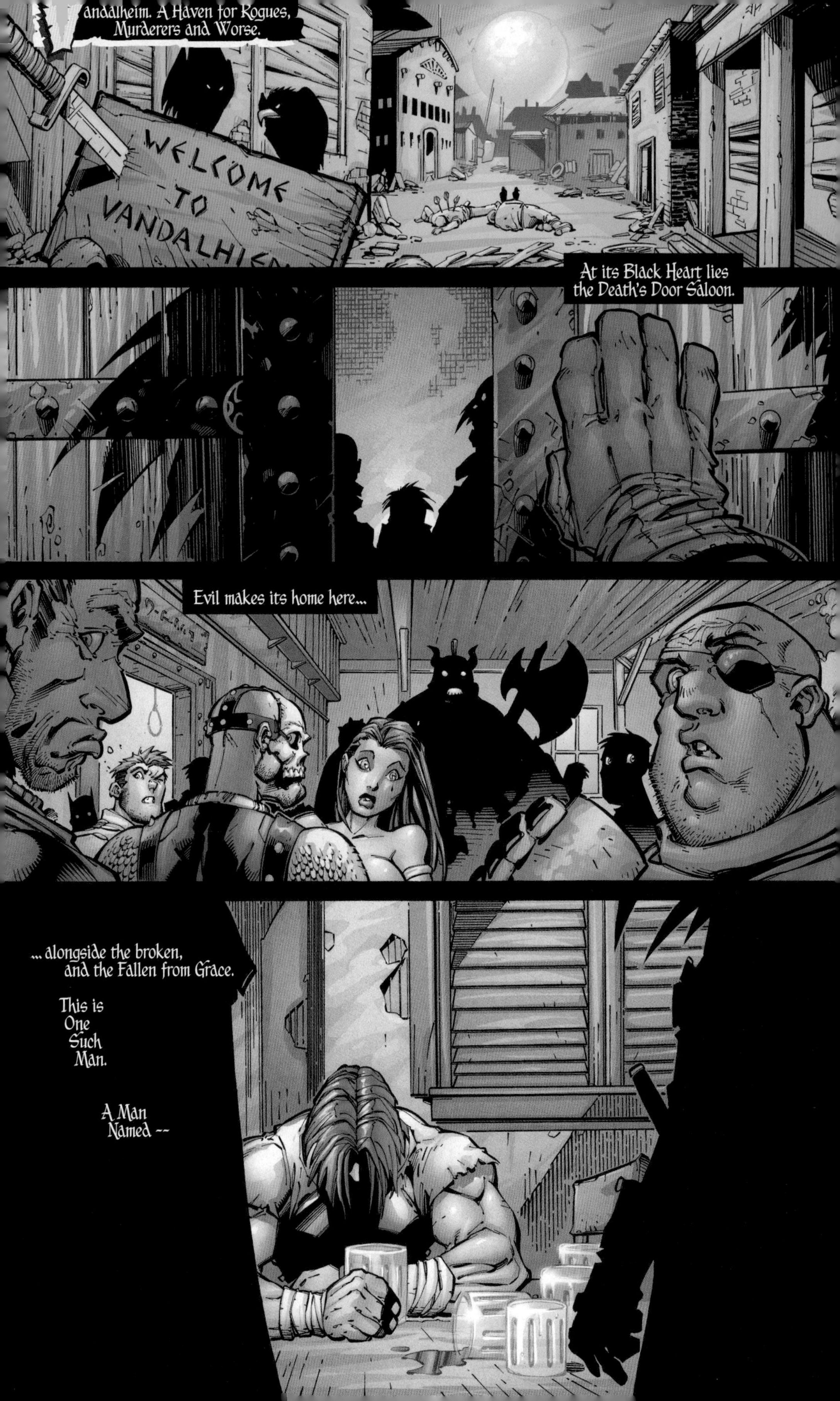

Vandalheim. A Haven for Rogues, Murderers and Worse.
WELCOME TO VANDALHIEM
At its Black Heart lies the Death's Door Saloon.
Evil makes its home here...
... alongside the broken, and the Fallen from Grace.
This is One Such Man.
A Man Named --

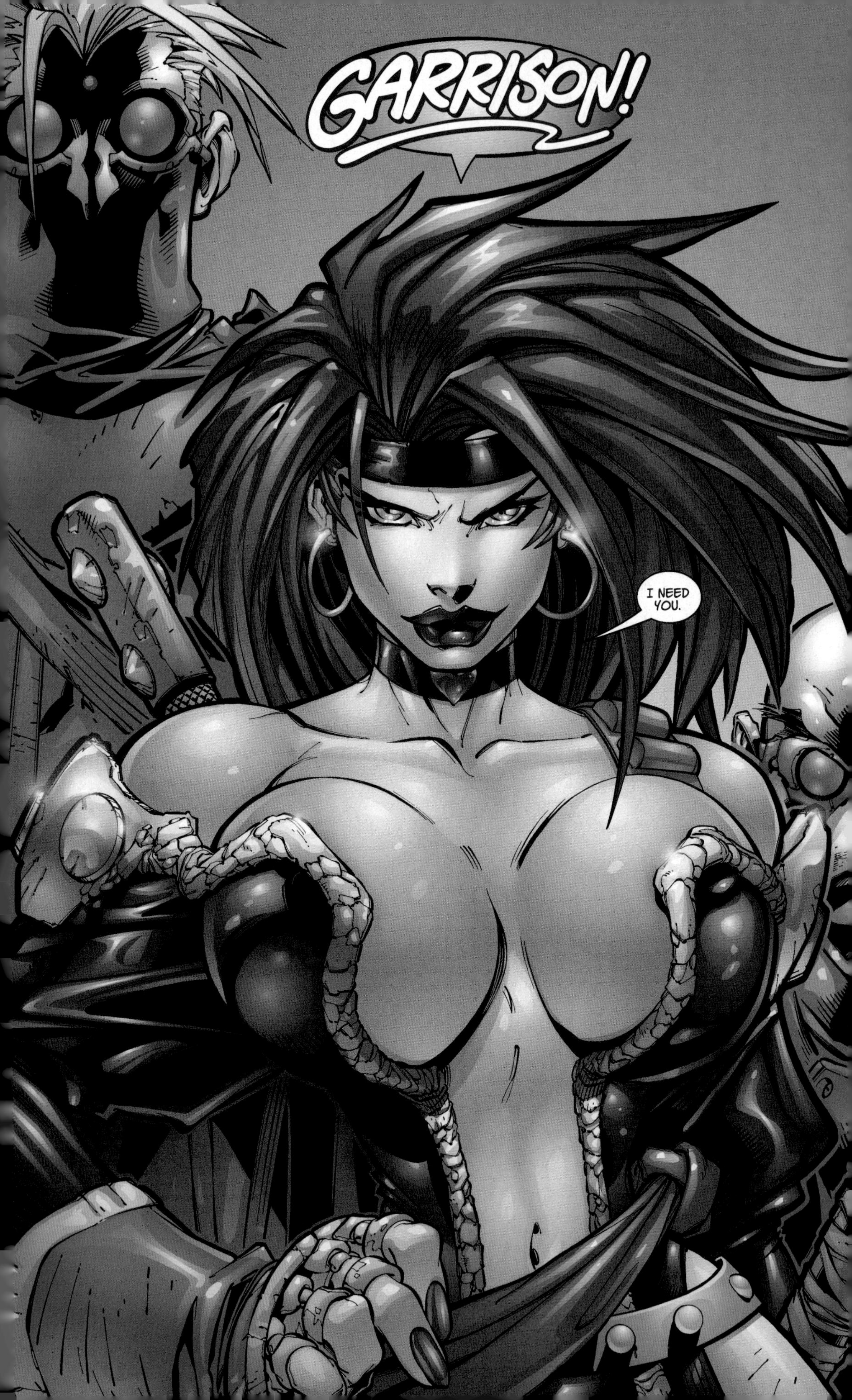
GARRISON!
I NEED YOU.

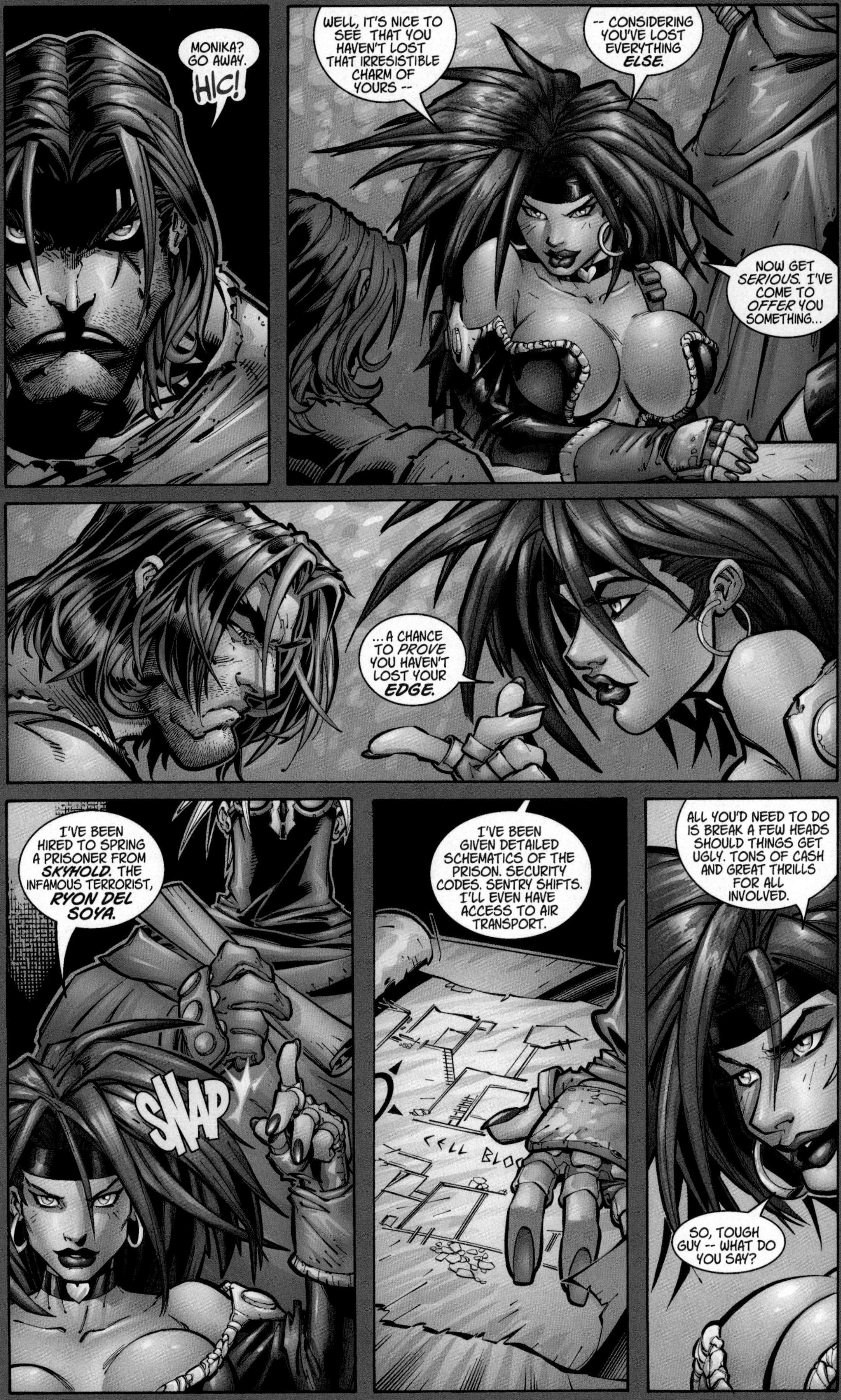
MONIKA? GO AWAY. HIC!
WELL, IT'S NICE TO SEE THAT YOU HAVEN'T LOST THAT IRRESISTIBLE CHARM OF YOURS --
-- CONSIDERING YOU'VE LOST EVERYTHING *ELSE*.
NOW GET *SERIOUS*. I'VE COME TO *OFFER* YOU SOMETHING...
...A CHANCE TO *PROVE* YOU HAVEN'T LOST YOUR *EDGE*.
I'VE BEEN HIRED TO SPRING A PRISONER FROM *SKYHOLD*. THE INFAMOUS TERRORIST, *RYON DEL SOYA*.
SNAP
I'VE BEEN GIVEN DETAILED SCHEMATICS OF THE PRISON. SECURITY CODES. SENTRY SHIFTS. I'LL EVEN HAVE ACCESS TO AIR TRANSPORT.
CELL BLO
ALL YOU'D NEED TO DO IS BREAK A FEW HEADS SHOULD THINGS GET UGLY. TONS OF CASH AND GREAT THRILLS FOR ALL INVOLVED.
SO, TOUGH GUY -- WHAT DO YOU SAY?

SKYHOLD? HAHAHAHA-- I HAVEN'T LAUGHED IN SO LONG, I THOUGHT I'D FORGOTTEN HOW!

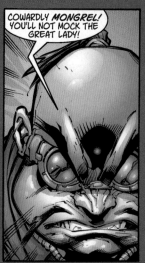

COWARDLY *MONGREL!* YOU'LL NOT MOCK THE GREAT LADY!

STOP.

THERE'S NO POINT IN BUSTIN' UP A DRUNKEN HAS-BEEN.

STICKS AND STONES... *GLUG GLUG*

PATHETIC.

THWAK

IS THIS WHAT YOUR LIFE HAS *BECOME?!*

THEN *END IT!!* GO ON!!

THUNK

DO IT, GARRISON. AND GO TO *HELL.*

...ALREADY THERE.

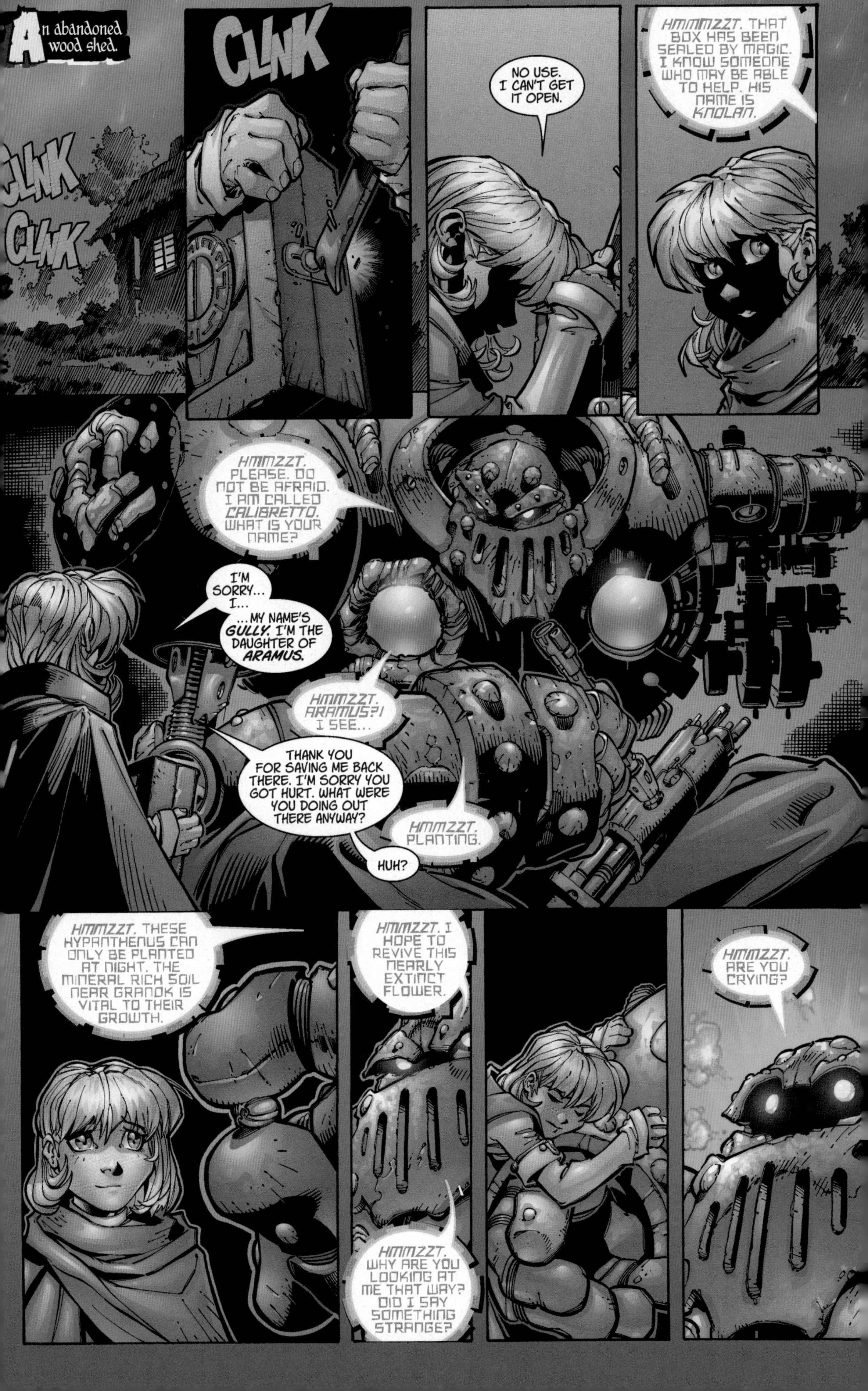
An abandoned wood shed.
CLINK
CLINK
CLINK
NO USE. I CAN'T GET IT OPEN.
HMMMZZT. THAT BOX HAS BEEN SEALED BY MAGIC. I KNOW SOMEONE WHO MAY BE ABLE TO HELP. HIS NAME IS KNOLAN.
HMMZZT. PLEASE. DO NOT BE AFRAID. I AM CALLED CALIBRETTO. WHAT IS YOUR NAME?
I'M SORRY... I... ...MY NAME'S GULLY. I'M THE DAUGHTER OF ARAMUS.
HMMZZT. ARAMUS?! I SEE...
THANK YOU FOR SAVING ME BACK THERE. I'M SORRY YOU GOT HURT. WHAT WERE YOU DOING OUT THERE ANYWAY?
HMMZZT. PLANTING.
HUH?
HMMZZT. THESE HYPANTHENUS CAN ONLY BE PLANTED AT NIGHT. THE MINERAL RICH SOIL NEAR GRANOK IS VITAL TO THEIR GROWTH.
HMMZZT. I HOPE TO REVIVE THIS NEARLY EXTINCT FLOWER.
HMMZZT. WHY ARE YOU LOOKING AT ME THAT WAY? DID I SAY SOMETHING STRANGE?
HMMZZT. ARE YOU CRYING?

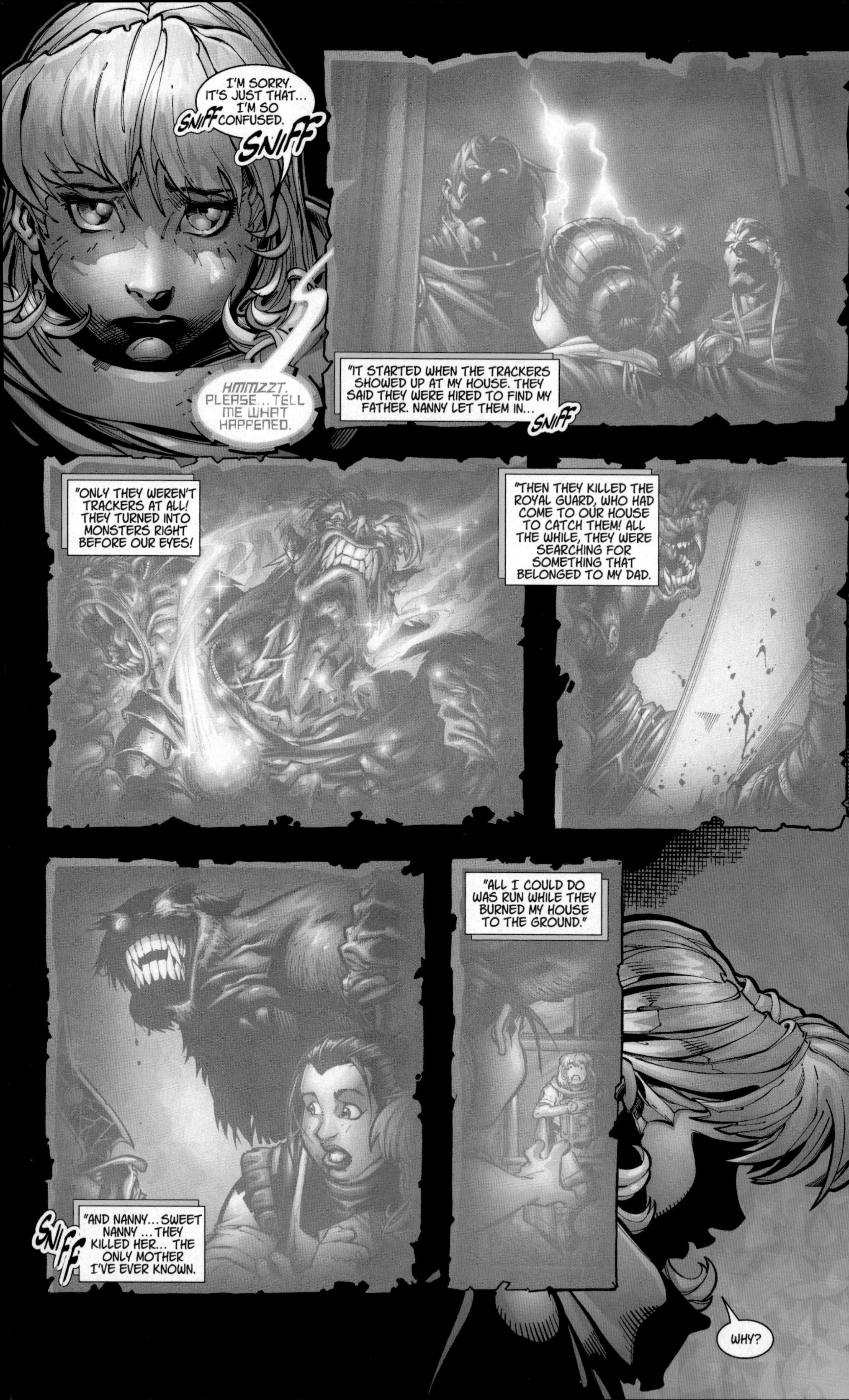
I'M SORRY. IT'S JUST THAT... I'M SO CONFUSED.
SNIFF
SNIFF
HMMZZT. PLEASE... TELL ME WHAT HAPPENED.
"IT STARTED WHEN THE TRACKERS SHOWED UP AT MY HOUSE. THEY SAID THEY WERE HIRED TO FIND MY FATHER. NANNY LET THEM IN...
SNIFF
"ONLY THEY WEREN'T TRACKERS AT ALL! THEY TURNED INTO MONSTERS RIGHT BEFORE OUR EYES!
"THEN THEY KILLED THE ROYAL GUARD, WHO HAD COME TO OUR HOUSE TO CATCH THEM! ALL THE WHILE, THEY WERE SEARCHING FOR SOMETHING THAT BELONGED TO MY DAD.
SNIFF
"AND NANNY... SWEET NANNY... THEY KILLED HER... THE ONLY MOTHER I'VE EVER KNOWN.
"ALL I COULD DO WAS RUN WHILE THEY BURNED MY HOUSE TO THE GROUND."
WHY?

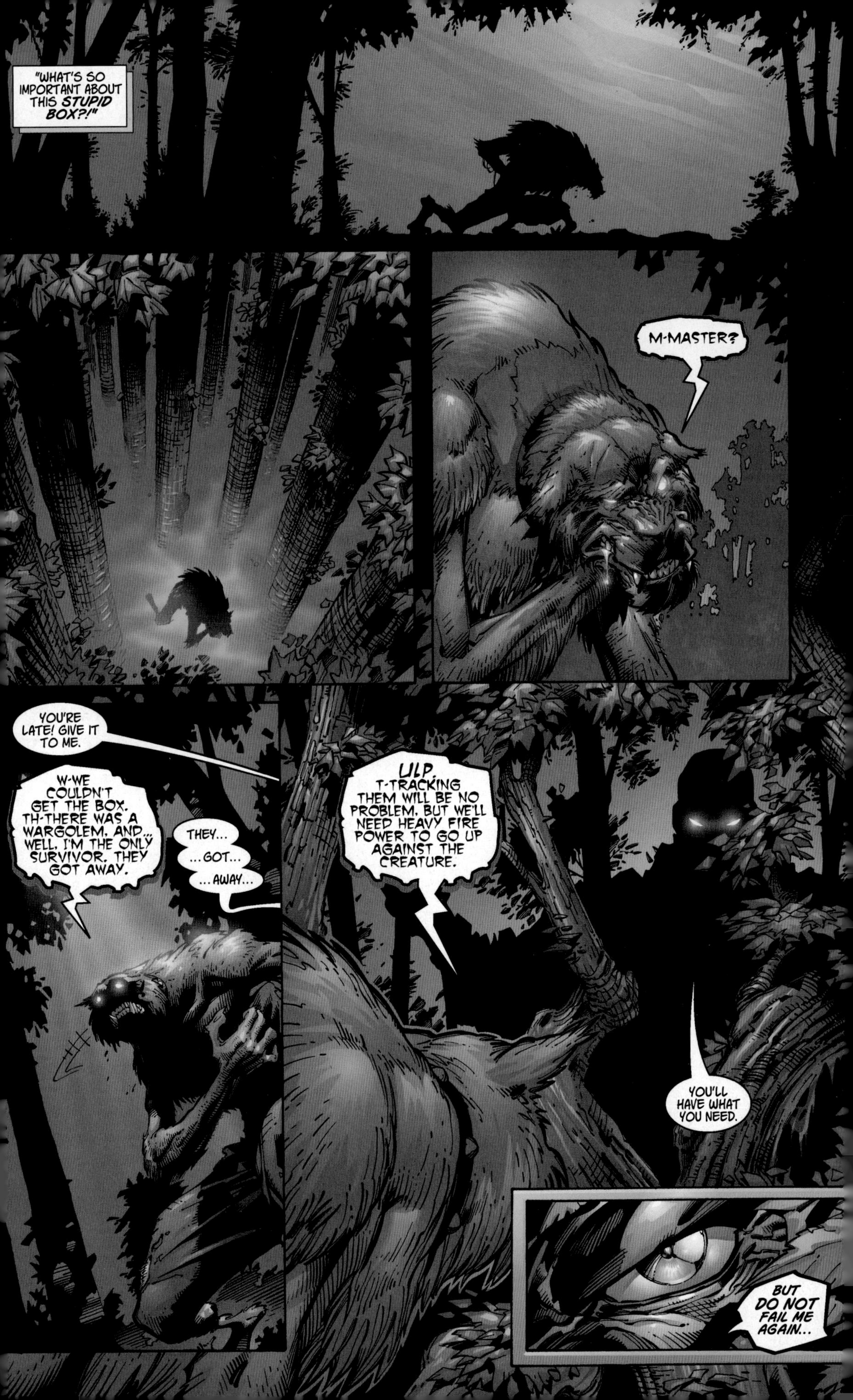
"WHAT'S SO IMPORTANT ABOUT THIS STUPID BOX?!"
M-MASTER?
YOU'RE LATE! GIVE IT TO ME.
W-WE COULDN'T GET THE BOX. TH-THERE WAS A WARGOLEM. AND... WELL, I'M THE ONLY SURVIVOR. THEY GOT AWAY.
THEY...
...GOT...
...AWAY...
ULP.
T-TRACKING THEM WILL BE NO PROBLEM. BUT WE'LL NEED HEAVY FIRE POWER TO GO UP AGAINST THE CREATURE.
YOU'LL HAVE WHAT YOU NEED.
BUT DO NOT FAIL ME AGAIN...

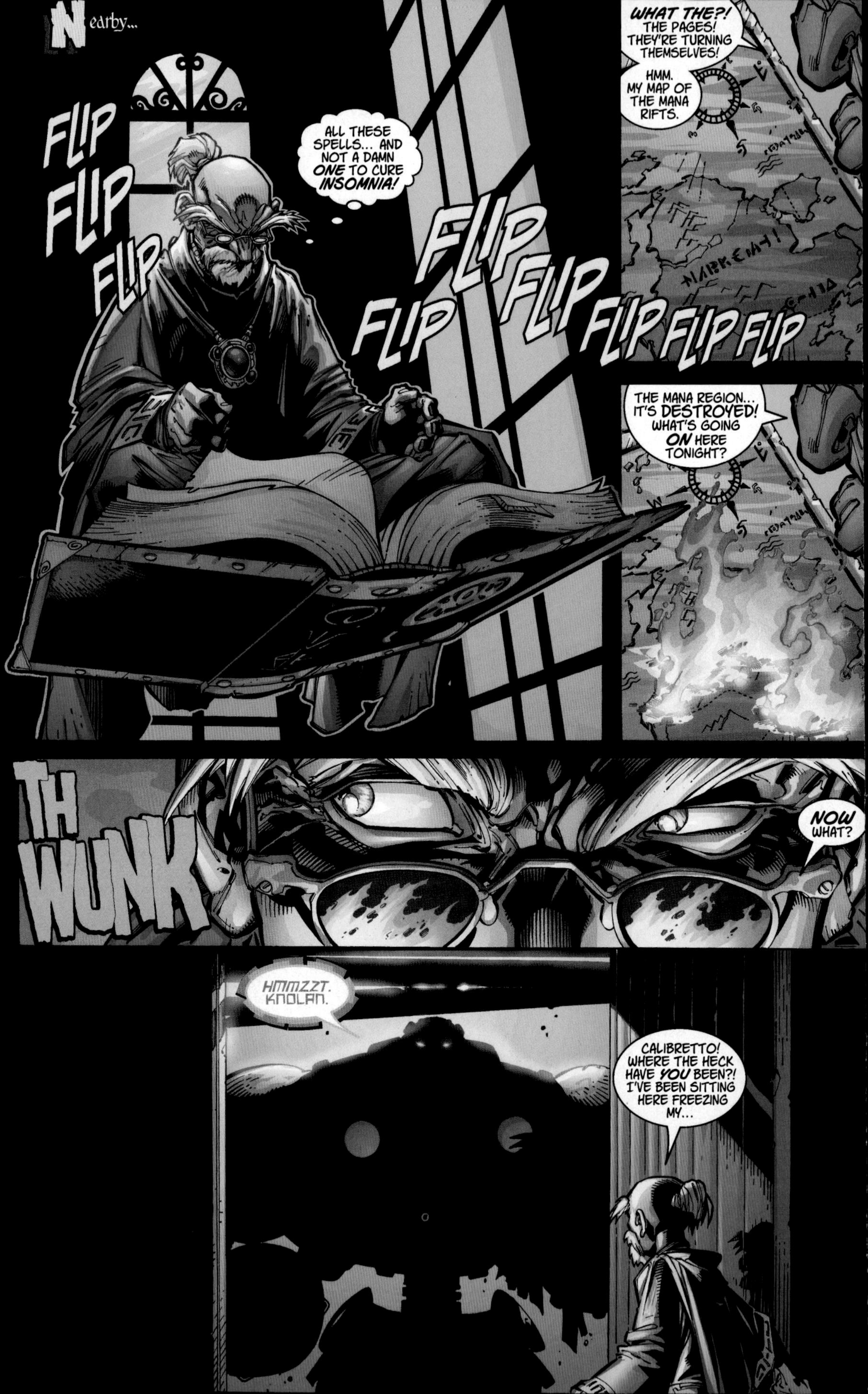
Nearby...
FLIP FLIP FLIP
ALL THESE SPELLS... AND NOT A DAMN ONE TO CURE INSOMNIA!
FLIP FLIP FLIP FLIP FLIP FLIP
WHAT THE?! THE PAGES! THEY'RE TURNING THEMSELVES!
HMM. MY MAP OF THE MANA RIFTS.
THE MANA REGION... IT'S DESTROYED! WHAT'S GOING ON HERE TONIGHT?
TH WUNK
NOW WHAT?
HMMZZT. KNOLAN.
CALIBRETTO! WHERE THE HECK HAVE YOU BEEN?! I'VE BEEN SITTING HERE FREEZING MY...

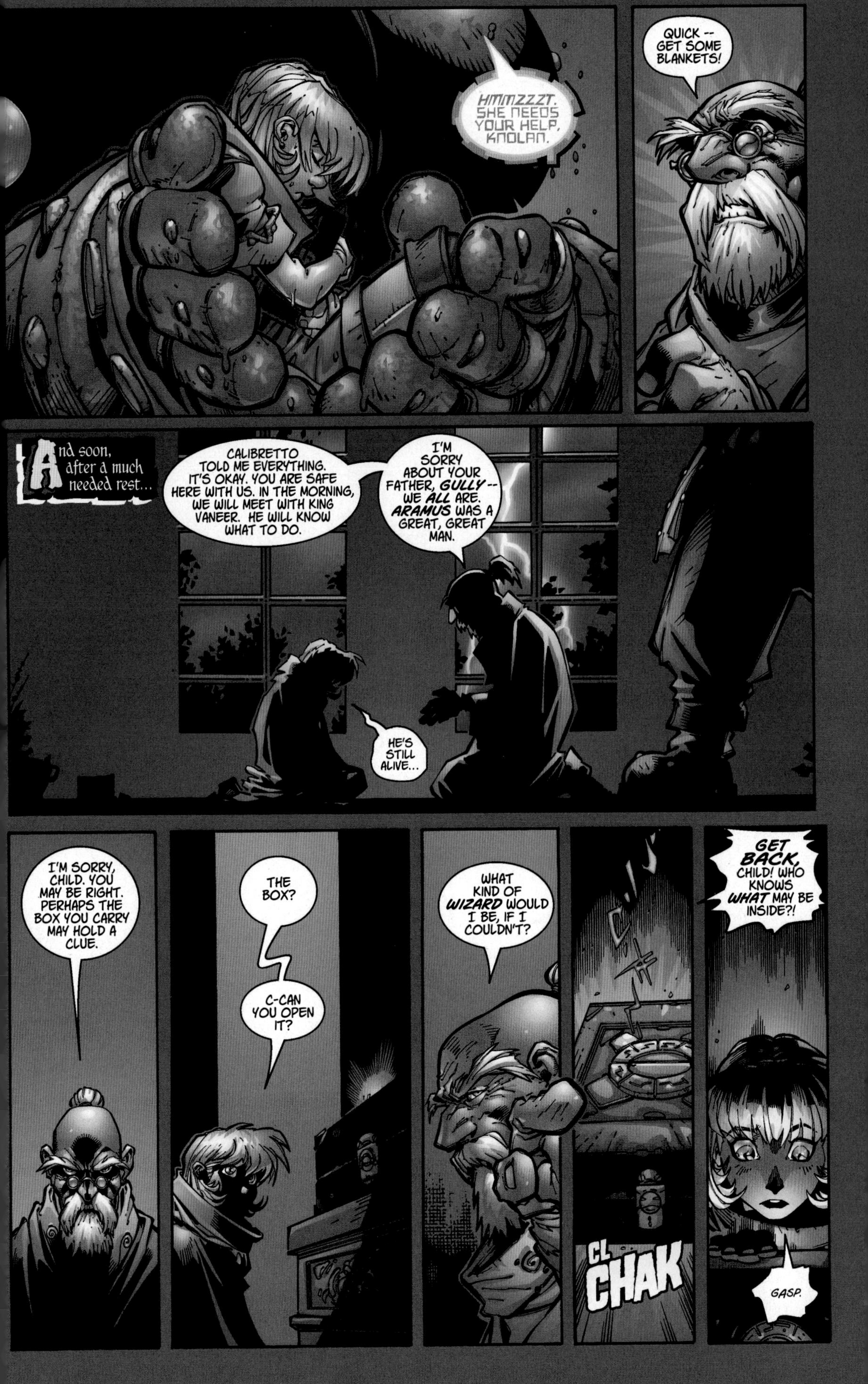
HMMZZZT. SHE NEEDS YOUR HELP, KNOLAN.
QUICK -- GET SOME BLANKETS!
And soon, after a much needed rest...
CALIBRETTO TOLD ME EVERYTHING. IT'S OKAY. YOU ARE SAFE HERE WITH US. IN THE MORNING, WE WILL MEET WITH KING VANEER. HE WILL KNOW WHAT TO DO.
I'M SORRY ABOUT YOUR FATHER, GULLY -- WE ALL ARE. ARAMUS WAS A GREAT, GREAT MAN.
HE'S STILL ALIVE...
I'M SORRY, CHILD. YOU MAY BE RIGHT. PERHAPS THE BOX YOU CARRY MAY HOLD A CLUE.
THE BOX?
C-CAN YOU OPEN IT?
WHAT KIND OF WIZARD WOULD I BE, IF I COULDN'T?
CL CHAK
GET BACK, CHILD! WHO KNOWS WHAT MAY BE INSIDE?!
GASP.

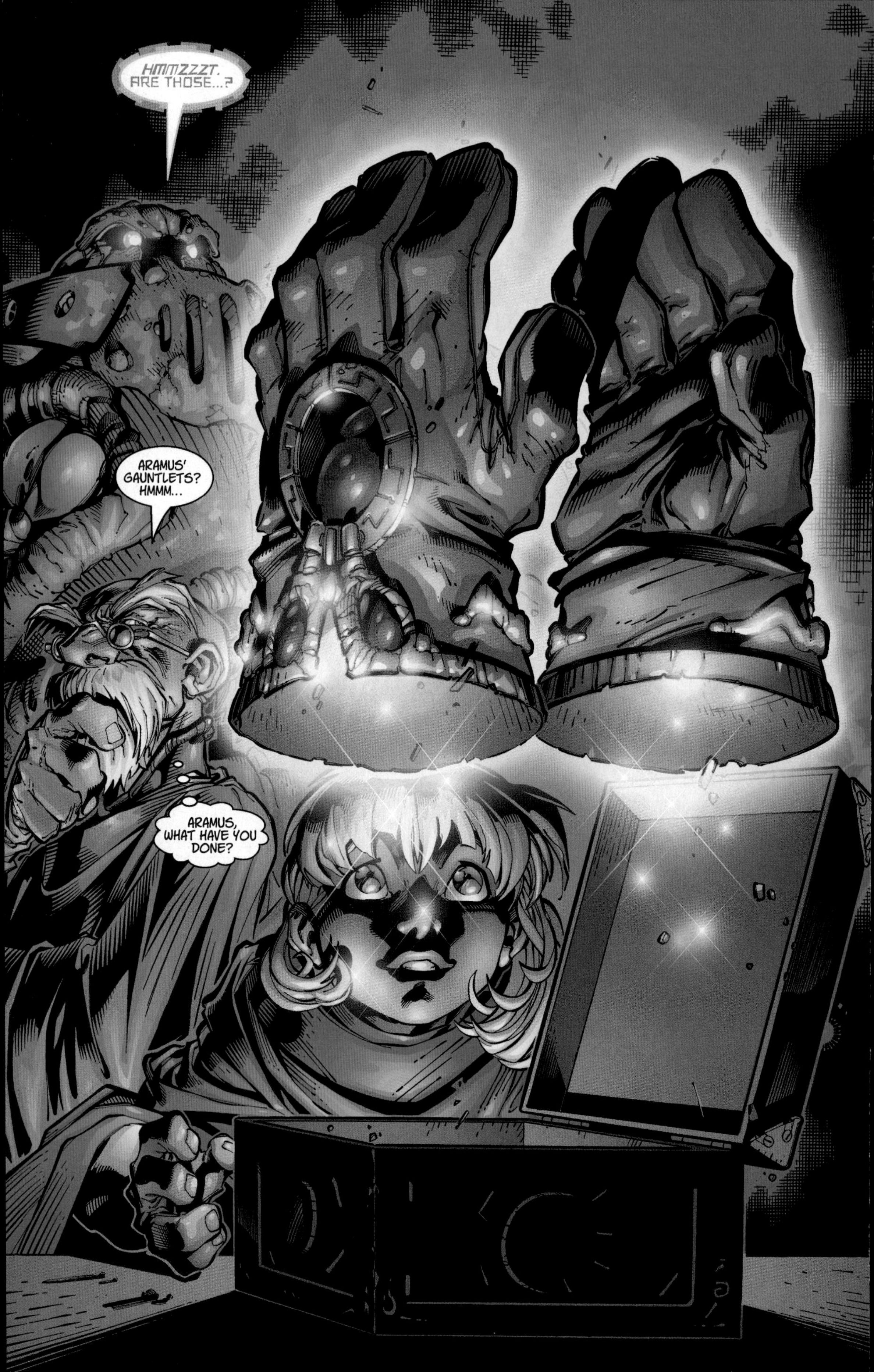
HMMZZZT. ARE THOSE...?
ARAMUS' GAUNTLETS? HMMM...
ARAMUS, WHAT HAVE YOU DONE?

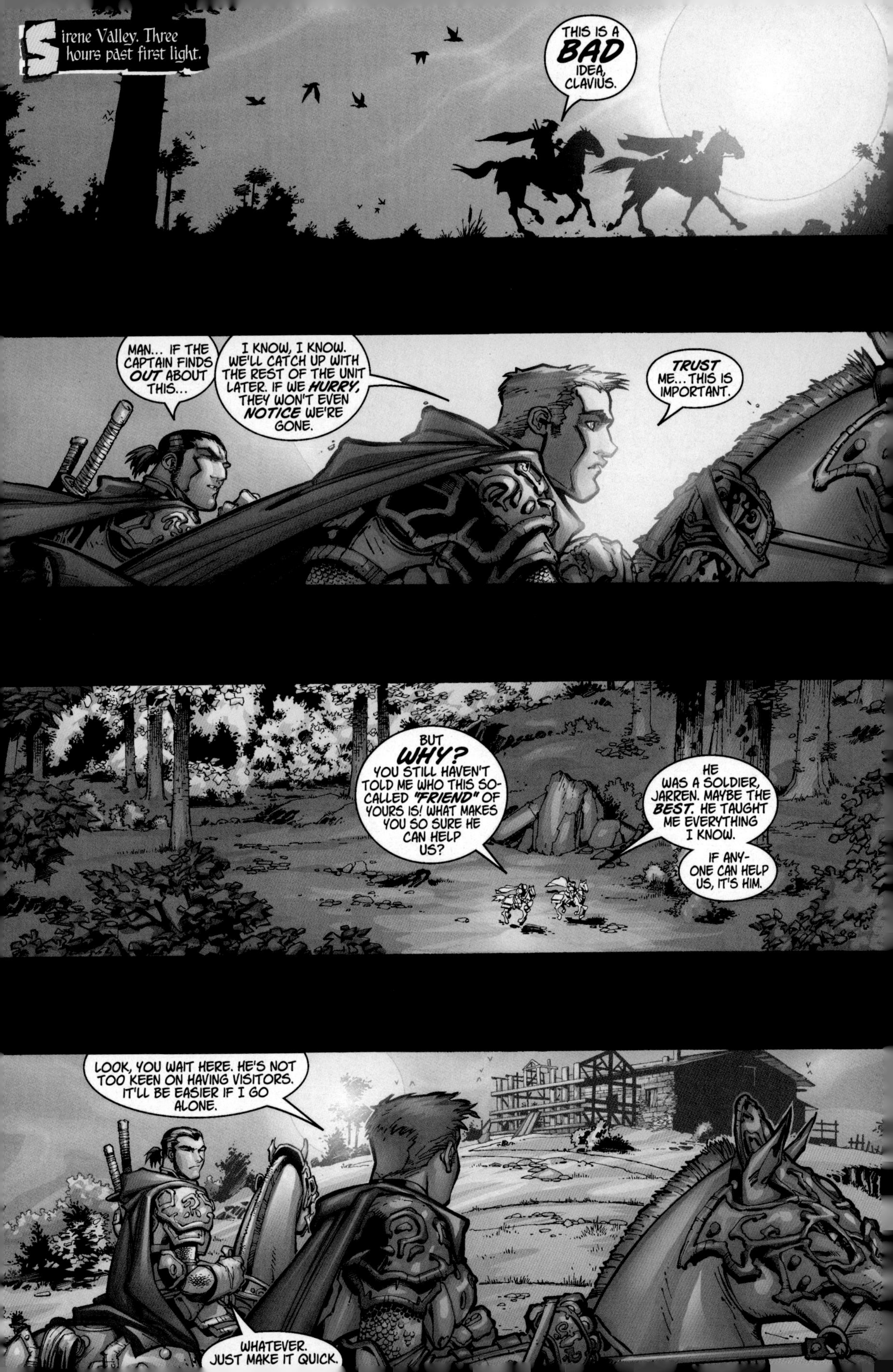
Sirene Valley. Three hours past first light.
THIS IS A BAD IDEA, CLAVIUS.
MAN... IF THE CAPTAIN FINDS OUT ABOUT THIS...
I KNOW, I KNOW. WE'LL CATCH UP WITH THE REST OF THE UNIT LATER. IF WE HURRY, THEY WON'T EVEN NOTICE WE'RE GONE.
TRUST ME... THIS IS IMPORTANT.
BUT WHY? YOU STILL HAVEN'T TOLD ME WHO THIS SO-CALLED "FRIEND" OF YOURS IS! WHAT MAKES YOU SO SURE HE CAN HELP US?
HE WAS A SOLDIER, JARREN. MAYBE THE BEST. HE TAUGHT ME EVERYTHING I KNOW.
IF ANYONE CAN HELP US, IT'S HIM.
LOOK, YOU WAIT HERE. HE'S NOT TOO KEEN ON HAVING VISITORS. IT'LL BE EASIER IF I GO ALONE.
WHATEVER. JUST MAKE IT QUICK.

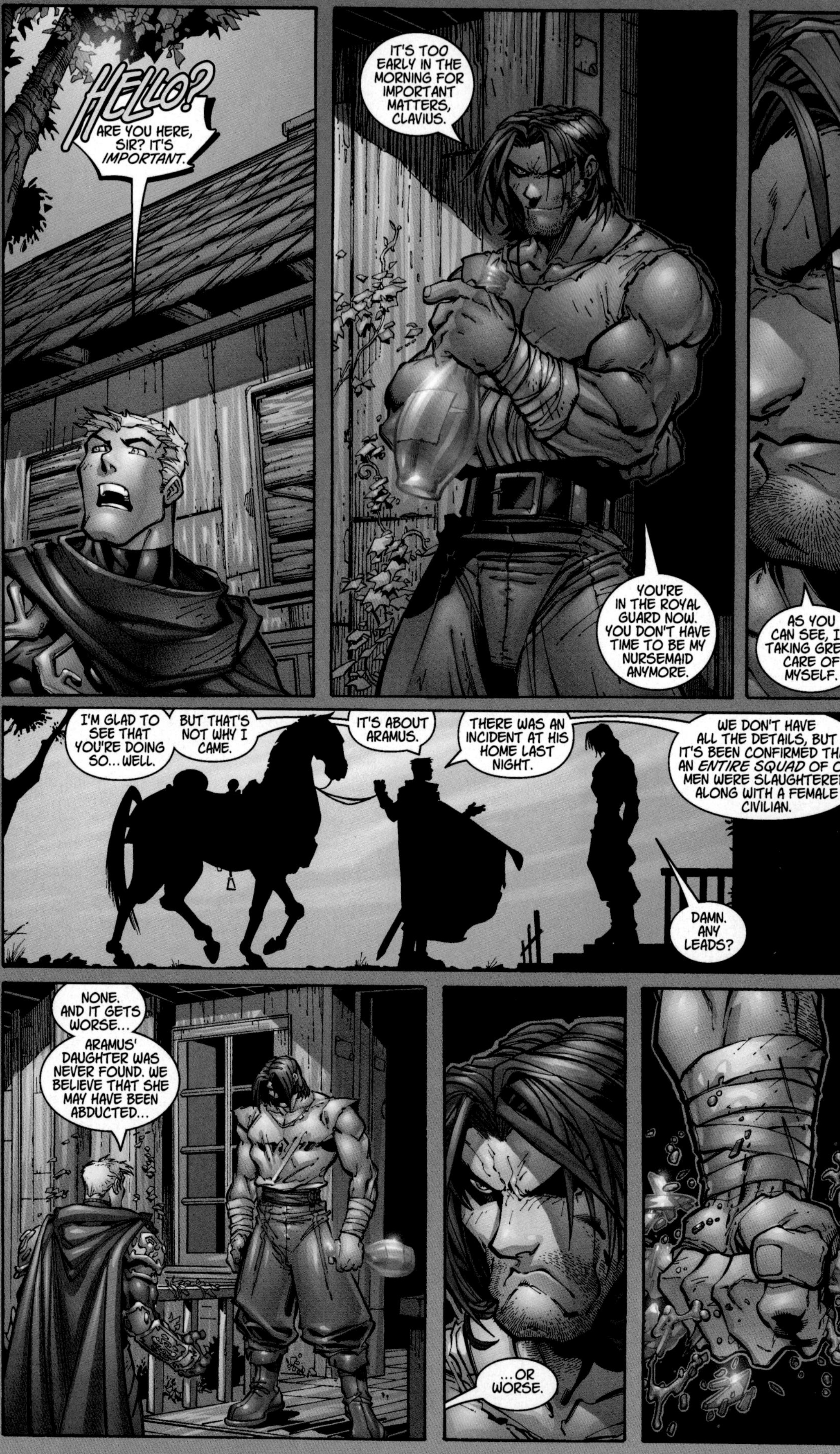
HELLO?
ARE YOU HERE, SIR? IT'S IMPORTANT.
IT'S TOO EARLY IN THE MORNING FOR IMPORTANT MATTERS, CLAVIUS.
YOU'RE IN THE ROYAL GUARD NOW. YOU DON'T HAVE TIME TO BE MY NURSEMAID ANYMORE.
AS YOU CAN SEE, I'M TAKING GREAT CARE OF MYSELF.
I'M GLAD TO SEE THAT YOU'RE DOING SO... WELL.
BUT THAT'S NOT WHY I CAME.
IT'S ABOUT ARAMUS.
THERE WAS AN INCIDENT AT HIS HOME LAST NIGHT.
WE DON'T HAVE ALL THE DETAILS, BUT IT'S BEEN CONFIRMED THAT AN ENTIRE SQUAD OF OUR MEN WERE SLAUGHTERED, ALONG WITH A FEMALE CIVILIAN.
DAMN. ANY LEADS?
NONE. AND IT GETS WORSE...
ARAMUS' DAUGHTER WAS NEVER FOUND. WE BELIEVE THAT SHE MAY HAVE BEEN ABDUCTED...
...OR WORSE.

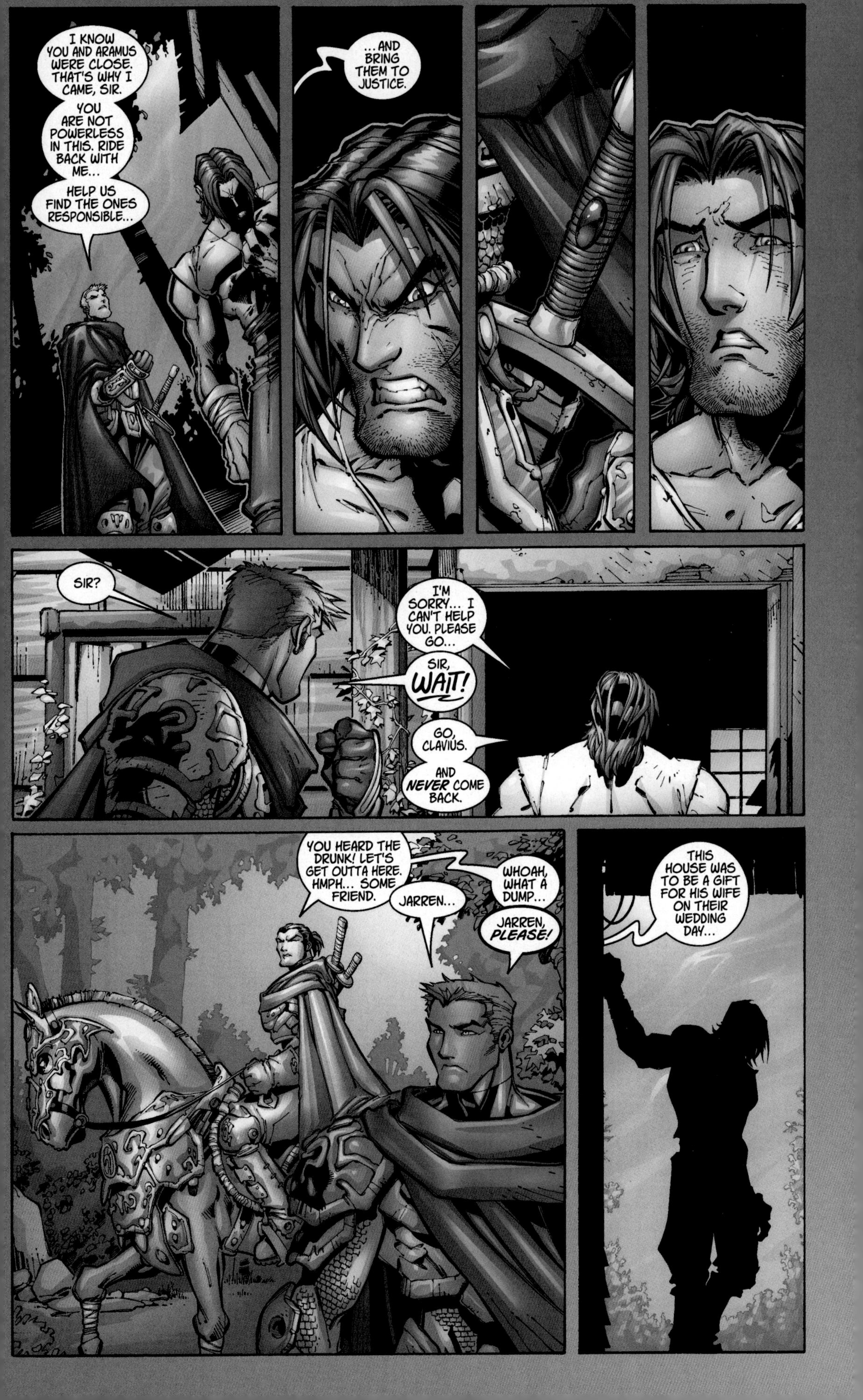
I KNOW YOU AND ARAMUS WERE CLOSE. THAT'S WHY I CAME, SIR.
YOU ARE NOT POWERLESS IN THIS. RIDE BACK WITH ME...
HELP US FIND THE ONES RESPONSIBLE...
...AND BRING THEM TO JUSTICE.
SIR?
I'M SORRY... I CAN'T HELP YOU. PLEASE GO...
SIR, WAIT!
GO, CLAVIUS.
AND NEVER COME BACK.
YOU HEARD THE DRUNK! LET'S GET OUTTA HERE. HMPH... SOME FRIEND.
JARREN...
WHOAH, WHAT A DUMP...
JARREN, PLEASE!
THIS HOUSE WAS TO BE A GIFT FOR HIS WIFE ON THEIR WEDDING DAY...

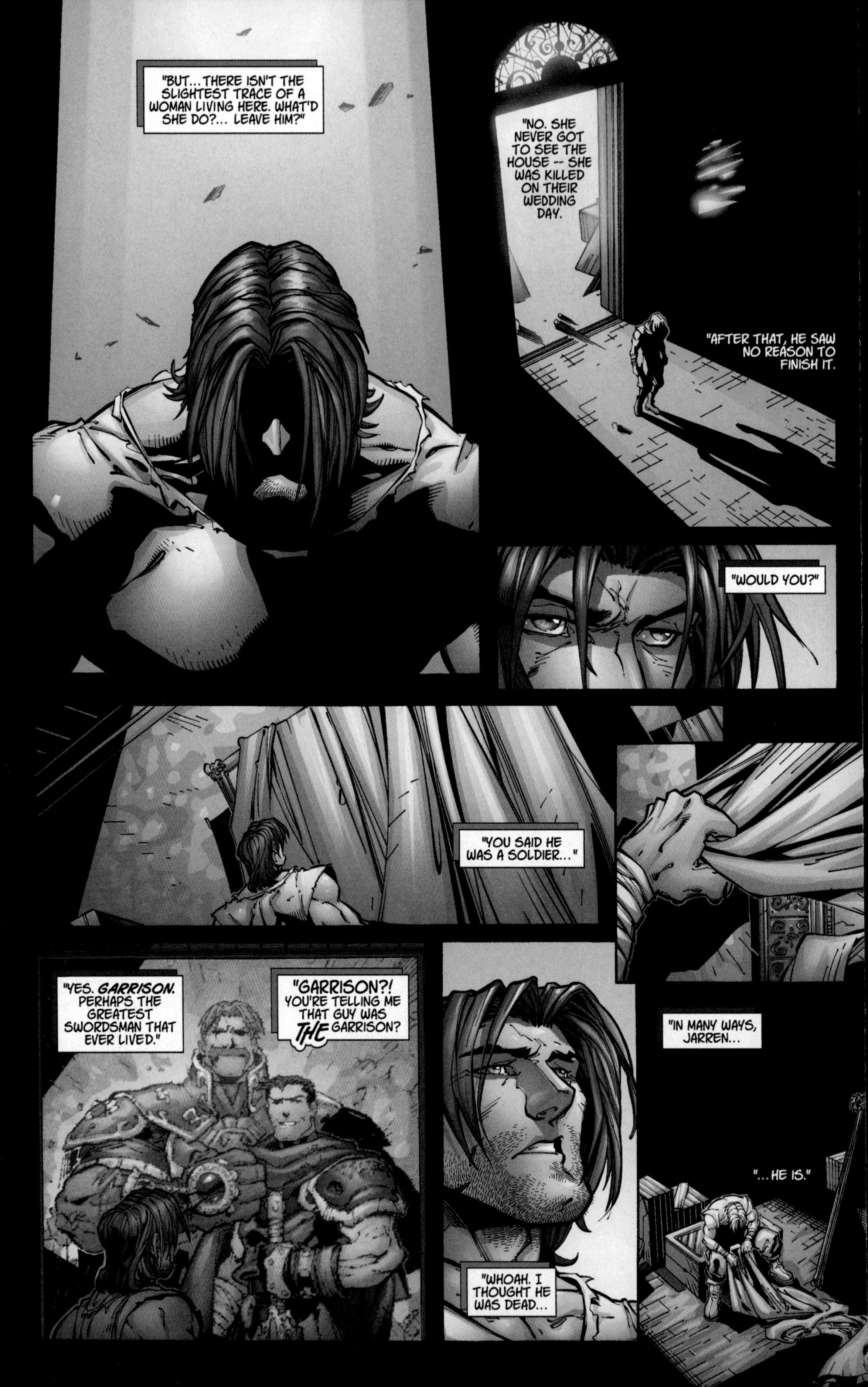
"BUT... THERE ISN'T THE SLIGHTEST TRACE OF A WOMAN LIVING HERE. WHAT'D SHE DO?... LEAVE HIM?"
"NO. SHE NEVER GOT TO SEE THE HOUSE -- SHE WAS KILLED ON THEIR WEDDING DAY.
"AFTER THAT, HE SAW NO REASON TO FINISH IT.
"WOULD YOU?"
"YOU SAID HE WAS A SOLDIER..."
"YES. GARRISON. PERHAPS THE GREATEST SWORDSMAN THAT EVER LIVED."
"GARRISON?! YOU'RE TELLING ME THAT GUY WAS THE GARRISON?
"WHOAH. I THOUGHT HE WAS DEAD...
"IN MANY WAYS, JARREN...
"...HE IS."

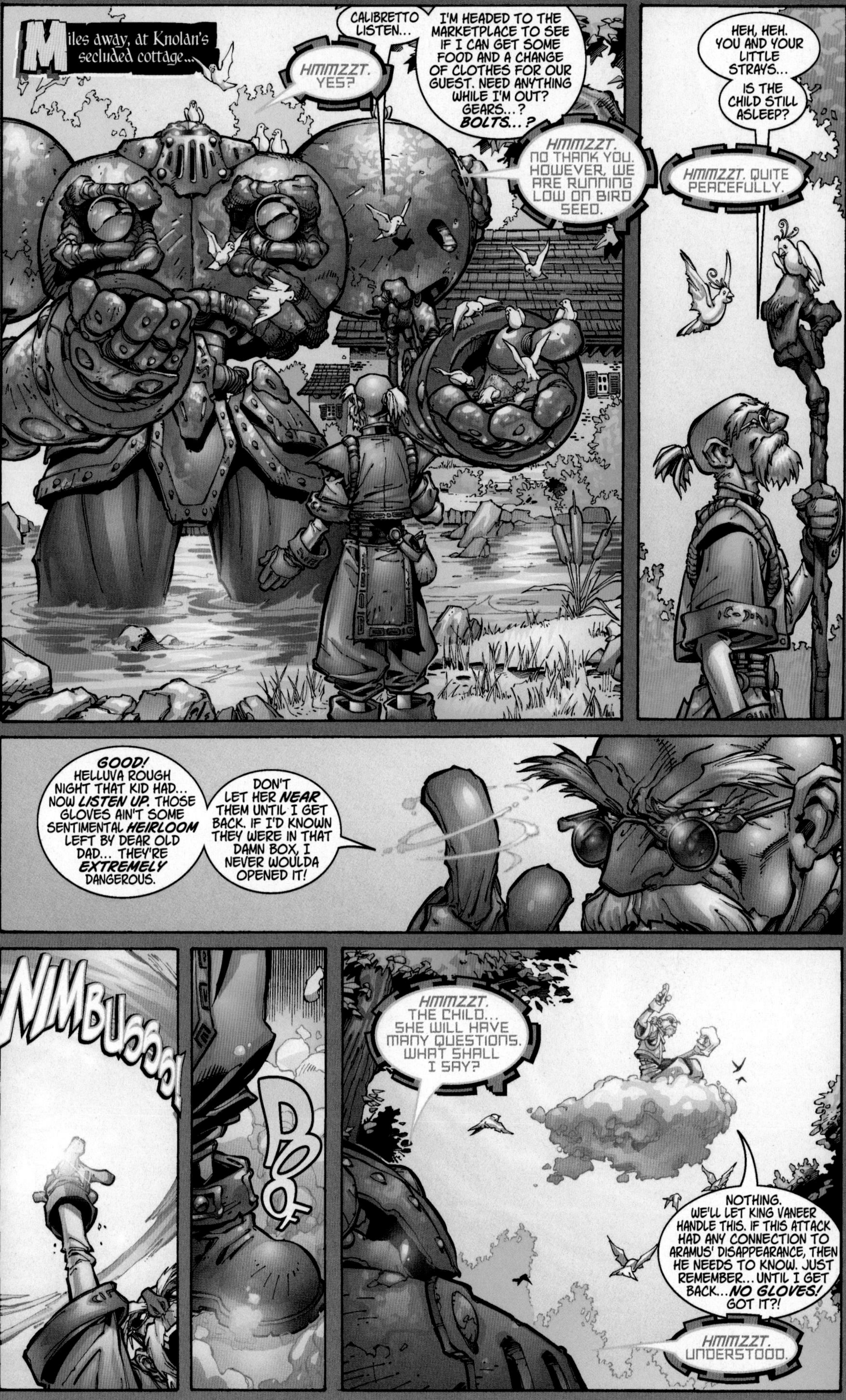

Miles away, at Knolan's secluded cottage...
CALIBRETTO LISTEN...
HMMZZT. YES?
I'M HEADED TO THE MARKETPLACE TO SEE IF I CAN GET SOME FOOD AND A CHANGE OF CLOTHES FOR OUR GUEST. NEED ANYTHING WHILE I'M OUT? GEARS...? BOLTS...?
HMMZZT. NO THANK YOU. HOWEVER, WE ARE RUNNING LOW ON BIRD SEED.
HEH, HEH. YOU AND YOUR LITTLE STRAYS...
IS THE CHILD STILL ASLEEP?
HMMZZT. QUITE PEACEFULLY.
GOOD! HELLUVA ROUGH NIGHT THAT KID HAD... NOW LISTEN UP. THOSE GLOVES AIN'T SOME SENTIMENTAL HEIRLOOM LEFT BY DEAR OLD DAD... THEY'RE EXTREMELY DANGEROUS.
DON'T LET HER NEAR THEM UNTIL I GET BACK. IF I'D KNOWN THEY WERE IN THAT DAMN BOX, I NEVER WOULDA OPENED IT!
NIMBUSSS!
BOOF
HMMZZT. THE CHILD... SHE WILL HAVE MANY QUESTIONS. WHAT SHALL I SAY?
NOTHING. WE'LL LET KING VANEER HANDLE THIS. IF THIS ATTACK HAD ANY CONNECTION TO ARAMUS' DISAPPEARANCE, THEN HE NEEDS TO KNOW. JUST REMEMBER... UNTIL I GET BACK... NO GLOVES! GOT IT?!
HMMZZT. UNDERSTOOD.

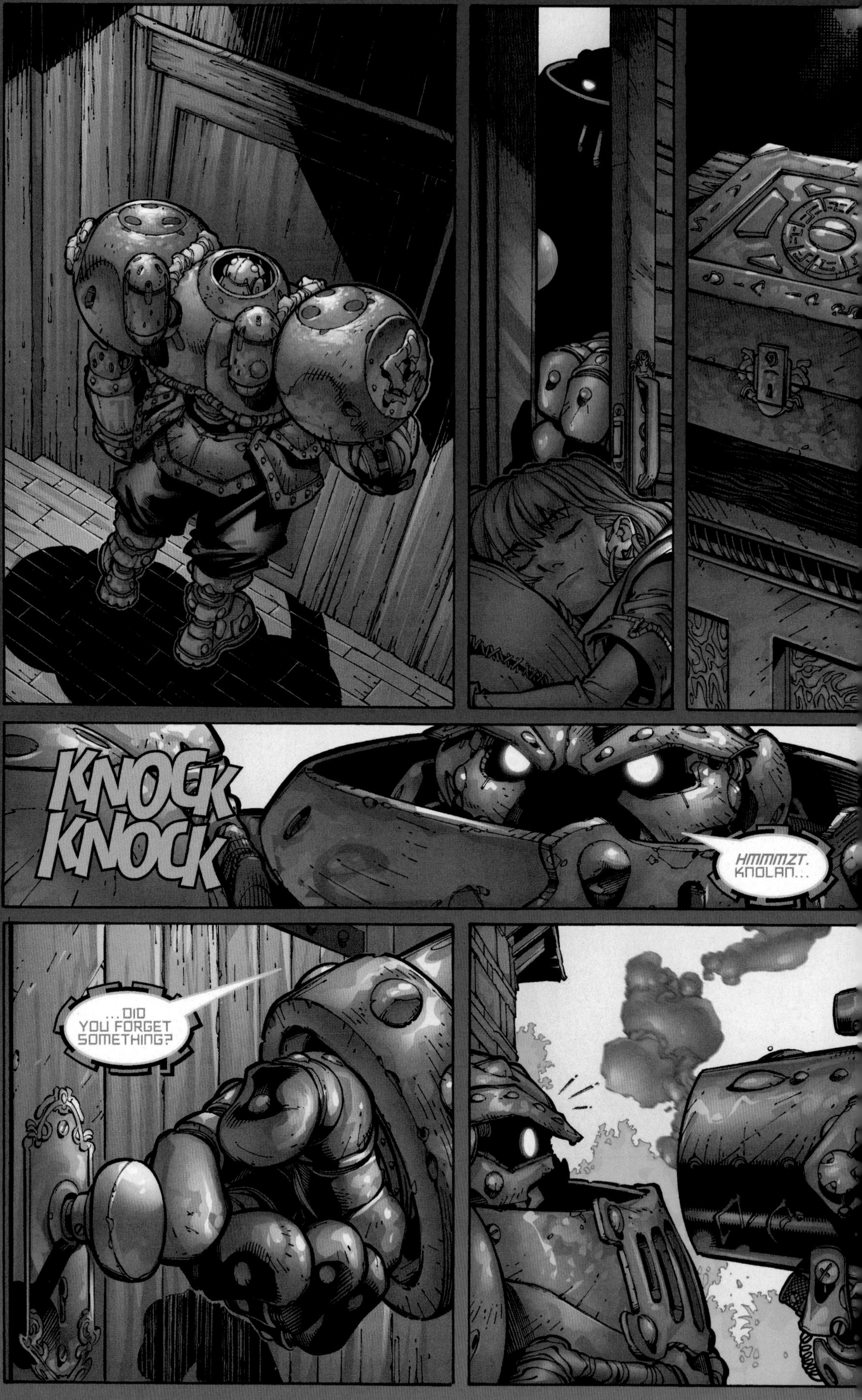
KNOCK KNOCK
HMMMZT. KNOLAN...
...DID YOU FORGET SOMETHING?

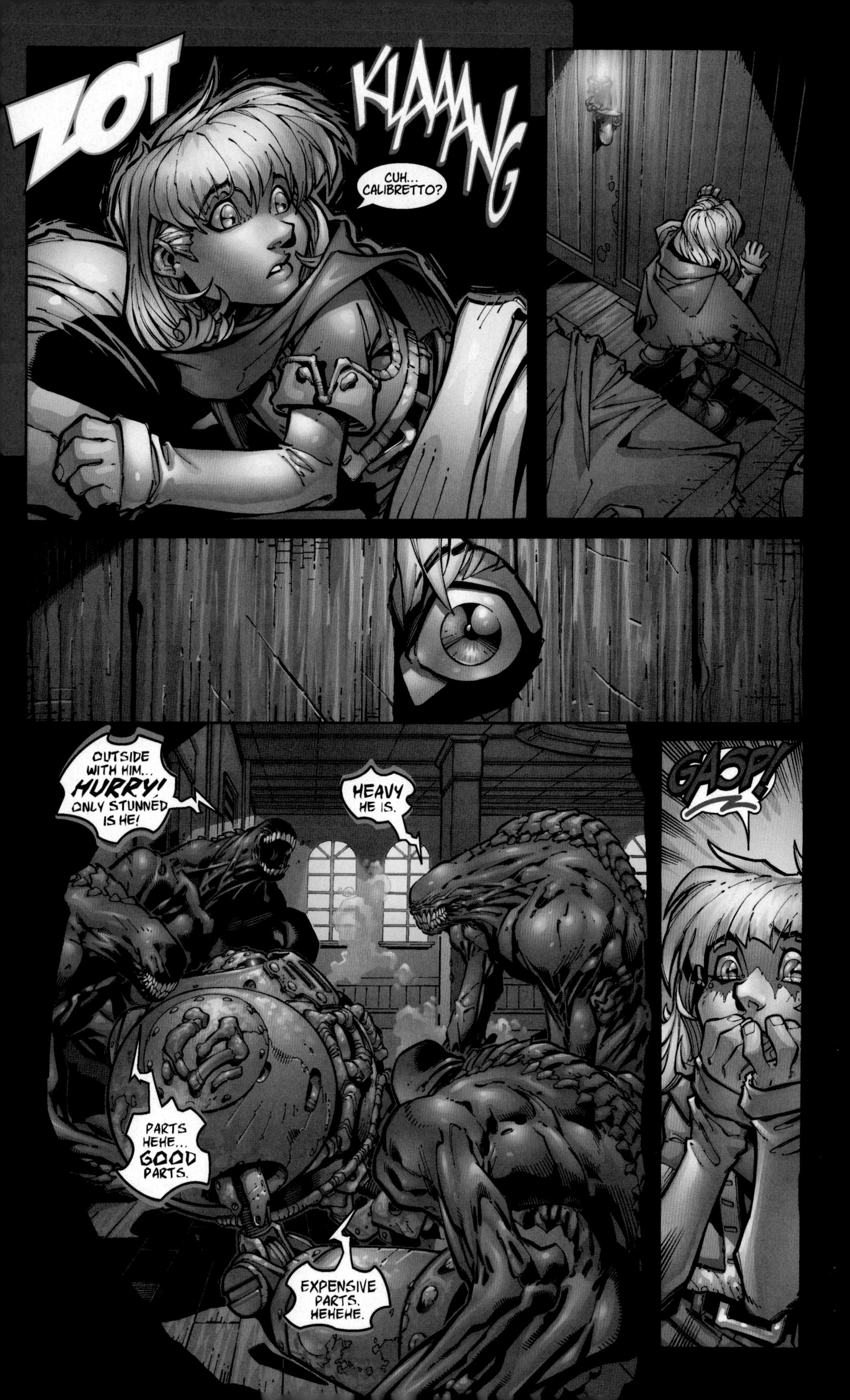
ZOT
KLAAAANG
CUH... CALIBRETTO?
OUTSIDE WITH HIM... HURRY! ONLY STUNNED IS HE!
HEAVY HE IS.
PARTS HEHE... GOOD PARTS.
EXPENSIVE PARTS. HEHEHE.
GASP!

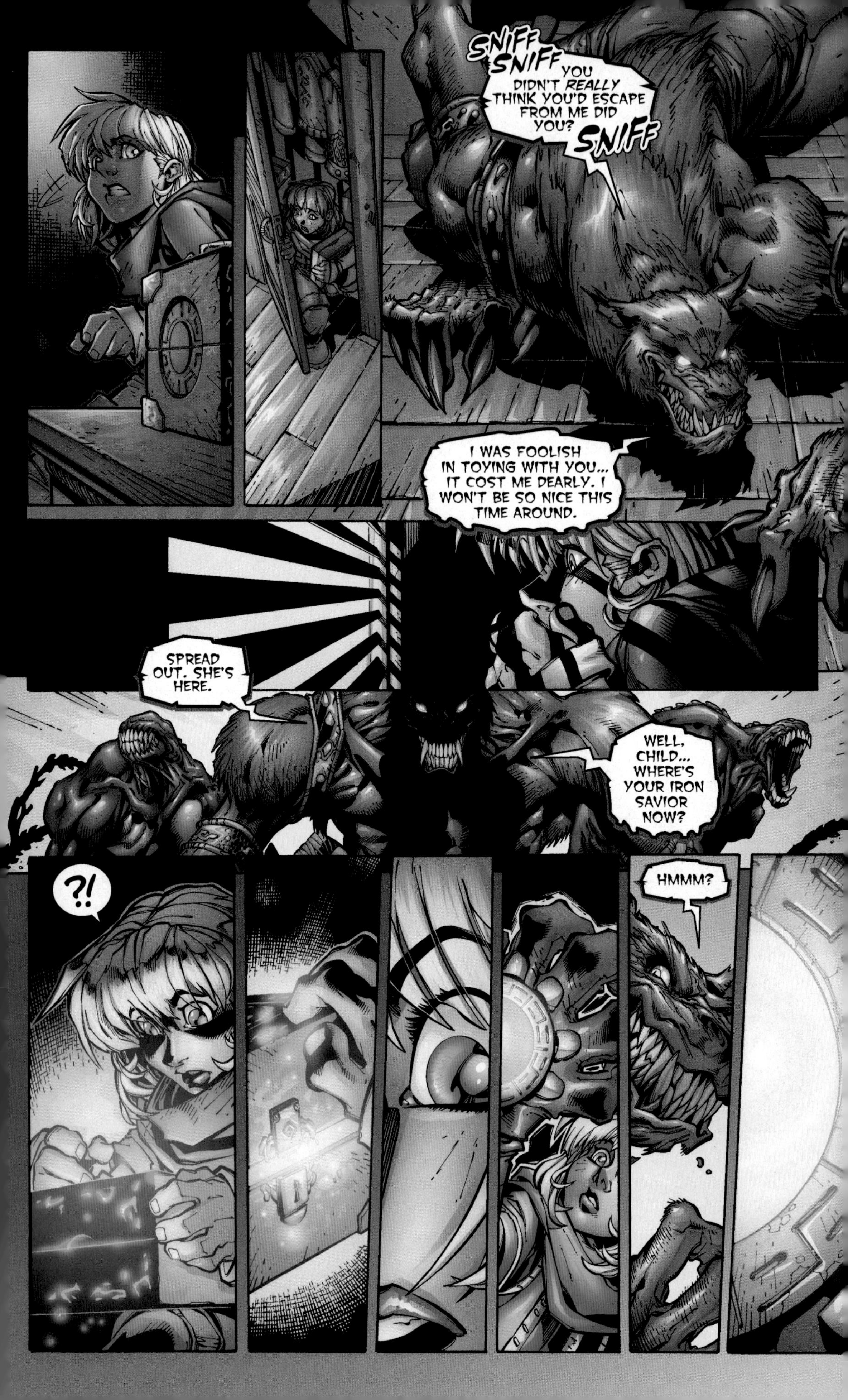
SNIFF SNIFF
YOU DIDN'T REALLY THINK YOU'D ESCAPE FROM ME DID YOU?
SNIFF
I WAS FOOLISH IN TOYING WITH YOU... IT COST ME DEARLY. I WON'T BE SO NICE THIS TIME AROUND.
SPREAD OUT. SHE'S HERE.
WELL, CHILD... WHERE'S YOUR IRON SAVIOR NOW?
?!
HMMM?

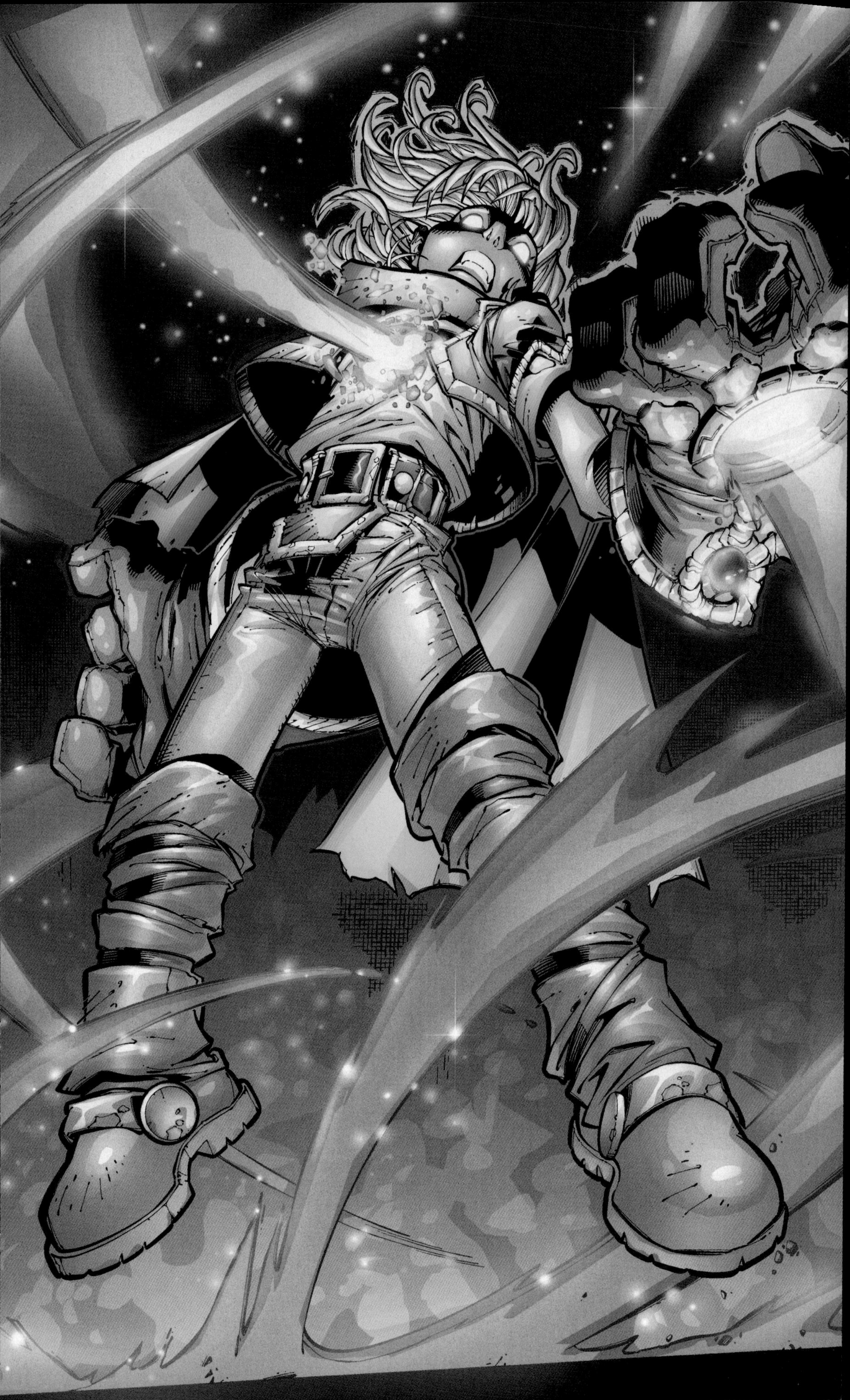

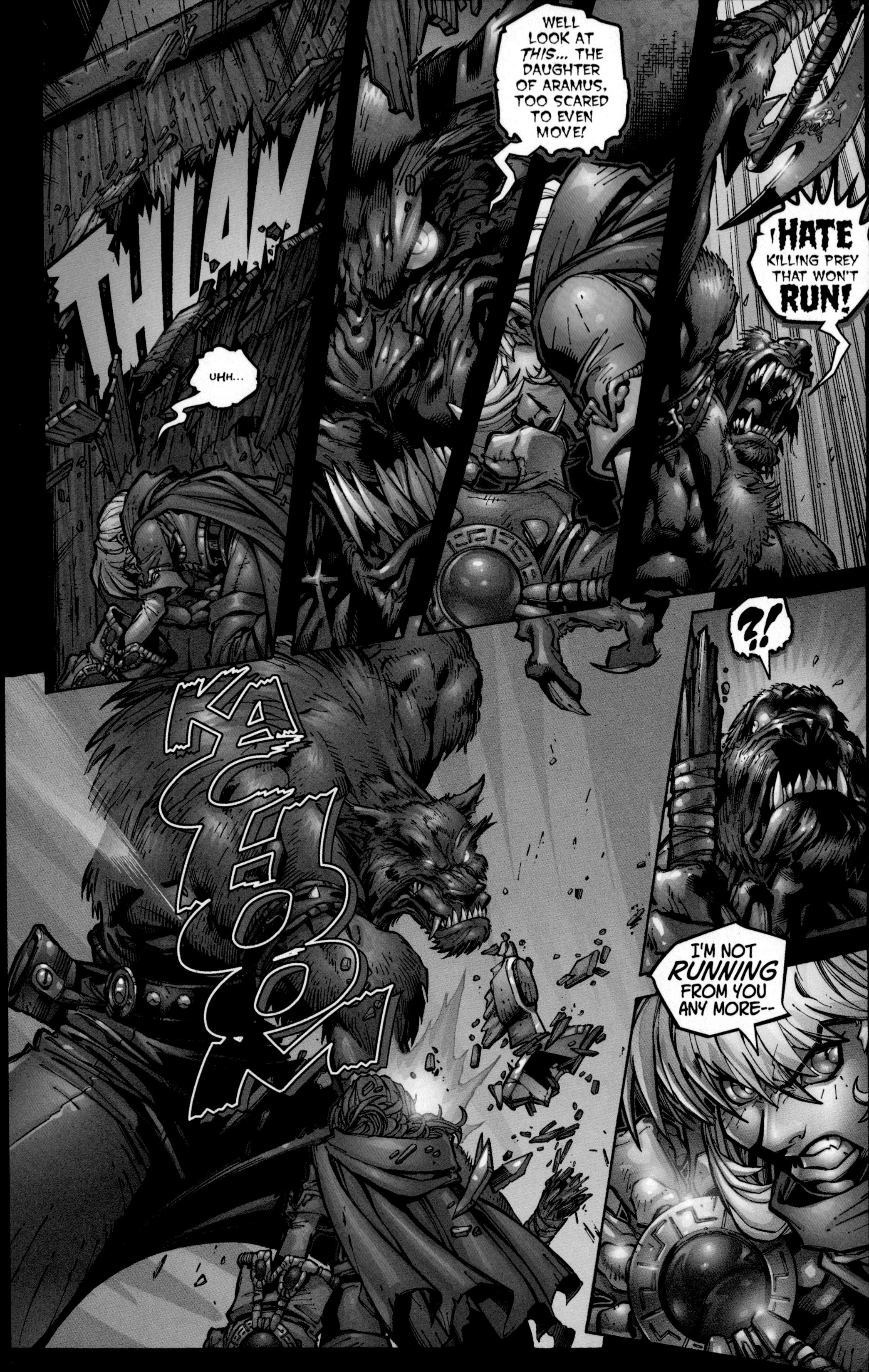
THAM
WELL LOOK AT THIS... THE DAUGHTER OF ARAMUS, TOO SCARED TO EVEN MOVE!
UHH...
'HATE KILLING PREY THAT WON'T RUN!
KA-CHOOM
?!
I'M NOT RUNNING FROM YOU ANY MORE--

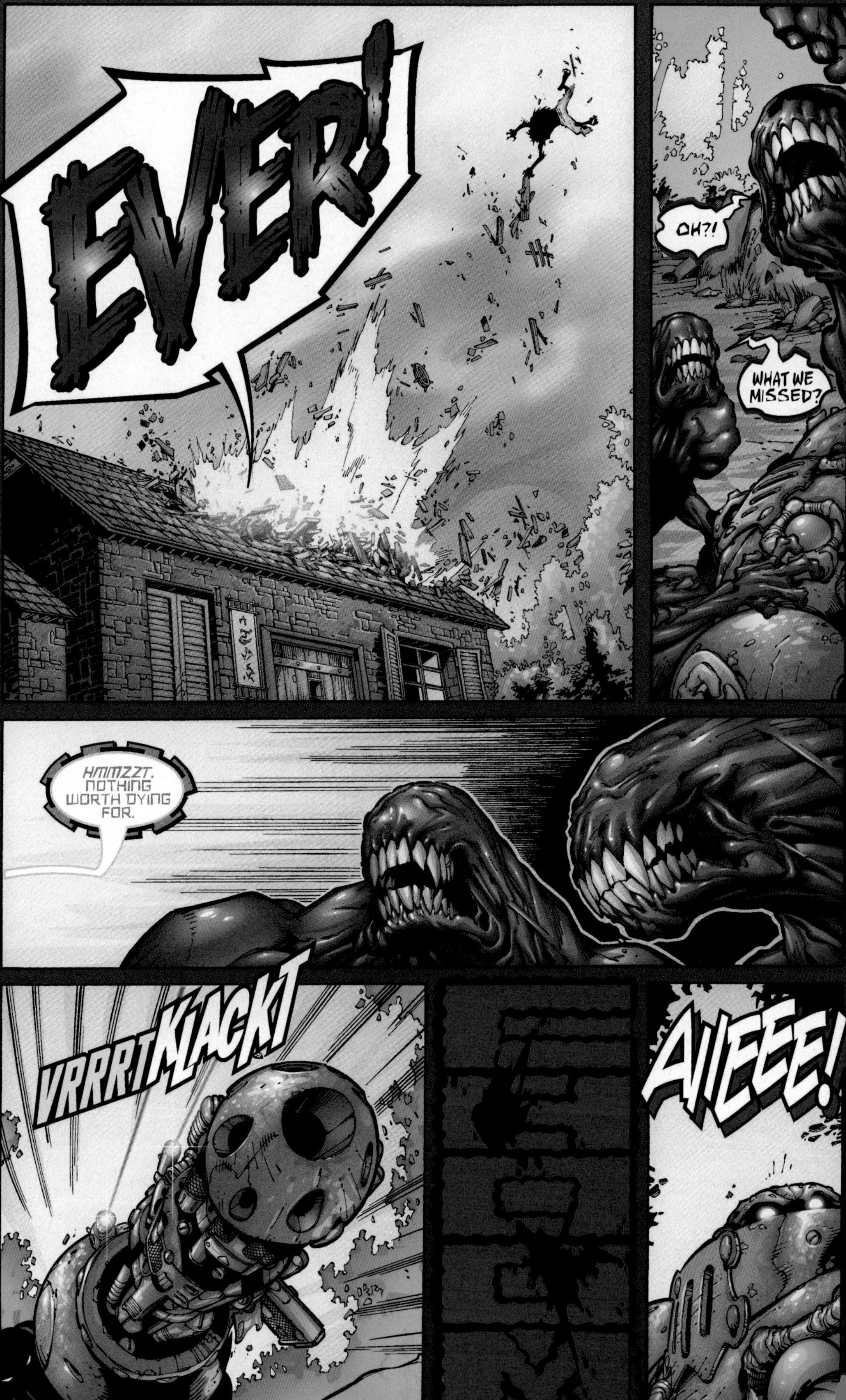
EVER!
OH?!
WHAT WE MISSED?
HMMZZT. NOTHING WORTH DYING FOR.
VRRRTKLACKT
AIEEE!

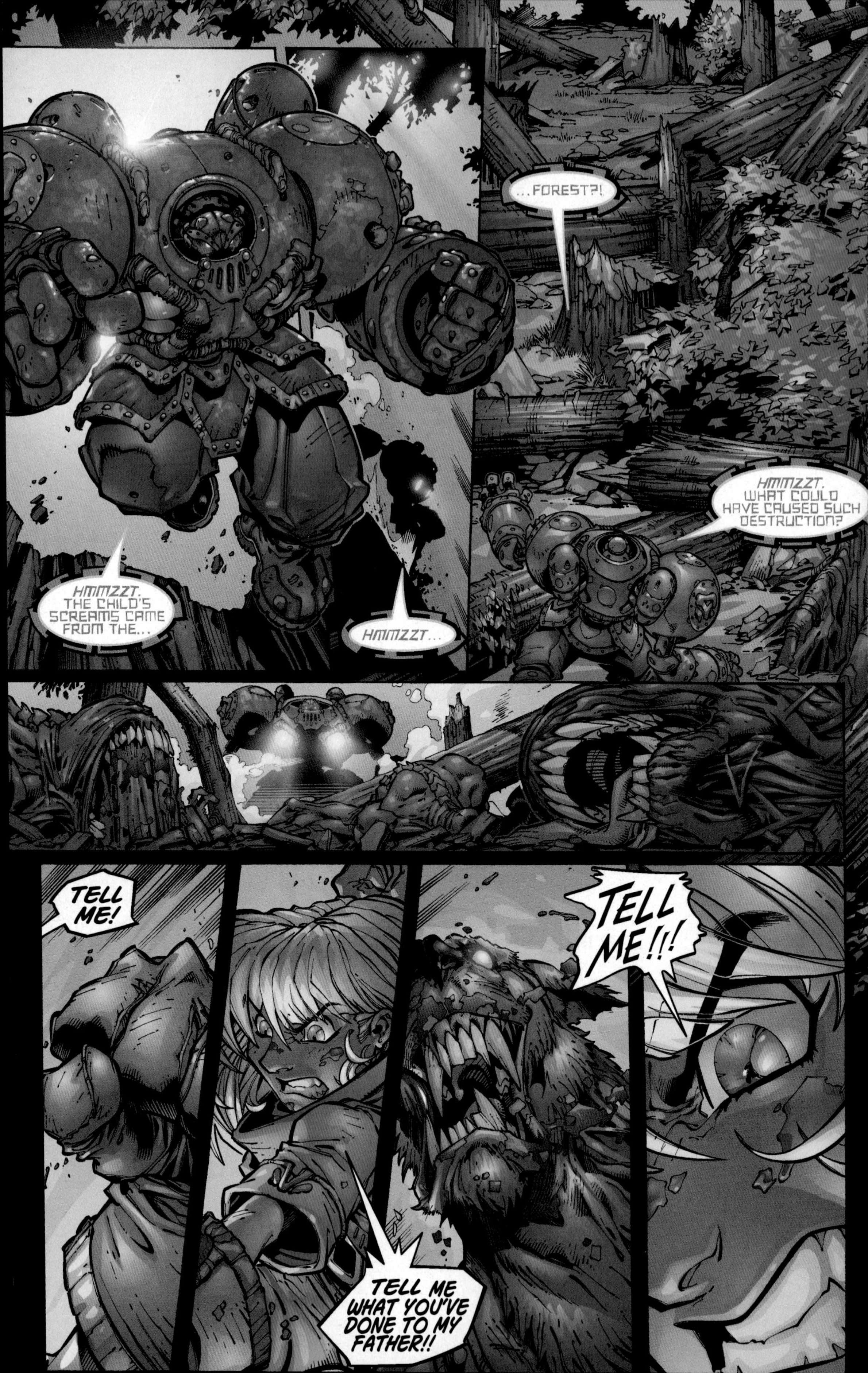
HMMZZT. THE CHILD'S SCREAMS CAME FROM THE...
HMMZZT...
...FOREST?!
HMMZZT. WHAT COULD HAVE CAUSED SUCH DESTRUCTION?
TELL ME!
TELL ME WHAT YOU'VE DONE TO MY FATHER!!
TELL ME!!!

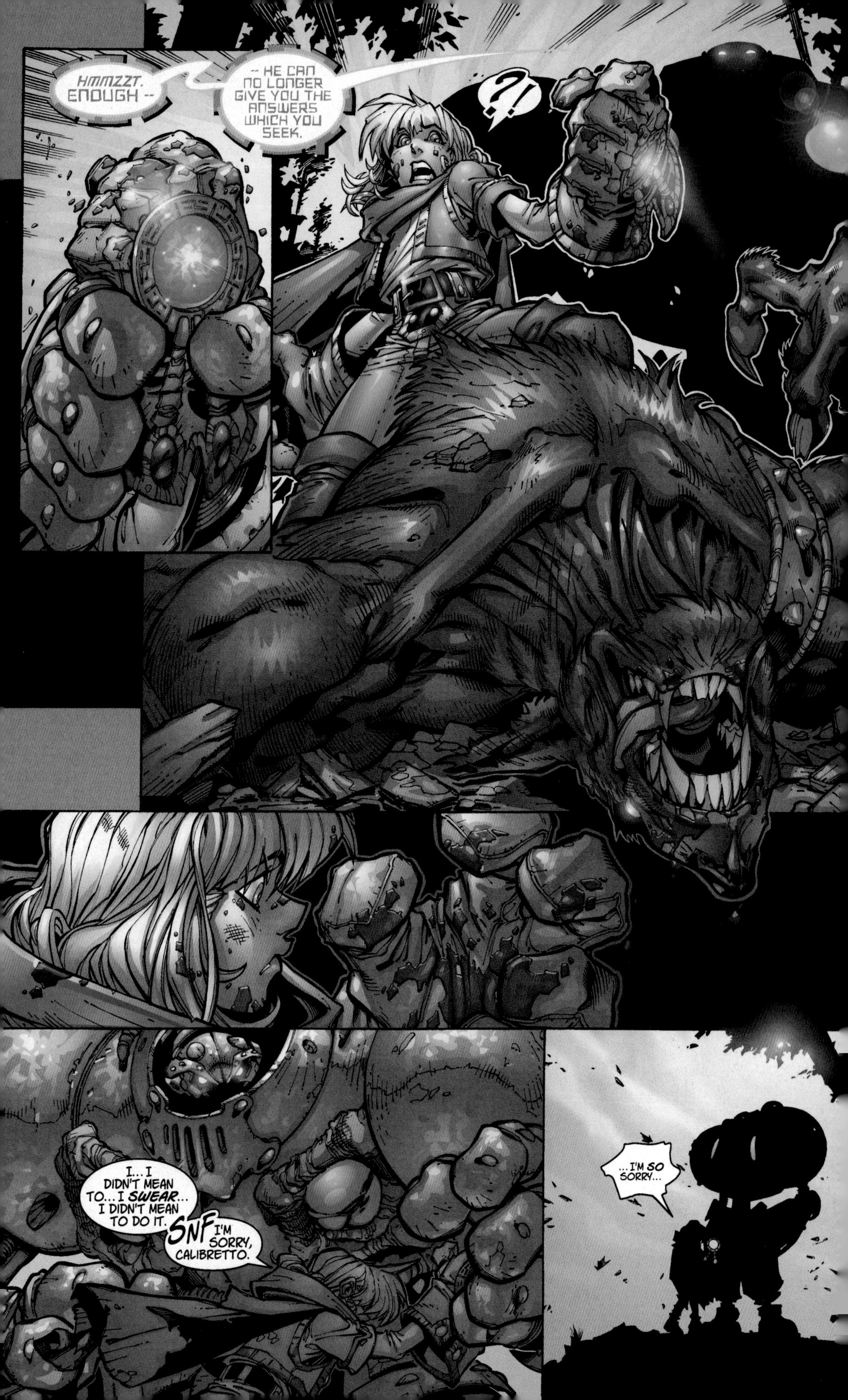
HMMZZT. ENOUGH --
-- HE CAN NO LONGER GIVE YOU THE ANSWERS WHICH YOU SEEK.
?!
I... I DIDN'T MEAN TO... I SWEAR... I DIDN'T MEAN TO DO IT.
SNF
I'M SORRY, CALIBRETTO.
...I'M SO SORRY...

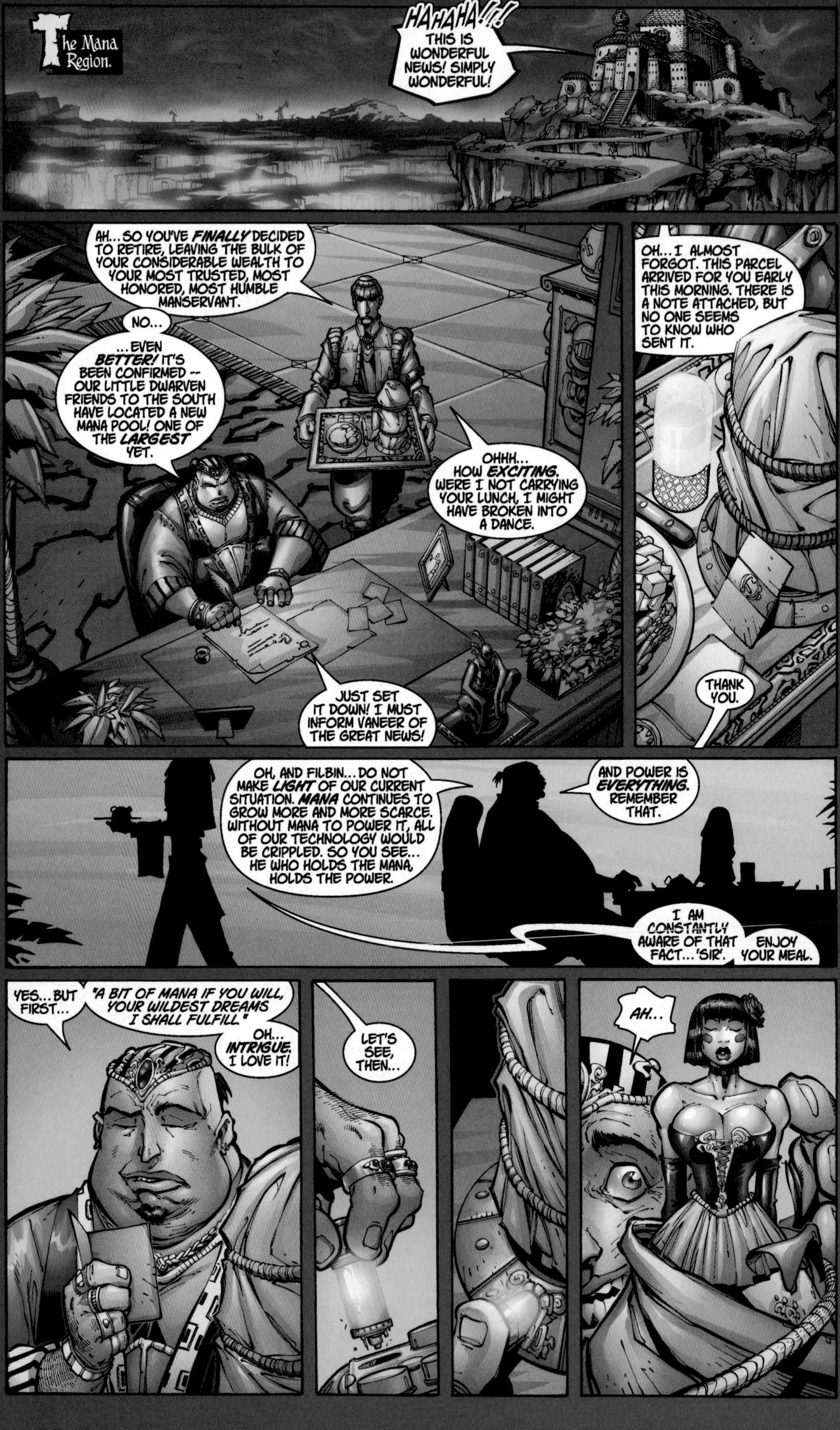
The Mana Region.
HAHAHA!!!
THIS IS WONDERFUL NEWS! SIMPLY WONDERFUL!
AH... SO YOU'VE FINALLY DECIDED TO RETIRE, LEAVING THE BULK OF YOUR CONSIDERABLE WEALTH TO YOUR MOST TRUSTED, MOST HONORED, MOST HUMBLE MANSERVANT.
NO...
...EVEN BETTER! IT'S BEEN CONFIRMED -- OUR LITTLE DWARVEN FRIENDS TO THE SOUTH HAVE LOCATED A NEW MANA POOL! ONE OF THE LARGEST YET.
OHHH... HOW EXCITING. WERE I NOT CARRYING YOUR LUNCH, I MIGHT HAVE BROKEN INTO A DANCE.
JUST SET IT DOWN! I MUST INFORM VANEER OF THE GREAT NEWS!
OH... I ALMOST FORGOT. THIS PARCEL ARRIVED FOR YOU EARLY THIS MORNING. THERE IS A NOTE ATTACHED, BUT NO ONE SEEMS TO KNOW WHO SENT IT.
THANK YOU.
OH, AND FILBIN... DO NOT MAKE LIGHT OF OUR CURRENT SITUATION. MANA CONTINUES TO GROW MORE AND MORE SCARCE. WITHOUT MANA TO POWER IT, ALL OF OUR TECHNOLOGY WOULD BE CRIPPLED. SO YOU SEE... HE WHO HOLDS THE MANA, HOLDS THE POWER.
AND POWER IS EVERYTHING. REMEMBER THAT.
I AM CONSTANTLY AWARE OF THAT FACT... 'SIR'.
ENJOY YOUR MEAL.
YES... BUT FIRST...
"A BIT OF MANA IF YOU WILL, YOUR WILDEST DREAMS I SHALL FULFILL."
OH... INTRIGUE. I LOVE IT!
LET'S SEE, THEN...
AH...

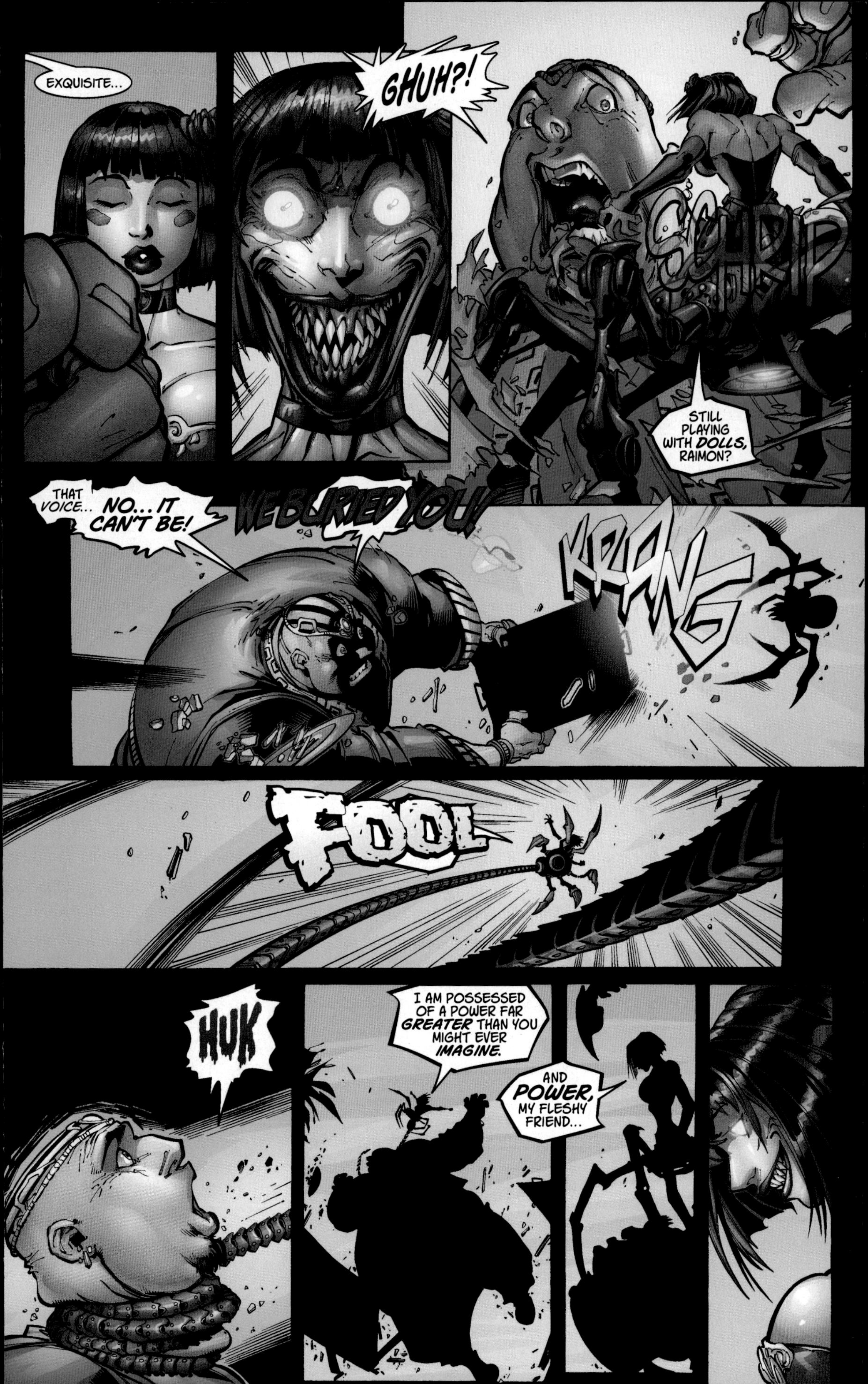
EXQUISITE...
GHUH?!
SCHRIP
STILL PLAYING WITH DOLLS, RAIMON?
THAT VOICE... NO... IT CAN'T BE!
WE BURIED YOU!
KRANG
FOOL
HUK
I AM POSSESSED OF A POWER FAR GREATER THAN YOU MIGHT EVER IMAGINE.
AND POWER, MY FLESHY FRIEND...

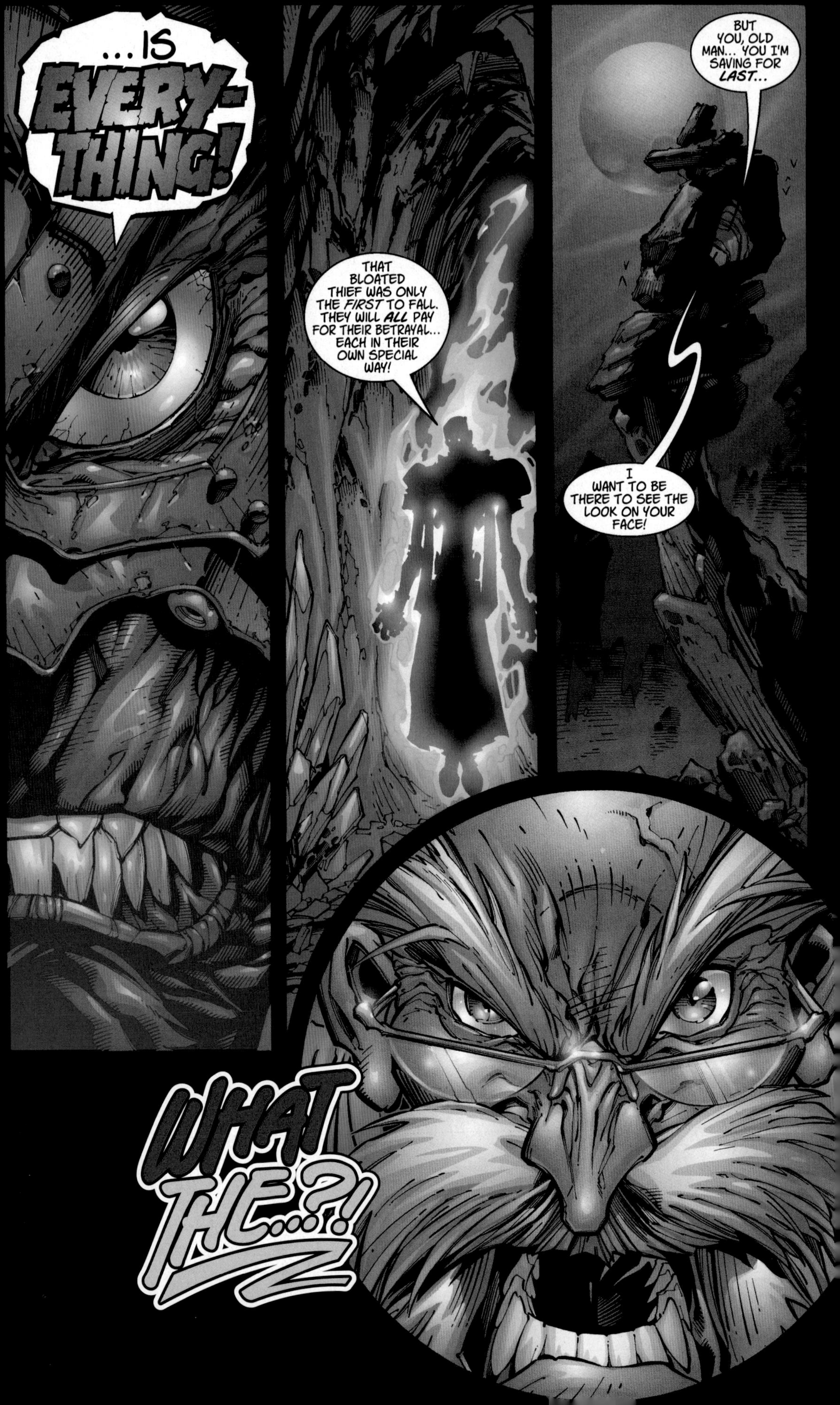
...IS EVERY-THING!
THAT BLOATED THIEF WAS ONLY THE FIRST TO FALL. THEY WILL ALL PAY FOR THEIR BETRAYAL... EACH IN THEIR OWN SPECIAL WAY!
BUT YOU, OLD MAN... YOU I'M SAVING FOR LAST...
I WANT TO BE THERE TO SEE THE LOOK ON YOUR FACE!
WHAT THE...?!

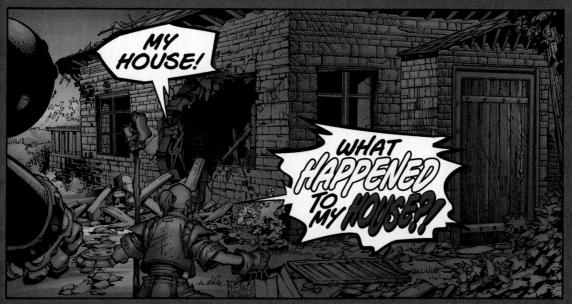

MY HOUSE!

WHAT HAPPENED TO MY HOUSE?!

HMMZZT. PLEASE TRY TO STAY CALM. THE GLOVES, THEY...

THE GLOVES?

THE GLOVES?!

HMMZZT. I WILL EXPLAIN, BUT YOU MUST CALM DOWN! YOUR TEMPER TANTRUM IS AFFECTING THE ENVIRONMENT...

IT'S ABOUT TO AFFECT SOMETHING ELSE IF YOU DON'T START TALKIN'--

-- AND FAST!

HMMMMMZZZT. THELYCELOTRETURNED ONLYTHISTIMEITBROUGHT ALONGABANDOFGRINNERS WHOMANAGEDTOINCAPACITATE MEMOMENTARILYUSINGSOME SORTOFMAGNETICPULSE CANNON...

OKAY...

...WHICHLEFT THECHILDTO FENDFORHER SELFONLYSHE USEDTHE GLOVES...

OKAY!

...AND PROCEEDED TODESTROY THEIRENTIRE NUMBERASWELL ASTHEHOUSE THERELAS ...HI...

OKAY!!

KTAANG

WHERE IS SHE?!

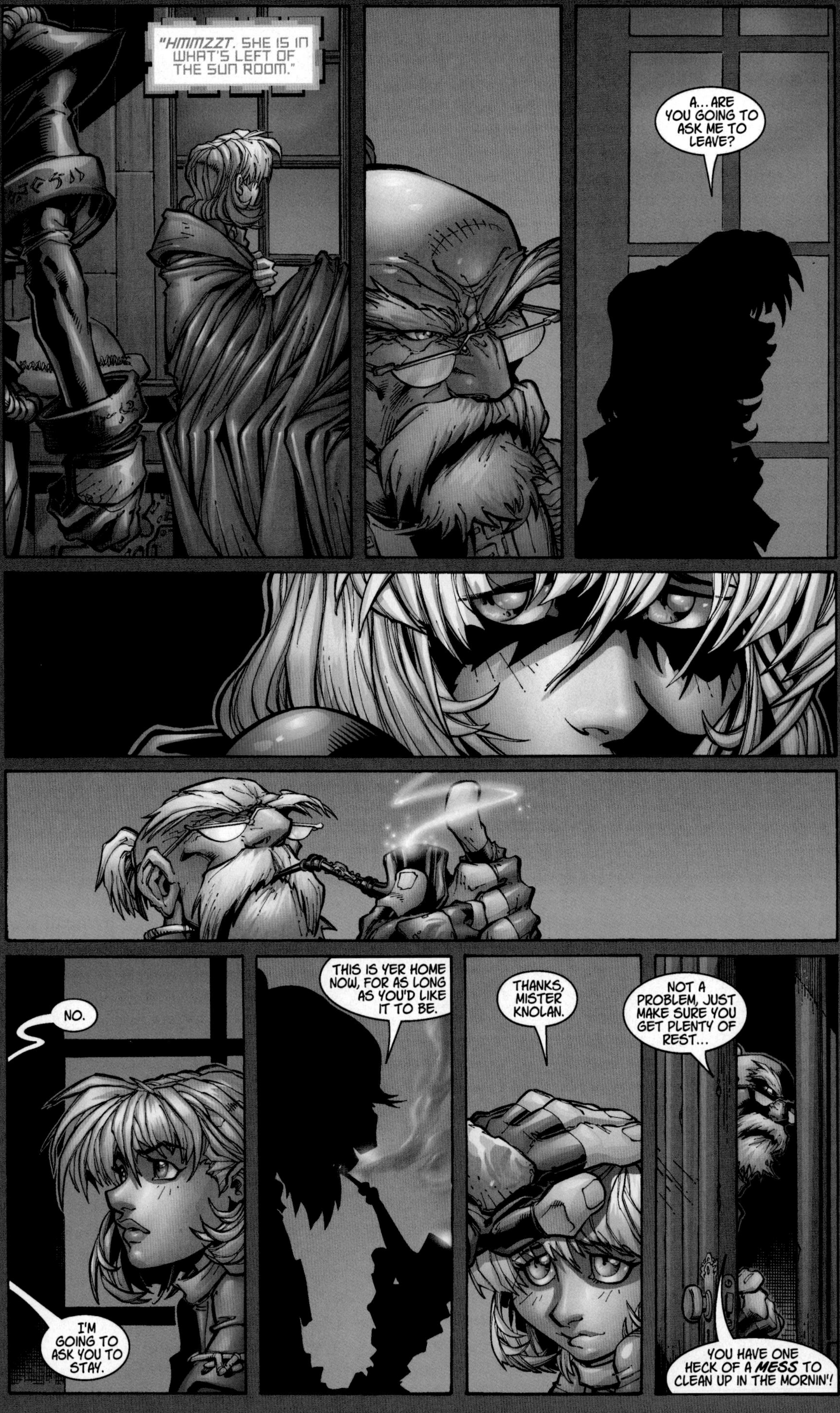
"HMMZZT. SHE IS IN WHAT'S LEFT OF THE SUN ROOM."
A... ARE YOU GOING TO ASK ME TO LEAVE?
NO.
I'M GOING TO ASK YOU TO STAY.
THIS IS YER HOME NOW, FOR AS LONG AS YOU'D LIKE IT TO BE.
THANKS, MISTER KNOLAN.
NOT A PROBLEM, JUST MAKE SURE YOU GET PLENTY OF REST...
YOU HAVE ONE HECK OF A MESS TO CLEAN UP IN THE MORNIN'!

ELSEWHERE...

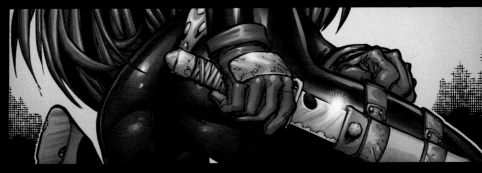

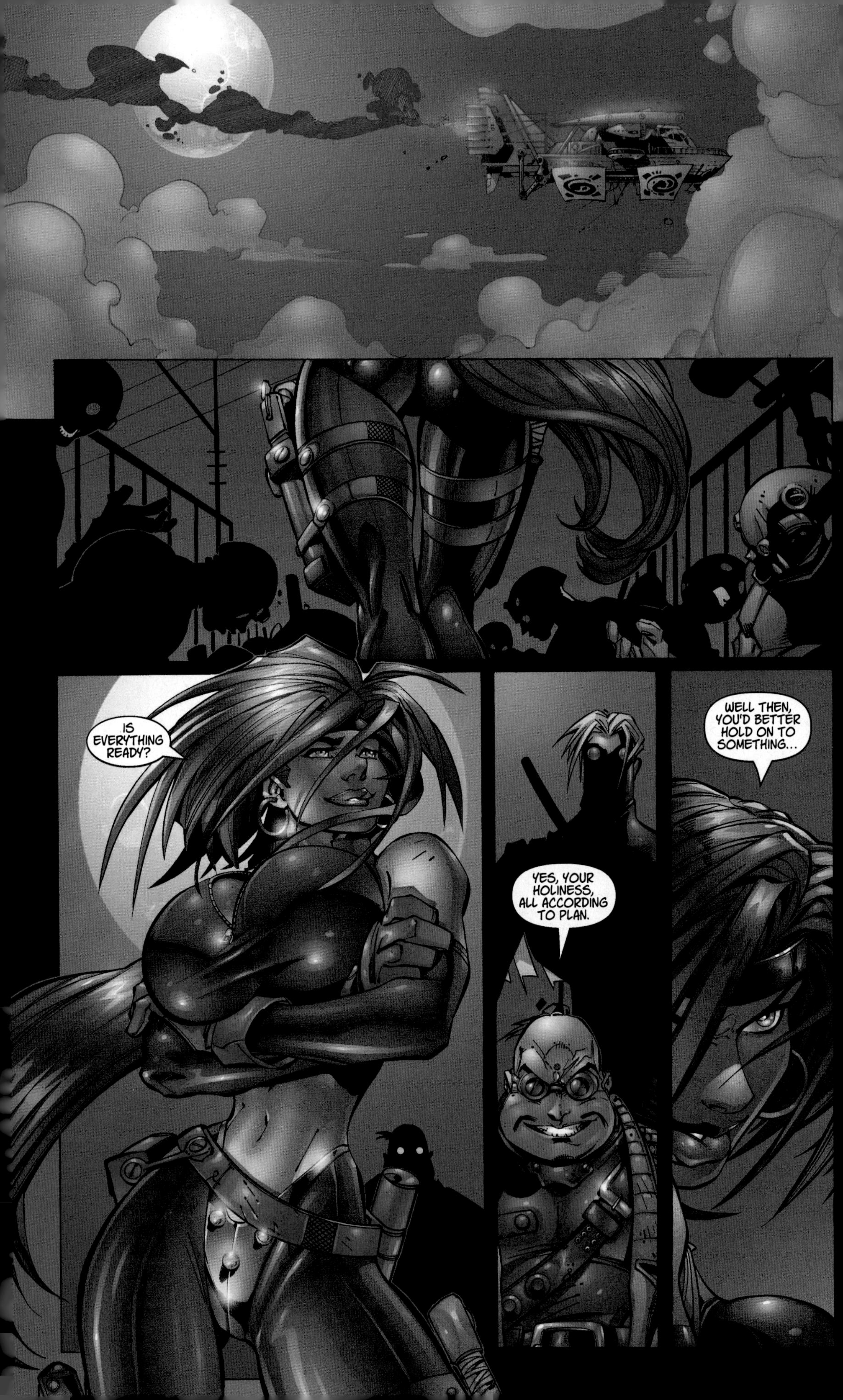
IS EVERYTHING READY?
YES, YOUR HOLINESS, ALL ACCORDING TO PLAN.
WELL THEN, YOU'D BETTER HOLD ON TO SOMETHING...

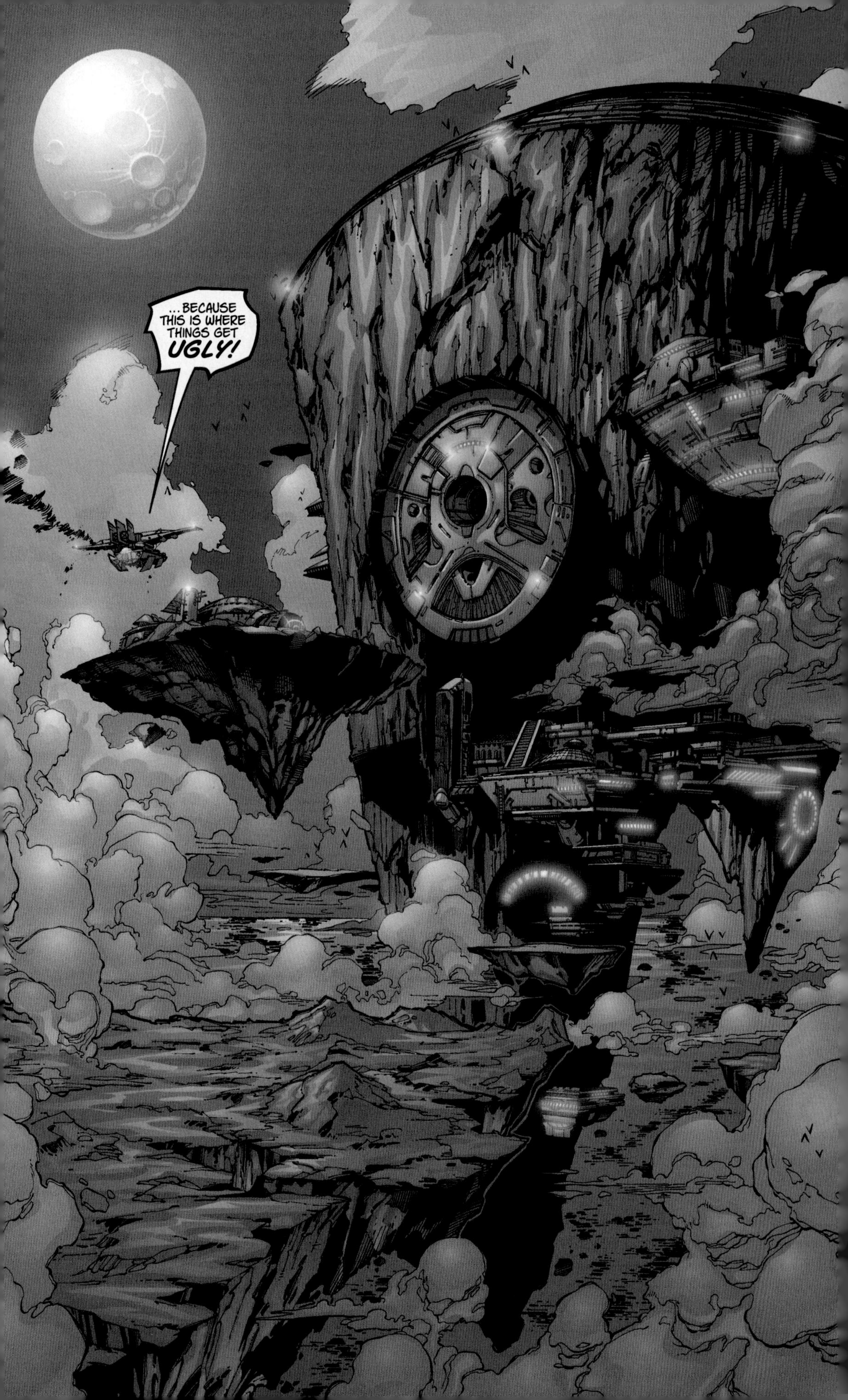
...BECAUSE THIS IS WHERE THINGS GET UGLY!

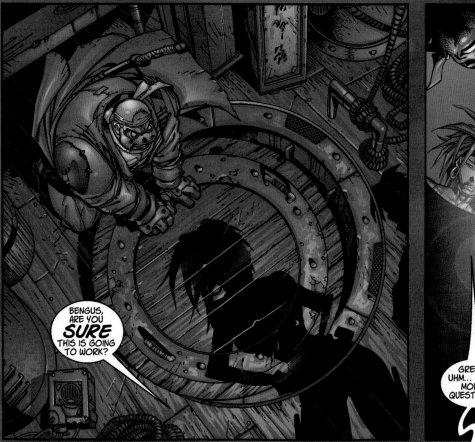

LIKE A WELL-OILED MACHINE.

BENGUS, ARE YOU **SURE** THIS IS GOING TO WORK?

GREAT, UHM... **ONE** MORE QUESTION...

...DO THEY **BITE?!**

OH, THEY'RE QUITE HARMLESS. UNLESS THEY'RE EXPOSED TO UNNATURAL LIGHT... **THEN** THEY GET **MEAN!**

HEHEHE... SORRY. EH... MAYBE NOW WOULD BE A GOOD TIME TO GO OVER THE PLAN.

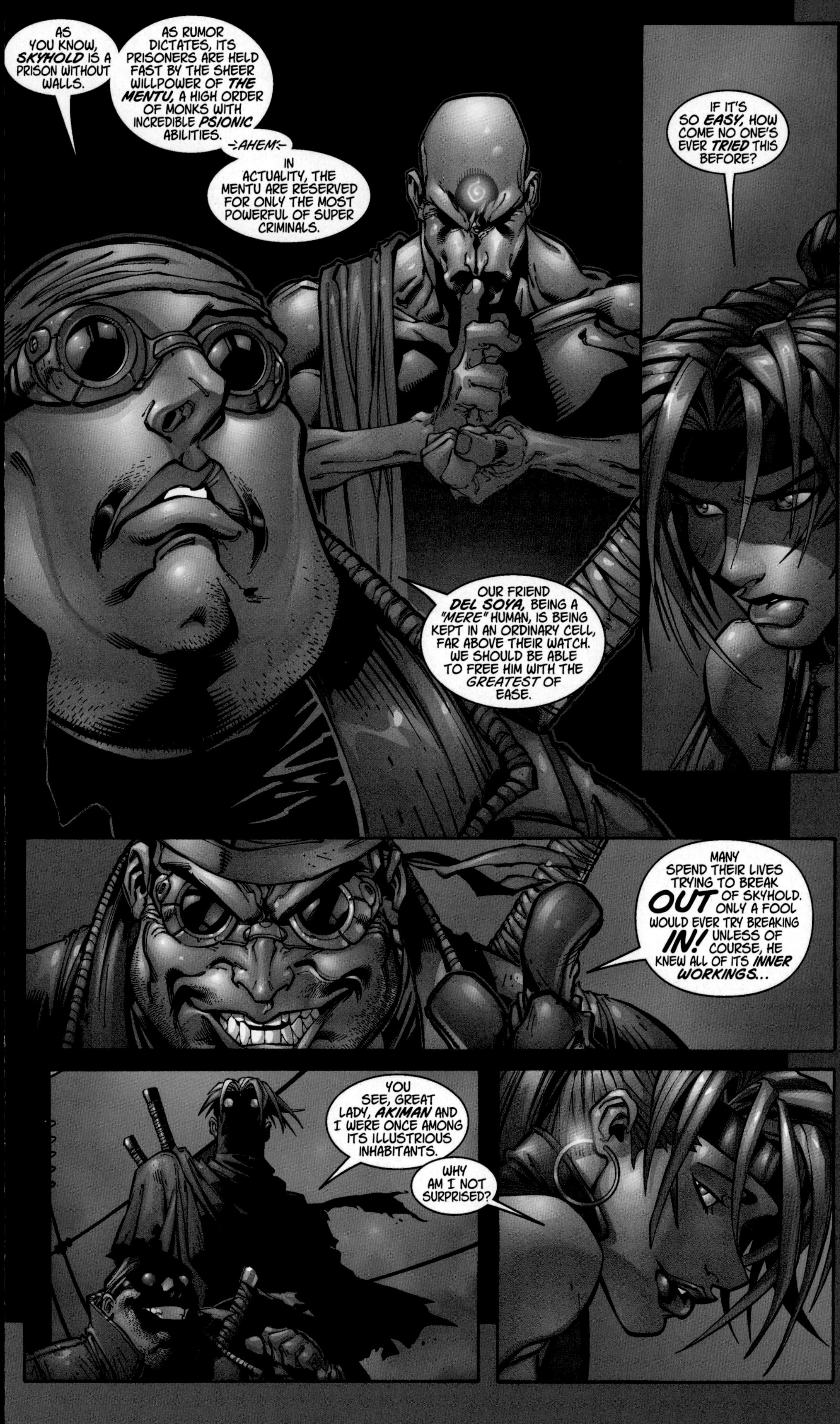
AS YOU KNOW, SKYHOLD IS A PRISON WITHOUT WALLS.
AS RUMOR DICTATES, ITS PRISONERS ARE HELD FAST BY THE SHEER WILLPOWER OF THE MENTU, A HIGH ORDER OF MONKS WITH INCREDIBLE PSIONIC ABILITIES.
-AHEM-
IN ACTUALITY, THE MENTU ARE RESERVED FOR ONLY THE MOST POWERFUL OF SUPER CRIMINALS.
IF IT'S SO EASY, HOW COME NO ONE'S EVER TRIED THIS BEFORE?
OUR FRIEND DEL SOYA, BEING A "MERE" HUMAN, IS BEING KEPT IN AN ORDINARY CELL, FAR ABOVE THEIR WATCH. WE SHOULD BE ABLE TO FREE HIM WITH THE GREATEST OF EASE.
MANY SPEND THEIR LIVES TRYING TO BREAK OUT OF SKYHOLD. ONLY A FOOL WOULD EVER TRY BREAKING IN! UNLESS OF COURSE, HE KNEW ALL OF ITS INNER WORKINGS...
YOU SEE, GREAT LADY, AKIMAN AND I WERE ONCE AMONG ITS ILLUSTRIOUS INHABITANTS.
WHY AM I NOT SURPRISED?

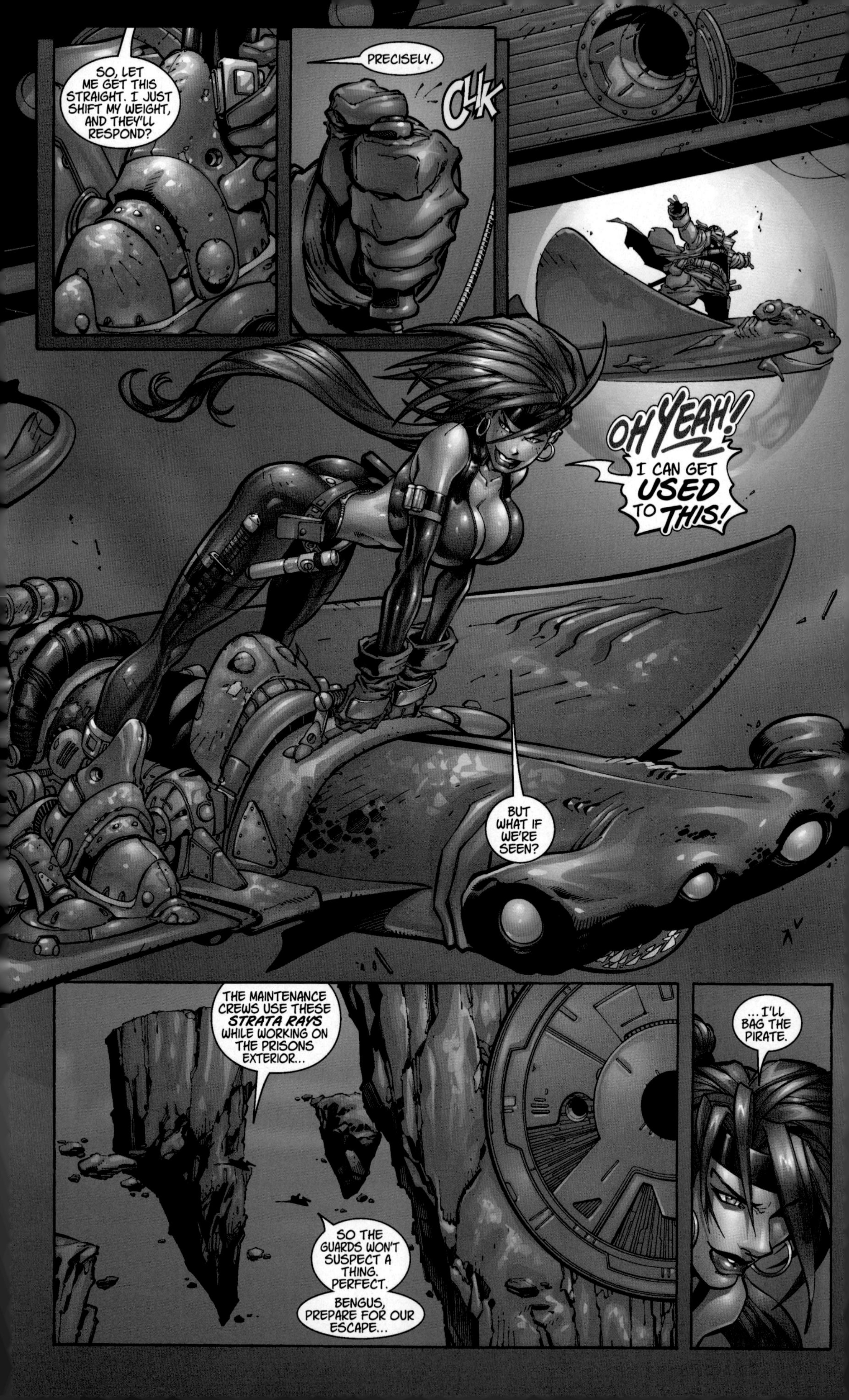

SO, LET ME GET THIS STRAIGHT. I JUST SHIFT MY WEIGHT, AND THEY'LL RESPOND?
PRECISELY.
CLIK
OH YEAH! I CAN GET USED TO THIS!
BUT WHAT IF WE'RE SEEN?
THE MAINTENANCE CREWS USE THESE STRATA RAYS WHILE WORKING ON THE PRISONS EXTERIOR...
SO THE GUARDS WON'T SUSPECT A THING. PERFECT.
BENGUS, PREPARE FOR OUR ESCAPE...
...I'LL BAG THE PIRATE.

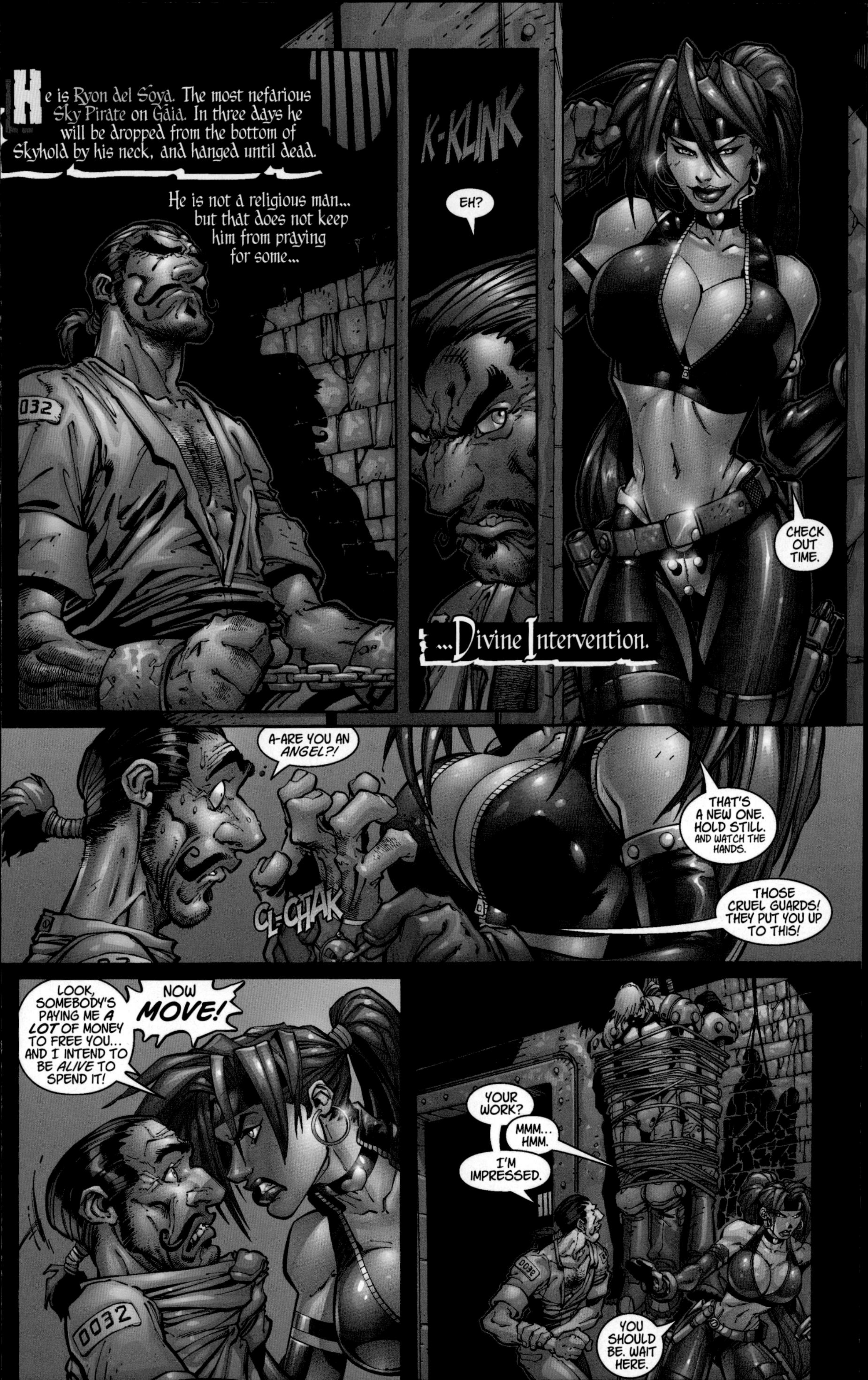
He is Ryon del Soya. The most nefarious Sky Pirate on Gaia. In three days he will be dropped from the bottom of Skyhold by his neck, and hanged until dead.
He is not a religious man... but that does not keep him from praying for some...
K-KLINK
EH?
...Divine Intervention.
CHECK OUT TIME.
A-ARE YOU AN ANGEL?!
THAT'S A NEW ONE. HOLD STILL. AND WATCH THE HANDS.
CL-CHAK
THOSE CRUEL GUARDS! THEY PUT YOU UP TO THIS!
LOOK, SOMEBODY'S PAYING ME A LOT OF MONEY TO FREE YOU... AND I INTEND TO BE ALIVE TO SPEND IT!
NOW MOVE!
YOUR WORK?
MMM... HMM.
I'M IMPRESSED.
YOU SHOULD BE. WAIT HERE.

West Gun tower.

HAIL, *DUNRIC.* ANYTHING TO REPORT?

NOPE. ALL'S QUIET.

WELL, THIS IS STRANGE. THAT *STRATA RAY* OUT THERE... IT'S BEEN CIRCLING AROUND WITHOUT A RIDER FOR THE LAST TEN MINUTES...

HMM... I'M SURE IT'S JUST A STRAY, BUT I'D BETTER CALL IT IN, JUST IN CASE...

I'M AFRAID I CAN'T LET YOU DO THAT, GENTLEMEN.

WHAT THE...?!

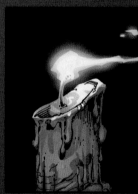

SHIING

CHUK

CHING

FREEZE!

KL CHAK

YOU SO MUCH AS *BREATHE* AND I'LL...

KRUNCH

YUM.

WH... WHAT *THE HELL* ARE YOU?

HUNGRY.

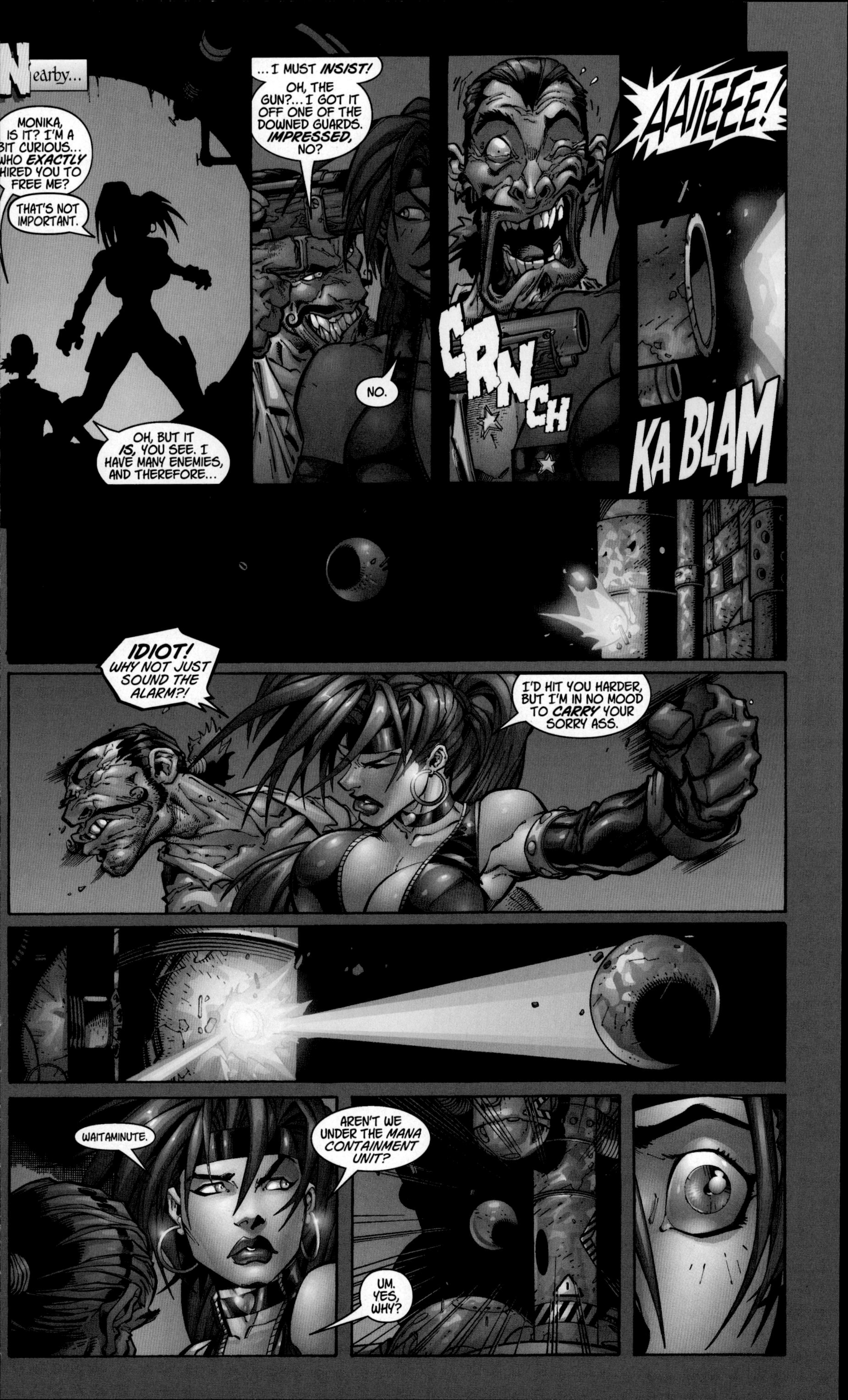
Nearby...
MONIKA, IS IT? I'M A BIT CURIOUS... WHO EXACTLY HIRED YOU TO FREE ME?
THAT'S NOT IMPORTANT.
OH, BUT IT IS, YOU SEE. I HAVE MANY ENEMIES, AND THEREFORE...
...I MUST INSIST! OH, THE GUN?... I GOT IT OFF ONE OF THE DOWNED GUARDS. IMPRESSED, NO?
NO.
CRNCH
AAIIEEE!
KA BLAM
IDIOT! WHY NOT JUST SOUND THE ALARM?!
I'D HIT YOU HARDER, BUT I'M IN NO MOOD TO CARRY YOUR SORRY ASS.
WAITAMINUTE.
AREN'T WE UNDER THE MANA CONTAINMENT UNIT?
UM. YES, WHY?

PTWOM

One mile below.

HHHMMMM

HMM

HMM?!

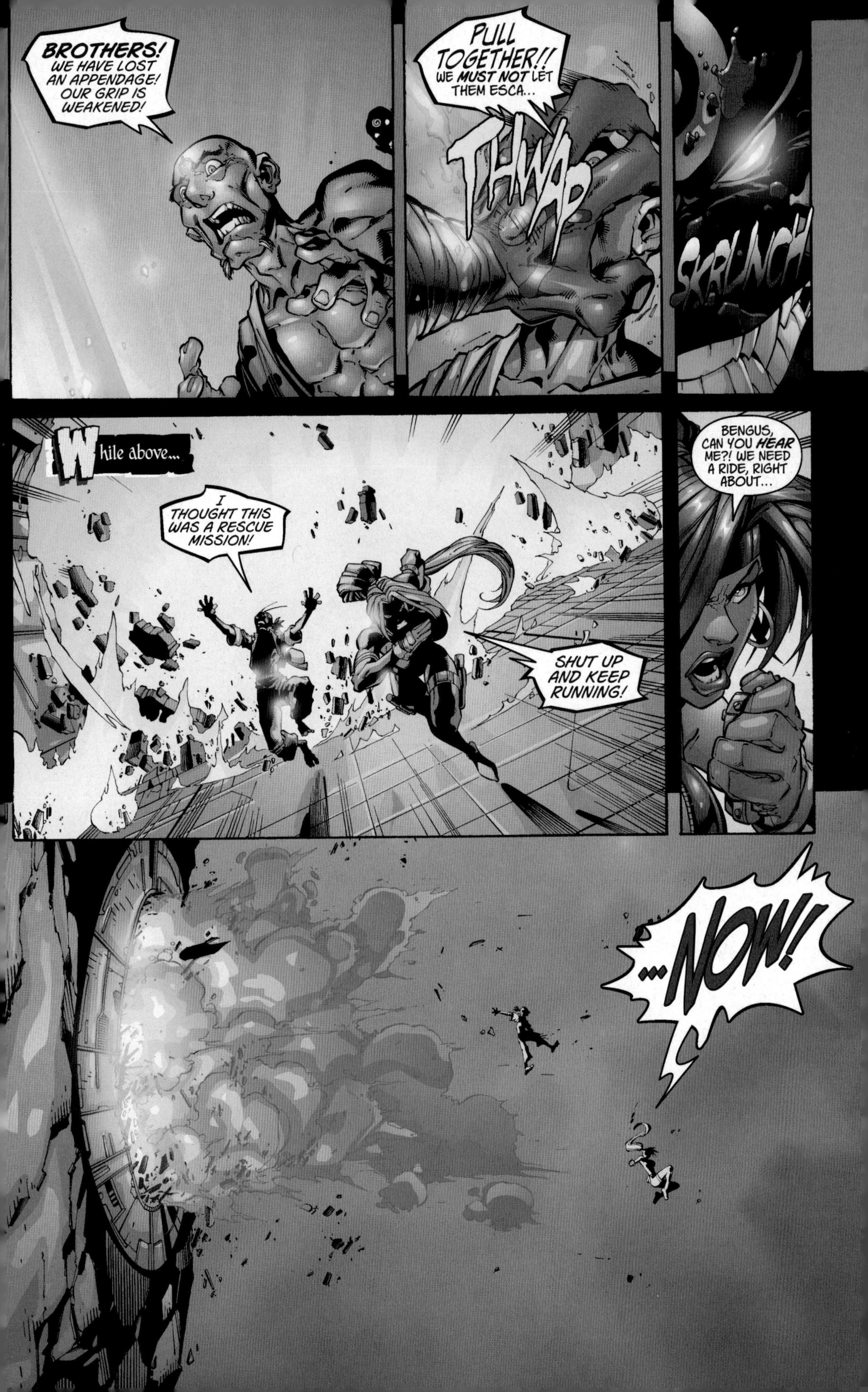
BROTHERS! WE HAVE LOST AN APPENDAGE! OUR GRIP IS WEAKENED!
PULL TOGETHER!! WE MUST NOT LET THEM ESCA...
THWAP
SKRUNCH
While above...
I THOUGHT THIS WAS A RESCUE MISSION!
SHUT UP AND KEEP RUNNING!
BENGUS, CAN YOU HEAR ME?! WE NEED A RIDE, RIGHT ABOUT...
...NOW!

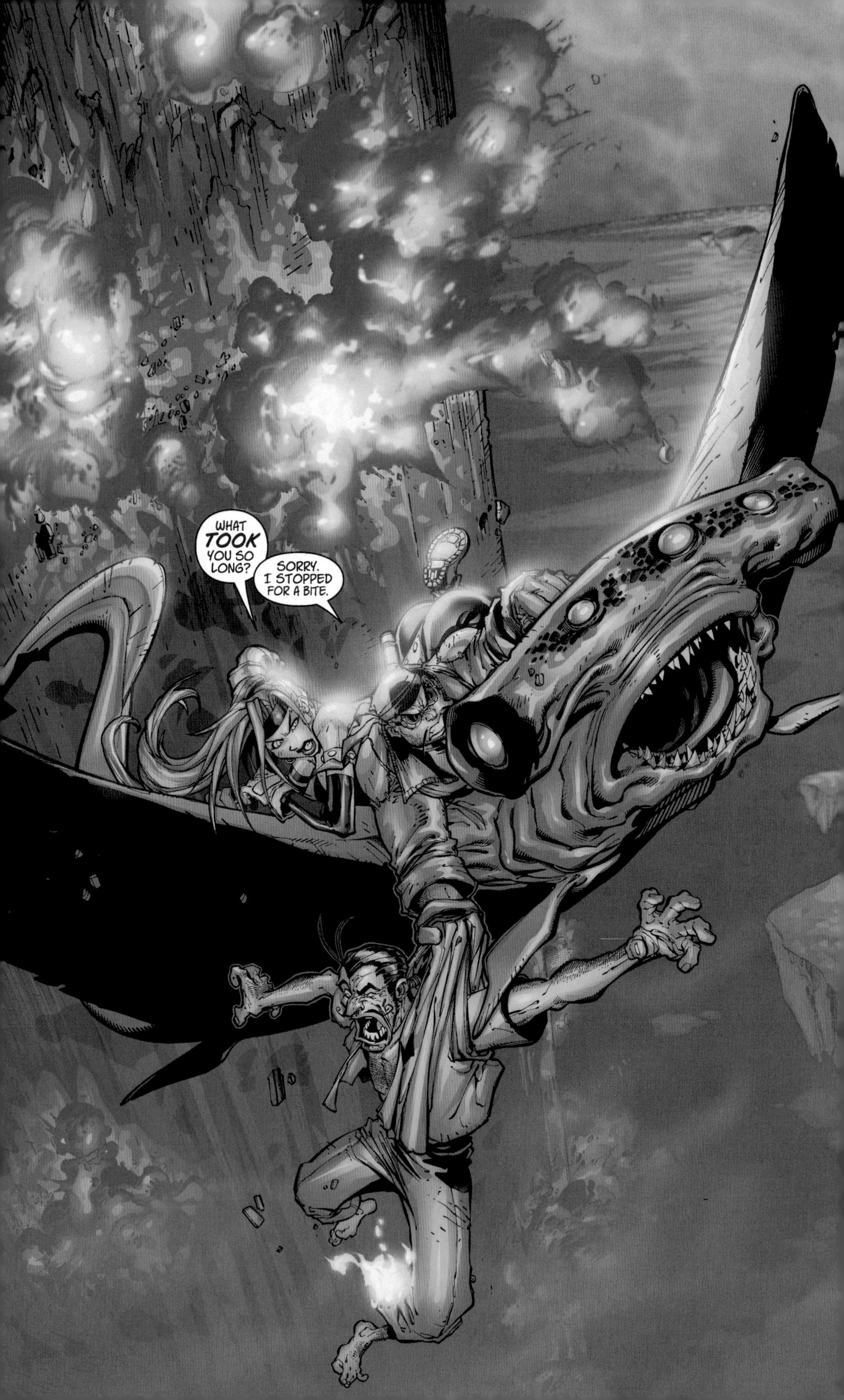
WHAT TOOK YOU SO LONG?
SORRY. I STOPPED FOR A BITE.

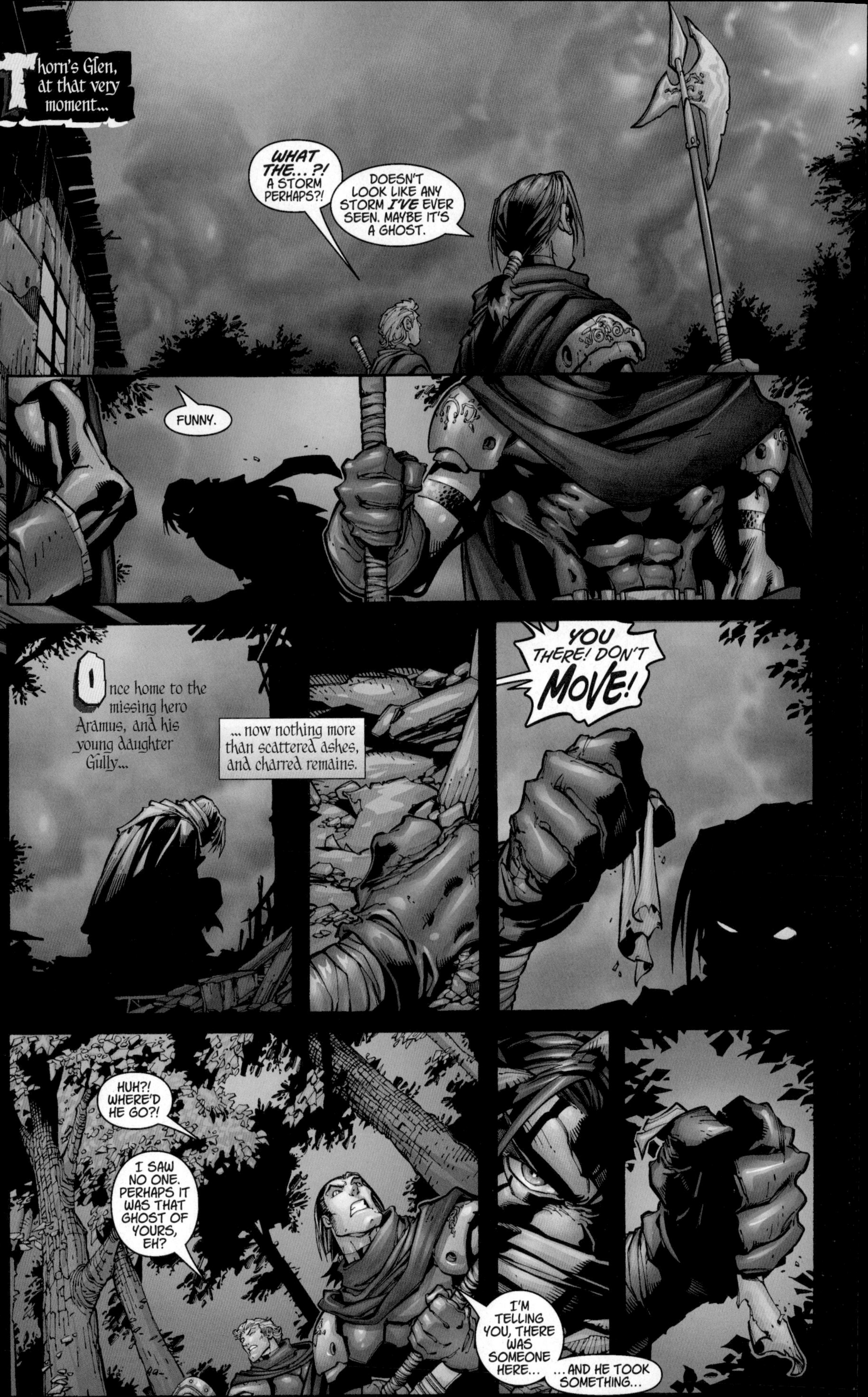
Thorn's Glen, at that very moment...
WHAT THE...?! A STORM PERHAPS?!
DOESN'T LOOK LIKE ANY STORM I'VE EVER SEEN. MAYBE IT'S A GHOST.
FUNNY.
Once home to the missing hero Aramus, and his young daughter Gully...
...now nothing more than scattered ashes, and charred remains.
YOU THERE! DON'T MOVE!
HUH?! WHERE'D HE GO?!
I SAW NO ONE. PERHAPS IT WAS THAT GHOST OF YOURS, EH?
I'M TELLING YOU, THERE WAS SOMEONE HERE...
...AND HE TOOK SOMETHING...

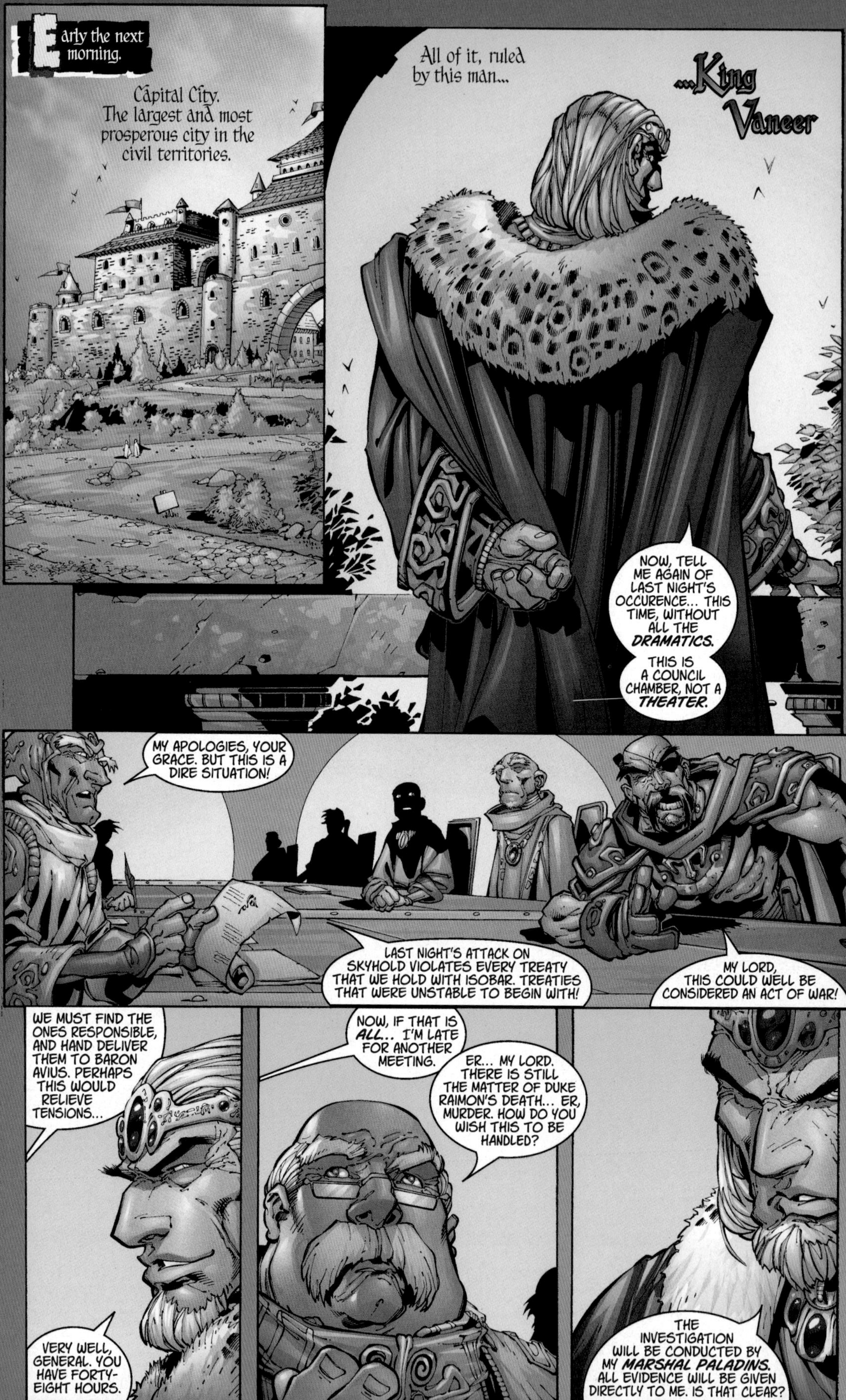
Early the next morning.
Capital City. The largest and most prosperous city in the civil territories.
All of it, ruled by this man...
...King Vaneer
NOW, TELL ME AGAIN OF LAST NIGHT'S OCCURENCE... THIS TIME, WITHOUT ALL THE DRAMATICS.
THIS IS A COUNCIL CHAMBER, NOT A THEATER.
MY APOLOGIES, YOUR GRACE. BUT THIS IS A DIRE SITUATION!
LAST NIGHT'S ATTACK ON SKYHOLD VIOLATES EVERY TREATY THAT WE HOLD WITH ISOBAR. TREATIES THAT WERE UNSTABLE TO BEGIN WITH!
MY LORD, THIS COULD WELL BE CONSIDERED AN ACT OF WAR!
WE MUST FIND THE ONES RESPONSIBLE, AND HAND DELIVER THEM TO BARON AVIUS. PERHAPS THIS WOULD RELIEVE TENSIONS...
VERY WELL, GENERAL. YOU HAVE FORTY-EIGHT HOURS.
NOW, IF THAT IS ALL... I'M LATE FOR ANOTHER MEETING.
ER... MY LORD. THERE IS STILL THE MATTER OF DUKE RAIMON'S DEATH... ER, MURDER. HOW DO YOU WISH THIS TO BE HANDLED?
THE INVESTIGATION WILL BE CONDUCTED BY MY MARSHAL PALADINS. ALL EVIDENCE WILL BE GIVEN DIRECTLY TO ME. IS THAT CLEAR?

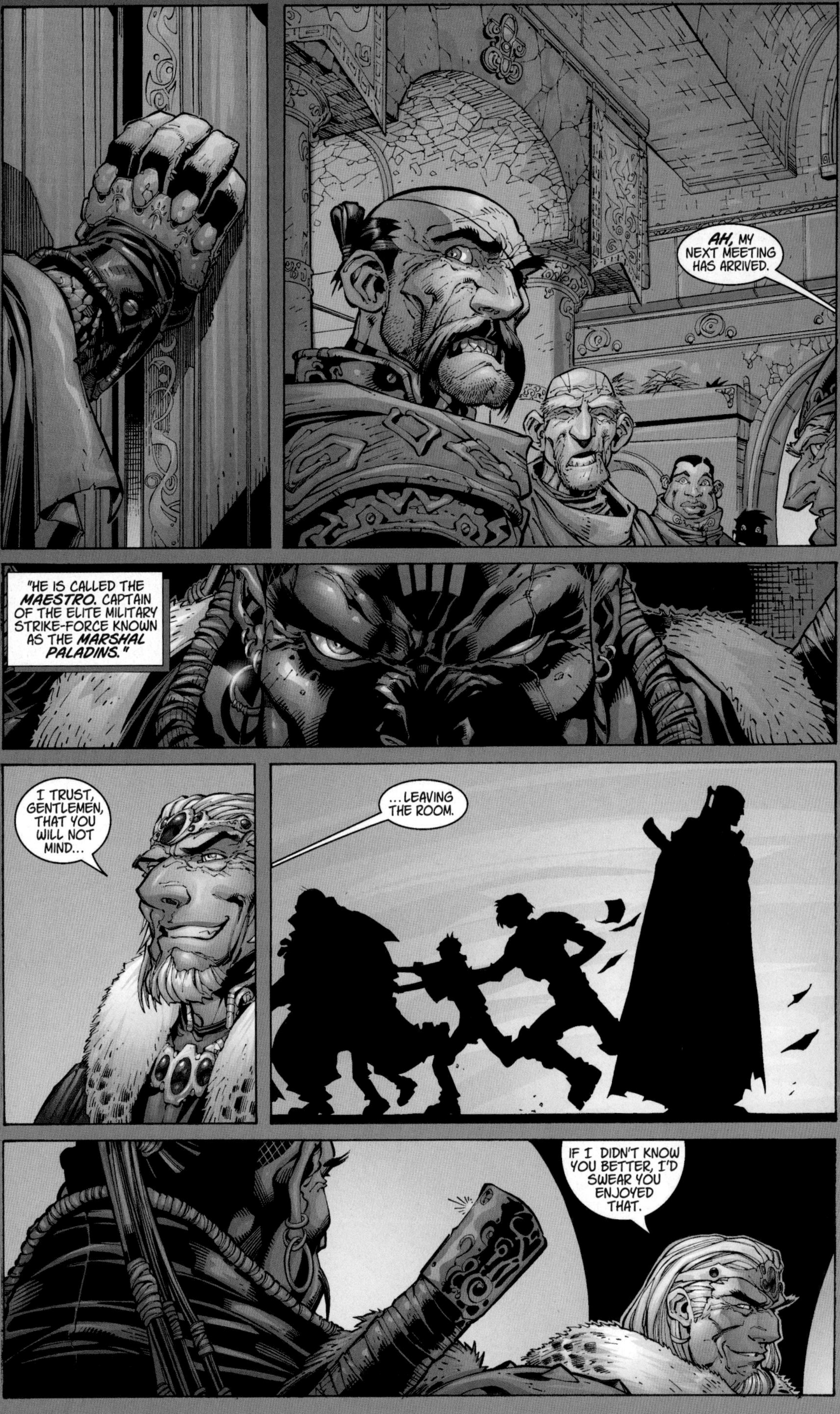
AH, MY NEXT MEETING HAS ARRIVED.
"HE IS CALLED THE MAESTRO. CAPTAIN OF THE ELITE MILITARY STRIKE-FORCE KNOWN AS THE MARSHAL PALADINS."
I TRUST, GENTLEMEN, THAT YOU WILL NOT MIND...
...LEAVING THE ROOM.
IF I DIDN'T KNOW YOU BETTER, I'D SWEAR YOU ENJOYED THAT.

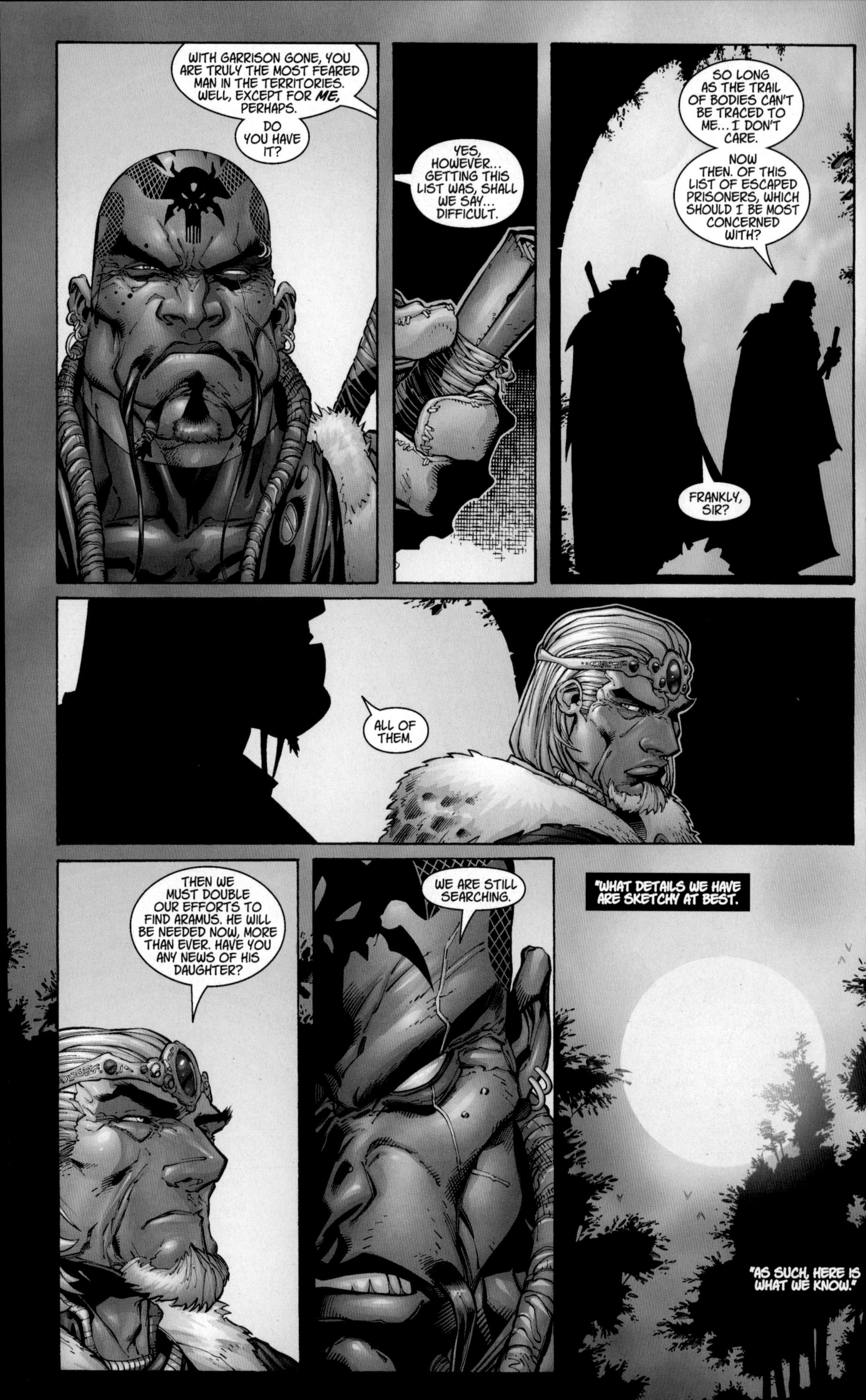
WITH GARRISON GONE, YOU ARE TRULY THE MOST FEARED MAN IN THE TERRITORIES. WELL, EXCEPT FOR *ME,* PERHAPS.
DO YOU HAVE IT?
YES, HOWEVER... GETTING THIS LIST WAS, SHALL WE SAY... DIFFICULT.
SO LONG AS THE TRAIL OF BODIES CAN'T BE TRACED TO ME... I DON'T CARE.
NOW THEN. OF THIS LIST OF ESCAPED PRISONERS, WHICH SHOULD I BE MOST CONCERNED WITH?
FRANKLY, SIR?
ALL OF THEM.
THEN WE MUST DOUBLE OUR EFFORTS TO FIND ARAMUS. HE WILL BE NEEDED NOW, MORE THAN EVER. HAVE YOU ANY NEWS OF HIS DAUGHTER?
WE ARE STILL SEARCHING.
"WHAT DETAILS WE HAVE ARE SKETCHY AT BEST.
"AS SUCH, HERE IS WHAT WE KNOW."

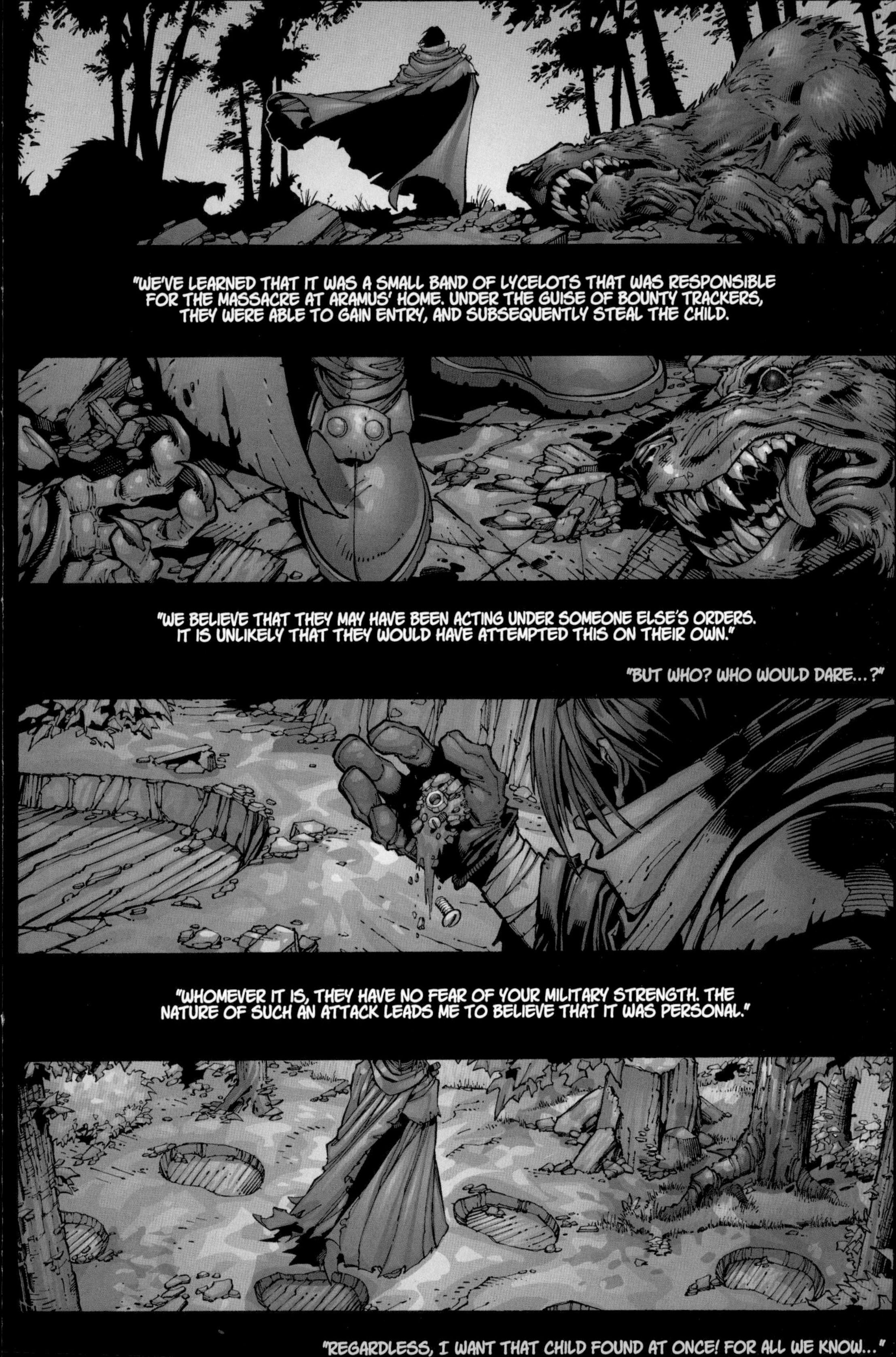
"WE'VE LEARNED THAT IT WAS A SMALL BAND OF LYCELOTS THAT WAS RESPONSIBLE FOR THE MASSACRE AT ARAMUS' HOME. UNDER THE GUISE OF BOUNTY TRACKERS, THEY WERE ABLE TO GAIN ENTRY, AND SUBSEQUENTLY STEAL THE CHILD.
"WE BELIEVE THAT THEY MAY HAVE BEEN ACTING UNDER SOMEONE ELSE'S ORDERS. IT IS UNLIKELY THAT THEY WOULD HAVE ATTEMPTED THIS ON THEIR OWN."
"BUT WHO? WHO WOULD DARE...?"
"WHOMEVER IT IS, THEY HAVE NO FEAR OF YOUR MILITARY STRENGTH. THE NATURE OF SUCH AN ATTACK LEADS ME TO BELIEVE THAT IT WAS PERSONAL."
"REGARDLESS, I WANT THAT CHILD FOUND AT ONCE! FOR ALL WE KNOW..."

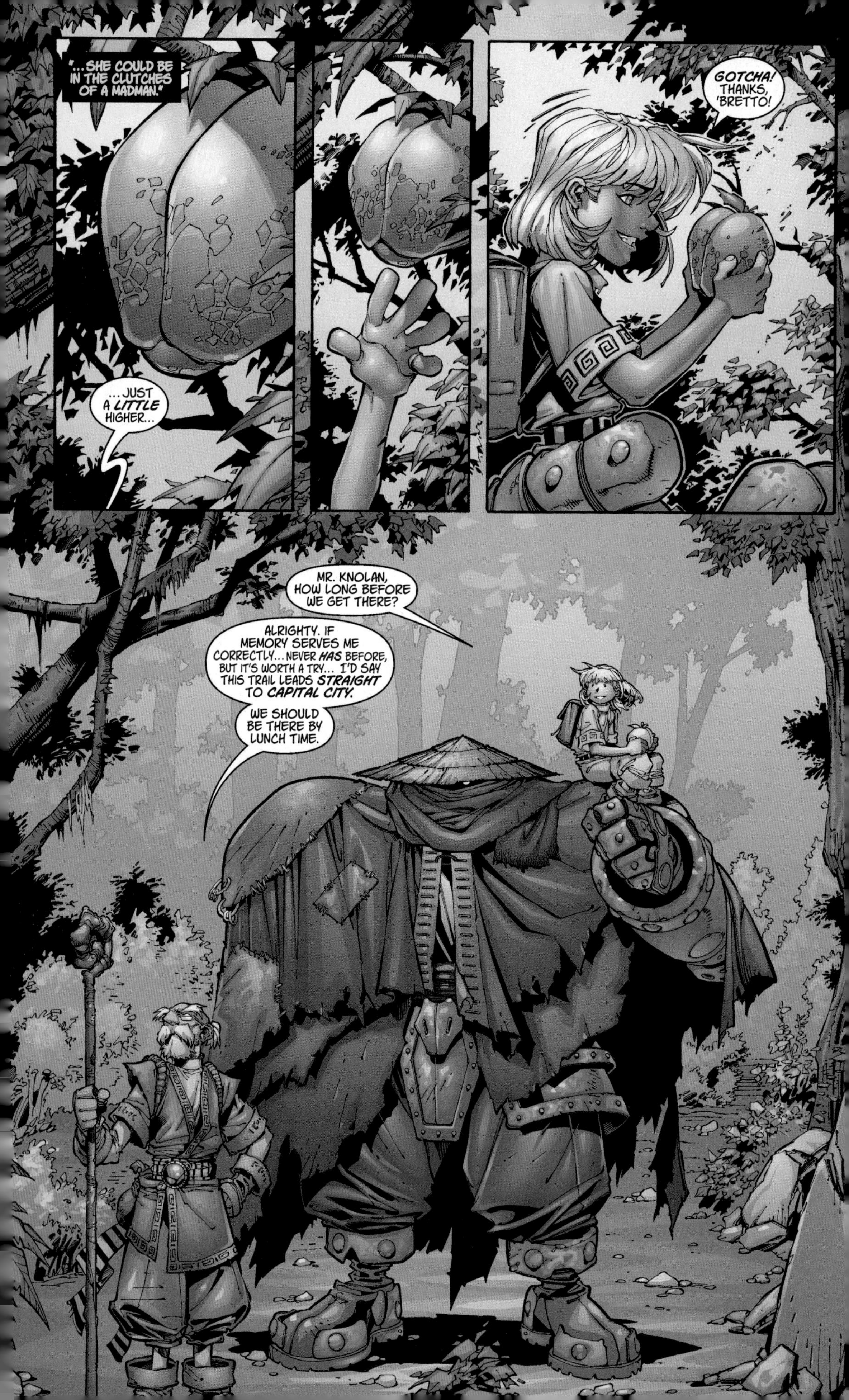
"...SHE COULD BE IN THE CLUTCHES OF A MADMAN."
...JUST A *LITTLE* HIGHER...
GOTCHA! THANKS, 'BRETTO!
MR. KNOLAN, HOW LONG BEFORE WE GET THERE?
ALRIGHTY. IF MEMORY SERVES ME CORRECTLY... NEVER *HAS* BEFORE, BUT IT'S WORTH A TRY... I'D SAY THIS TRAIL LEADS *STRAIGHT* TO *CAPITAL CITY.*
WE SHOULD BE THERE BY LUNCH TIME.

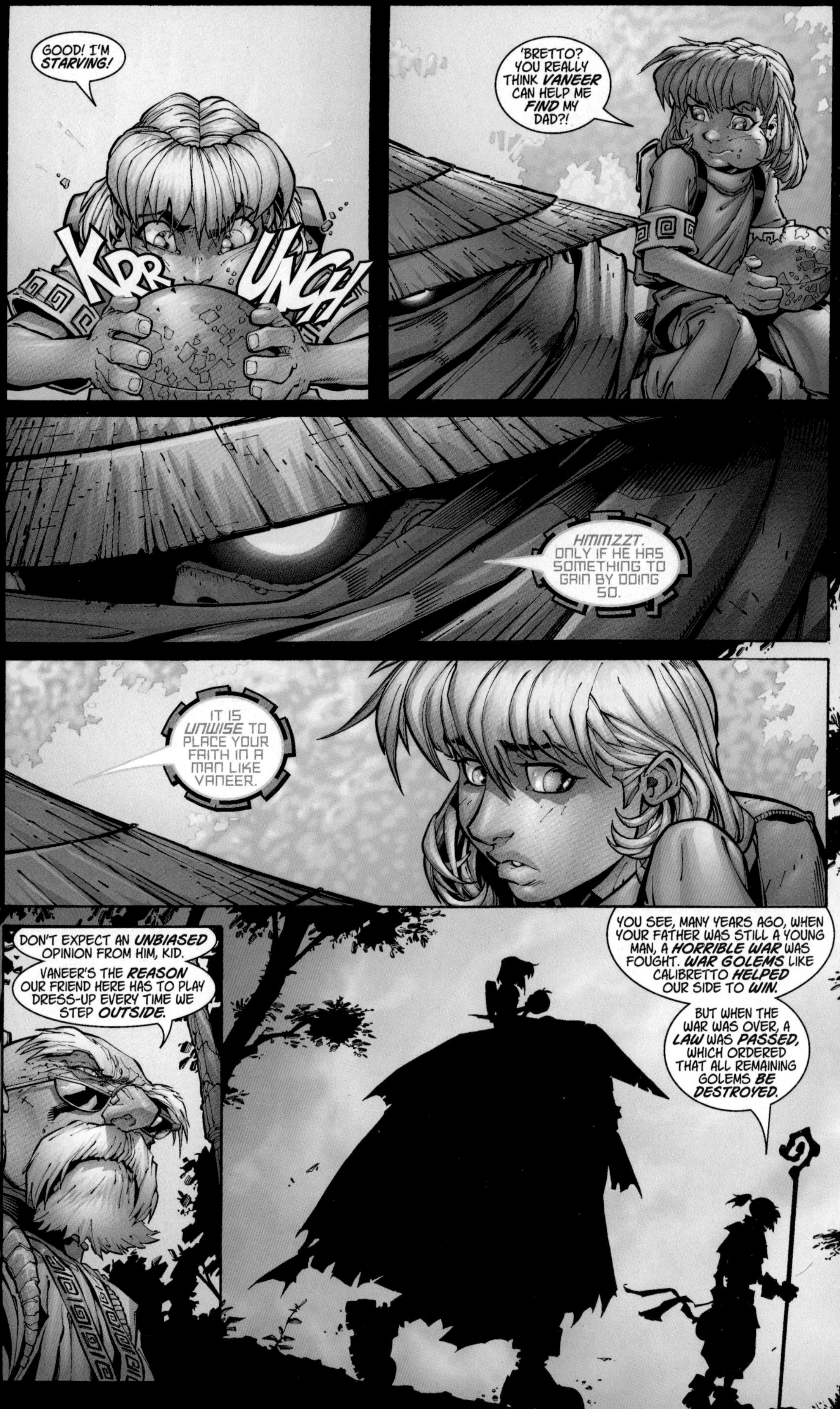
GOOD! I'M STARVING!
KRR UNCH
'BRETTO? YOU REALLY THINK VANEER CAN HELP ME FIND MY DAD?!
HMMZZT. ONLY IF HE HAS SOMETHING TO GAIN BY DOING SO.
IT IS UNWISE TO PLACE YOUR FAITH IN A MAN LIKE VANEER.
DON'T EXPECT AN UNBIASED OPINION FROM HIM, KID.
VANEER'S THE REASON OUR FRIEND HERE HAS TO PLAY DRESS-UP EVERY TIME WE STEP OUTSIDE.
YOU SEE, MANY YEARS AGO, WHEN YOUR FATHER WAS STILL A YOUNG MAN, A HORRIBLE WAR WAS FOUGHT. WAR GOLEMS LIKE CALIBRETTO HELPED OUR SIDE TO WIN.
BUT WHEN THE WAR WAS OVER, A LAW WAS PASSED, WHICH ORDERED THAT ALL REMAINING GOLEMS BE DESTROYED.

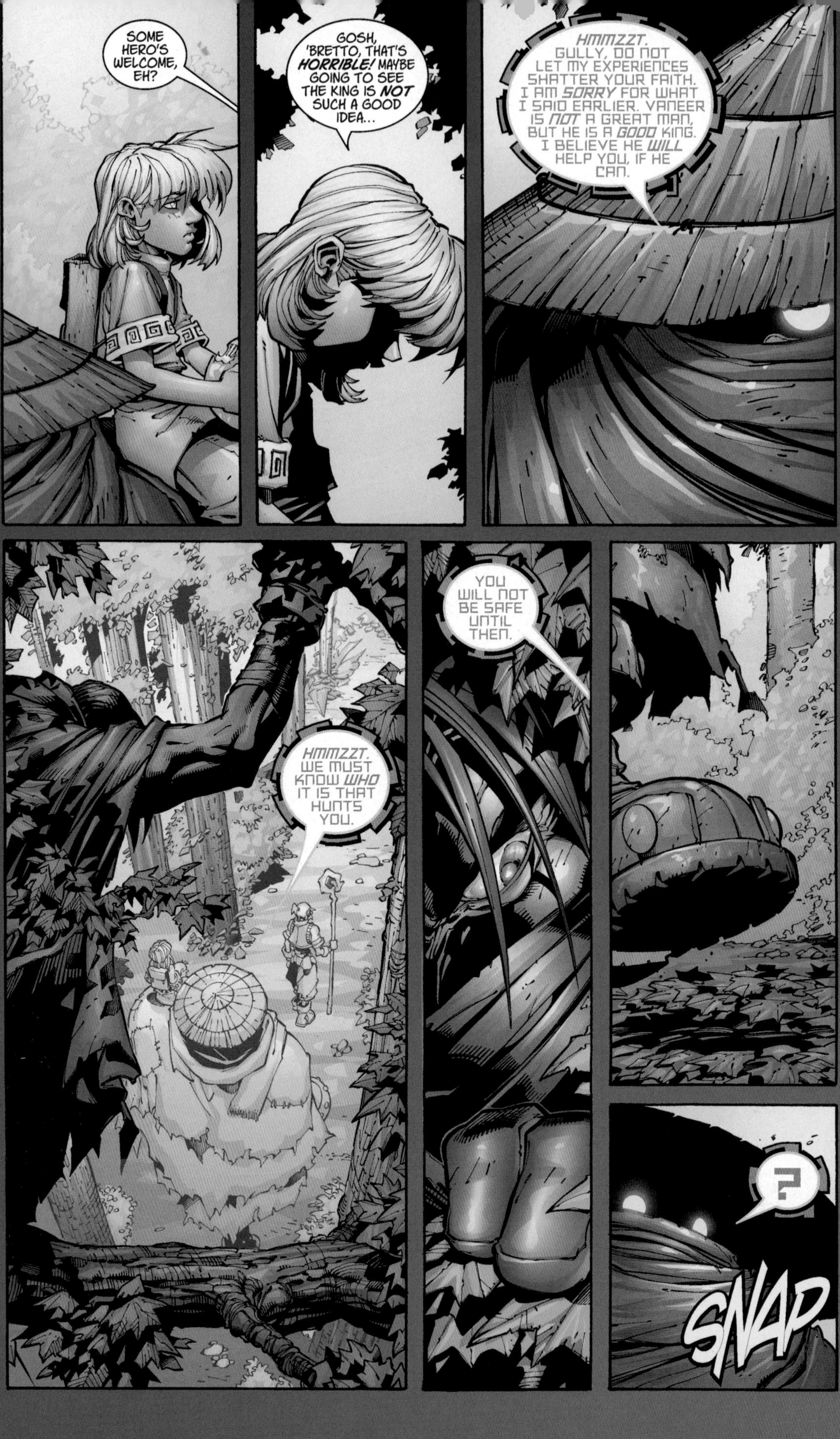
SOME HERO'S WELCOME, EH?
GOSH, 'BRETTO, THAT'S HORRIBLE! MAYBE GOING TO SEE THE KING IS NOT SUCH A GOOD IDEA...
HMMZZT. GULLY, DO NOT LET MY EXPERIENCES SHATTER YOUR FAITH. I AM SORRY FOR WHAT I SAID EARLIER. VANEER IS NOT A GREAT MAN, BUT HE IS A GOOD KING. I BELIEVE HE WILL HELP YOU, IF HE CAN.
HMMZZT. WE MUST KNOW WHO IT IS THAT HUNTS YOU.
YOU WILL NOT BE SAFE UNTIL THEN.
?
SNAP

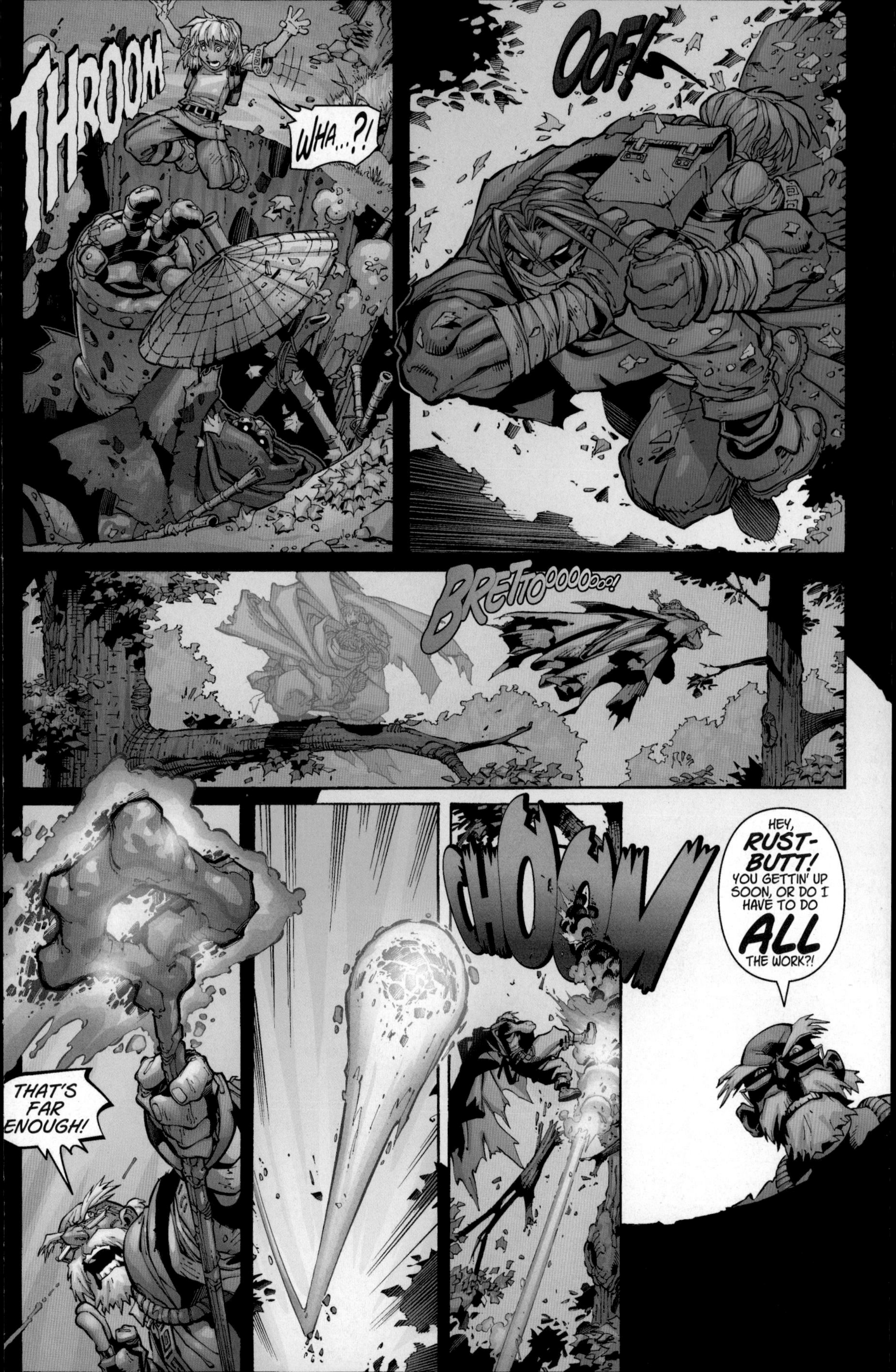
THROOM
WHA...?!
OOF!
BRETTOoooooo!
THAT'S FAR ENOUGH!
CHOOM
HEY, RUST-BUTT! YOU GETTIN' UP SOON, OR DO I HAVE TO DO ALL THE WORK?!

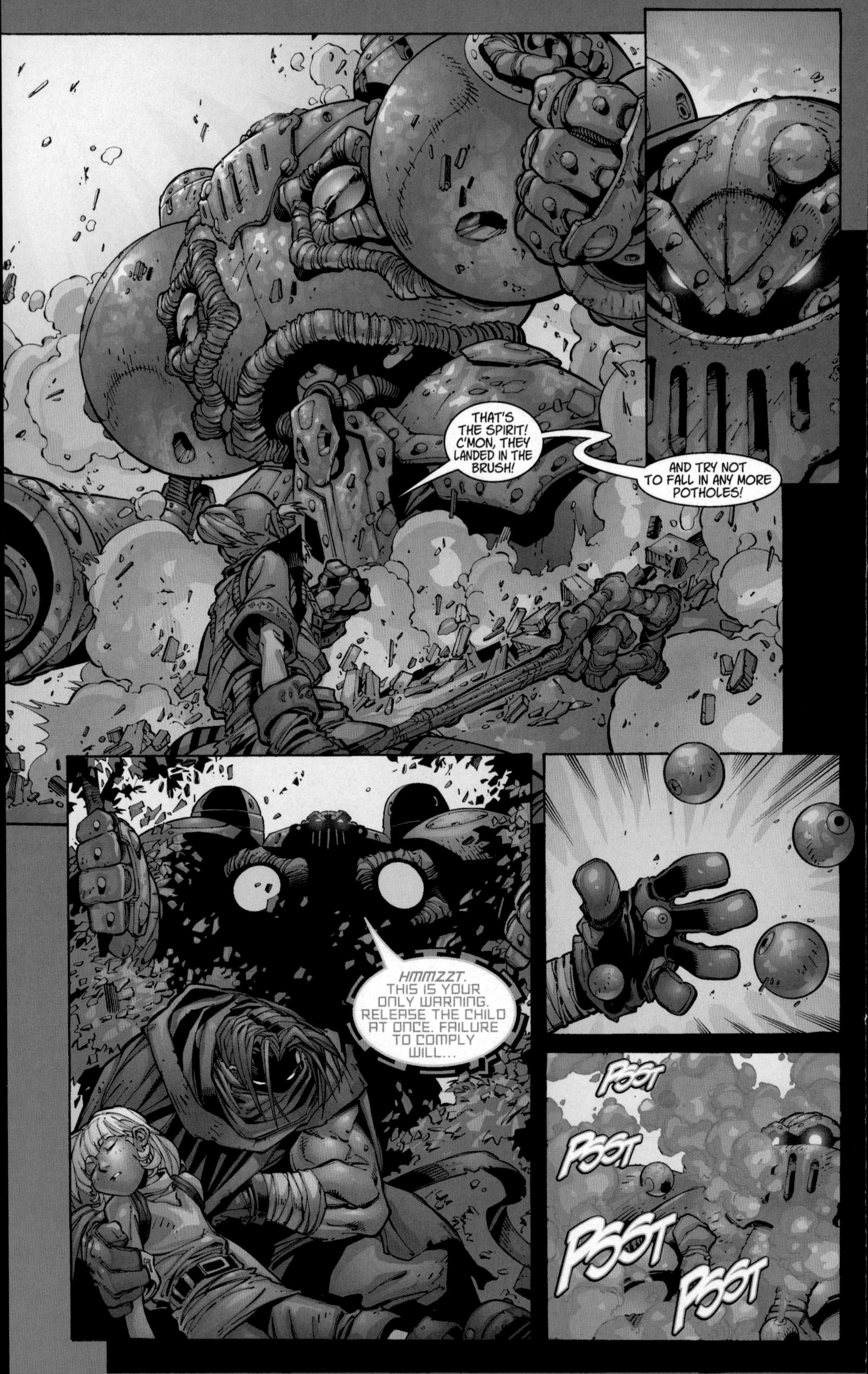
THAT'S THE SPIRIT! C'MON, THEY LANDED IN THE BRUSH!
AND TRY NOT TO FALL IN ANY MORE POTHOLES!
HMMZZT. THIS IS YOUR ONLY WARNING. RELEASE THE CHILD AT ONCE. FAILURE TO COMPLY WILL...
PSST
PSST
PSST
PSST

CALIBRETTO! I'VE GOT THE CHILD! SHE'S *OKAY!*

HMMZZT. GET HER TO SAFETY...

...I WILL DEAL WITH THIS VERMIN!

VRRTT

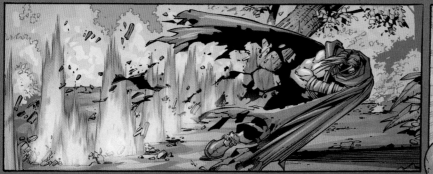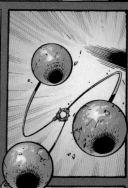

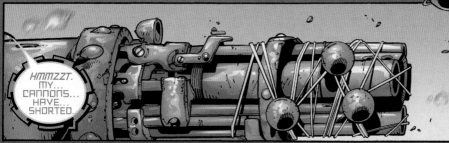

HMMZZT. MY... CANNONS... HAVE... SHORTED.

FRROOMM

ENOUGH! I HAVE NOT KILLED A MAN IN MANY YEARS, BUT I WILL IF I MUST, TO PROTECT THIS CHILD!

THEN OLD MAN...

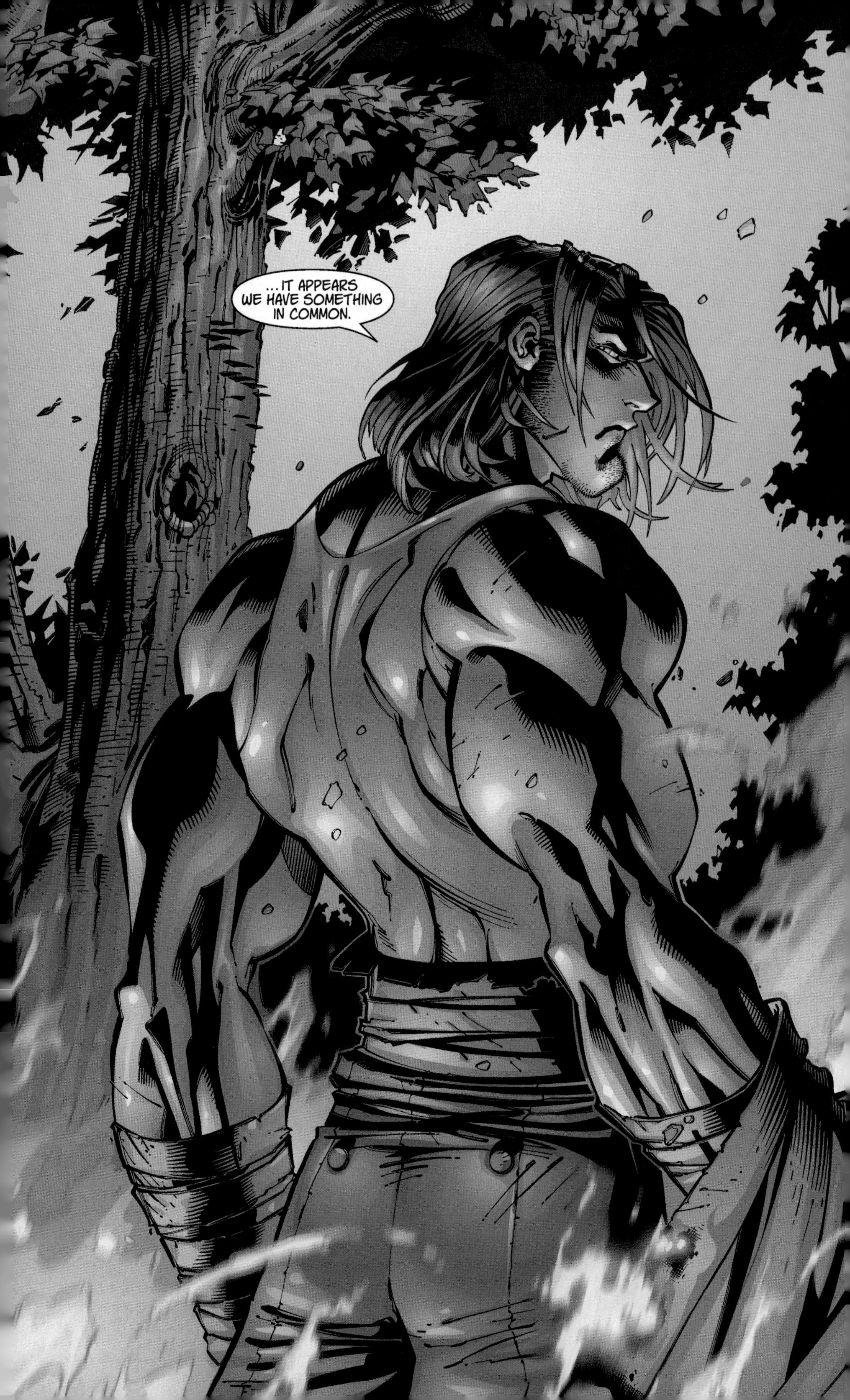
...IT APPEARS WE HAVE SOMETHING IN COMMON.

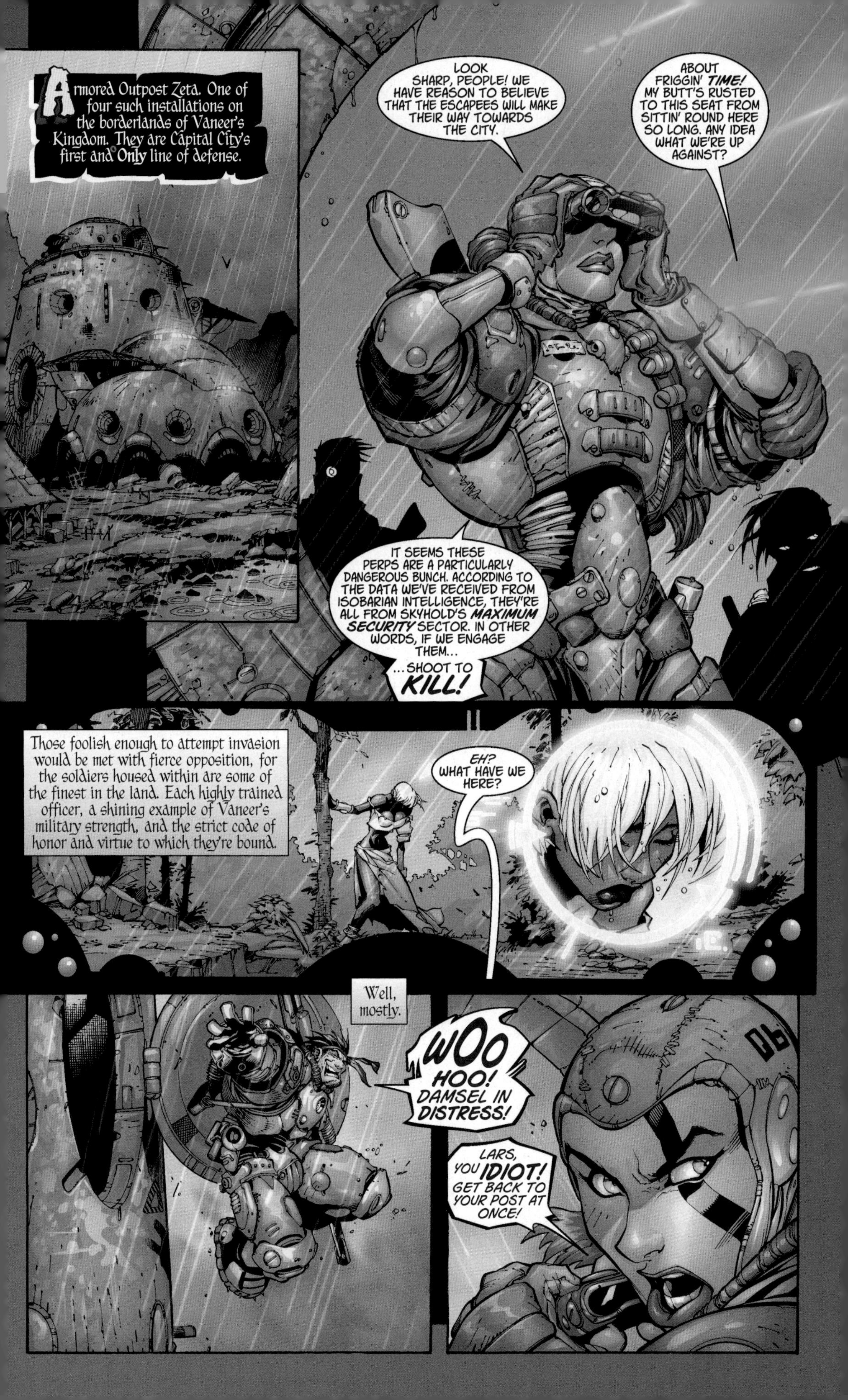
Armored Outpost Zeta. One of four such installations on the borderlands of Vaneer's Kingdom. They are Capital City's first and Only line of defense.
LOOK SHARP, PEOPLE! WE HAVE REASON TO BELIEVE THAT THE ESCAPEES WILL MAKE THEIR WAY TOWARDS THE CITY.
ABOUT FRIGGIN' TIME! MY BUTT'S RUSTED TO THIS SEAT FROM SITTIN' ROUND HERE SO LONG. ANY IDEA WHAT WE'RE UP AGAINST?
IT SEEMS THESE PERPS ARE A PARTICULARLY DANGEROUS BUNCH. ACCORDING TO THE DATA WE'VE RECEIVED FROM ISOBARIAN INTELLIGENCE, THEY'RE ALL FROM SKYHOLD'S MAXIMUM SECURITY SECTOR. IN OTHER WORDS, IF WE ENGAGE THEM...
...SHOOT TO KILL!
Those foolish enough to attempt invasion would be met with fierce opposition, for the soldiers housed within are some of the finest in the land. Each highly trained officer, a shining example of Vaneer's military strength, and the strict code of honor and virtue to which they're bound.
EH? WHAT HAVE WE HERE?
Well, mostly.
WOO HOO! DAMSEL IN DISTRESS!
LARS, YOU IDIOT! GET BACK TO YOUR POST AT ONCE!

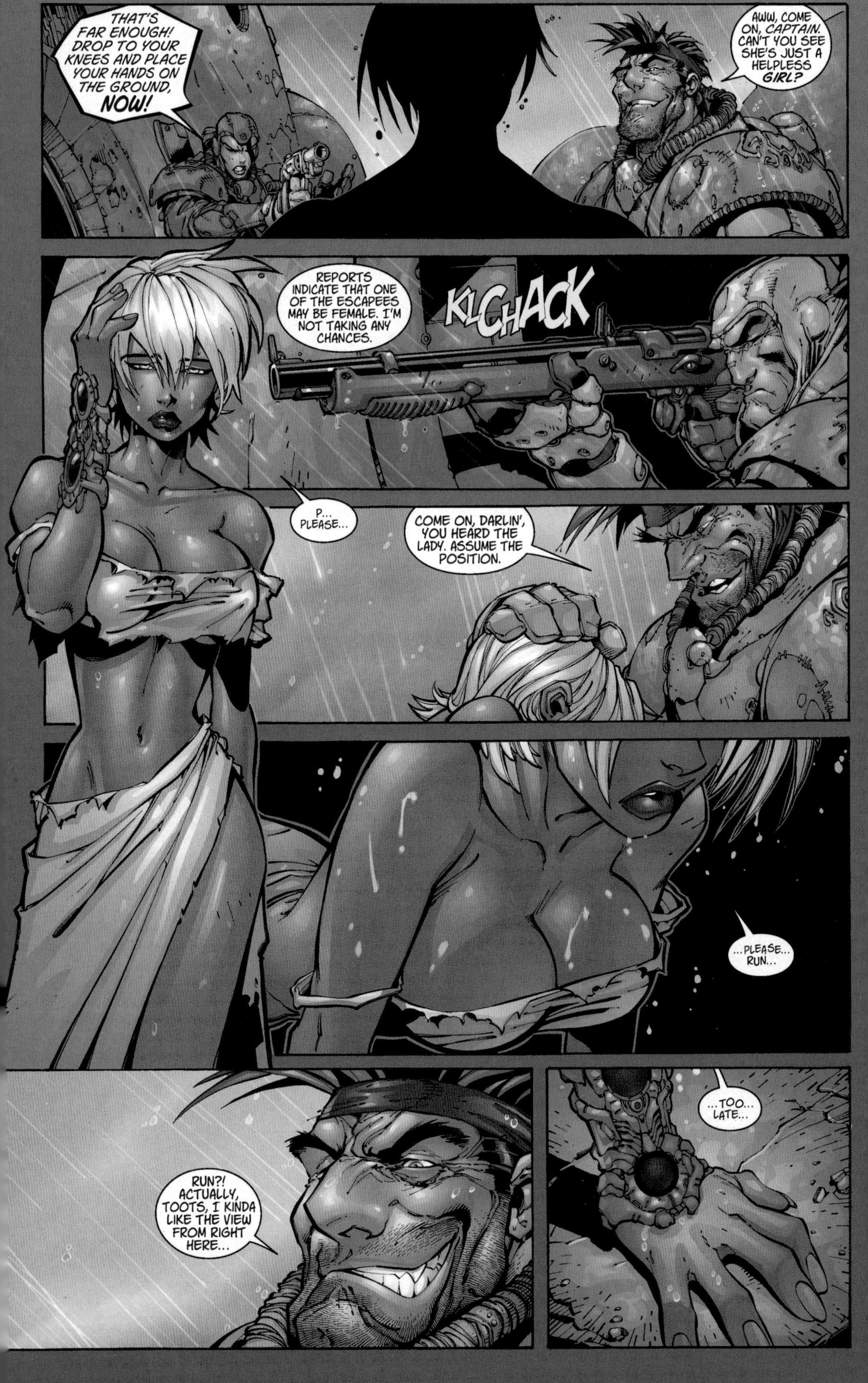
THAT'S FAR ENOUGH! DROP TO YOUR KNEES AND PLACE YOUR HANDS ON THE GROUND, NOW!
AWW, COME ON, CAPTAIN. CAN'T YOU SEE SHE'S JUST A HELPLESS GIRL?
REPORTS INDICATE THAT ONE OF THE ESCAPEES MAY BE FEMALE. I'M NOT TAKING ANY CHANCES.
KLCHACK
P... PLEASE...
COME ON, DARLIN', YOU HEARD THE LADY. ASSUME THE POSITION.
...PLEASE... RUN...
RUN?! ACTUALLY, TOOTS, I KINDA LIKE THE VIEW FROM RIGHT HERE...
...TOO... LATE...

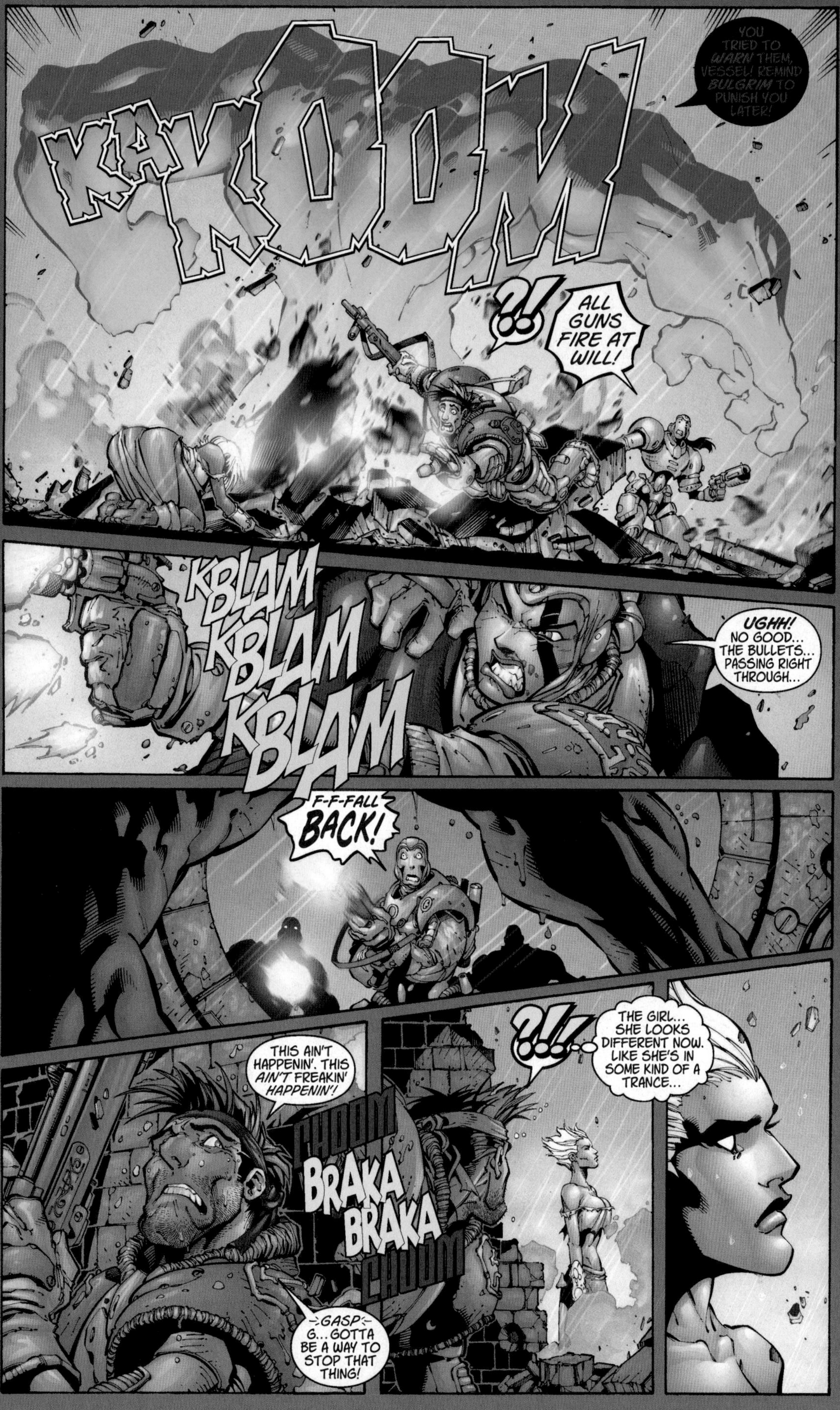
YOU TRIED TO WARN THEM, VESSEL! REMIND BULGRIM TO PUNISH YOU LATER!
KAKOOM
?!
ALL GUNS FIRE AT WILL!
KBLAM KBLAM KBLAM
UGHH! NO GOOD... THE BULLETS... PASSING RIGHT THROUGH...
F-F-FALL BACK!
THIS AIN'T HAPPENIN'. THIS AIN'T FREAKIN' HAPPENIN'!
CHOOM
BRAKA BRAKA
CHOOM
-GASP- G... GOTTA BE A WAY TO STOP THAT THING!
?!!...
THE GIRL... SHE LOOKS DIFFERENT NOW. LIKE SHE'S IN SOME KIND OF A TRANCE...

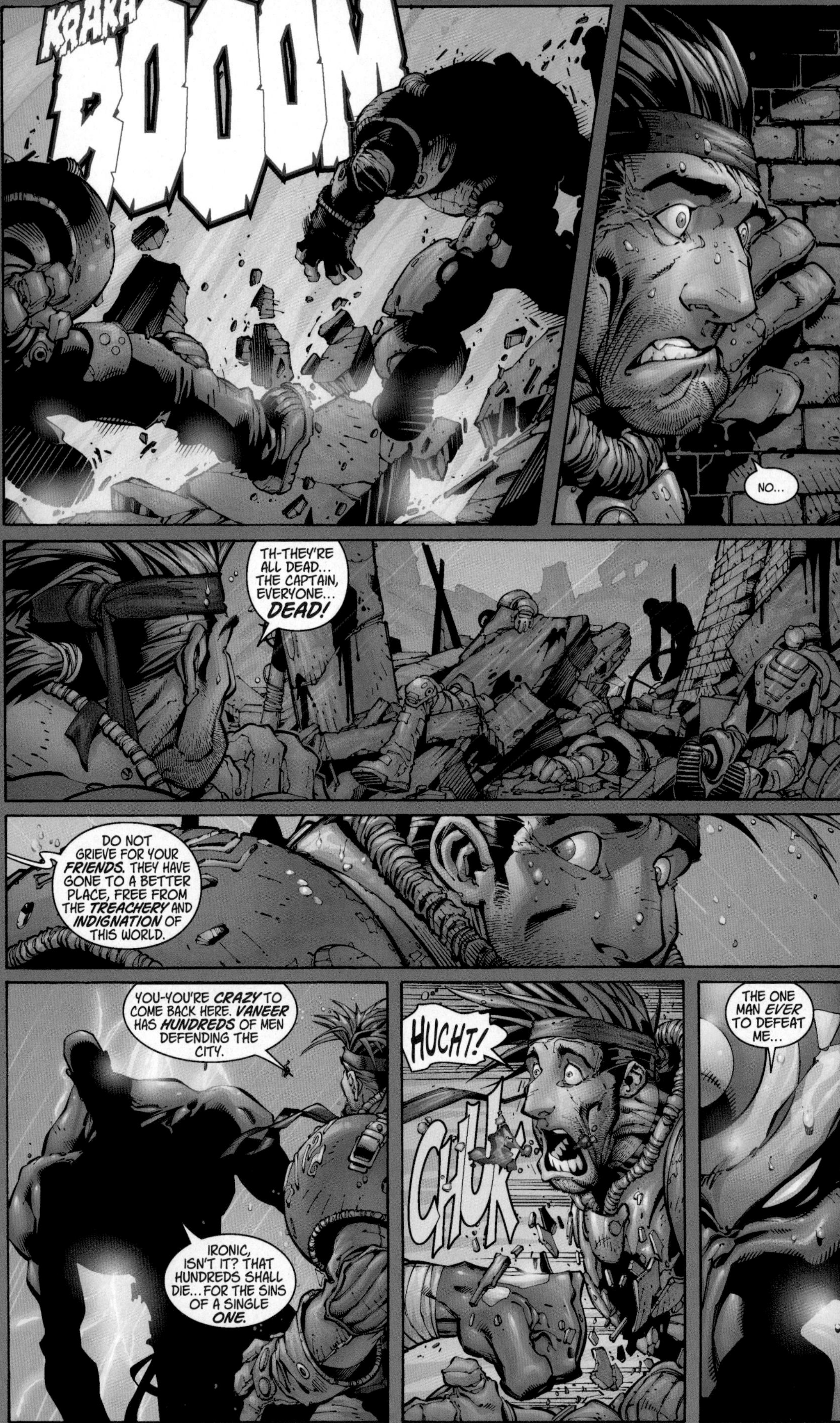
KRAKA
BOOOM
NO...
TH-THEY'RE ALL DEAD... THE CAPTAIN, EVERYONE... DEAD!
DO NOT GRIEVE FOR YOUR FRIENDS. THEY HAVE GONE TO A BETTER PLACE, FREE FROM THE TREACHERY AND INDIGNATION OF THIS WORLD.
YOU-YOU'RE CRAZY TO COME BACK HERE. VANEER HAS HUNDREDS OF MEN DEFENDING THE CITY.
IRONIC, ISN'T IT? THAT HUNDREDS SHALL DIE...FOR THE SINS OF A SINGLE ONE.
HUCHT!
CHUK
THE ONE MAN EVER TO DEFEAT ME...

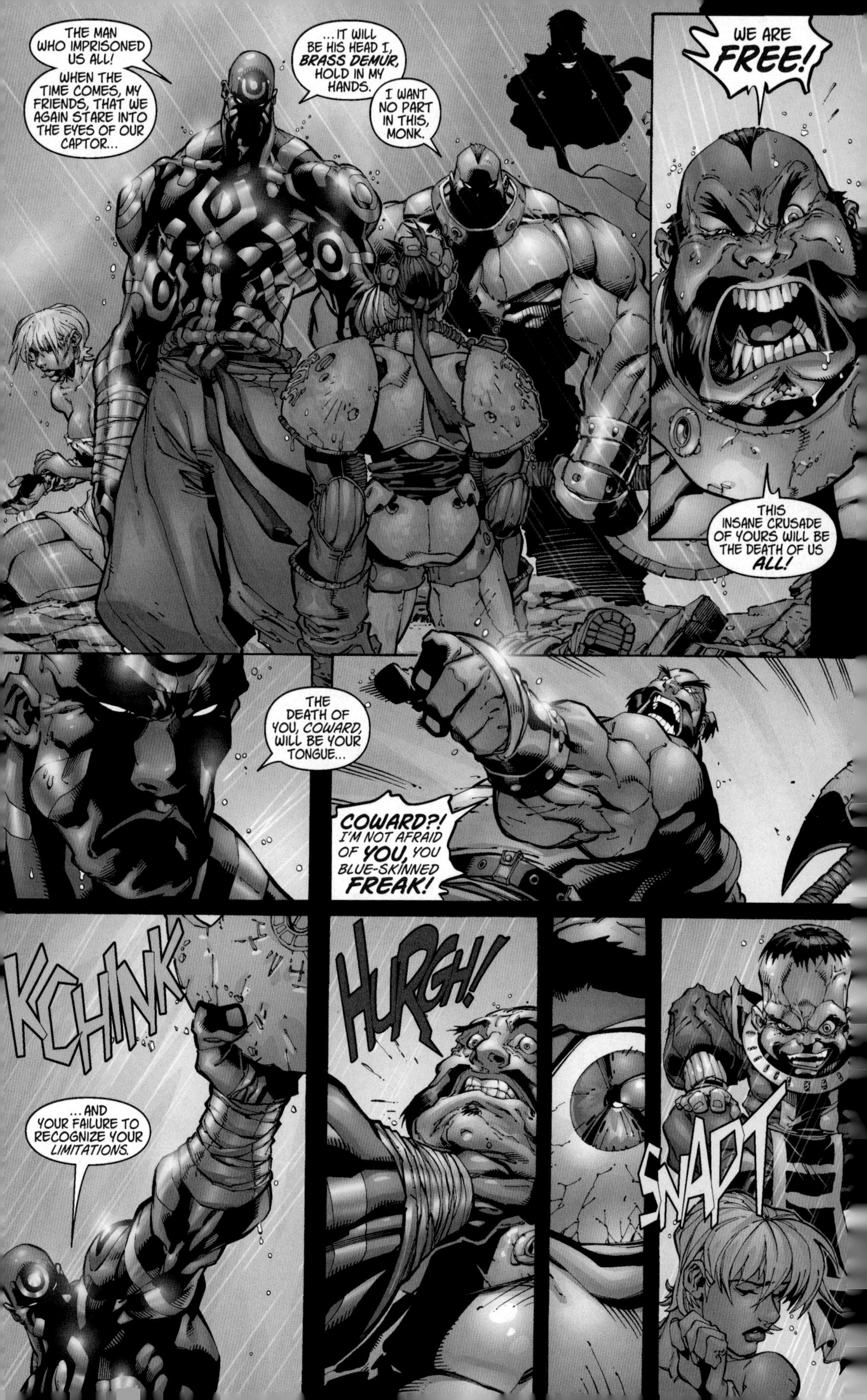
THE MAN WHO IMPRISONED US ALL!
WHEN THE TIME COMES, MY FRIENDS, THAT WE AGAIN STARE INTO THE EYES OF OUR CAPTOR...
...IT WILL BE HIS HEAD I, BRASS DEMUR, HOLD IN MY HANDS.
I WANT NO PART IN THIS, MONK.
WE ARE FREE!
THIS INSANE CRUSADE OF YOURS WILL BE THE DEATH OF US ALL!
THE DEATH OF YOU, COWARD, WILL BE YOUR TONGUE...
COWARD?! I'M NOT AFRAID OF YOU, YOU BLUE-SKINNED FREAK!
KCHINK
...AND YOUR FAILURE TO RECOGNIZE YOUR LIMITATIONS.
HURGH!
SNAP

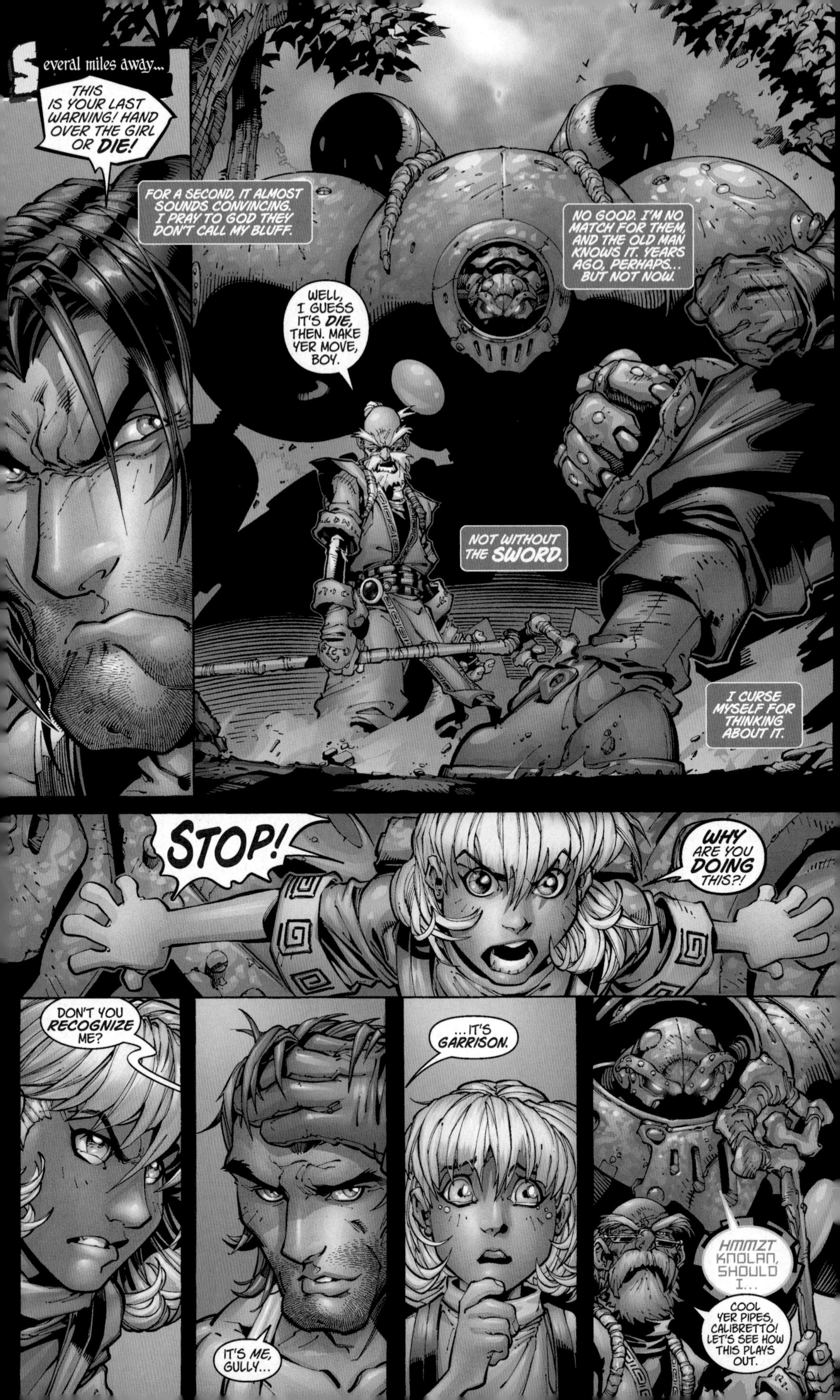
Several miles away...
THIS IS YOUR LAST WARNING! HAND OVER THE GIRL OR DIE!
FOR A SECOND, IT ALMOST SOUNDS CONVINCING. I PRAY TO GOD THEY DON'T CALL MY BLUFF.
WELL, I GUESS IT'S DIE, THEN. MAKE YER MOVE, BOY.
NO GOOD. I'M NO MATCH FOR THEM, AND THE OLD MAN KNOWS IT. YEARS AGO, PERHAPS... BUT NOT NOW.
NOT WITHOUT THE SWORD.
I CURSE MYSELF FOR THINKING ABOUT IT.
STOP!
WHY ARE YOU DOING THIS?!
DON'T YOU RECOGNIZE ME?
IT'S ME, GULLY...
...IT'S GARRISON.
HMMZT KNOLAN, SHOULD I...
COOL YER PIPES, CALIBRETTO! LET'S SEE HOW THIS PLAYS OUT.

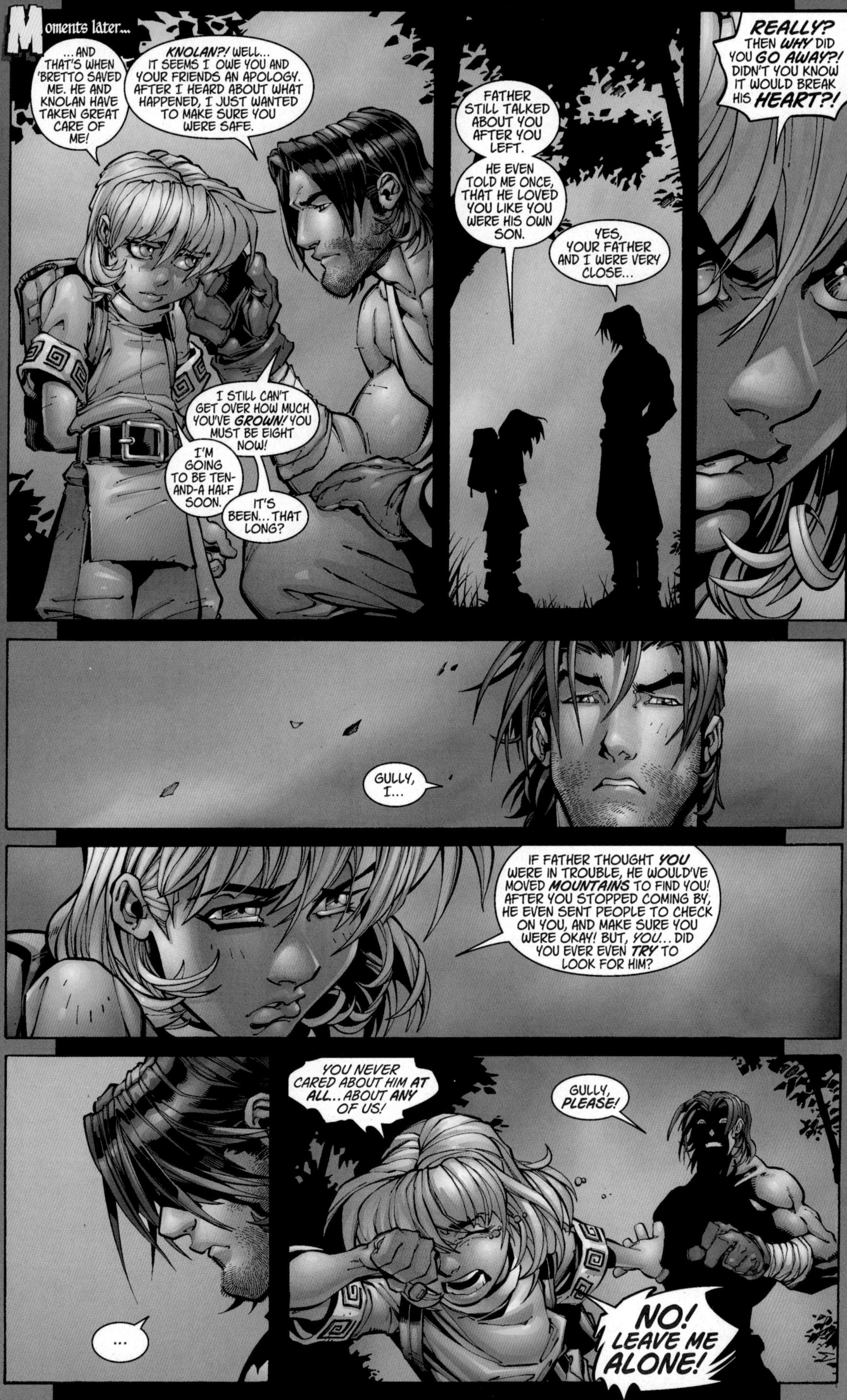

Moments later...
...AND THAT'S WHEN 'BRETTO SAVED ME. HE AND KNOLAN HAVE TAKEN GREAT CARE OF ME!
KNOLAN?! WELL... IT SEEMS I OWE YOU AND YOUR FRIENDS AN APOLOGY. AFTER I HEARD ABOUT WHAT HAPPENED, I JUST WANTED TO MAKE SURE YOU WERE SAFE.
I STILL CAN'T GET OVER HOW MUCH YOU'VE GROWN! YOU MUST BE EIGHT NOW!
I'M GOING TO BE TEN-AND-A HALF SOON.
IT'S BEEN... THAT LONG?
FATHER STILL TALKED ABOUT YOU AFTER YOU LEFT.
HE EVEN TOLD ME ONCE, THAT HE LOVED YOU LIKE YOU WERE HIS OWN SON.
YES, YOUR FATHER AND I WERE VERY CLOSE...
REALLY? THEN WHY DID YOU GO AWAY?! DIDN'T YOU KNOW IT WOULD BREAK HIS HEART?!
GULLY, I...
IF FATHER THOUGHT YOU WERE IN TROUBLE, HE WOULD'VE MOVED MOUNTAINS TO FIND YOU! AFTER YOU STOPPED COMING BY, HE EVEN SENT PEOPLE TO CHECK ON YOU, AND MAKE SURE YOU WERE OKAY! BUT, YOU... DID YOU EVER EVEN TRY TO LOOK FOR HIM?
...
YOU NEVER CARED ABOUT HIM AT ALL... ABOUT ANY OF US!
GULLY, PLEASE!
NO! LEAVE ME ALONE!

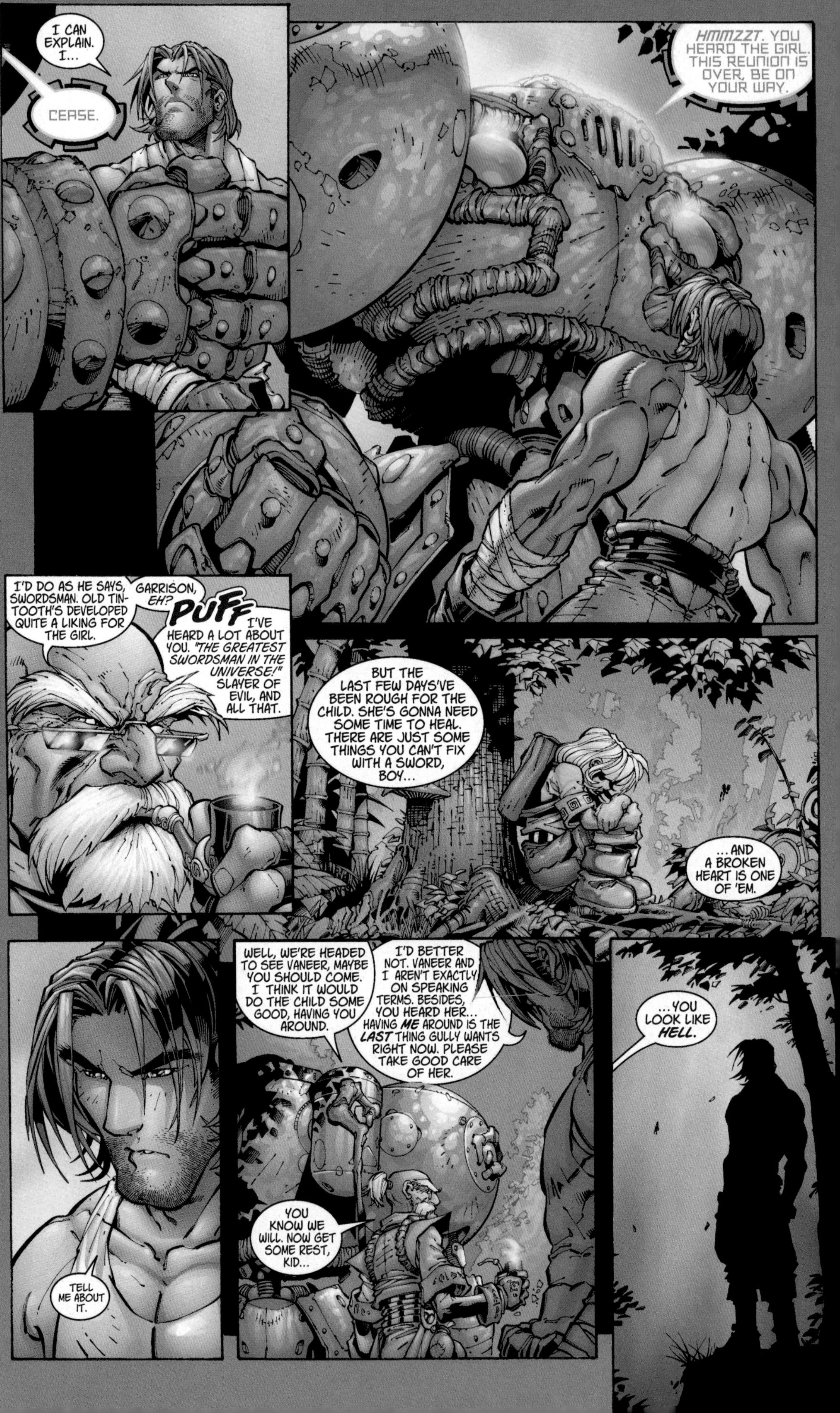
I CAN EXPLAIN. I...
CEASE.
HMMZZT. YOU HEARD THE GIRL. THIS REUNION IS OVER. BE ON YOUR WAY.
I'D DO AS HE SAYS, SWORDSMAN. OLD TIN-TOOTH'S DEVELOPED QUITE A LIKING FOR THE GIRL.
GARRISON, EH?
PUFF
I'VE HEARD A LOT ABOUT YOU. "THE GREATEST SWORDSMAN IN THE UNIVERSE!" SLAYER OF EVIL, AND ALL THAT.
BUT THE LAST FEW DAYS'VE BEEN ROUGH FOR THE CHILD. SHE'S GONNA NEED SOME TIME TO HEAL. THERE ARE JUST SOME THINGS YOU CAN'T FIX WITH A SWORD, BOY...
...AND A BROKEN HEART IS ONE OF 'EM.
TELL ME ABOUT IT.
WELL, WE'RE HEADED TO SEE VANEER, MAYBE YOU SHOULD COME. I THINK IT WOULD DO THE CHILD SOME GOOD, HAVING YOU AROUND.
I'D BETTER NOT. VANEER AND I AREN'T EXACTLY ON SPEAKING TERMS. BESIDES, YOU HEARD HER... HAVING ME AROUND IS THE LAST THING GULLY WANTS RIGHT NOW. PLEASE TAKE GOOD CARE OF HER.
YOU KNOW WE WILL. NOW GET SOME REST, KID...
...YOU LOOK LIKE HELL.

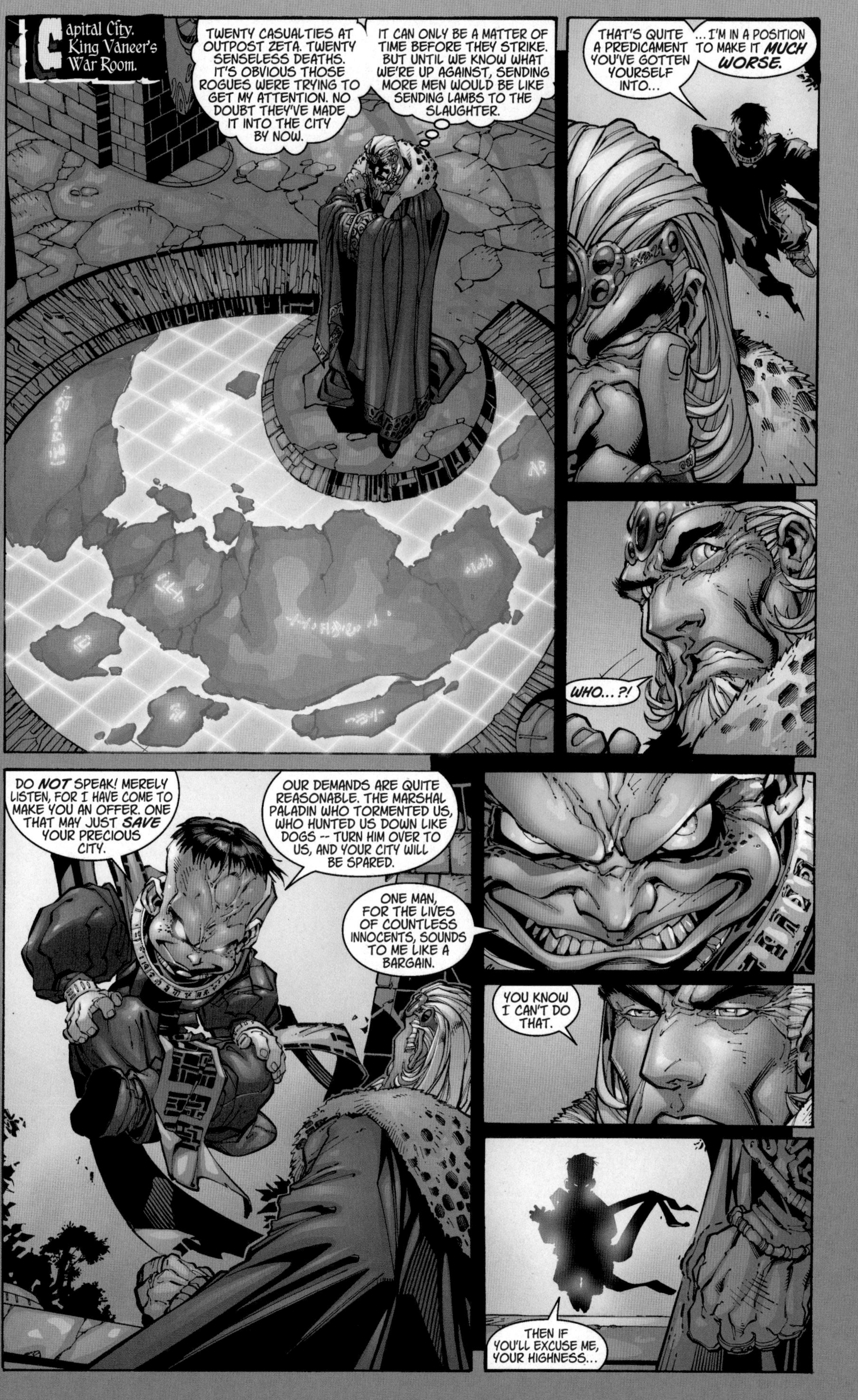
Capital City. King Vaneer's War Room.
TWENTY CASUALTIES AT OUTPOST ZETA. TWENTY SENSELESS DEATHS. IT'S OBVIOUS THOSE ROGUES WERE TRYING TO GET MY ATTENTION. NO DOUBT THEY'VE MADE IT INTO THE CITY BY NOW.
IT CAN ONLY BE A MATTER OF TIME BEFORE THEY STRIKE. BUT UNTIL WE KNOW WHAT WE'RE UP AGAINST, SENDING MORE MEN WOULD BE LIKE SENDING LAMBS TO THE SLAUGHTER.
THAT'S QUITE A PREDICAMENT YOU'VE GOTTEN YOURSELF INTO...
... I'M IN A POSITION TO MAKE IT MUCH WORSE.
WHO...?!
DO NOT SPEAK! MERELY LISTEN, FOR I HAVE COME TO MAKE YOU AN OFFER. ONE THAT MAY JUST SAVE YOUR PRECIOUS CITY.
OUR DEMANDS ARE QUITE REASONABLE. THE MARSHAL PALADIN WHO TORMENTED US, WHO HUNTED US DOWN LIKE DOGS -- TURN HIM OVER TO US, AND YOUR CITY WILL BE SPARED.
ONE MAN, FOR THE LIVES OF COUNTLESS INNOCENTS, SOUNDS TO ME LIKE A BARGAIN.
YOU KNOW I CAN'T DO THAT.
THEN IF YOU'LL EXCUSE ME, YOUR HIGHNESS...

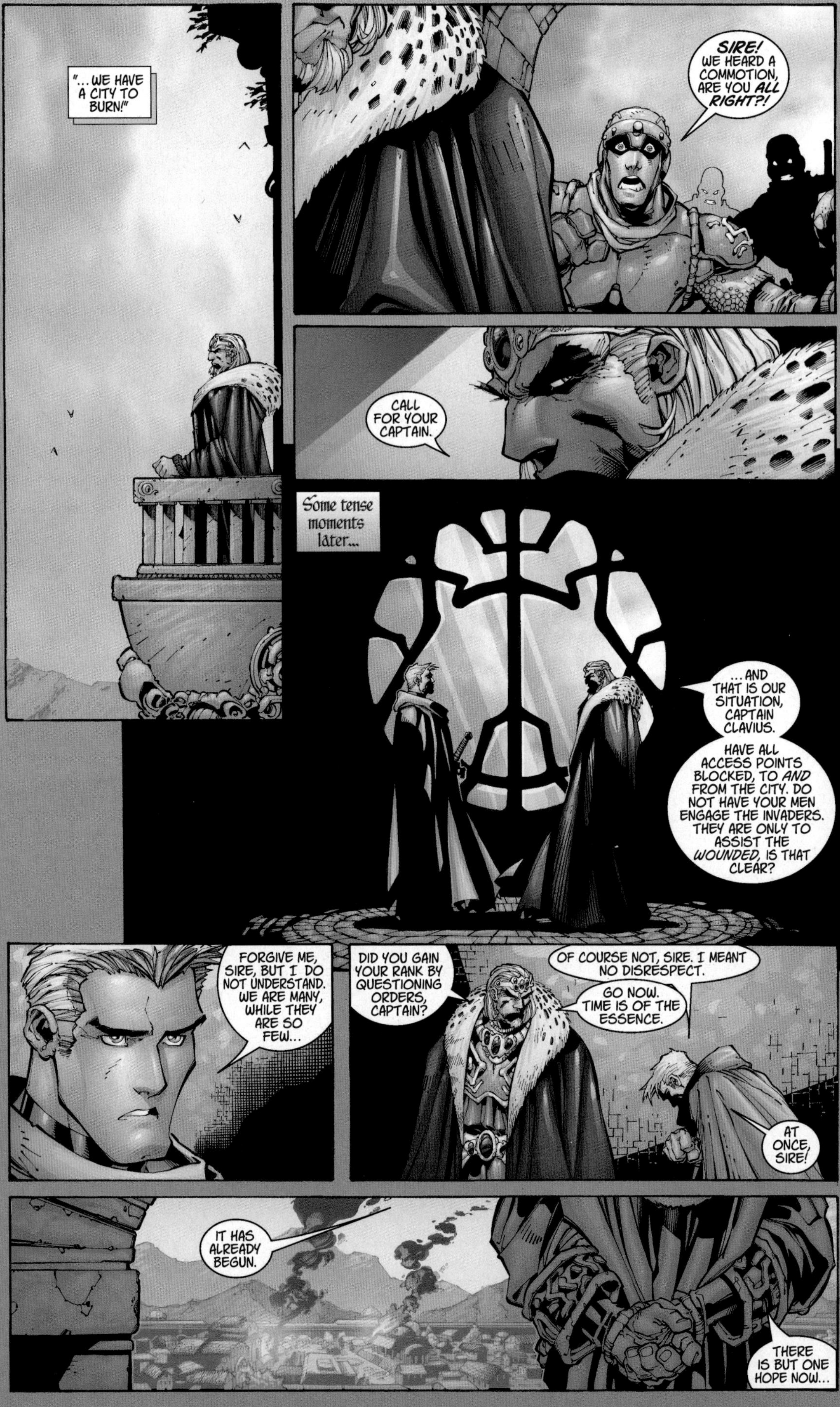
"...WE HAVE A CITY TO BURN!"
SIRE! WE HEARD A COMMOTION, ARE YOU ALL RIGHT?!
CALL FOR YOUR CAPTAIN.
Some tense moments later...
...AND THAT IS OUR SITUATION, CAPTAIN CLAVIUS.
HAVE ALL ACCESS POINTS BLOCKED, TO AND FROM THE CITY. DO NOT HAVE YOUR MEN ENGAGE THE INVADERS. THEY ARE ONLY TO ASSIST THE WOUNDED, IS THAT CLEAR?
FORGIVE ME, SIRE, BUT I DO NOT UNDERSTAND. WE ARE MANY, WHILE THEY ARE SO FEW...
DID YOU GAIN YOUR RANK BY QUESTIONING ORDERS, CAPTAIN?
OF COURSE NOT, SIRE. I MEANT NO DISRESPECT.
GO NOW. TIME IS OF THE ESSENCE.
AT ONCE, SIRE!
IT HAS ALREADY BEGUN.
THERE IS BUT ONE HOPE NOW...

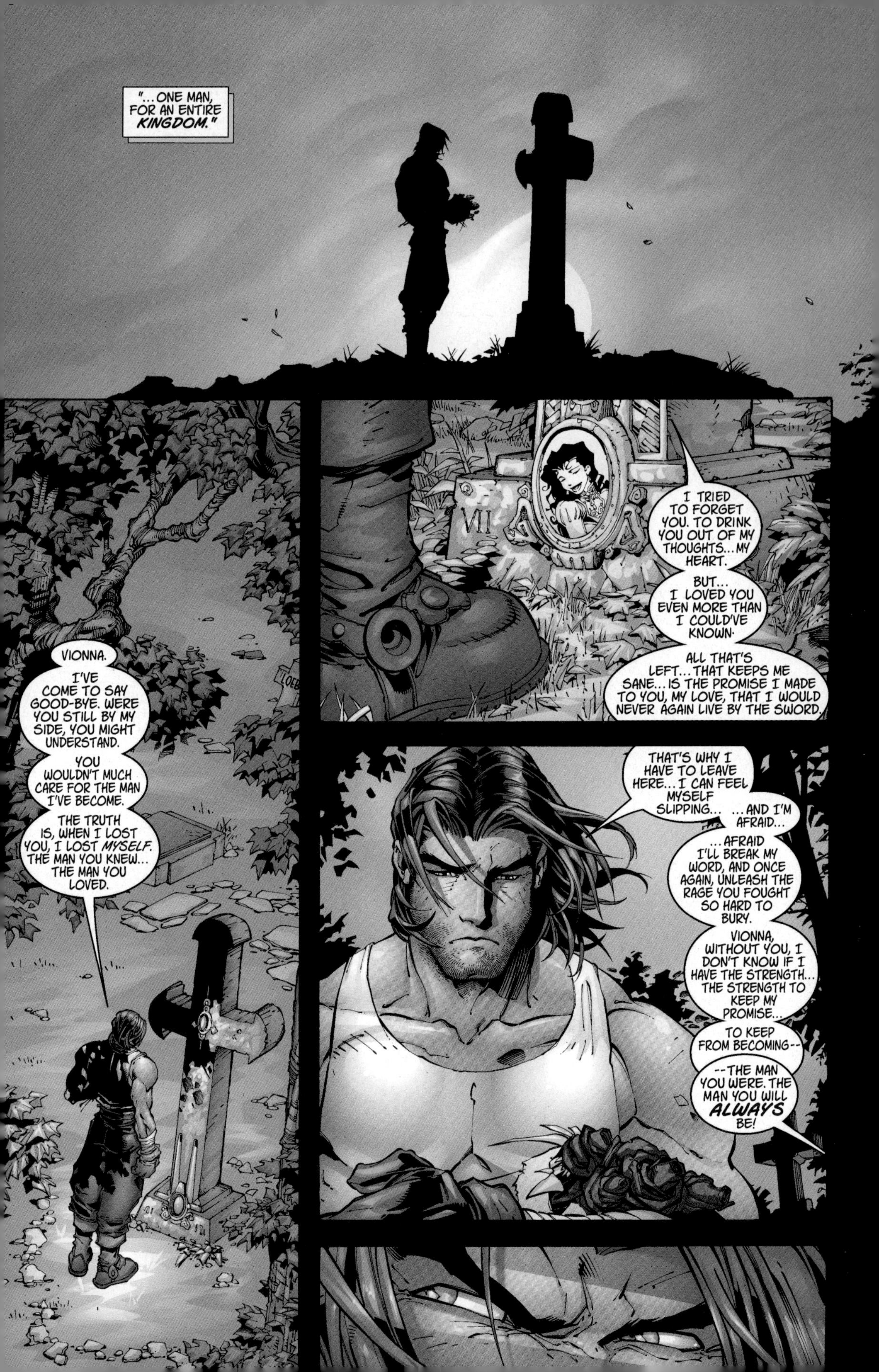
"...ONE MAN, FOR AN ENTIRE *KINGDOM.*"
I TRIED TO FORGET YOU. TO DRINK YOU OUT OF MY THOUGHTS... MY HEART.
BUT... I LOVED YOU EVEN MORE THAN I COULD'VE KNOWN.
ALL THAT'S LEFT... THAT KEEPS ME SANE... IS THE PROMISE I MADE TO YOU, MY LOVE, THAT I WOULD NEVER AGAIN LIVE BY THE SWORD.
VIONNA.
I'VE COME TO SAY GOOD-BYE. WERE YOU STILL BY MY SIDE, YOU MIGHT UNDERSTAND.
YOU WOULDN'T MUCH CARE FOR THE MAN I'VE BECOME.
THE TRUTH IS, WHEN I LOST YOU, I LOST *MYSELF.* THE MAN YOU KNEW... THE MAN YOU LOVED.
THAT'S WHY I HAVE TO LEAVE HERE... I CAN FEEL MYSELF SLIPPING...
...AND I'M AFRAID...
...AFRAID I'LL BREAK MY WORD, AND ONCE AGAIN, UNLEASH THE RAGE YOU FOUGHT SO HARD TO BURY.
VIONNA, WITHOUT YOU, I DON'T KNOW IF I HAVE THE STRENGTH... THE STRENGTH TO KEEP MY PROMISE...
TO KEEP FROM BECOMING--
--THE MAN YOU WERE. THE MAN YOU WILL ***ALWAYS*** BE!

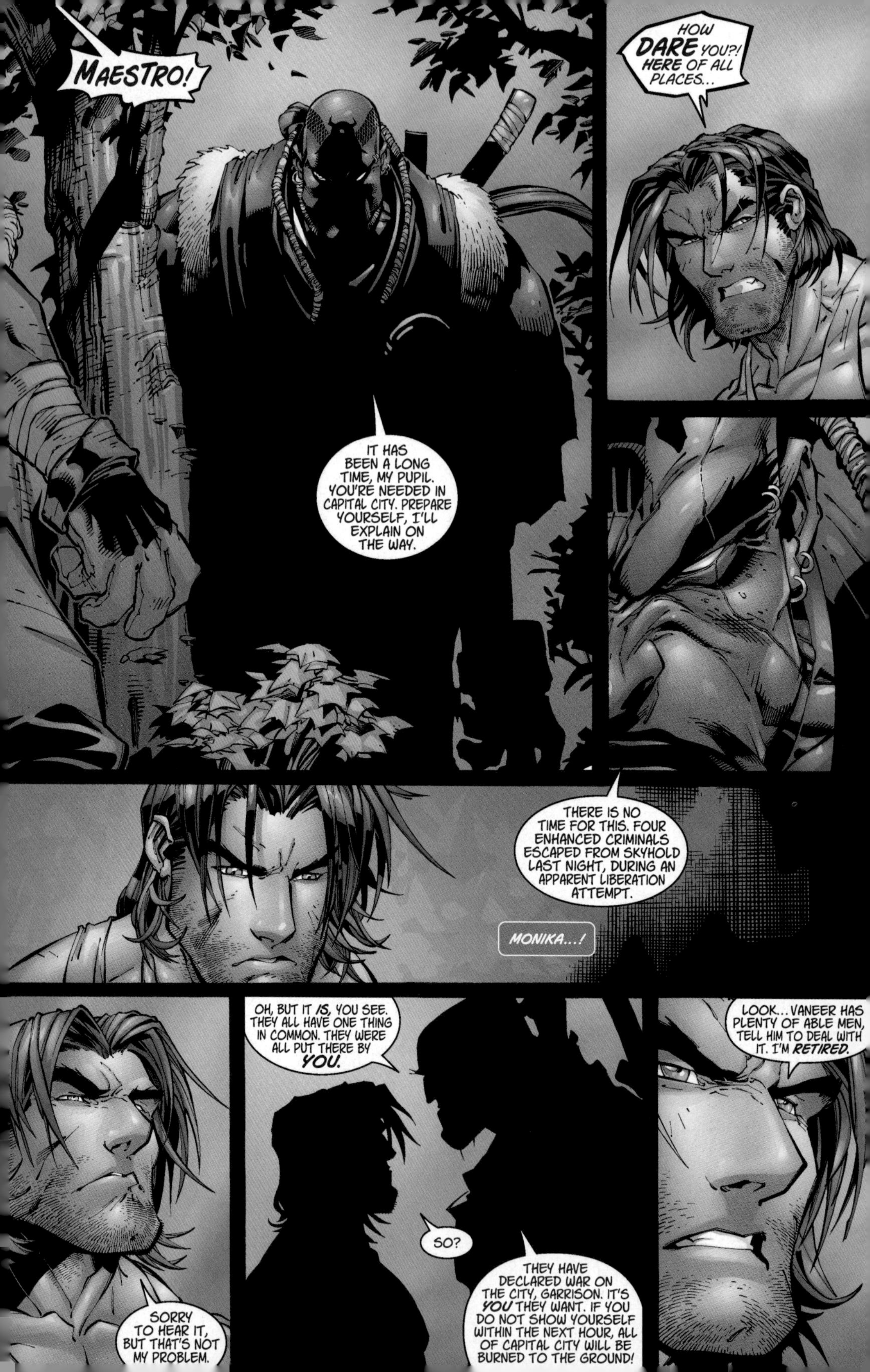
MAESTRO!
HOW DARE YOU?! HERE OF ALL PLACES...
IT HAS BEEN A LONG TIME, MY PUPIL. YOU'RE NEEDED IN CAPITAL CITY. PREPARE YOURSELF, I'LL EXPLAIN ON THE WAY.
THERE IS NO TIME FOR THIS. FOUR ENHANCED CRIMINALS ESCAPED FROM SKYHOLD LAST NIGHT, DURING AN APPARENT LIBERATION ATTEMPT.
MONIKA...!
SORRY TO HEAR IT, BUT THAT'S NOT MY PROBLEM.
OH, BUT IT IS, YOU SEE. THEY ALL HAVE ONE THING IN COMMON. THEY WERE ALL PUT THERE BY YOU.
SO?
THEY HAVE DECLARED WAR ON THE CITY, GARRISON. IT'S YOU THEY WANT. IF YOU DO NOT SHOW YOURSELF WITHIN THE NEXT HOUR, ALL OF CAPITAL CITY WILL BE BURNED TO THE GROUND!
LOOK... VANEER HAS PLENTY OF ABLE MEN, TELL HIM TO DEAL WITH IT. I'M RETIRED.

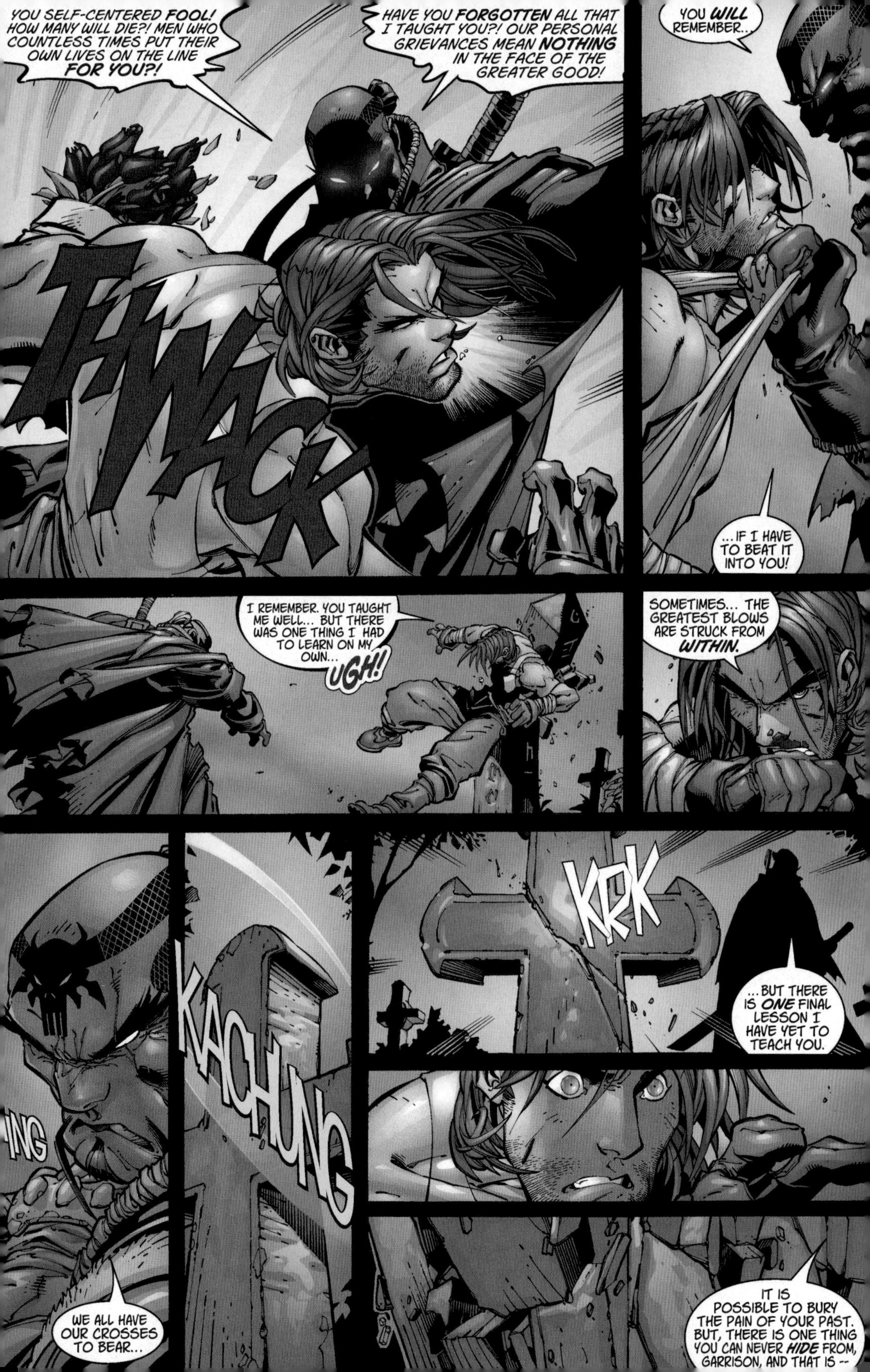

YOU SELF-CENTERED FOOL! HOW MANY WILL DIE?! MEN WHO COUNTLESS TIMES PUT THEIR OWN LIVES ON THE LINE FOR YOU?!
HAVE YOU FORGOTTEN ALL THAT I TAUGHT YOU?! OUR PERSONAL GRIEVANCES MEAN NOTHING IN THE FACE OF THE GREATER GOOD!
THWACK
YOU WILL REMEMBER...
...IF I HAVE TO BEAT IT INTO YOU!
I REMEMBER. YOU TAUGHT ME WELL... BUT THERE WAS ONE THING I HAD TO LEARN ON MY OWN...
UGH!
SOMETIMES... THE GREATEST BLOWS ARE STRUCK FROM WITHIN.
KACHUNG
WE ALL HAVE OUR CROSSES TO BEAR...
KRK
...BUT THERE IS ONE FINAL LESSON I HAVE YET TO TEACH YOU.
IT IS POSSIBLE TO BURY THE PAIN OF YOUR PAST. BUT, THERE IS ONE THING YOU CAN NEVER HIDE FROM, GARRISON, AND THAT IS --

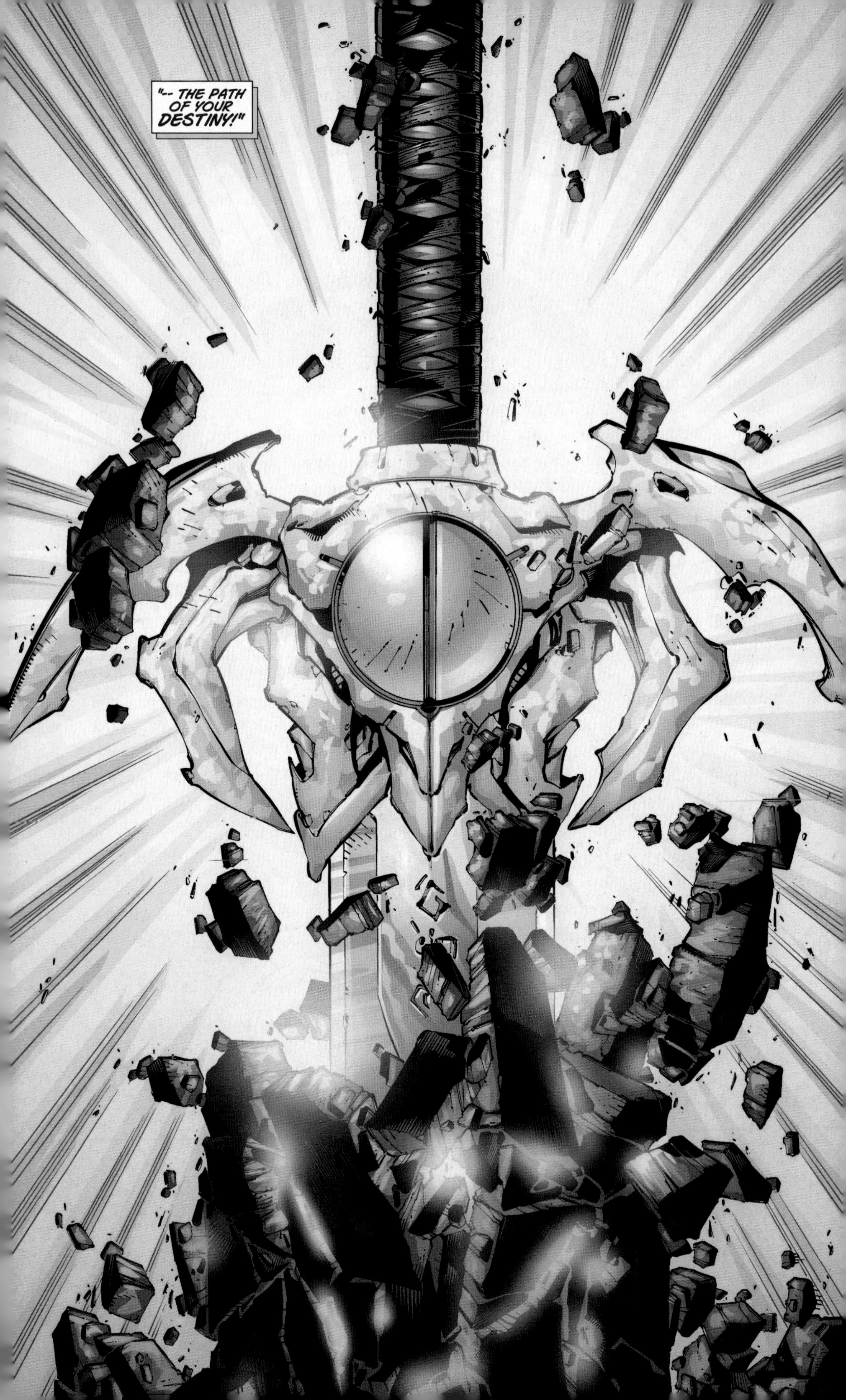
"-- THE PATH OF YOUR DESTINY!"

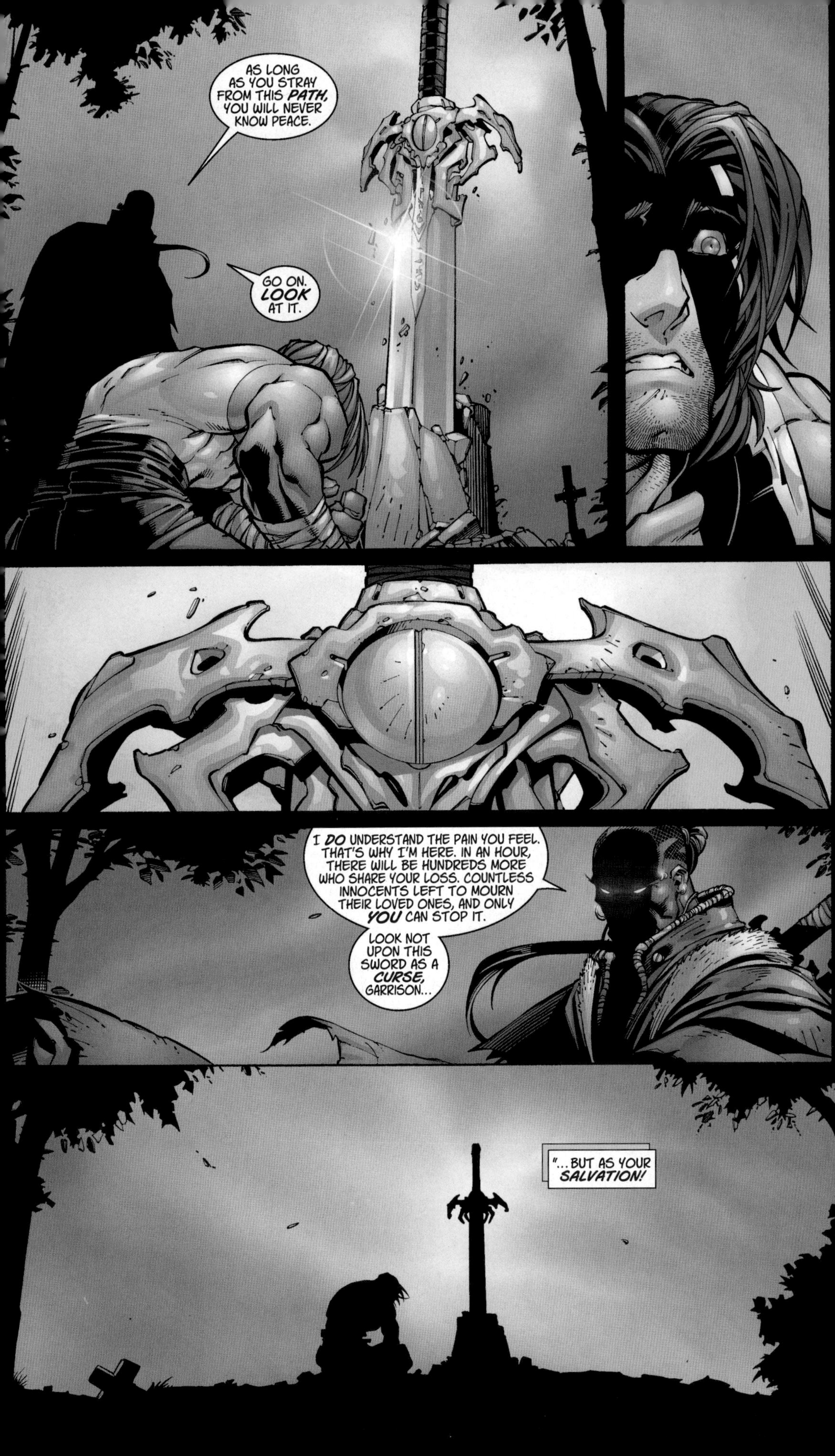
AS LONG AS YOU STRAY FROM THIS PATH, YOU WILL NEVER KNOW PEACE.
GO ON. LOOK AT IT.
I DO UNDERSTAND THE PAIN YOU FEEL. THAT'S WHY I'M HERE. IN AN HOUR, THERE WILL BE HUNDREDS MORE WHO SHARE YOUR LOSS. COUNTLESS INNOCENTS LEFT TO MOURN THEIR LOVED ONES, AND ONLY YOU CAN STOP IT.
LOOK NOT UPON THIS SWORD AS A CURSE, GARRISON...
"...BUT AS YOUR SALVATION!

While, at the city...

FINALLY, WE'RE...!

HERE?!

KNOLAN! *THE CITY!*

EITHER THIS CITY IS UNDER ATTACK, OR VANEER'S GOT ONE *HECK* OF A FIREWORKS DISPLAY!

LET'S GO!

And soon...

HMMZZT. KNOLAN, THERE IS DEFINITELY A *HOSTILE* PRESENCE WITHIN THE CITY.

I THINK WE'VE GOT *THAT* PART FIGURED OUT, SHELL-SHORTS! HOW'S ABOUT A *WHO*, AND *WHY?!*

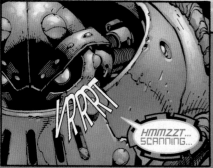

VRRRT

HMMZZT... SCANNING...

CLK

HMMZZT. THE ATTACKS ALL SEEM TO COME FROM A SINGLE, HIGH-LEVEL MAGIC USER.

MAGIC?! THAT'S *YOUR* DEPARTMENT, MR. KNOLAN! YOU'VE *GOTTA* DO SOMETHING!

WHAT DO I LOOK LIKE, KID? SOME KIND OF *SUPER-HERO?!*

I DON'T *SAVE* THE DAY, I JUST TRY TO *ENJOY* IT!

THOUGH AT THIS RATE, I *MAY* NOT HAVE MANY LEFT!

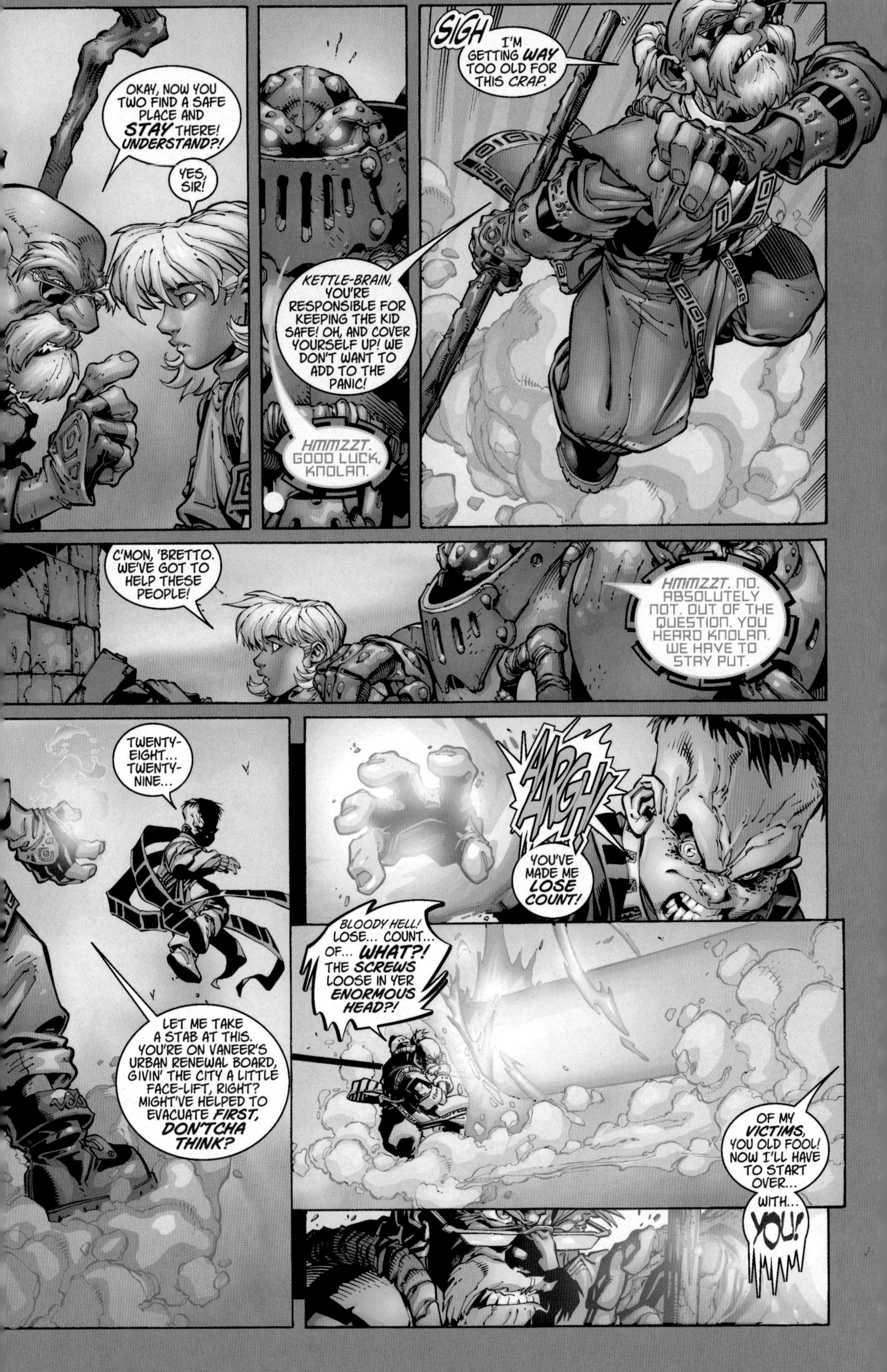
OKAY, NOW YOU TWO FIND A SAFE PLACE AND STAY THERE! UNDERSTAND?!
YES, SIR!
!
KETTLE-BRAIN, YOU'RE RESPONSIBLE FOR KEEPING THE KID SAFE! OH, AND COVER YOURSELF UP! WE DON'T WANT TO ADD TO THE PANIC!
HMMZZT. GOOD LUCK, KNOLAN.
SIGH
I'M GETTING WAY TOO OLD FOR THIS CRAP.
C'MON, 'BRETTO. WE'VE GOT TO HELP THESE PEOPLE!
HMMZZT. NO. ABSOLUTELY NOT. OUT OF THE QUESTION. YOU HEARD KNOLAN. WE HAVE TO STAY PUT.
TWENTY-EIGHT... TWENTY-NINE...
LET ME TAKE A STAB AT THIS. YOU'RE ON VANEER'S URBAN RENEWAL BOARD, GIVIN' THE CITY A LITTLE FACE-LIFT, RIGHT? MIGHT'VE HELPED TO EVACUATE FIRST, DON'TCHA THINK?
AARGH!
YOU'VE MADE ME LOSE COUNT!
BLOODY HELL! LOSE... COUNT... OF... WHAT?! THE SCREWS LOOSE IN YER ENORMOUS HEAD?!
OF MY VICTIMS, YOU OLD FOOL! NOW I'LL HAVE TO START OVER...
WITH...
YOU!

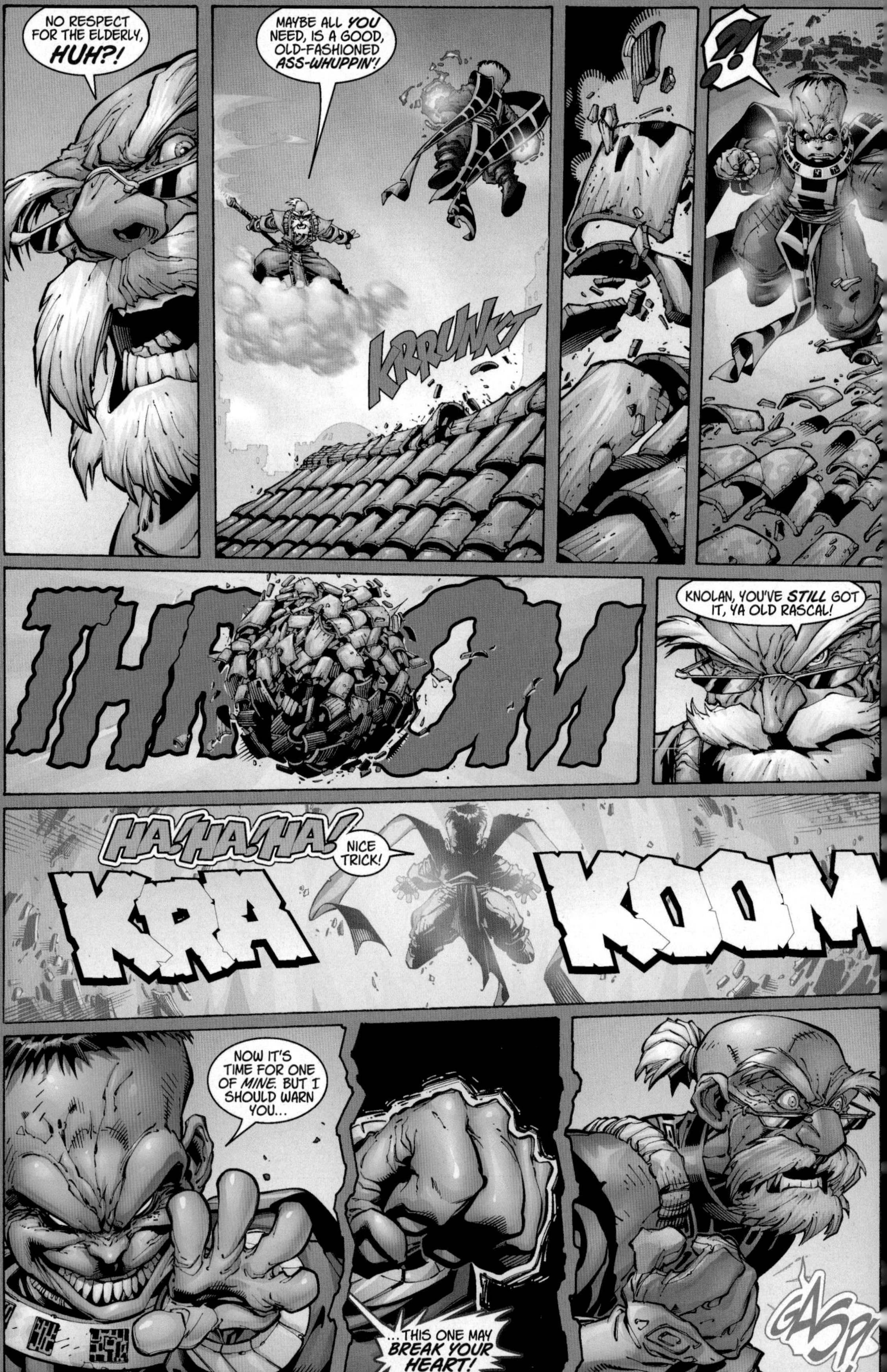
NO RESPECT FOR THE ELDERLY, HUH?!
MAYBE ALL YOU NEED, IS A GOOD, OLD-FASHIONED ASS-WHUPPIN'!
KRRUNKT
THROOM
KNOLAN, YOU'VE STILL GOT IT, YA OLD RASCAL!
HA! HA! HA!
NICE TRICK!
KRAKOOM
NOW IT'S TIME FOR ONE OF MINE. BUT I SHOULD WARN YOU...
...THIS ONE MAY BREAK YOUR HEART!
GASP!

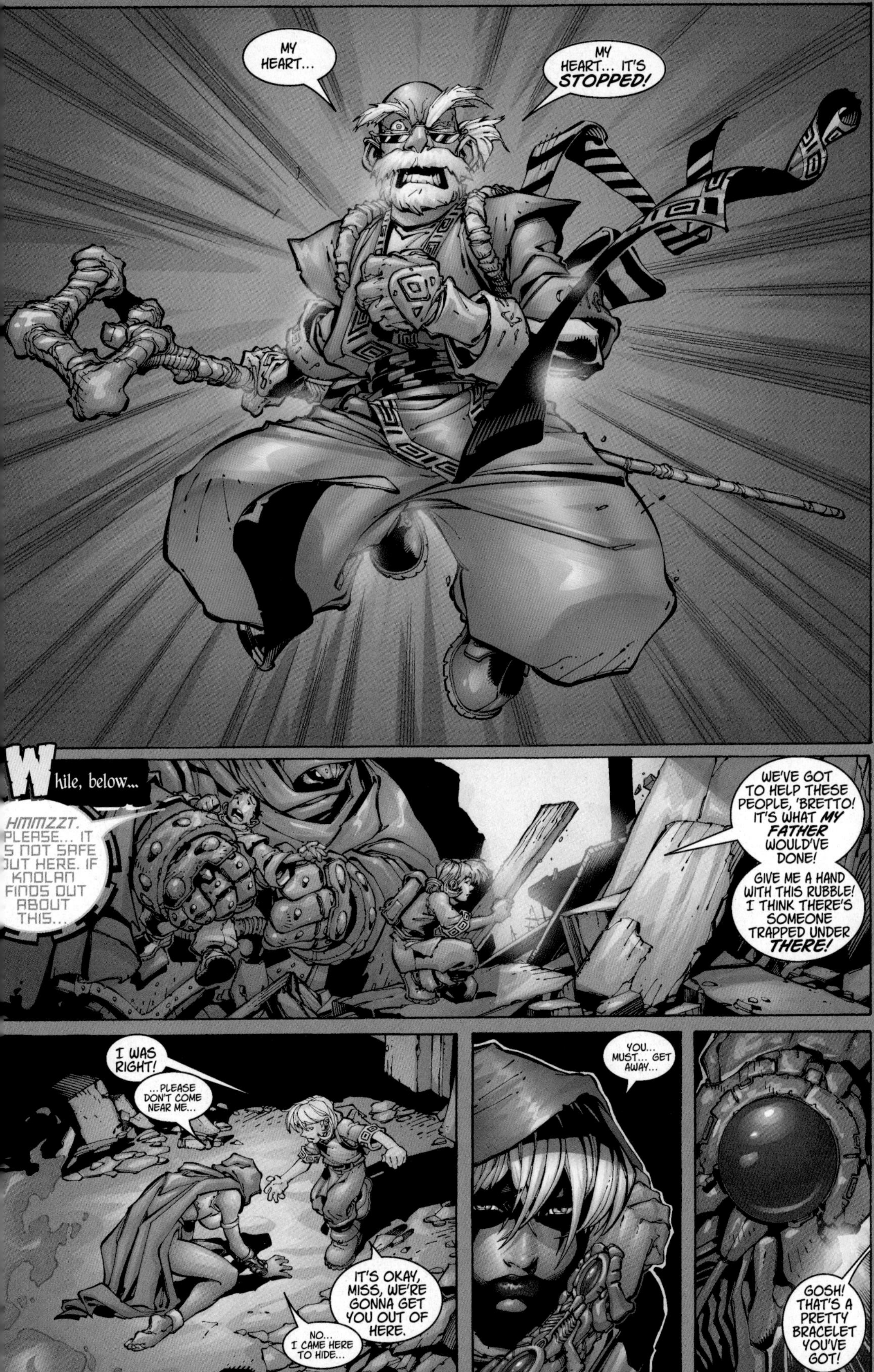
MY HEART...
MY HEART... IT'S STOPPED!
While, below...
HMMZZT. PLEASE... IT'S NOT SAFE OUT HERE. IF KNOLAN FINDS OUT ABOUT THIS...
WE'VE GOT TO HELP THESE PEOPLE, 'BRETTO! IT'S WHAT MY FATHER WOULD'VE DONE!
GIVE ME A HAND WITH THIS RUBBLE! I THINK THERE'S SOMEONE TRAPPED UNDER THERE!
I WAS RIGHT!
...PLEASE DON'T COME NEAR ME...
IT'S OKAY, MISS, WE'RE GONNA GET YOU OUT OF HERE.
NO... I CAME HERE TO HIDE...
YOU... MUST... GET AWAY...
GOSH! THAT'S A PRETTY BRACELET YOU'VE GOT!

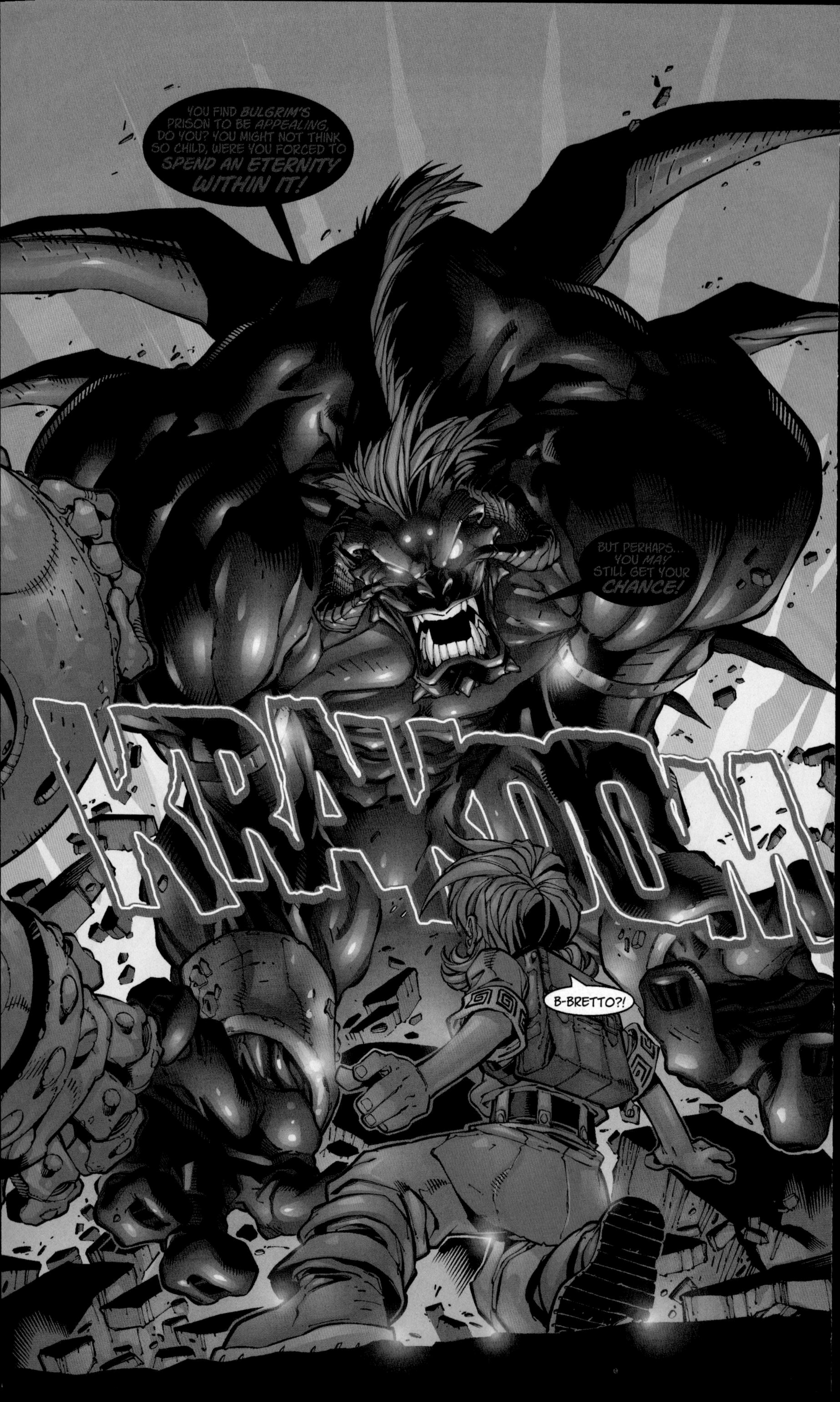
YOU FIND BULGRIM'S PRISON TO BE APPEALING, DO YOU? YOU MIGHT NOT THINK SO CHILD, WERE YOU FORCED TO SPEND AN ETERNITY WITHIN IT!
BUT PERHAPS... YOU MAY STILL GET YOUR CHANCE!
B-BRETTO?!

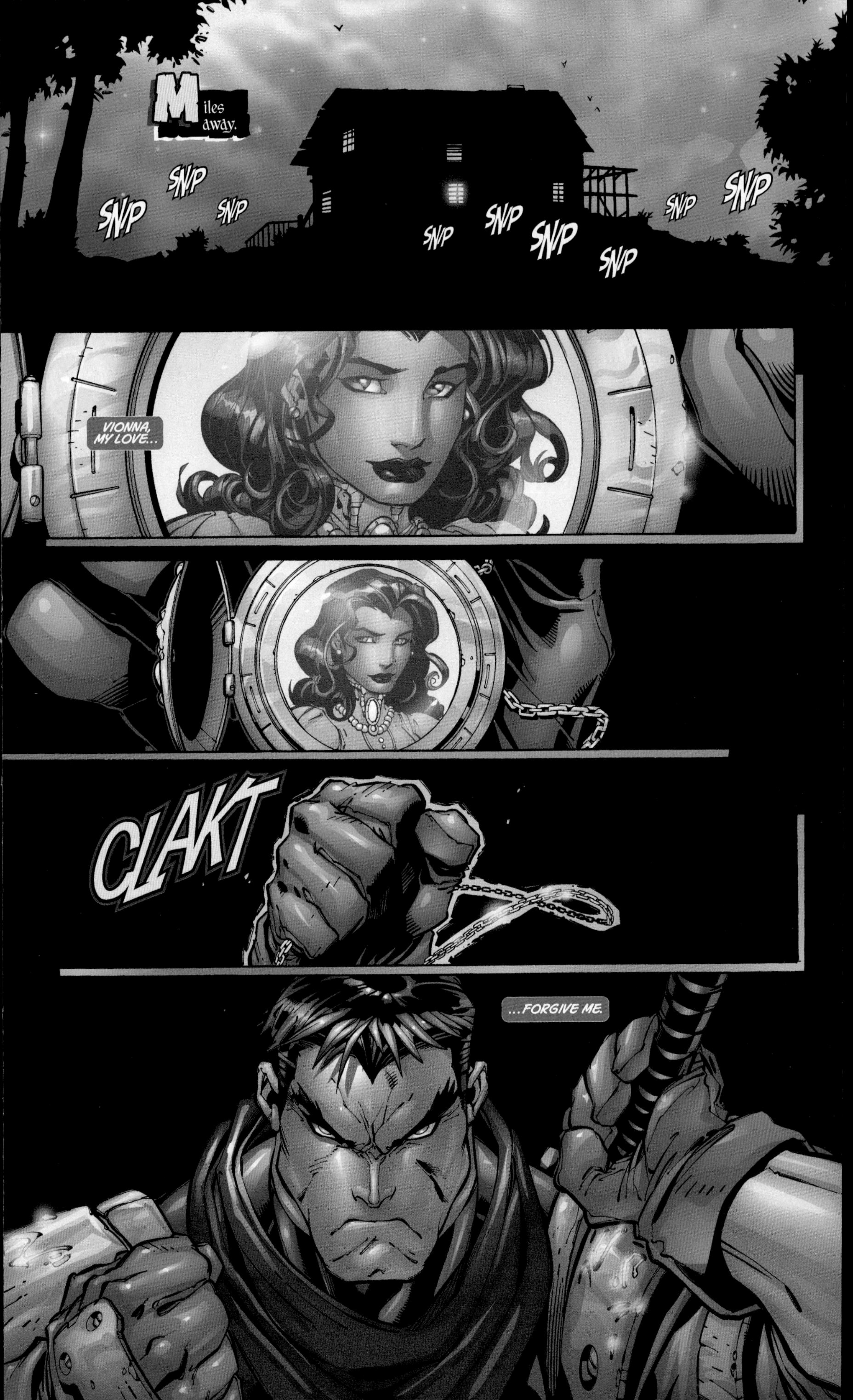
Miles Mawdy.
SNIP SNIP SNIP SNIP SNIP SNIP SNIP SNIP SNIP
VIONNA, MY LOVE...
CLAKT
...FORGIVE ME.

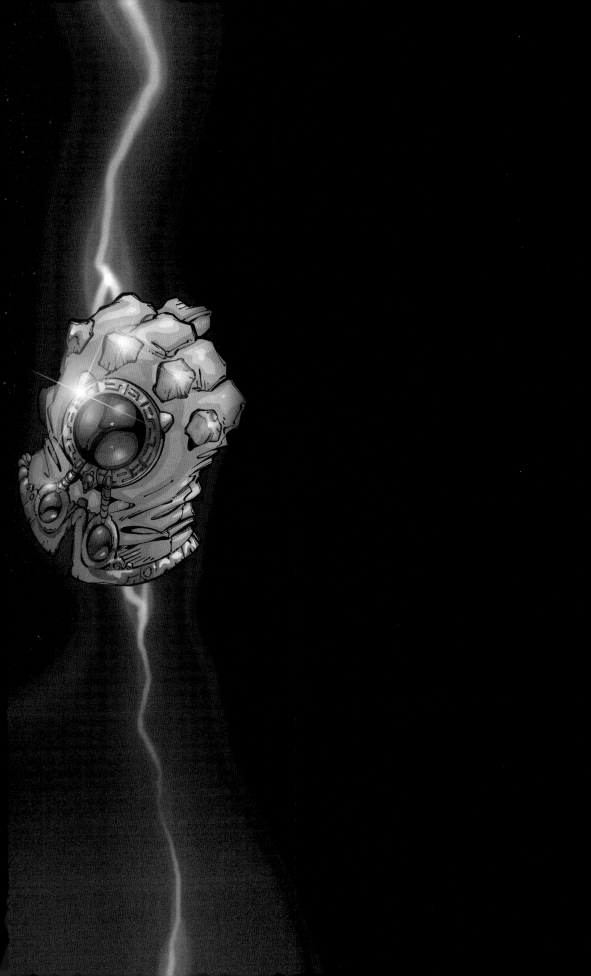

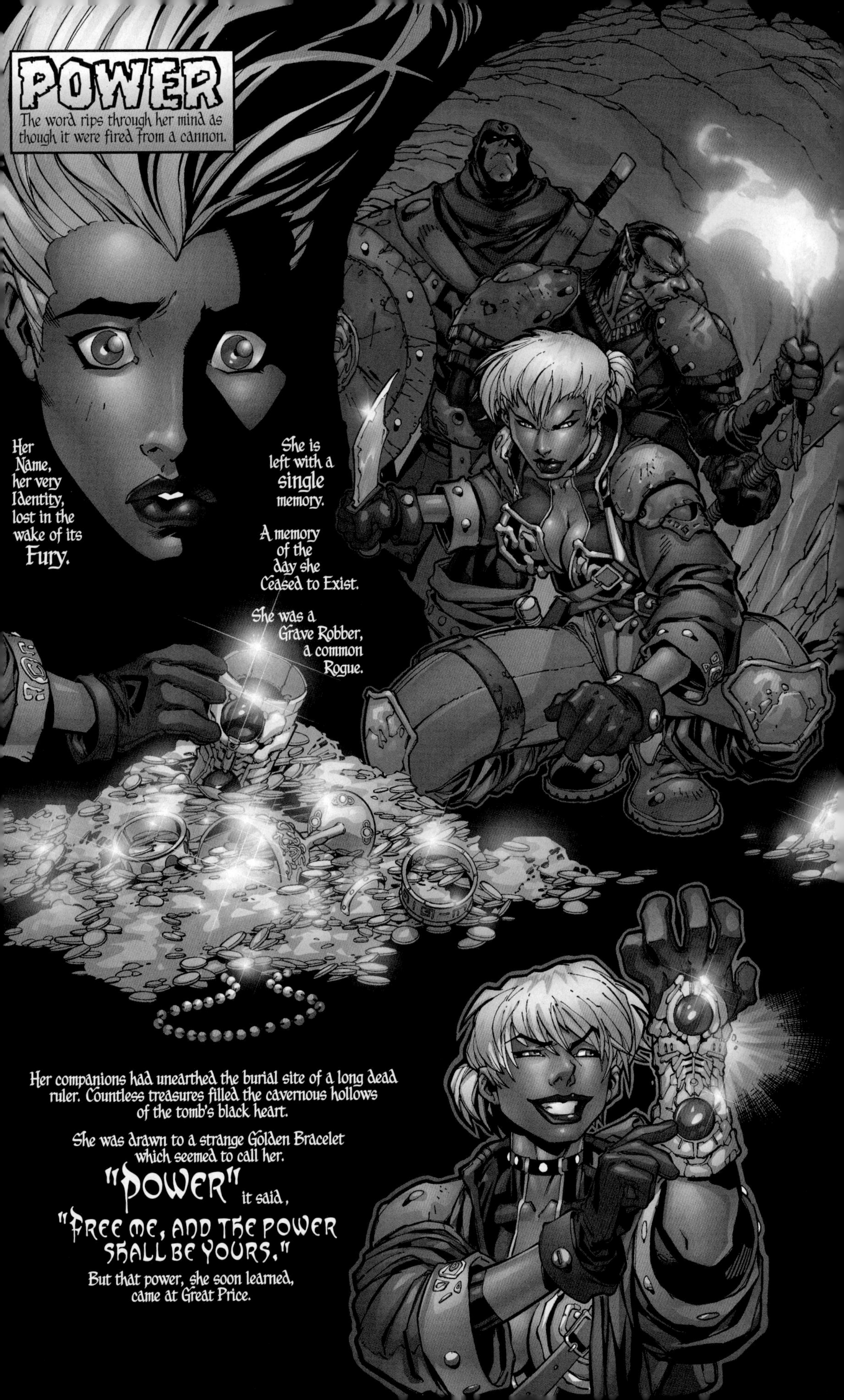
POWER
The word rips through her mind as though it were fired from a cannon.
Her Name, her very Identity, lost in the wake of its Fury.
She is left with a single memory.
A memory of the day she Ceased to Exist.
She was a Grave Robber, a common Rogue.
Her companions had unearthed the burial site of a long dead ruler. Countless treasures filled the cavernous hollows of the tomb's black heart.
She was drawn to a strange Golden Bracelet which seemed to call her.
"POWER" it said,
"FREE ME, AND THE POWER SHALL BE YOURS."
But that power, she soon learned, came at Great Price.

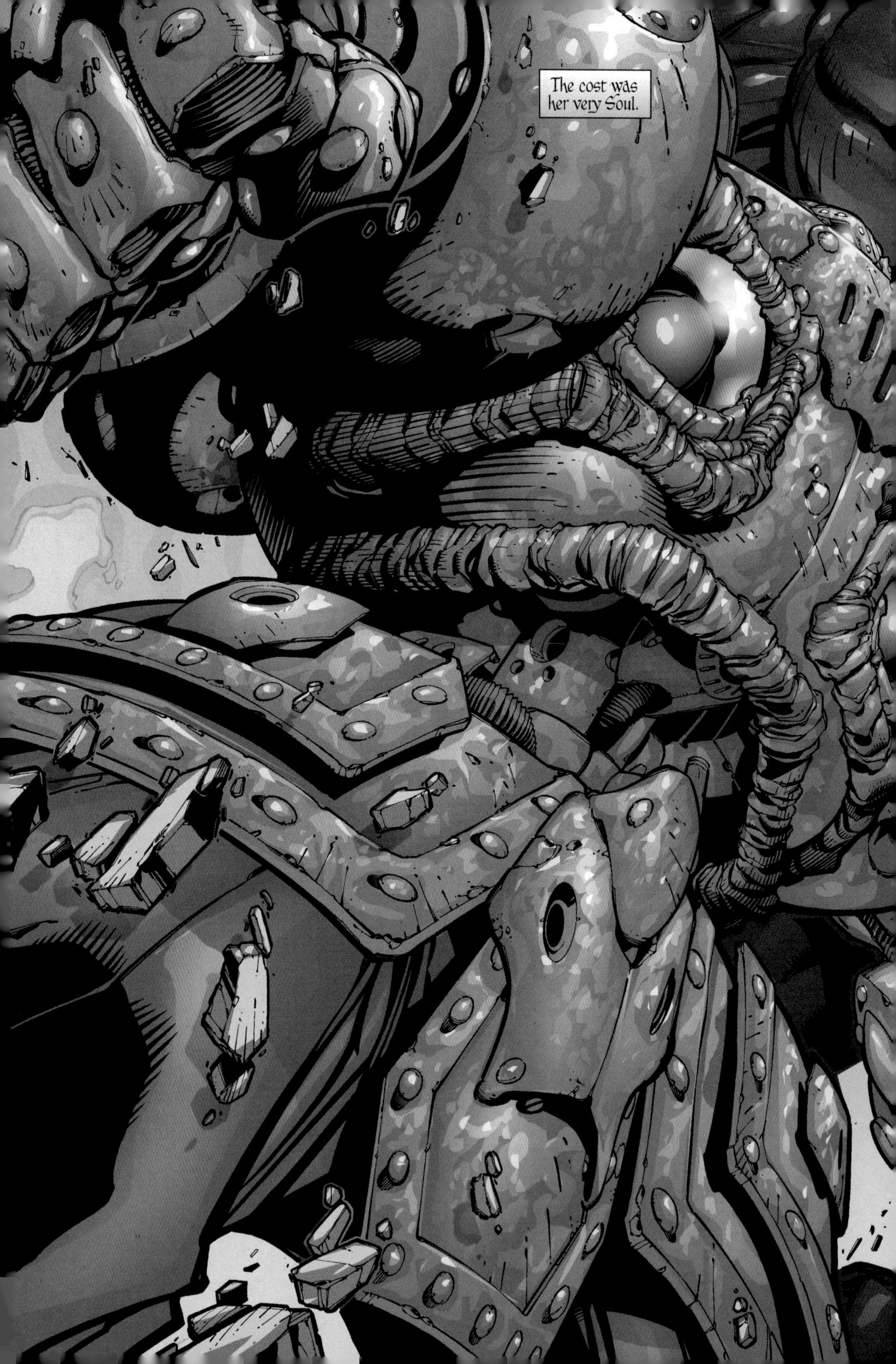
The cost was
her very Soul.

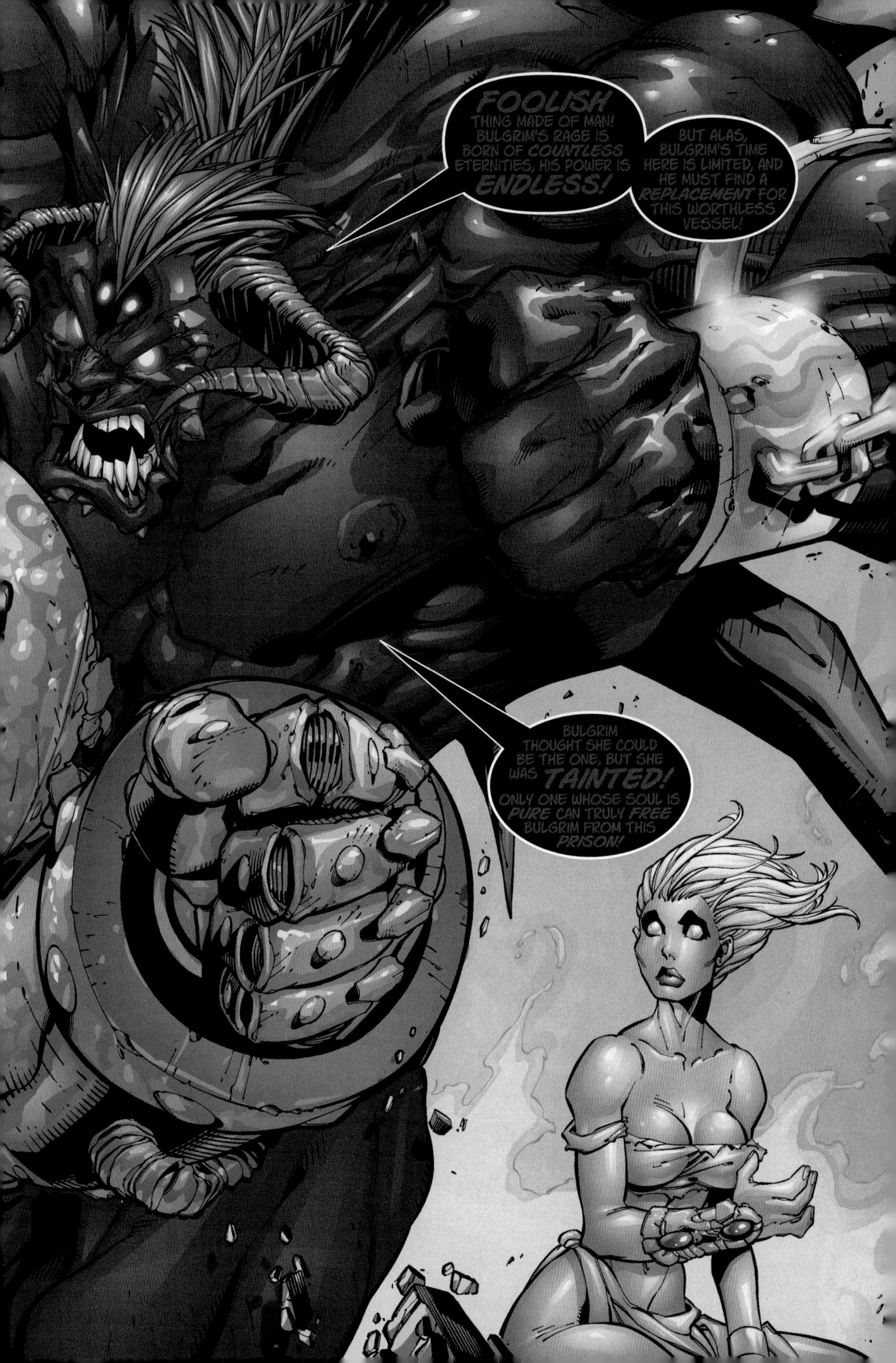
FOOLISH THING MADE OF MAN! BULGRIM'S RAGE IS BORN OF COUNTLESS ETERNITIES, HIS POWER IS ENDLESS!
BUT ALAS, BULGRIM'S TIME HERE IS LIMITED, AND HE MUST FIND A REPLACEMENT FOR THIS WORTHLESS VESSEL!
BULGRIM THOUGHT SHE COULD BE THE ONE, BUT SHE WAS TAINTED! ONLY ONE WHOSE SOUL IS PURE CAN TRULY FREE BULGRIM FROM THIS PRISON!

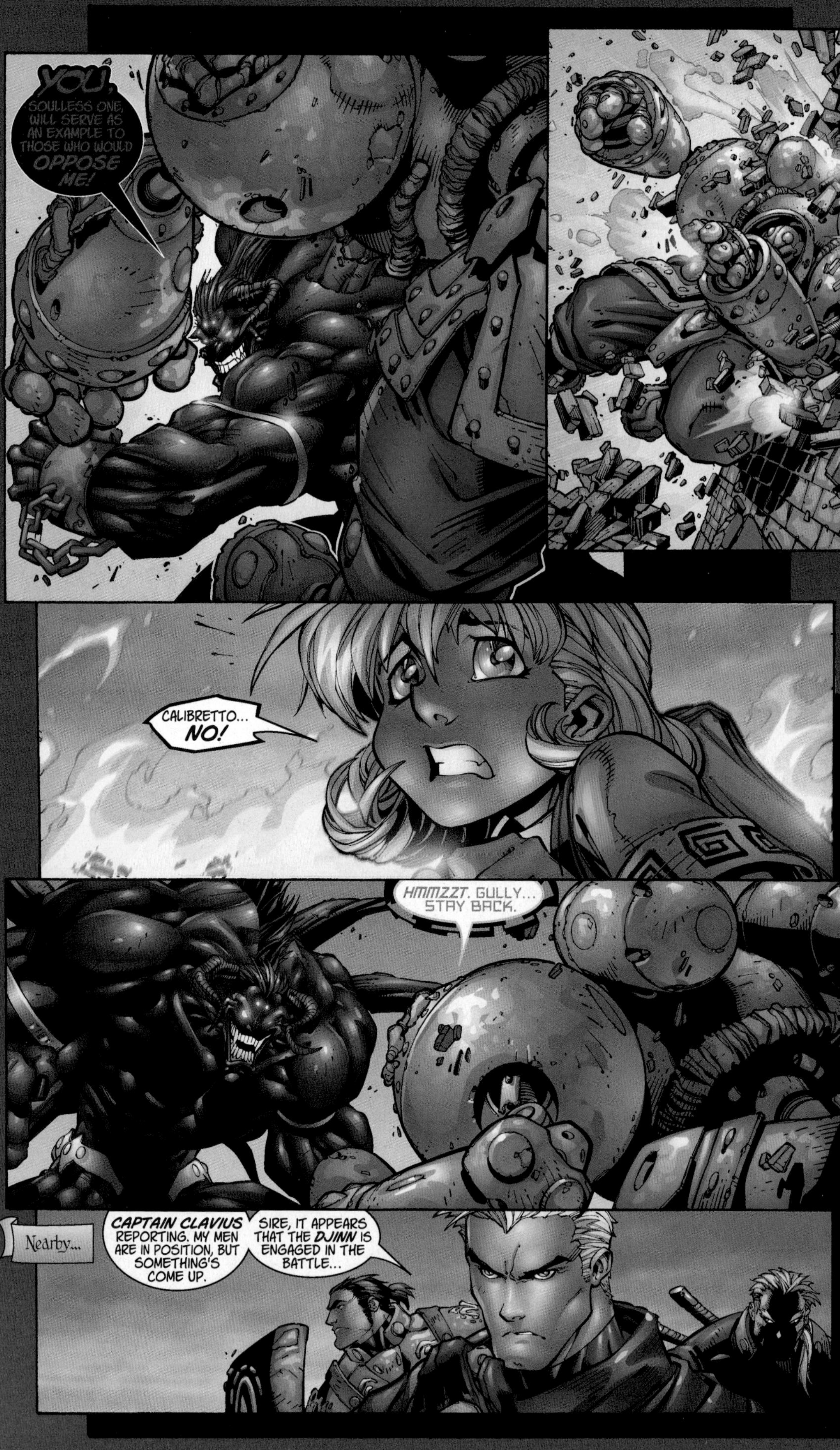
YOU, SOULLESS ONE, WILL SERVE AS AN EXAMPLE TO THOSE WHO WOULD OPPOSE ME!
CALIBRETTO... NO!
HMMZZT. GULLY... STAY BACK.
Nearby...
CAPTAIN CLAVIUS REPORTING. MY MEN ARE IN POSITION, BUT SOMETHING'S COME UP.
SIRE, IT APPEARS THAT THE DJINN IS ENGAGED IN THE BATTLE...

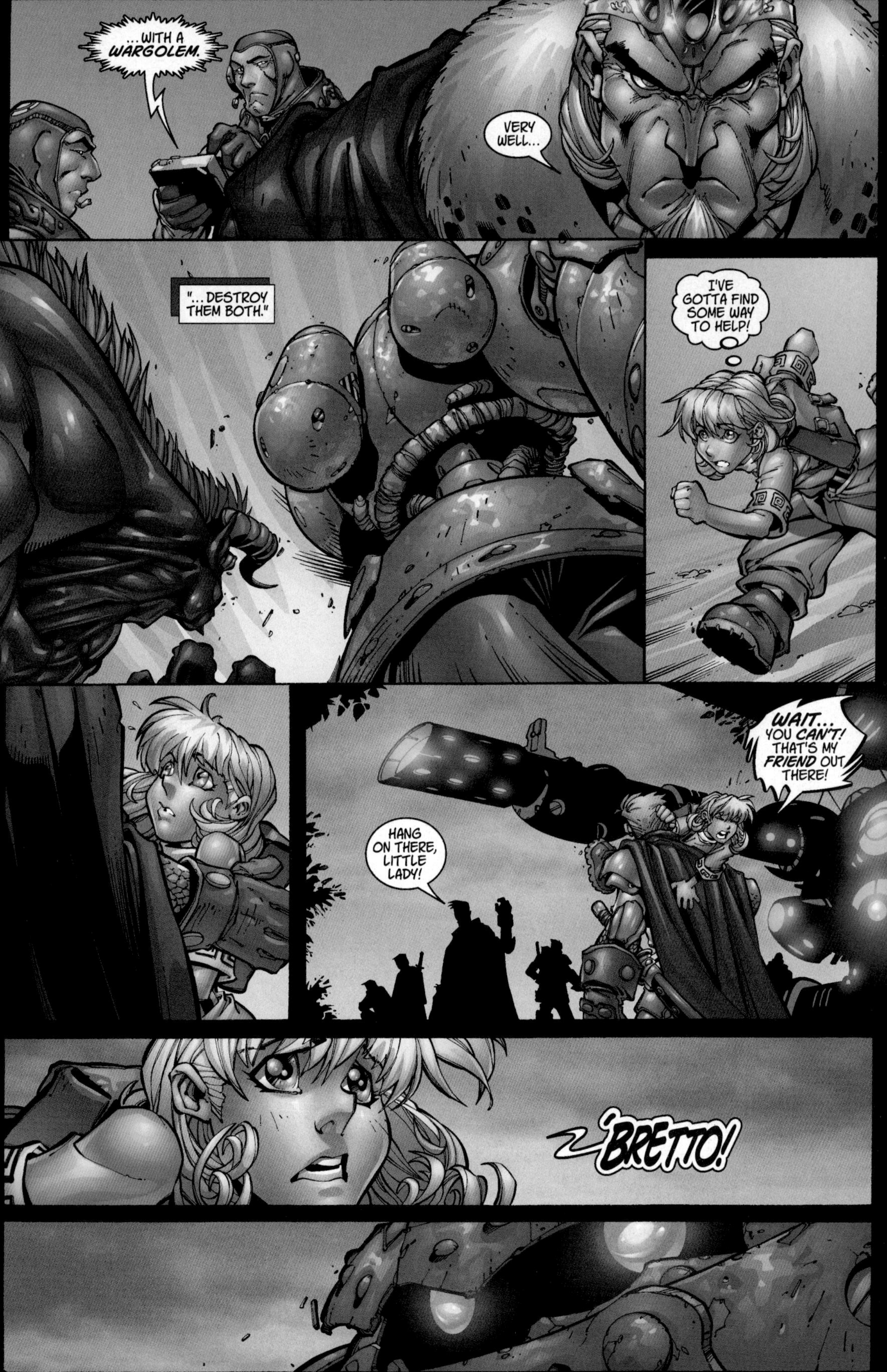
...WITH A WARGOLEM.
VERY WELL...
"...DESTROY THEM BOTH."
I'VE GOTTA FIND SOME WAY TO HELP!
WAIT... YOU CAN'T! THAT'S MY FRIEND OUT THERE!
HANG ON THERE, LITTLE LADY!
BRETTO!

NO!

FOOLS!

WEAPONS MADE BY THE HANDS OF MEN HAVE *NO* AFFECT ON *BULGRIM!*

LET *GO* OF ME!

HEY! COME BACK HERE!

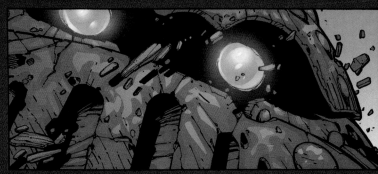

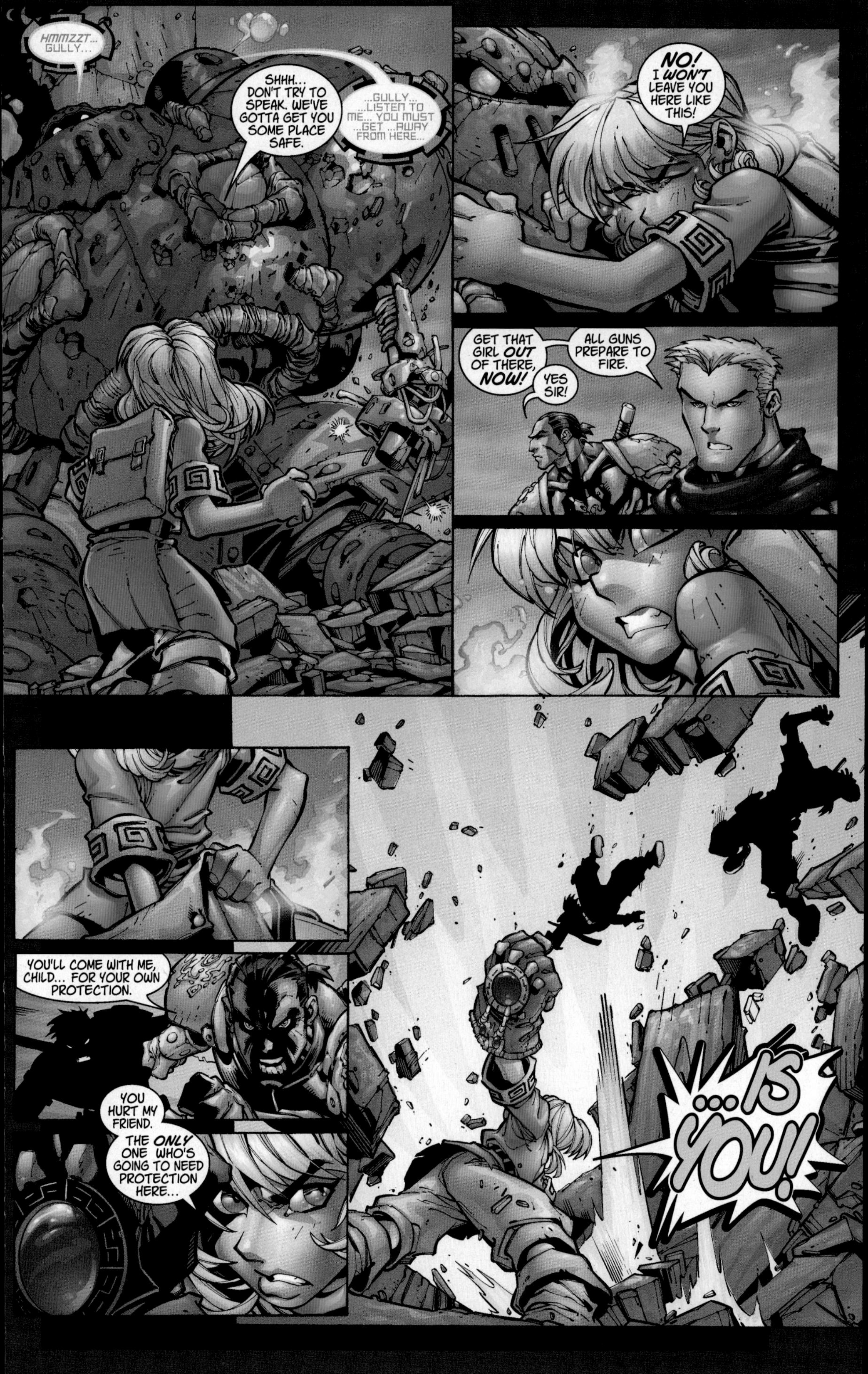
HMMZZT... GULLY...
SHHH... DON'T TRY TO SPEAK. WE'VE GOTTA GET YOU SOME PLACE SAFE.
...GULLY... ...LISTEN TO ME... YOU MUST ...GET ...AWAY FROM HERE...
NO! I WON'T LEAVE YOU HERE LIKE THIS!
GET THAT GIRL OUT OF THERE, NOW!
YES SIR!
ALL GUNS PREPARE TO FIRE.
YOU'LL COME WITH ME, CHILD... FOR YOUR OWN PROTECTION.
YOU HURT MY FRIEND.
THE ONLY ONE WHO'S GOING TO NEED PROTECTION HERE...
...IS YOU!

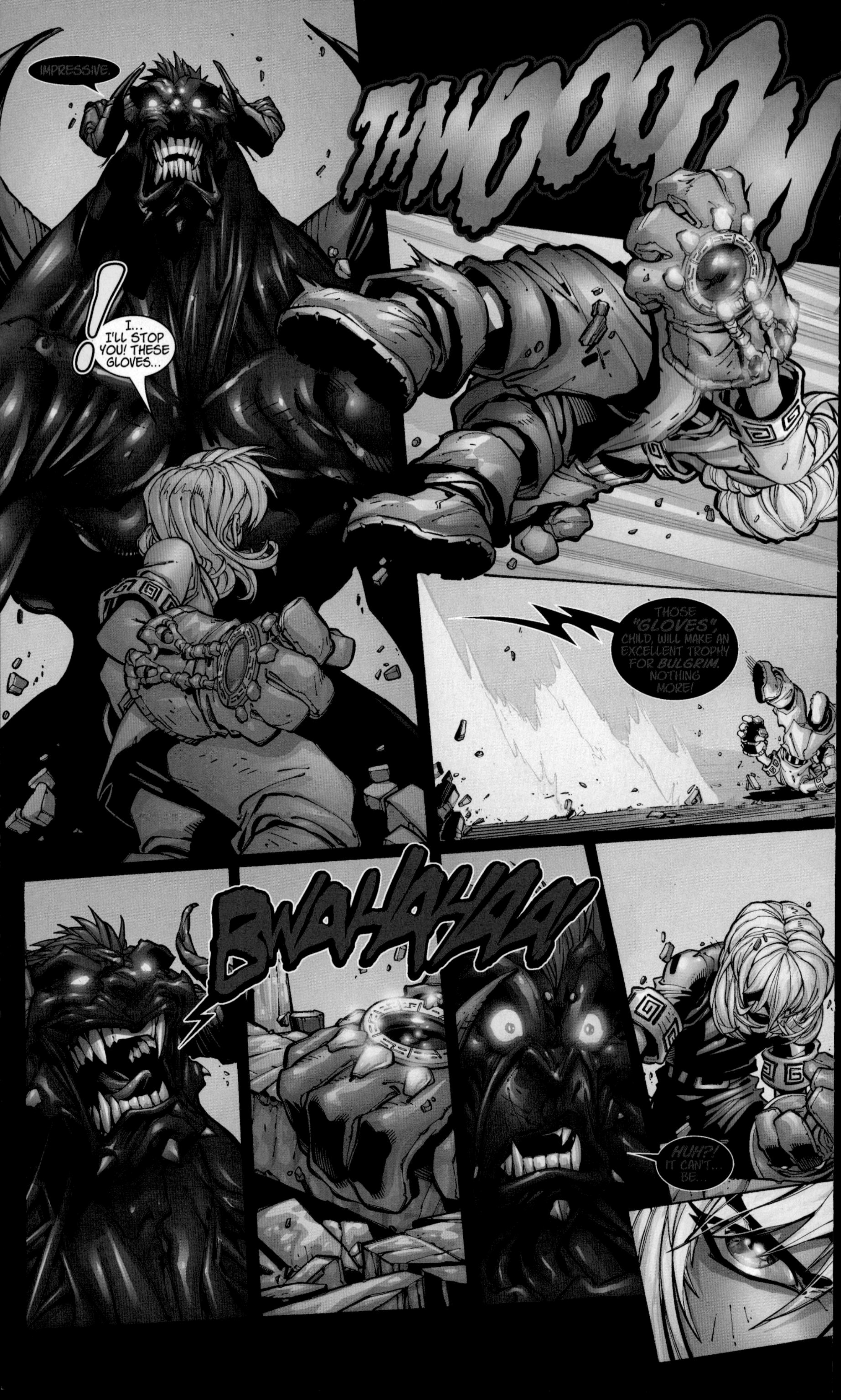
IMPRESSIVE.
THOOOOM
!
I... I'LL STOP YOU! THESE GLOVES...
THOSE "GLOVES", CHILD, WILL MAKE AN EXCELLENT TROPHY FOR BULGRIM. NOTHING MORE!
BWAHAHAA!
HUH?! IT CAN'T... BE...

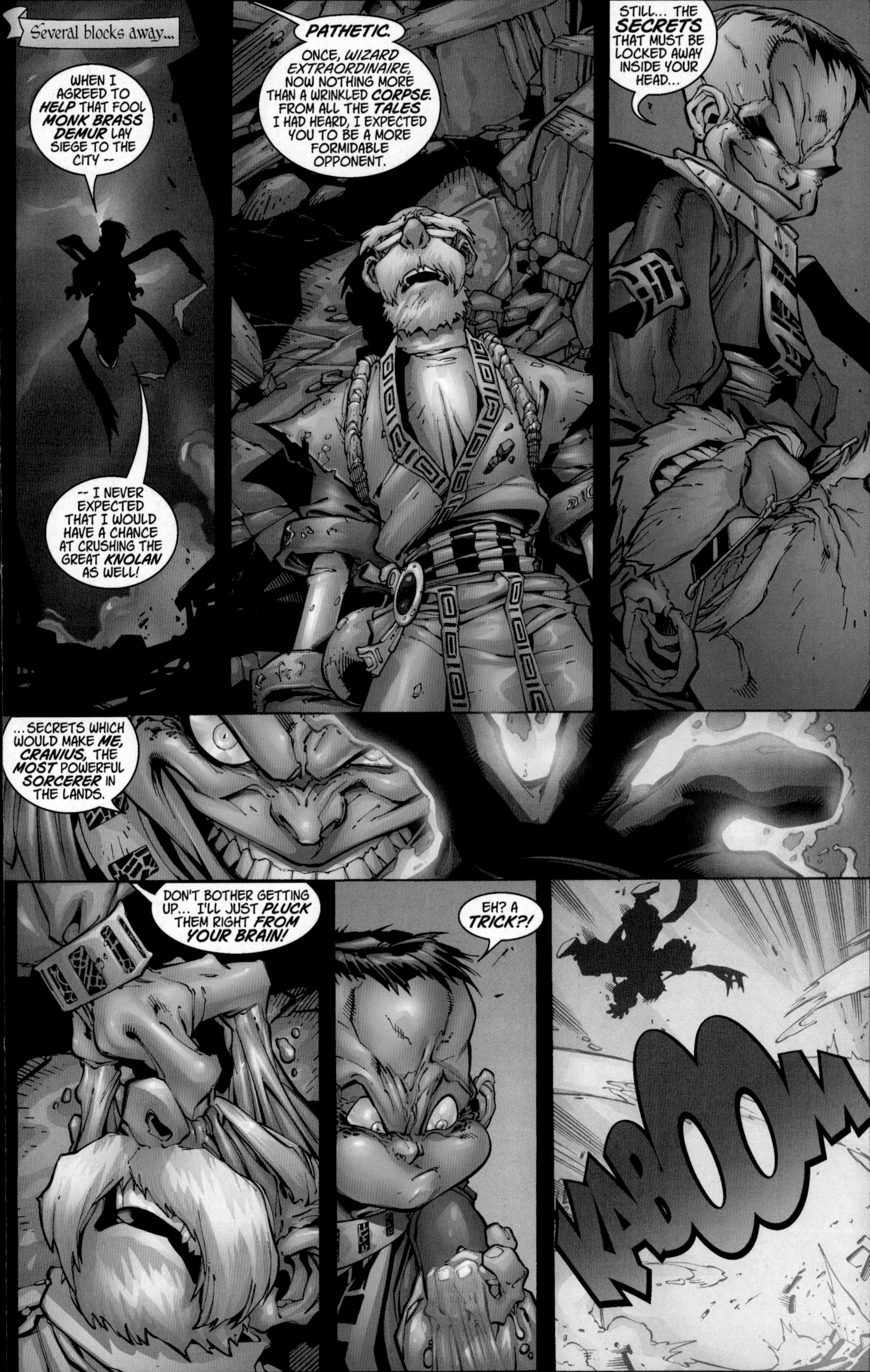
Several blocks away...
WHEN I AGREED TO HELP THAT FOOL MONK BRASS DEMUR LAY SIEGE TO THE CITY --
-- I NEVER EXPECTED THAT I WOULD HAVE A CHANCE AT CRUSHING THE GREAT KNOLAN AS WELL!
PATHETIC.
ONCE, WIZARD EXTRAORDINAIRE, NOW NOTHING MORE THAN A WRINKLED CORPSE. FROM ALL THE TALES I HAD HEARD, I EXPECTED YOU TO BE A MORE FORMIDABLE OPPONENT.
STILL... THE SECRETS THAT MUST BE LOCKED AWAY INSIDE YOUR HEAD...
...SECRETS WHICH WOULD MAKE ME, CRANIUS, THE MOST POWERFUL SORCERER IN THE LANDS.
DON'T BOTHER GETTING UP... I'LL JUST PLUCK THEM RIGHT FROM YOUR BRAIN!
EH? A TRICK?!
KABOOM

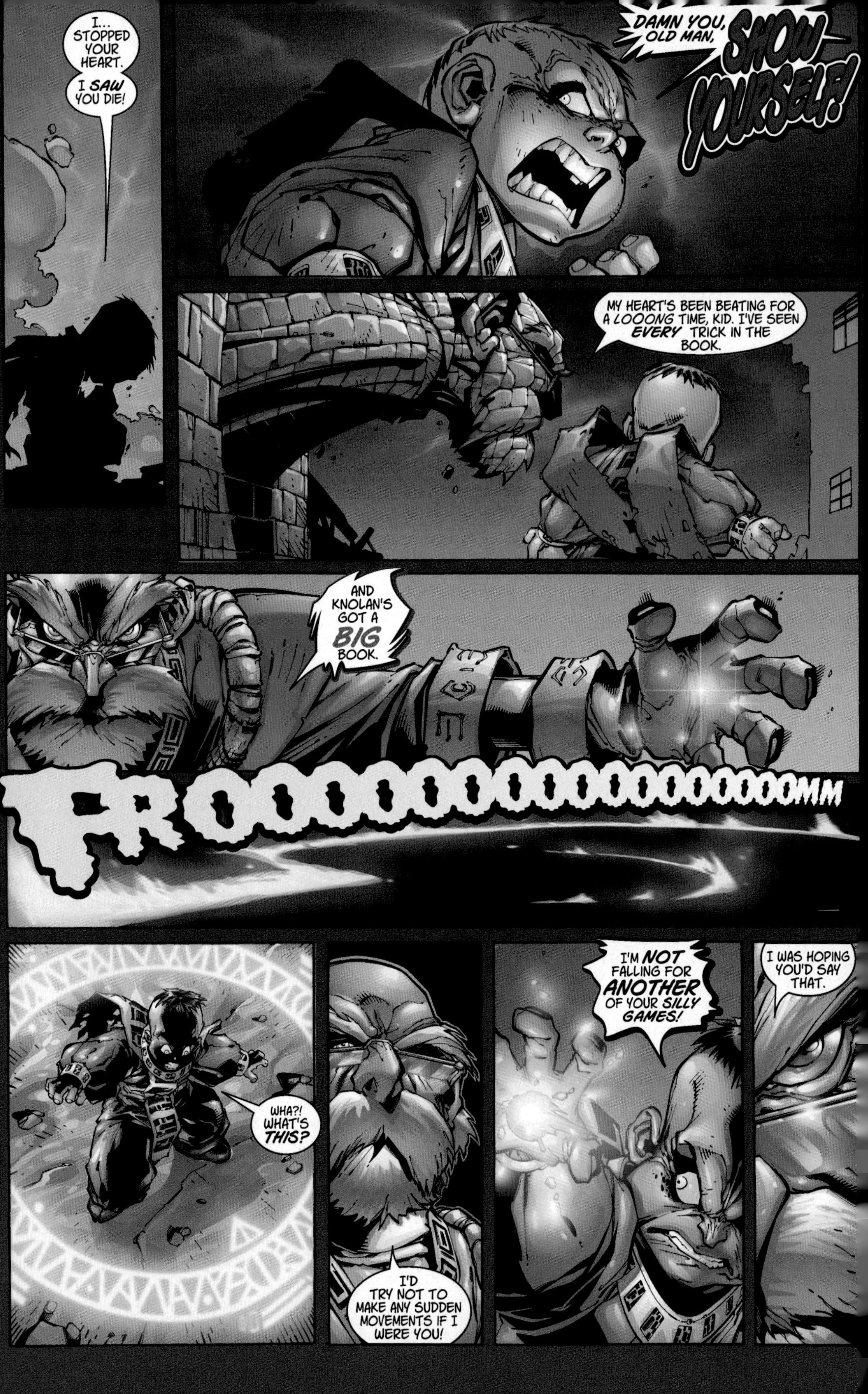

I... STOPPED YOUR HEART.
I SAW YOU DIE!
DAMN YOU, OLD MAN, SHOW YOURSELF!
MY HEART'S BEEN BEATING FOR A LOOONG TIME, KID. I'VE SEEN EVERY TRICK IN THE BOOK.
AND KNOLAN'S GOT A BIG BOOK.
FROOOOOOOOOOOOOOOOOOMM
WHA?! WHAT'S THIS?
I'D TRY NOT TO MAKE ANY SUDDEN MOVEMENTS IF I WERE YOU!
I'M NOT FALLING FOR ANOTHER OF YOUR SILLY GAMES!
I WAS HOPING YOU'D SAY THAT.

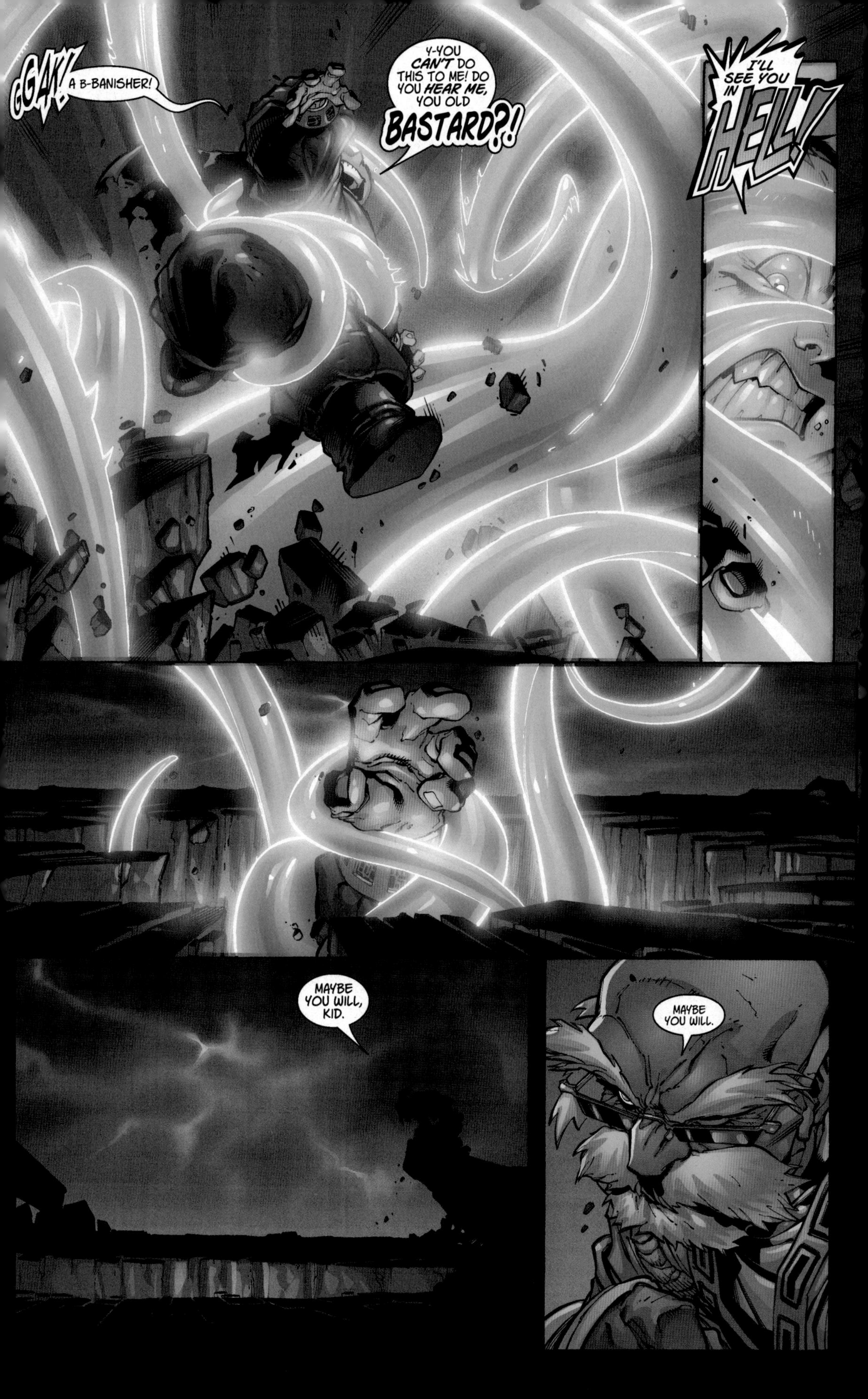
GGAK!
A B-BANISHER!
Y-YOU CAN'T DO THIS TO ME! DO YOU HEAR ME, YOU OLD BASTARD?!
I'LL SEE YOU IN HELL!
MAYBE YOU WILL, KID.
MAYBE YOU WILL.

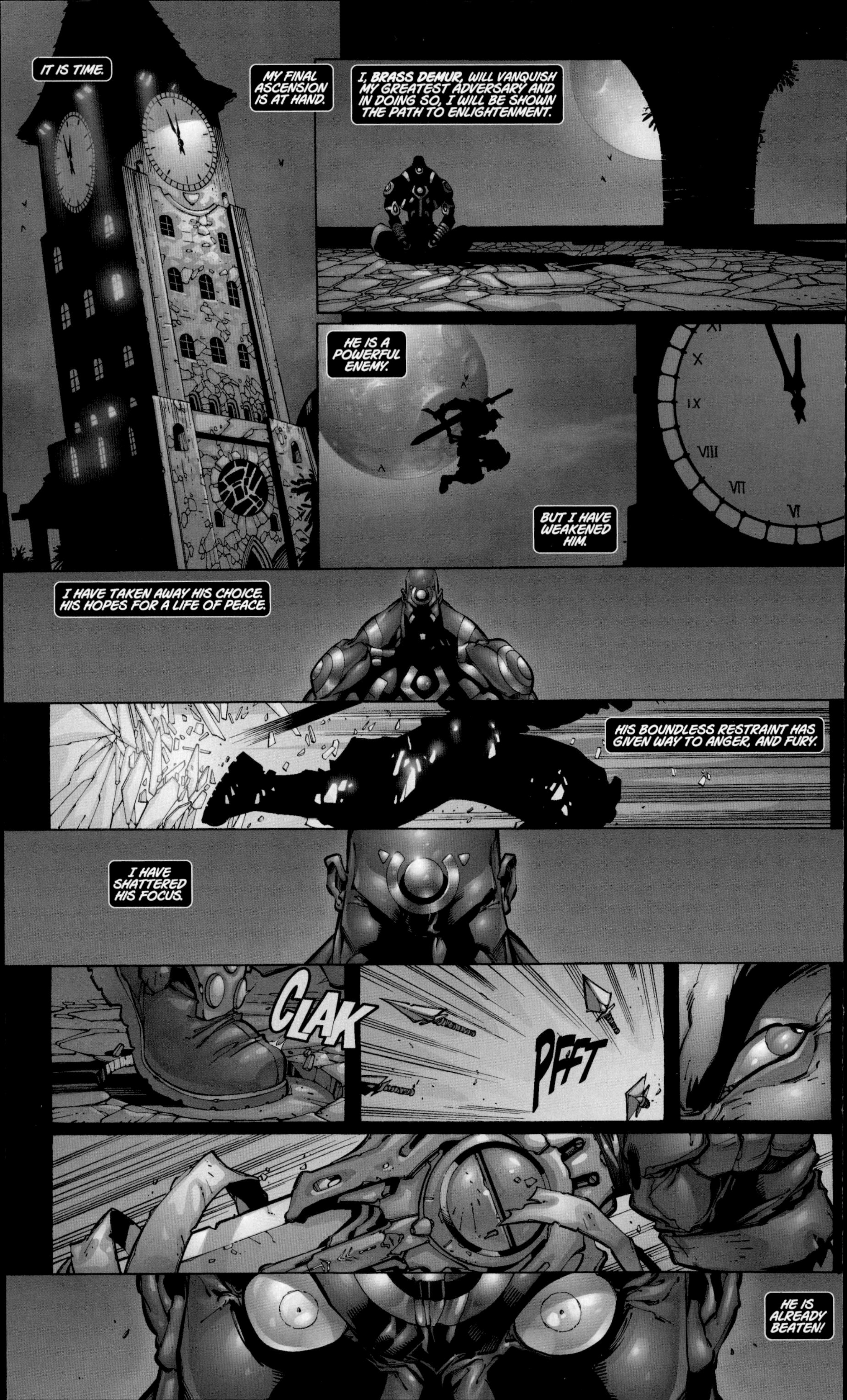
IT IS TIME.
MY FINAL ASCENSION IS AT HAND.
I, BRASS DEMUR, WILL VANQUISH MY GREATEST ADVERSARY AND IN DOING SO, I WILL BE SHOWN THE PATH TO ENLIGHTENMENT.
HE IS A POWERFUL ENEMY.
BUT I HAVE WEAKENED HIM.
I HAVE TAKEN AWAY HIS CHOICE. HIS HOPES FOR A LIFE OF PEACE.
HIS BOUNDLESS RESTRAINT HAS GIVEN WAY TO ANGER, AND FURY.
I HAVE SHATTERED HIS FOCUS.
CLAK
PFFT
HE IS ALREADY BEATEN!

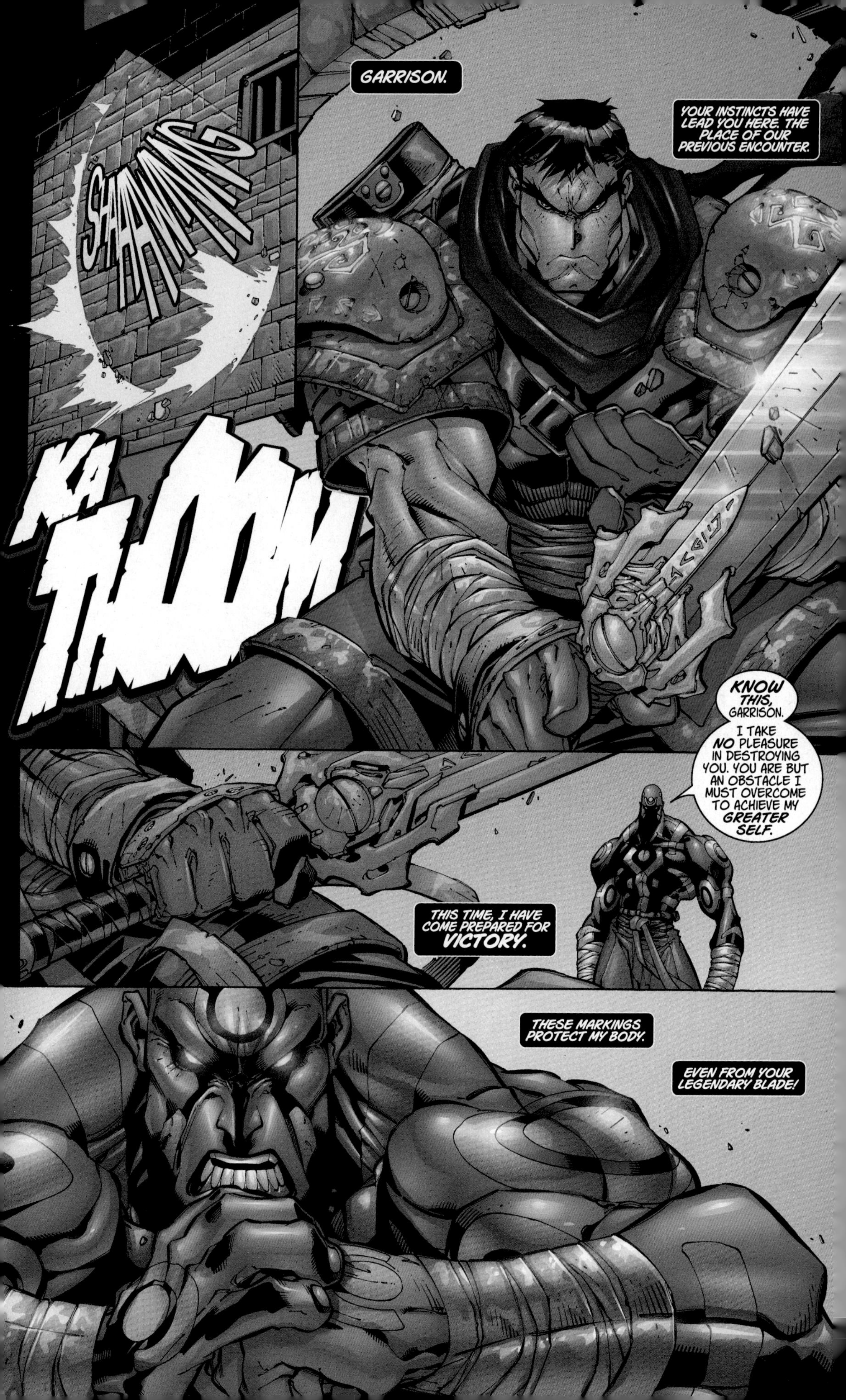
SHHHANNG
KA THOOM
GARRISON.
YOUR INSTINCTS HAVE LEAD YOU HERE. THE PLACE OF OUR PREVIOUS ENCOUNTER.
KNOW THIS, GARRISON.
I TAKE NO PLEASURE IN DESTROYING YOU. YOU ARE BUT AN OBSTACLE I MUST OVERCOME TO ACHIEVE MY GREATER SELF.
THIS TIME, I HAVE COME PREPARED FOR VICTORY.
THESE MARKINGS PROTECT MY BODY.
EVEN FROM YOUR LEGENDARY BLADE!

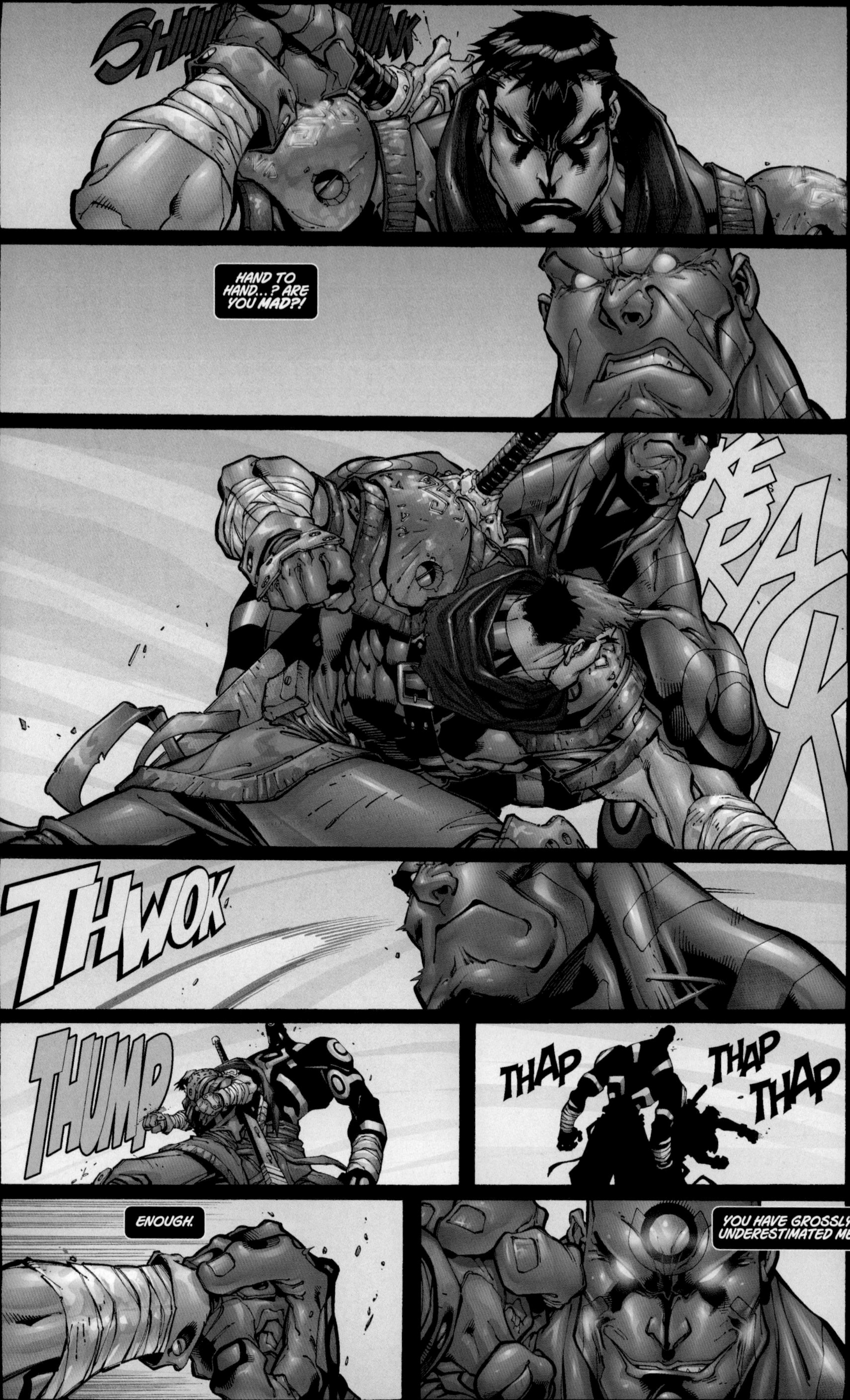
HAND TO HAND...? ARE YOU MAD?!
THWOK
THUMP
THAP
THAP
THAP
ENOUGH.
YOU HAVE GROSSLY UNDERESTIMATED ME.

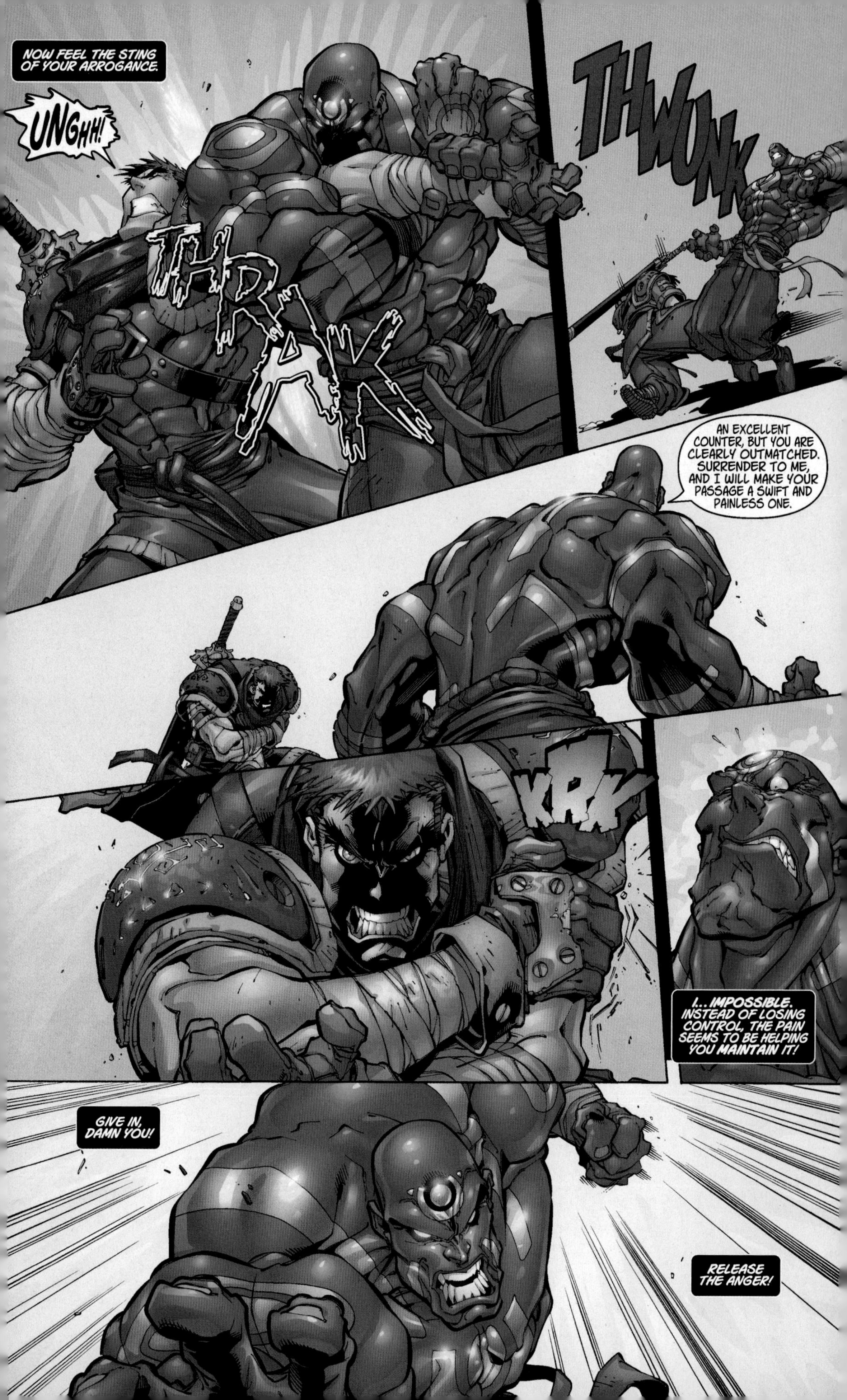
NOW FEEL THE STING OF YOUR ARROGANCE.
UNGHH!
THRAK
THWONK
AN EXCELLENT COUNTER, BUT YOU ARE CLEARLY OUTMATCHED. SURRENDER TO ME, AND I WILL MAKE YOUR PASSAGE A SWIFT AND PAINLESS ONE.
KRK
I... IMPOSSIBLE. INSTEAD OF LOSING CONTROL, THE PAIN SEEMS TO BE HELPING YOU MAINTAIN IT!
GIVE IN, DAMN YOU!
RELEASE THE ANGER!

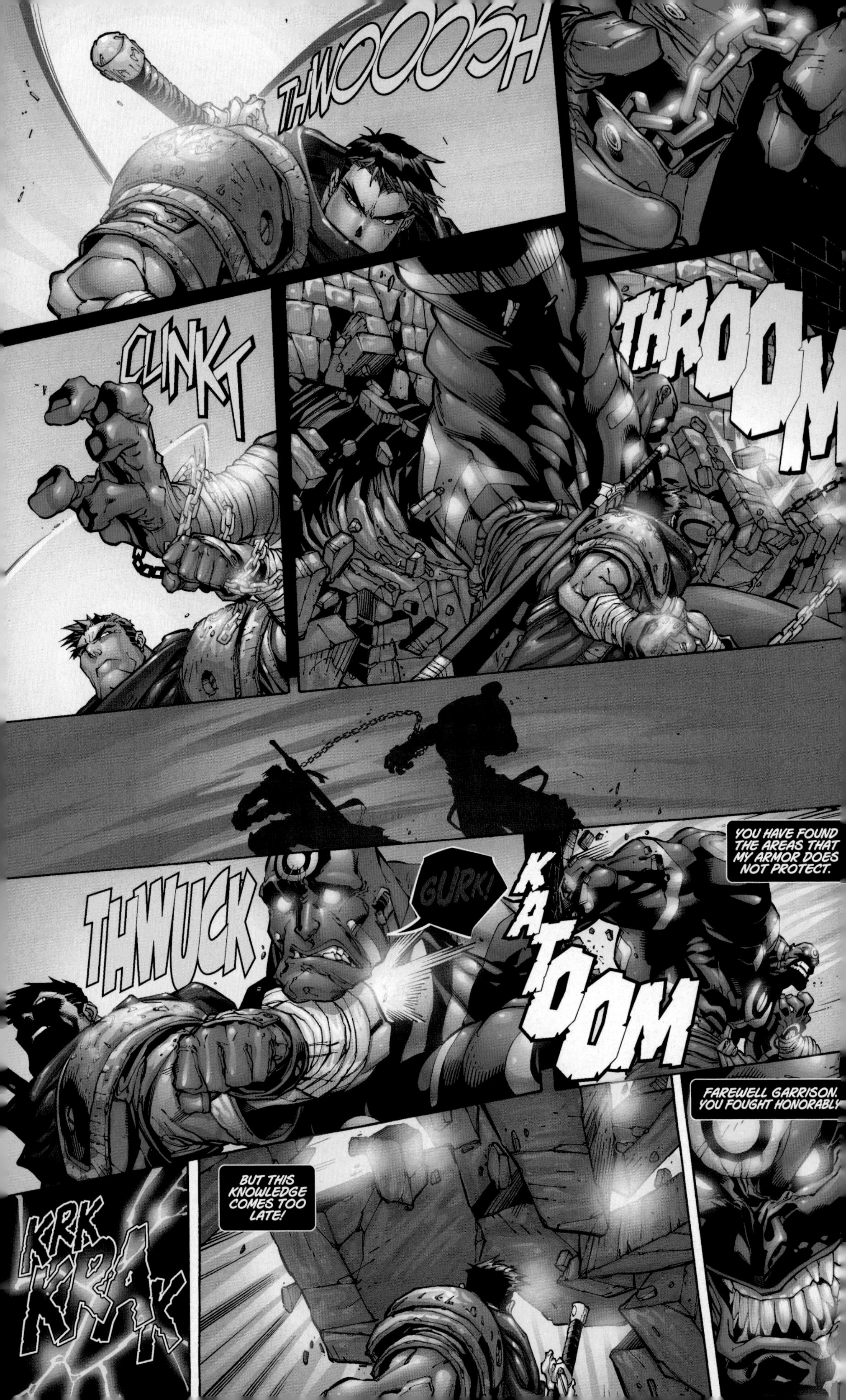
THWOOOSH
CLINKT
THROOM
THWUCK
GURK!
KA TOOM
YOU HAVE FOUND THE AREAS THAT MY ARMOR DOES NOT PROTECT.
KRK KRAK
BUT THIS KNOWLEDGE COMES TOO LATE!
FAREWELL GARRISON. YOU FOUGHT HONORABLY

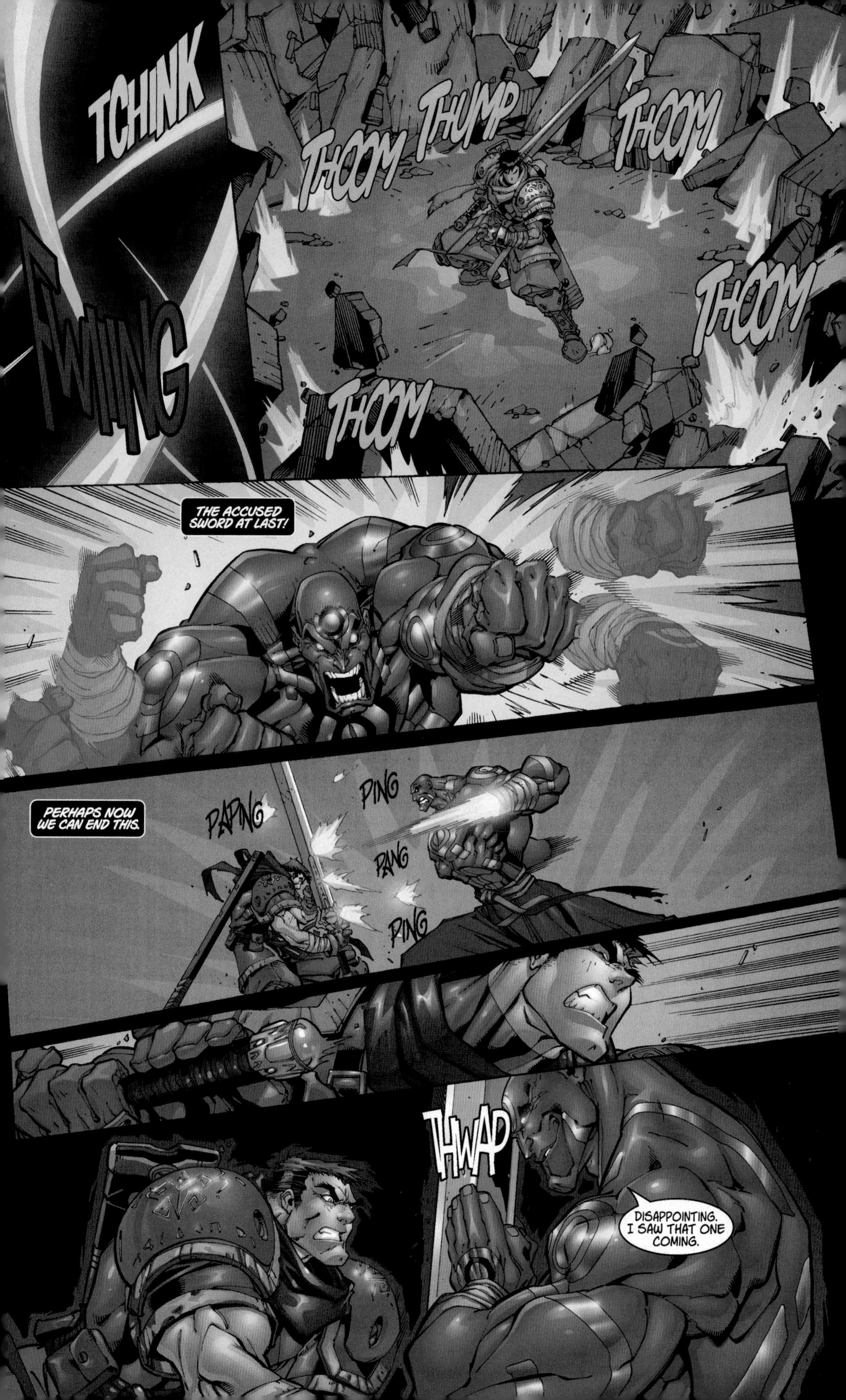
TCHINK
FWIIING
THOOM THUMP
THOOM
THOOM
THOOM
THE ACCUSED SWORD AT LAST!
PERHAPS NOW WE CAN END THIS.
PAPING
PING
PANG
PING
THWAP
DISAPPOINTING. I SAW THAT ONE COMING.

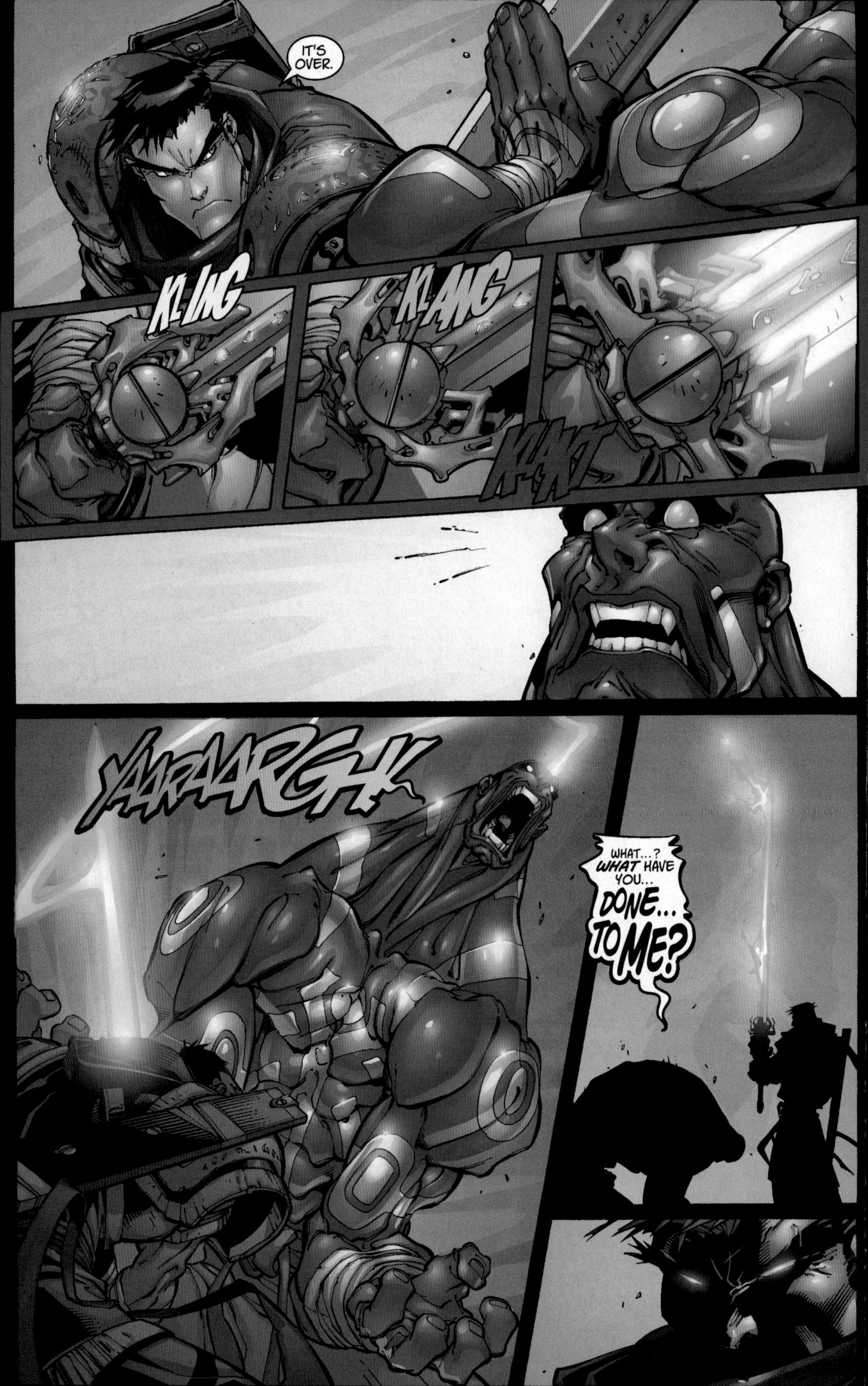
IT'S OVER.
KLING
KLANG
KLAKT
YAARAARGH!
WHAT...? WHAT HAVE YOU... DONE... TO ME?

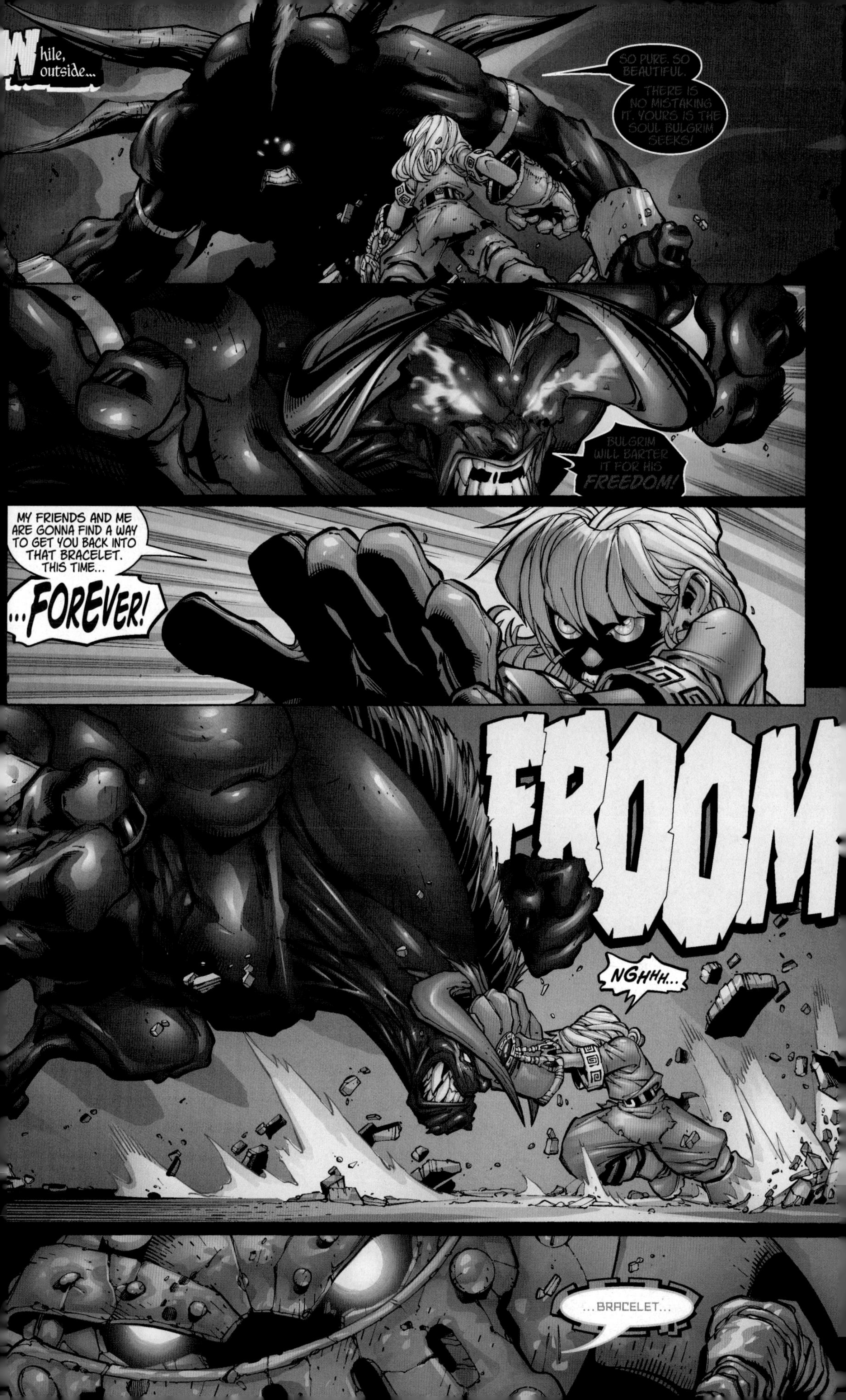
While, outside...
SO PURE. SO BEAUTIFUL.
THERE IS NO MISTAKING IT. YOURS IS THE SOUL BULGRIM SEEKS!
BULGRIM WILL BARTER IT FOR HIS FREEDOM!
MY FRIENDS AND ME ARE GONNA FIND A WAY TO GET YOU BACK INTO THAT BRACELET. THIS TIME...
...FOREVER!
FROOM
NGHHH...
...BRACELET...

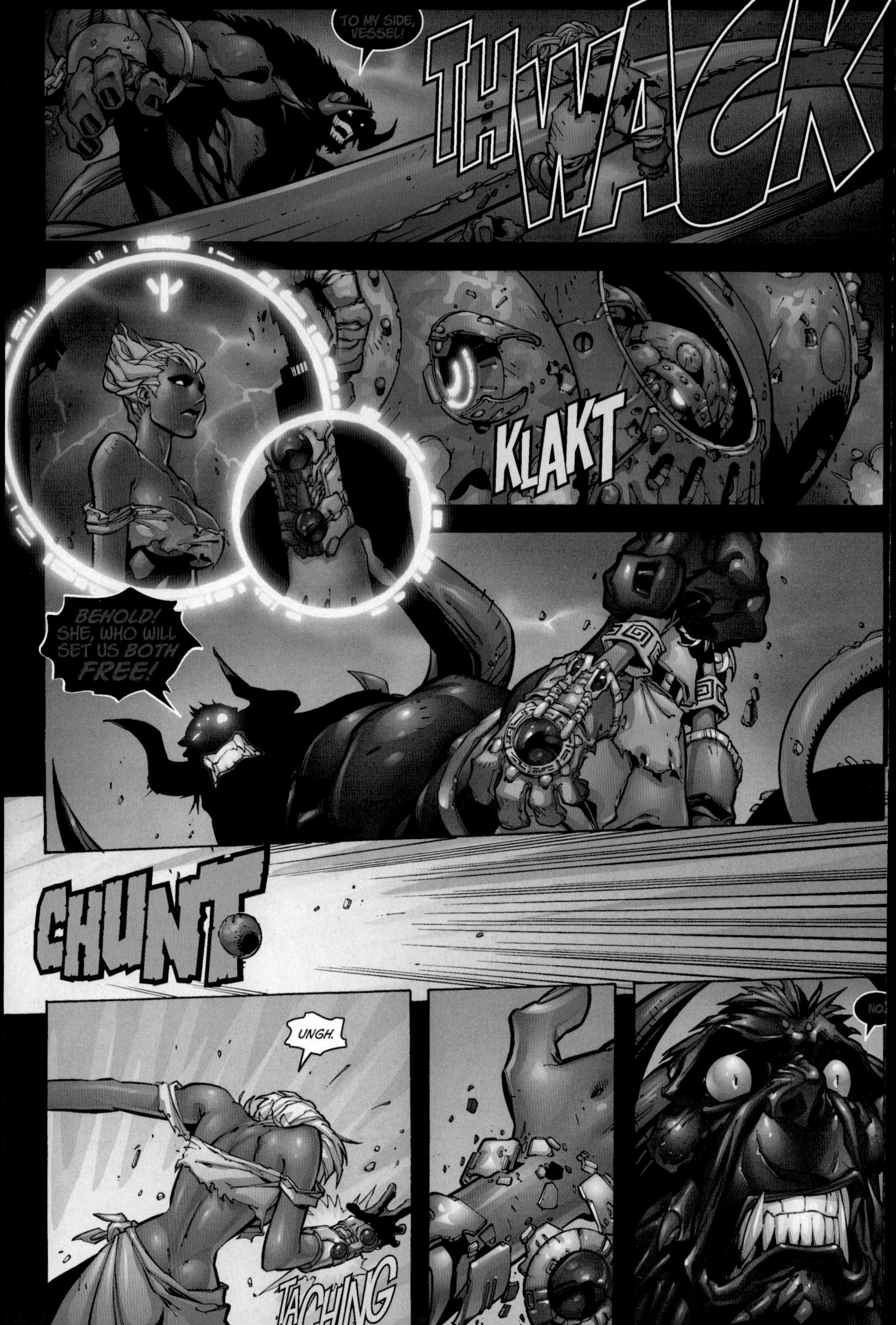
TO MY SIDE, VESSEL!
THWACK
KLAKT
BEHOLD! SHE, WHO WILL SET US BOTH FREE!
CHUNT
UNGH.
TACHING
NO

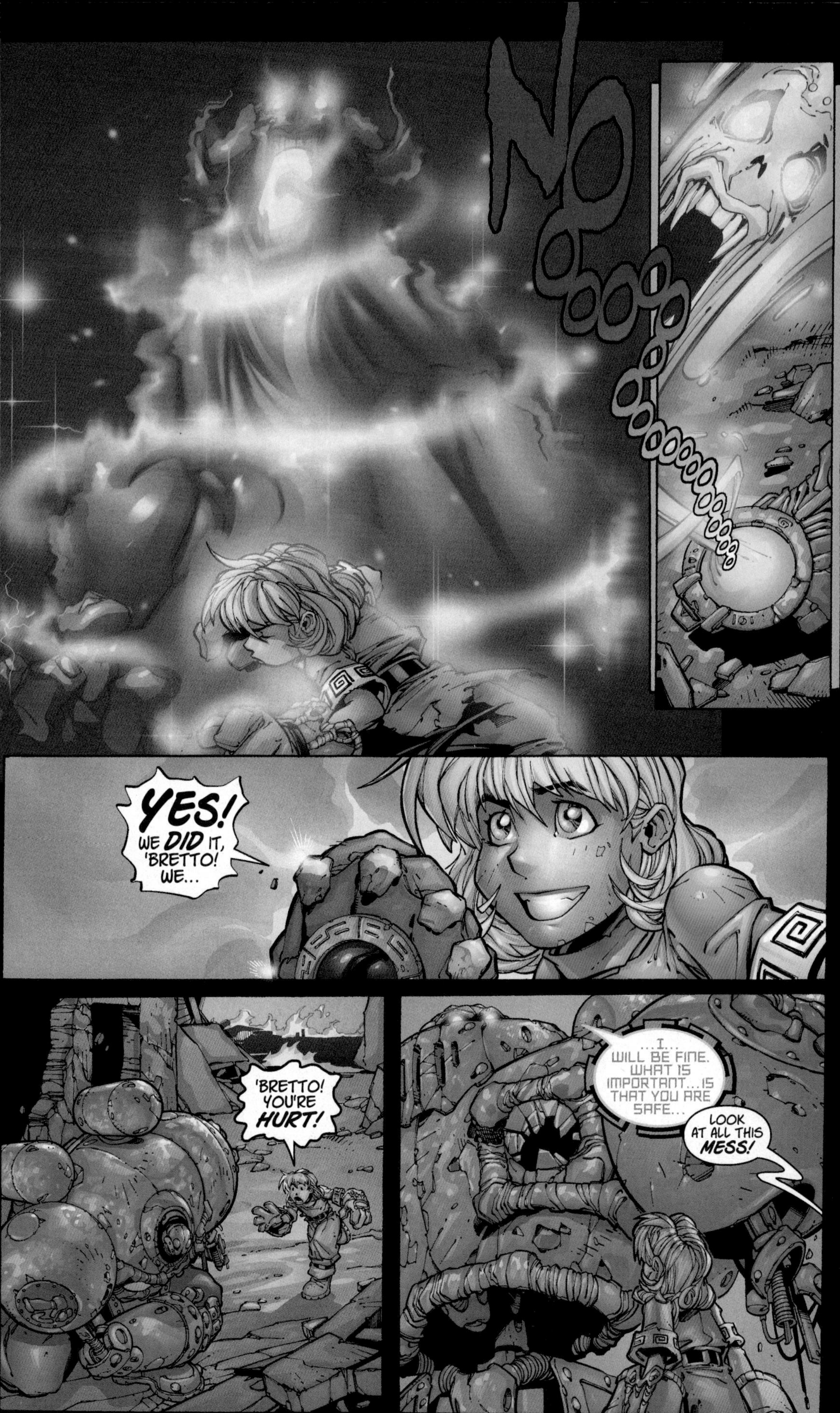
NOOOOOOOOOOOOOOOOOOOOOO
YES! WE DID IT, 'BRETTO! WE...
'BRETTO! YOU'RE HURT!
...I... WILL BE FINE. WHAT IS IMPORTANT... IS THAT YOU ARE SAFE...
LOOK AT ALL THIS MESS!

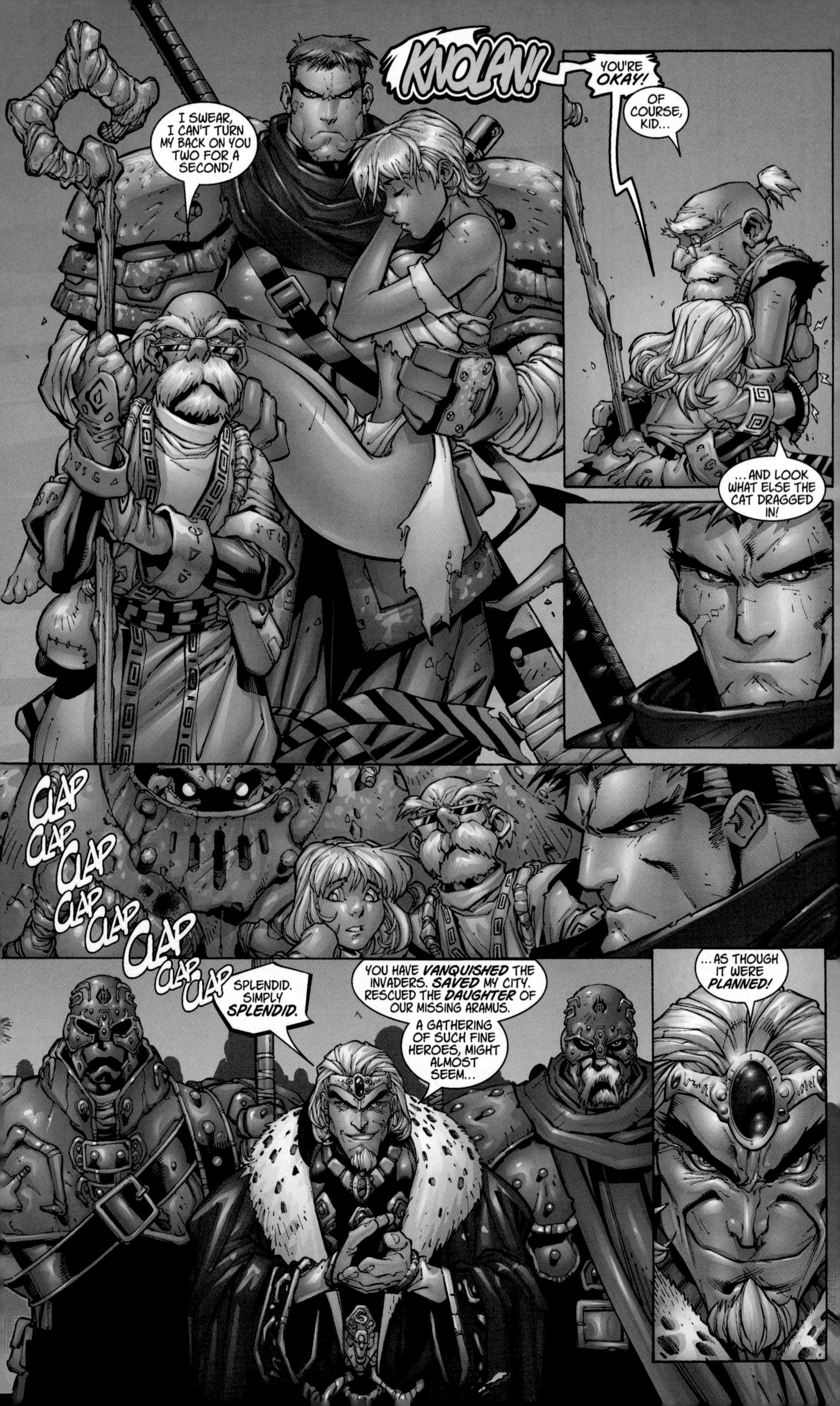

I SWEAR, I CAN'T TURN MY BACK ON YOU TWO FOR A SECOND!
KNOLAN!
YOU'RE OKAY!
OF COURSE, KID...
...AND LOOK WHAT ELSE THE CAT DRAGGED IN!
CLAP CLAP CLAP CLAP CLAP CLAP CLAP CLAP
SPLENDID. SIMPLY SPLENDID.
YOU HAVE VANQUISHED THE INVADERS. SAVED MY CITY. RESCUED THE DAUGHTER OF OUR MISSING ARAMUS.
A GATHERING OF SUCH FINE HEROES, MIGHT ALMOST SEEM...
...AS THOUGH IT WERE PLANNED!

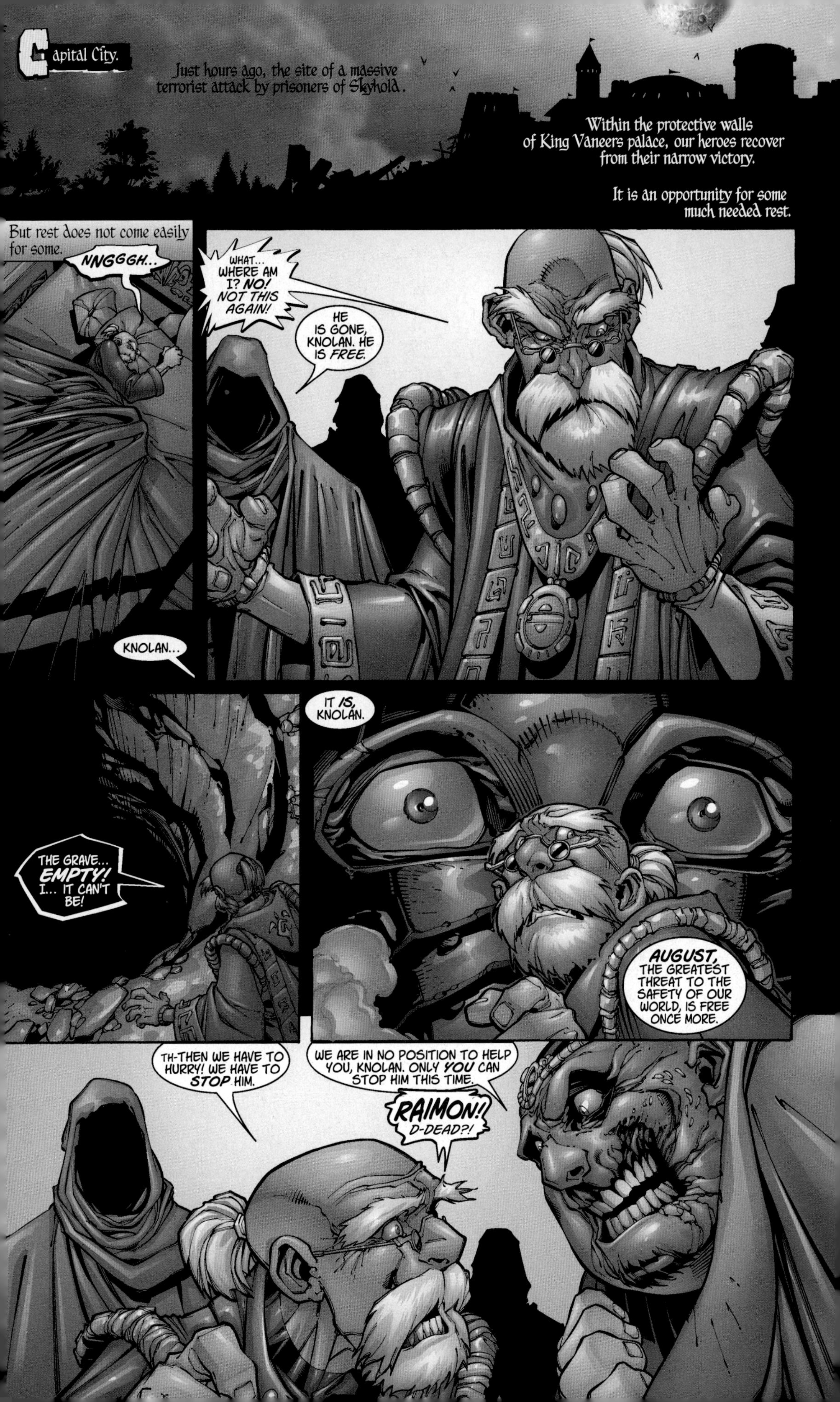
Capital City.
Just hours ago, the site of a massive terrorist attack by prisoners of Skyhold.
Within the protective walls of King Vaneers palace, our heroes recover from their narrow victory.
It is an opportunity for some much needed rest.
But rest does not come easily for some.
NNGGGH...
WHAT... WHERE AM I? NO! NOT THIS AGAIN!
HE IS GONE, KNOLAN. HE IS FREE.
KNOLAN...
IT IS, KNOLAN.
THE GRAVE... EMPTY! I... IT CAN'T BE!
AUGUST, THE GREATEST THREAT TO THE SAFETY OF OUR WORLD, IS FREE ONCE MORE.
TH-THEN WE HAVE TO HURRY! WE HAVE TO STOP HIM.
WE ARE IN NO POSITION TO HELP YOU, KNOLAN. ONLY YOU CAN STOP HIM THIS TIME.
RAIMON! D-DEAD?!

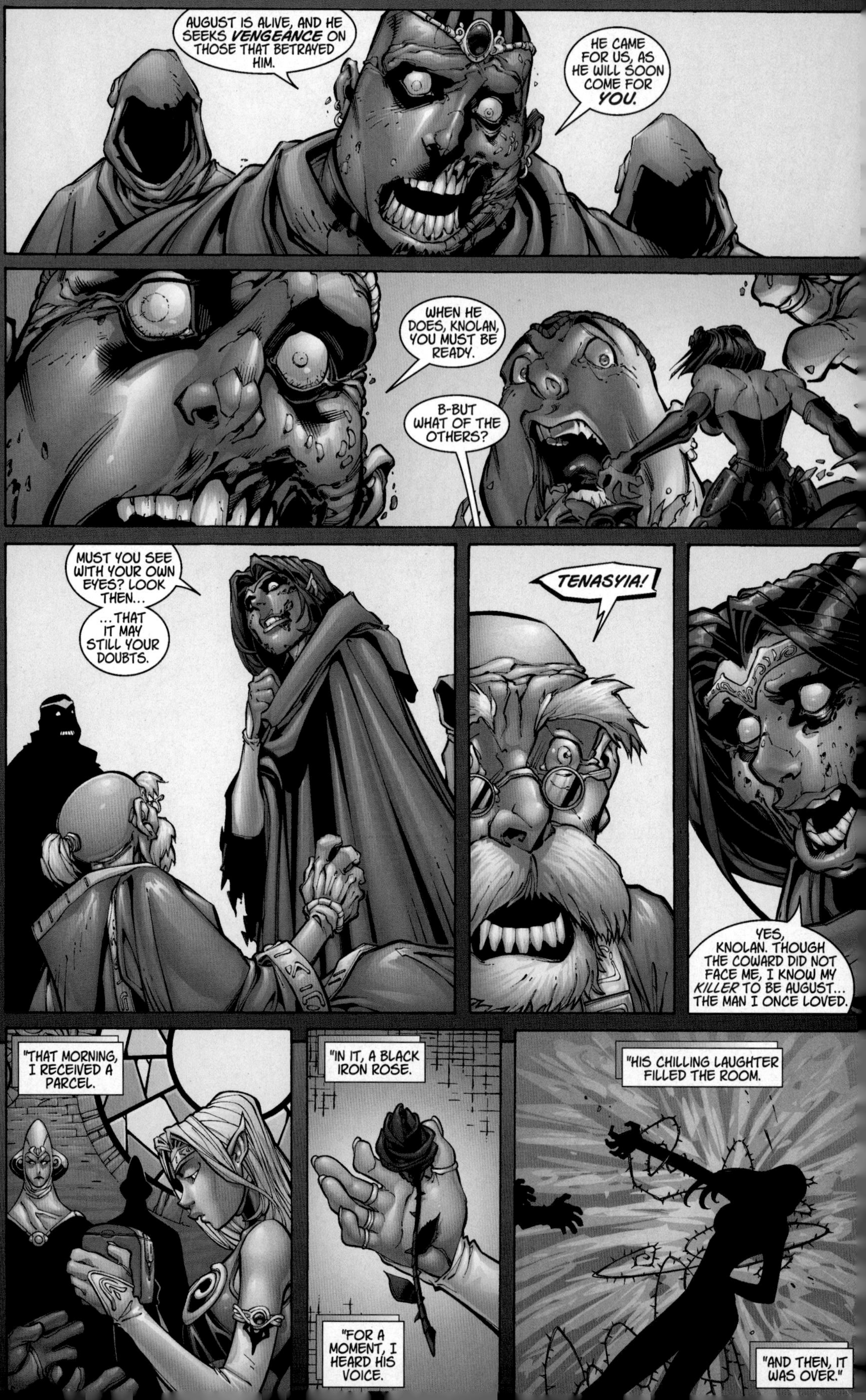
AUGUST IS ALIVE, AND HE SEEKS VENGEANCE ON THOSE THAT BETRAYED HIM.
HE CAME FOR US, AS HE WILL SOON COME FOR YOU.
WHEN HE DOES, KNOLAN, YOU MUST BE READY.
B-BUT WHAT OF THE OTHERS?
MUST YOU SEE WITH YOUR OWN EYES? LOOK THEN...
...THAT IT MAY STILL YOUR DOUBTS.
TENASYIA!
YES, KNOLAN. THOUGH THE COWARD DID NOT FACE ME, I KNOW MY KILLER TO BE AUGUST... THE MAN I ONCE LOVED.
"THAT MORNING, I RECEIVED A PARCEL.
"IN IT, A BLACK IRON ROSE.
"FOR A MOMENT, I HEARD HIS VOICE.
"HIS CHILLING LAUGHTER FILLED THE ROOM.
"AND THEN, IT WAS OVER."

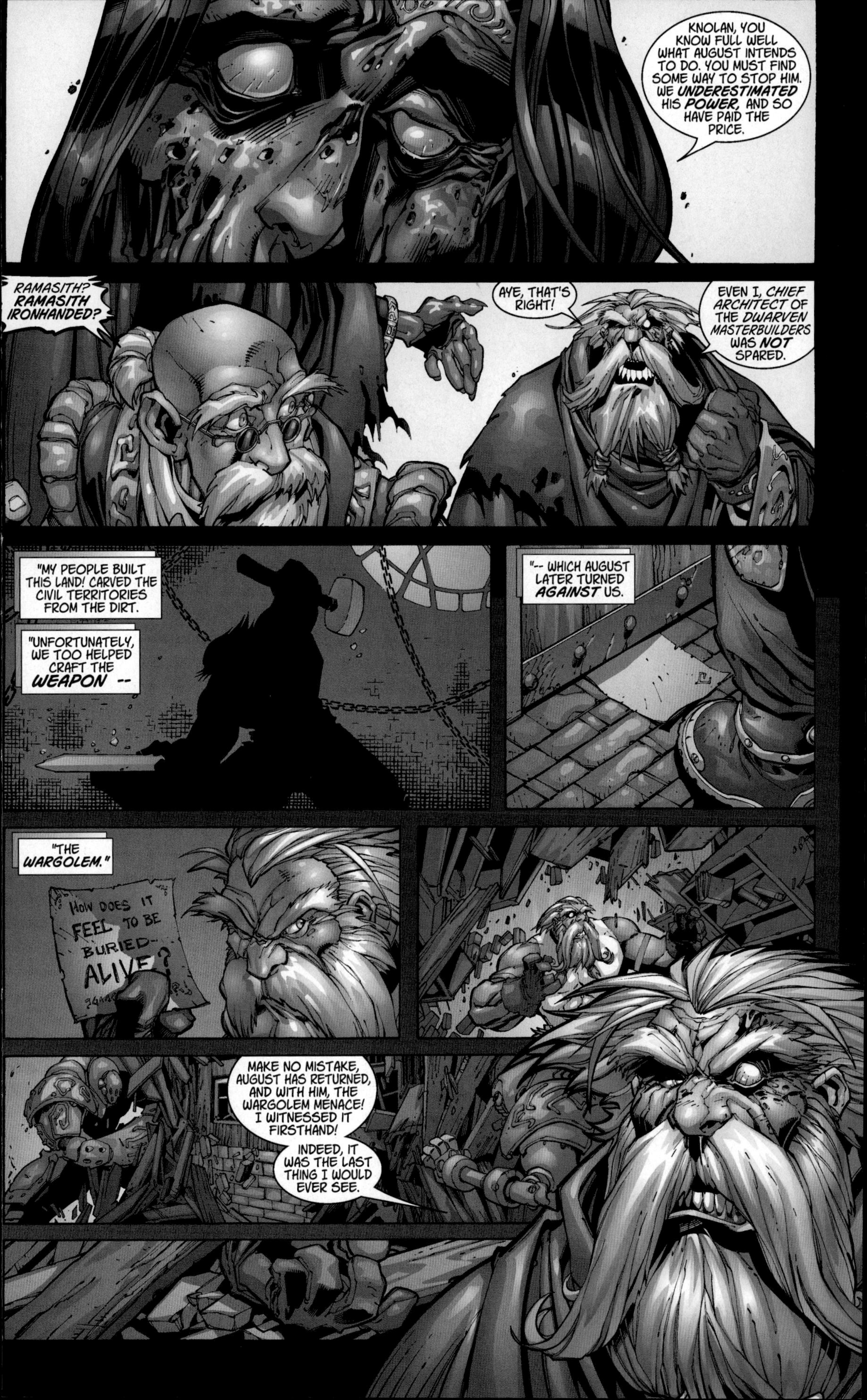
KNOLAN, YOU KNOW FULL WELL WHAT AUGUST INTENDS TO DO. YOU MUST FIND SOME WAY TO STOP HIM. WE UNDERESTIMATED HIS POWER, AND SO HAVE PAID THE PRICE.
RAMASITH? RAMASITH IRONHANDED?
AYE, THAT'S RIGHT!
EVEN I, CHIEF ARCHITECT OF THE DWARVEN MASTERBUILDERS WAS NOT SPARED.
"MY PEOPLE BUILT THIS LAND! CARVED THE CIVIL TERRITORIES FROM THE DIRT.
"UNFORTUNATELY, WE TOO HELPED CRAFT THE WEAPON --
"-- WHICH AUGUST LATER TURNED AGAINST US.
"THE WARGOLEM."
HOW DOES IT FEEL TO BE BURIED-- ALIVE?
MAKE NO MISTAKE, AUGUST HAS RETURNED, AND WITH HIM, THE WARGOLEM MENACE! I WITNESSED IT FIRSTHAND!
INDEED, IT WAS THE LAST THING I WOULD EVER SEE.

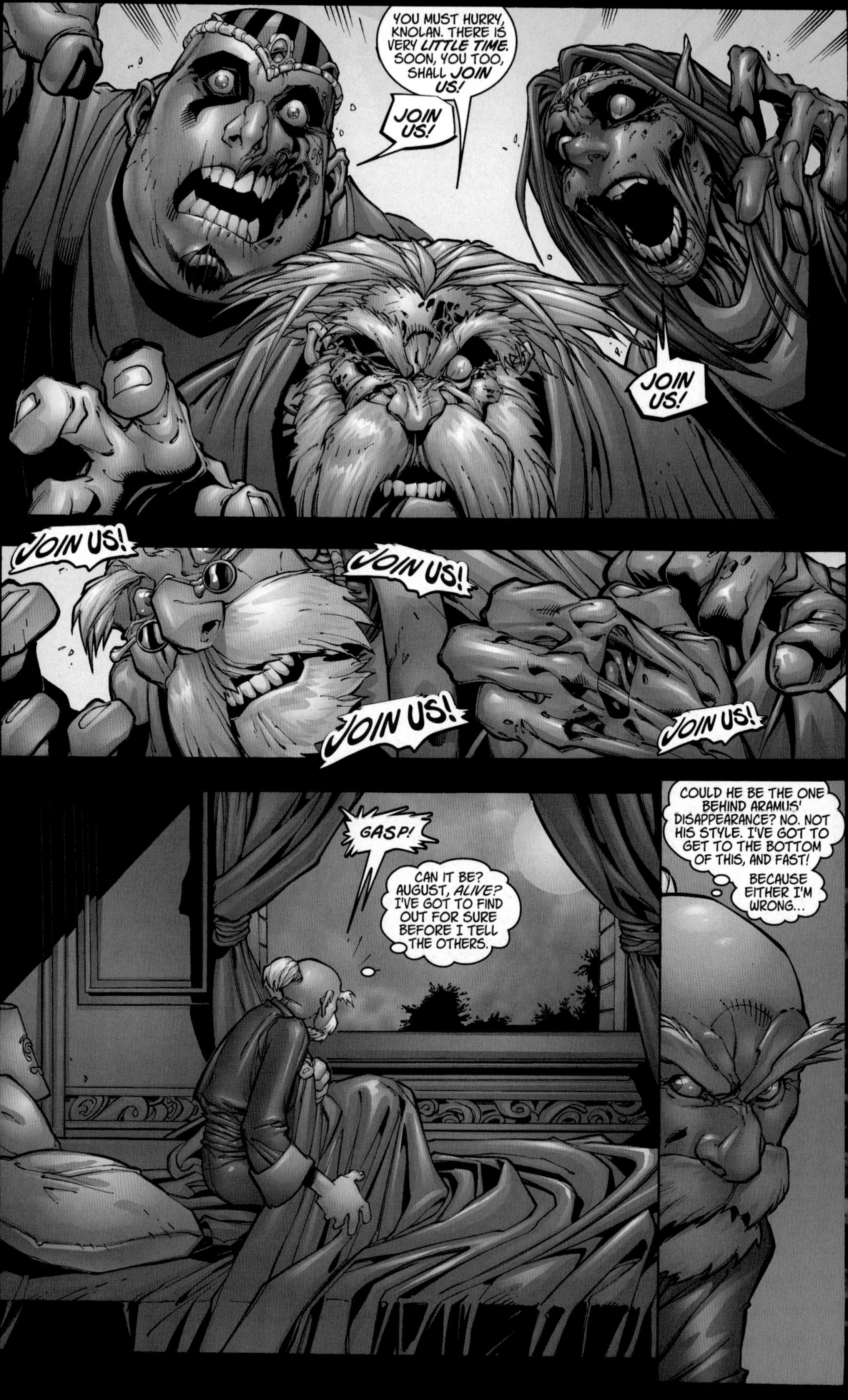
YOU MUST HURRY, KNOLAN. THERE IS VERY LITTLE TIME. SOON, YOU TOO, SHALL JOIN US!
JOIN US!
JOIN US!
JOIN US!
JOIN US!
JOIN US!
JOIN US!
GASP!
CAN IT BE? AUGUST, ALIVE? I'VE GOT TO FIND OUT FOR SURE BEFORE I TELL THE OTHERS.
COULD HE BE THE ONE BEHIND ARAMUS' DISAPPEARANCE? NO. NOT HIS STYLE. I'VE GOT TO GET TO THE BOTTOM OF THIS, AND FAST!
BECAUSE EITHER I'M WRONG...

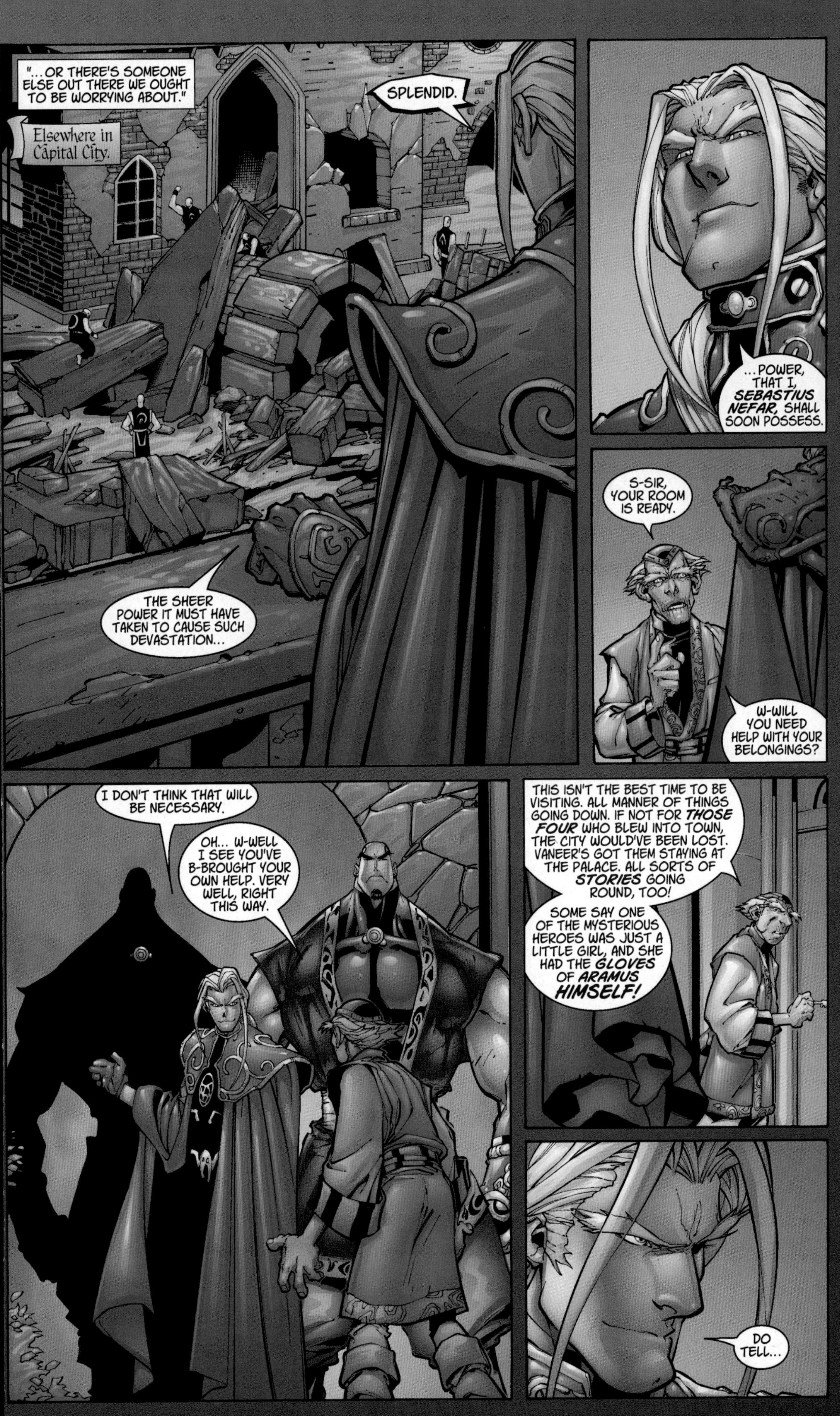
"...OR THERE'S SOMEONE ELSE OUT THERE WE OUGHT TO BE WORRYING ABOUT."
Elsewhere in Capital City.
SPLENDID.
THE SHEER POWER IT MUST HAVE TAKEN TO CAUSE SUCH DEVASTATION...
...POWER, THAT I, SEBASTIUS NEFAR, SHALL SOON POSSESS.
S-SIR, YOUR ROOM IS READY.
W-WILL YOU NEED HELP WITH YOUR BELONGINGS?
I DON'T THINK THAT WILL BE NECESSARY.
OH... W-WELL I SEE YOU'VE B-BROUGHT YOUR OWN HELP. VERY WELL, RIGHT THIS WAY.
THIS ISN'T THE BEST TIME TO BE VISITING. ALL MANNER OF THINGS GOING DOWN. IF NOT FOR THOSE FOUR WHO BLEW INTO TOWN, THE CITY WOULD'VE BEEN LOST. VANEER'S GOT THEM STAYING AT THE PALACE. ALL SORTS OF STORIES GOING ROUND, TOO!
SOME SAY ONE OF THE MYSTERIOUS HEROES WAS JUST A LITTLE GIRL, AND SHE HAD THE GLOVES OF ARAMUS HIMSELF!
DO TELL...

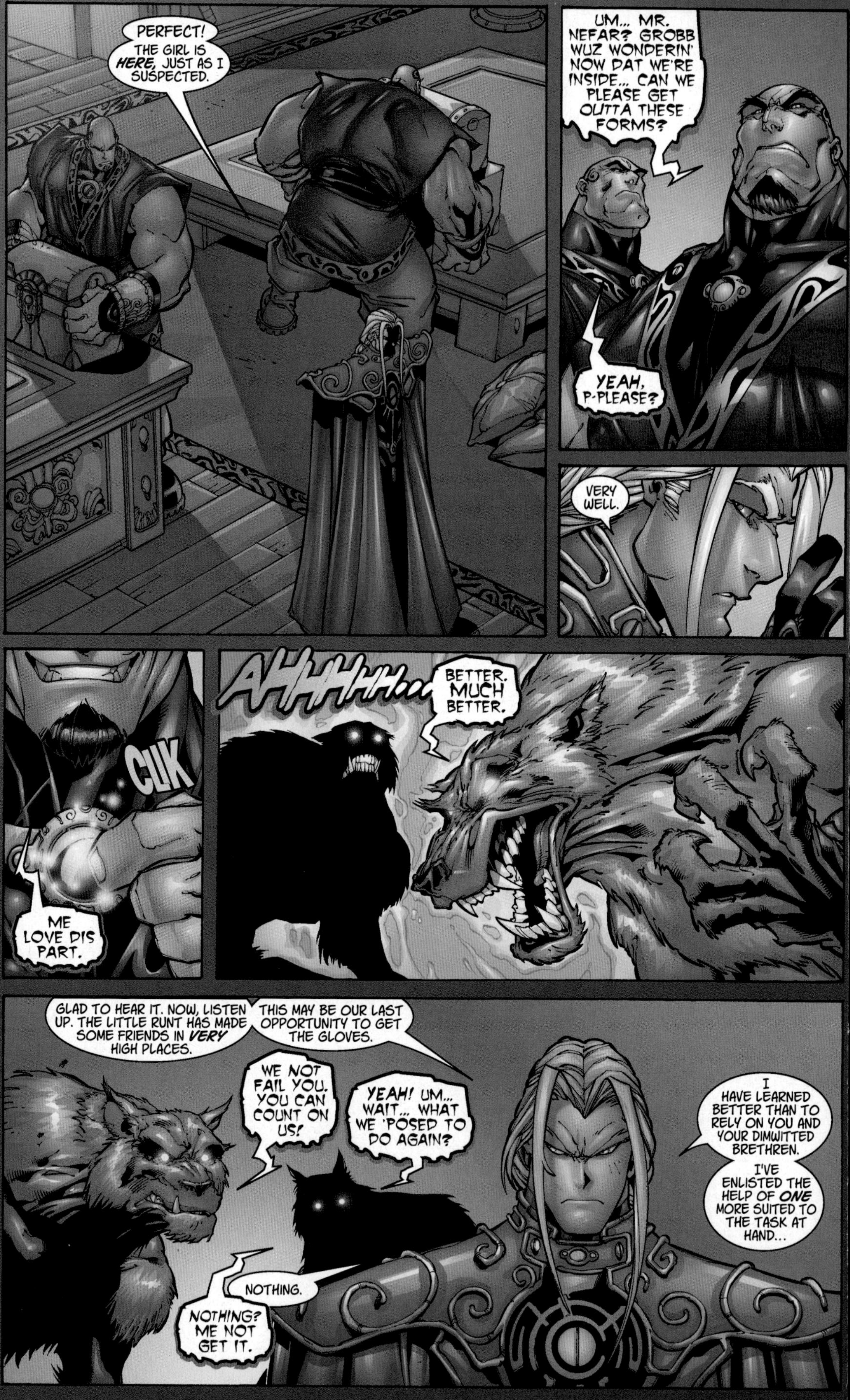
PERFECT! THE GIRL IS HERE, JUST AS I SUSPECTED.
UM... MR. NEFAR? GROBB WUZ WONDERIN' NOW DAT WE'RE INSIDE... CAN WE PLEASE GET OUTTA THESE FORMS?
YEAH, P-PLEASE?
VERY WELL.
CLIK
ME LOVE DIS PART.
AHHHHH...
BETTER. MUCH BETTER.
GLAD TO HEAR IT. NOW, LISTEN UP. THE LITTLE RUNT HAS MADE SOME FRIENDS IN VERY HIGH PLACES.
THIS MAY BE OUR LAST OPPORTUNITY TO GET THE GLOVES.
WE NOT FAIL YOU. YOU CAN COUNT ON US!
YEAH! UM... WAIT... WHAT WE 'POSED TO DO AGAIN?
I HAVE LEARNED BETTER THAN TO RELY ON YOU AND YOUR DIMWITTED BRETHREN.
I'VE ENLISTED THE HELP OF ONE MORE SUITED TO THE TASK AT HAND...
NOTHING.
NOTHING? ME NOT GET IT.

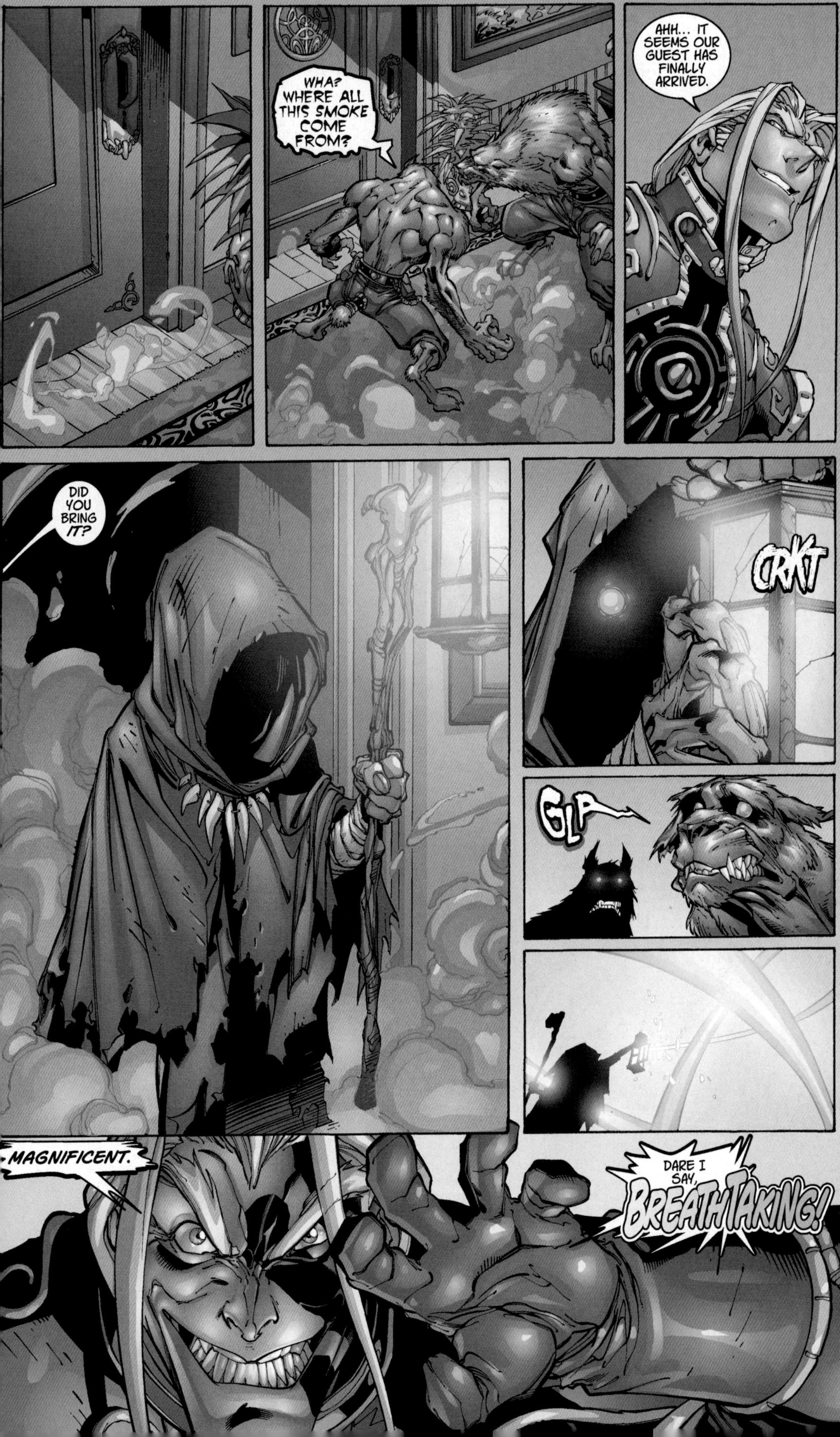
WHA? WHERE ALL THIS SMOKE COME FROM?
AHH... IT SEEMS OUR GUEST HAS FINALLY ARRIVED.
DID YOU BRING IT?
CRKT
GLP
MAGNIFICENT.
DARE I SAY, BREATHTAKING!

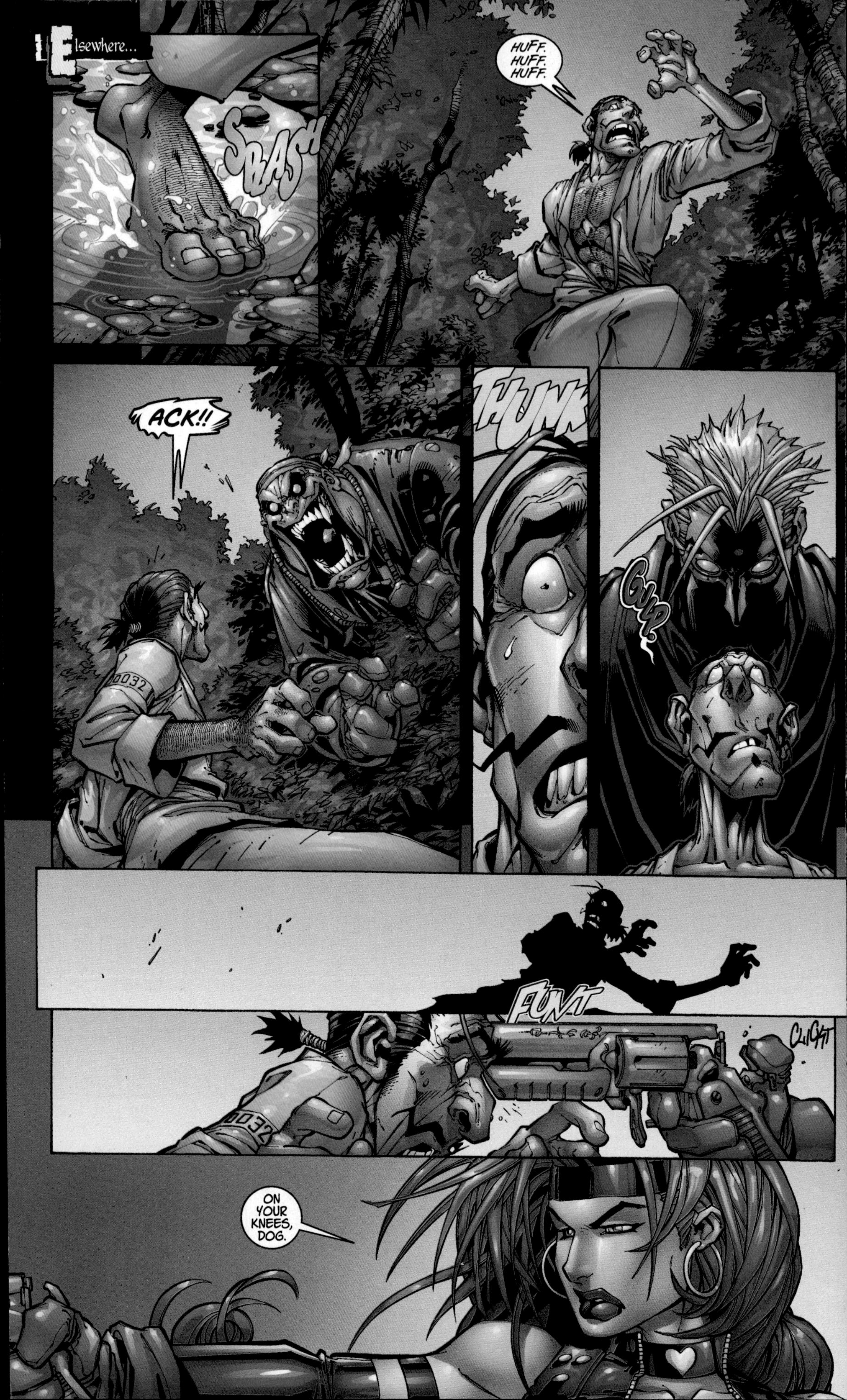
Elsewhere...
SPLASH
HUFF. HUFF. HUFF.
ACK!!
THUNK
GULP
FUNT
CLICK
ON YOUR KNEES, DOG.

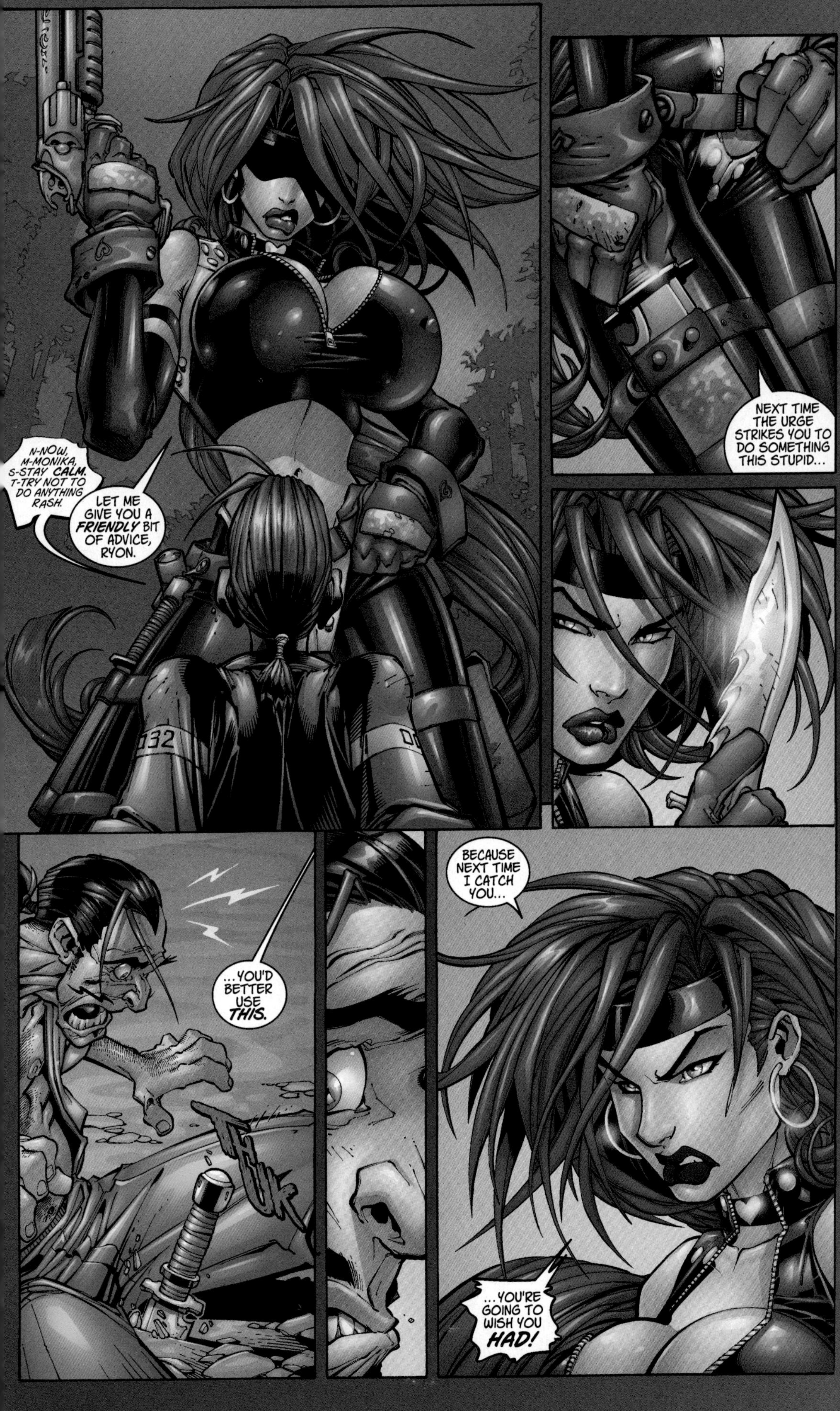
N-NOW, M-MONIKA, S-STAY CALM. T-TRY NOT TO DO ANYTHING RASH.
LET ME GIVE YOU A FRIENDLY BIT OF ADVICE, RYON.
NEXT TIME THE URGE STRIKES YOU TO DO SOMETHING THIS STUPID...
...YOU'D BETTER USE THIS.
BECAUSE NEXT TIME I CATCH YOU...
...YOU'RE GOING TO WISH YOU HAD!

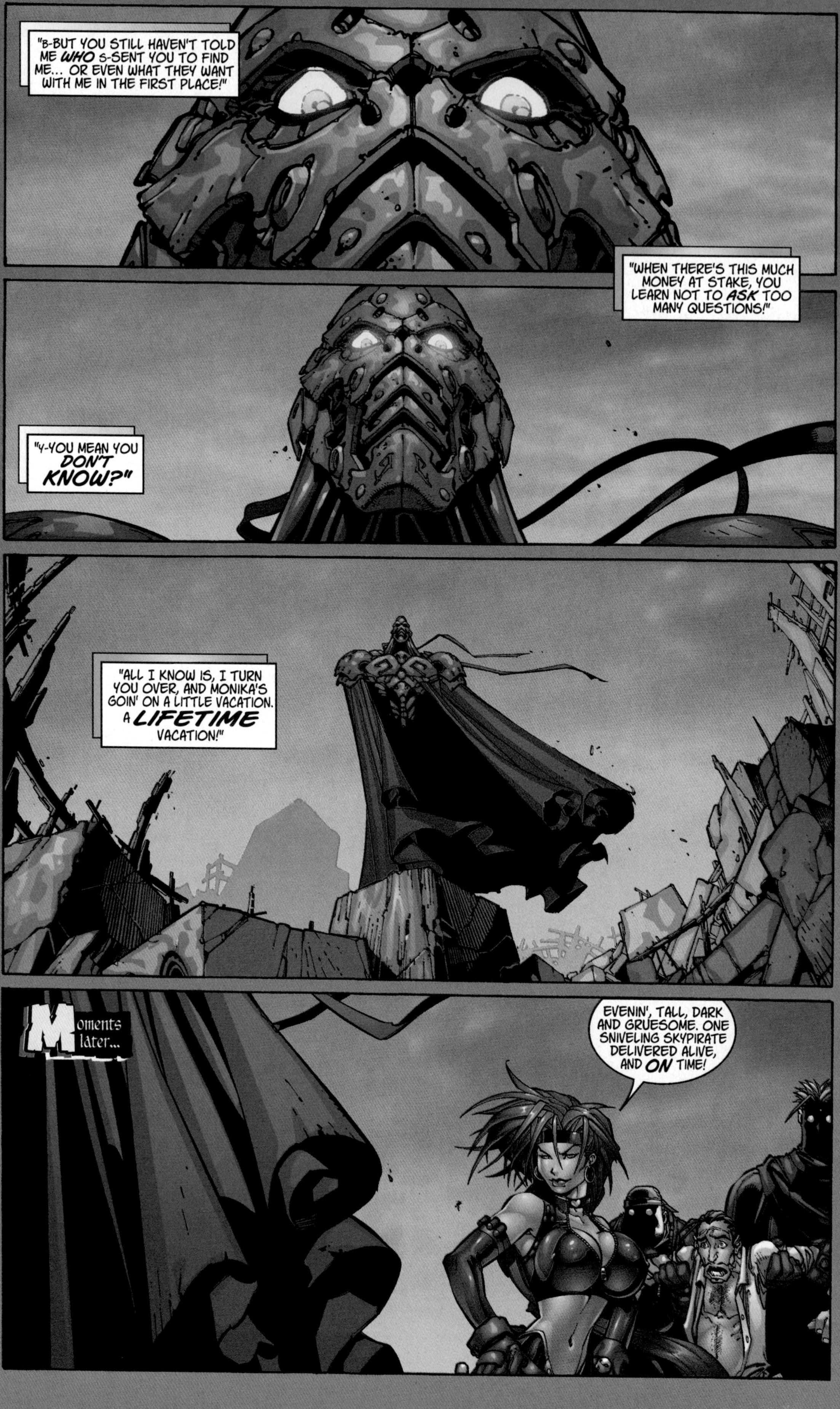
"B-BUT YOU STILL HAVEN'T TOLD ME WHO S-SENT YOU TO FIND ME... OR EVEN WHAT THEY WANT WITH ME IN THE FIRST PLACE!"
"WHEN THERE'S THIS MUCH MONEY AT STAKE, YOU LEARN NOT TO ASK TOO MANY QUESTIONS!"
"Y-YOU MEAN YOU DON'T KNOW?"
"ALL I KNOW IS, I TURN YOU OVER, AND MONIKA'S GOIN' ON A LITTLE VACATION. A LIFETIME VACATION!"
Moments later...
EVENIN', TALL, DARK AND GRUESOME. ONE SNIVELING SKYPIRATE DELIVERED ALIVE, AND ON TIME!

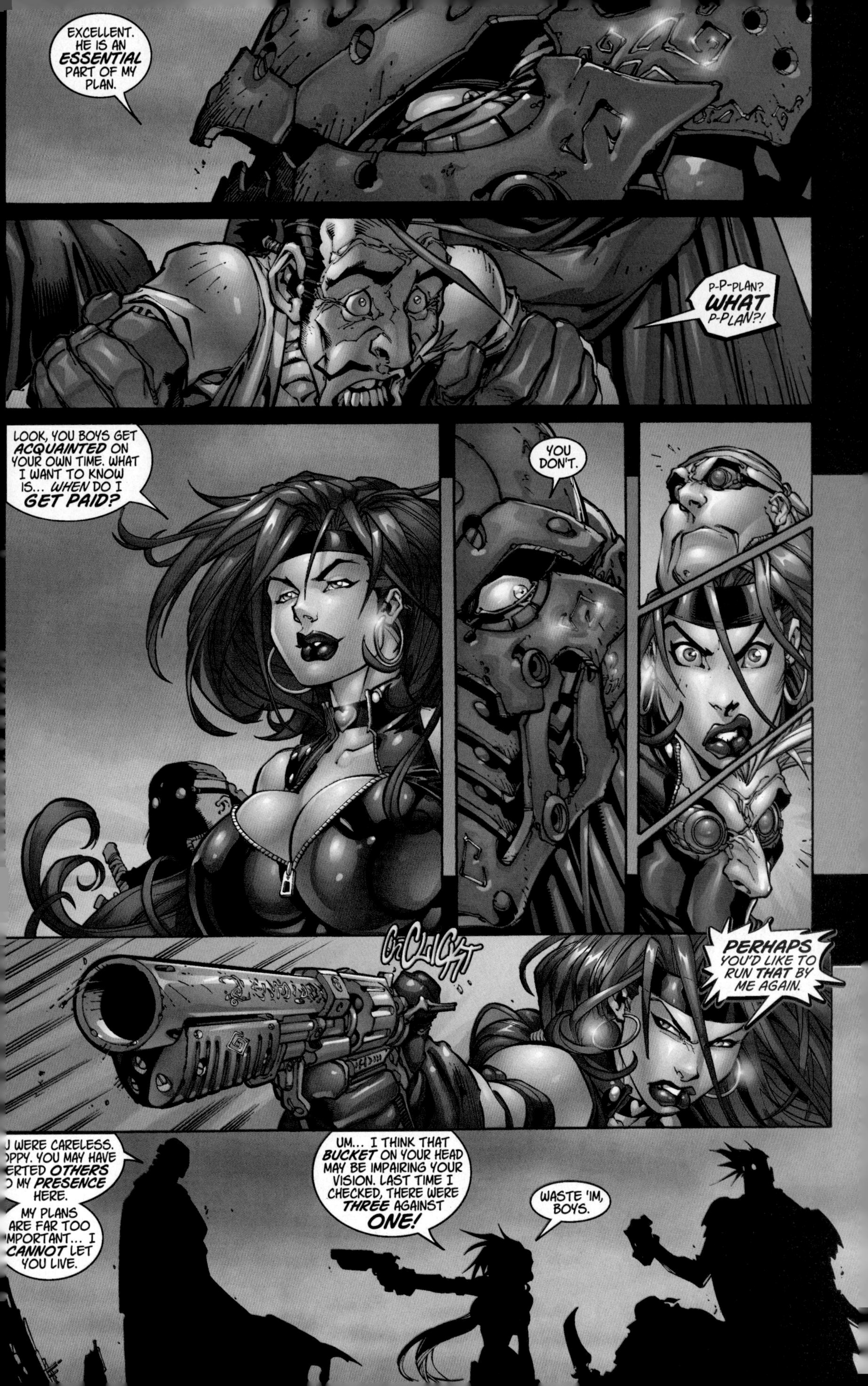
EXCELLENT. HE IS AN ESSENTIAL PART OF MY PLAN.
P-P-PLAN? WHAT P-PLAN?!
LOOK, YOU BOYS GET ACQUAINTED ON YOUR OWN TIME. WHAT I WANT TO KNOW IS... WHEN DO I GET PAID?
YOU DON'T.
CHCLICK
PERHAPS YOU'D LIKE TO RUN THAT BY ME AGAIN.
U WERE CARELESS. OPPY. YOU MAY HAVE ERTED OTHERS O MY PRESENCE HERE.
MY PLANS ARE FAR TOO MPORTANT... I CANNOT LET YOU LIVE.
UM... I THINK THAT BUCKET ON YOUR HEAD MAY BE IMPAIRING YOUR VISION. LAST TIME I CHECKED, THERE WERE THREE AGAINST ONE!
WASTE 'IM, BOYS.

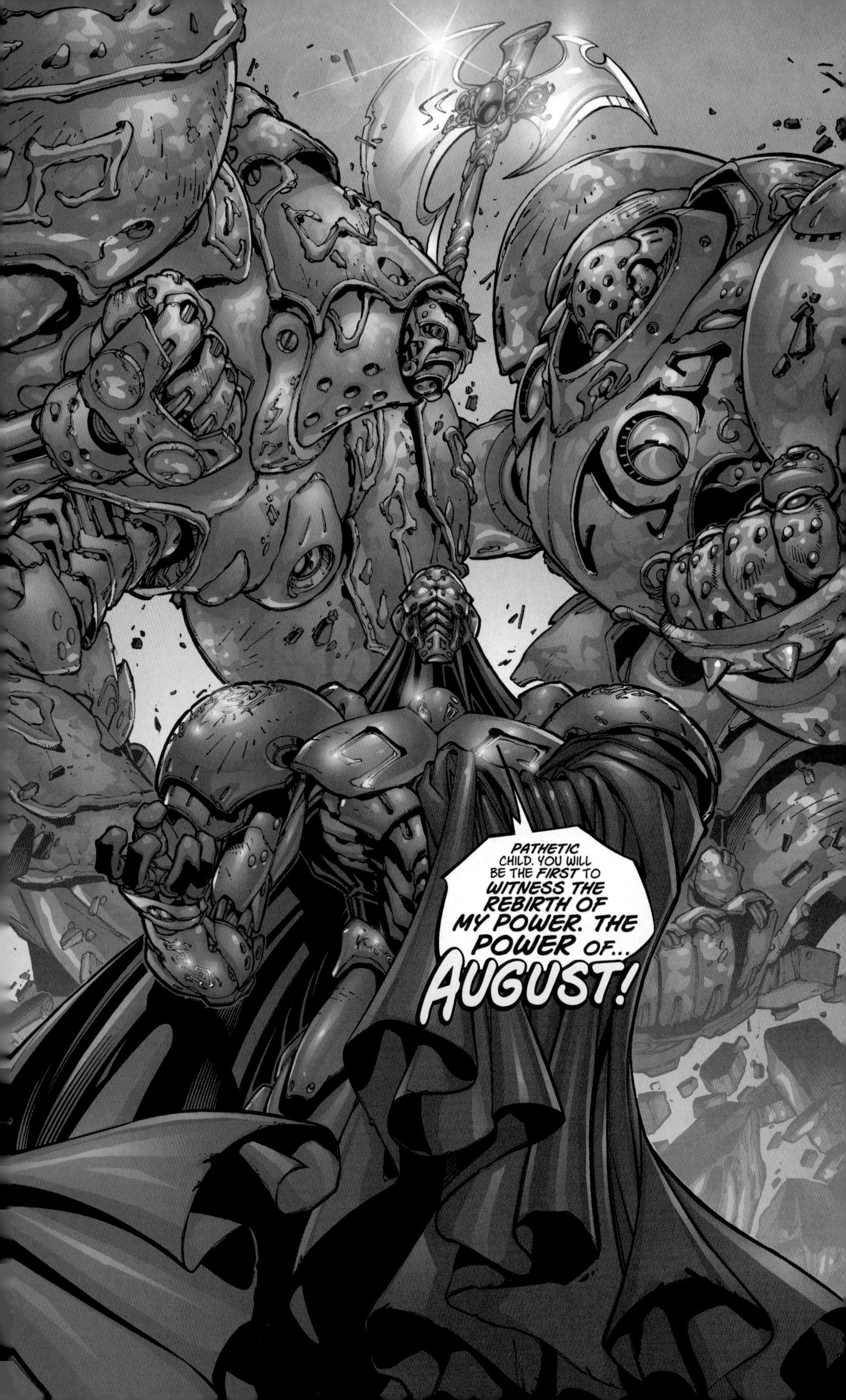
PATHETIC CHILD. YOU WILL BE THE FIRST TO WITNESS THE REBIRTH OF MY POWER. THE POWER OF... AUGUST!

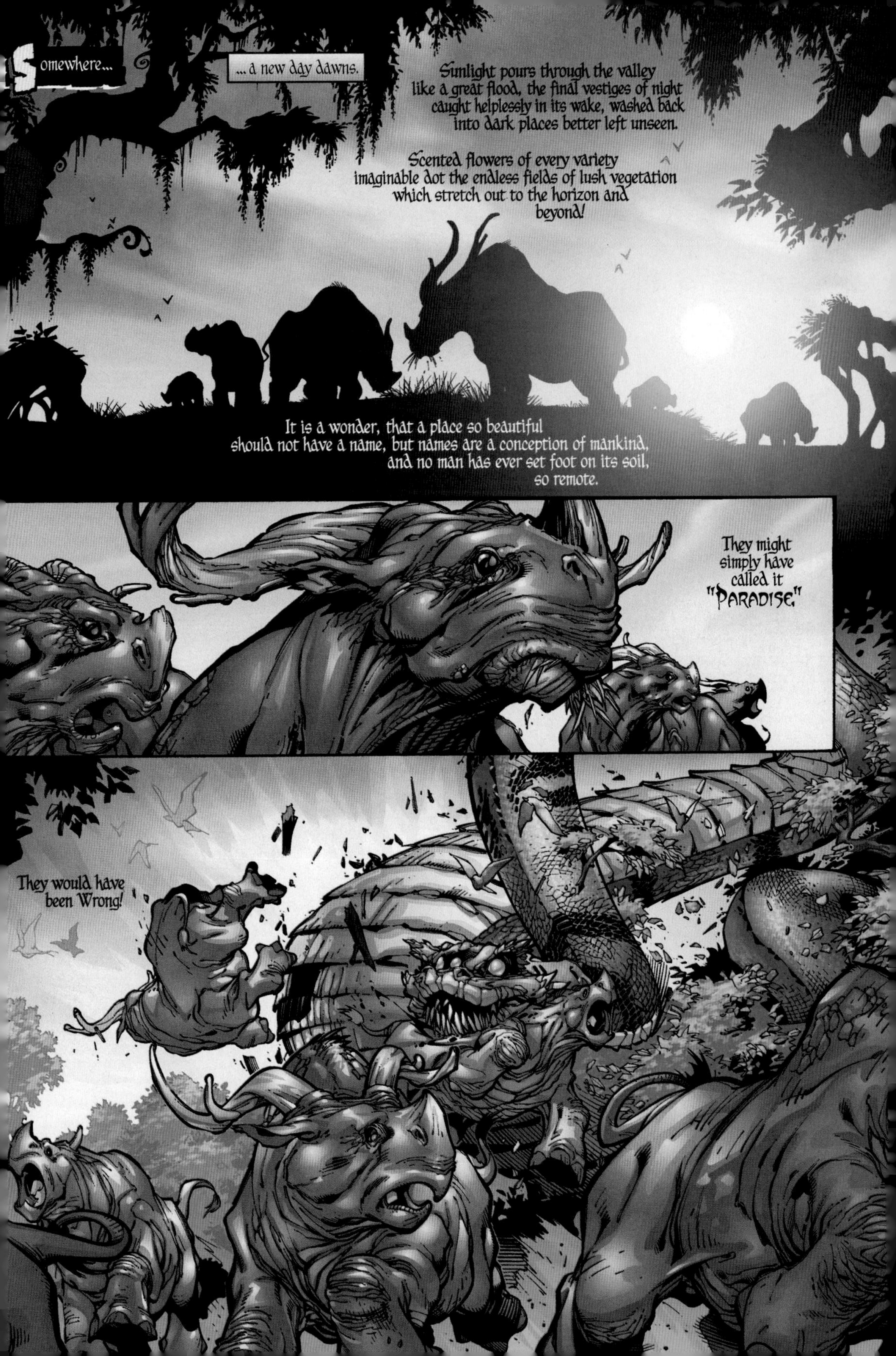
Somewhere...
... a new day dawns.
Sunlight pours through the valley like a great flood, the final vestiges of night caught helplessly in its wake, washed back into dark places better left unseen.
Scented flowers of every variety imaginable dot the endless fields of lush vegetation which stretch out to the horizon and beyond!
It is a wonder, that a place so beautiful should not have a name, but names are a conception of mankind, and no man has ever set foot on its soil, so remote.
They might simply have called it "Paradise."
They would have been Wrong!

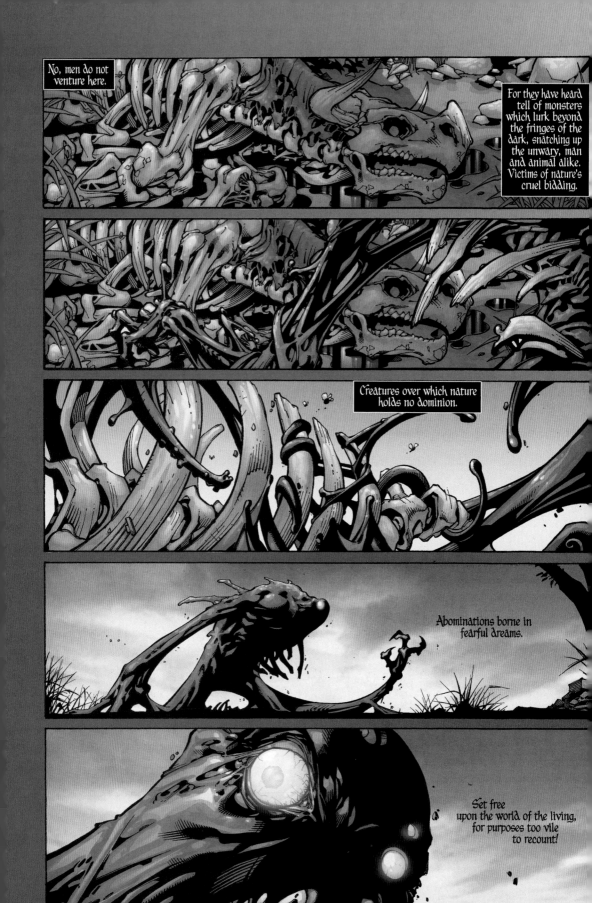

No, men do not venture here.

For they have heard tell of monsters which lurk beyond the fringes of the dark, snatching up the unwary, man and animal alike. Victims of nature's cruel bidding.

Creatures over which nature holds no dominion.

Abominations borne in fearful dreams.

Set free upon the world of the living, for purposes too vile to recount!

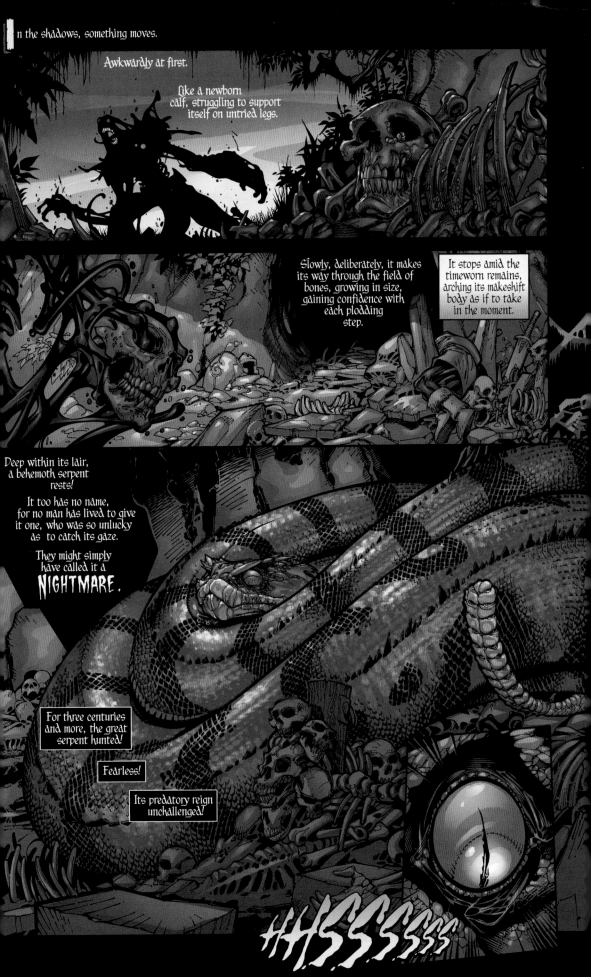

In the shadows, something moves.

Awkwardly at first.

Like a newborn calf, struggling to support itself on untried legs.

Slowly, deliberately, it makes its way through the field of bones, growing in size, gaining confidence with each plodding step.

It stops amid the timeworn remains, arching its makeshift body as if to take in the moment.

Deep within its lair, a behemoth serpent rests!

It too has no name, for no man has lived to give it one, who was so unlucky as to catch its gaze.

They might simply have called it a NIGHTMARE.

For three centuries and more, the great serpent hunted!

Fearless!

Its predatory reign unchallenged!

HHSSSSSS

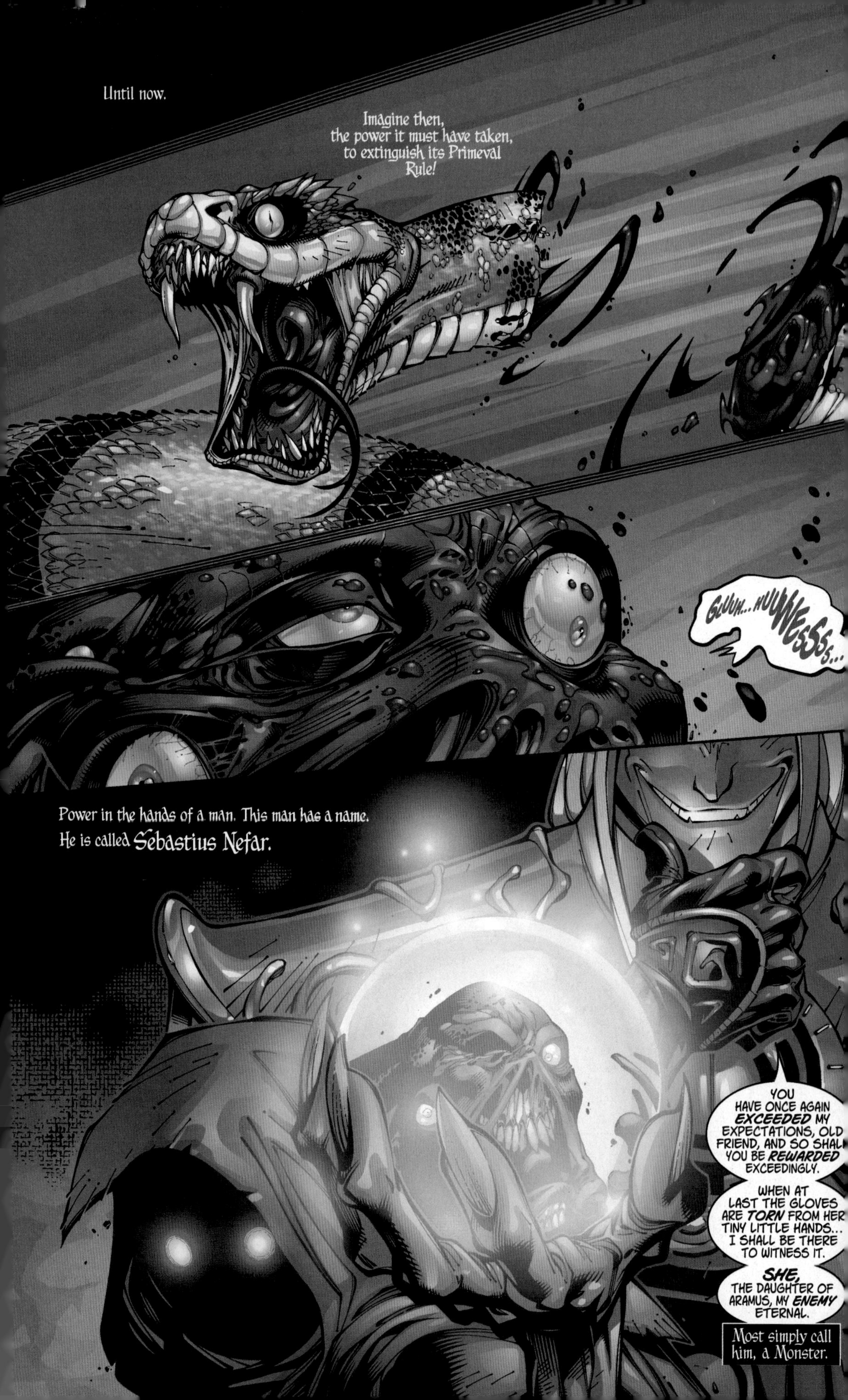
Until now.
Imagine then, the power it must have taken, to extinguish its Primeval Rule!
GLUUH...HUUWESSSs...
Power in the hands of a man. This man has a name. He is called Sebastius Nefar.
YOU HAVE ONCE AGAIN EXCEEDED MY EXPECTATIONS, OLD FRIEND, AND SO SHALL YOU BE REWARDED EXCEEDINGLY.
WHEN AT LAST THE GLOVES ARE TORN FROM HER TINY LITTLE HANDS... I SHALL BE THERE TO WITNESS IT.
SHE, THE DAUGHTER OF ARAMUS, MY ENEMY ETERNAL.
Most simply call him, a Monster.

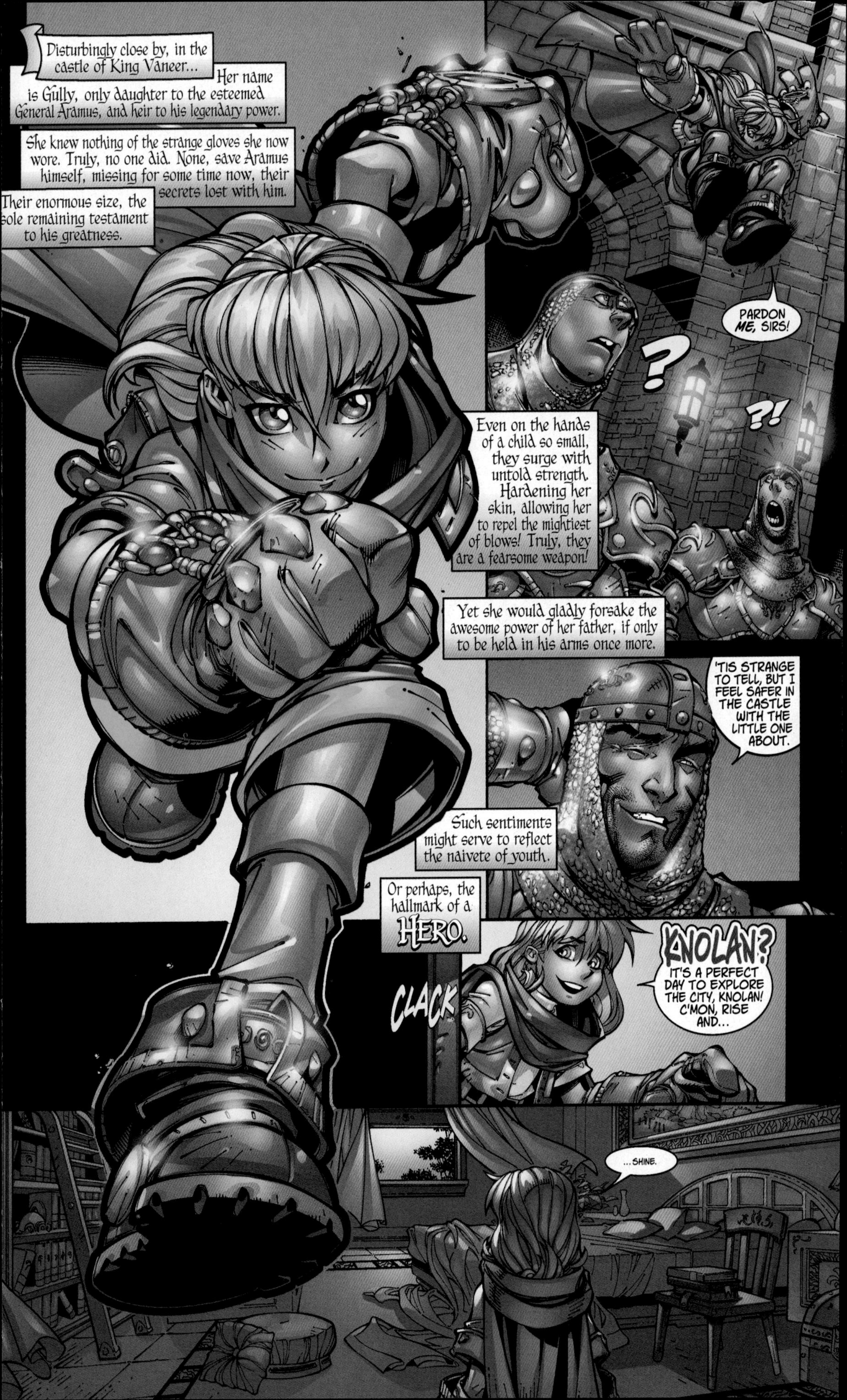
Disturbingly close by, in the castle of King Vaneer...
Her name is Gully, only daughter to the esteemed General Aramus, and heir to his legendary power.
She knew nothing of the strange gloves she now wore. Truly, no one did. None, save Aramus himself, missing for some time now, their secrets lost with him.
Their enormous size, the sole remaining testament to his greatness.
PARDON ME, SIRS!
?
?!
Even on the hands of a child so small, they surge with untold strength. Hardening her skin, allowing her to repel the mightiest of blows! Truly, they are a fearsome weapon!
Yet she would gladly forsake the awesome power of her father, if only to be held in his arms once more.
'TIS STRANGE TO TELL, BUT I FEEL SAFER IN THE CASTLE WITH THE LITTLE ONE ABOUT.
Such sentiments might serve to reflect the naivete of youth.
Or perhaps, the hallmark of a HERO.
CLACK
KNOLAN? IT'S A PERFECT DAY TO EXPLORE THE CITY, KNOLAN! C'MON, RISE AND...
...SHINE.

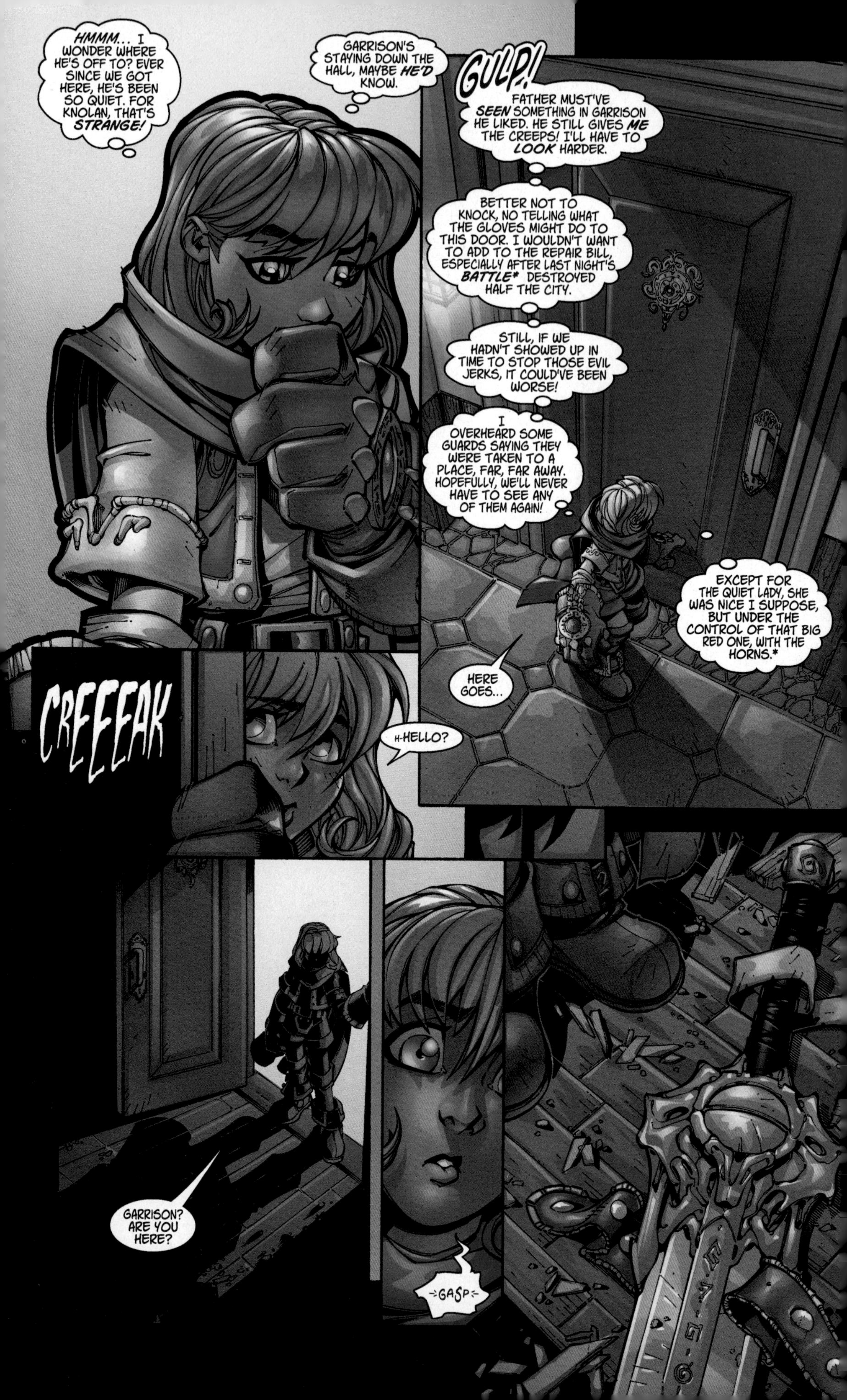
HMMM... I WONDER WHERE HE'S OFF TO? EVER SINCE WE GOT HERE, HE'S BEEN SO QUIET. FOR KNOLAN, THAT'S STRANGE!
GARRISON'S STAYING DOWN THE HALL, MAYBE HE'D KNOW.
GULP!
FATHER MUST'VE SEEN SOMETHING IN GARRISON HE LIKED. HE STILL GIVES ME THE CREEPS! I'LL HAVE TO LOOK HARDER.
BETTER NOT TO KNOCK, NO TELLING WHAT THE GLOVES MIGHT DO TO THIS DOOR. I WOULDN'T WANT TO ADD TO THE REPAIR BILL, ESPECIALLY AFTER LAST NIGHT'S BATTLE* DESTROYED HALF THE CITY.
STILL, IF WE HADN'T SHOWED UP IN TIME TO STOP THOSE EVIL JERKS, IT COULD'VE BEEN WORSE!
I OVERHEARD SOME GUARDS SAYING THEY WERE TAKEN TO A PLACE, FAR, FAR AWAY. HOPEFULLY, WE'LL NEVER HAVE TO SEE ANY OF THEM AGAIN!
EXCEPT FOR THE QUIET LADY, SHE WAS NICE I SUPPOSE, BUT UNDER THE CONTROL OF THAT BIG RED ONE, WITH THE HORNS.*
HERE GOES...
CREEEAK
H-HELLO?
GARRISON? ARE YOU HERE?
GASP

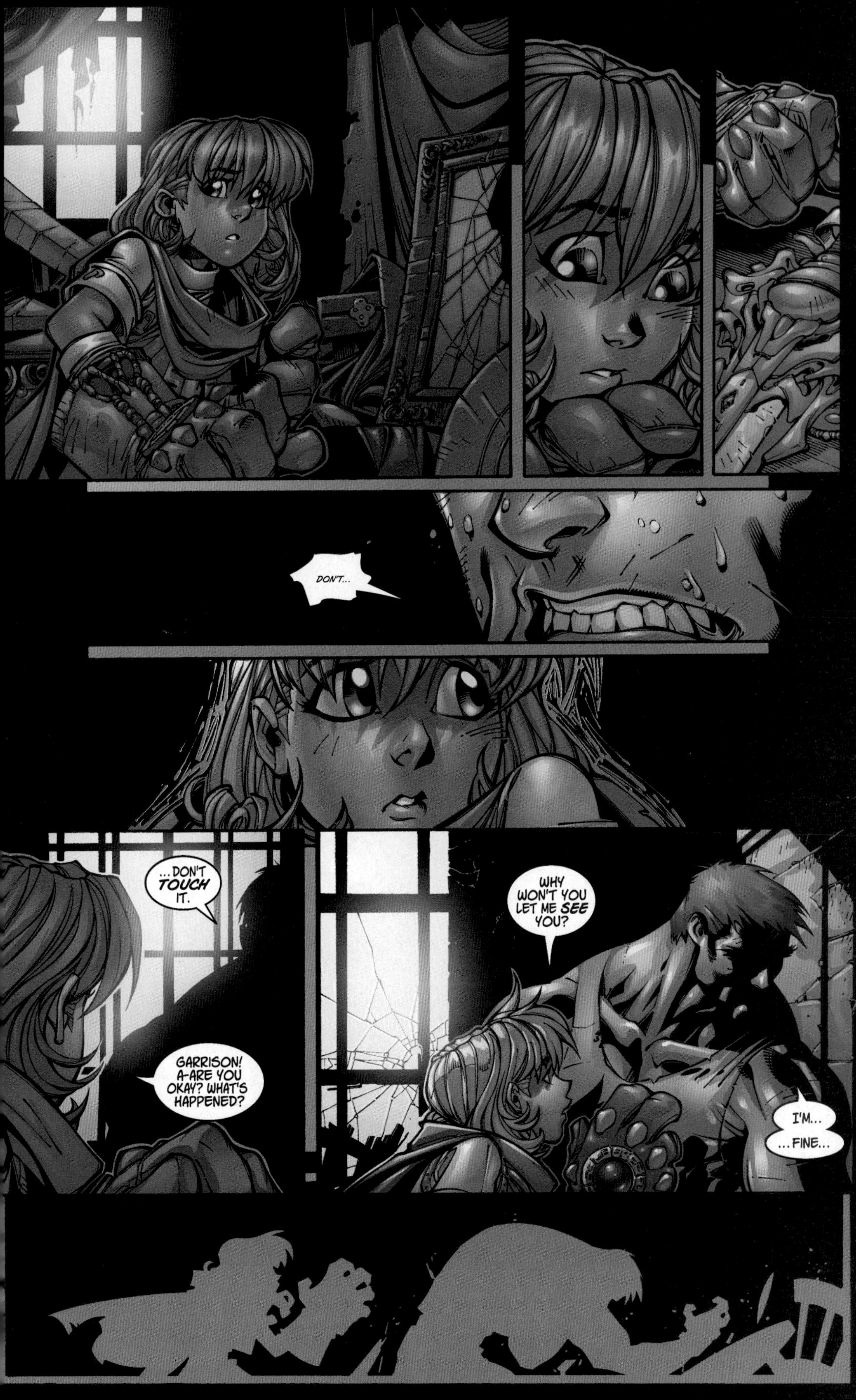
DON'T...
...DON'T TOUCH IT.
GARRISON! A-ARE YOU OKAY? WHAT'S HAPPENED?
WHY WON'T YOU LET ME SEE YOU?
I'M...
...FINE...

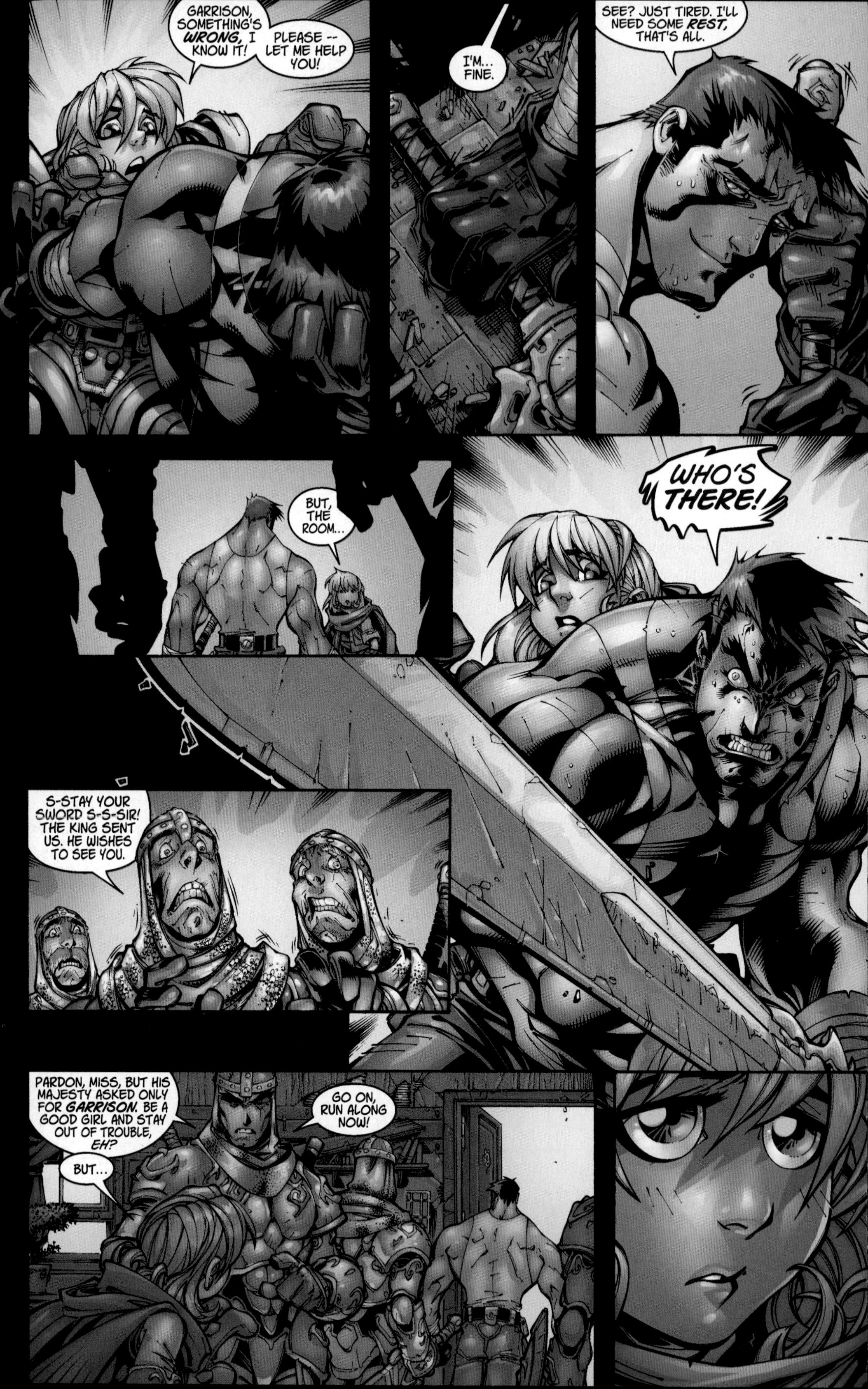
GARRISON, SOMETHING'S WRONG, I KNOW IT!
PLEASE -- LET ME HELP YOU!
I'M... FINE.
SEE? JUST TIRED. I'LL NEED SOME REST, THAT'S ALL.
BUT, THE ROOM...
WHO'S THERE!
S-STAY YOUR SWORD S-S-SIR! THE KING SENT US. HE WISHES TO SEE YOU.
PARDON, MISS, BUT HIS MAJESTY ASKED ONLY FOR GARRISON. BE A GOOD GIRL AND STAY OUT OF TROUBLE, EH?
GO ON, RUN ALONG NOW!
BUT...

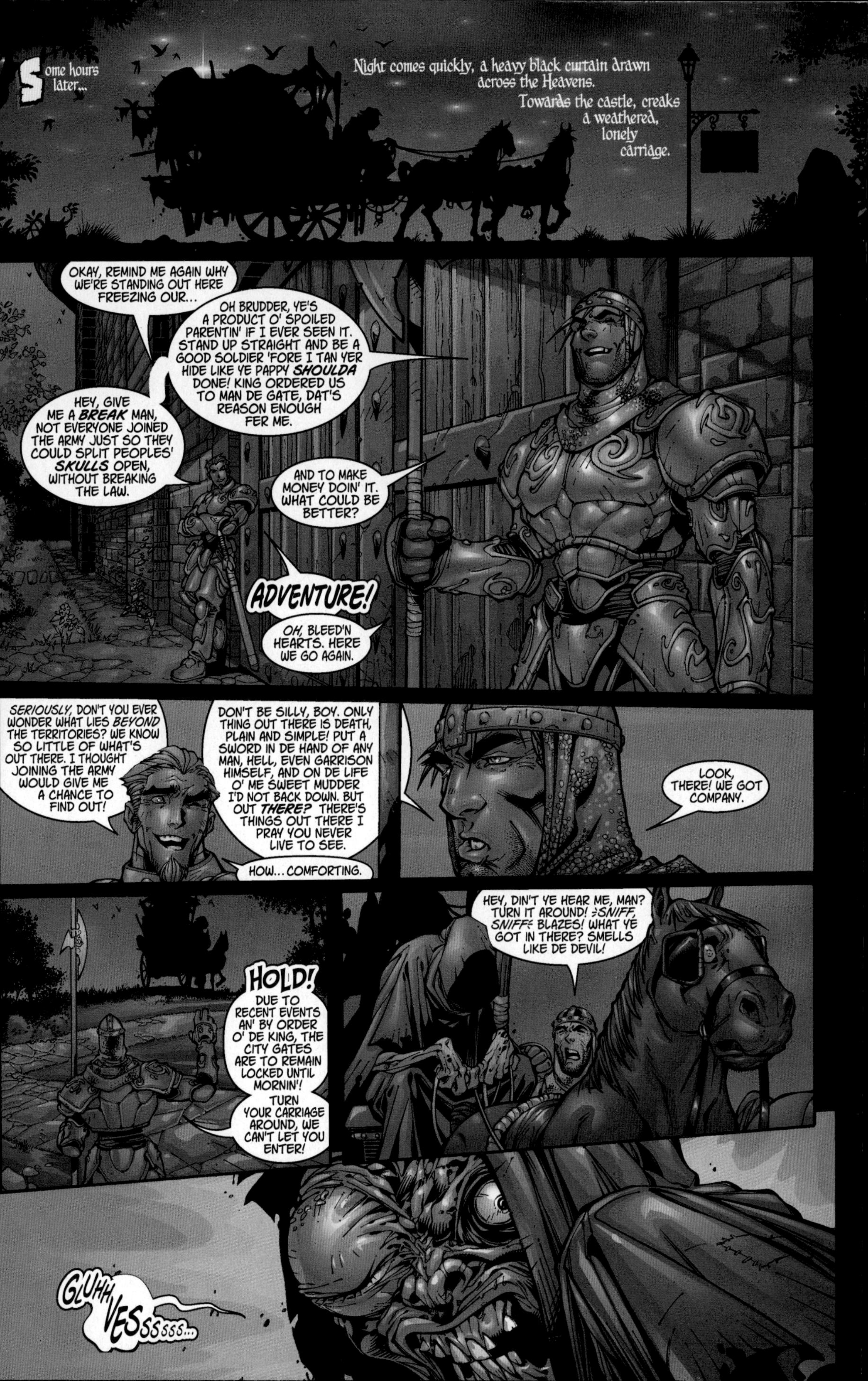
Some hours later...
Night comes quickly, a heavy black curtain drawn across the Heavens.
Towards the castle, creaks a weathered, lonely carriage.
OKAY, REMIND ME AGAIN WHY WE'RE STANDING OUT HERE FREEZING OUR...
OH BRUDDER, YE'S A PRODUCT O' SPOILED PARENTIN' IF I EVER SEEN IT. STAND UP STRAIGHT AND BE A GOOD SOLDIER 'FORE I TAN YER HIDE LIKE YE PAPPY SHOULDA DONE! KING ORDERED US TO MAN DE GATE, DAT'S REASON ENOUGH FER ME.
HEY, GIVE ME A BREAK MAN, NOT EVERYONE JOINED THE ARMY JUST SO THEY COULD SPLIT PEOPLES' SKULLS OPEN, WITHOUT BREAKING THE LAW.
AND TO MAKE MONEY DOIN' IT. WHAT COULD BE BETTER?
ADVENTURE!
OH, BLEED'N HEARTS. HERE WE GO AGAIN.
SERIOUSLY, DON'T YOU EVER WONDER WHAT LIES BEYOND THE TERRITORIES? WE KNOW SO LITTLE OF WHAT'S OUT THERE. I THOUGHT JOINING THE ARMY WOULD GIVE ME A CHANCE TO FIND OUT!
DON'T BE SILLY, BOY. ONLY THING OUT THERE IS DEATH, PLAIN AND SIMPLE! PUT A SWORD IN DE HAND OF ANY MAN, HELL, EVEN GARRISON HIMSELF, AND ON DE LIFE O' ME SWEET MUDDER I'D NOT BACK DOWN. BUT OUT THERE? THERE'S THINGS OUT THERE I PRAY YOU NEVER LIVE TO SEE.
HOW... COMFORTING.
LOOK, THERE! WE GOT COMPANY.
HOLD!
DUE TO RECENT EVENTS AN' BY ORDER O' DE KING, THE CITY GATES ARE TO REMAIN LOCKED UNTIL MORNIN'! TURN YOUR CARRIAGE AROUND, WE CAN'T LET YOU ENTER!
HEY, DIN'T YE HEAR ME, MAN? TURN IT AROUND! =SNIFF, SNIFF= BLAZES! WHAT YE GOT IN THERE? SMELLS LIKE DE DEVIL!
GLUHH VESSSSSS...

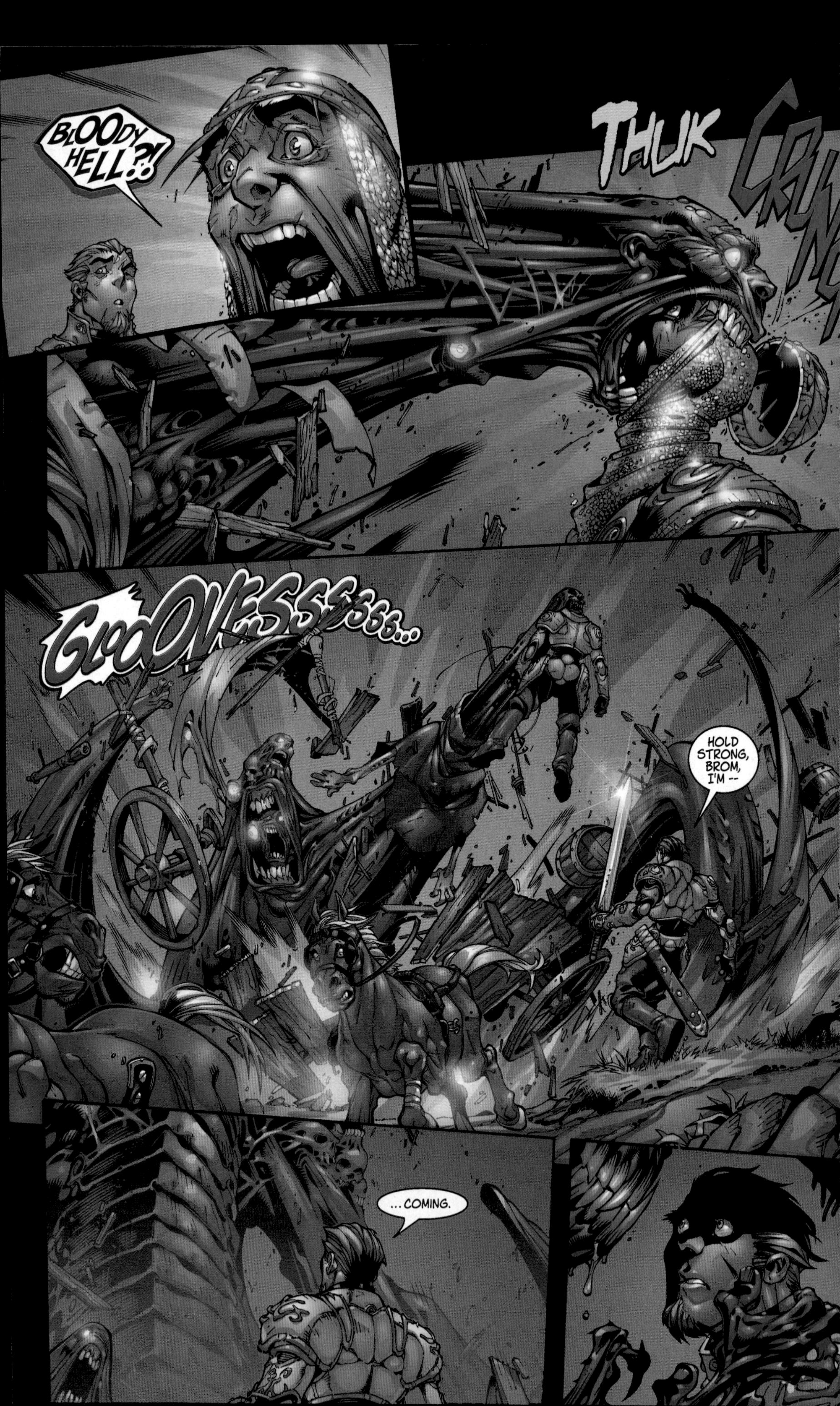
BLOODY HELL?!
THUK
GLOOOVESSSSSSS...
HOLD STRONG, BROM, I'M --
... COMING.

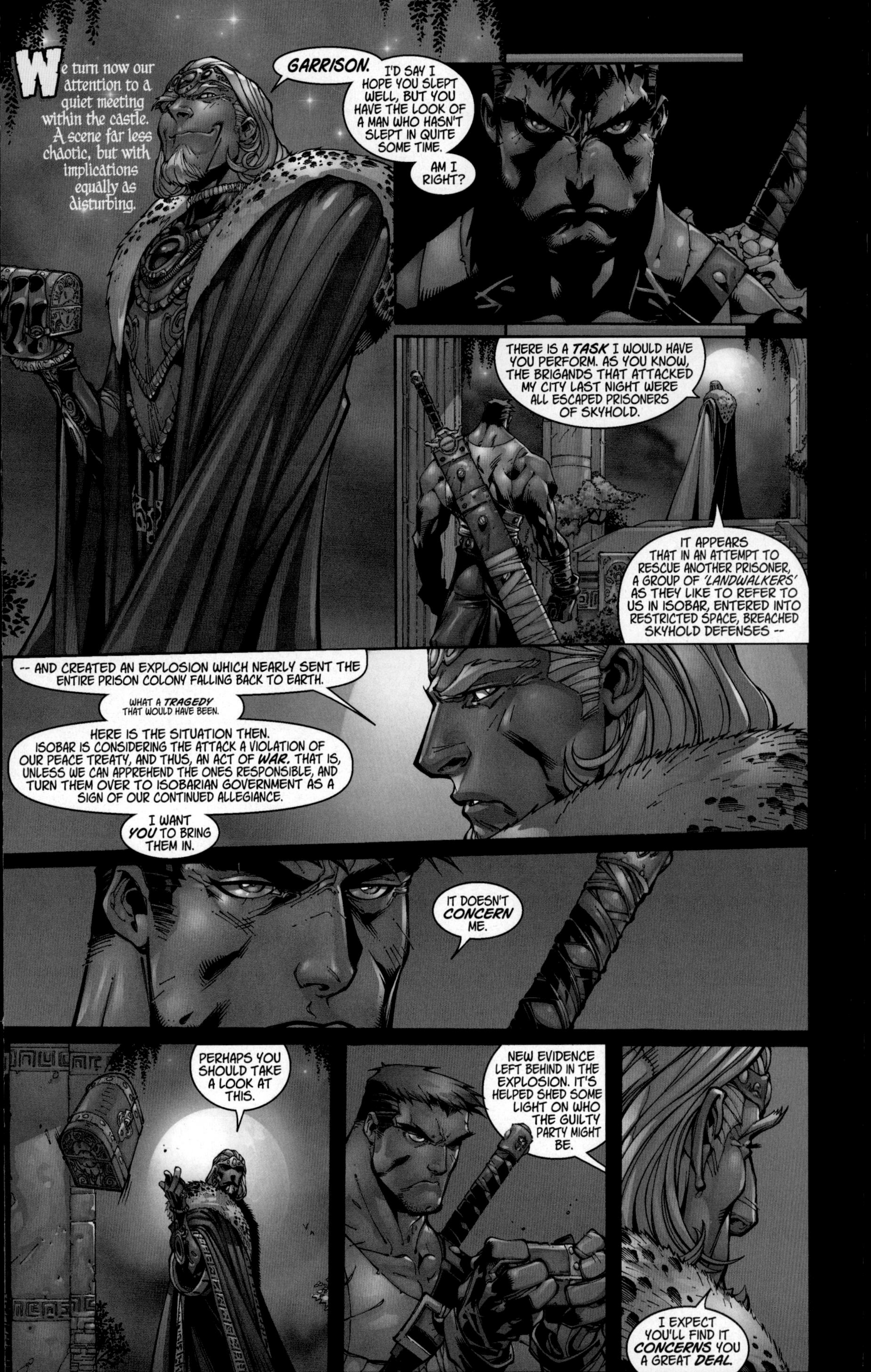
We turn now our attention to a quiet meeting within the castle. A scene far less chaotic, but with implications equally as disturbing.
GARRISON.
I'D SAY I HOPE YOU SLEPT WELL, BUT YOU HAVE THE LOOK OF A MAN WHO HASN'T SLEPT IN QUITE SOME TIME.
AM I RIGHT?
THERE IS A TASK I WOULD HAVE YOU PERFORM. AS YOU KNOW, THE BRIGANDS THAT ATTACKED MY CITY LAST NIGHT WERE ALL ESCAPED PRISONERS OF SKYHOLD.
IT APPEARS THAT IN AN ATTEMPT TO RESCUE ANOTHER PRISONER, A GROUP OF 'LANDWALKERS' AS THEY LIKE TO REFER TO US IN ISOBAR, ENTERED INTO RESTRICTED SPACE, BREACHED SKYHOLD DEFENSES --
-- AND CREATED AN EXPLOSION WHICH NEARLY SENT THE ENTIRE PRISON COLONY FALLING BACK TO EARTH.
WHAT A TRAGEDY THAT WOULD HAVE BEEN.
HERE IS THE SITUATION THEN. ISOBAR IS CONSIDERING THE ATTACK A VIOLATION OF OUR PEACE TREATY, AND THUS, AN ACT OF WAR. THAT IS, UNLESS WE CAN APPREHEND THE ONES RESPONSIBLE, AND TURN THEM OVER TO ISOBARIAN GOVERNMENT AS A SIGN OF OUR CONTINUED ALLEGIANCE.
I WANT YOU TO BRING THEM IN.
IT DOESN'T CONCERN ME.
PERHAPS YOU SHOULD TAKE A LOOK AT THIS.
NEW EVIDENCE LEFT BEHIND IN THE EXPLOSION. IT'S HELPED SHED SOME LIGHT ON WHO THE GUILTY PARTY MIGHT BE.
I EXPECT YOU'LL FIND IT CONCERNS YOU A GREAT DEAL.

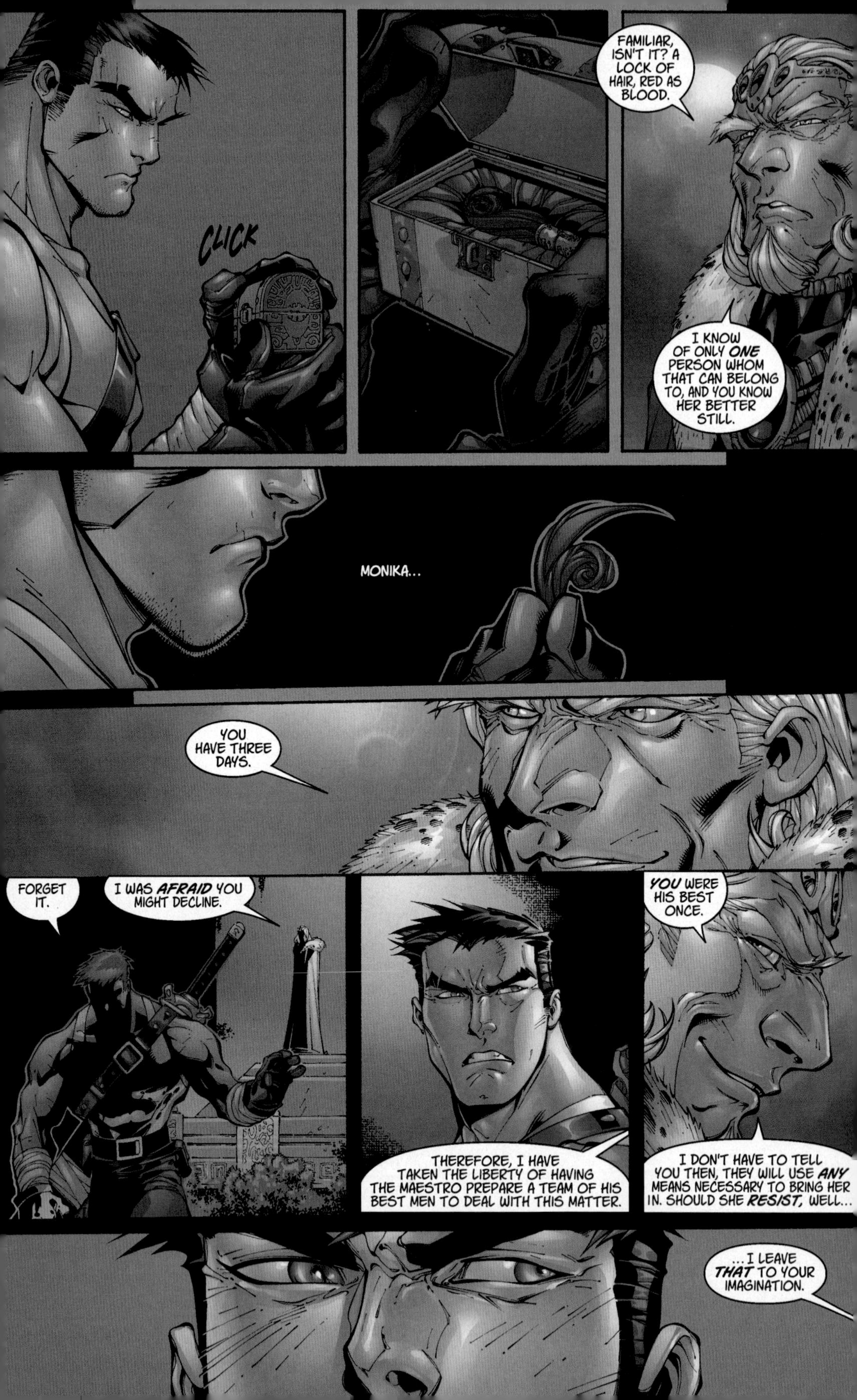
CLICK
FAMILIAR, ISN'T IT? A LOCK OF HAIR, RED AS BLOOD.
I KNOW OF ONLY ***ONE*** PERSON WHOM THAT CAN BELONG TO, AND YOU KNOW HER BETTER STILL.
MONIKA...
YOU HAVE THREE DAYS.
FORGET IT.
I WAS ***AFRAID*** YOU MIGHT DECLINE.
THEREFORE, I HAVE TAKEN THE LIBERTY OF HAVING THE MAESTRO PREPARE A TEAM OF HIS BEST MEN TO DEAL WITH THIS MATTER.
YOU WERE HIS BEST ONCE.
I DON'T HAVE TO TELL YOU THEN, THEY WILL USE ***ANY*** MEANS NECESSARY TO BRING HER IN. SHOULD SHE ***RESIST,*** WELL...
...I LEAVE ***THAT*** TO YOUR IMAGINATION.

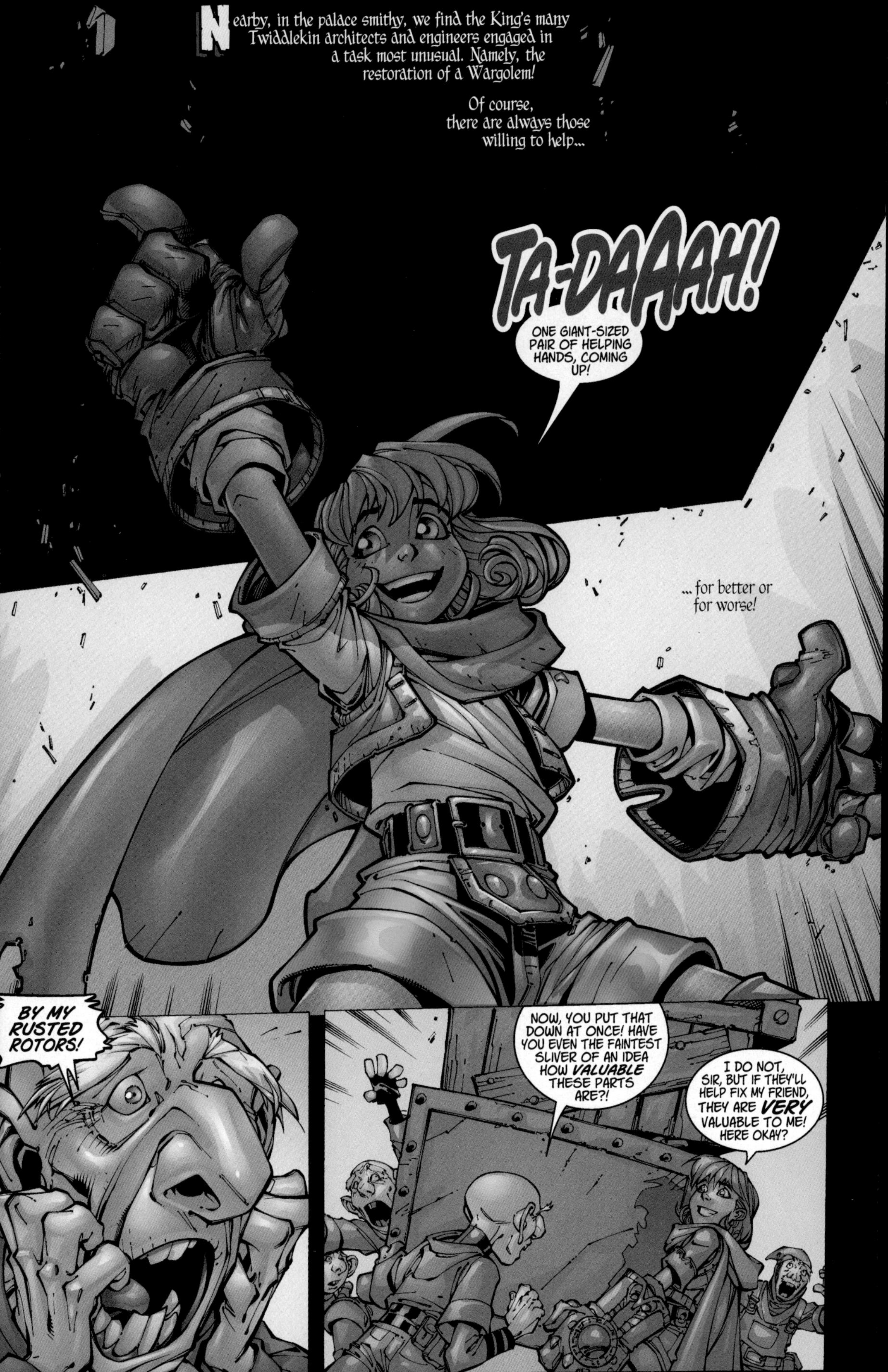
Nearby, in the palace smithy, we find the King's many Twiddlekin architects and engineers engaged in a task most unusual. Namely, the restoration of a Wargolem!
Of course, there are always those willing to help...
TA-DAAAH!
ONE GIANT-SIZED PAIR OF HELPING HANDS, COMING UP!
... for better or for worse!
BY MY RUSTED ROTORS!
NOW, YOU PUT THAT DOWN AT ONCE! HAVE YOU EVEN THE FAINTEST SLIVER OF AN IDEA HOW VALUABLE THESE PARTS ARE?!
I DO NOT, SIR, BUT IF THEY'LL HELP FIX MY FRIEND, THEY ARE VERY VALUABLE TO ME! HERE OKAY?

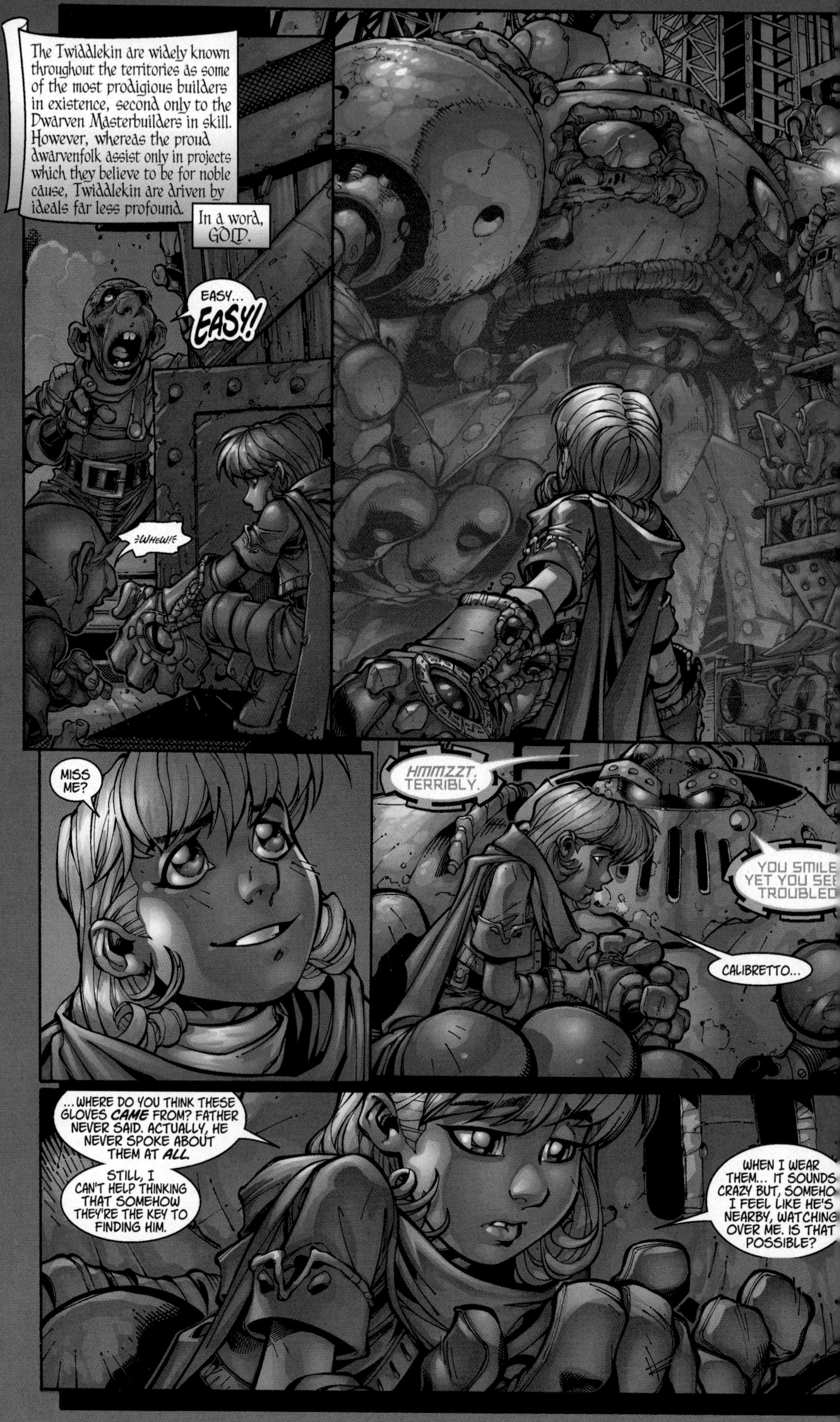

The Twiddlekin are widely known throughout the territories as some of the most prodigious builders in existence, second only to the Dwarven Masterbuilders in skill. However, whereas the proud dwarvenfolk assist only in projects which they believe to be for noble cause, Twiddlekin are driven by ideals far less profound.
In a word, GOLD.
EASY... EASY!
WHEW!
MISS ME?
HMMZZT. TERRIBLY.
YOU SMILE YET YOU SEE TROUBLED
CALIBRETTO...
...WHERE DO YOU THINK THESE GLOVES CAME FROM? FATHER NEVER SAID. ACTUALLY, HE NEVER SPOKE ABOUT THEM AT ALL.
STILL, I CAN'T HELP THINKING THAT SOMEHOW THEY'RE THE KEY TO FINDING HIM.
WHEN I WEAR THEM... IT SOUNDS CRAZY BUT, SOMEHO I FEEL LIKE HE'S NEARBY, WATCHING OVER ME. IS THAT POSSIBLE?

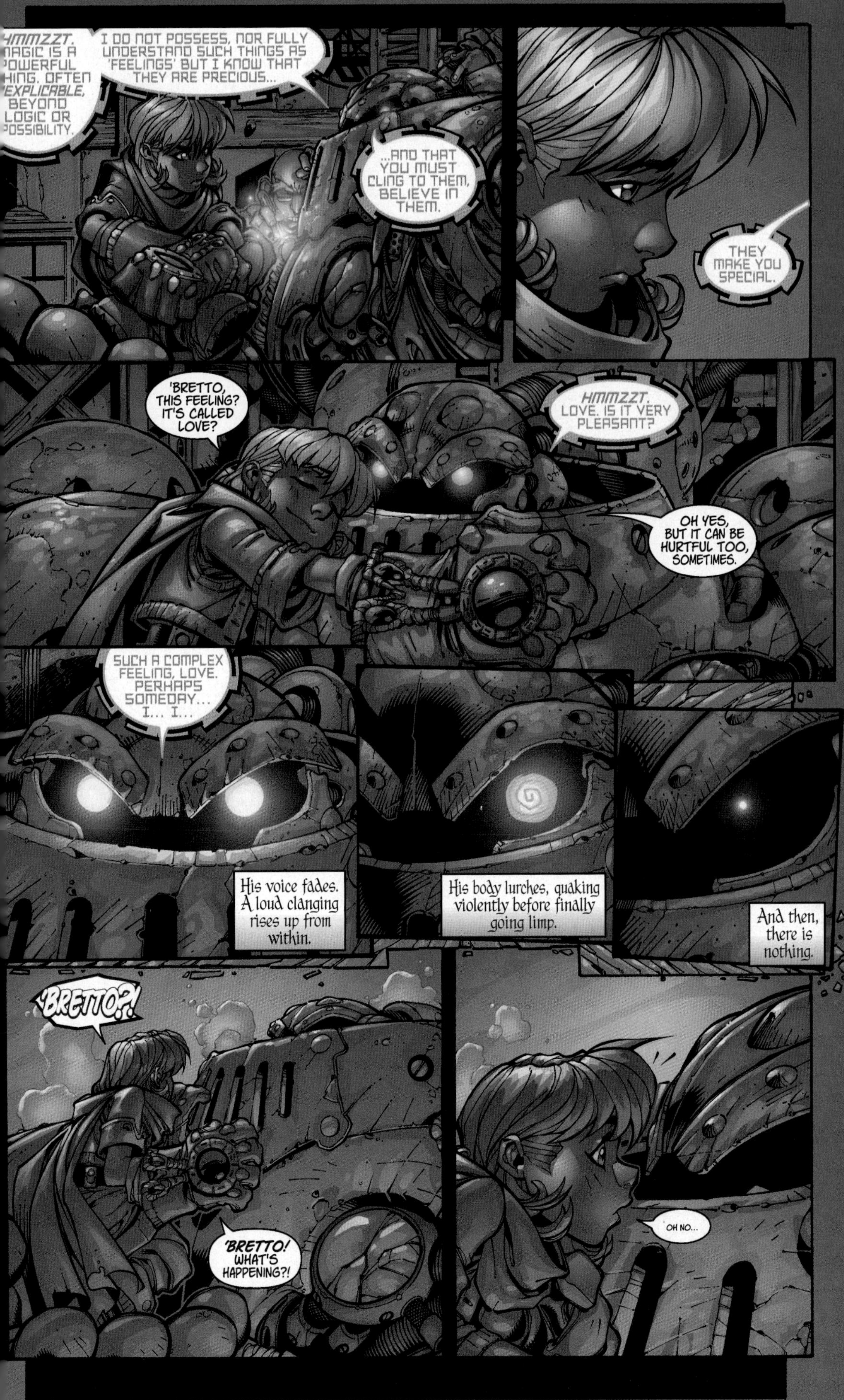
HMMZZT. MAGIC IS A POWERFUL THING. OFTEN INEXPLICABLE, BEYOND LOGIC OR POSSIBILITY.
I DO NOT POSSESS, NOR FULLY UNDERSTAND SUCH THINGS AS 'FEELINGS' BUT I KNOW THAT THEY ARE PRECIOUS...
...AND THAT YOU MUST CLING TO THEM, BELIEVE IN THEM.
THEY MAKE YOU SPECIAL.
'BRETTO, THIS FEELING? IT'S CALLED LOVE?
HMMZZT. LOVE. IS IT VERY PLEASANT?
OH YES, BUT IT CAN BE HURTFUL TOO, SOMETIMES.
SUCH A COMPLEX FEELING, LOVE. PERHAPS SOMEDAY... I... I...
His voice fades. A loud clanging rises up from within.
His body lurches, quaking violently before finally going limp.
And then, there is nothing.
'BRETTO?!
'BRETTO! WHAT'S HAPPENING?!
OH NO...

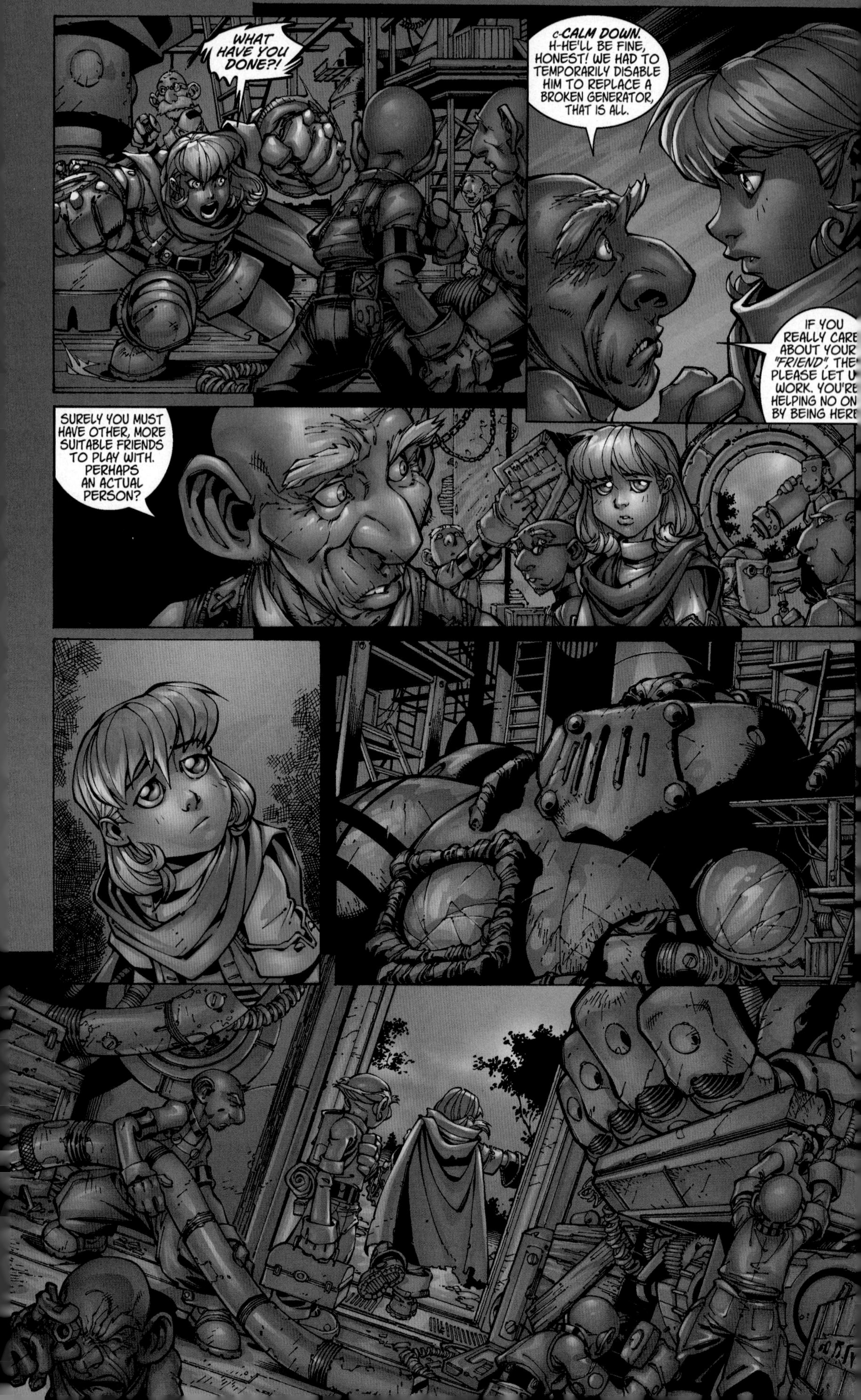
WHAT HAVE YOU DONE?!
c-CALM DOWN. H-HE'LL BE FINE, HONEST! WE HAD TO TEMPORARILY DISABLE HIM TO REPLACE A BROKEN GENERATOR, THAT IS ALL.
IF YOU REALLY CARE ABOUT YOUR "FRIEND", THEN PLEASE LET US WORK. YOU'RE HELPING NO ONE BY BEING HERE.
SURELY YOU MUST HAVE OTHER, MORE SUITABLE FRIENDS TO PLAY WITH. PERHAPS AN ACTUAL PERSON?

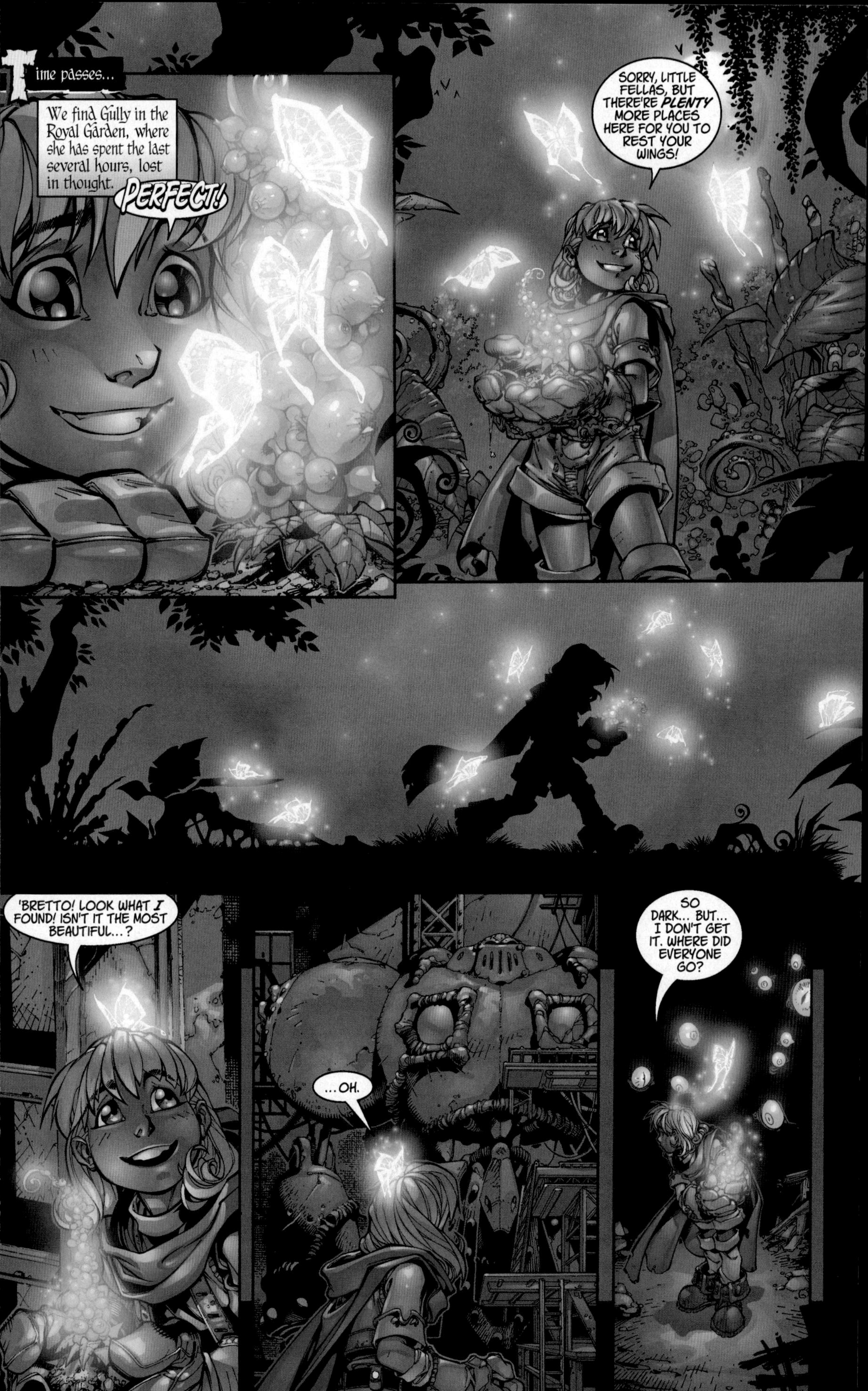
Time passes...
We find Gully in the Royal Garden, where she has spent the last several hours, lost in thought.
PERFECT!
SORRY, LITTLE FELLAS, BUT THERE'RE PLENTY MORE PLACES HERE FOR YOU TO REST YOUR WINGS!
'BRETTO! LOOK WHAT I FOUND! ISN'T IT THE MOST BEAUTIFUL...?
...OH.
SO DARK... BUT... I DON'T GET IT. WHERE DID EVERYONE GO?

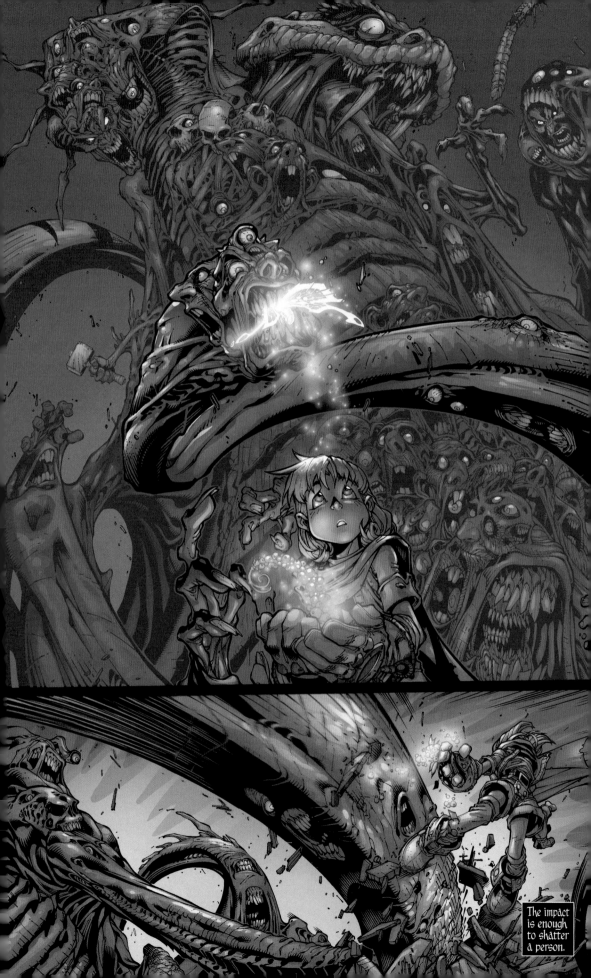

The impact is enough to shatter a person.

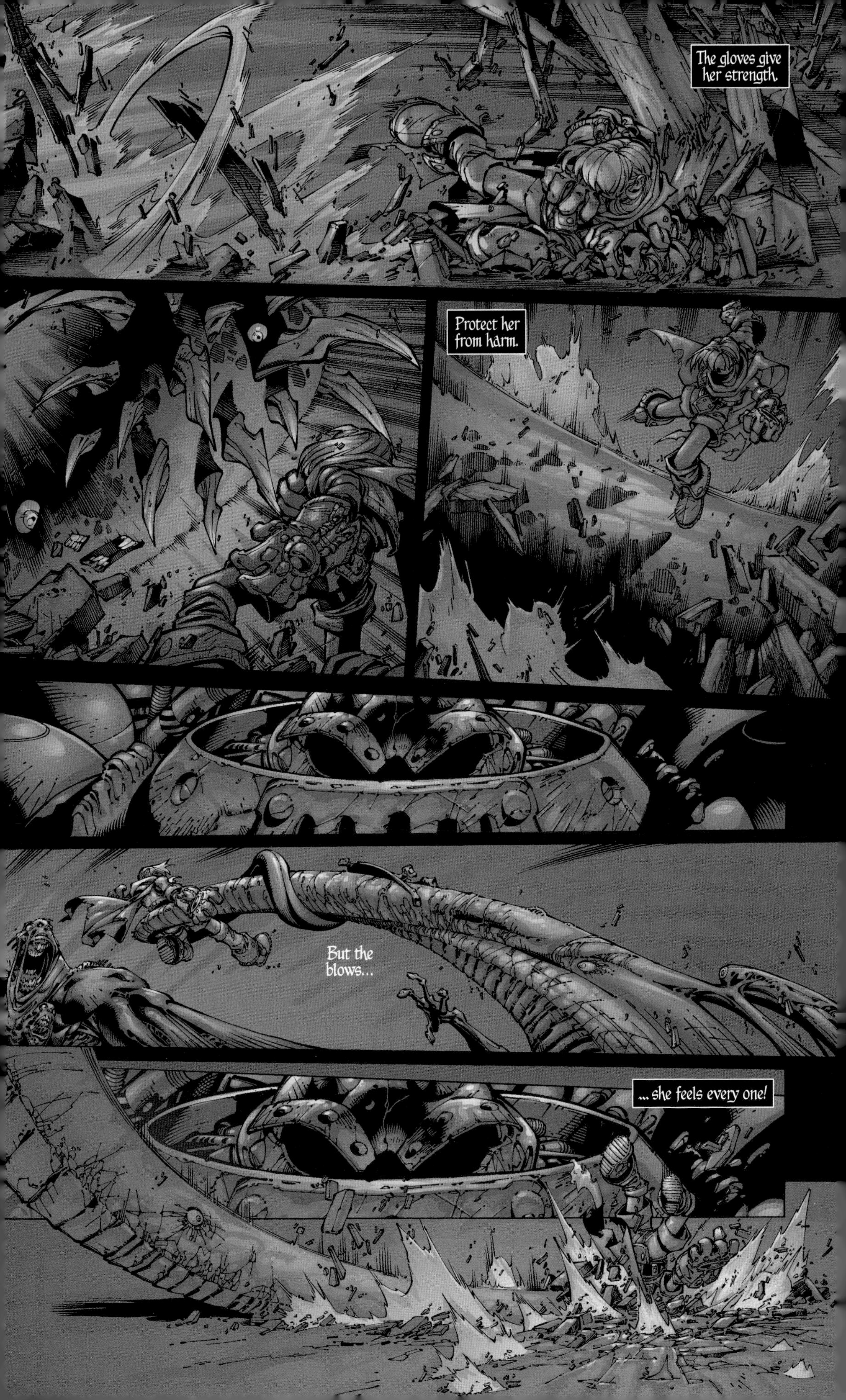
The gloves give her strength.
Protect her from harm.
But the blows...
...she feels every one!

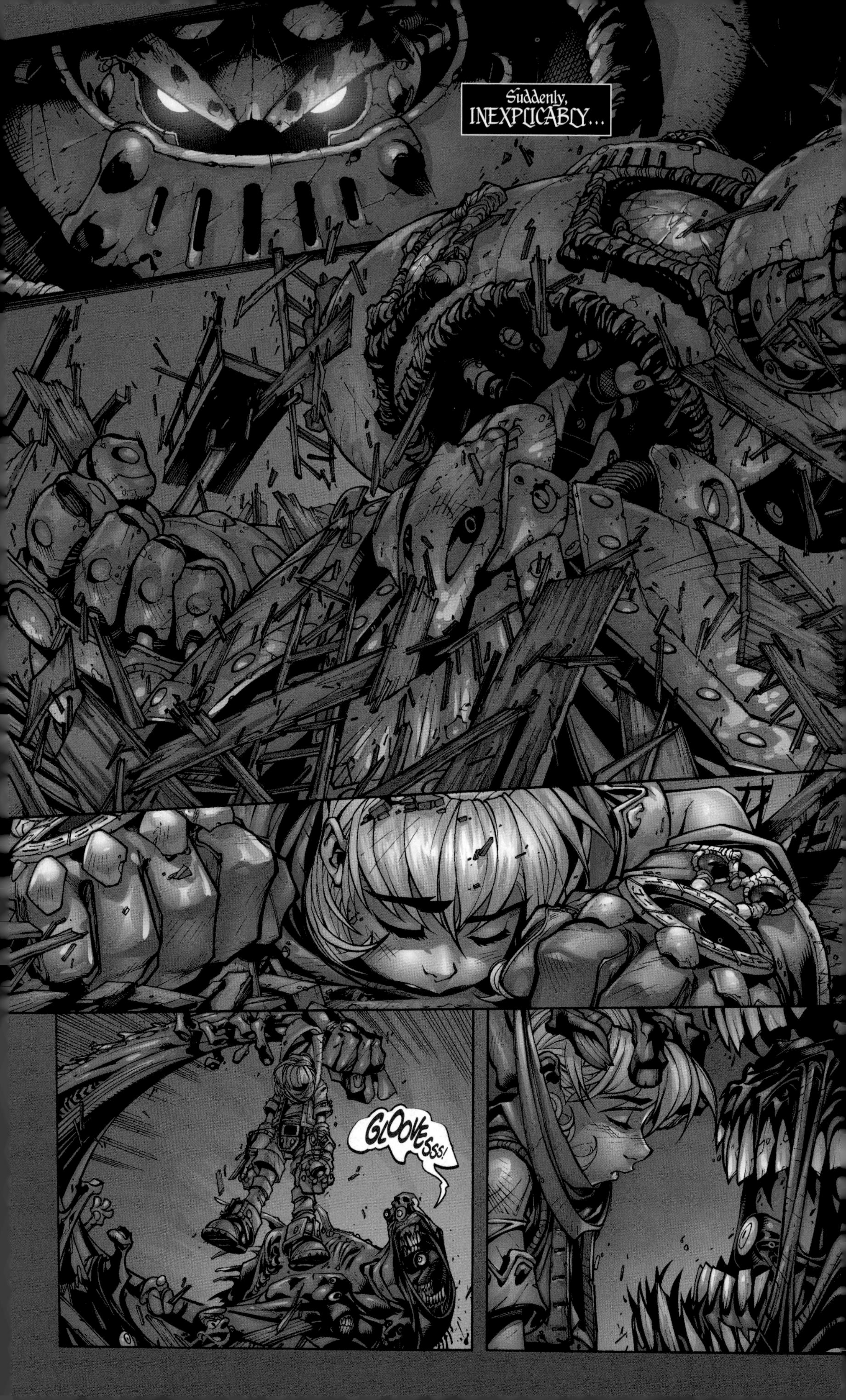
Suddenly,
INEXPLICABLY...
GLOOVEsss!

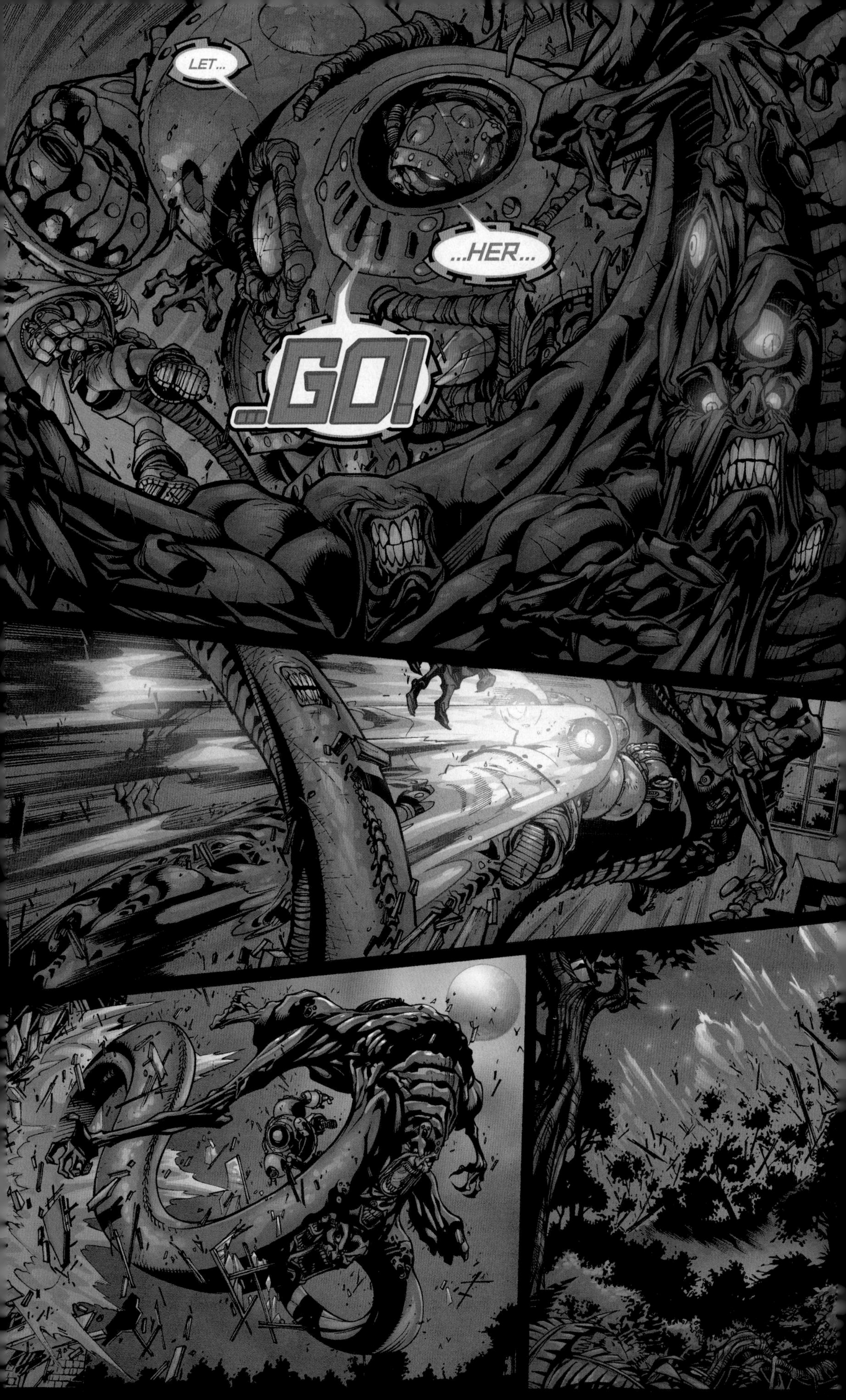
LET...
...HER...
...GO!

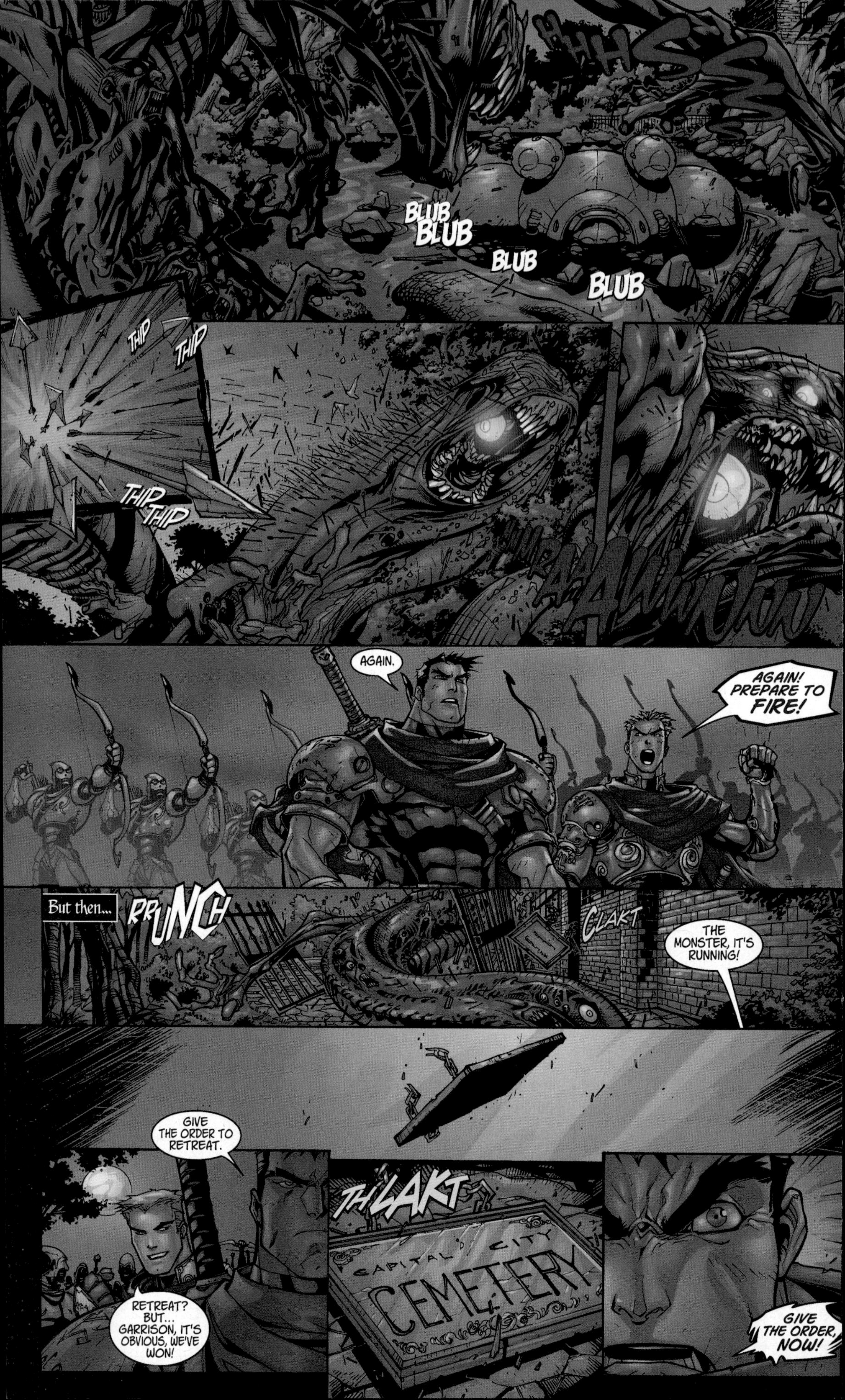
HHHSSSS
BLUB
BLUB
BLUB
BLUB
THIP
THIP
THIP THIP
AGAIN.
AGAIN! PREPARE TO FIRE!
But then...
RRUNCH
CLAKT
THE MONSTER, IT'S RUNNING!
GIVE THE ORDER TO RETREAT.
RETREAT? BUT... GARRISON, IT'S OBVIOUS, WE'VE WON!
THLAKT
CAPITAL CITY
CEMETERY
GIVE THE ORDER, NOW!

ime stands still.

The image, forever burned into their minds.

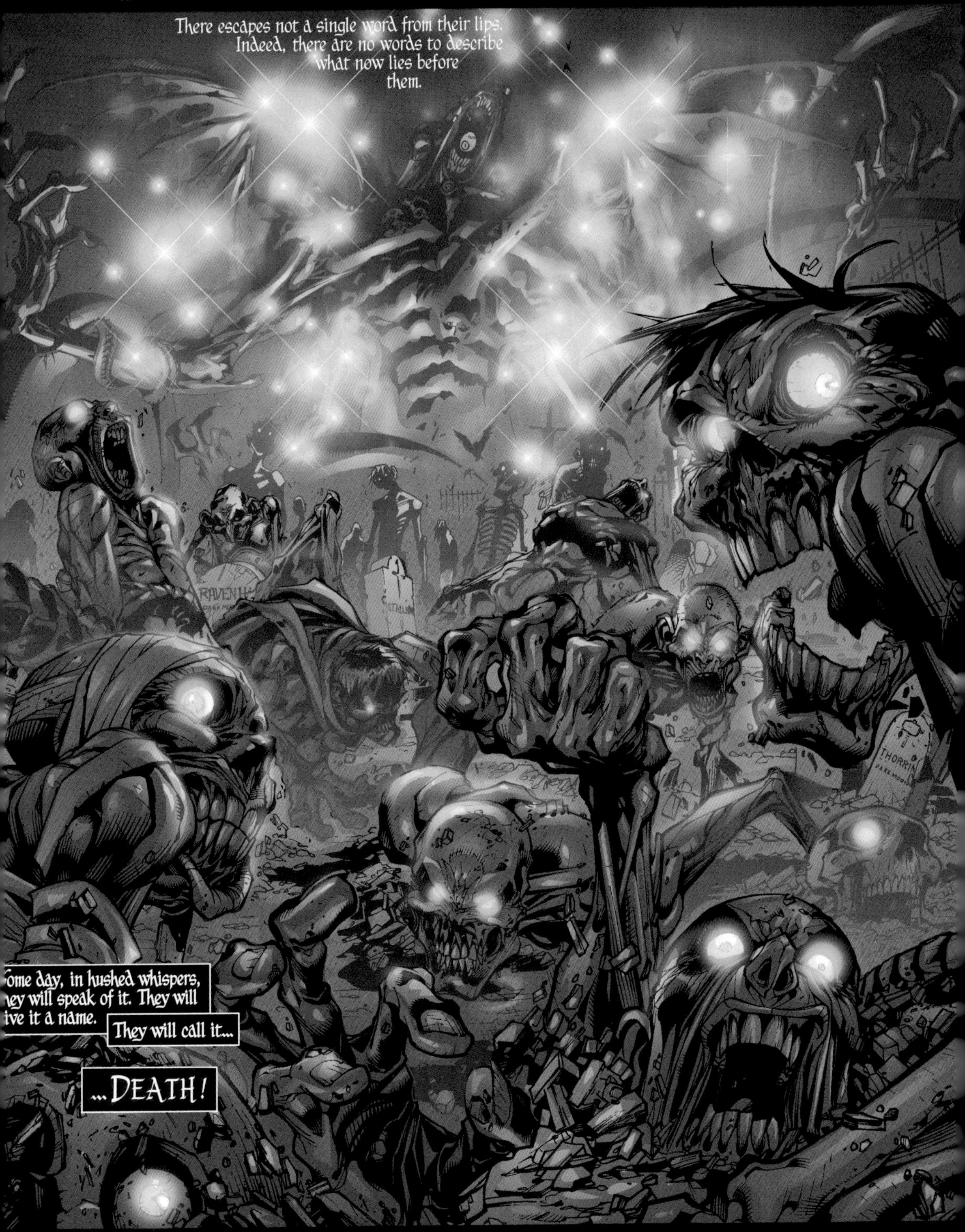

There escapes not a single word from their lips. Indeed, there are no words to describe what now lies before them.
ome day, in hushed whispers, ıey will speak of it. They will ive it a name.
They will call it...
...DEATH!

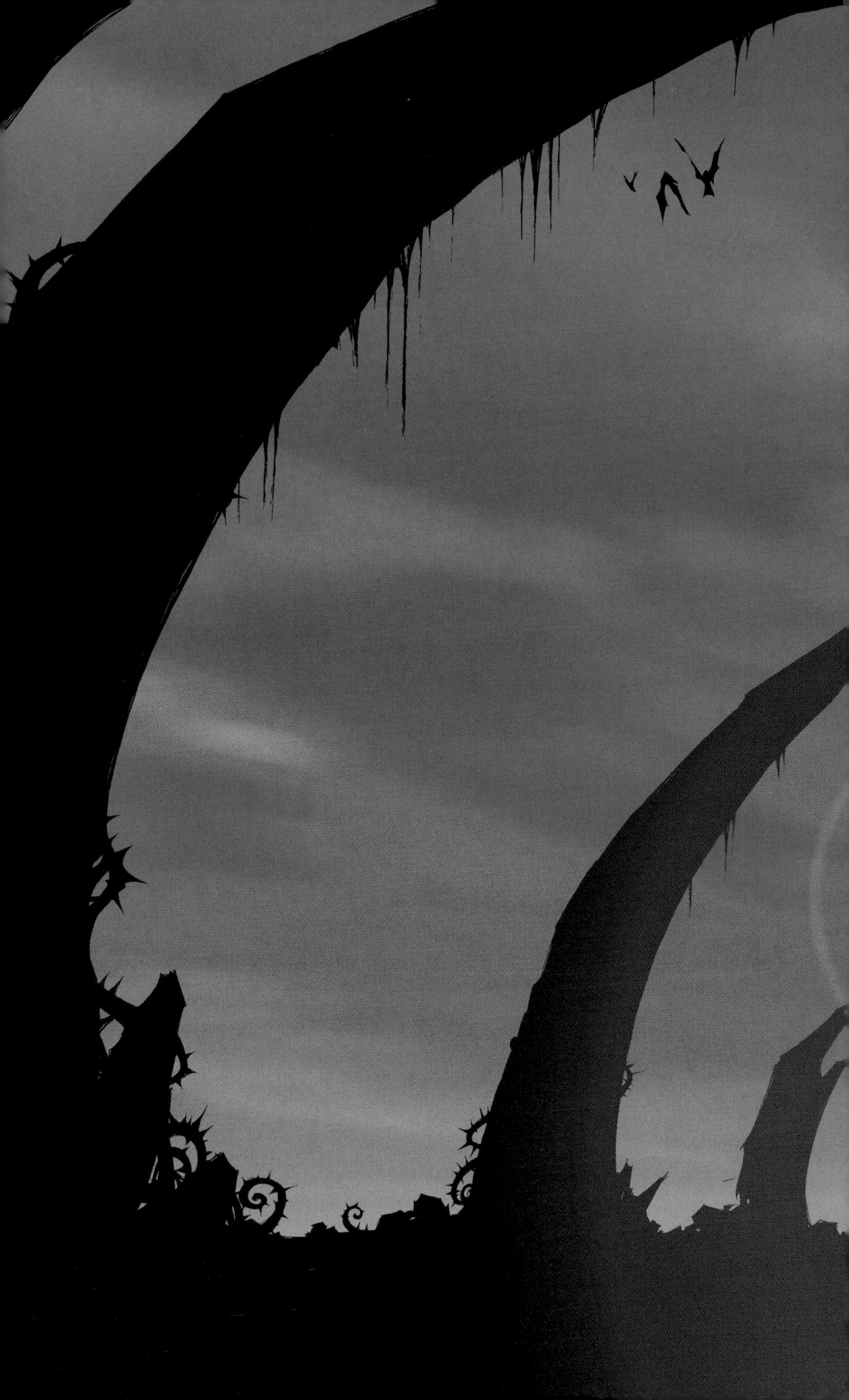

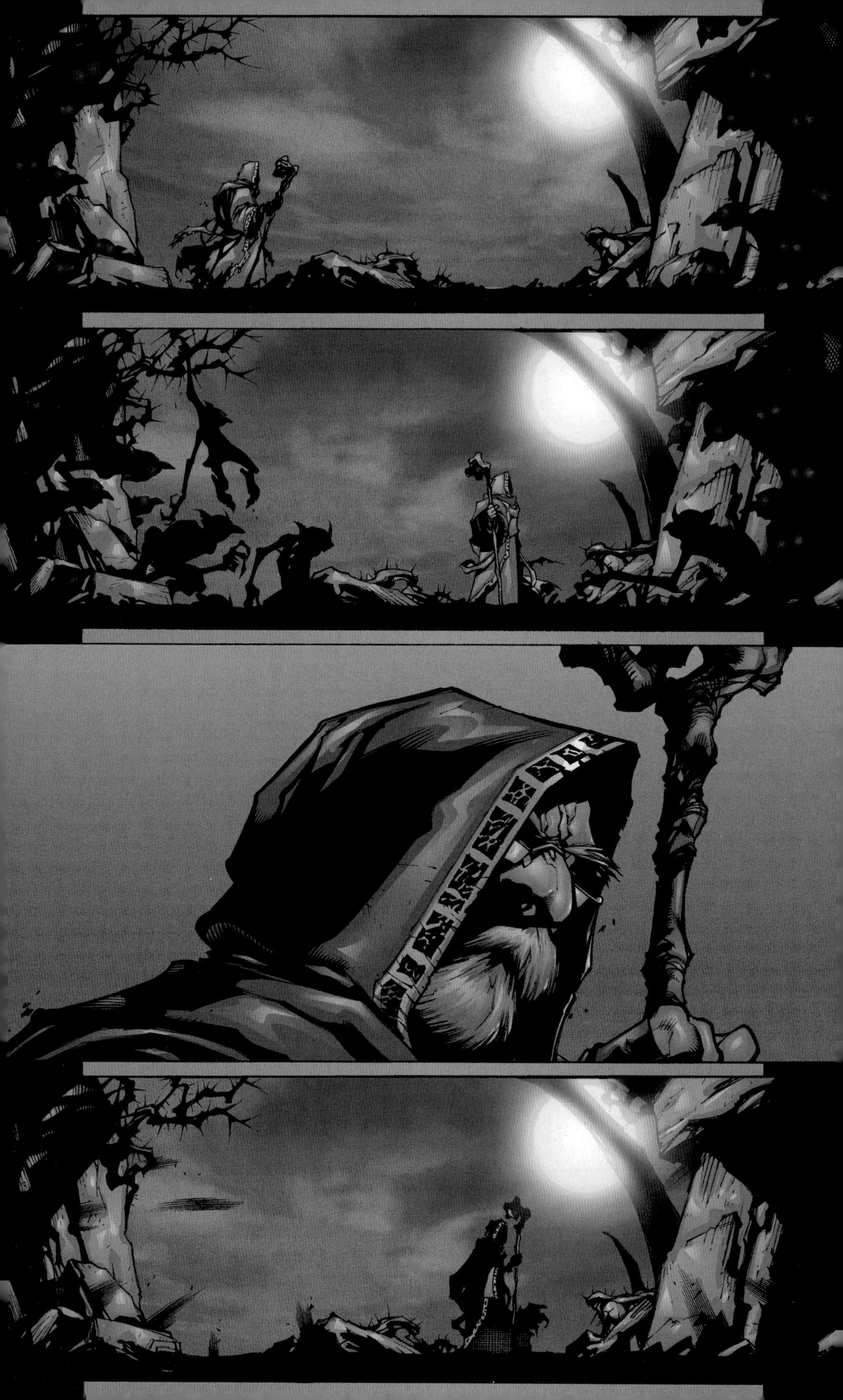

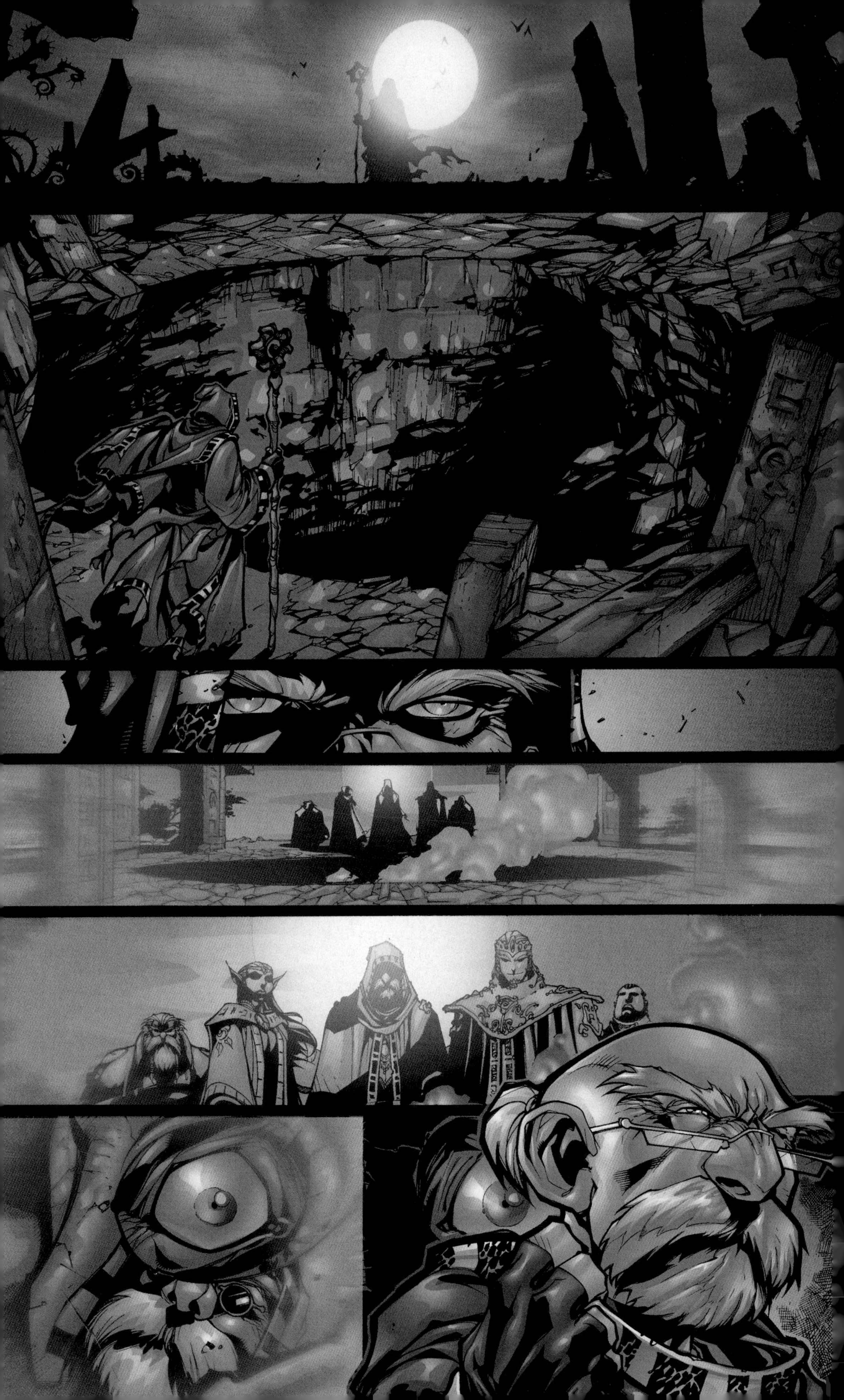

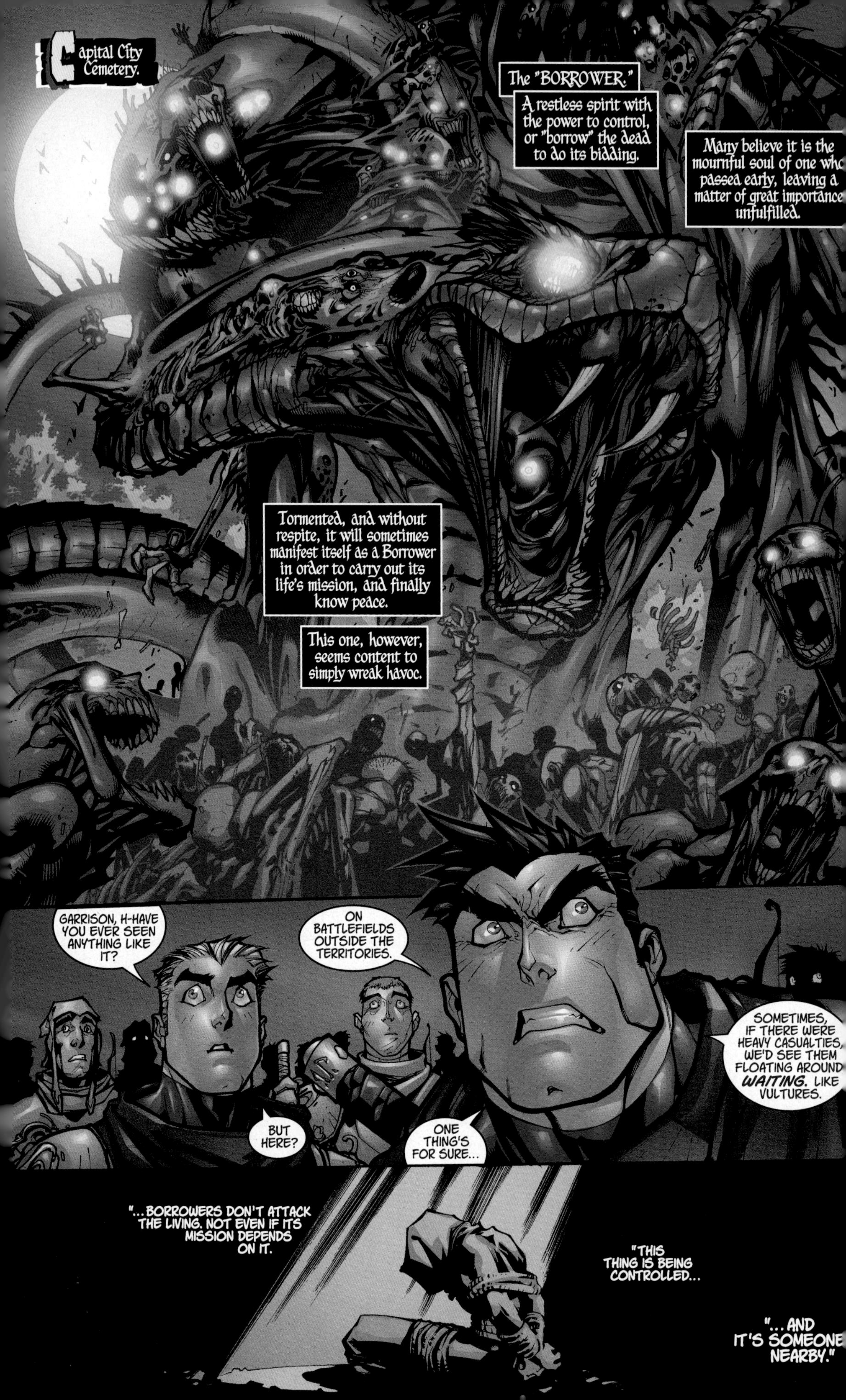
Capital City Cemetery.
The "BORROWER."
A restless spirit with the power to control, or "borrow" the dead to do its bidding.
Many believe it is the mournful soul of one who passed early, leaving a matter of great importance unfulfilled.
Tormented, and without respite, it will sometimes manifest itself as a Borrower in order to carry out its life's mission, and finally know peace.
This one, however, seems content to simply wreak havoc.
GARRISON, H-HAVE YOU EVER SEEN ANYTHING LIKE IT?
ON BATTLEFIELDS OUTSIDE THE TERRITORIES.
SOMETIMES, IF THERE WERE HEAVY CASUALTIES, WE'D SEE THEM FLOATING AROUND *WAITING.* LIKE VULTURES.
BUT HERE?
ONE THING'S FOR SURE...
"...BORROWERS DON'T ATTACK THE LIVING. NOT EVEN IF ITS MISSION DEPENDS ON IT.
"THIS THING IS BEING CONTROLLED...
"...AND IT'S SOMEONE NEARBY."

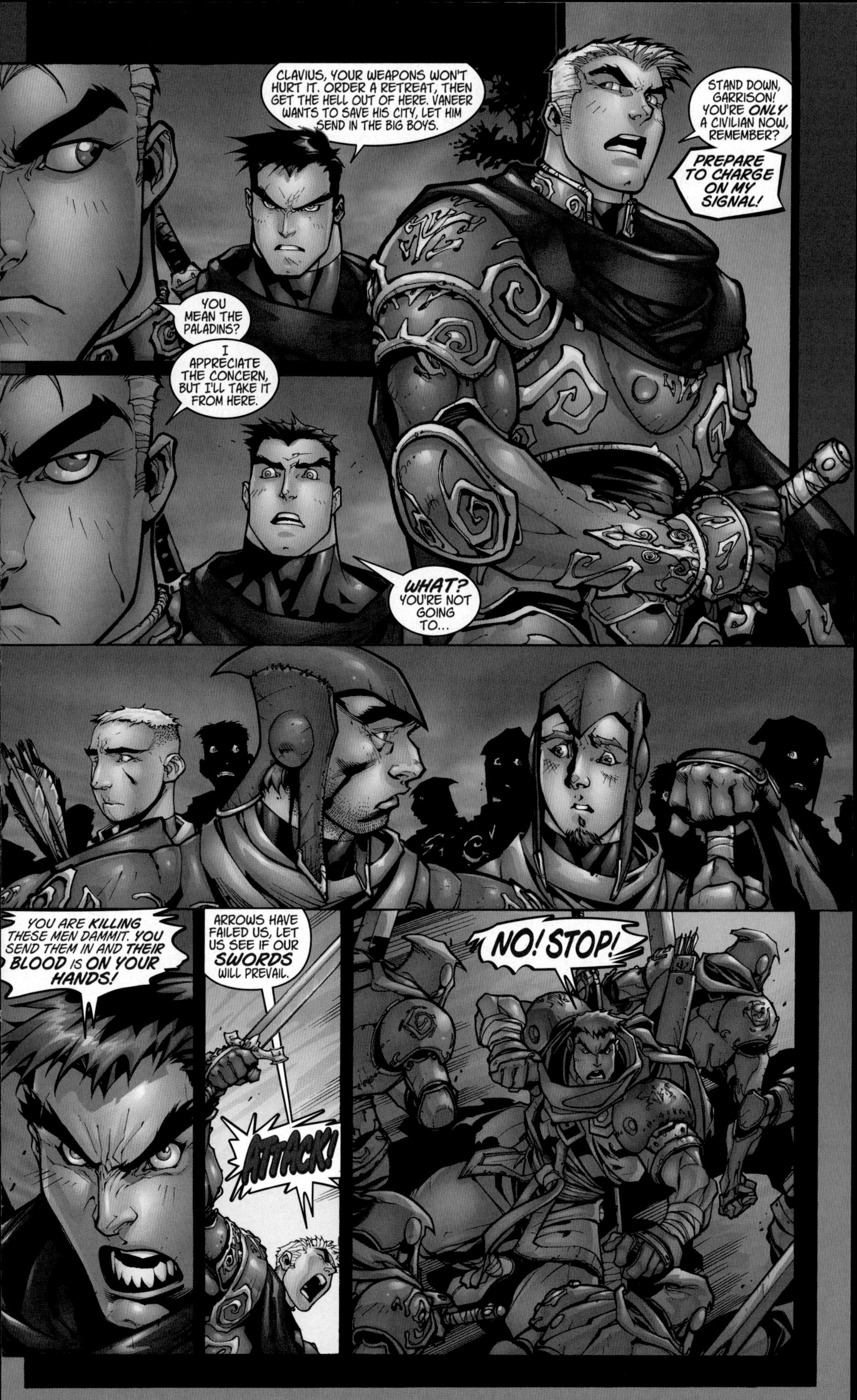
CLAVIUS, YOUR WEAPONS WON'T HURT IT. ORDER A RETREAT, THEN GET THE HELL OUT OF HERE. VANEER WANTS TO SAVE HIS CITY, LET HIM SEND IN THE BIG BOYS.
STAND DOWN, GARRISON! YOU'RE ONLY A CIVILIAN NOW, REMEMBER?
PREPARE TO CHARGE ON MY SIGNAL!
YOU MEAN THE PALADINS?
I APPRECIATE THE CONCERN, BUT I'LL TAKE IT FROM HERE.
WHAT? YOU'RE NOT GOING TO...
YOU ARE KILLING THESE MEN DAMMIT. YOU SEND THEM IN AND THEIR BLOOD IS ON YOUR HANDS!
ARROWS HAVE FAILED US, LET US SEE IF OUR SWORDS WILL PREVAIL.
ATTACK!
NO! STOP!

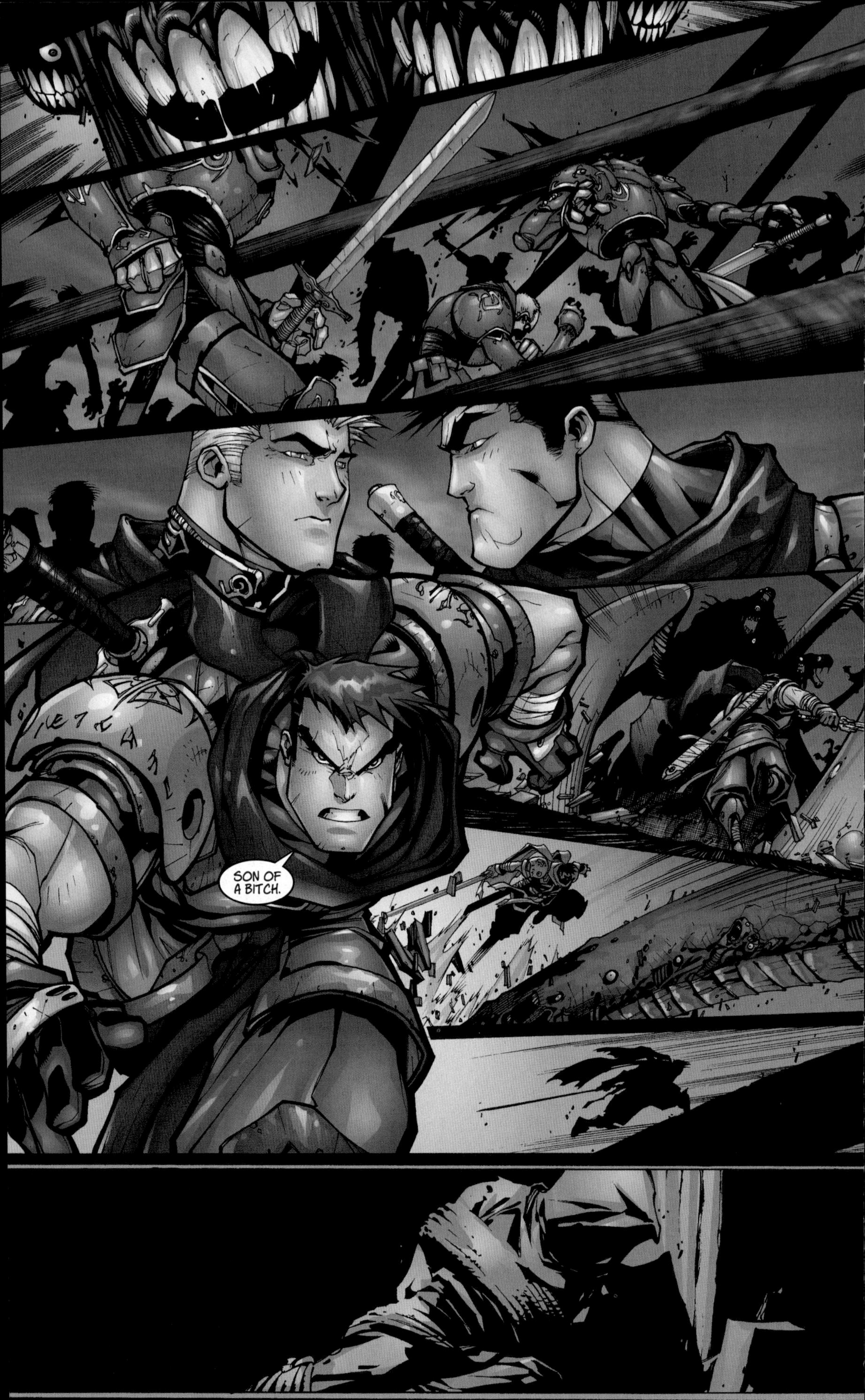
SON OF A BITCH.

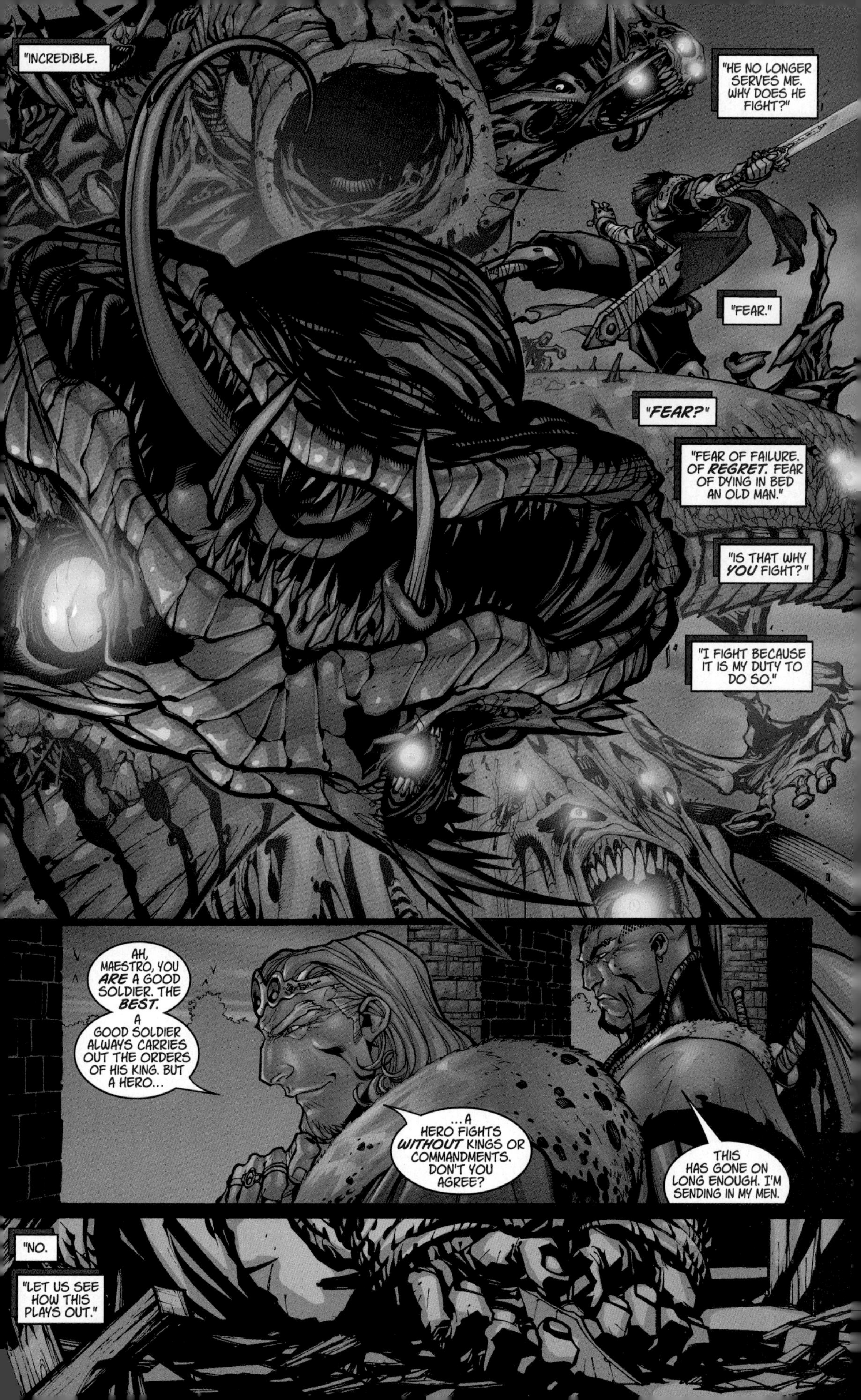
"INCREDIBLE.
"HE NO LONGER SERVES ME. WHY DOES HE FIGHT?"
"FEAR."
"FEAR?"
"FEAR OF FAILURE. OF REGRET. FEAR OF DYING IN BED AN OLD MAN."
"IS THAT WHY YOU FIGHT?"
"I FIGHT BECAUSE IT IS MY DUTY TO DO SO."
AH, MAESTRO, YOU ARE A GOOD SOLDIER. THE BEST.
A GOOD SOLDIER ALWAYS CARRIES OUT THE ORDERS OF HIS KING. BUT A HERO...
...A HERO FIGHTS WITHOUT KINGS OR COMMANDMENTS. DON'T YOU AGREE?
THIS HAS GONE ON LONG ENOUGH. I'M SENDING IN MY MEN.
"NO.
"LET US SEE HOW THIS PLAYS OUT."

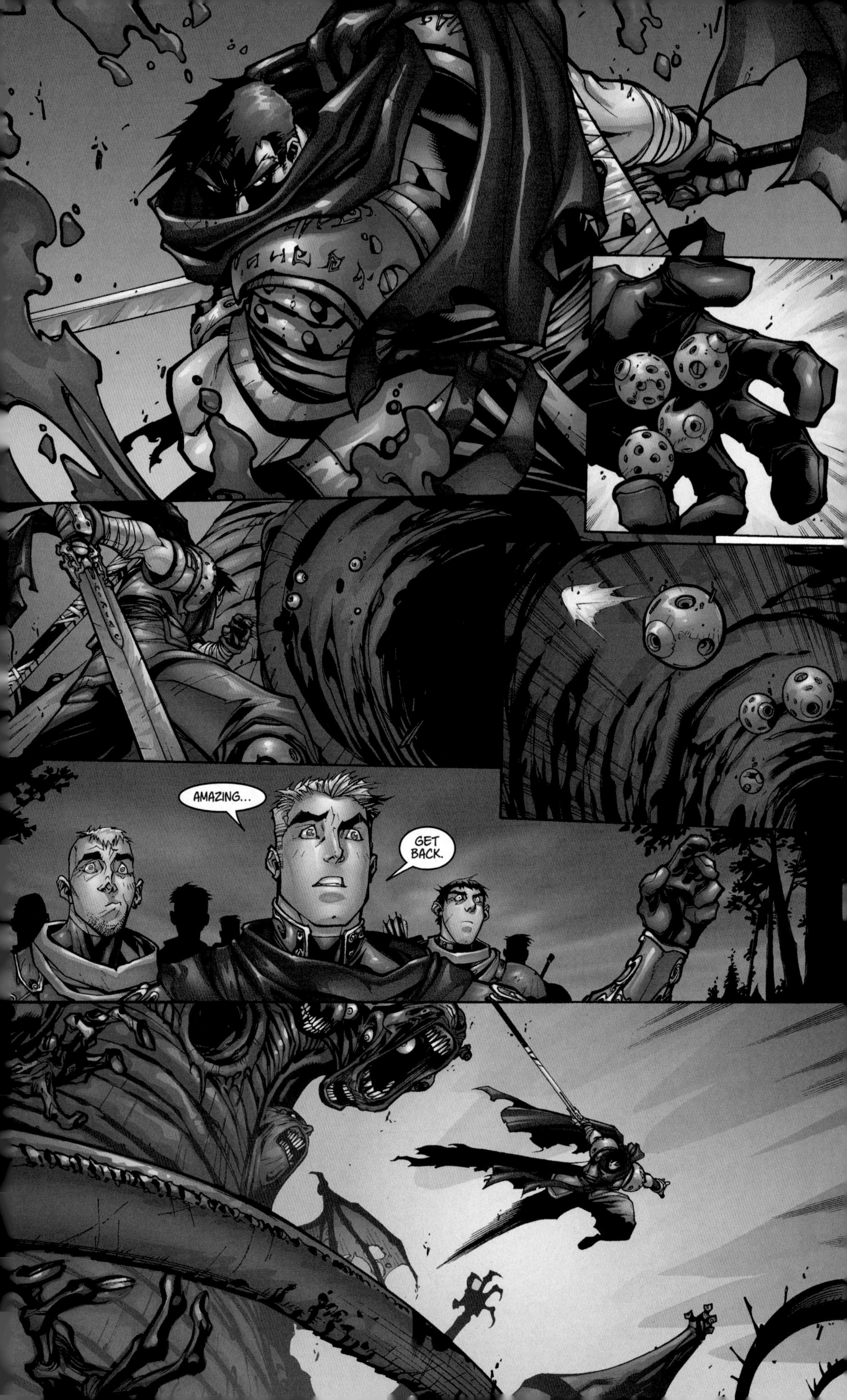
AMAZING...
GET BACK.

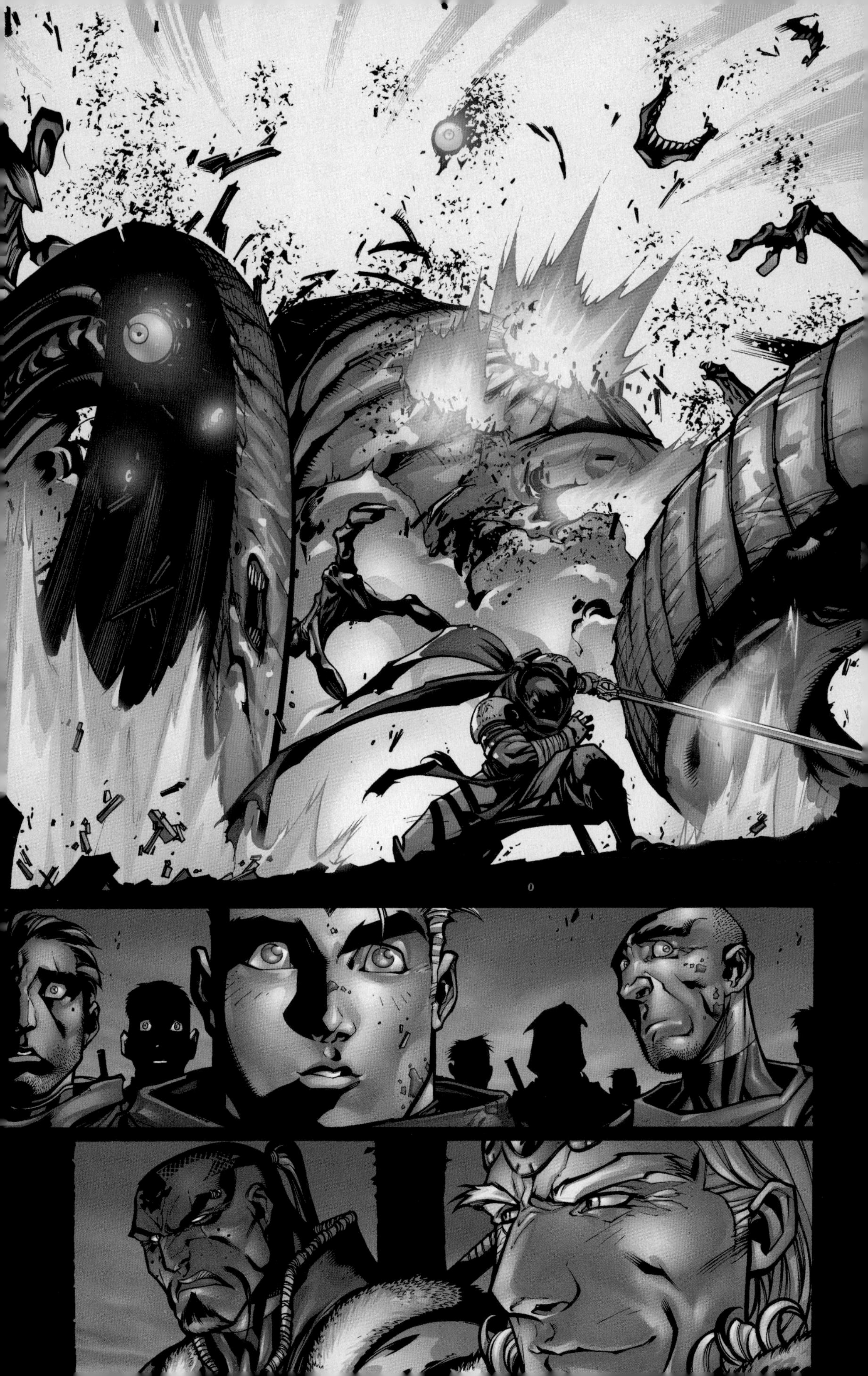

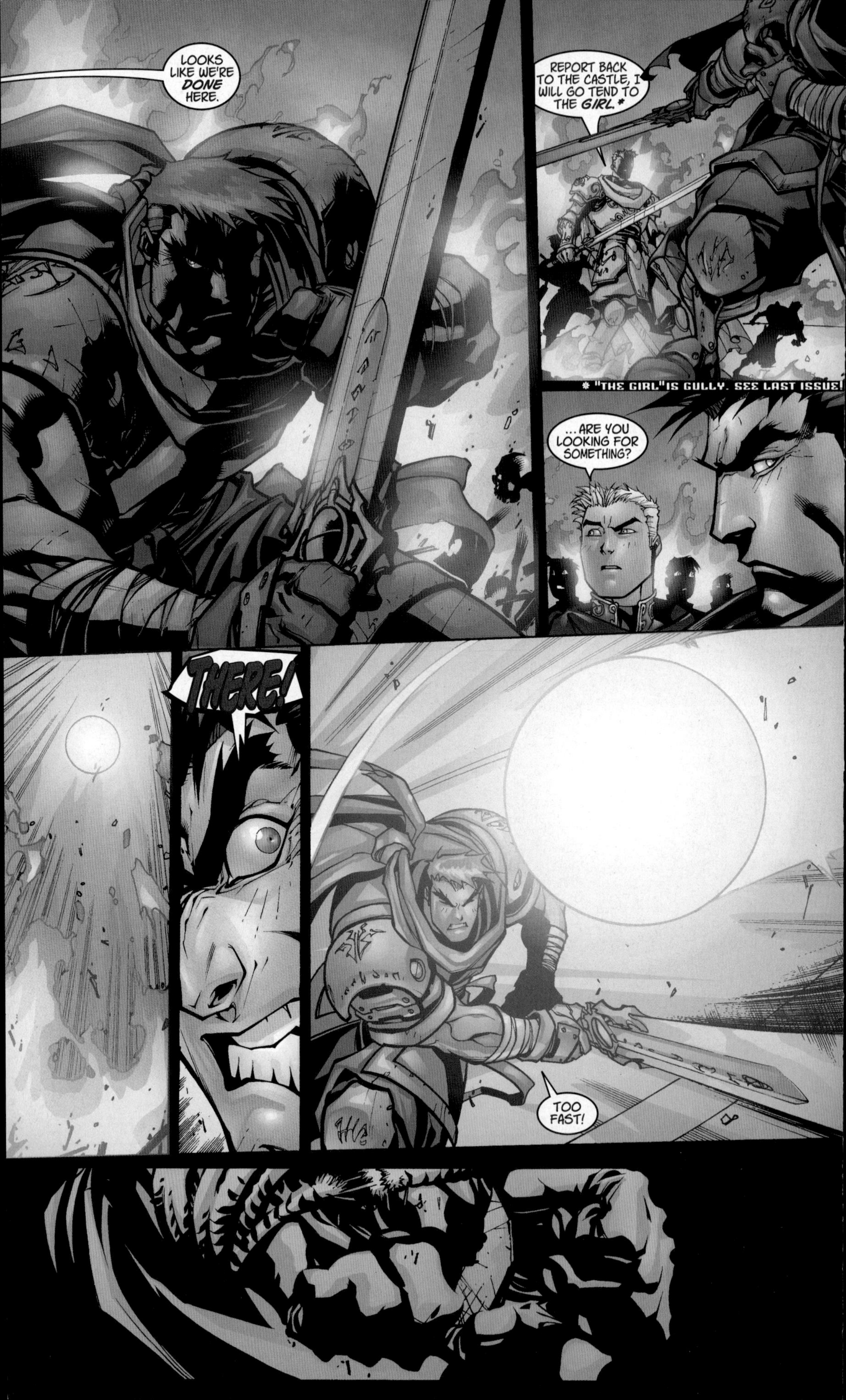
LOOKS LIKE WE'RE DONE HERE.
REPORT BACK TO THE CASTLE, I WILL GO TEND TO THE GIRL.*
* "THE GIRL" IS GULLY. SEE LAST ISSUE!
...ARE YOU LOOKING FOR SOMETHING?
THERE!
TOO FAST!

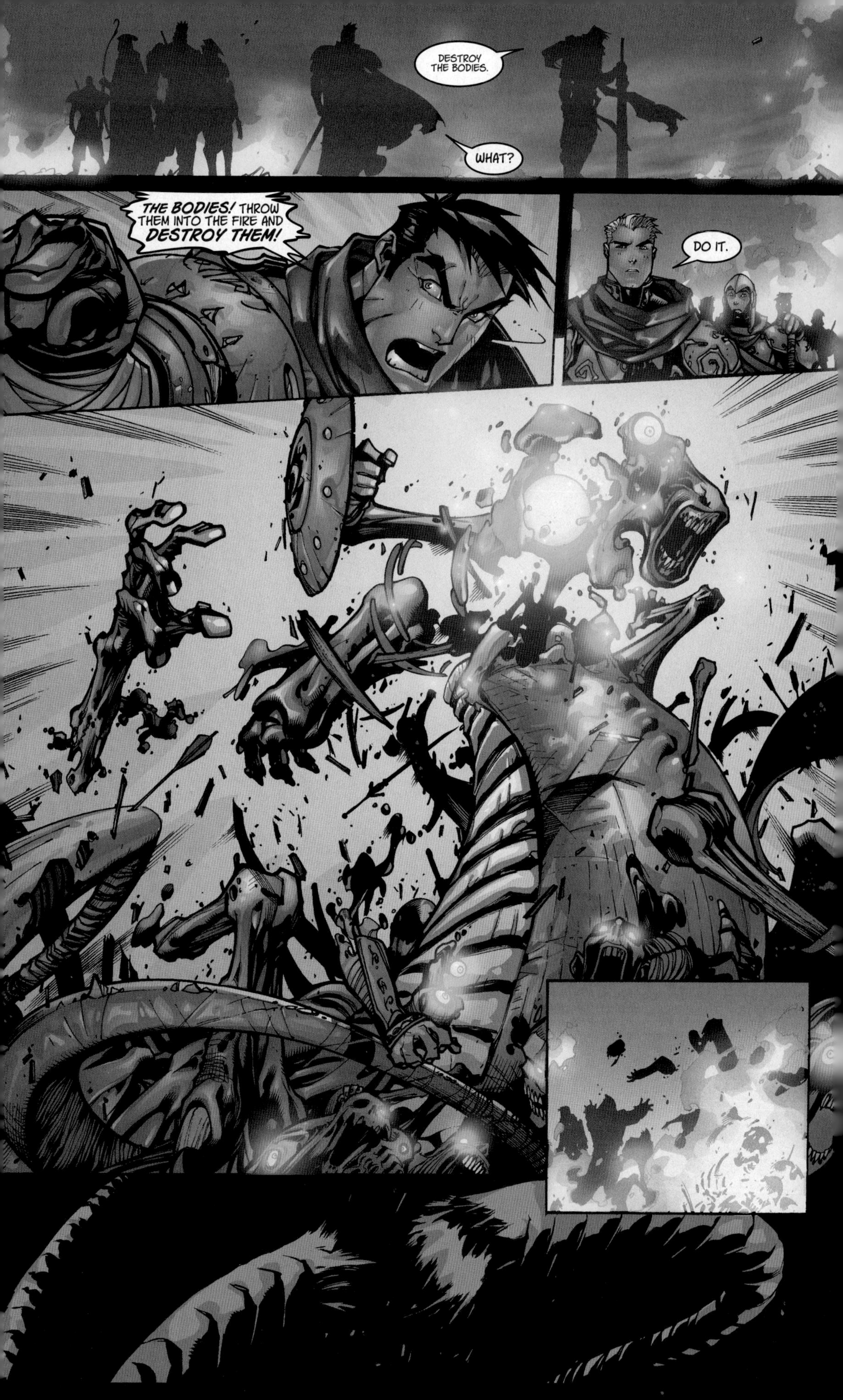
DESTROY THE BODIES.
WHAT?
THE BODIES! THROW THEM INTO THE FIRE AND DESTROY THEM!
DO IT.

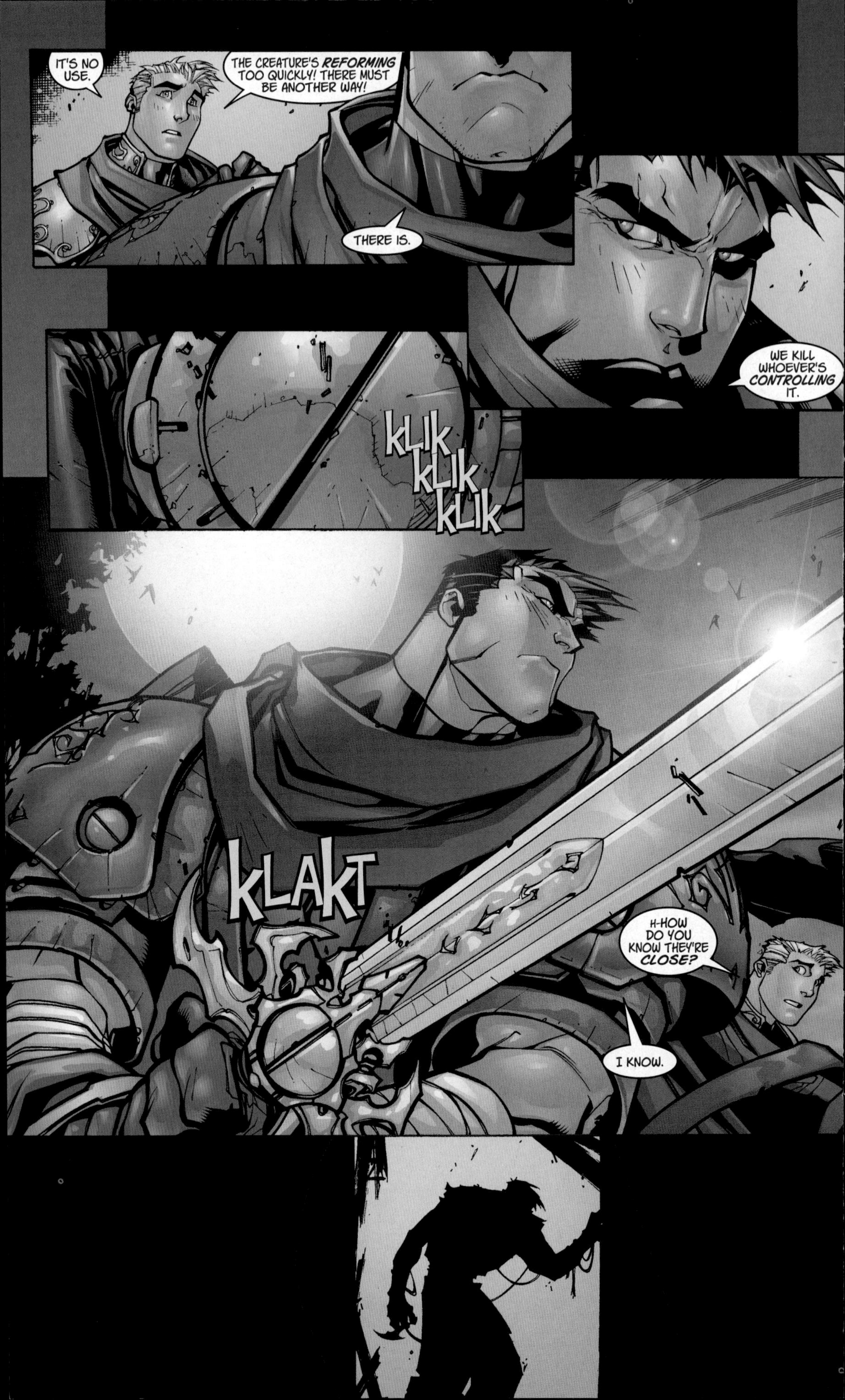
IT'S NO USE.
THE CREATURE'S REFORMING TOO QUICKLY! THERE MUST BE ANOTHER WAY!
THERE IS.
WE KILL WHOEVER'S CONTROLLING IT.
KLIK KLIK KLIK
KLAKT
H-HOW DO YOU KNOW THEY'RE CLOSE?
I KNOW.

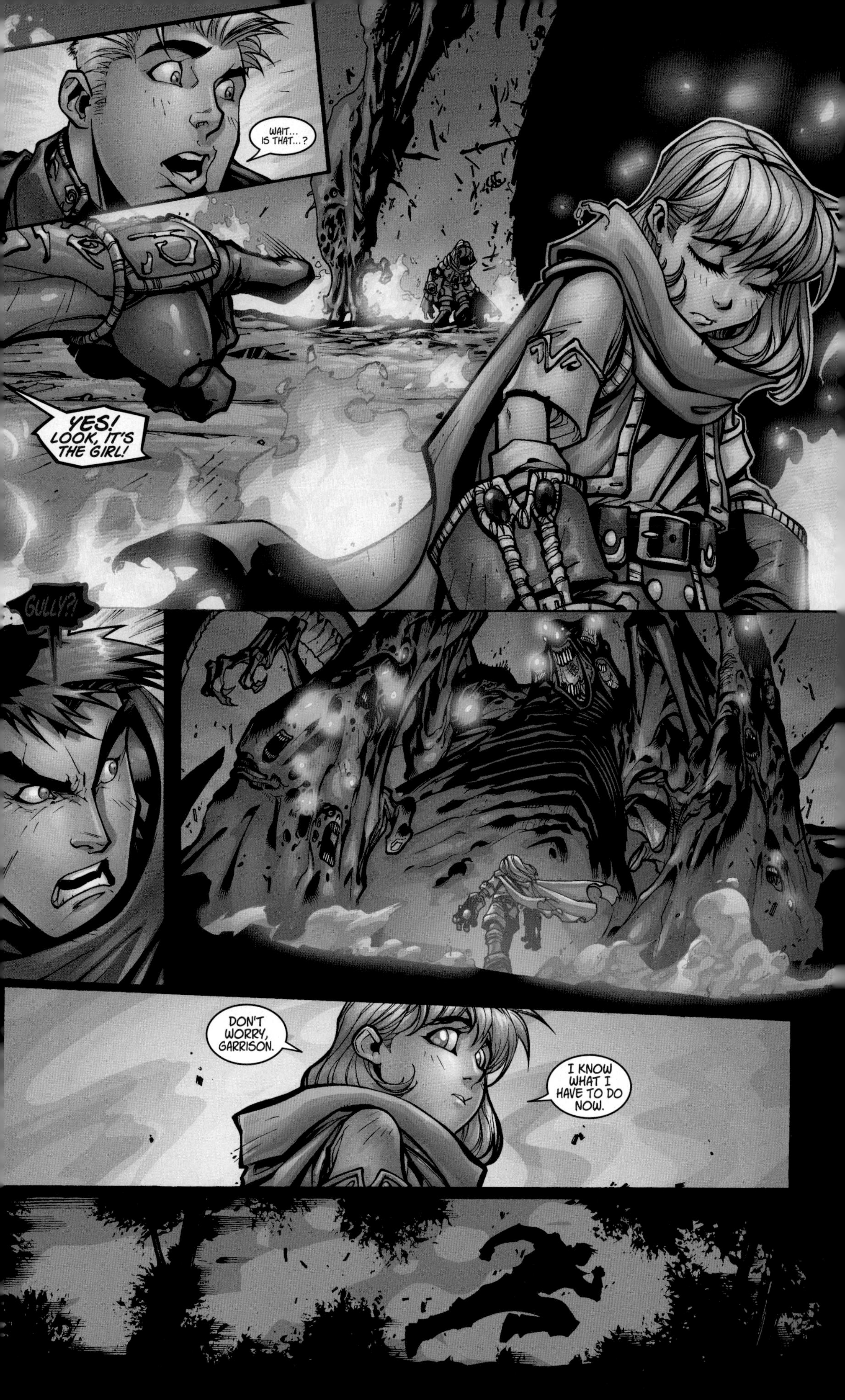
WAIT... IS THAT...?
YES! LOOK, IT'S THE GIRL!
GULLY?!
DON'T WORRY, GARRISON.
I KNOW WHAT I HAVE TO DO NOW.

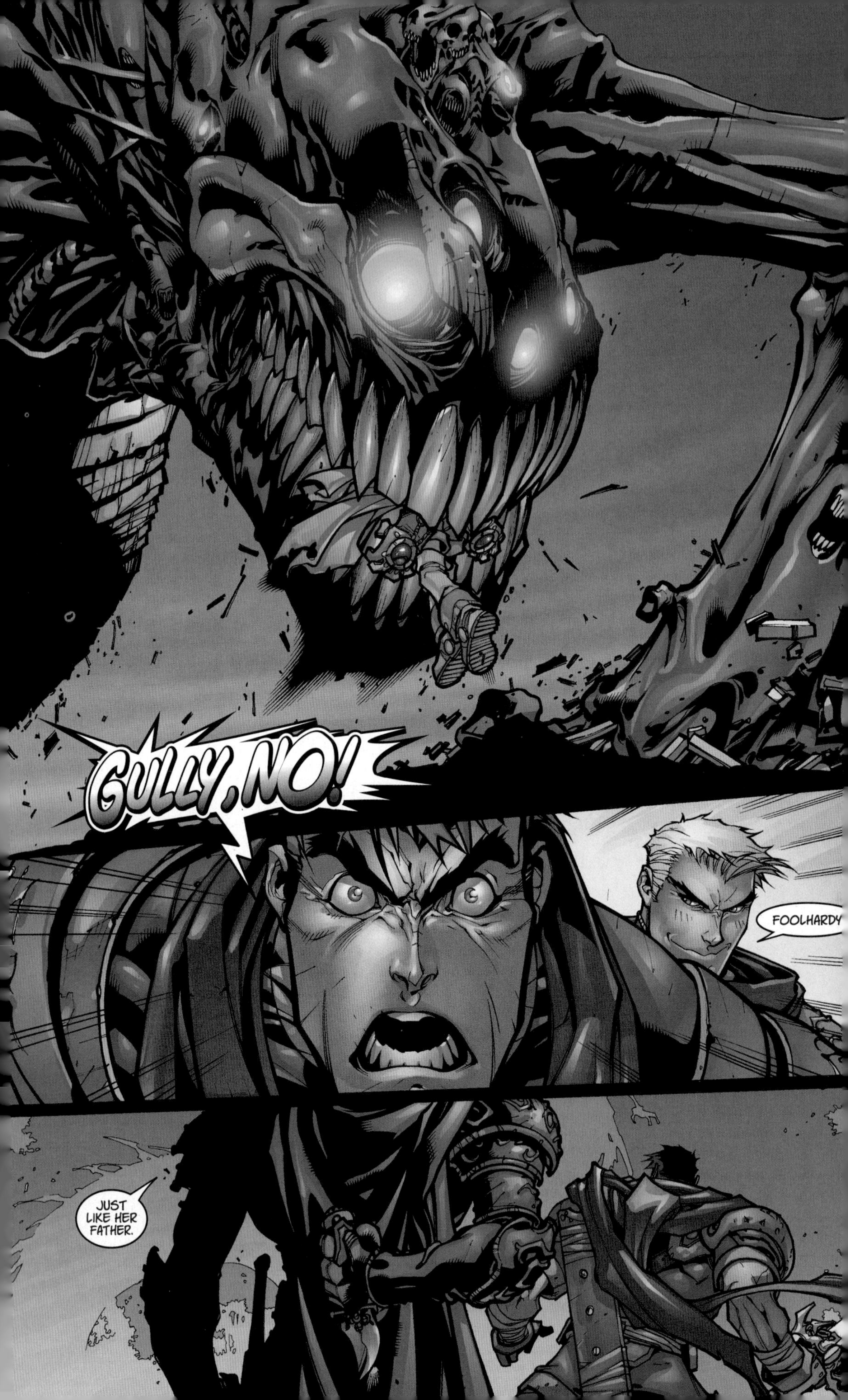
GULLY, NO!
FOOLHARDY
JUST LIKE HER FATHER.

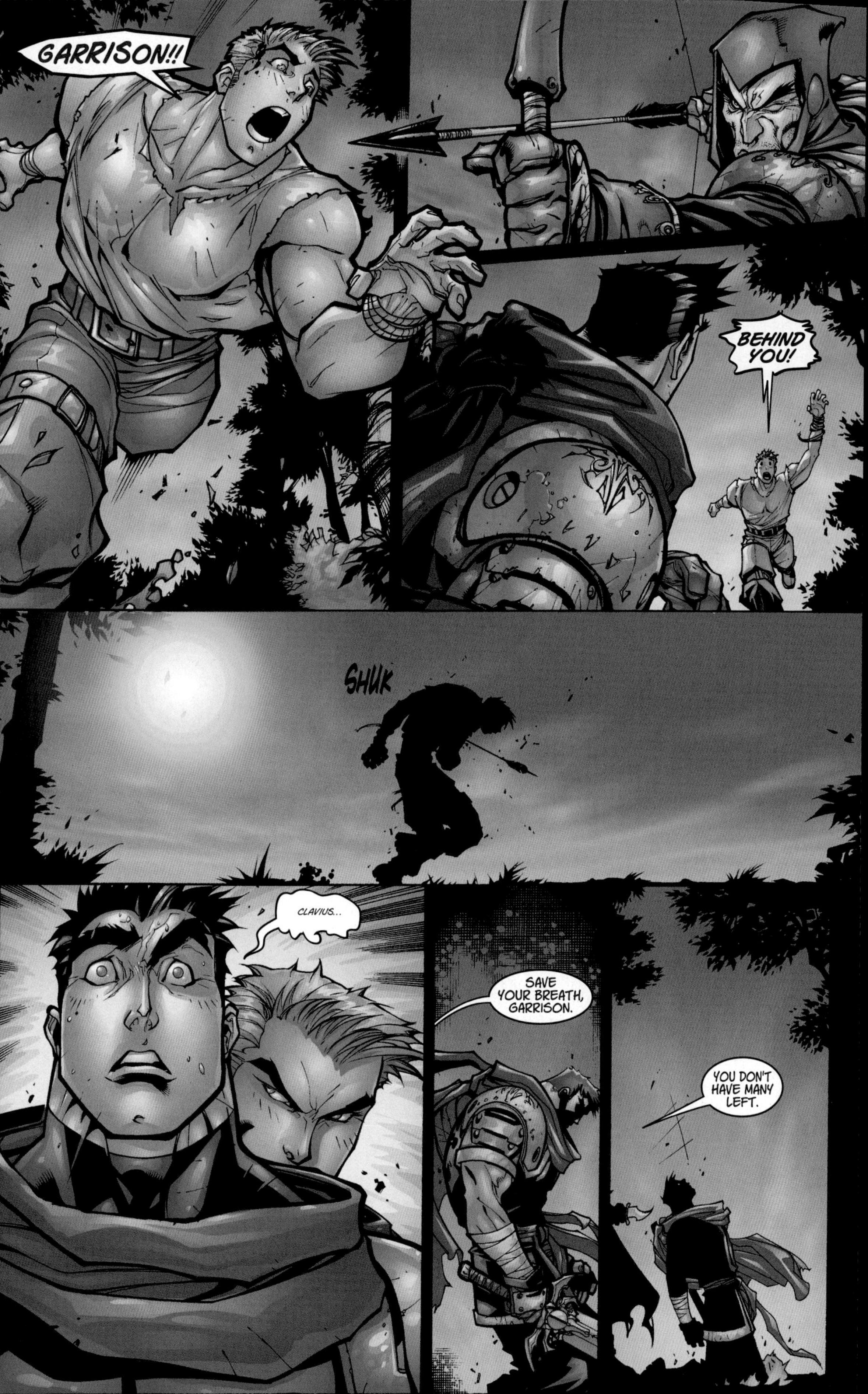
GARRISON!!
BEHIND YOU!
SHUK
CLAVIUS...
SAVE YOUR BREATH, GARRISON.
YOU DON'T HAVE MANY LEFT.

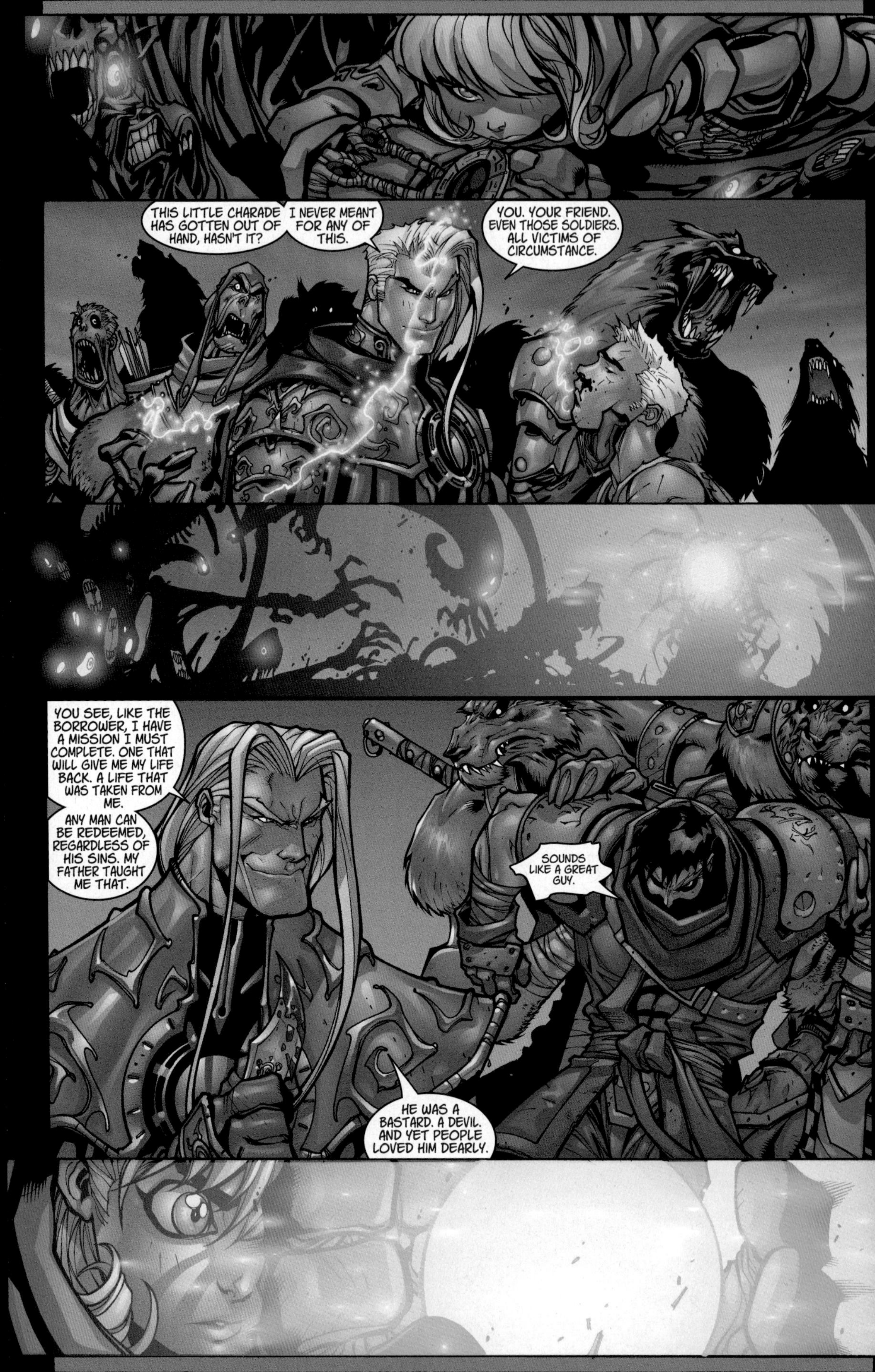
THIS LITTLE CHARADE HAS GOTTEN OUT OF HAND, HASN'T IT?
I NEVER MEANT FOR ANY OF THIS.
YOU. YOUR FRIEND. EVEN THOSE SOLDIERS. ALL VICTIMS OF CIRCUMSTANCE.
YOU SEE, LIKE THE BORROWER, I HAVE A MISSION I MUST COMPLETE. ONE THAT WILL GIVE ME MY LIFE BACK. A LIFE THAT WAS TAKEN FROM ME.
ANY MAN CAN BE REDEEMED, REGARDLESS OF HIS SINS. MY FATHER TAUGHT ME THAT.
SOUNDS LIKE A GREAT GUY.
HE WAS A BASTARD. A DEVIL. AND YET PEOPLE LOVED HIM DEARLY.

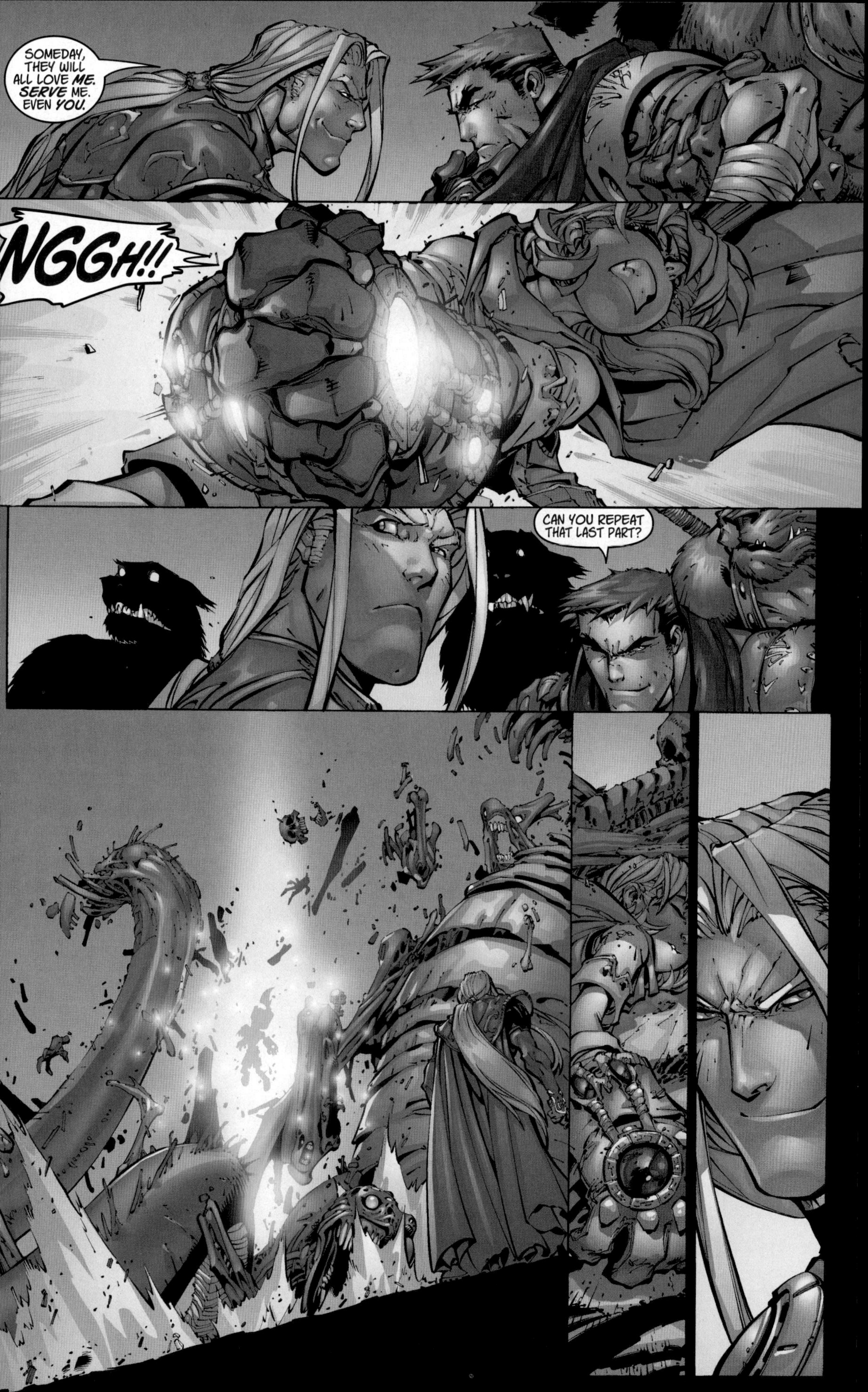
SOMEDAY, THEY WILL ALL LOVE ME. SERVE ME. EVEN YOU.
NGGH!!
CAN YOU REPEAT THAT LAST PART?

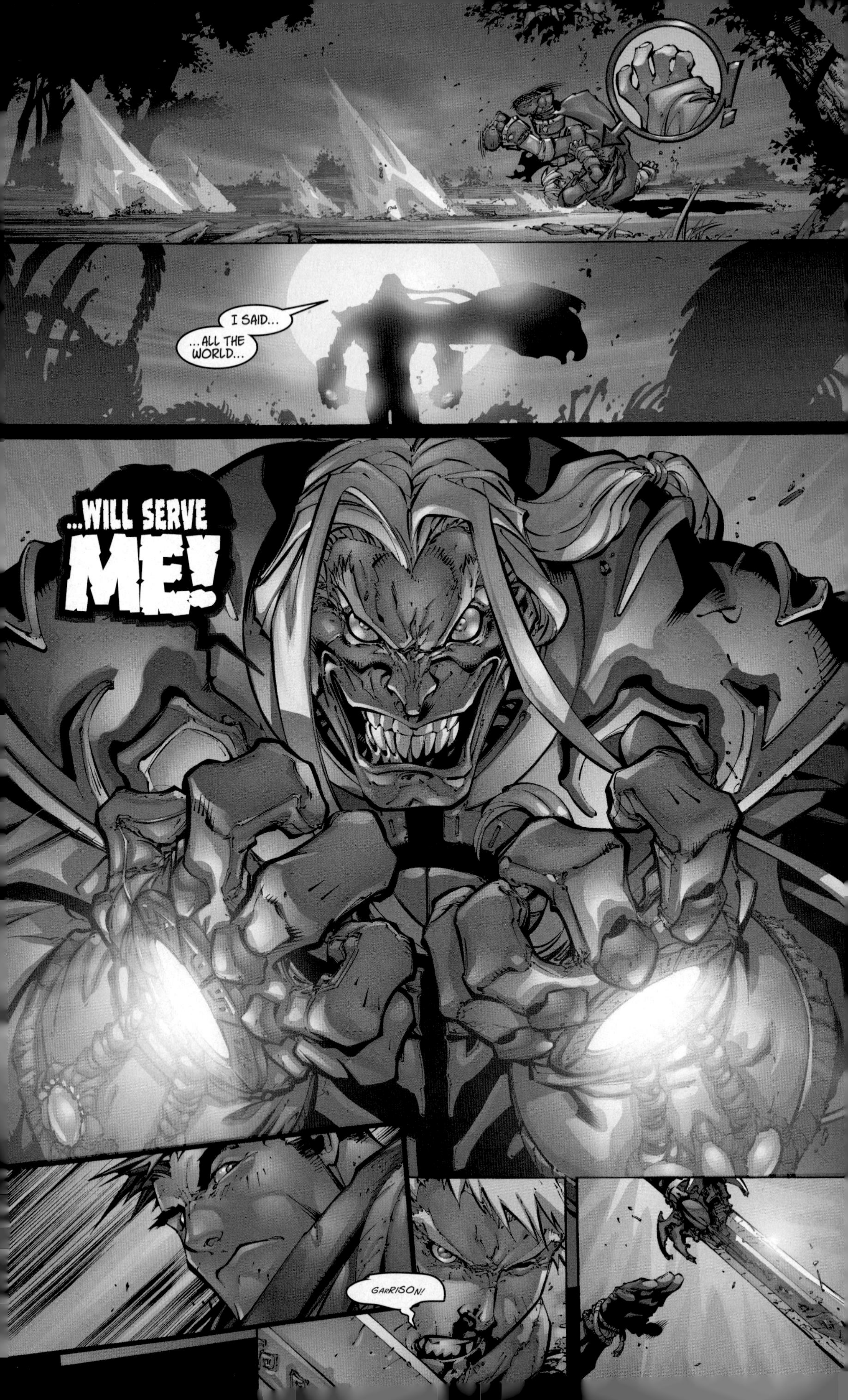
I SAID...
...ALL THE WORLD...
...WILL SERVE ME!
GARRISON!

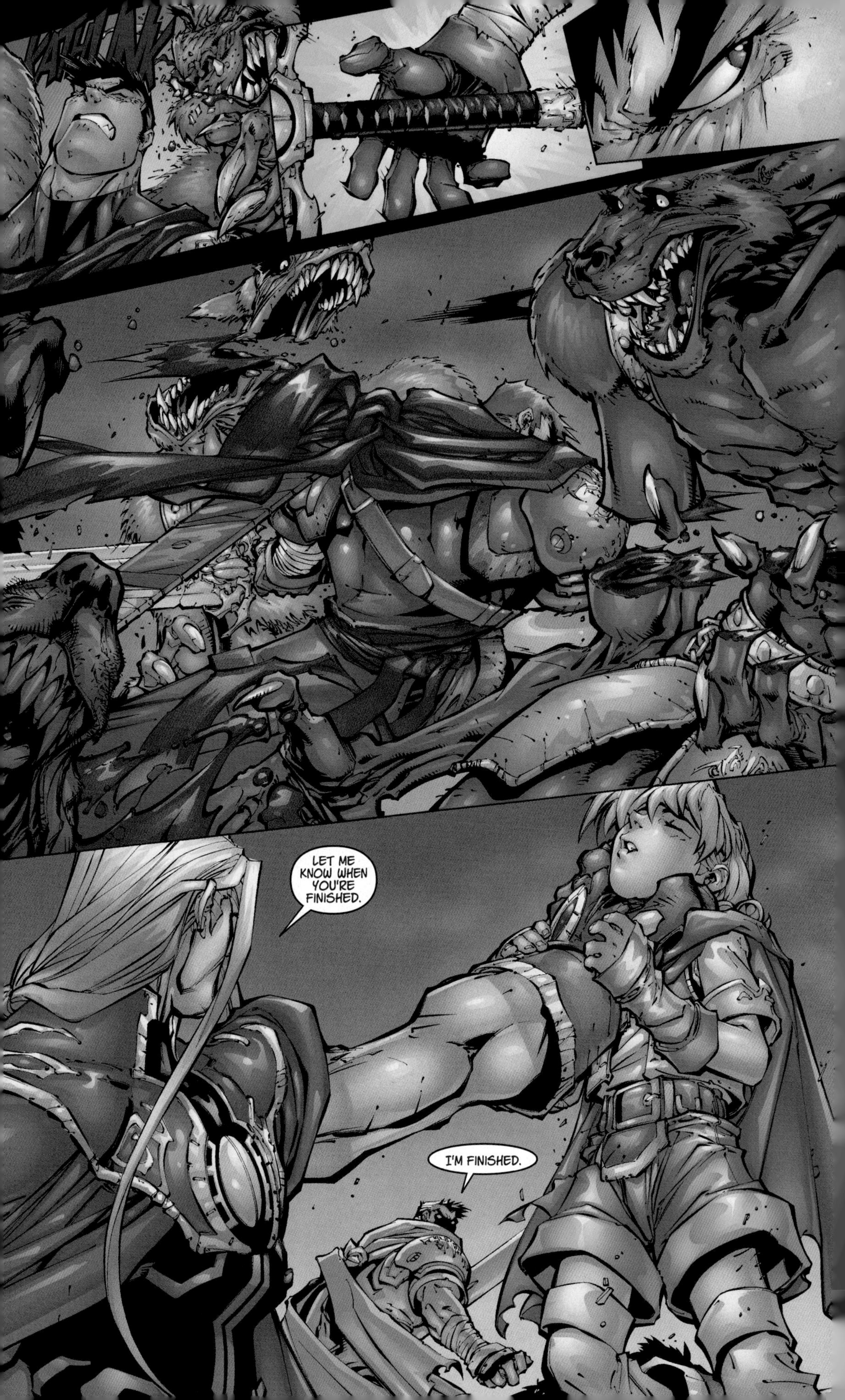
LET ME KNOW WHEN YOU'RE FINISHED.
I'M FINISHED.

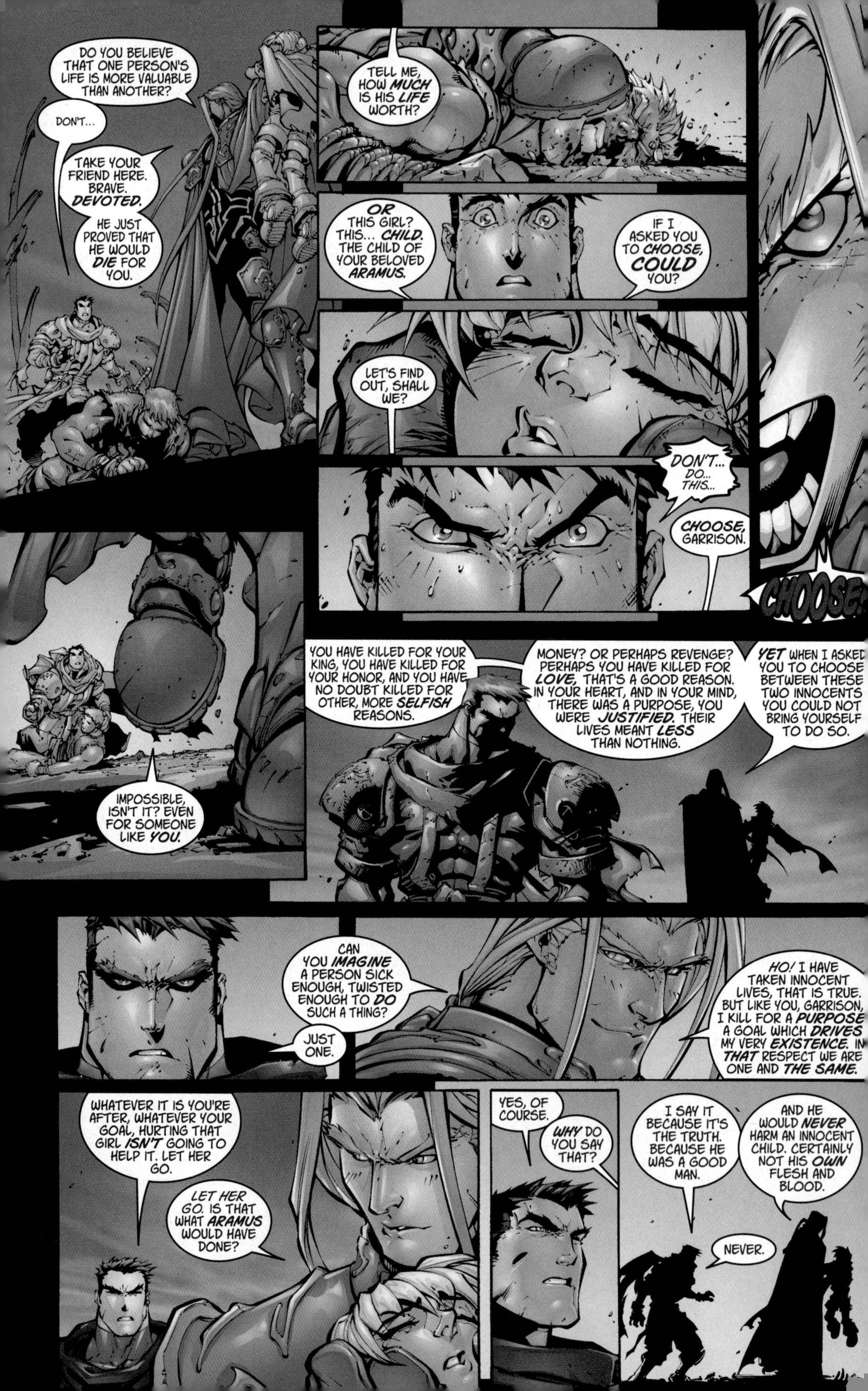
DO YOU BELIEVE THAT ONE PERSON'S LIFE IS MORE VALUABLE THAN ANOTHER?
DON'T...
TAKE YOUR FRIEND HERE. BRAVE. DEVOTED.
HE JUST PROVED THAT HE WOULD DIE FOR YOU.
TELL ME, HOW MUCH IS HIS LIFE WORTH?
OR THIS GIRL? THIS... CHILD. THE CHILD OF YOUR BELOVED ARAMUS.
IF I ASKED YOU TO CHOOSE, COULD YOU?
LET'S FIND OUT, SHALL WE?
DON'T... DO... THIS...
CHOOSE, GARRISON.
CHOOSE!
IMPOSSIBLE, ISN'T IT? EVEN FOR SOMEONE LIKE YOU.
YOU HAVE KILLED FOR YOUR KING, YOU HAVE KILLED FOR YOUR HONOR, AND YOU HAVE NO DOUBT KILLED FOR OTHER, MORE SELFISH REASONS.
MONEY? OR PERHAPS REVENGE? PERHAPS YOU HAVE KILLED FOR LOVE, THAT'S A GOOD REASON. IN YOUR HEART, AND IN YOUR MIND, THERE WAS A PURPOSE, YOU WERE JUSTIFIED. THEIR LIVES MEANT LESS THAN NOTHING.
YET WHEN I ASKED YOU TO CHOOSE BETWEEN THESE TWO INNOCENTS YOU COULD NOT BRING YOURSELF TO DO SO.
CAN YOU IMAGINE A PERSON SICK ENOUGH, TWISTED ENOUGH TO DO SUCH A THING?
JUST ONE.
HO! I HAVE TAKEN INNOCENT LIVES, THAT IS TRUE. BUT LIKE YOU, GARRISON, I KILL FOR A PURPOSE. A GOAL WHICH DRIVES MY VERY EXISTENCE. IN THAT RESPECT WE ARE ONE AND THE SAME.
WHATEVER IT IS YOU'RE AFTER, WHATEVER YOUR GOAL, HURTING THAT GIRL ISN'T GOING TO HELP IT. LET HER GO.
LET HER GO. IS THAT WHAT ARAMUS WOULD HAVE DONE?
YES, OF COURSE.
WHY DO YOU SAY THAT?
I SAY IT BECAUSE IT'S THE TRUTH. BECAUSE HE WAS A GOOD MAN.
AND HE WOULD NEVER HARM AN INNOCENT CHILD. CERTAINLY NOT HIS OWN FLESH AND BLOOD.
NEVER.

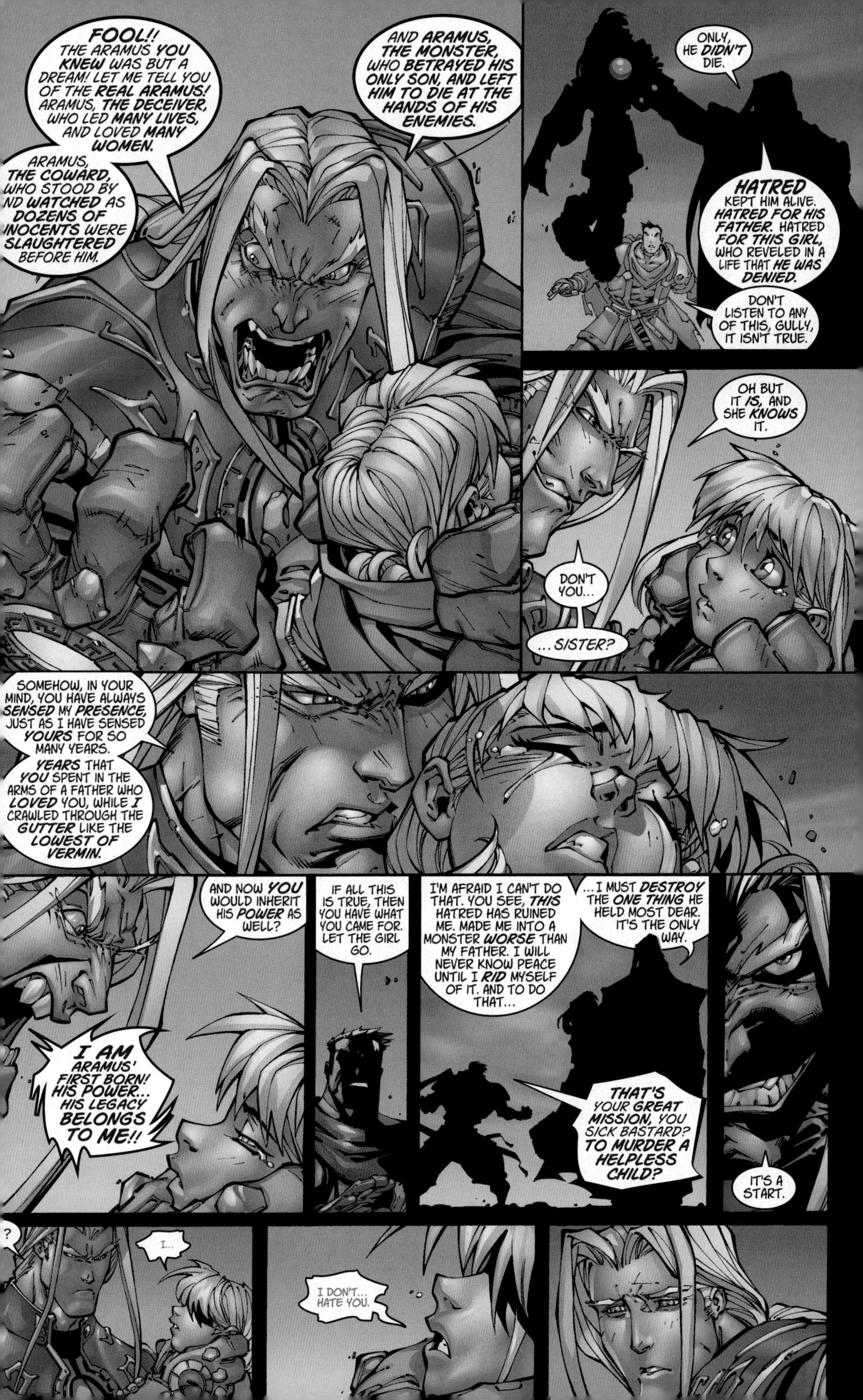
FOOL!! THE ARAMUS YOU KNEW WAS BUT A DREAM! LET ME TELL YOU OF THE REAL ARAMUS! ARAMUS, THE DECEIVER, WHO LED MANY LIVES, AND LOVED MANY WOMEN.
ARAMUS, THE COWARD, WHO STOOD BY ND WATCHED AS DOZENS OF INOCENTS WERE SLAUGHTERED BEFORE HIM.
AND ARAMUS, THE MONSTER, WHO BETRAYED HIS ONLY SON, AND LEFT HIM TO DIE AT THE HANDS OF HIS ENEMIES.
ONLY, HE DIDN'T DIE.
HATRED KEPT HIM ALIVE. HATRED FOR HIS FATHER. HATRED FOR THIS GIRL, WHO REVELED IN A LIFE THAT HE WAS DENIED.
DON'T LISTEN TO ANY OF THIS, GULLY, IT ISN'T TRUE.
OH BUT IT IS, AND SHE KNOWS IT.
DON'T YOU...
...SISTER?
SOMEHOW, IN YOUR MIND, YOU HAVE ALWAYS SENSED MY PRESENCE, JUST AS I HAVE SENSED YOURS FOR SO MANY YEARS.
YEARS THAT YOU SPENT IN THE ARMS OF A FATHER WHO LOVED YOU, WHILE I CRAWLED THROUGH THE GUTTER LIKE THE LOWEST OF VERMIN.
AND NOW YOU WOULD INHERIT HIS POWER AS WELL?
I AM ARAMUS' FIRST BORN! HIS POWER... HIS LEGACY BELONGS TO ME!!
IF ALL THIS IS TRUE, THEN YOU HAVE WHAT YOU CAME FOR. LET THE GIRL GO.
I'M AFRAID I CAN'T DO THAT. YOU SEE, THIS HATRED HAS RUINED ME. MADE ME INTO A MONSTER WORSE THAN MY FATHER. I WILL NEVER KNOW PEACE UNTIL I RID MYSELF OF IT. AND TO DO THAT...
...I MUST DESTROY THE ONE THING HE HELD MOST DEAR. IT'S THE ONLY WAY.
THAT'S YOUR GREAT MISSION, YOU SICK BASTARD? TO MURDER A HELPLESS CHILD?
IT'S A START.
I...
I DON'T... HATE YOU.

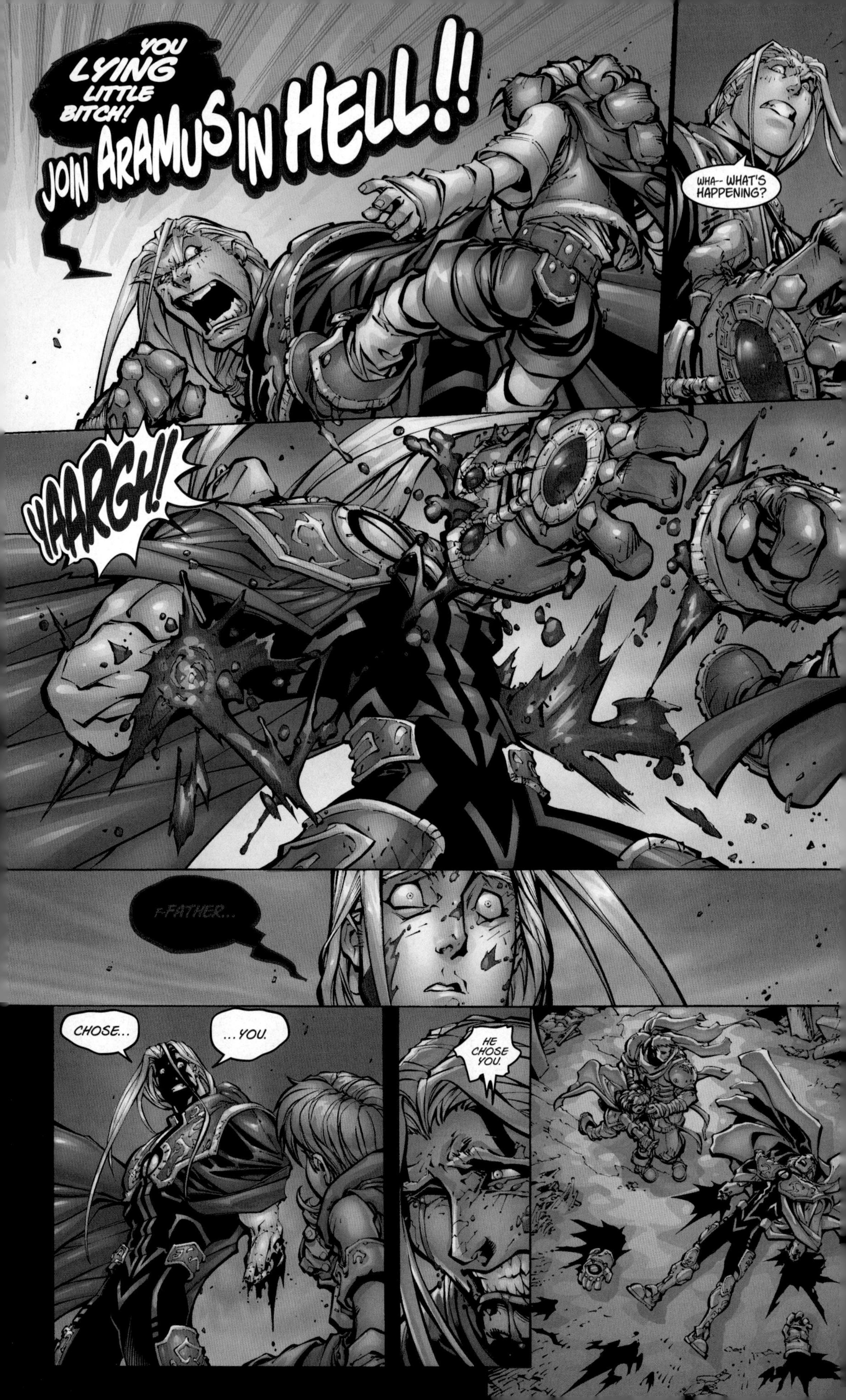
YOU LYING LITTLE BITCH! JOIN ARAMUS IN HELL!!
WHA-- WHAT'S HAPPENING?
YAARGH!!
F-FATHER...
CHOSE...
...YOU.
HE CHOSE YOU.

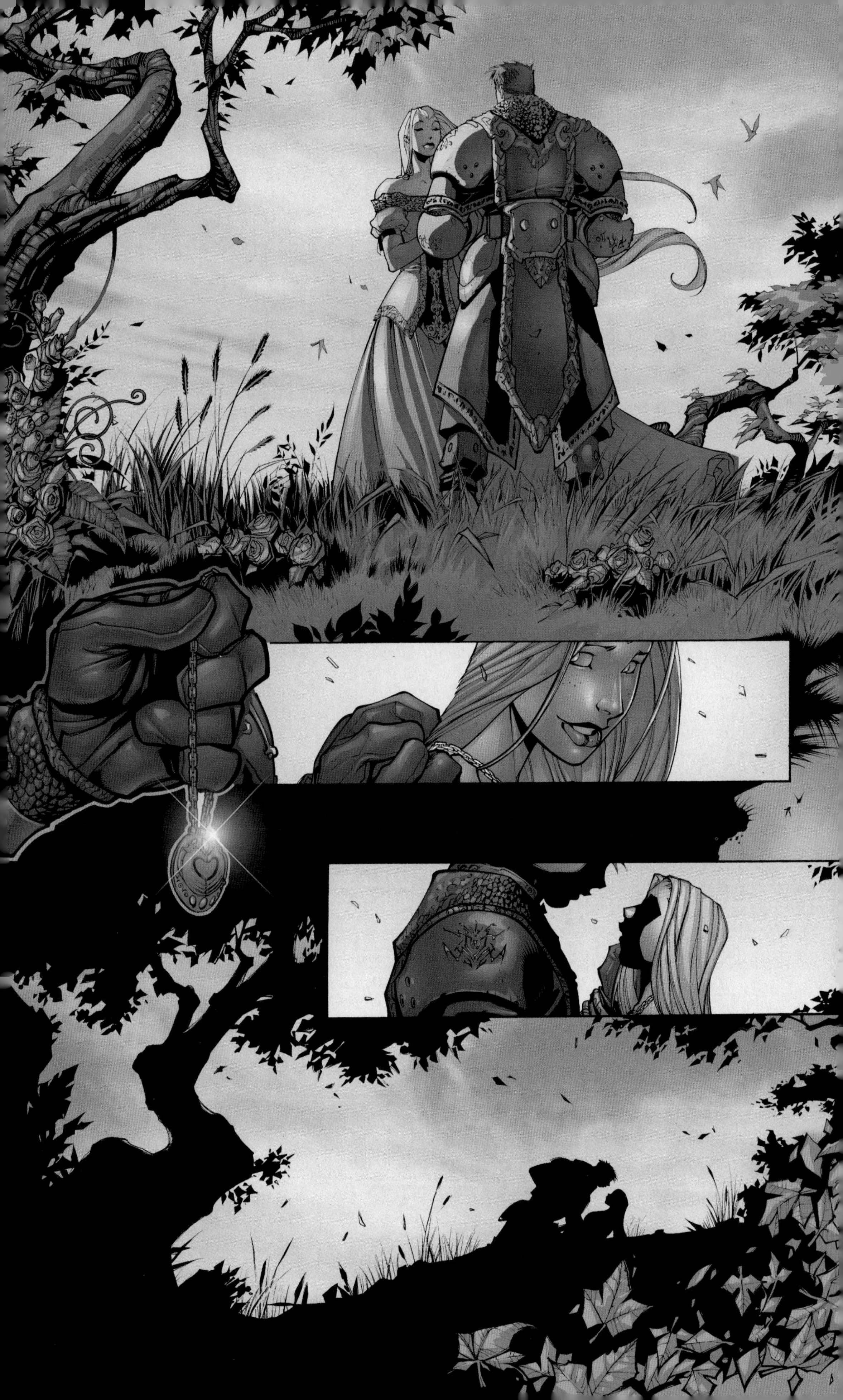

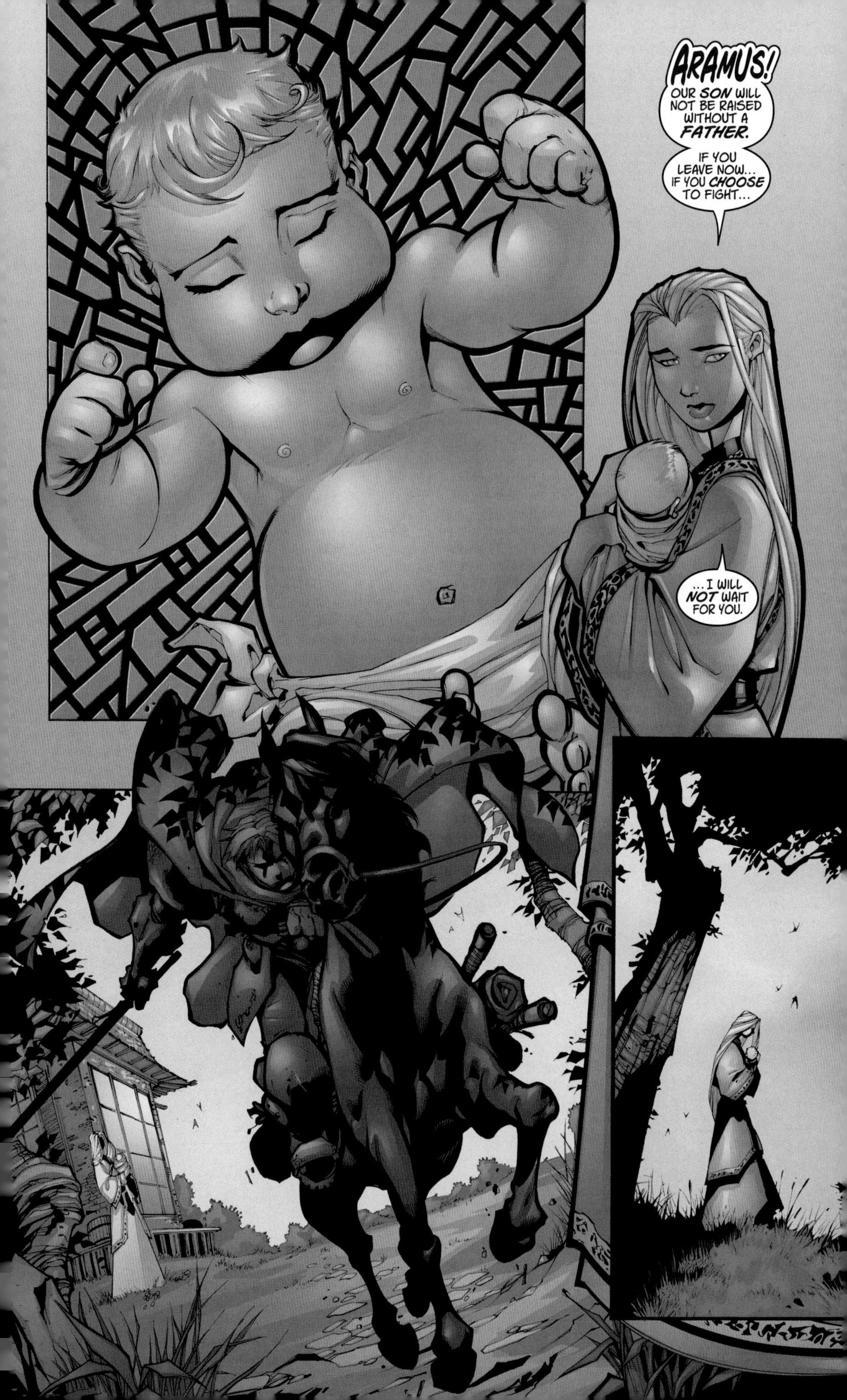
ARAMUS!
OUR SON WILL NOT BE RAISED WITHOUT A FATHER.
IF YOU LEAVE NOW... IF YOU CHOOSE TO FIGHT...
...I WILL NOT WAIT FOR YOU.

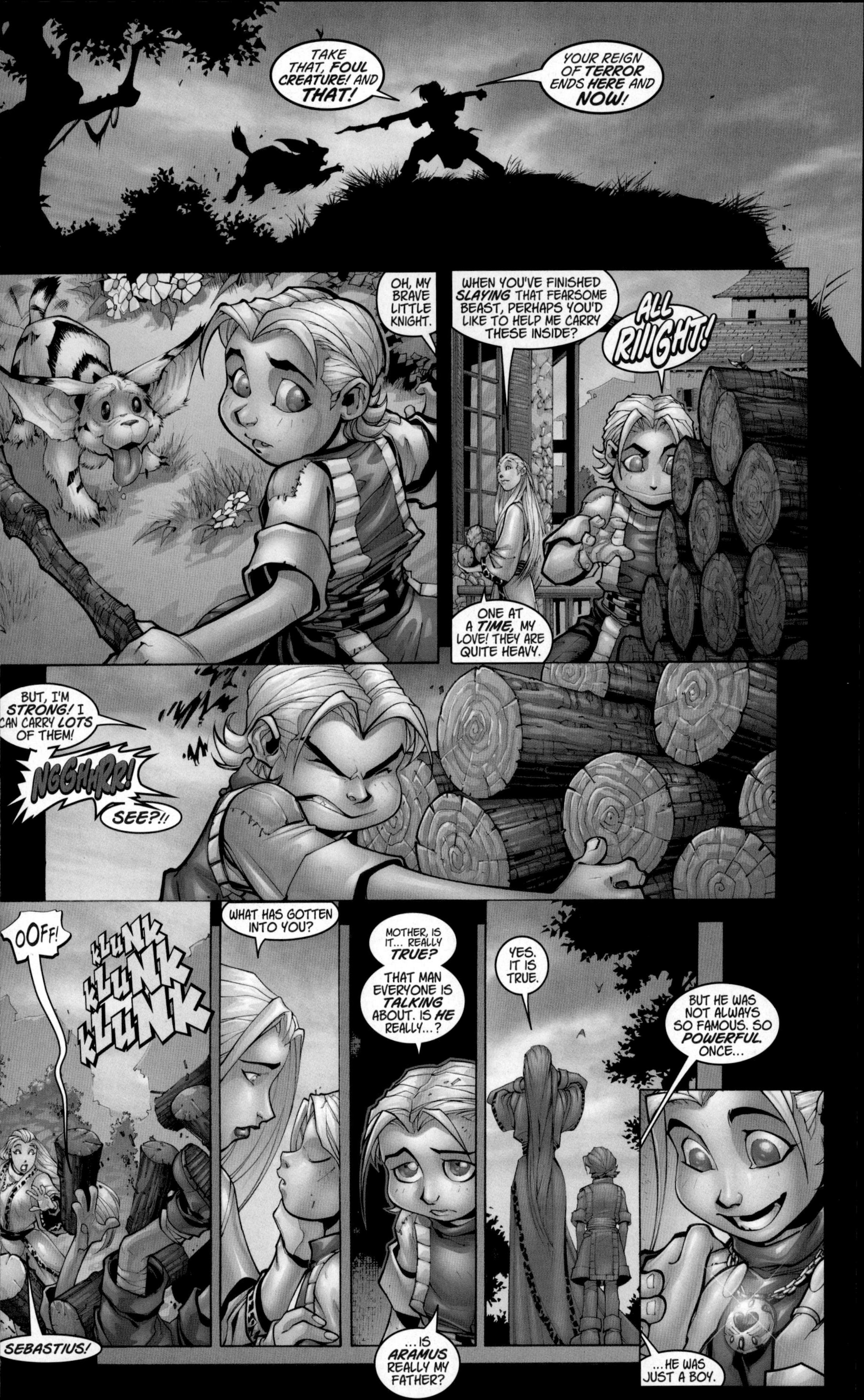
TAKE THAT, FOUL CREATURE! AND THAT!
YOUR REIGN OF TERROR ENDS HERE AND NOW!
OH, MY BRAVE LITTLE KNIGHT.
WHEN YOU'VE FINISHED SLAYING THAT FEARSOME BEAST, PERHAPS YOU'D LIKE TO HELP ME CARRY THESE INSIDE?
ALL RIIIGHT!
ONE AT A TIME, MY LOVE! THEY ARE QUITE HEAVY.
BUT, I'M STRONG! I CAN CARRY LOTS OF THEM!
NGGHHRR!
SEE?!!
OOFF!
KLUNK KLUNK KLUNK
SEBASTIUS!
WHAT HAS GOTTEN INTO YOU?
MOTHER, IS IT... REALLY TRUE?
THAT MAN EVERYONE IS TALKING ABOUT. IS HE REALLY...?
...IS ARAMUS REALLY MY FATHER?
YES. IT IS TRUE.
BUT HE WAS NOT ALWAYS SO FAMOUS. SO POWERFUL. ONCE...
...HE WAS JUST A BOY.

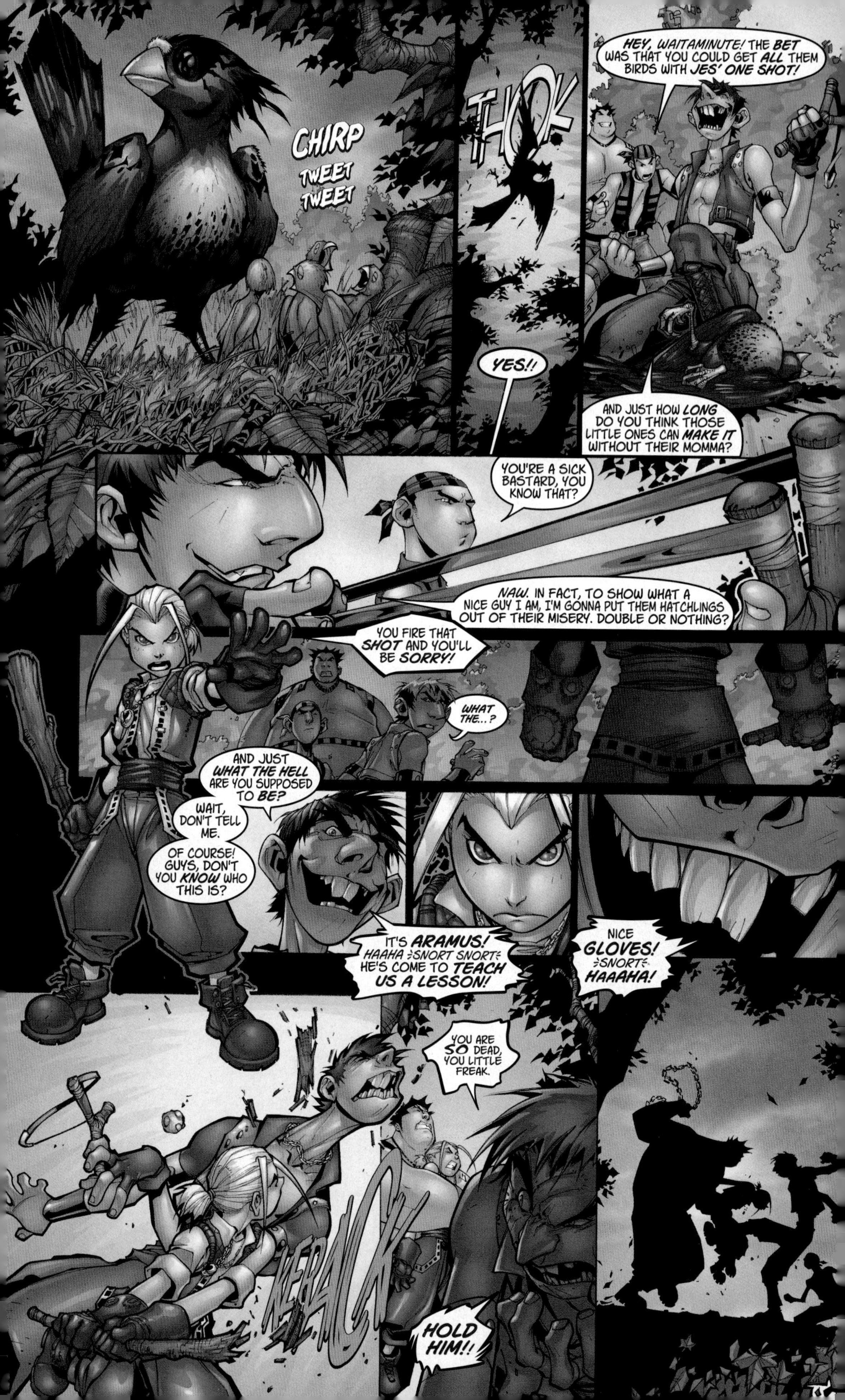
CHIRP
TWEET
TWEET
THOK
YES!!
HEY, WAITAMINUTE! THE BET WAS THAT YOU COULD GET ALL THEM BIRDS WITH JES' ONE SHOT!
AND JUST HOW LONG DO YOU THINK THOSE LITTLE ONES CAN MAKE IT WITHOUT THEIR MOMMA?
YOU'RE A SICK BASTARD, YOU KNOW THAT?
NAW. IN FACT, TO SHOW WHAT A NICE GUY I AM, I'M GONNA PUT THEM HATCHLINGS OUT OF THEIR MISERY. DOUBLE OR NOTHING?
YOU FIRE THAT SHOT AND YOU'LL BE SORRY!
WHAT THE...?
AND JUST WHAT THE HELL ARE YOU SUPPOSED TO BE?
WAIT, DON'T TELL ME.
OF COURSE! GUYS, DON'T YOU KNOW WHO THIS IS?
IT'S ARAMUS! HAAHA SNORT SNORT HE'S COME TO TEACH US A LESSON!
NICE GLOVES! SNORT HAAAHA!
YOU ARE SO DEAD, YOU LITTLE FREAK.
KERACK
HOLD HIM!!

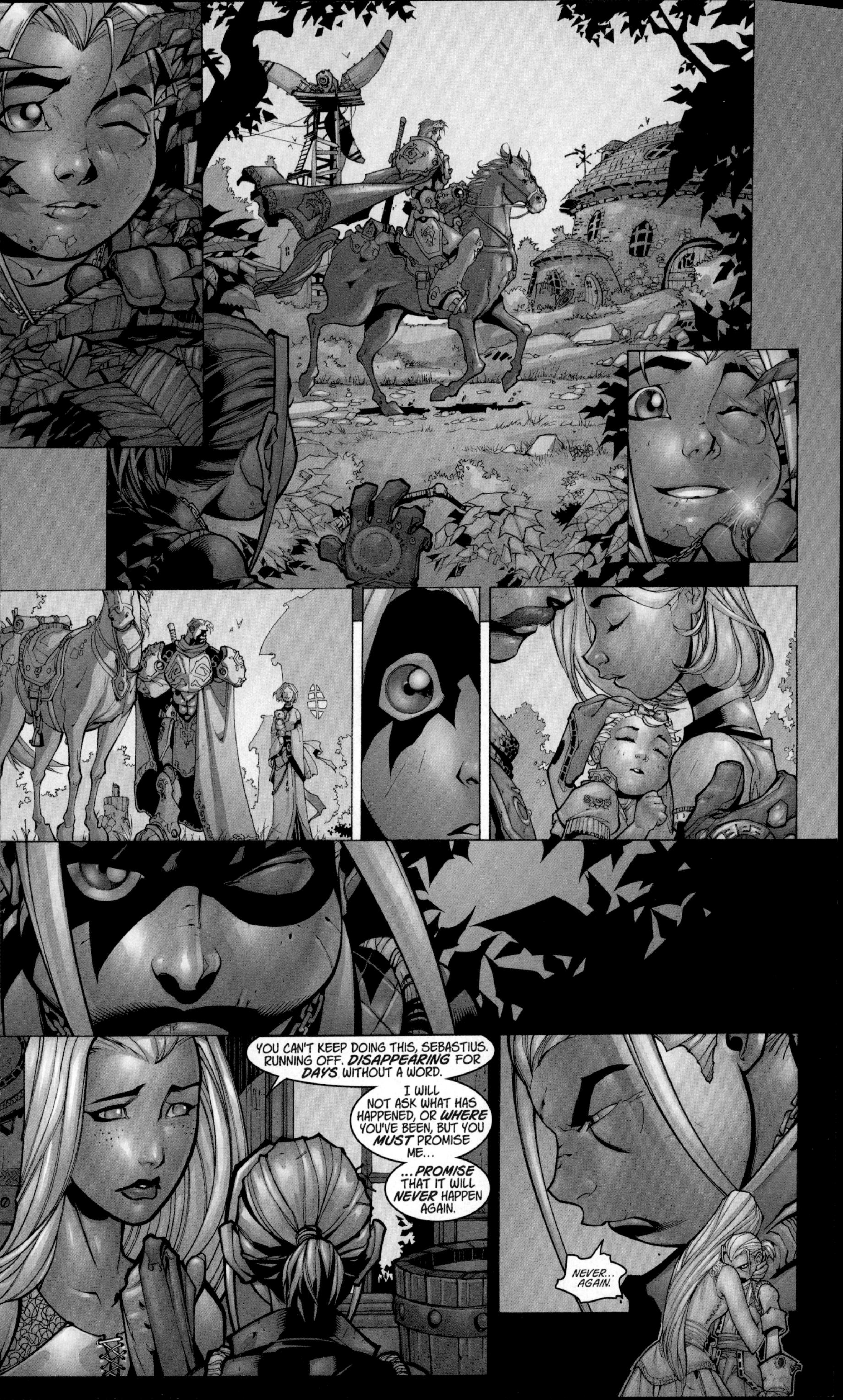
YOU CAN'T KEEP DOING THIS, SEBASTIUS. RUNNING OFF. DISAPPEARING FOR DAYS WITHOUT A WORD.
I WILL NOT ASK WHAT HAS HAPPENED, OR WHERE YOU'VE BEEN, BUT YOU MUST PROMISE ME...
...PROMISE THAT IT WILL NEVER HAPPEN AGAIN.
NEVER... AGAIN.

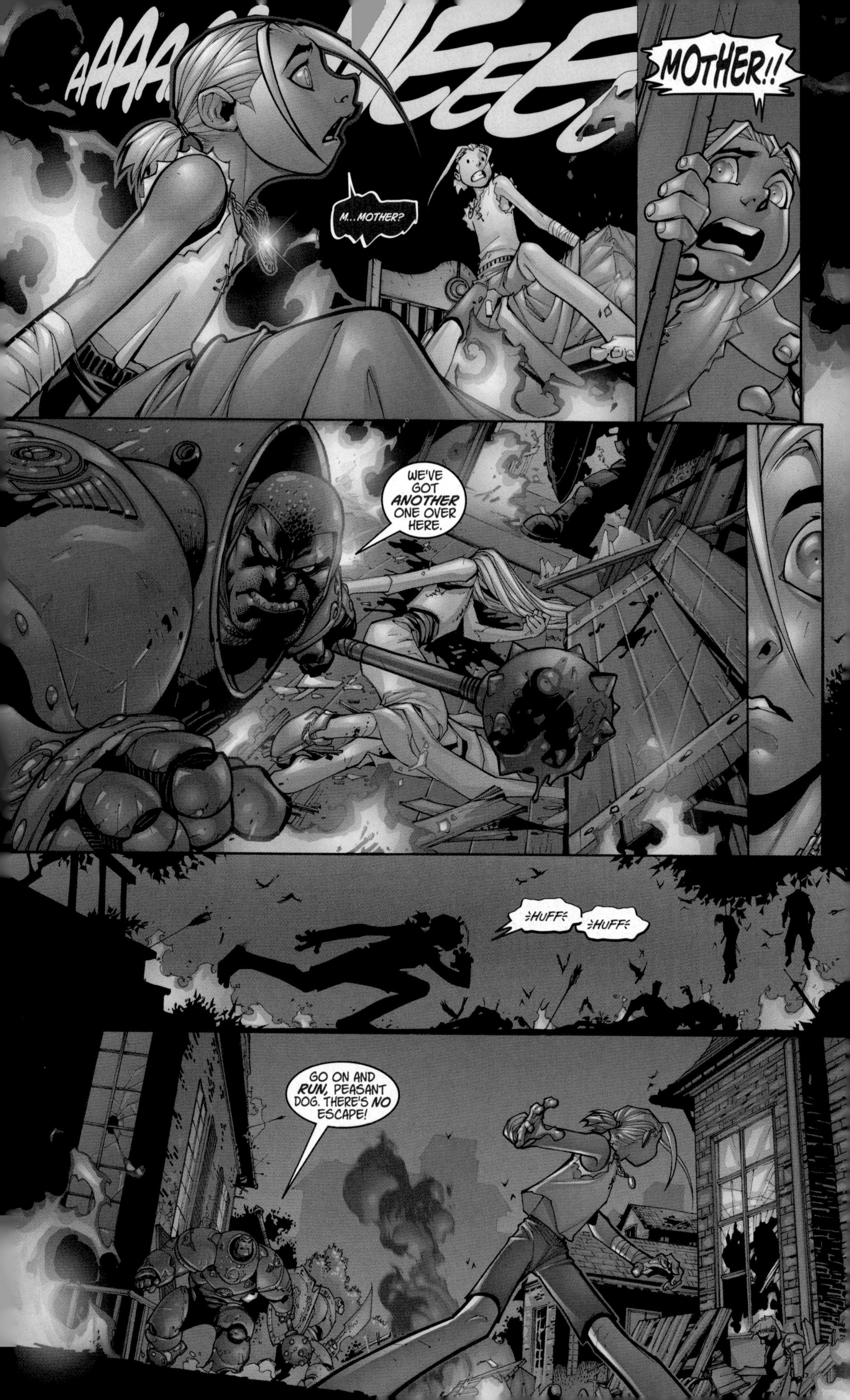
M...MOTHER?
MOTHER!!
WE'VE GOT ANOTHER ONE OVER HERE.
HUFF
HUFF
GO ON AND RUN, PEASANT DOG. THERE'S NO ESCAPE!

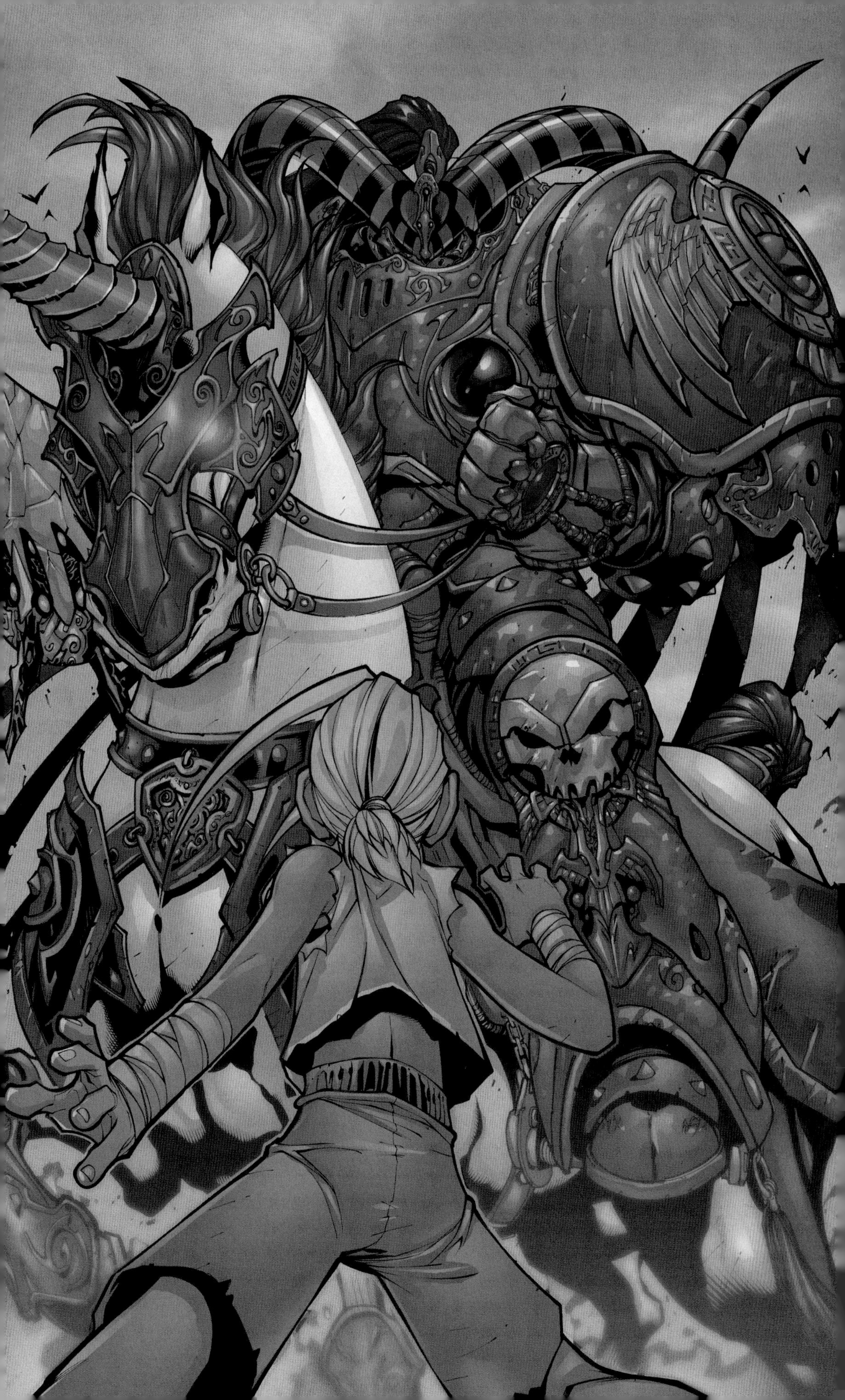

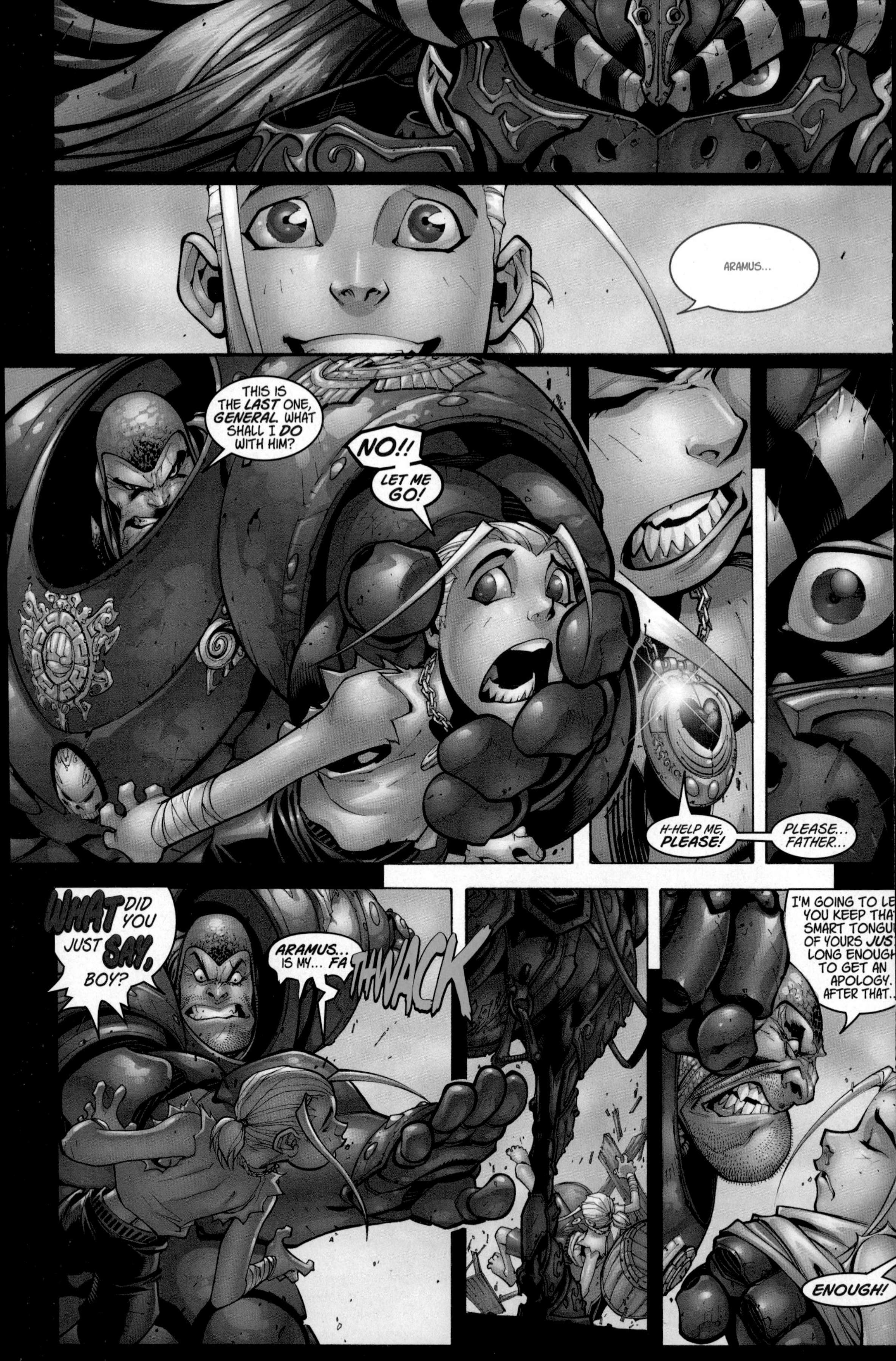
ARAMUS...
THIS IS THE LAST ONE, GENERAL. WHAT SHALL I DO WITH HIM?
NO!!
LET ME GO!
H-HELP ME, PLEASE!
PLEASE... FATHER...
WHAT DID YOU JUST SAY, BOY?
ARAMUS... IS MY... FA
THWACK
I'M GOING TO LE YOU KEEP THAT SMART TONGU OF YOURS JUS LONG ENOUGH TO GET AN APOLOGY. AFTER THAT...
ENOUGH!

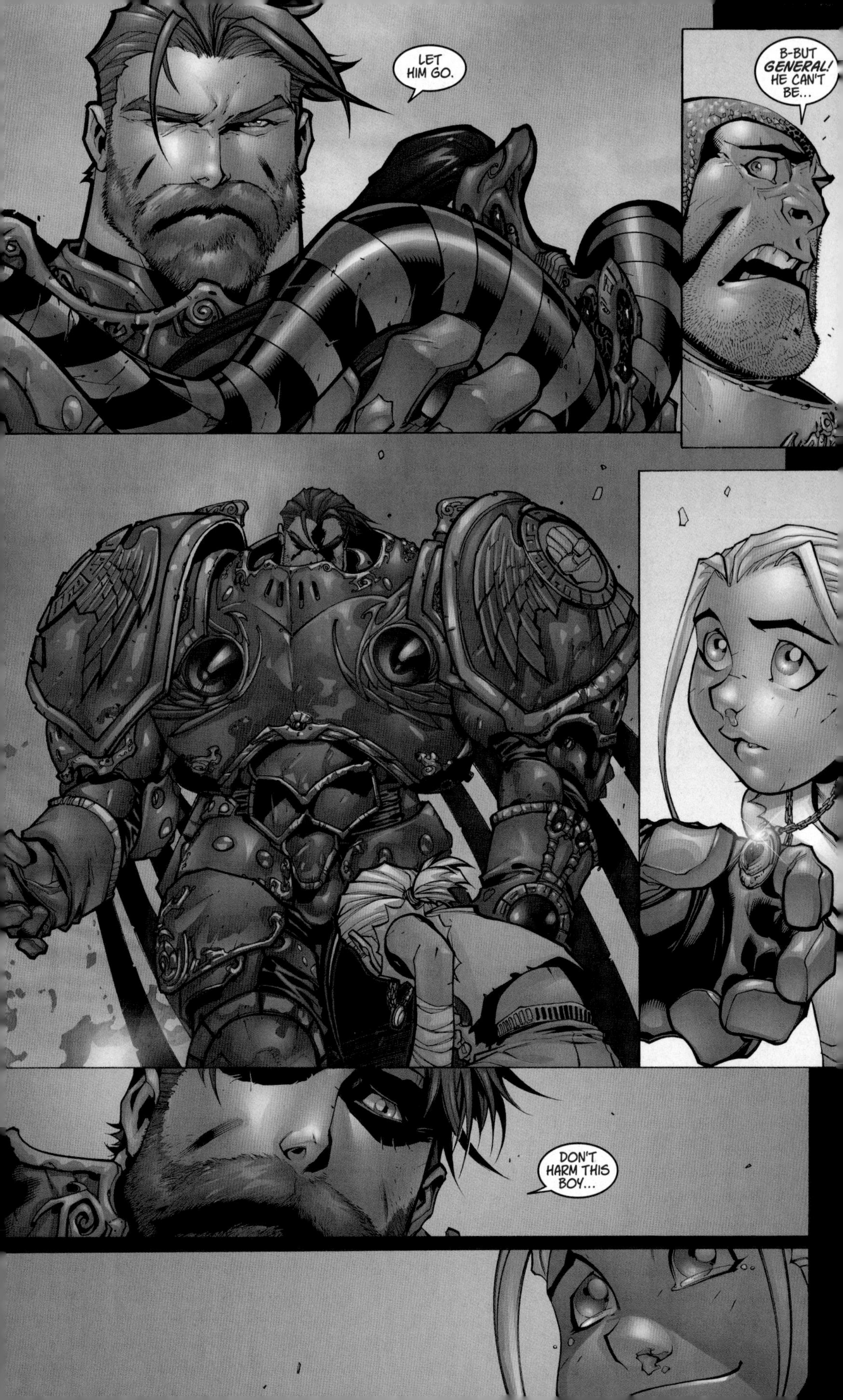
LET HIM GO.
B-BUT GENERAL! HE CAN'T BE...
DON'T HARM THIS BOY...

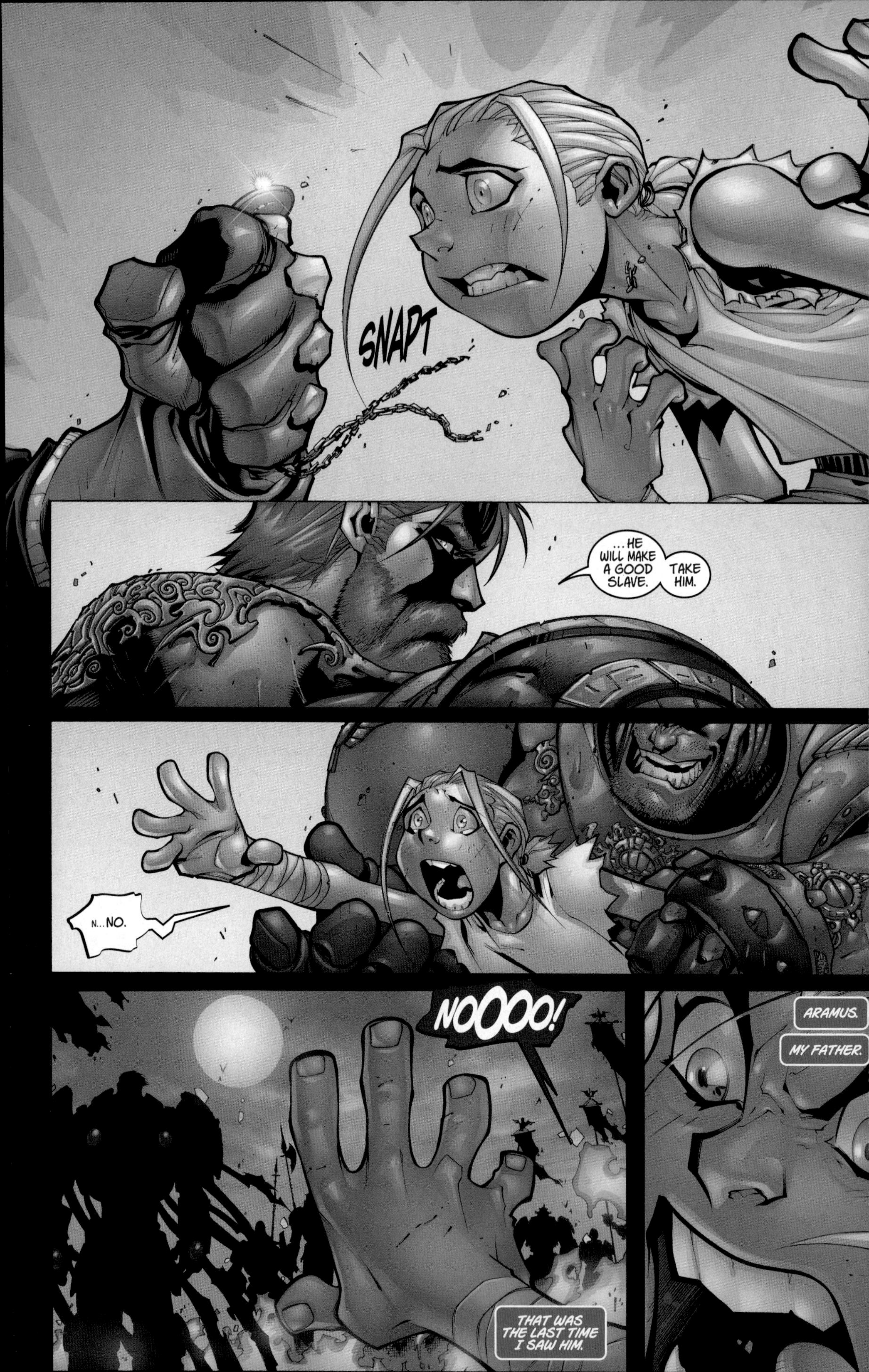
SNAPT
...HE WILL MAKE A GOOD SLAVE.
TAKE HIM.
N...NO.
NOOOO!
ARAMUS.
MY FATHER.
THAT WAS THE LAST TIME I SAW HIM.

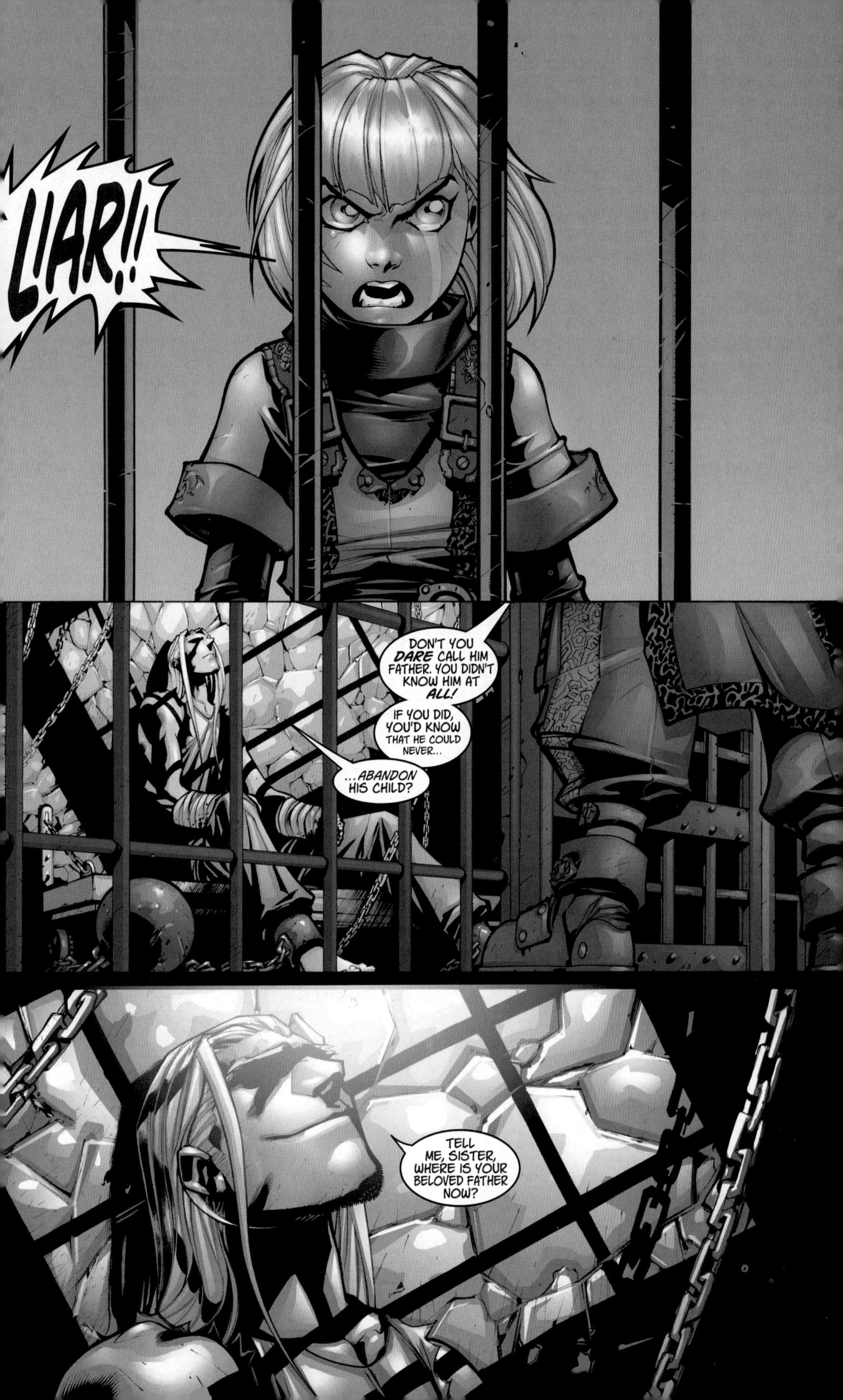
LIAR!!
DON'T YOU DARE CALL HIM FATHER. YOU DIDN'T KNOW HIM AT ALL!
IF YOU DID, YOU'D KNOW THAT HE COULD NEVER...
...ABANDON HIS CHILD?
TELL ME, SISTER, WHERE IS YOUR BELOVED FATHER NOW?

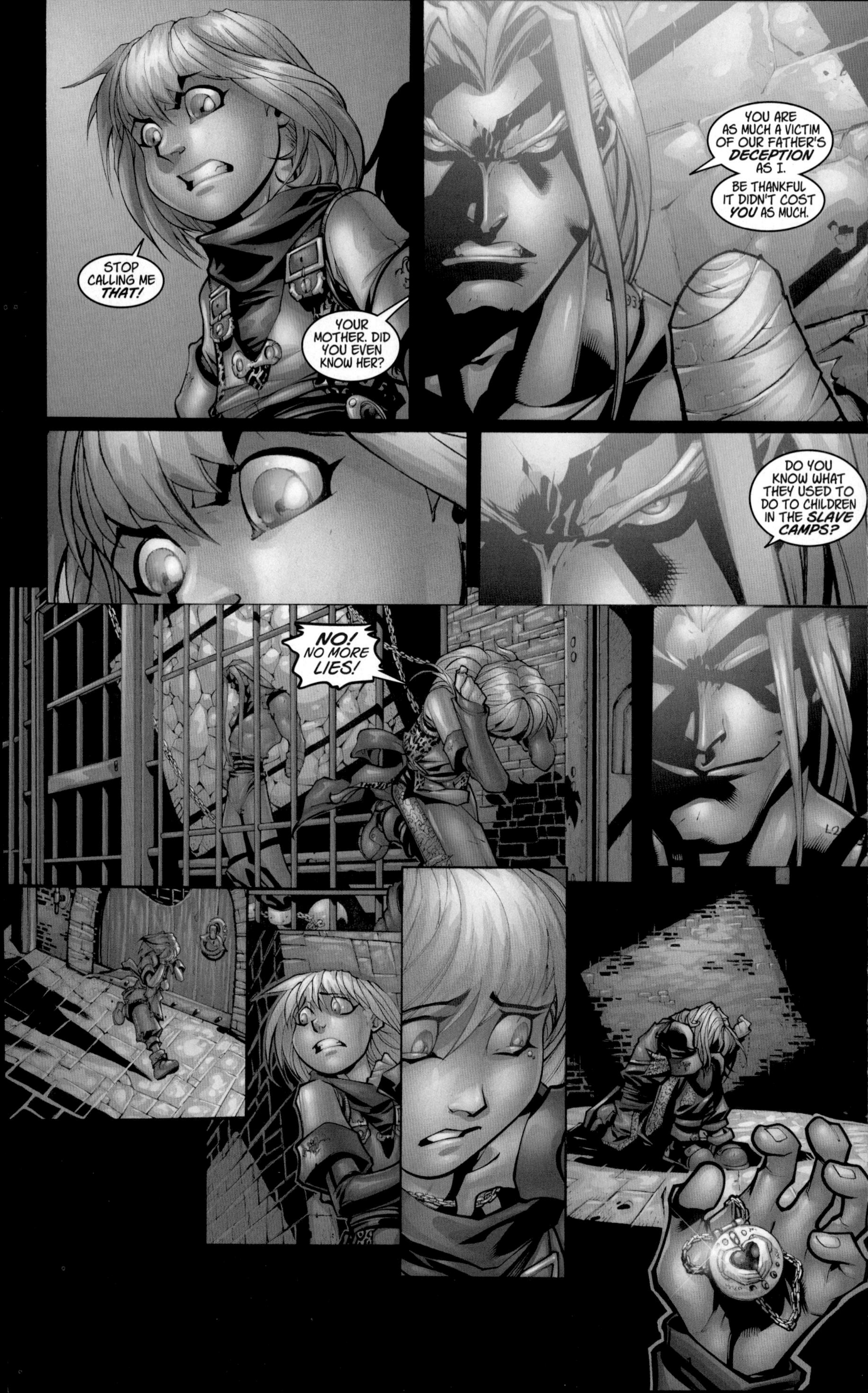

STOP CALLING ME THAT!
YOU ARE AS MUCH A VICTIM OF OUR FATHER'S DECEPTION AS I.
BE THANKFUL IT DIDN'T COST YOU AS MUCH.
YOUR MOTHER. DID YOU EVEN KNOW HER?
DO YOU KNOW WHAT THEY USED TO DO TO CHILDREN IN THE SLAVE CAMPS?
NO! NO MORE LIES!

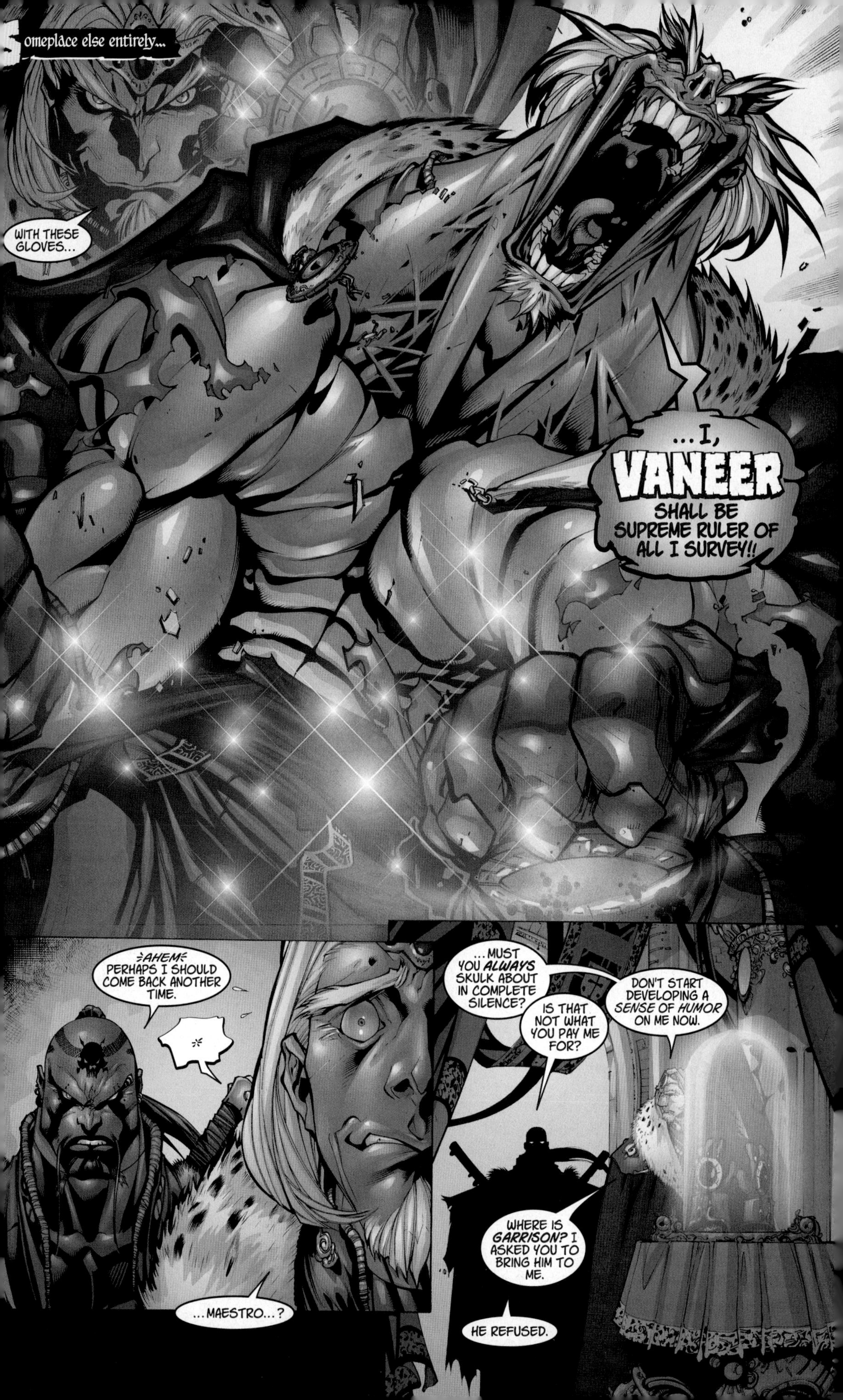
Someplace else entirely...
WITH THESE GLOVES...
...I, VANEER SHALL BE SUPREME RULER OF ALL I SURVEY!!
≈AHEM≈ PERHAPS I SHOULD COME BACK ANOTHER TIME.
...MAESTRO...?
...MUST YOU ALWAYS SKULK ABOUT IN COMPLETE SILENCE?
IS THAT NOT WHAT YOU PAY ME FOR?
DON'T START DEVELOPING A SENSE OF HUMOR ON ME NOW.
WHERE IS GARRISON? I ASKED YOU TO BRING HIM TO ME.
HE REFUSED.

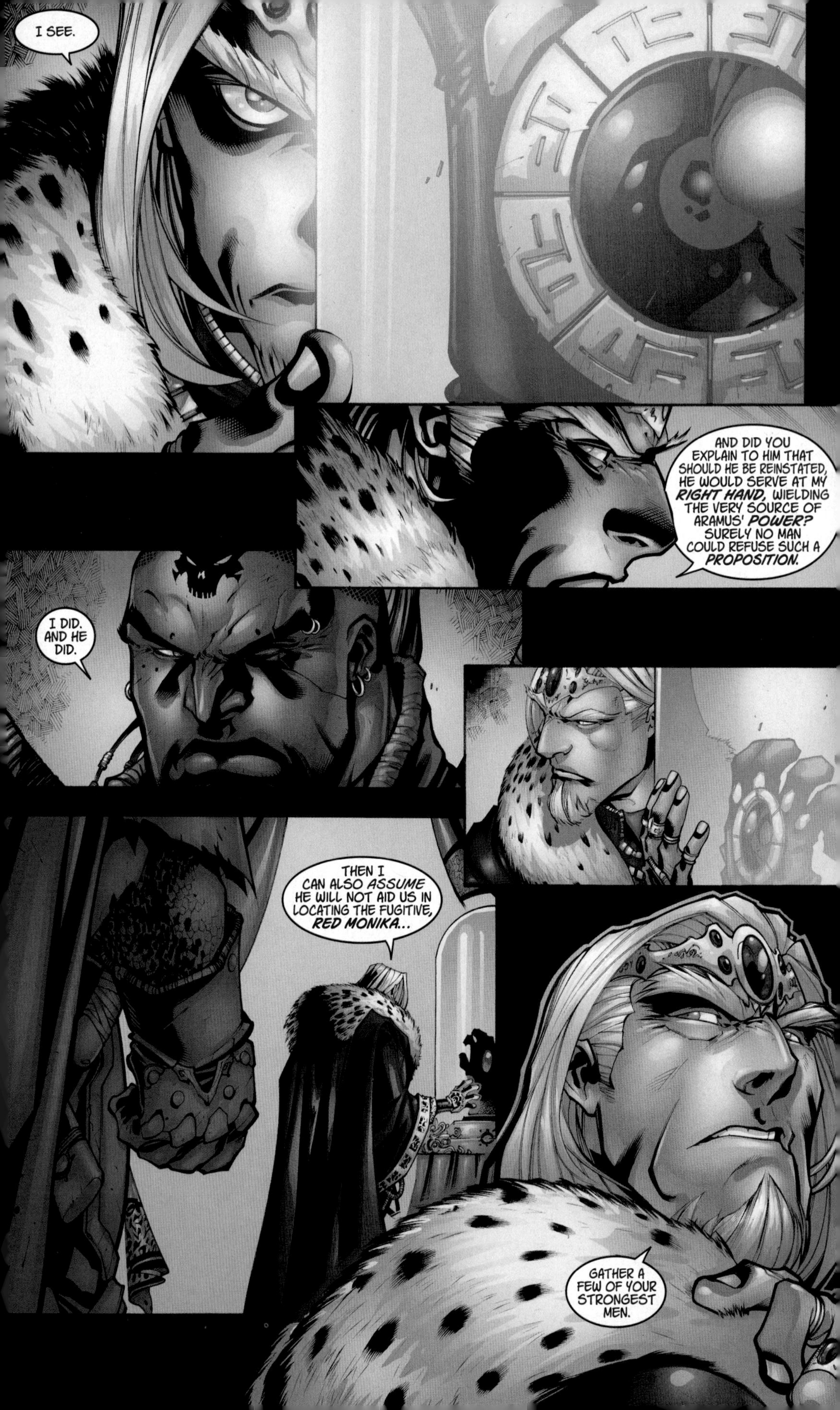
I SEE.
AND DID YOU EXPLAIN TO HIM THAT SHOULD HE BE REINSTATED, HE WOULD SERVE AT MY RIGHT HAND, WIELDING THE VERY SOURCE OF ARAMUS' POWER? SURELY NO MAN COULD REFUSE SUCH A PROPOSITION.
I DID. AND HE DID.
THEN I CAN ALSO ASSUME HE WILL NOT AID US IN LOCATING THE FUGITIVE, RED MONIKA...
GATHER A FEW OF YOUR STRONGEST MEN.

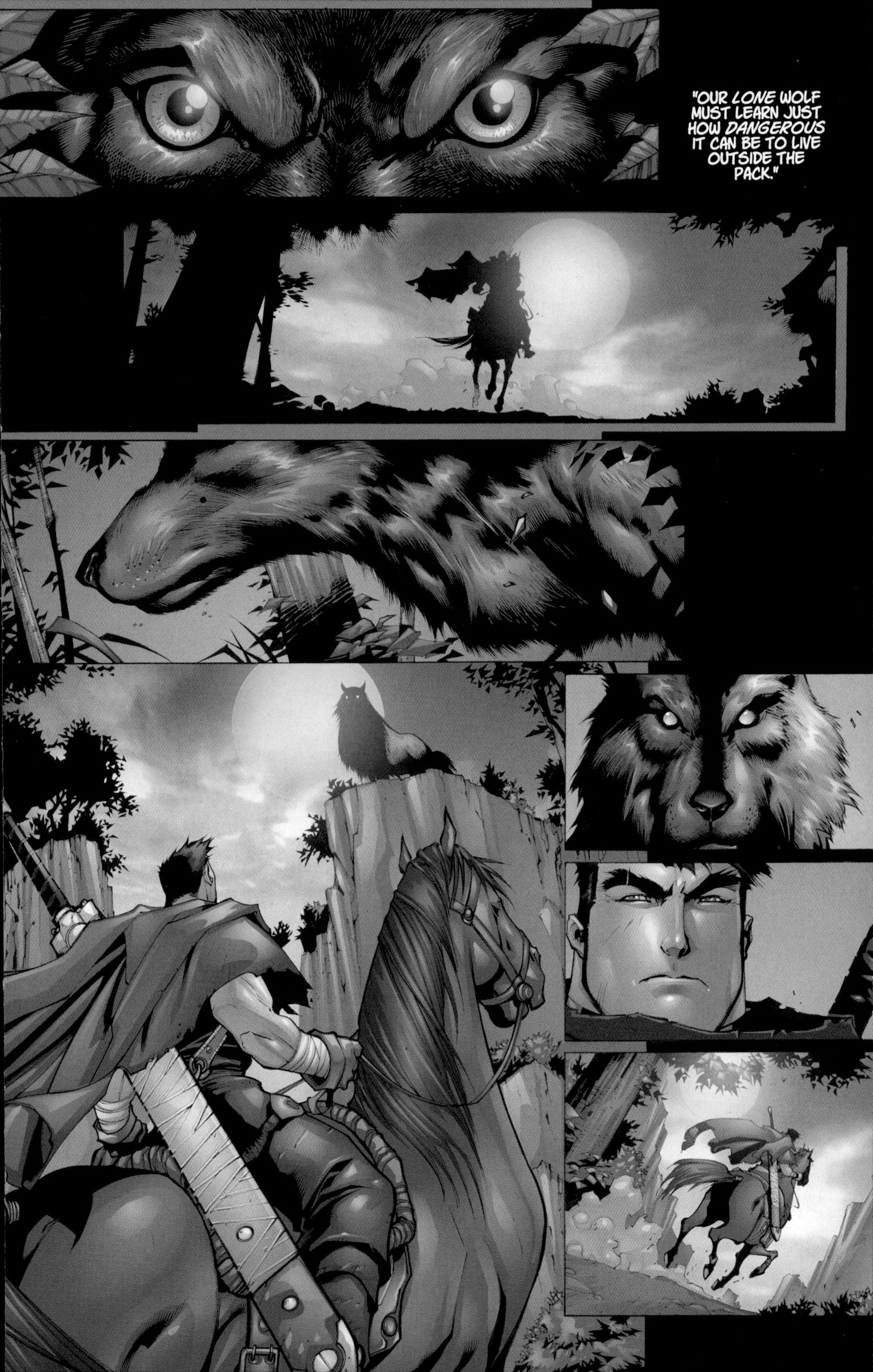
"OUR LONE WOLF MUST LEARN JUST HOW DANGEROUS IT CAN BE TO LIVE OUTSIDE THE PACK."

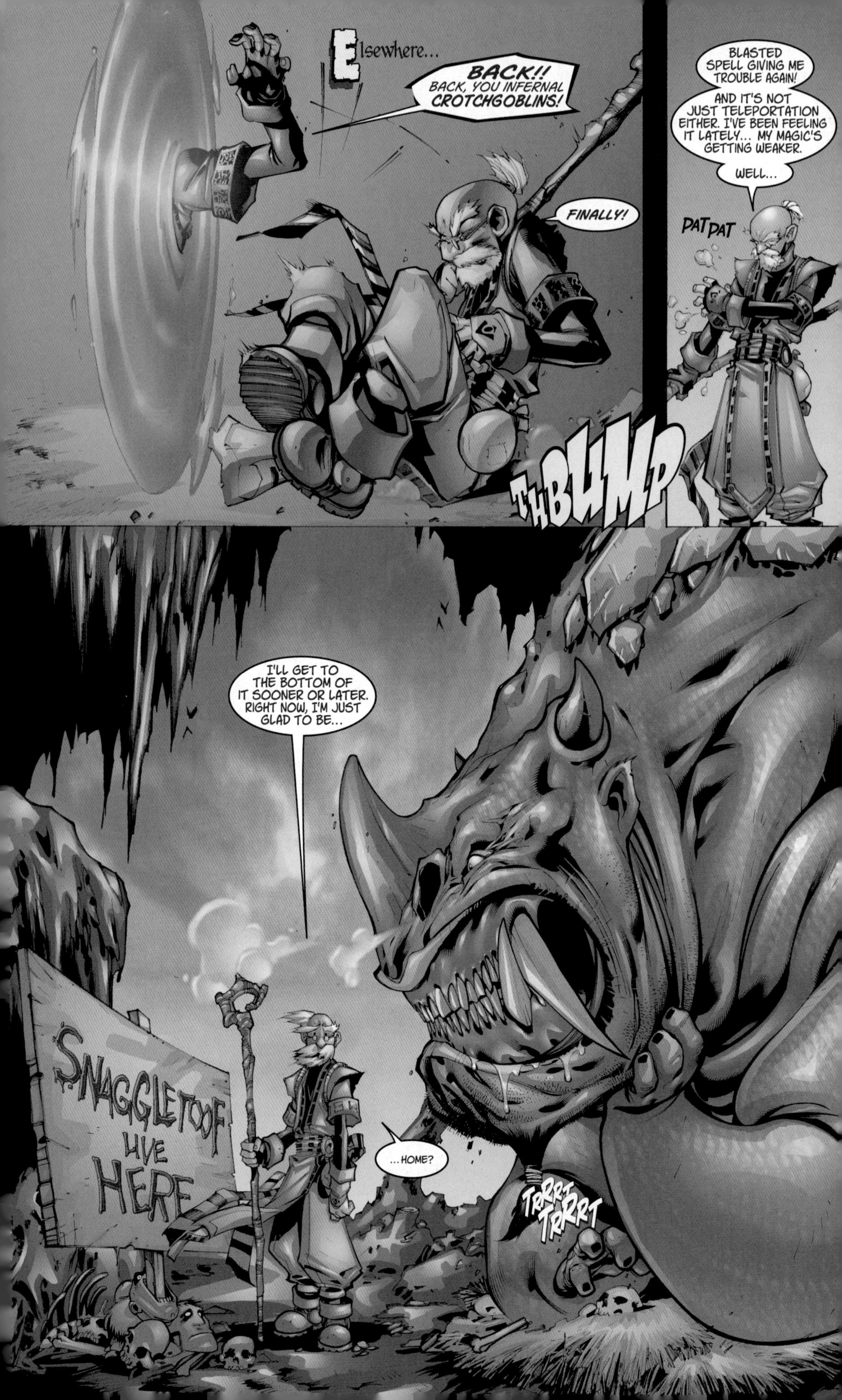
Elsewhere...
BACK!! BACK, YOU INFERNAL CROTCHGOBLINS!
FINALLY!
THBUMP
BLASTED SPELL GIVING ME TROUBLE AGAIN!
AND IT'S NOT JUST TELEPORTATION EITHER. I'VE BEEN FEELING IT LATELY... MY MAGIC'S GETTING WEAKER.
WELL...
PAT PAT
I'LL GET TO THE BOTTOM OF IT SOONER OR LATER. RIGHT NOW, I'M JUST GLAD TO BE...
SNAGGLETOOF LIVE HERE
...HOME?
TRRRT TRRRT

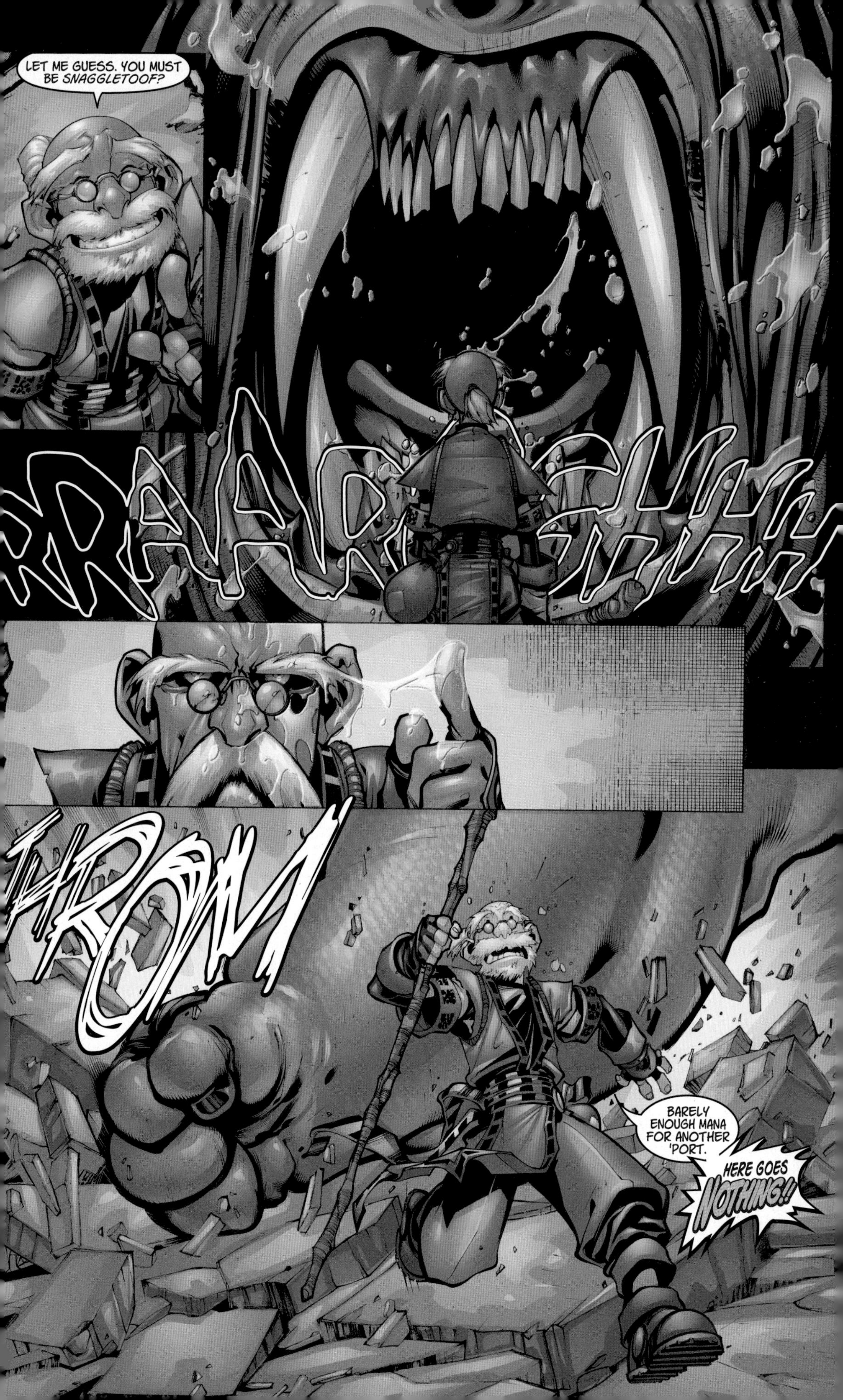
LET ME GUESS. YOU MUST BE SNAGGLETOOF?
RRAAARGHHH
THROOM
BARELY ENOUGH MANA FOR ANOTHER 'PORT.
HERE GOES NOTHING!!

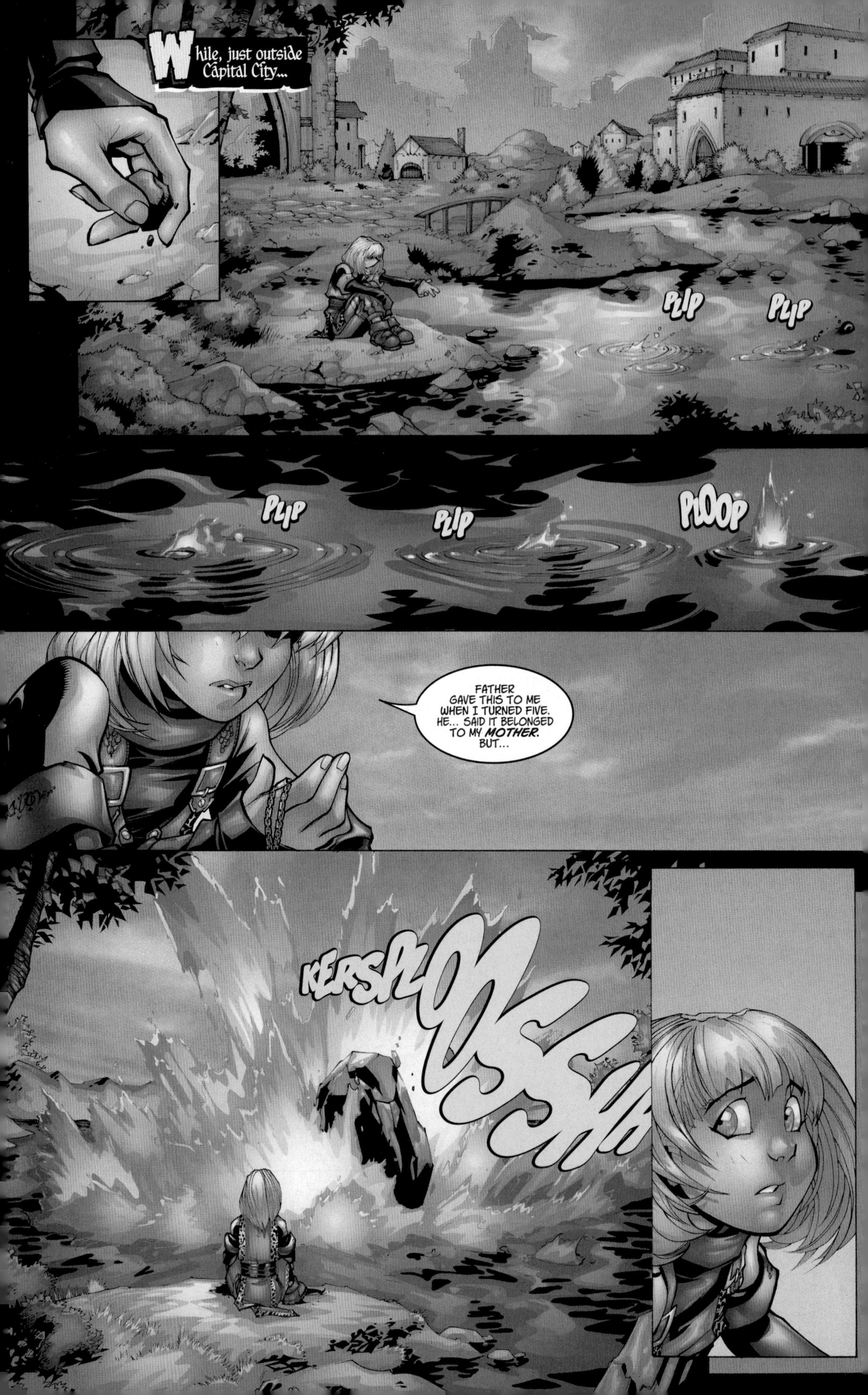
While, just outside Capital City...
PLIP
PLIP
PLIP
PLIP
PLOOP
FATHER GAVE THIS TO ME WHEN I TURNED FIVE. HE... SAID IT BELONGED TO MY *MOTHER.* BUT...
KERSPLOOSCH

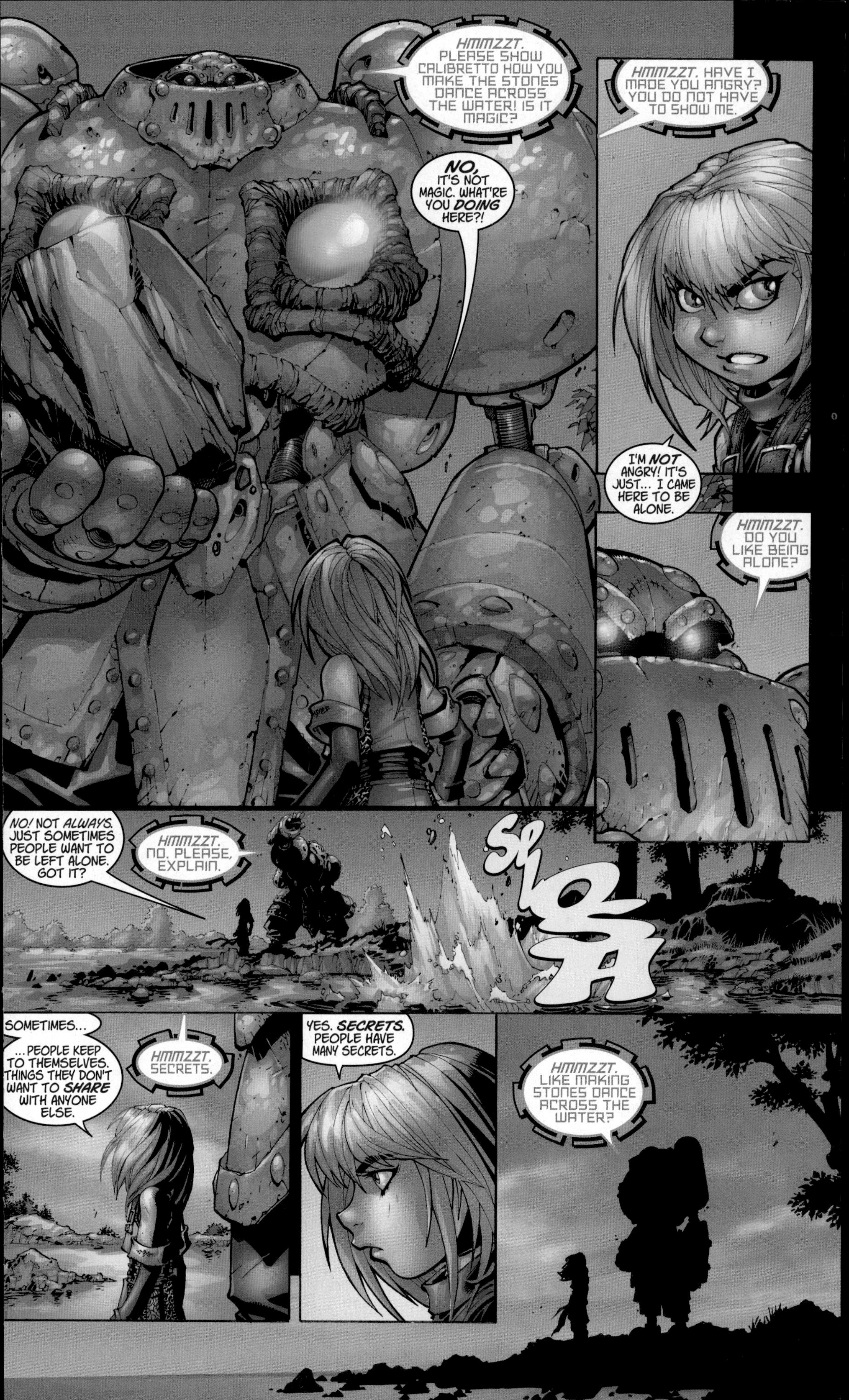
HMMZZT. PLEASE SHOW CALIBRETTO HOW YOU MAKE THE STONES DANCE ACROSS THE WATER! IS IT MAGIC?
NO, IT'S NOT MAGIC. WHAT'RE YOU DOING HERE?!
HMMZZT. HAVE I MADE YOU ANGRY? YOU DO NOT HAVE TO SHOW ME.
I'M NOT ANGRY! IT'S JUST... I CAME HERE TO BE ALONE.
HMMZZT. DO YOU LIKE BEING ALONE?
NO! NOT ALWAYS. JUST SOMETIMES PEOPLE WANT TO BE LEFT ALONE. GOT IT?
HMMZZT. NO. PLEASE, EXPLAIN.
SPLOSA
SOMETIMES...
...PEOPLE KEEP TO THEMSELVES. THINGS THEY DON'T WANT TO SHARE WITH ANYONE ELSE.
HMMZZT. SECRETS.
YES. SECRETS. PEOPLE HAVE MANY SECRETS.
HMMZZT. LIKE MAKING STONES DANCE ACROSS THE WATER?

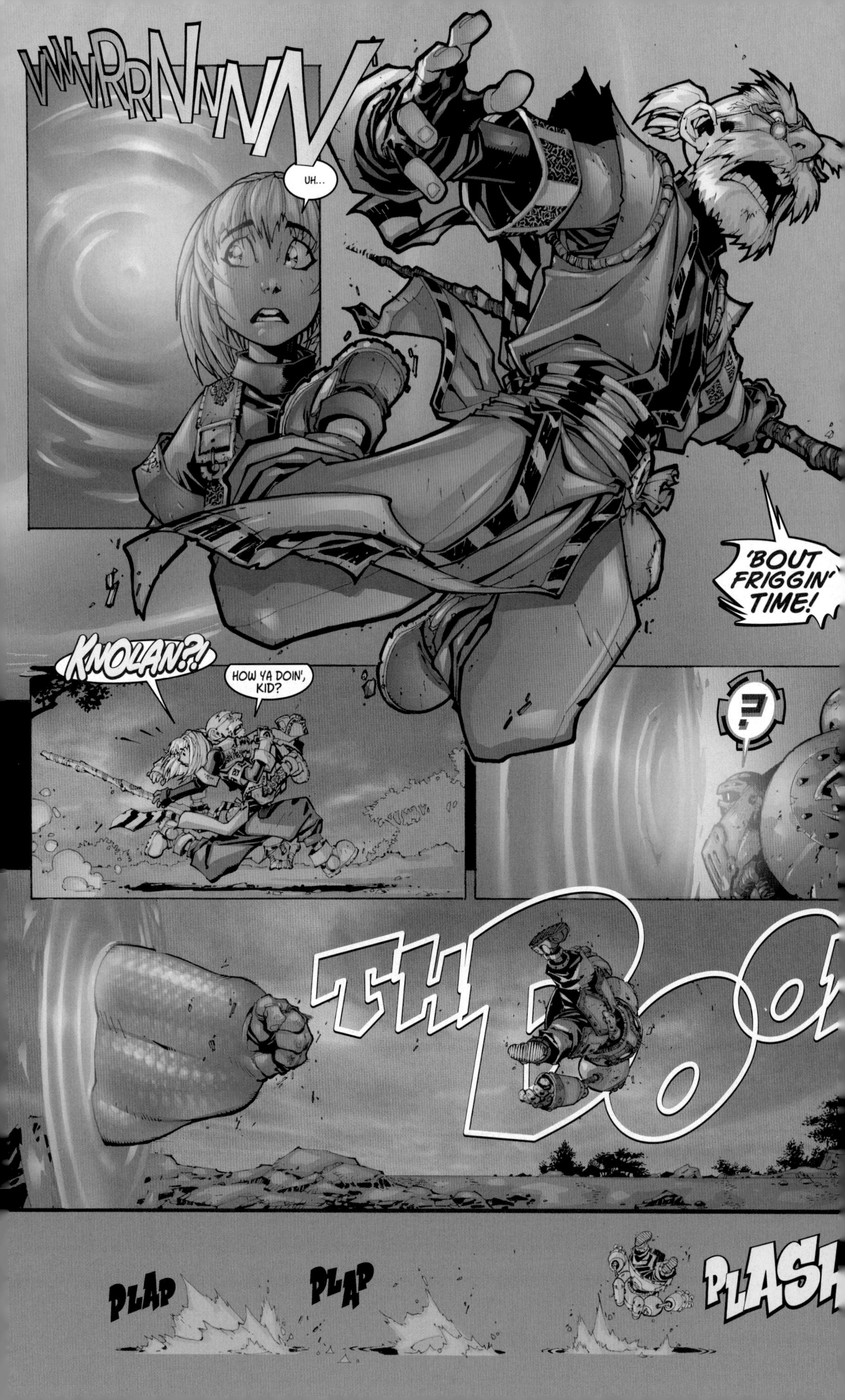
VVVVVRRRNNNNN
UH...
'BOUT FRIGGIN' TIME!
KNOLAN?!
HOW YA DOIN', KID?
?
THBOO
PLAP
PLAP
PLASH

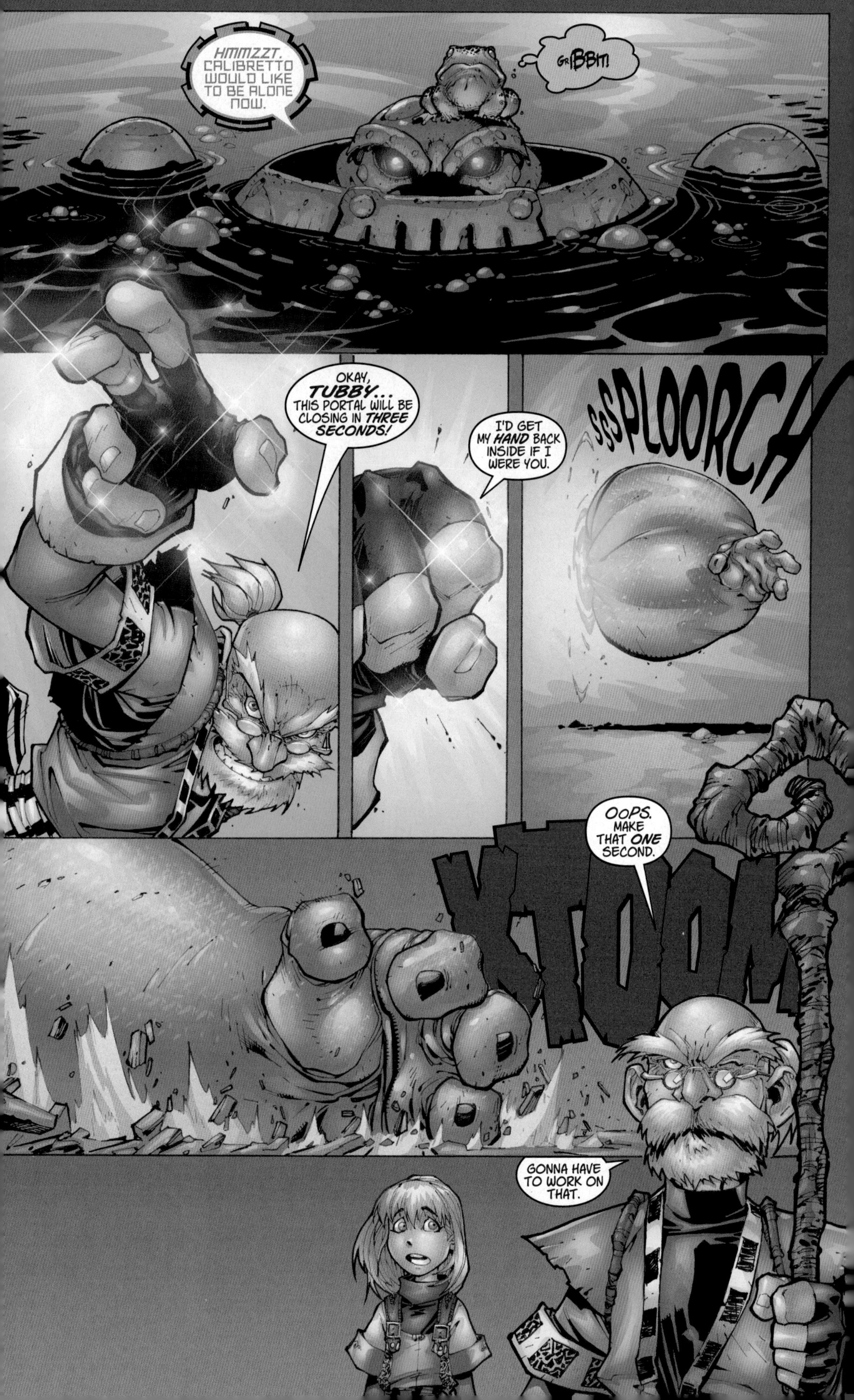
HMMZZT. CALIBRETTO WOULD LIKE TO BE ALONE NOW.
GRIBBIT!
OKAY, TUBBY... THIS PORTAL WILL BE CLOSING IN THREE SECONDS!
I'D GET MY HAND BACK INSIDE IF I WERE YOU.
SSSPLOORCH
OOPS. MAKE THAT ONE SECOND.
KTOOM
GONNA HAVE TO WORK ON THAT.

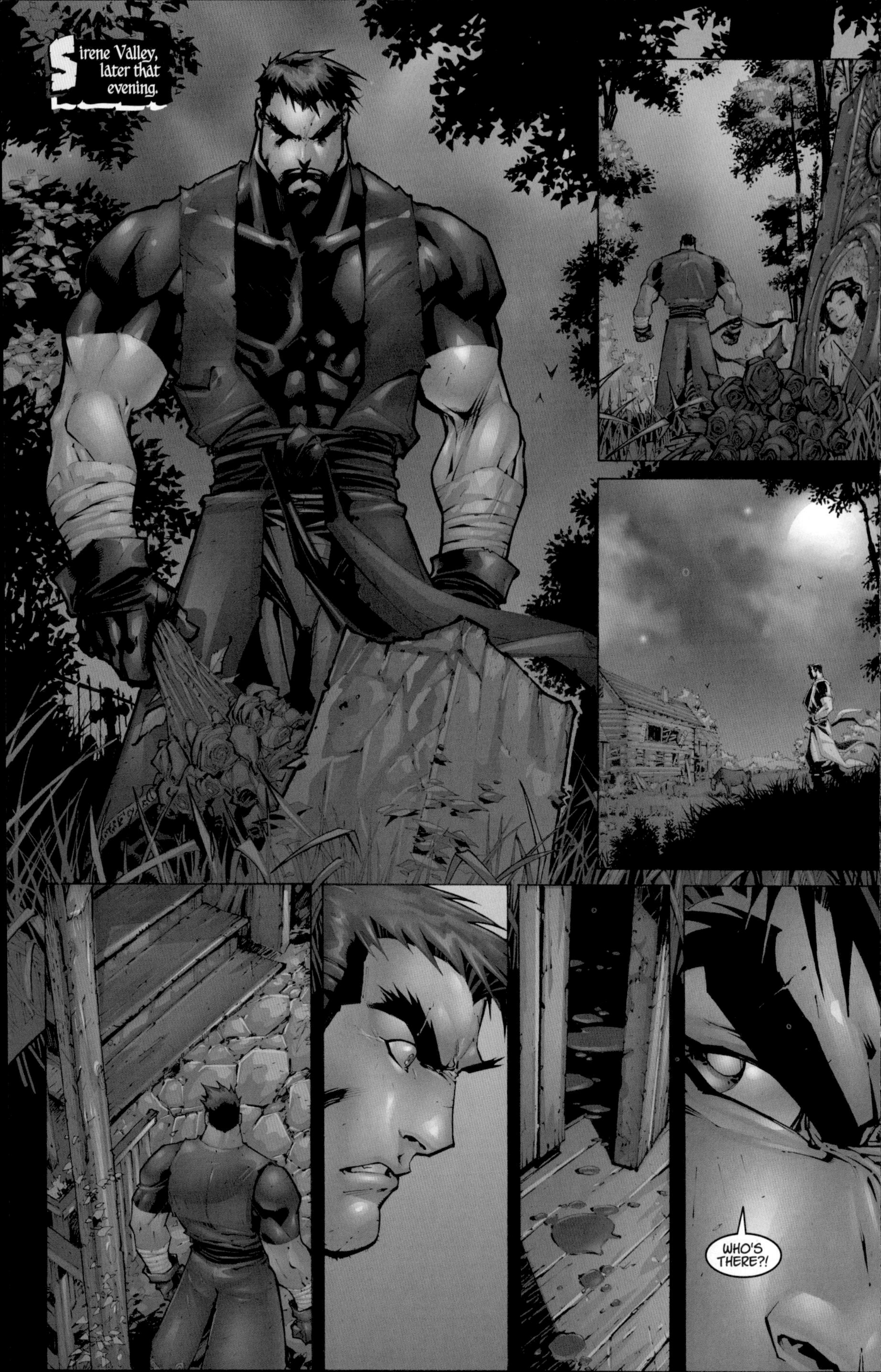
Sirene Valley, later that evening.
WHO'S THERE?!

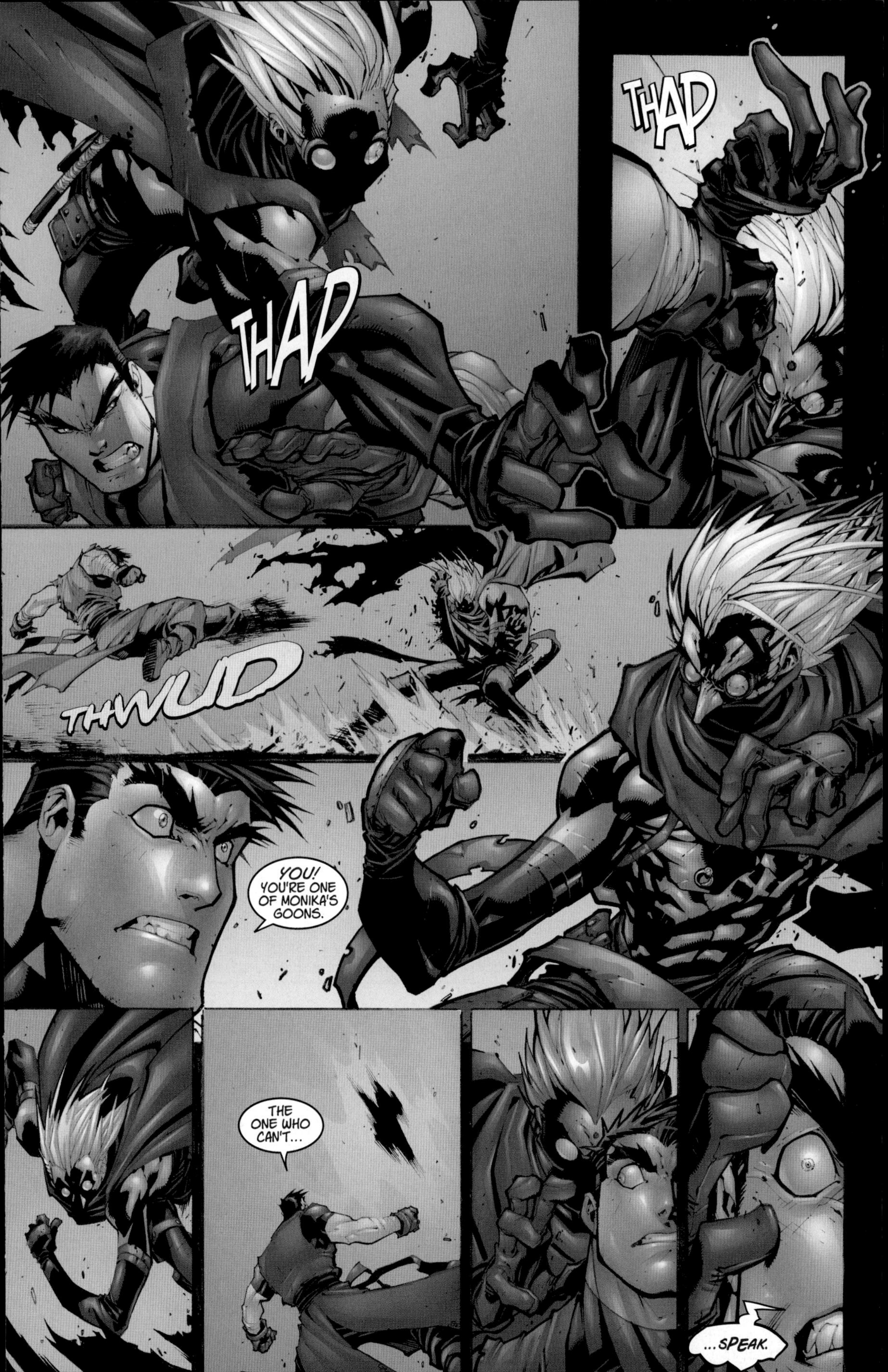
THAP
THAP
THWUD
YOU! YOU'RE ONE OF MONIKA'S GOONS.
THE ONE WHO CAN'T...
...SPEAK.

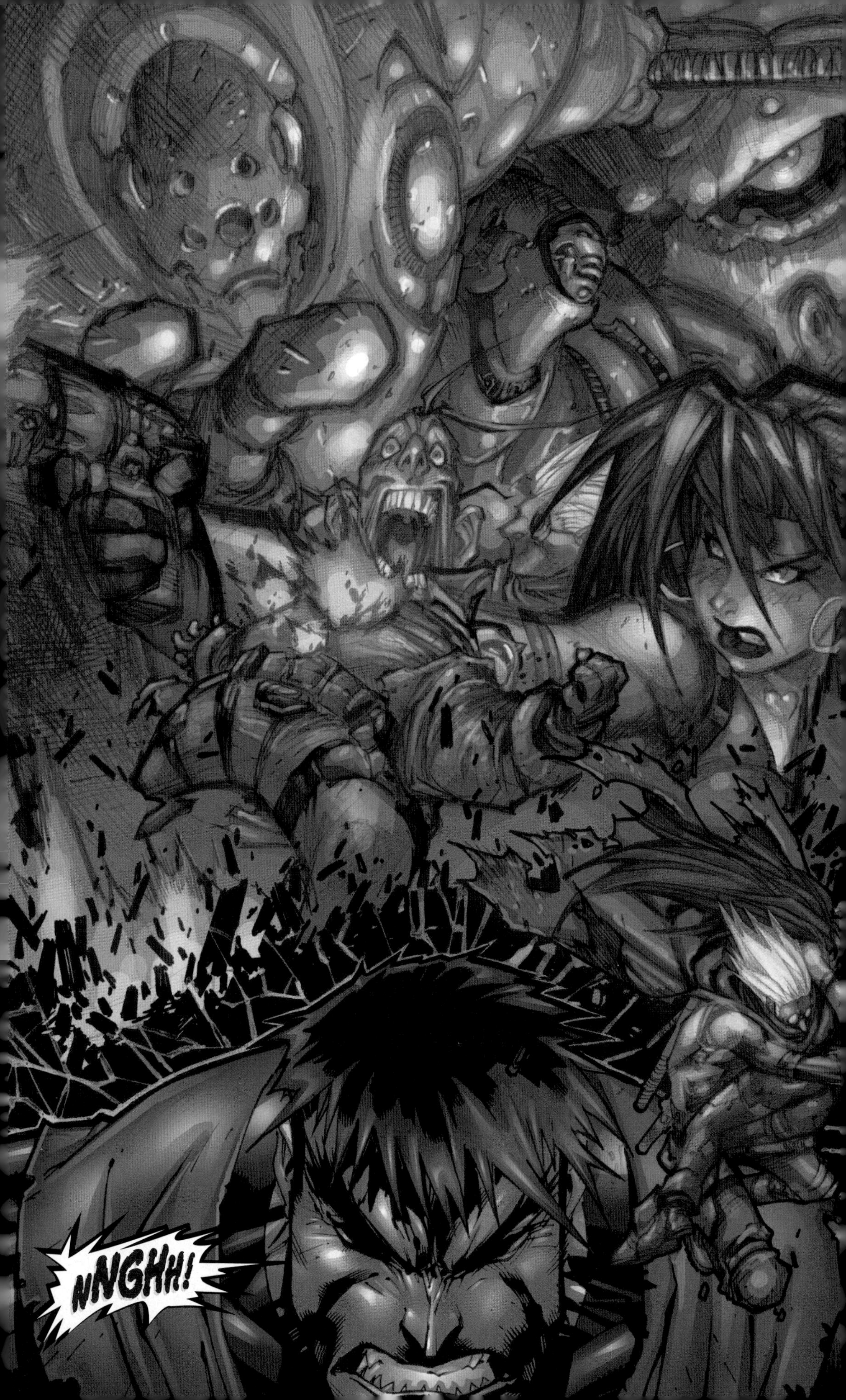
NNGHH!

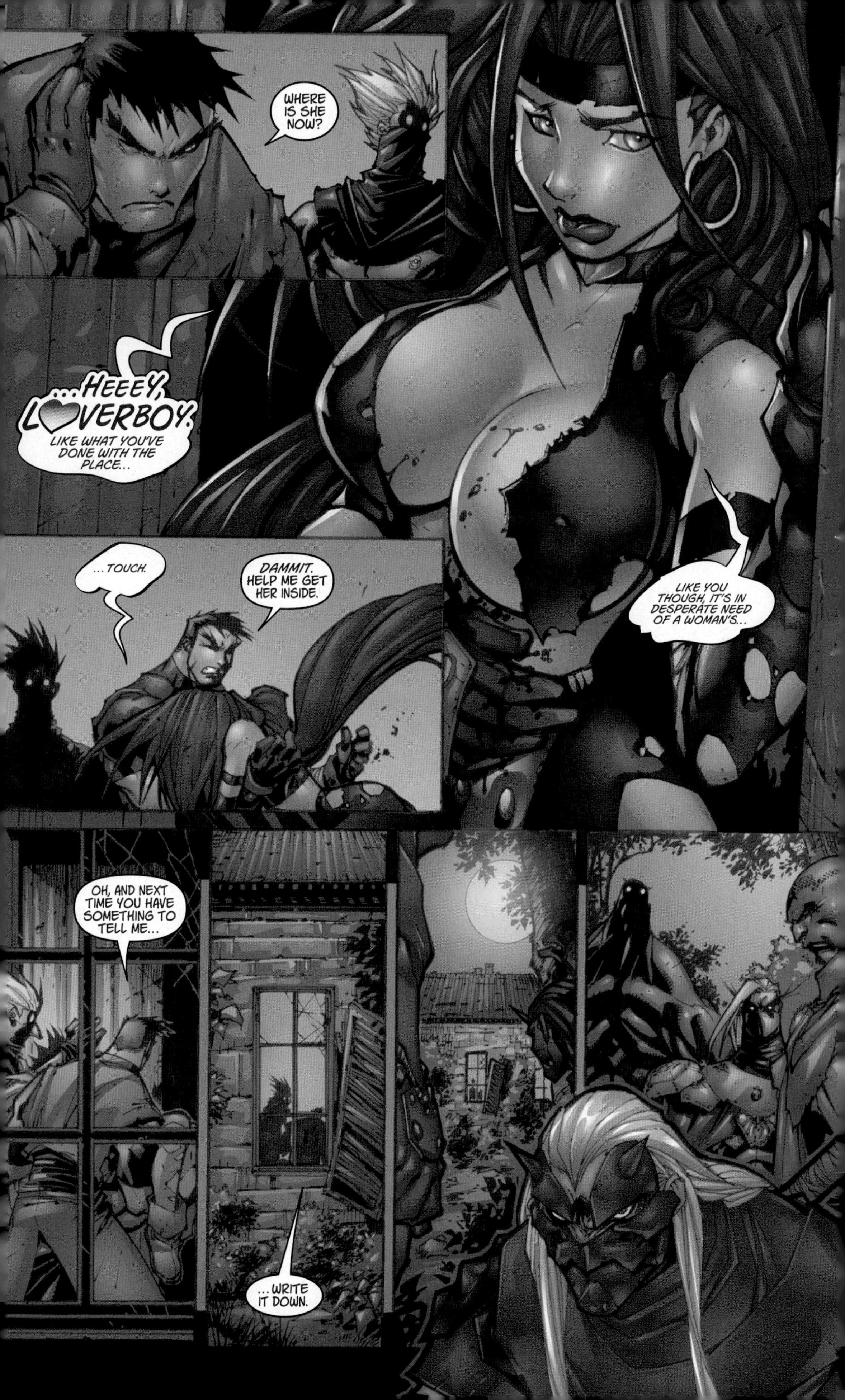
WHERE IS SHE NOW?
...HEEEY, LOVERBOY.
LIKE WHAT YOU'VE DONE WITH THE PLACE...
LIKE YOU THOUGH, IT'S IN DESPERATE NEED OF A WOMAN'S...
...TOUCH.
DAMMIT. HELP ME GET HER INSIDE.
OH, AND NEXT TIME YOU HAVE SOMETHING TO TELL ME...
...WRITE IT DOWN.

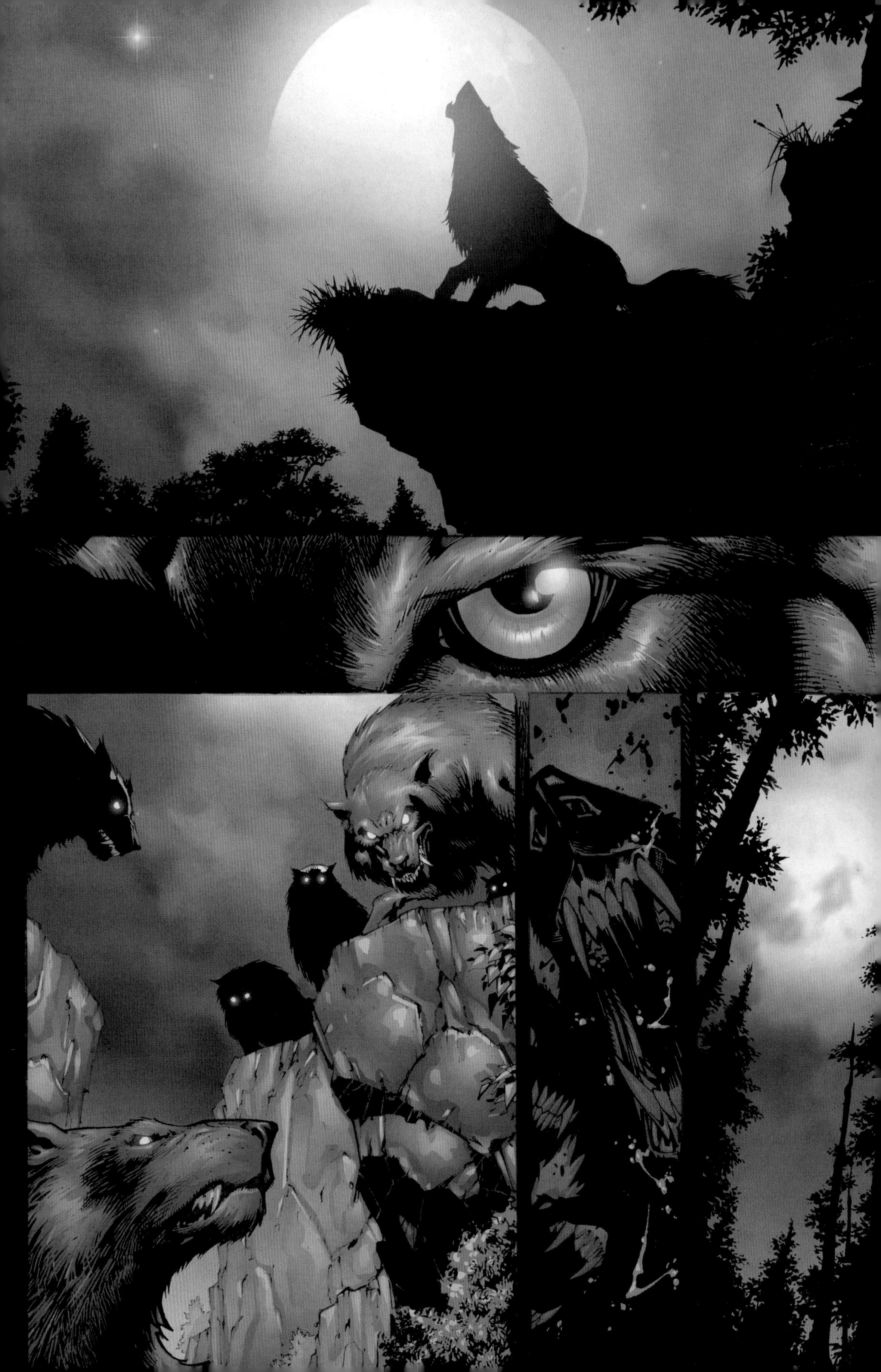

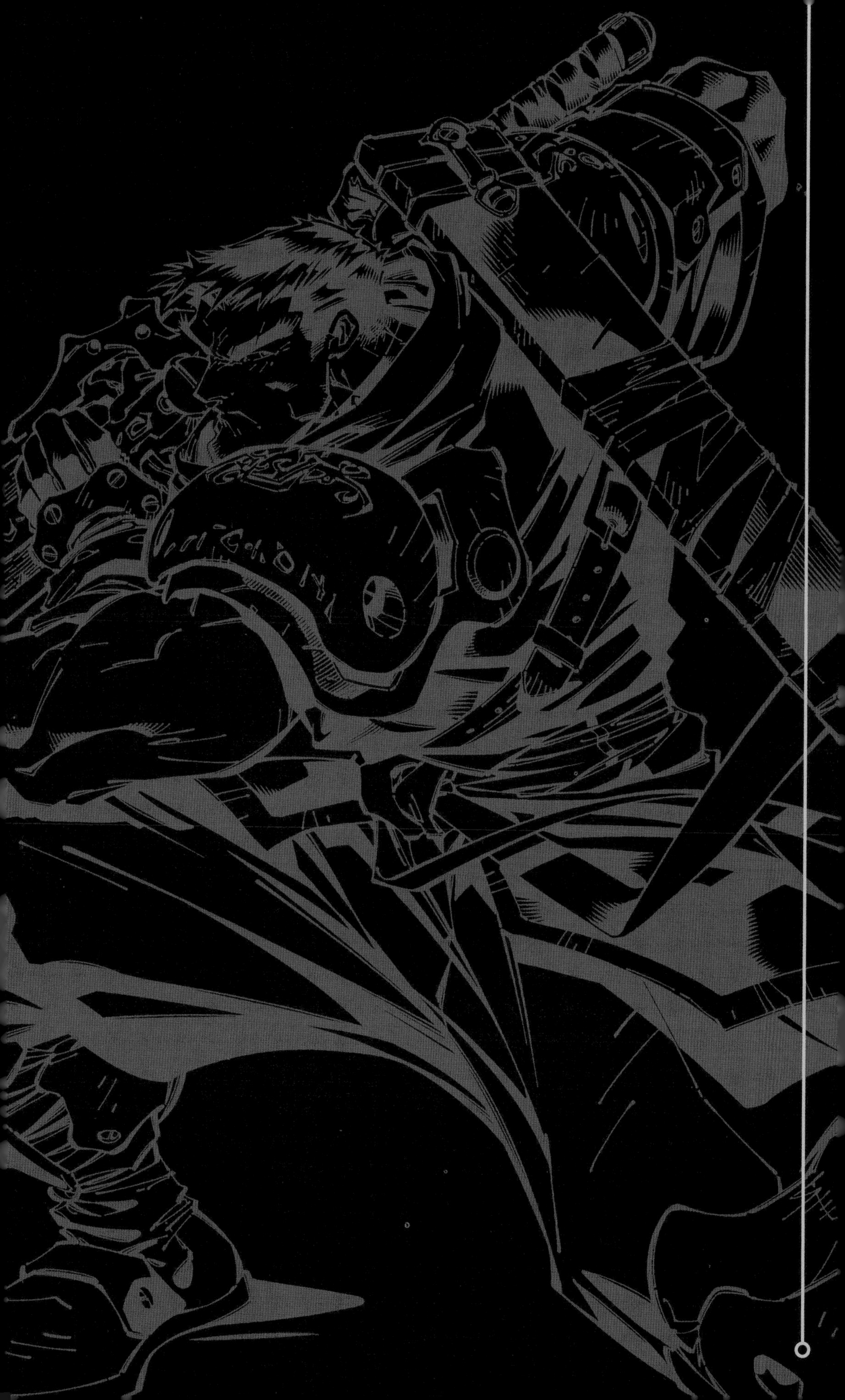

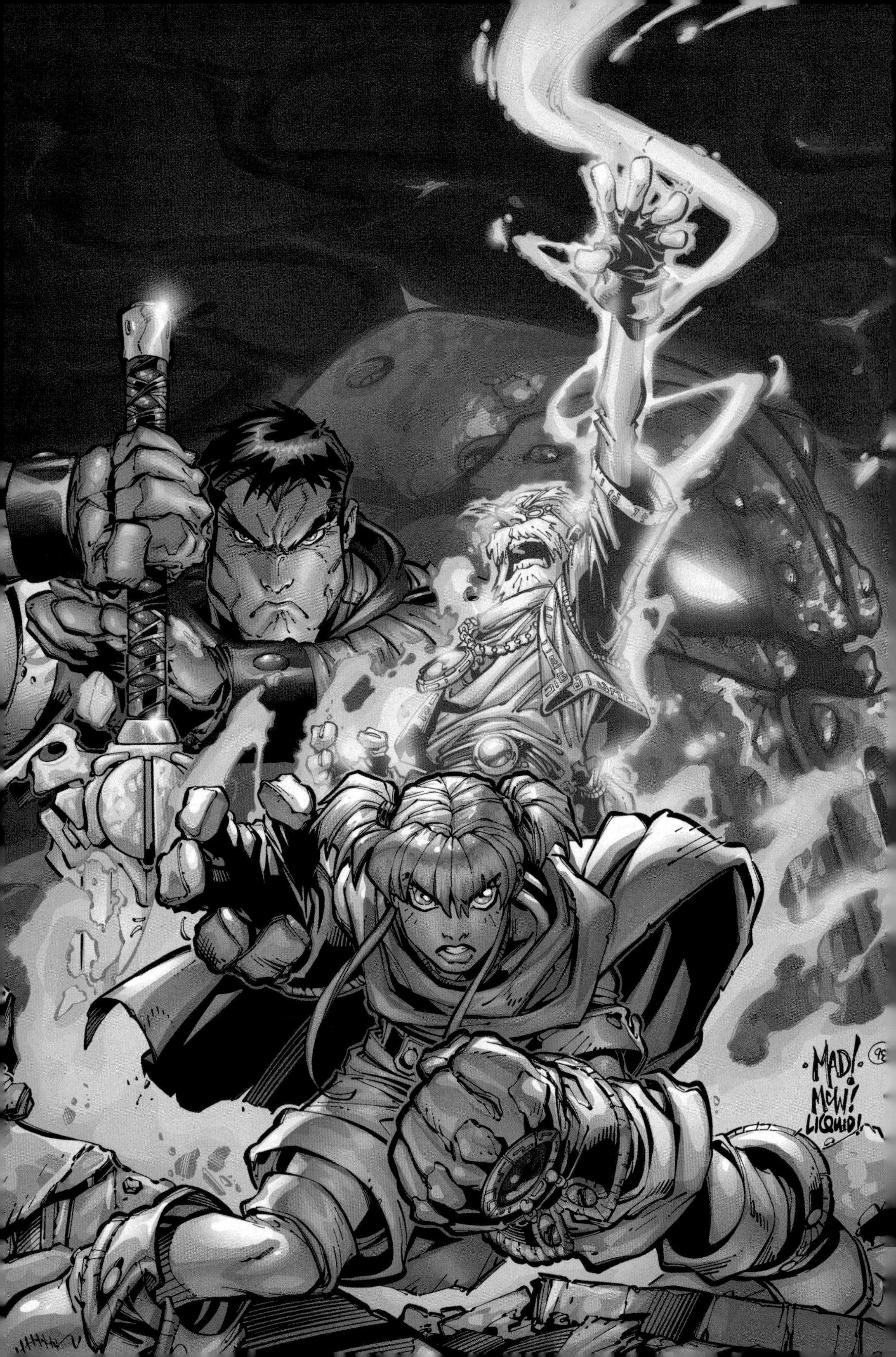
MAD! 98
McW!
LIQUID!

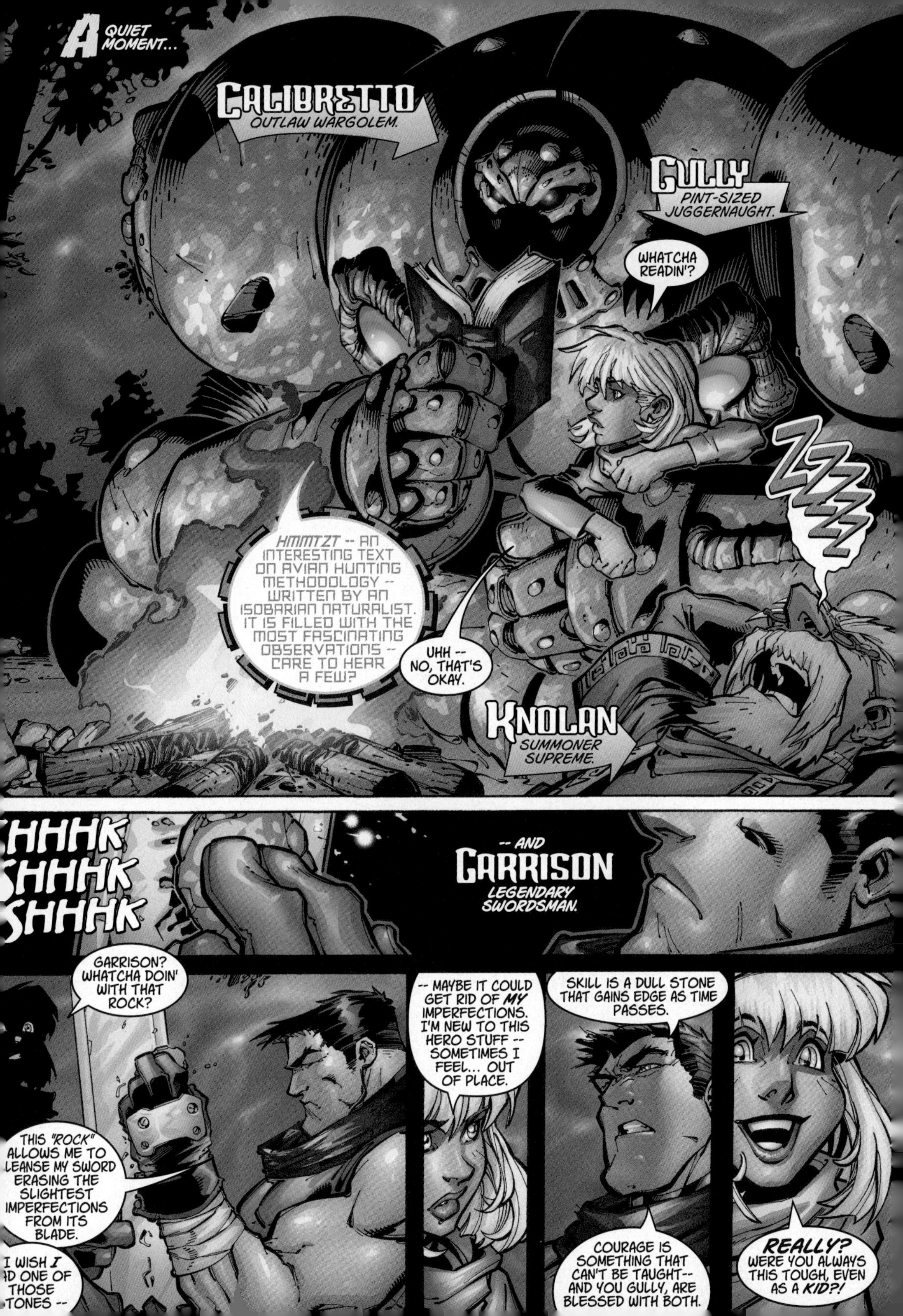
A QUIET MOMENT...
CALIBRETTO
OUTLAW WARGOLEM.
GULLY
PINT-SIZED JUGGERNAUGHT.
WHATCHA READIN'?
HMMTZT -- AN INTERESTING TEXT ON AVIAN HUNTING METHODOLOGY -- WRITTEN BY AN ISOBARIAN NATURALIST. IT IS FILLED WITH THE MOST FASCINATING OBSERVATIONS -- CARE TO HEAR A FEW?
UHH -- NO, THAT'S OKAY.
ZZZZ
KNOLAN
SUMMONER SUPREME.
SHHHK SHHHK SHHHK
-- AND
GARRISON
LEGENDARY SWORDSMAN.
GARRISON? WHATCHA DOIN' WITH THAT ROCK?
THIS "ROCK" ALLOWS ME TO CLEANSE MY SWORD ERASING THE SLIGHTEST IMPERFECTIONS FROM ITS BLADE.
I WISH I HAD ONE OF THOSE STONES --
-- MAYBE IT COULD GET RID OF MY IMPERFECTIONS. I'M NEW TO THIS HERO STUFF -- SOMETIMES I FEEL... OUT OF PLACE.
SKILL IS A DULL STONE THAT GAINS EDGE AS TIME PASSES.
COURAGE IS SOMETHING THAT CAN'T BE TAUGHT-- AND YOU GULLY, ARE BLESSED WITH BOTH.
REALLY? WERE YOU ALWAYS THIS TOUGH, EVEN AS A KID?!

IT'S NOT ALWAYS WHO'S THE TOUGHEST, GULLY. AS A MARTIAL PALADIN, I'VE BEEN TRAINED IN ALL FORMS OF COMBAT.

-- AND HAVE ENDURED ENDLESS HOURS OF PHYSICAL CONDITIONING -- BUT GOING WITH YOUR *GUT* WAS NOT IN THE CURRICULUM -- IN FACT, IT WAS FROWNED UPON. MY FINAL TRAINING MISSION WAS TO HUNT DOWN AND KILL A RAMPAGING BEAST CALLED THE *LUNDARA*. DURING OUR BATTLE, CERTAIN PIECES DIDN'T SEEM TO FIT -- SO I TRUSTED MY INSTINCTS, AND LOWERED MY GUARD, STOPPING THE FIGHT. THE MONSTER WE HAD THOUGHT HIM TO BE, BUT A PEACEFUL, INTELLIGENT CREATURE WHOSE ACTIONS WERE GREATLY MISUNDERSTOOD. I WAS REPRIMANDED FOR DISOBEYING ORDERS -- BUT THAT DAY, I ALSO *GAINED* SOMETHING. TO THIS DAY, THE LUNDARA REMAINS MY MOST CHERISHED AND TRUSTED FRIEND. SO YOU SEE, GULLY, KNOWING *WHEN* TO FIGHT IS AS IMPORTANT AS KNOWING *HOW* TO FIGHT!

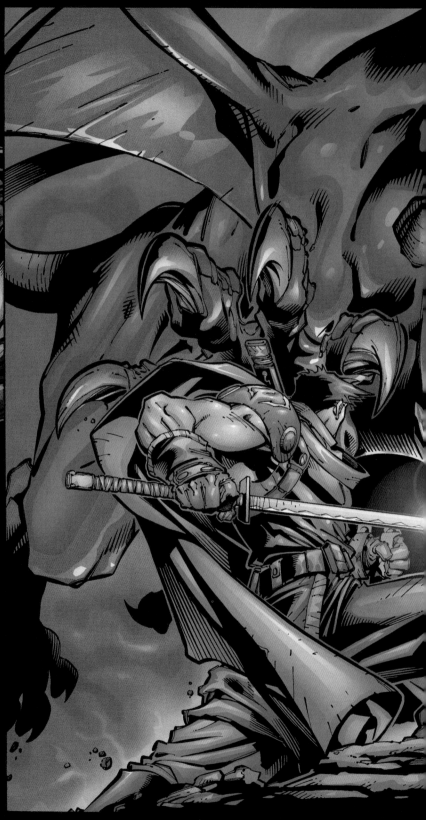

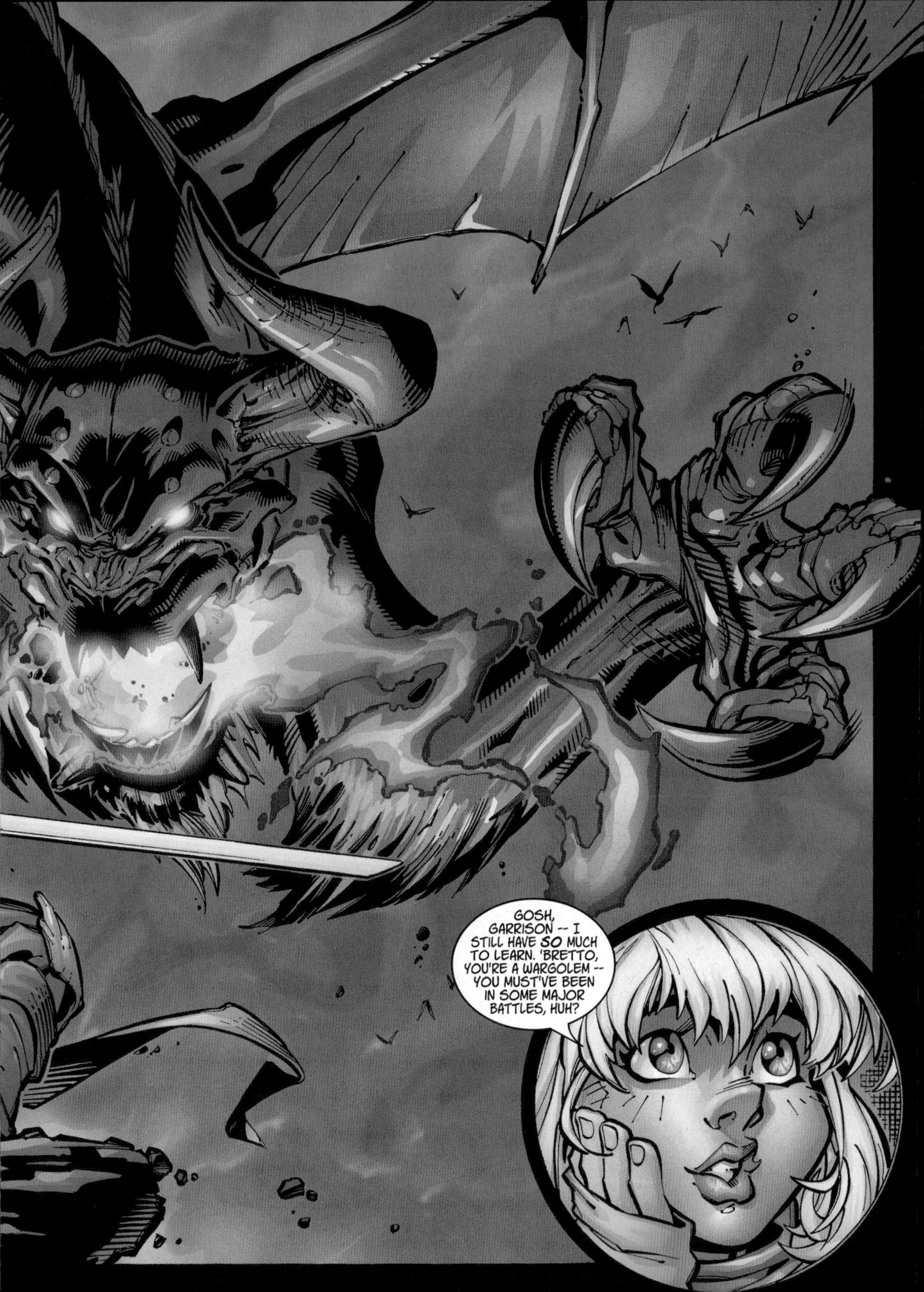
GOSH, GARRISON -- I STILL HAVE SO MUCH TO LEARN. 'BRETTO, YOU'RE A WARGOLEM -- YOU MUST'VE BEEN IN SOME MAJOR BATTLES, HUH?

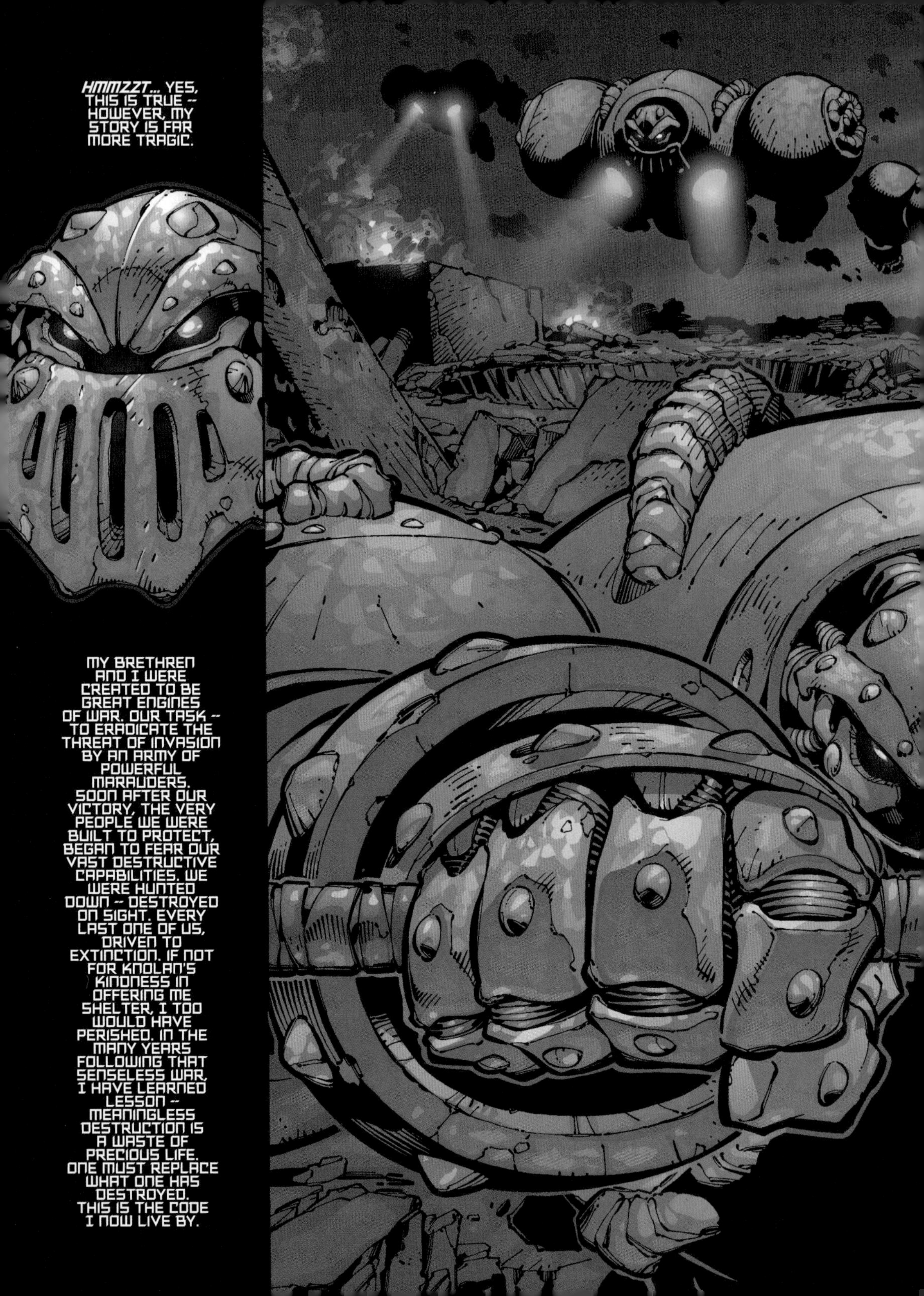
HMMZZT... YES, THIS IS TRUE -- HOWEVER, MY STORY IS FAR MORE TRAGIC.
MY BRETHREN AND I WERE CREATED TO BE GREAT ENGINES OF WAR. OUR TASK -- TO ERADICATE THE THREAT OF INVASION BY AN ARMY OF POWERFUL MARAUDERS. SOON AFTER OUR VICTORY, THE VERY PEOPLE WE WERE BUILT TO PROTECT, BEGAN TO FEAR OUR VAST DESTRUCTIVE CAPABILITIES. WE WERE HUNTED DOWN -- DESTROYED ON SIGHT. EVERY LAST ONE OF US, DRIVEN TO EXTINCTION. IF NOT FOR KNOLAN'S KINDNESS IN OFFERING ME SHELTER, I TOO WOULD HAVE PERISHED. IN THE MANY YEARS FOLLOWING THAT SENSELESS WAR, I HAVE LEARNED LESSON -- MEANINGLESS DESTRUCTION IS A WASTE OF PRECIOUS LIFE. ONE MUST REPLACE WHAT ONE HAS DESTROYED. THIS IS THE CODE I NOW LIVE BY.

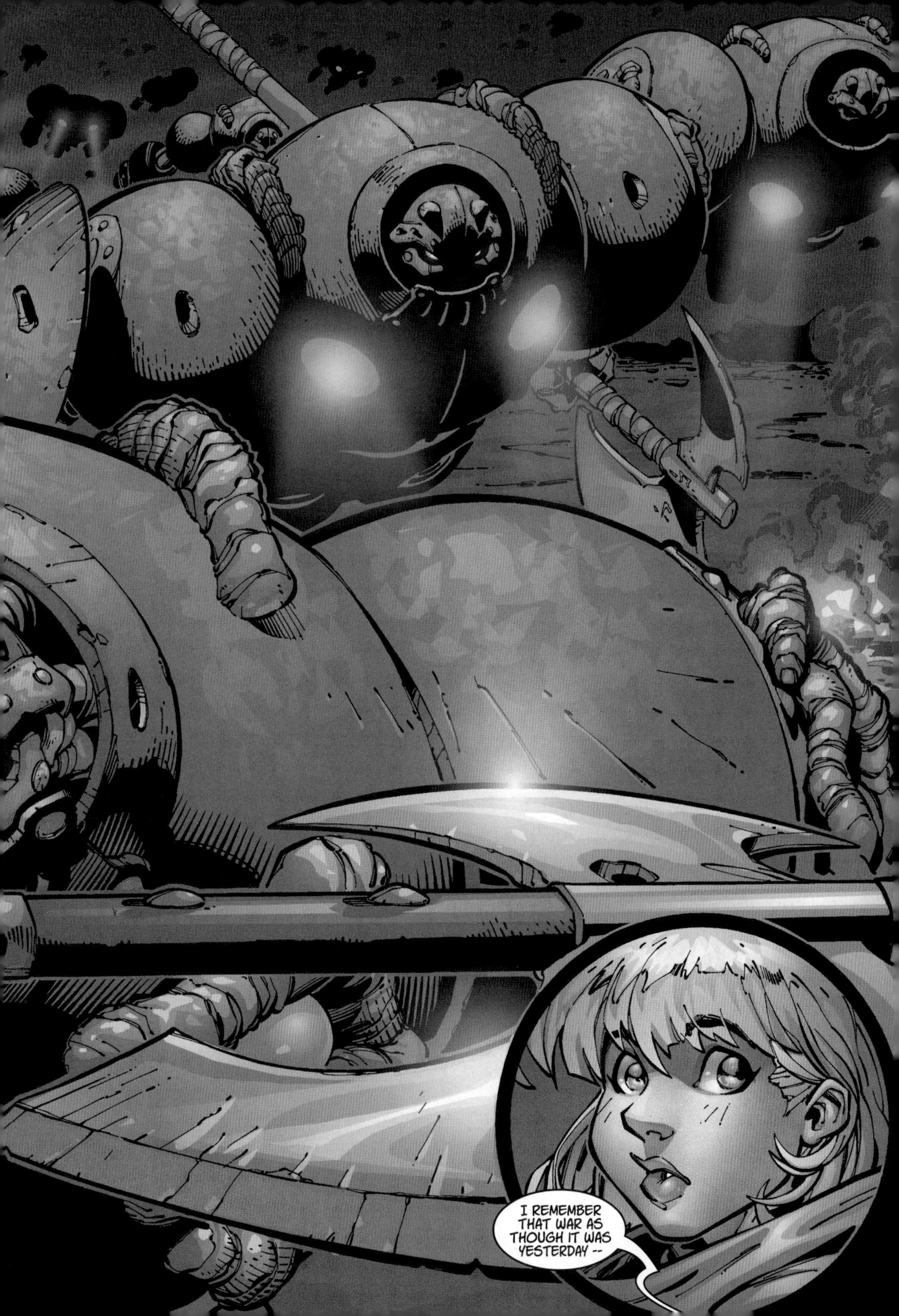
I REMEMBER THAT WAR AS THOUGH IT WAS YESTERDAY --

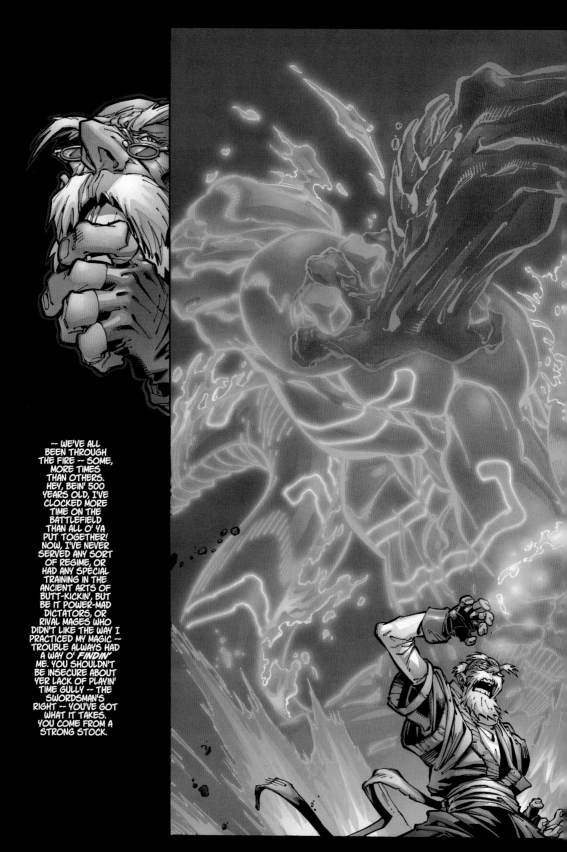

-- WE'VE ALL BEEN THROUGH THE FIRE -- SOME, MORE TIMES THAN OTHERS. HEY, BEIN' 500 YEARS OLD, I'VE CLOCKED MORE TIME ON THE BATTLEFIELD THAN ALL O' YA PUT TOGETHER! NOW, I'VE NEVER SERVED ANY SORT OF REGIME, OR HAD ANY SPECIAL TRAINING IN THE ANCIENT ARTS OF BUTT-KICKIN', BUT BE IT POWER-MAD DICTATORS, OR RIVAL MAGES WHO DIDN'T LIKE THE WAY I PRACTICED MY MAGIC -- TROUBLE ALWAYS HAD A WAY O' *FINDIN'* ME. YOU SHOULDN'T BE INSECURE ABOUT YER LACK OF PLAYIN' TIME GULLY -- THE SWORDSMAN'S RIGHT -- YOU'VE GOT WHAT IT TAKES. YOU COME FROM A STRONG STOCK.

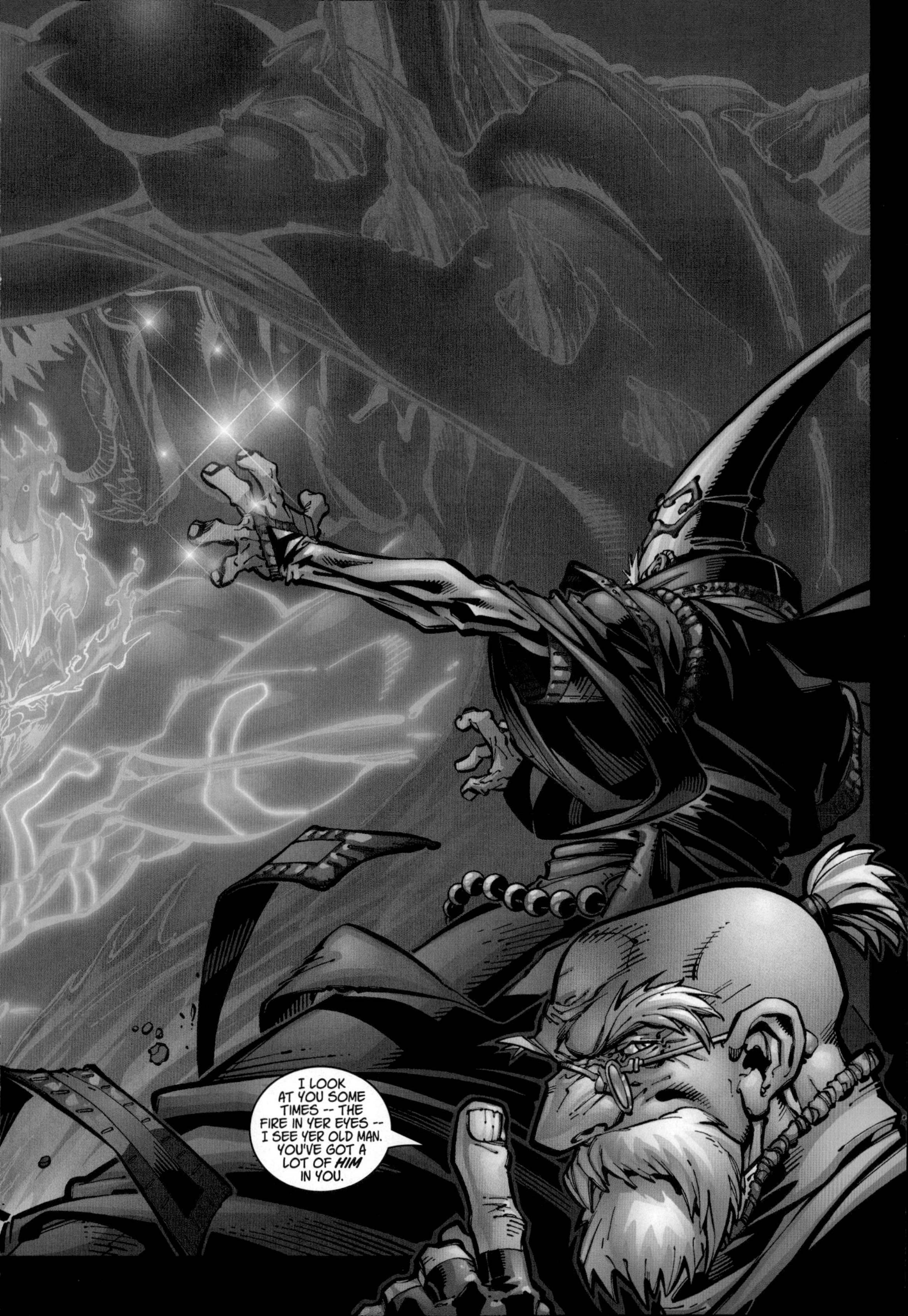
I LOOK AT YOU SOME TIMES -- THE FIRE IN YER EYES -- I SEE YER OLD MAN. YOU'VE GOT A LOT OF *HIM* IN YOU.

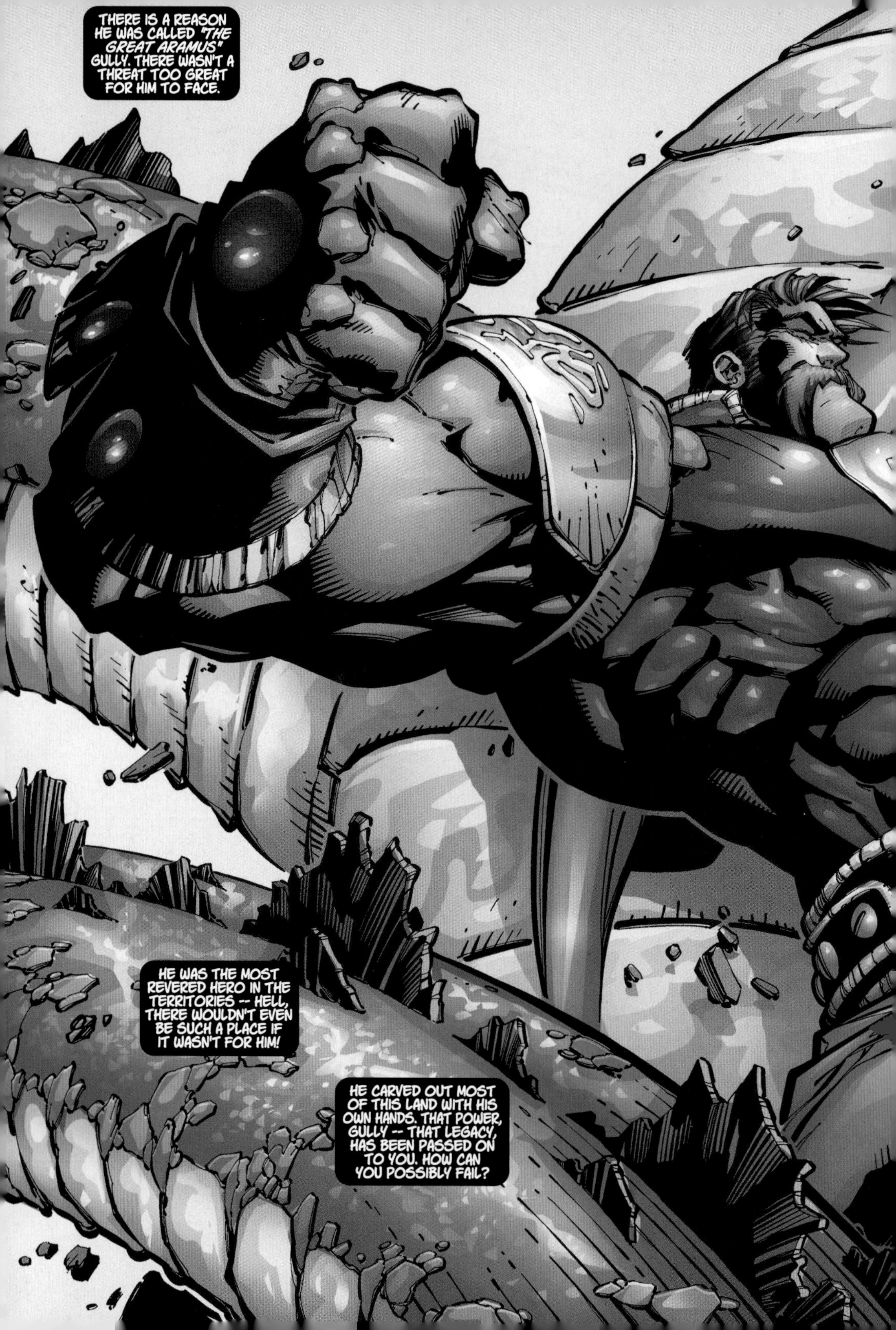
THERE IS A REASON HE WAS CALLED "THE GREAT ARAMUS" GULLY. THERE WASN'T A THREAT TOO GREAT FOR HIM TO FACE.
HE WAS THE MOST REVERED HERO IN THE TERRITORIES -- HELL, THERE WOULDN'T EVEN BE SUCH A PLACE IF IT WASN'T FOR HIM!
HE CARVED OUT MOST OF THIS LAND WITH HIS OWN HANDS. THAT POWER, GULLY -- THAT LEGACY, HAS BEEN PASSED ON TO YOU. HOW CAN YOU POSSIBLY FAIL?

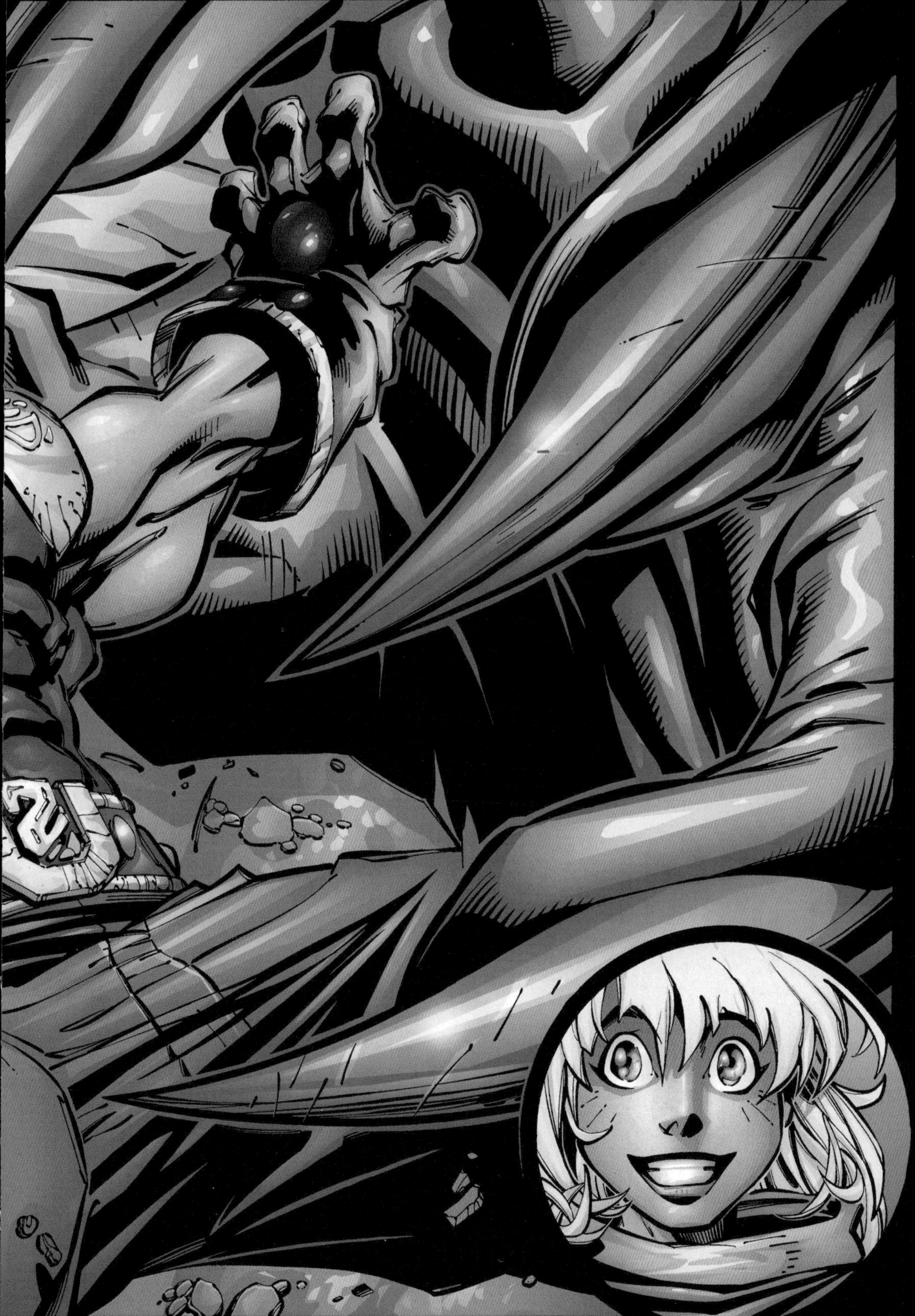

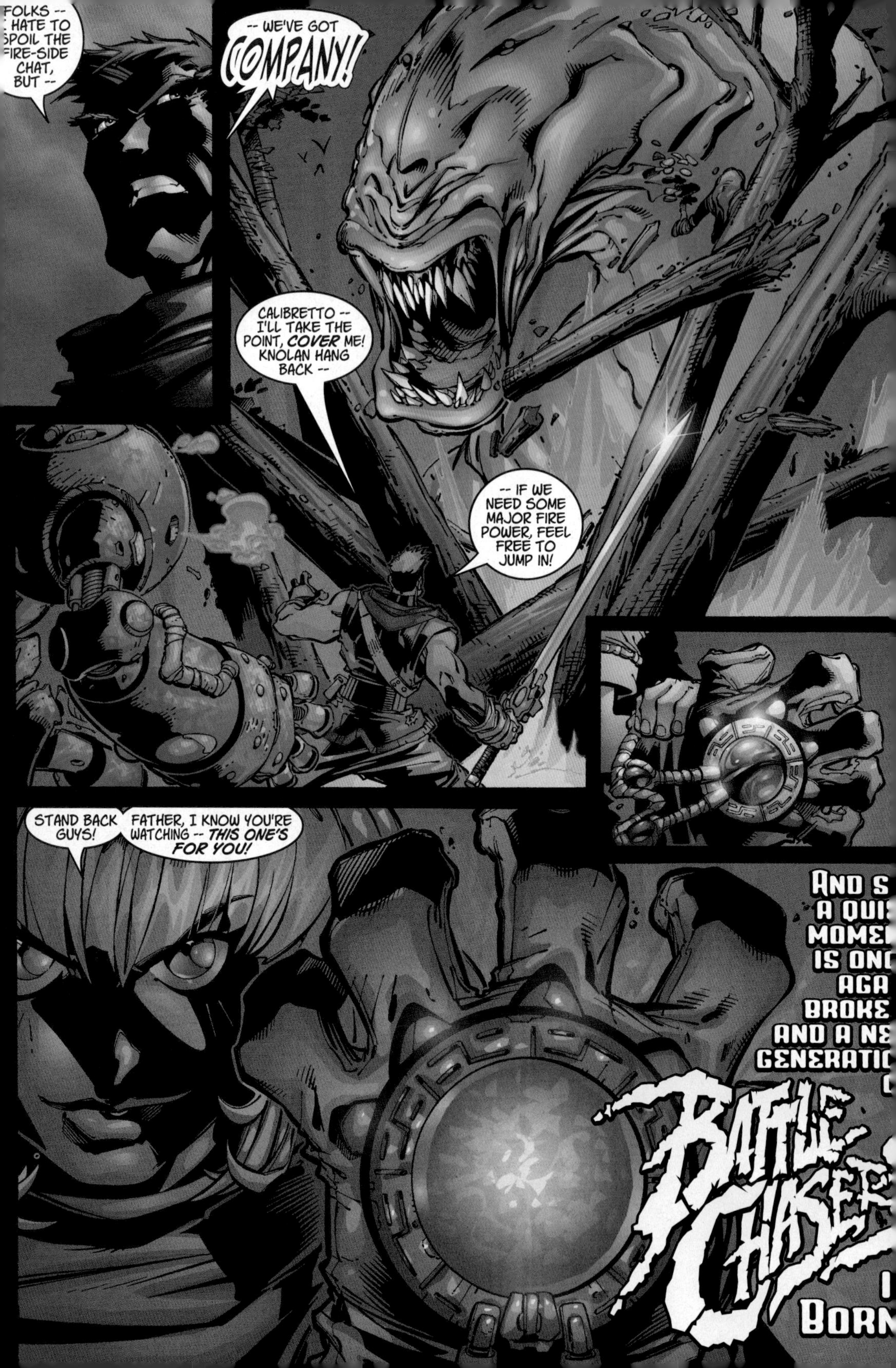
FOLKS -- I HATE TO SPOIL THE FIRE-SIDE CHAT, BUT --
-- WE'VE GOT COMPANY!
CALIBRETTO -- I'LL TAKE THE POINT, COVER ME! KNOLAN HANG BACK --
-- IF WE NEED SOME MAJOR FIRE POWER, FEEL FREE TO JUMP IN!
STAND BACK GUYS!
FATHER, I KNOW YOU'RE WATCHING -- THIS ONE'S FOR YOU!
AND S
A QUI
MOME
IS ONC
AGA
BROKE
AND A NE
GENERATIC
BATTLE CHASER
I
BORN

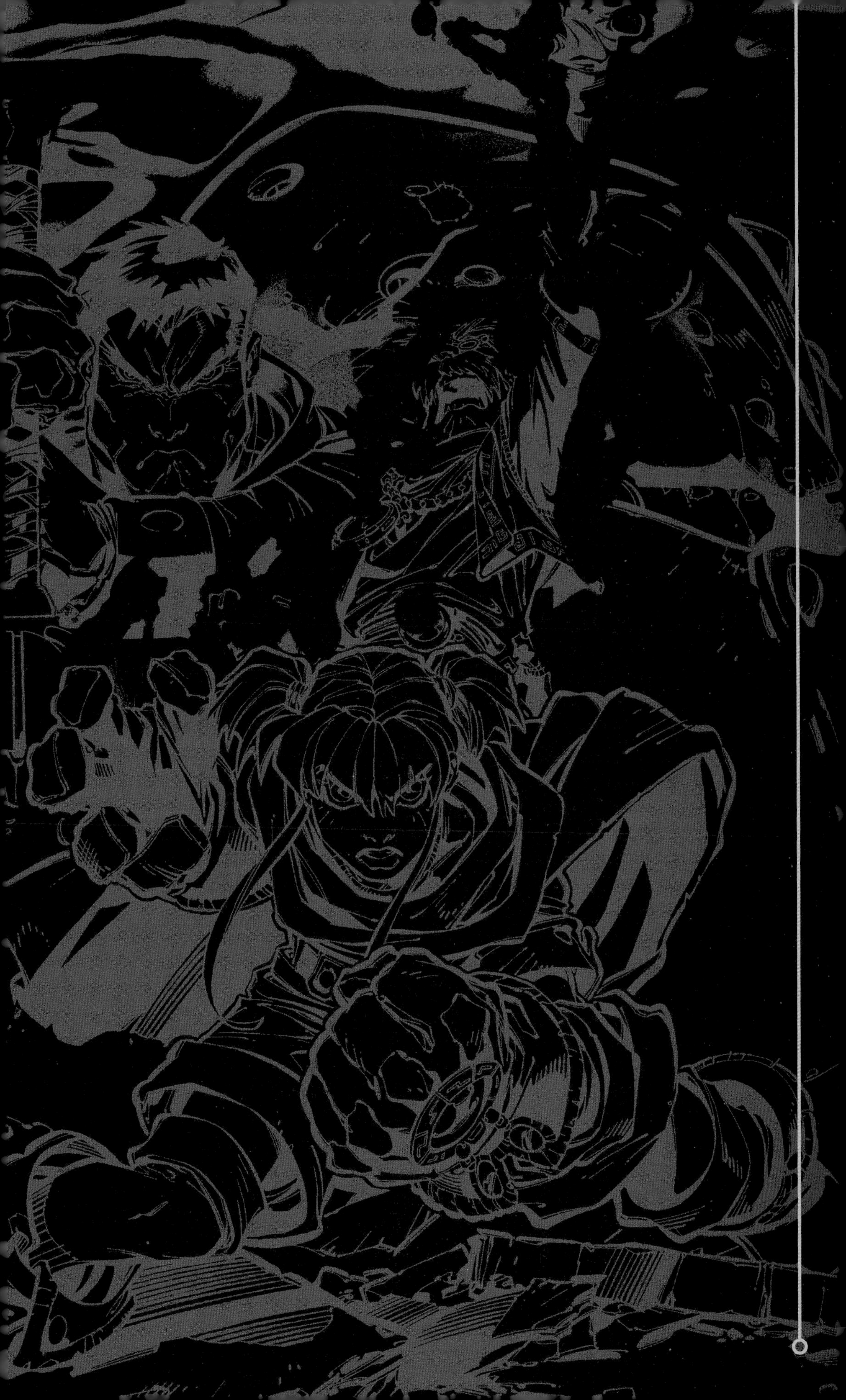

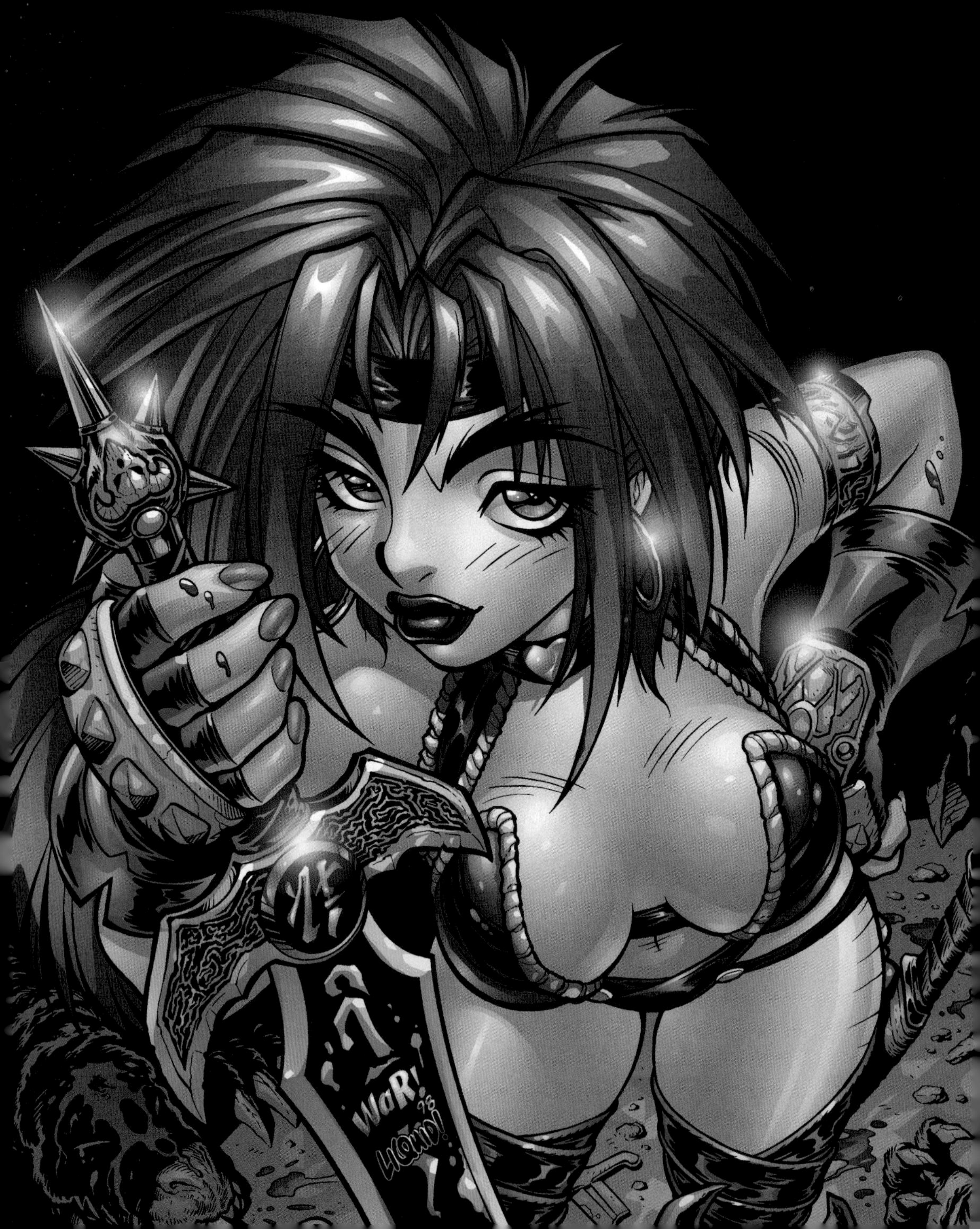
WaR! 98
LIQUID!

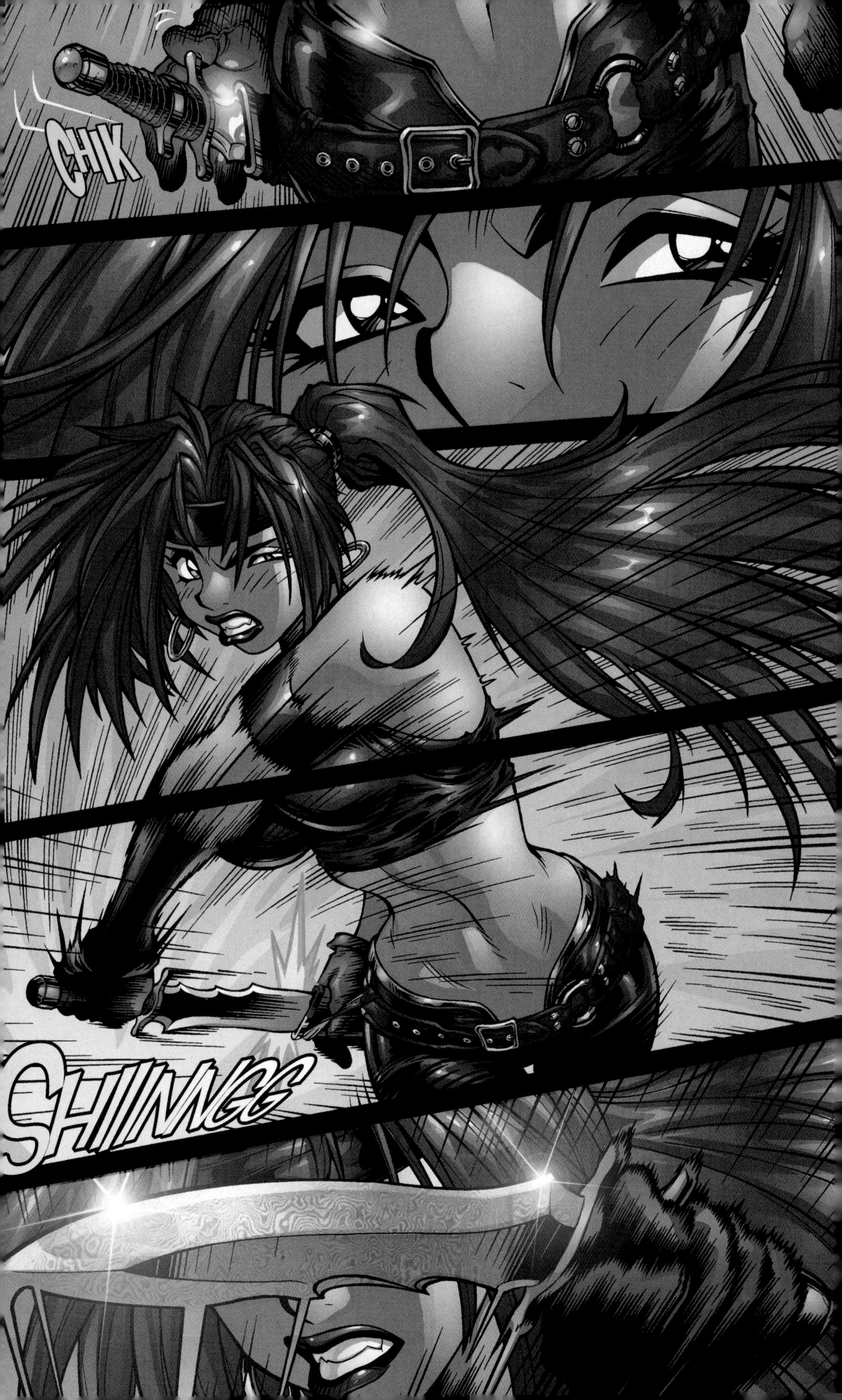
CHIK
SHIINGG

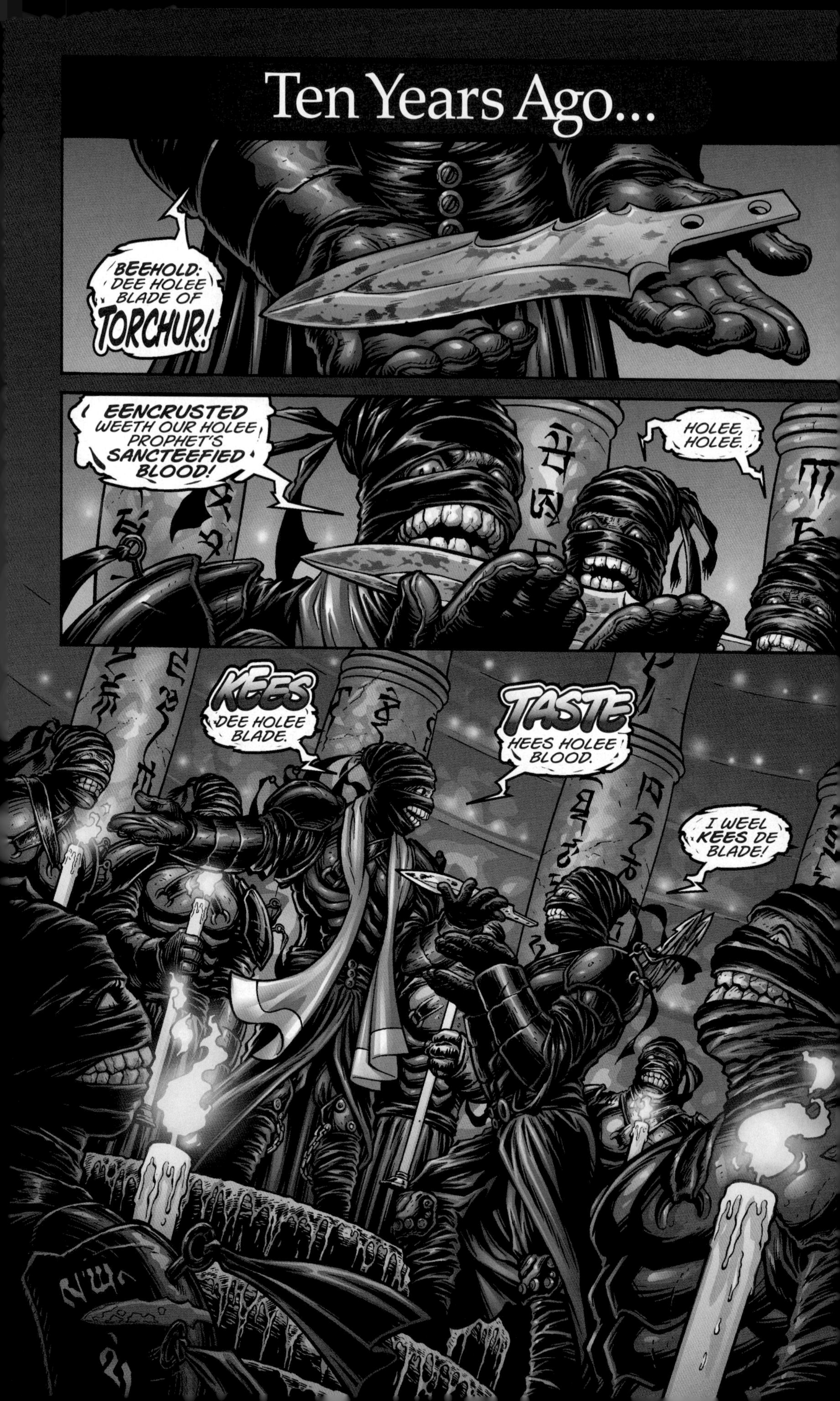

Ten Years Ago...
BEEHOLD: DEE HOLEE BLADE OF TORCHUR!
EENCRUSTED WEETH OUR HOLEE PROPHET'S SANCTEEFIED BLOOD!
HOLEE, HOLEE.
KEES DEE HOLEE BLADE.
TASTE HEES HOLEE BLOOD.
I WEEL KEES DE BLADE!

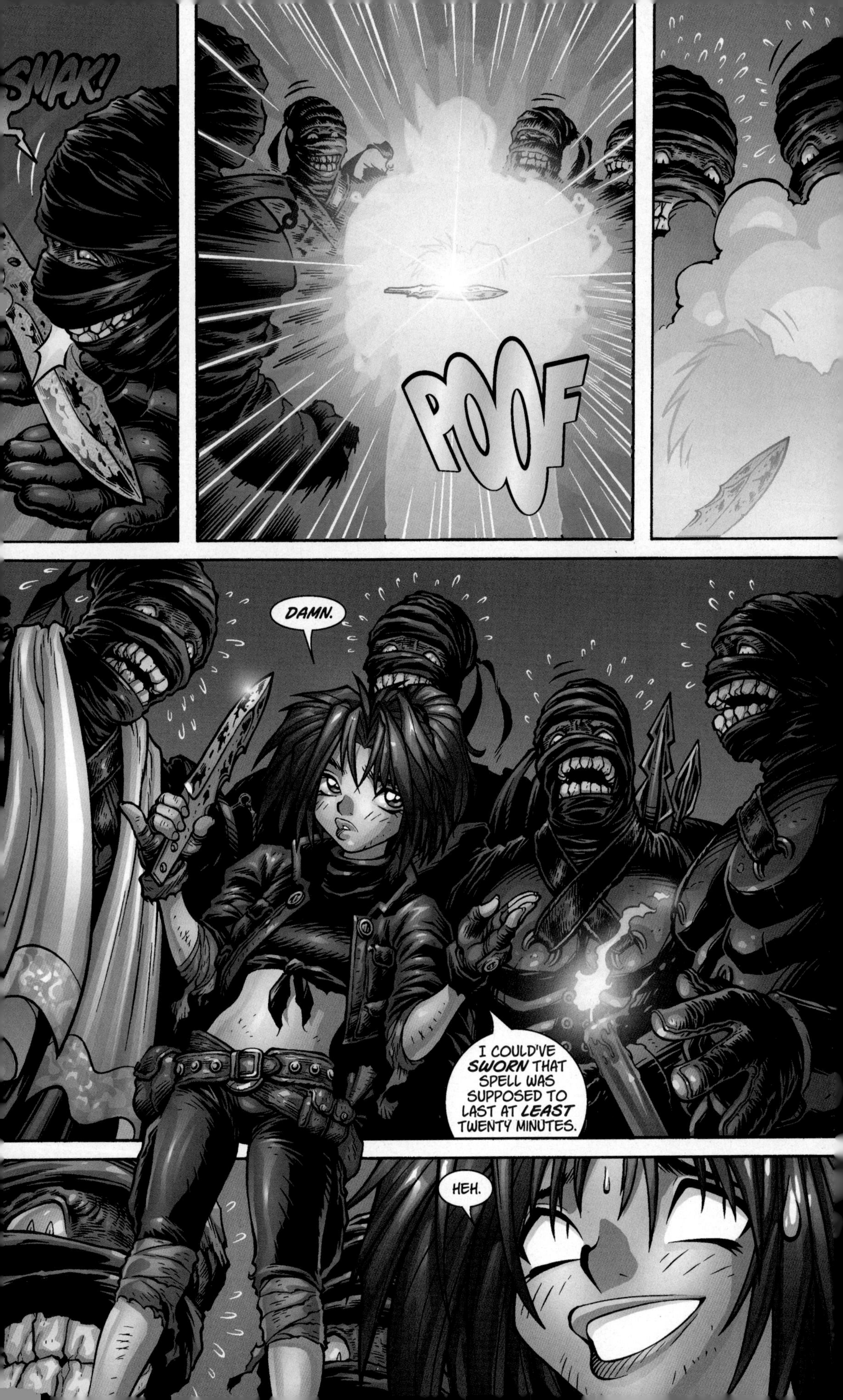
SMAK!
POOF
DAMN.
I COULD'VE SWORN THAT SPELL WAS SUPPOSED TO LAST AT LEAST TWENTY MINUTES.
HEH.

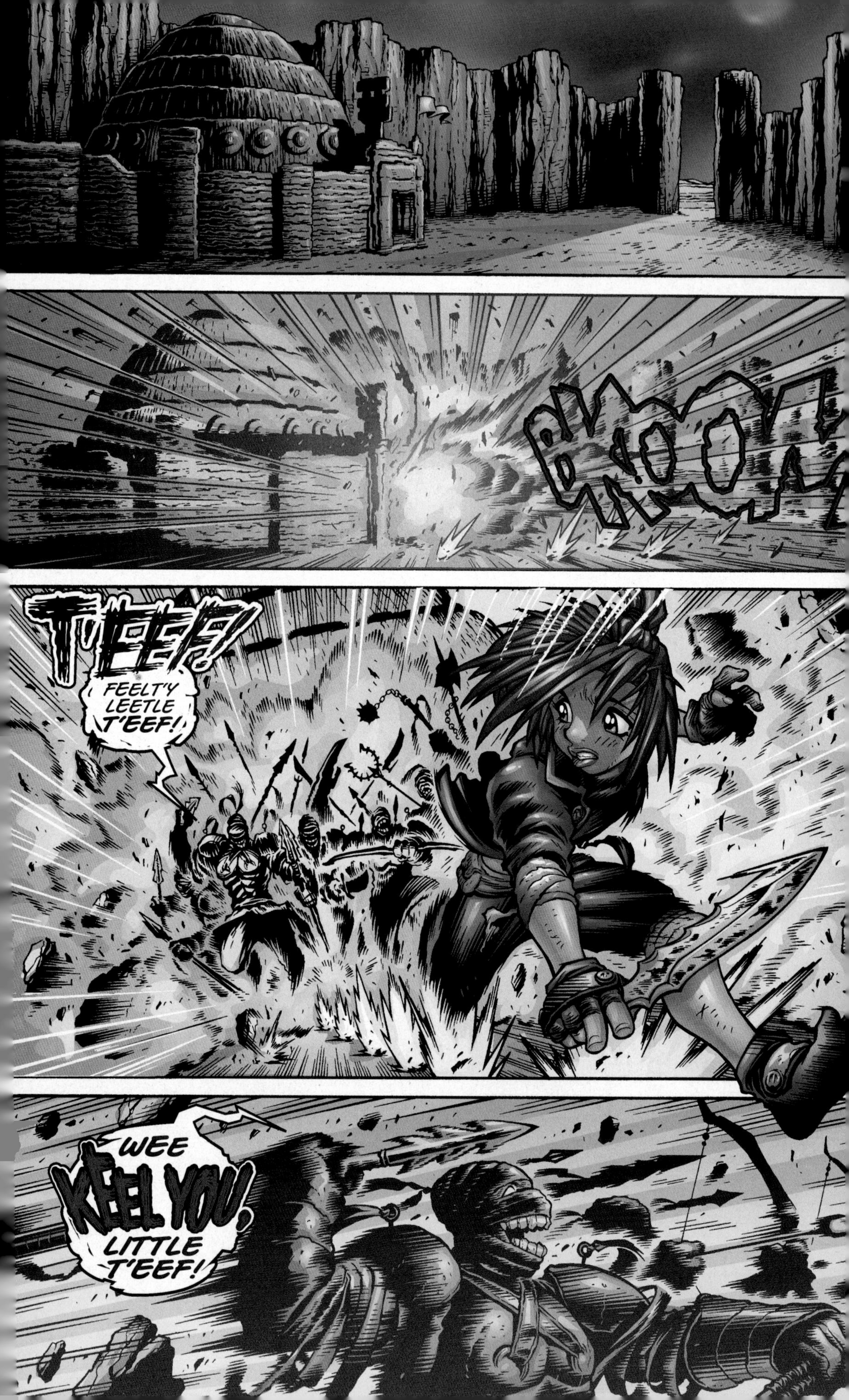
T'EEF!
FEELT'Y LEETLE T'EEF!
WEE KEEL YOU, LITTLE T'EEF!

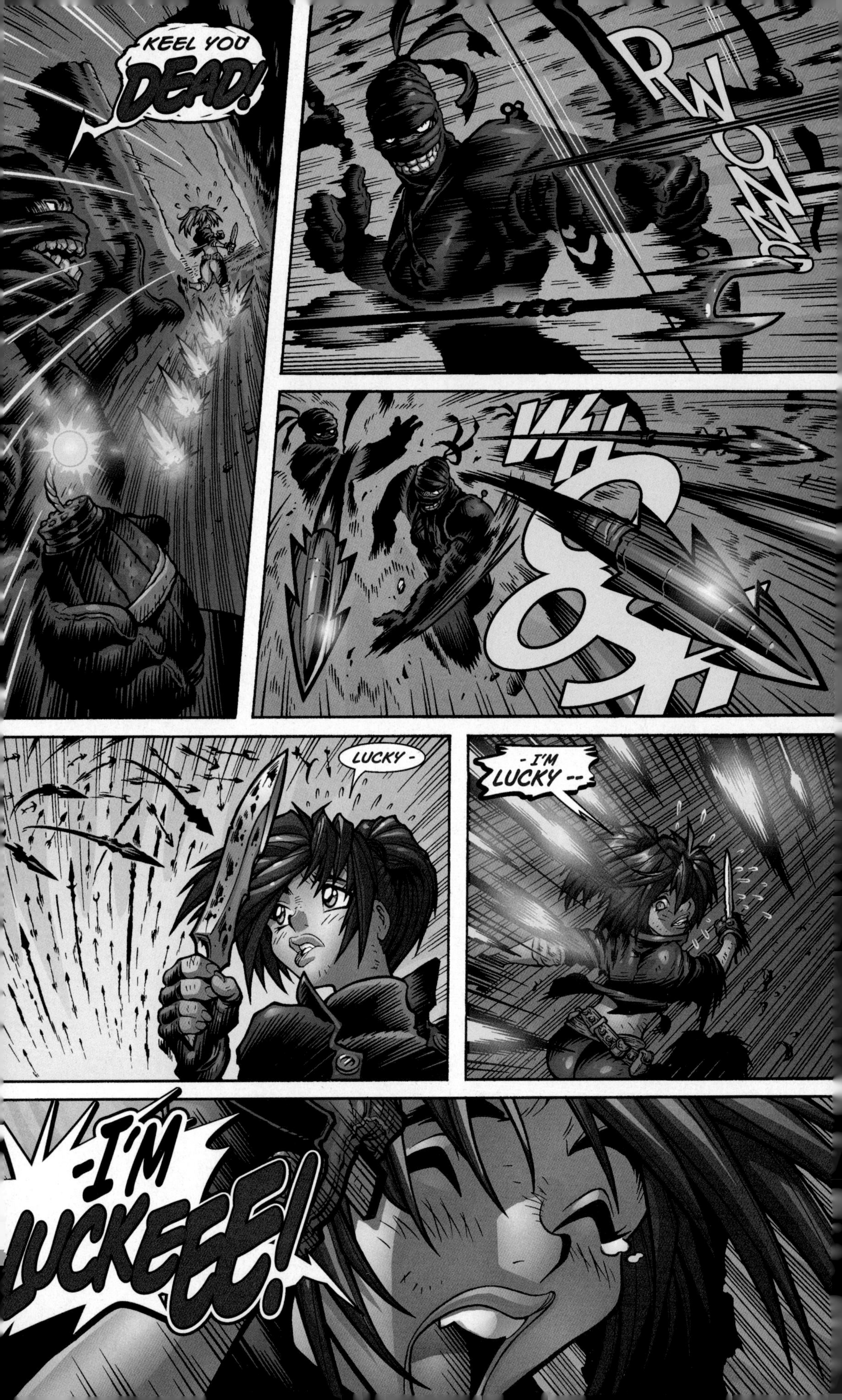
KEEL YOU DEAD!
RWOWZZ
WHOOSH
LUCKY -
- I'M LUCKY --
-I'M LUCKEEE!

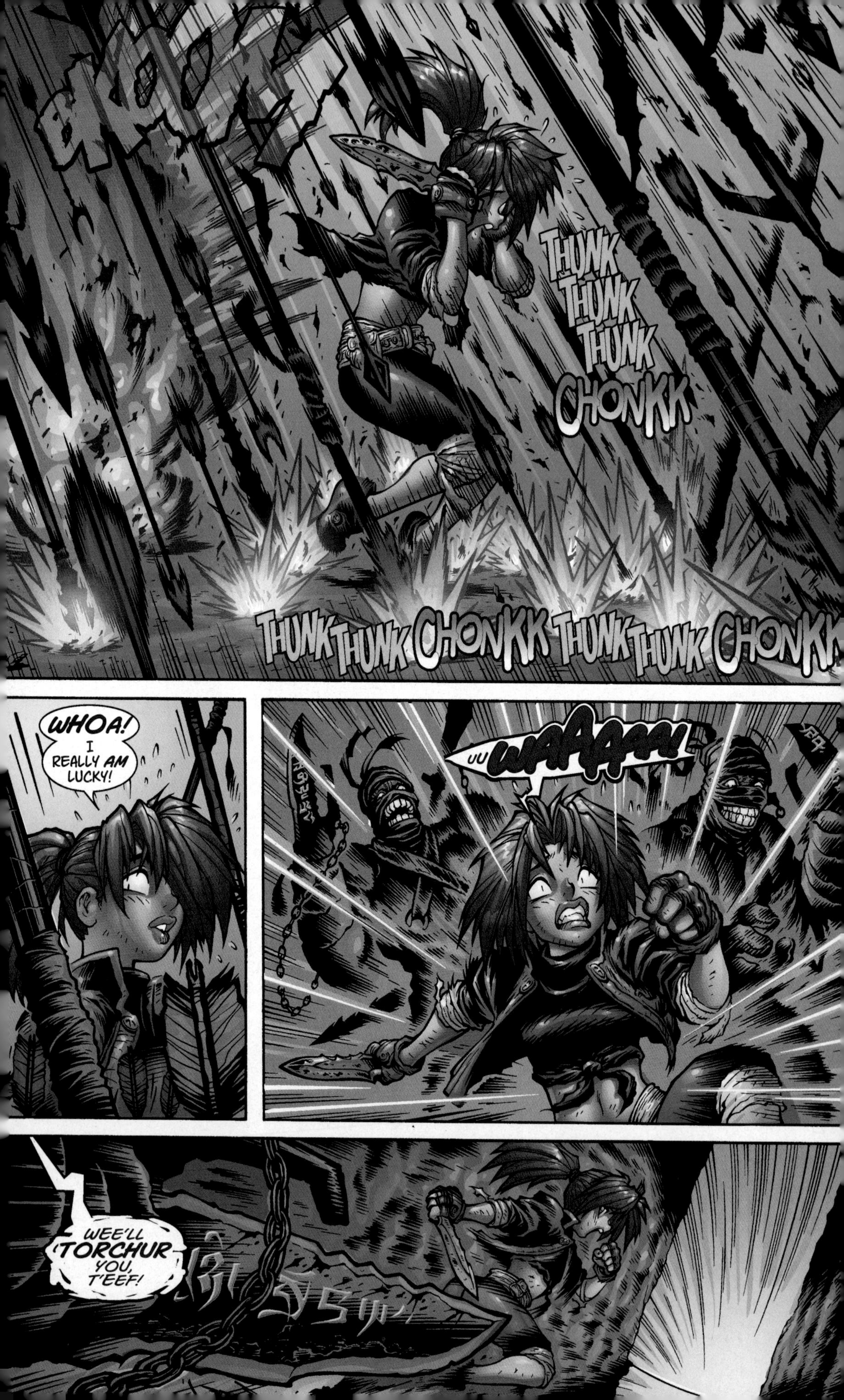
THUNK
THUNK
THUNK
CHONKK
THUNK THUNK CHONKK THUNK THUNK CHONKK
WHOA! I REALLY AM LUCKY!
UU WAAAAA!
WEE'LL TORCHUR YOU, T'EEF!

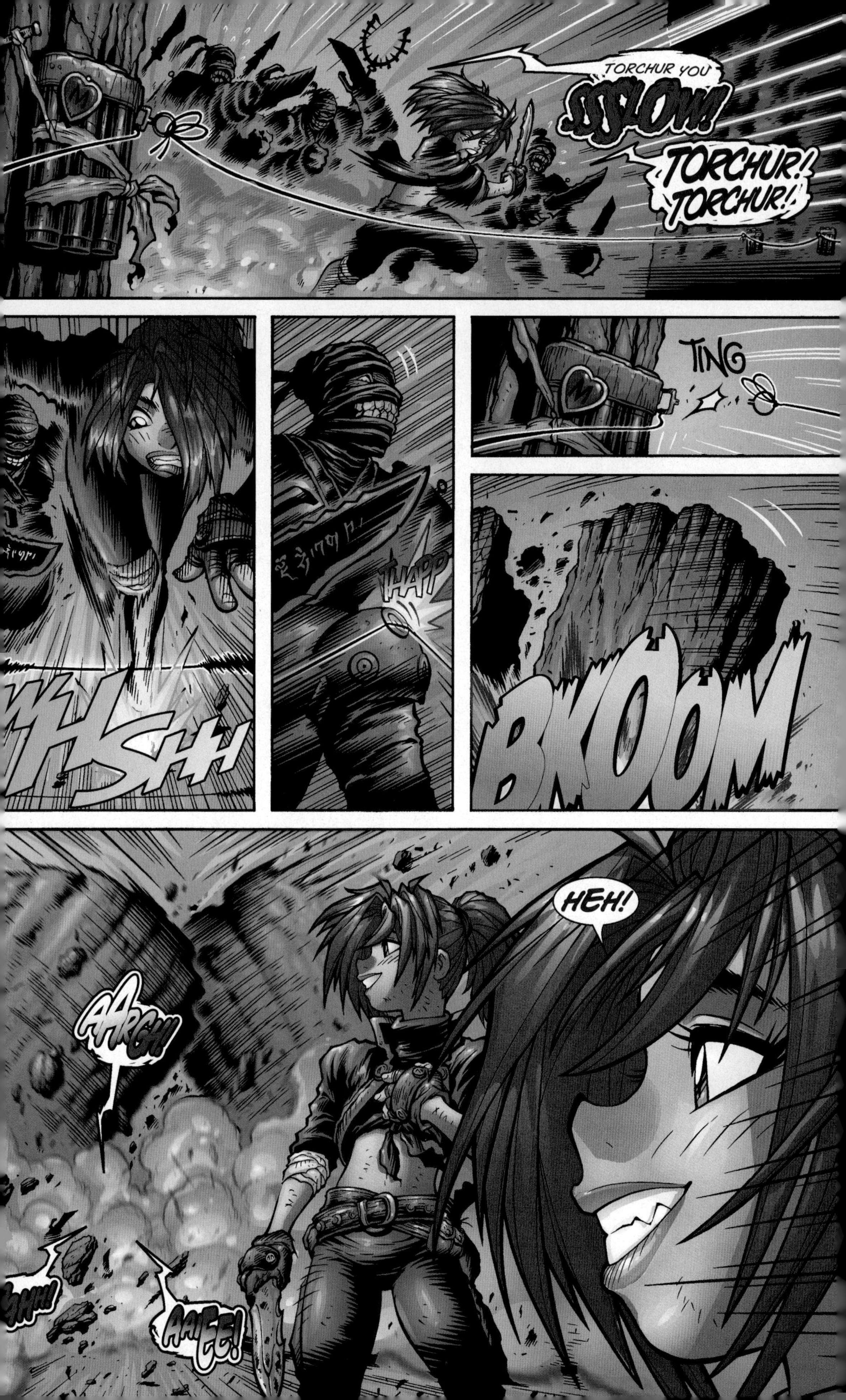
TORCHUR YOU
SSSLOW!
TORCHUR! TORCHUR!
TING
THAPP
WHSHH
BKOOM
HEH!
AARGH!
AHHH
AAIEE!

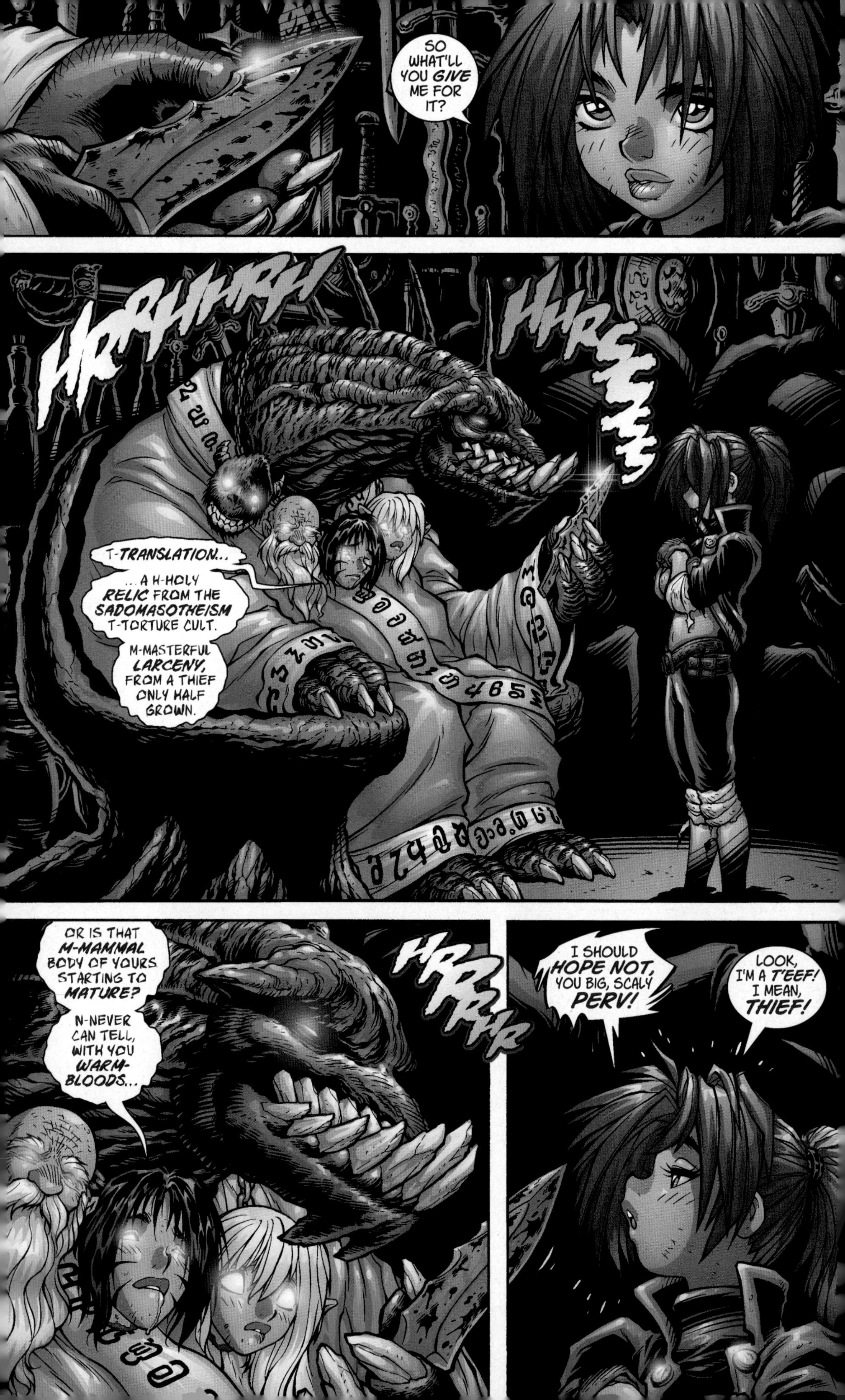

SO WHAT'LL YOU GIVE ME FOR IT?
HRRHHRH
HHRRRMM
T-TRANSLATION...
...A H-HOLY RELIC FROM THE SADOMASOTHEISM T-TORTURE CULT.
M-MASTERFUL LARCENY, FROM A THIEF ONLY HALF GROWN.
OR IS THAT M-MAMMAL BODY OF YOURS STARTING TO MATURE?
N-NEVER CAN TELL, WITH YOU WARM-BLOODS...
HRRRHR
I SHOULD HOPE NOT, YOU BIG, SCALY PERV!
LOOK, I'M A T'EEF! I MEAN, THIEF!

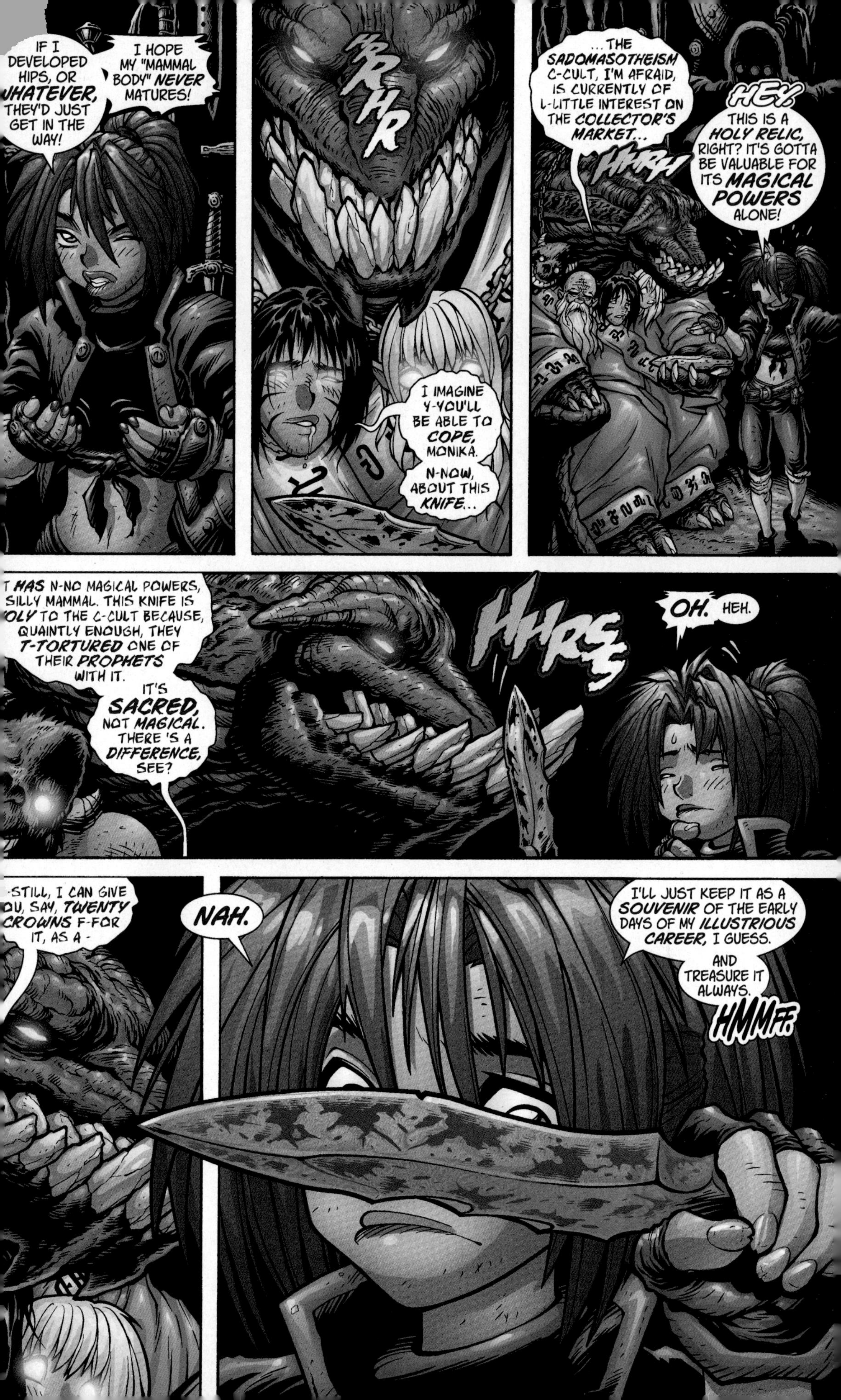

IF I DEVELOPED HIPS, OR WHATEVER, THEY'D JUST GET IN THE WAY!
I HOPE MY "MAMMAL BODY" NEVER MATURES!
HRHR
I IMAGINE Y-YOU'LL BE ABLE TO COPE, MONIKA.
N-NOW, ABOUT THIS KNIFE...
...THE SADOMASOTHEISM C-CULT, I'M AFRAID, IS CURRENTLY OF L-LITTLE INTEREST ON THE COLLECTOR'S MARKET...
HHRH
HEY!
THIS IS A HOLY RELIC, RIGHT? IT'S GOTTA BE VALUABLE FOR ITS MAGICAL POWERS ALONE!
T HAS N-NO MAGICAL POWERS, SILLY MAMMAL. THIS KNIFE IS OLY TO THE C-CULT BECAUSE, QUAINTLY ENOUGH, THEY T-TORTURED ONE OF THEIR PROPHETS WITH IT.
IT'S SACRED, NOT MAGICAL. THERE'S A DIFFERENCE, SEE?
HHRS
OH. HEH.
-STILL, I CAN GIVE OU, SAY, TWENTY CROWNS F-FOR IT, AS A -
NAH.
I'LL JUST KEEP IT AS A SOUVENIR OF THE EARLY DAYS OF MY ILLUSTRIOUS CAREER, I GUESS.
AND TREASURE IT ALWAYS.
HMMFF.

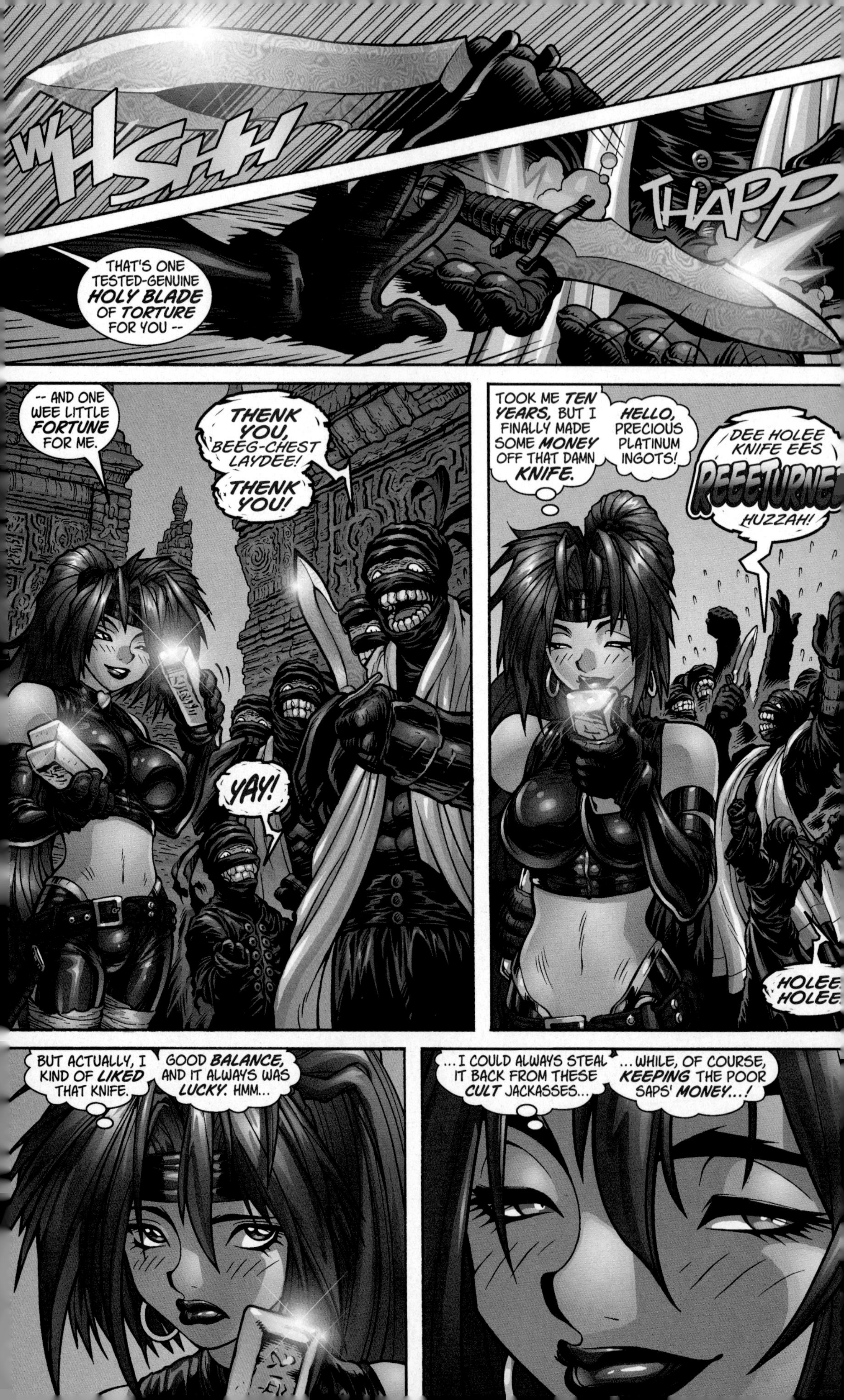
WHSHH
THAPP
THAT'S ONE TESTED-GENUINE HOLY BLADE OF TORTURE FOR YOU --
-- AND ONE WEE LITTLE FORTUNE FOR ME.
THENK YOU, BEEG-CHEST LAYDEE!
THENK YOU!
YAY!
TOOK ME TEN YEARS, BUT I FINALLY MADE SOME MONEY OFF THAT DAMN KNIFE.
HELLO, PRECIOUS PLATINUM INGOTS!
DEE HOLEE KNIFE EES
HUZZAH!
HOLEE HOLEE
BUT ACTUALLY, I KIND OF LIKED THAT KNIFE.
GOOD BALANCE, AND IT ALWAYS WAS LUCKY. HMM...
...I COULD ALWAYS STEAL IT BACK FROM THESE CULT JACKASSES...
...WHILE, OF COURSE, KEEPING THE POOR SAPS' MONEY...!

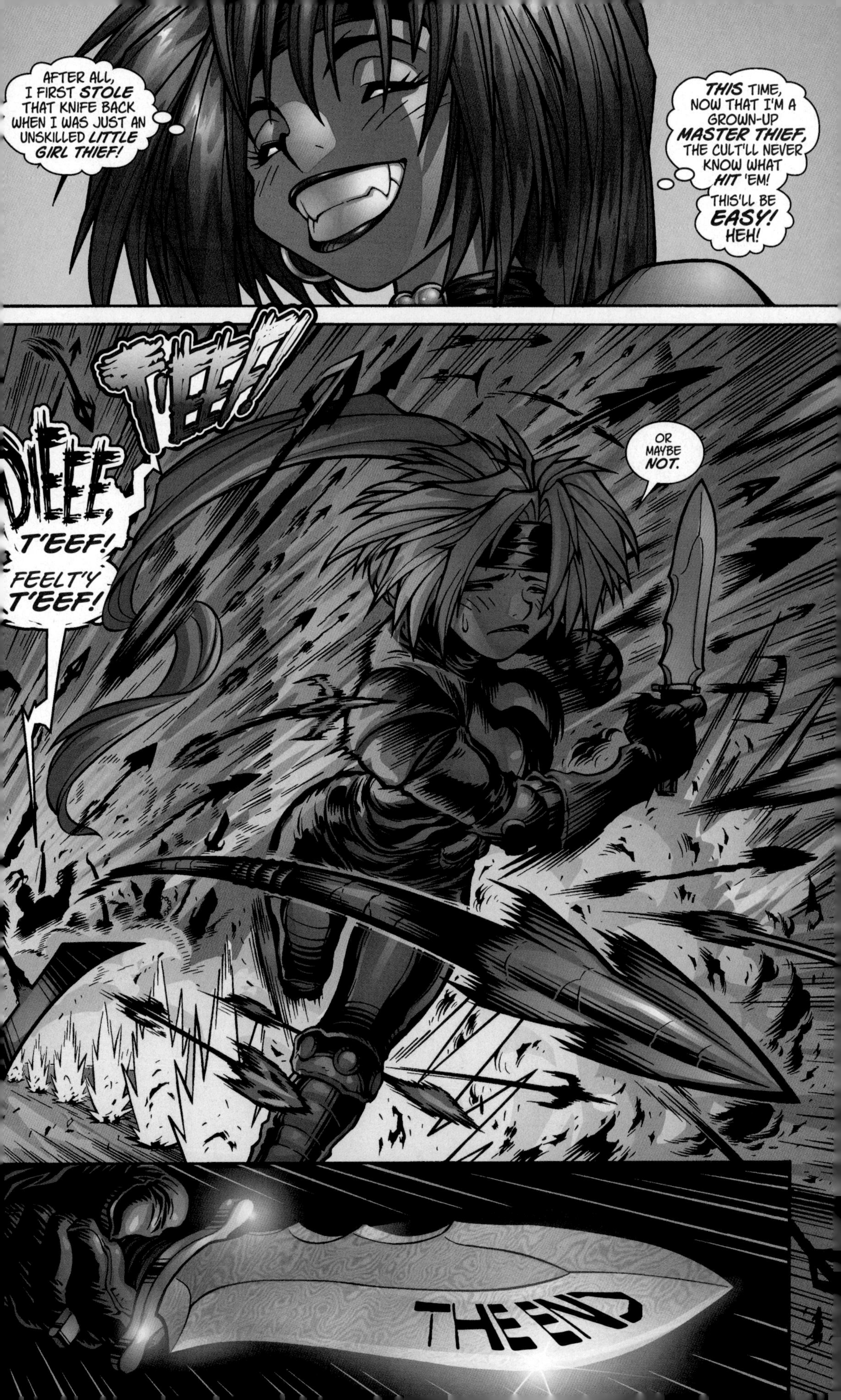
AFTER ALL, I FIRST STOLE THAT KNIFE BACK WHEN I WAS JUST AN UNSKILLED LITTLE GIRL THIEF!
THIS TIME, NOW THAT I'M A GROWN-UP MASTER THIEF, THE CULT'LL NEVER KNOW WHAT HIT 'EM!
THIS'LL BE EASY! HEH!
T'EEF!
DIEEE, T'EEF!
FEELT'Y T'EEF!
OR MAYBE NOT.
THE END

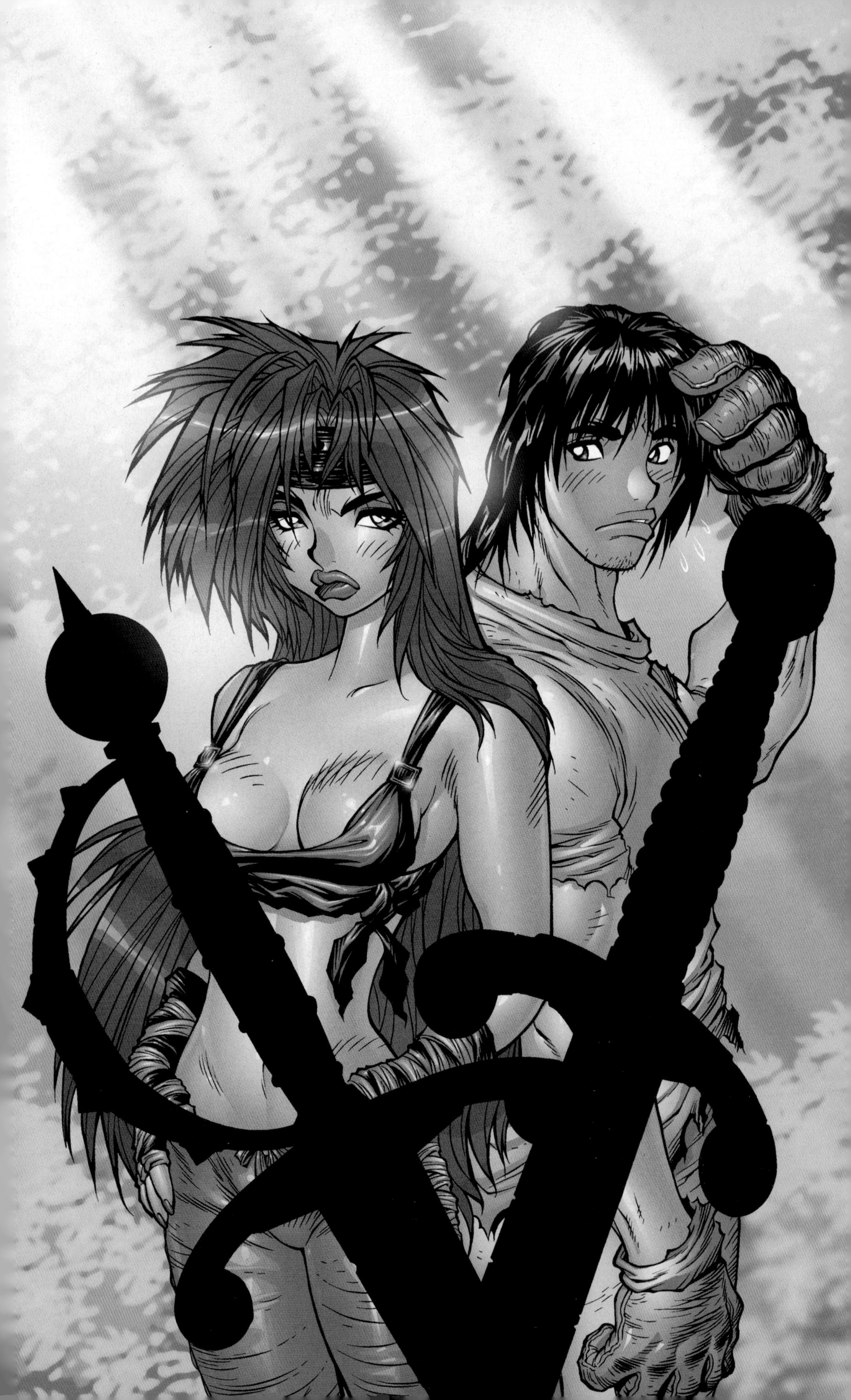

6 YEARS AGO...

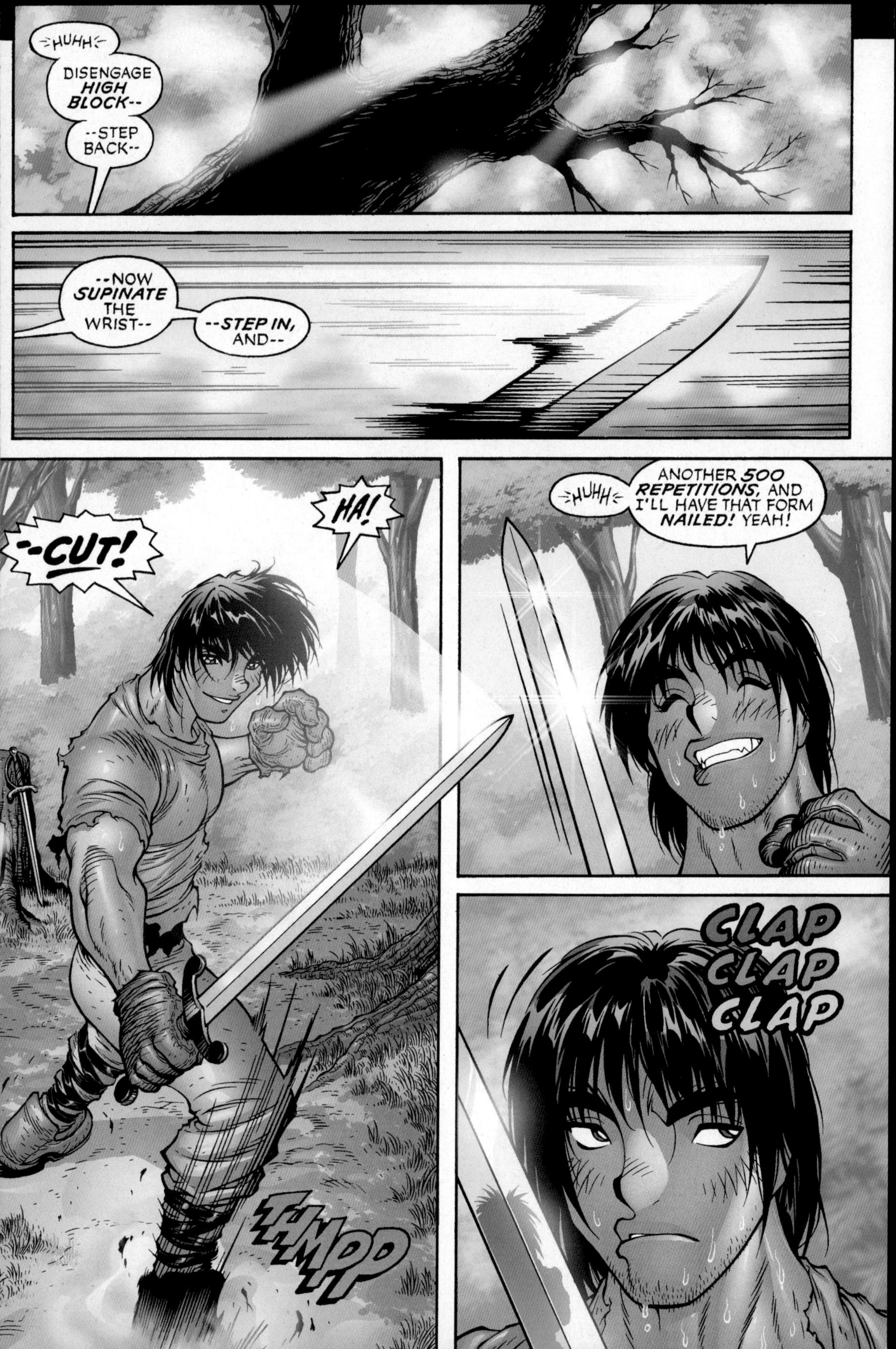
HUHH
DISENGAGE HIGH BLOCK--
--STEP BACK--
--NOW SUPINATE THE WRIST--
--STEP IN, AND--
--CUT!
HA!
THMPP
HUHH
ANOTHER 500 REPETITIONS, AND I'LL HAVE THAT FORM NAILED! YEAH!
CLAP
CLAP
CLAP

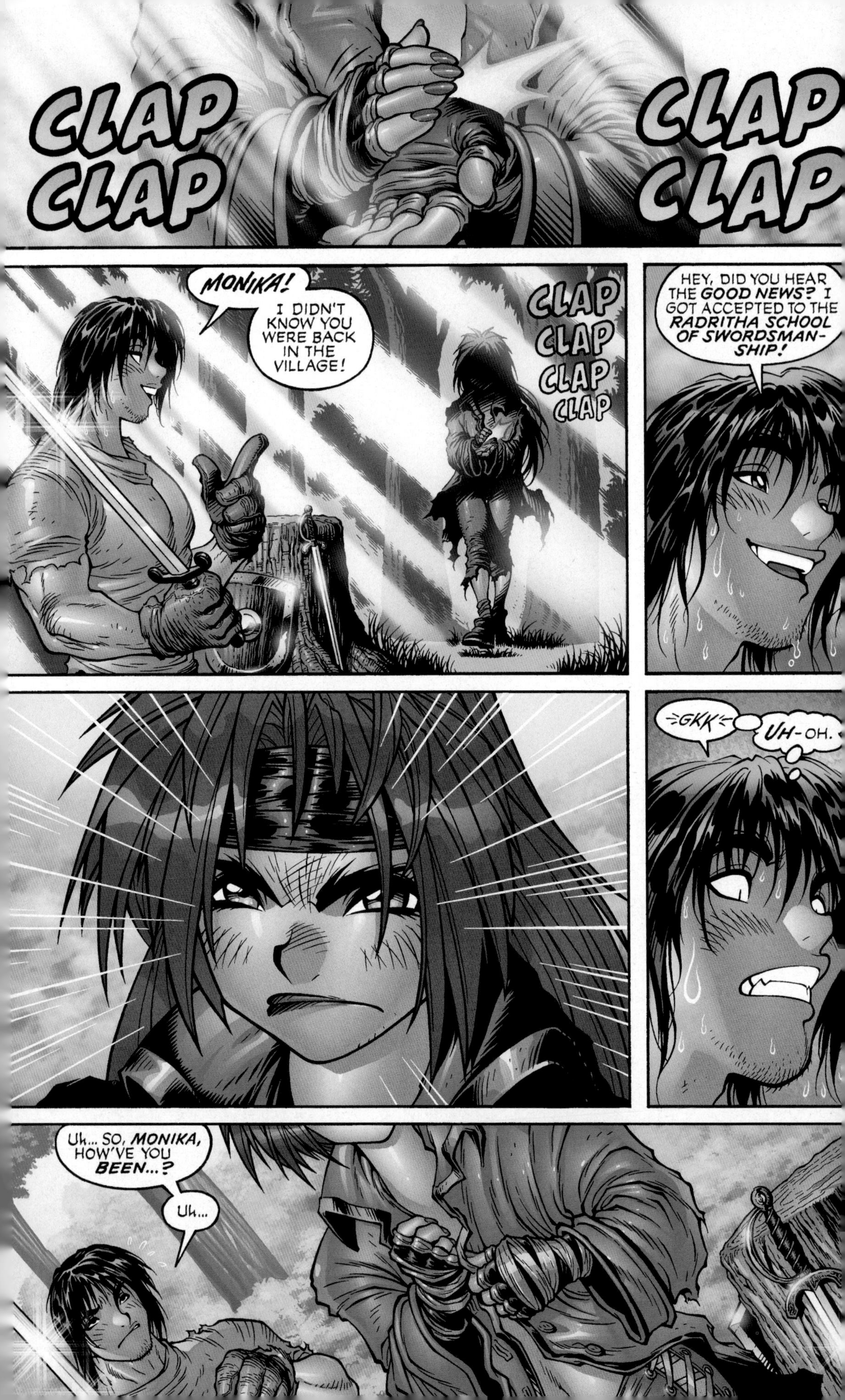
CLAP CLAP
CLAP CLAP
MONIKA! I DIDN'T KNOW YOU WERE BACK IN THE VILLAGE!
CLAP CLAP CLAP CLAP
HEY, DID YOU HEAR THE GOOD NEWS? I GOT ACCEPTED TO THE RADRITHA SCHOOL OF SWORDSMAN-SHIP!
=GKK=
UH-OH.
Uh... SO, MONIKA, HOW'VE YOU BEEN...?
Uh...

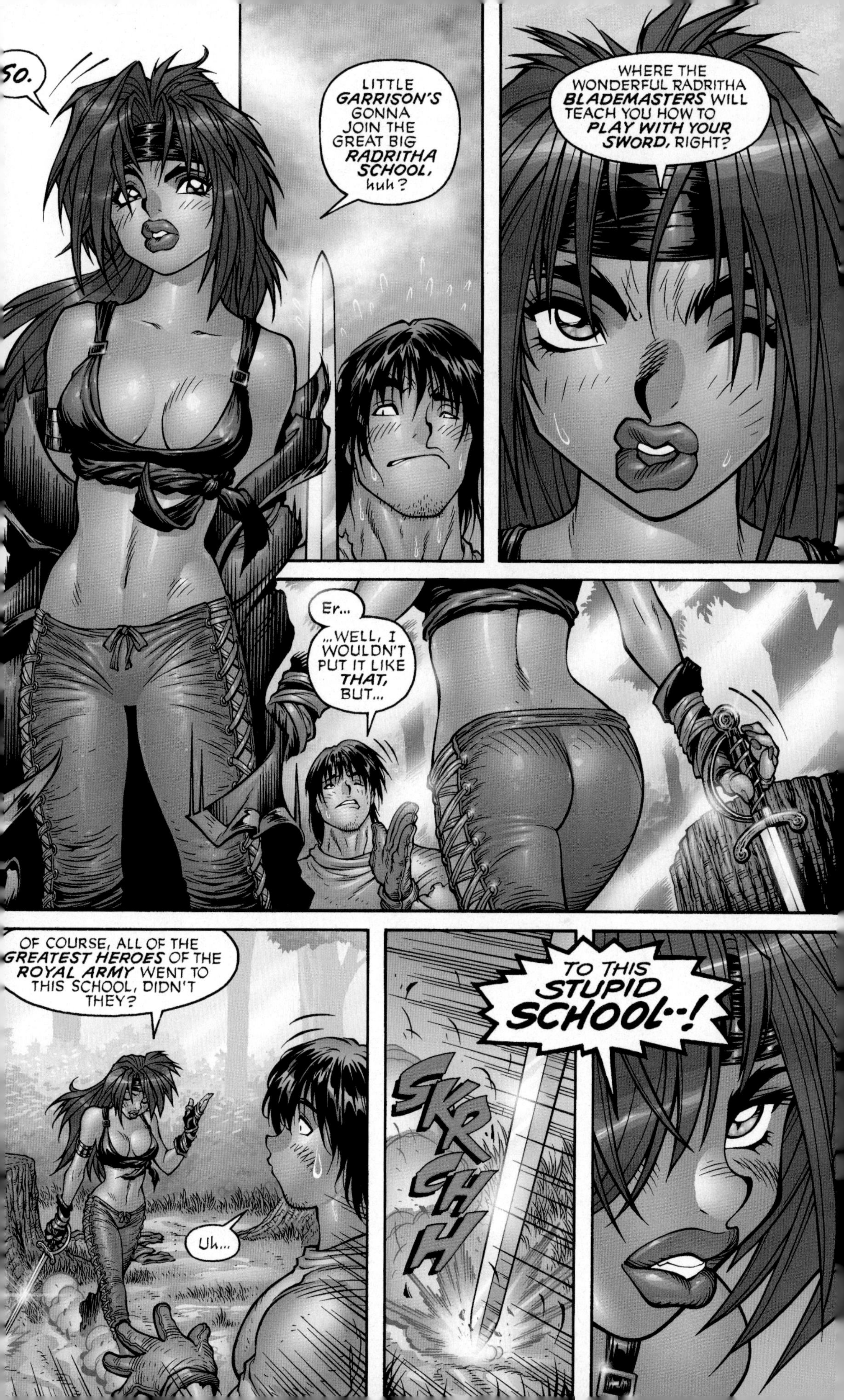
SO.
LITTLE GARRISON'S GONNA JOIN THE GREAT BIG RADRITHA SCHOOL, huh?
WHERE THE WONDERFUL RADRITHA BLADEMASTERS WILL TEACH YOU HOW TO PLAY WITH YOUR SWORD, RIGHT?
Er...
...WELL, I WOULDN'T PUT IT LIKE THAT, BUT...
OF COURSE, ALL OF THE GREATEST HEROES OF THE ROYAL ARMY WENT TO THIS SCHOOL, DIDN'T THEY?
Uh...
TO THIS STUPID SCHOOL--!
SKRCHHH

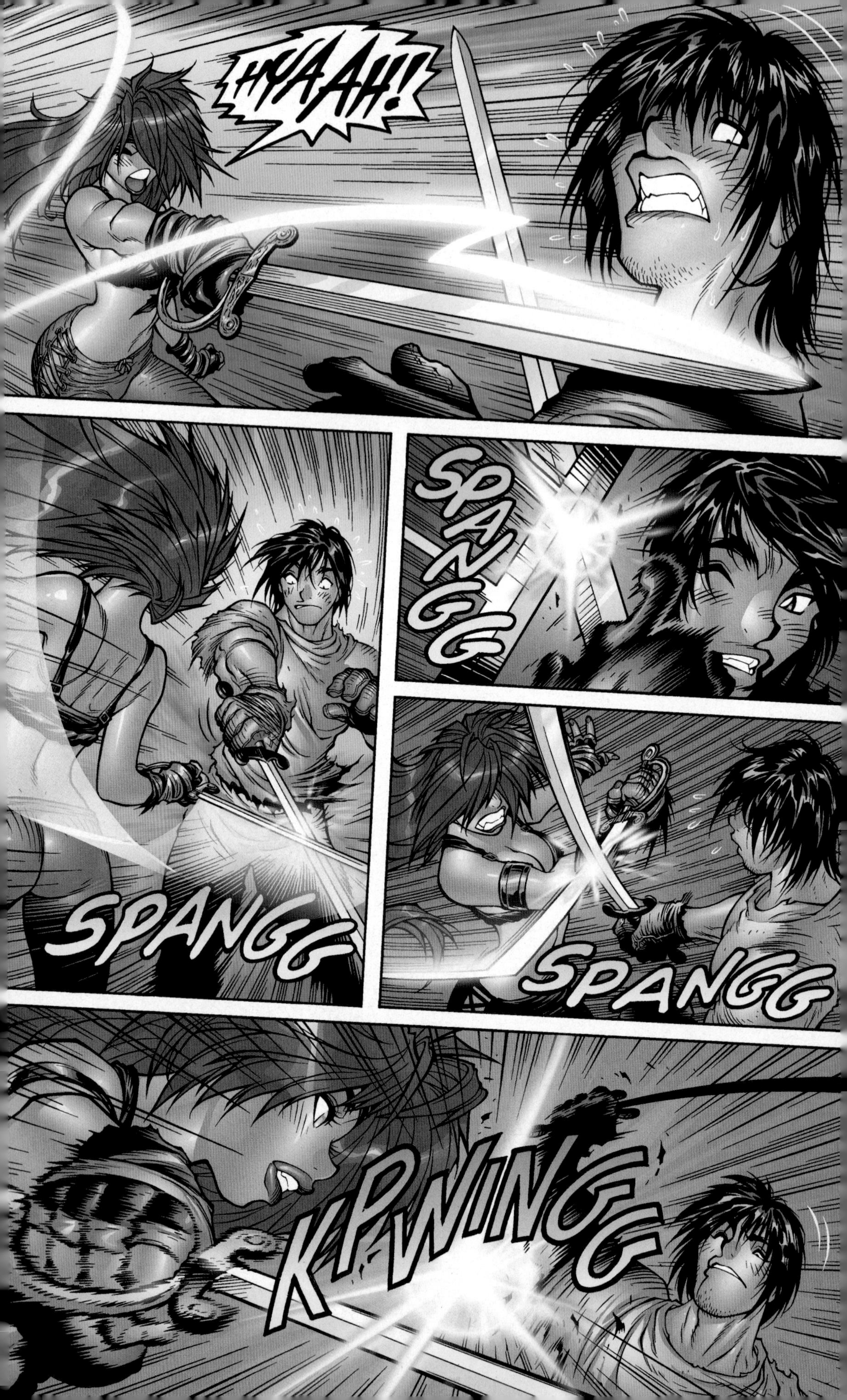
HYAAH!
SPANGG
SPANGG
SPANGG
KPWINGG

HAHH HAHH

HUHH HUHH

HUHH

M-MONIKA... WHY THE **HELL** ARE YOU--

SEE?

ANY-ONE CAN SWING A DAMN SWORD!

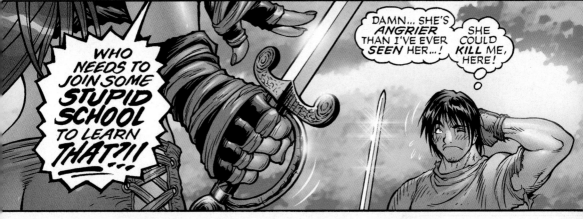

WHO NEEDS TO JOIN SOME **STUPID SCHOOL** TO LEARN **THAT?!!**...

DAMN... SHE'S **ANGRIER** THAN I'VE EVER **SEEN** HER...!

SHE COULD **KILL** ME, HERE!

BETTER PUT MY **LESSONS** INTO ACTION, NOW... MAKE MY "**WILL INTO STEEL**," LIKE MAESTRO SAYS...

ALL SO YOU CAN, WHAT, BE **ELIGIBLE** TO JOIN THE KING'S **MARSHAL PALADINS?**

ALL RIGHT... DON'T MAKE **EYE CONTACT**... KEEP YOUR GAZE ON THE **TORSO**, SO YOUR AWARENESS ENCOMPASSES YOUR OPPONENT'S **ENTIRE BODY**...

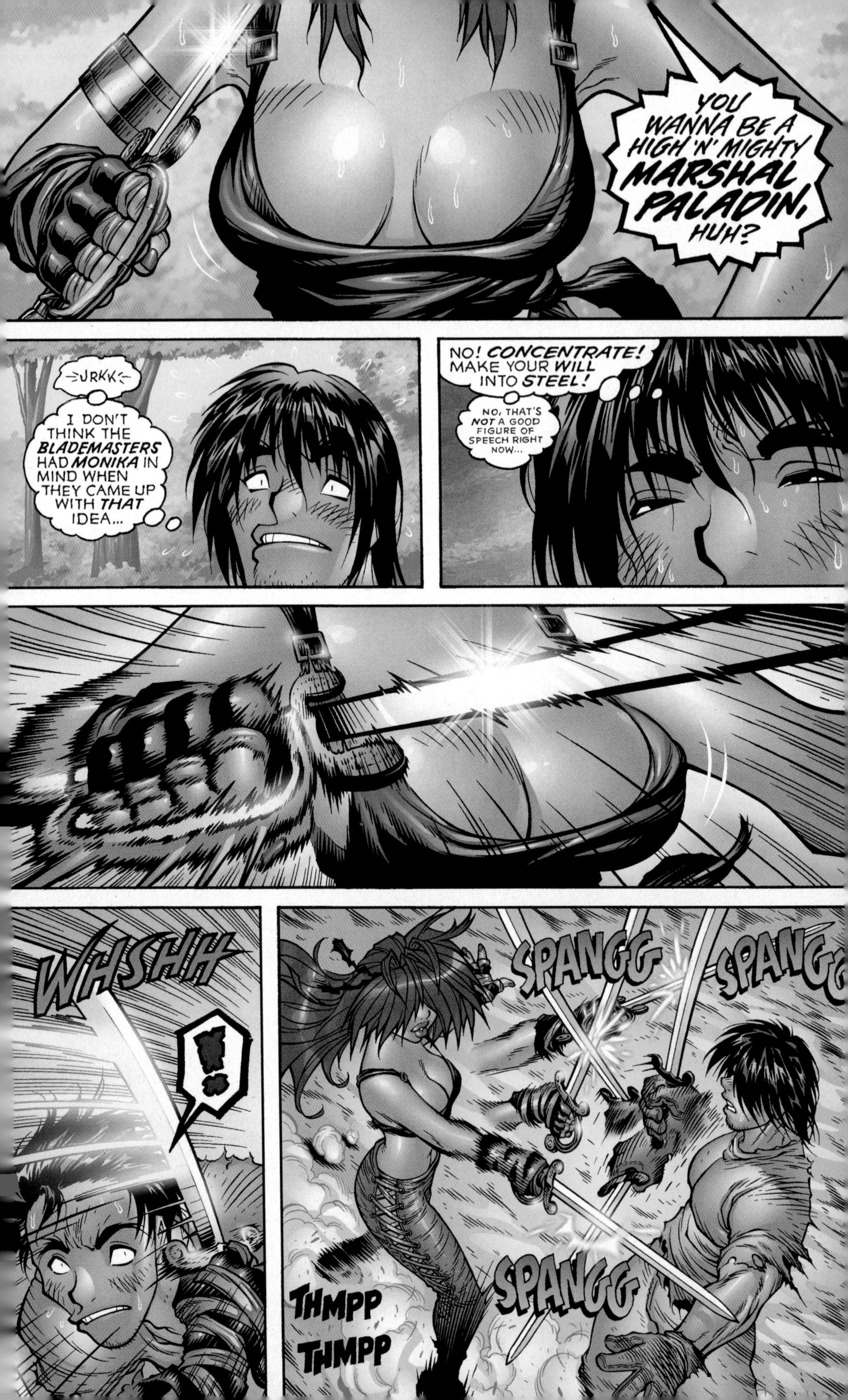
YOU WANNA BE A HIGH 'N' MIGHTY MARSHAL PALADIN, HUH?
=URKK=
I DON'T THINK THE BLADEMASTERS HAD MONIKA IN MIND WHEN THEY CAME UP WITH THAT IDEA...
NO! CONCENTRATE! MAKE YOUR WILL INTO STEEL!
NO, THAT'S NOT A GOOD FIGURE OF SPEECH RIGHT NOW...
WHSHH
!!
SPANGG
SPANGG
SPANGG
THMPP
THMPP

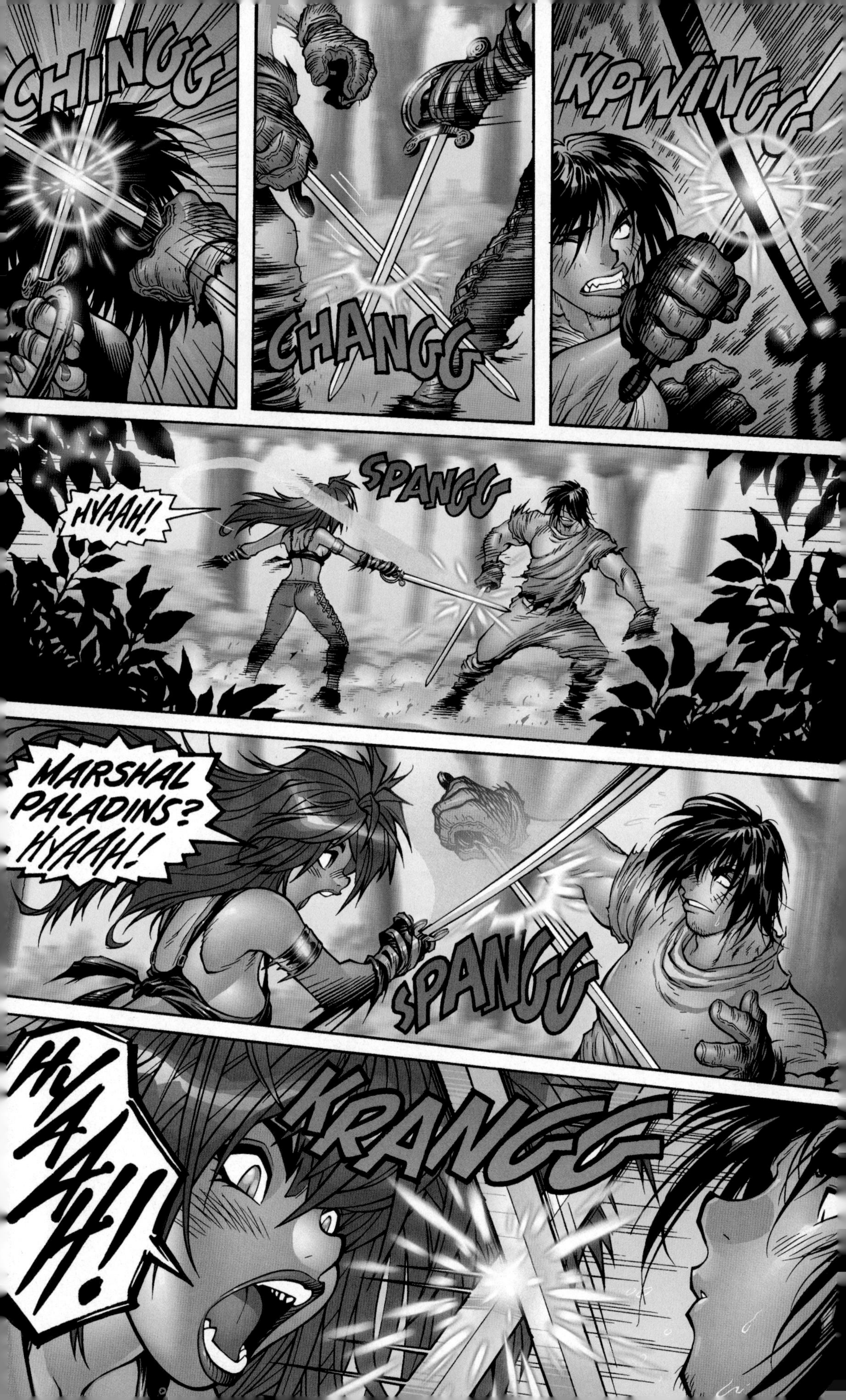
CHINGG
CHANGG
KPWINGG
HYAAH!
SPANGG
MARSHAL PALADINS? HYAAH!
SPANGG
HYAAAH!
KRANGG

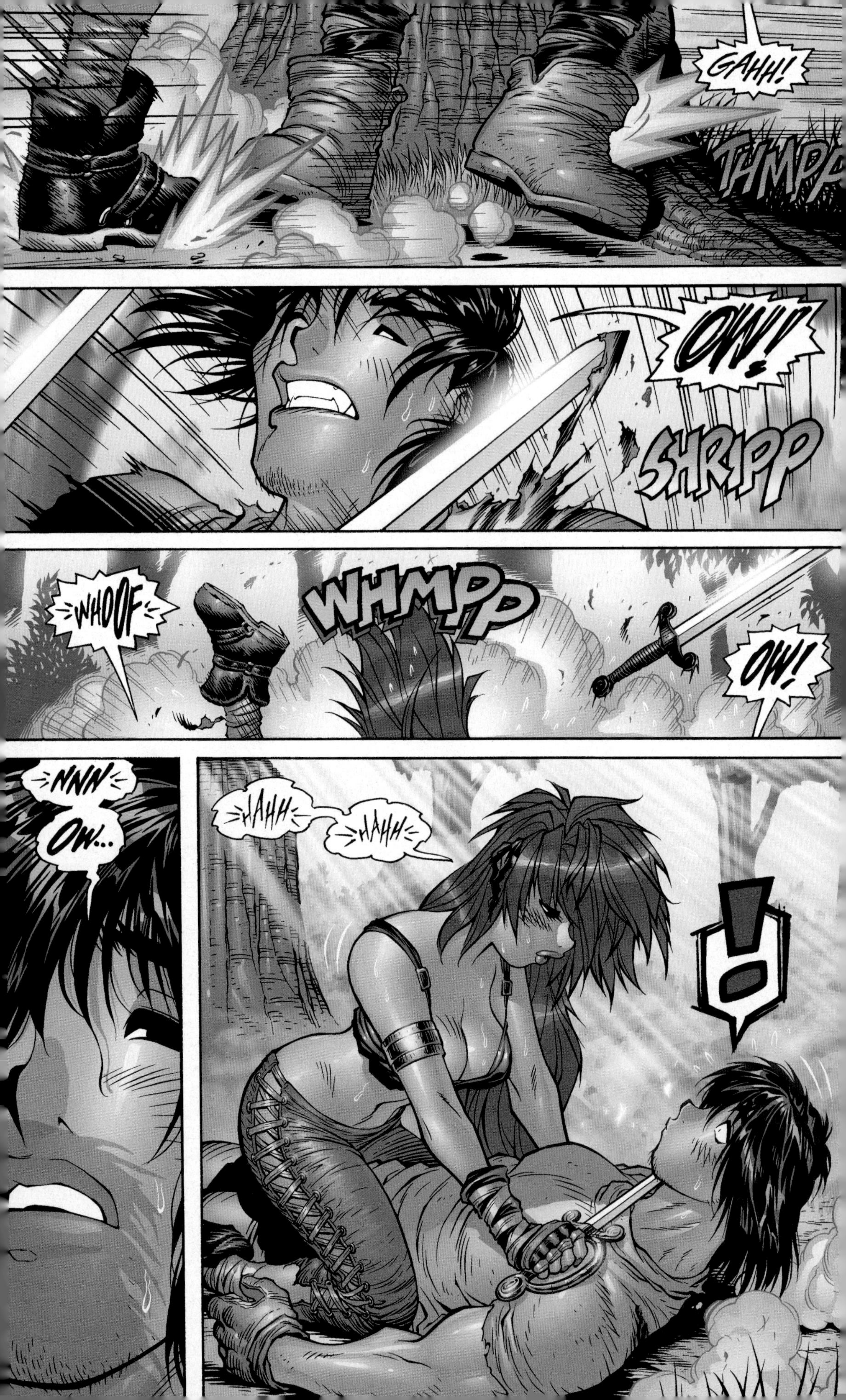
GAHH!
THMPP
OW!
SHRIPP
WHOOF
WHMPP
OW!
NNN
OW...
HAHH
HAHH
!

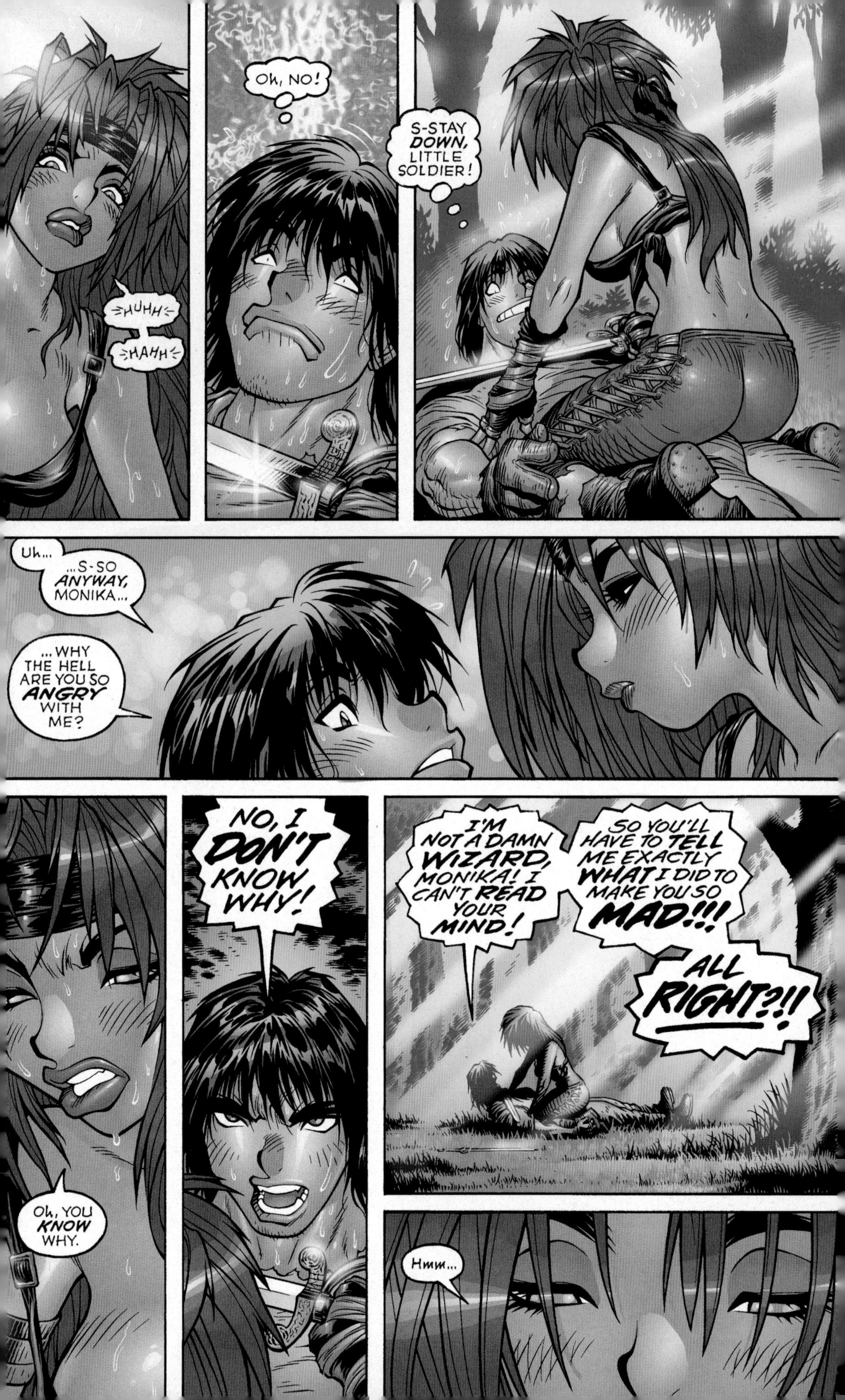

Oh, NO!
S-STAY DOWN, LITTLE SOLDIER!
HUHH
HAHH
Uh...
...S-SO ANYWAY, MONIKA...
...WHY THE HELL ARE YOU SO ANGRY WITH ME?
Oh, YOU KNOW WHY.
NO, I DON'T KNOW WHY!
I'M NOT A DAMN WIZARD, MONIKA! I CAN'T READ YOUR MIND!
SO YOU'LL HAVE TO TELL ME EXACTLY WHAT I DID TO MAKE YOU SO MAD!!!
ALL RIGHT?!!
Hmm...

OKAY, THEN. YOU'VE JOINED THE *RADRITHA* SCHOOL OF *SWORDSMANSHIP*, RIGHT?

Uh... *YEAH?*

GOT TO CALM DOWN... KEEP YOUR EYES ON HER *FACE*... THINK OF SOMETHING *ELSE*...

WELL, EVERYONE KNOWS THAT YOU NEED *RADRITHA SCHOOLING* TO GET INTO ELITE ROYAL UNITS, SUCH AS THE *MARSHAL PALADINS*...

THINK OF... *GRONAR ELM DISEASE*...

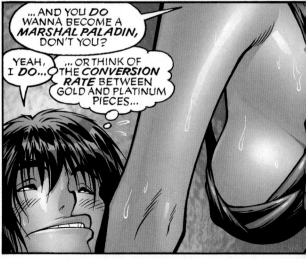

... AND YOU *DO* WANNA BECOME A *MARSHAL PALADIN*, DON'T YOU?

YEAH, I *DO*...

... OR THINK OF... THE *CONVERSION RATE* BETWEEN GOLD AND PLATINUM PIECES...

BUT D'YOU KNOW WHAT THE PALADINS *DO*, WHEN THEY'RE NOT OUT *KILLING FOREIGNERS?*

... OR THINK OF... *WHY IS THE SKY BLUE?*

THEY HUNT DOWN *LAWBREAKERS*. EVEN *KILL* 'EM SOMETIMES.

THEY HUNT DOWN *THIEVES*, GARRISON. *I'M* A THIEF, REMEMBER?

AH...

WILL *YOU* HUNT ME DOWN, WHEN *YOU'RE* A MARSHAL PALADIN?

WILL YOU LET THEM *KILL* ME, GARRISON?

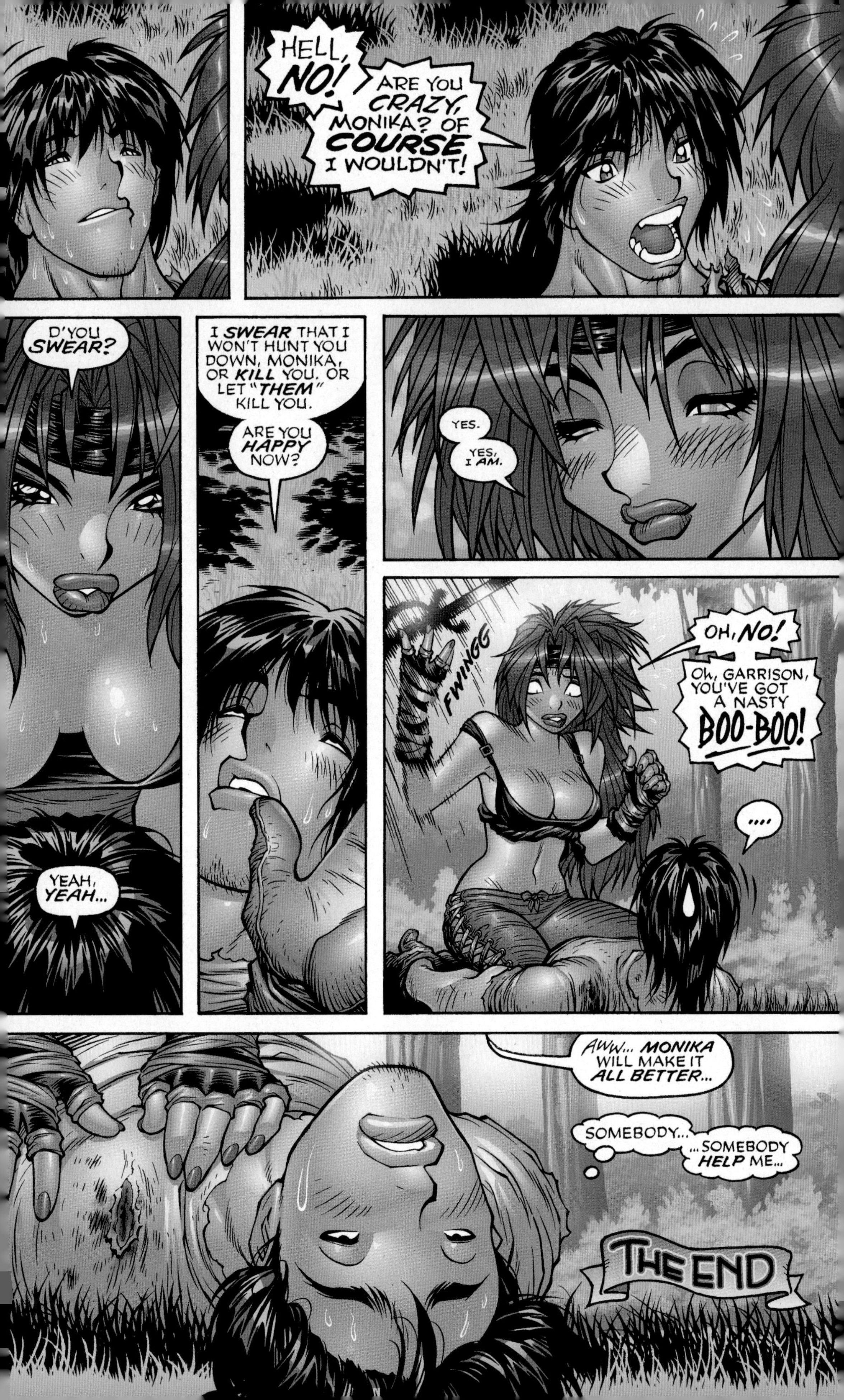
HELL, NO!
ARE YOU CRAZY, MONIKA? OF COURSE I WOULDN'T!
D'YOU SWEAR?
I SWEAR THAT I WON'T HUNT YOU DOWN, MONIKA, OR KILL YOU. OR LET "THEM" KILL YOU.
ARE YOU HAPPY NOW?
YEAH, YEAH...
YES.
YES, I AM.
FWINGG
OH, NO!
OH, GARRISON, YOU'VE GOT A NASTY BOO-BOO!
....
AWW... MONIKA WILL MAKE IT ALL BETTER...
SOMEBODY... ...SOMEBODY HELP ME...
THE END

ISSUE 10

ART FROM THE UNFINISHED ISSUE

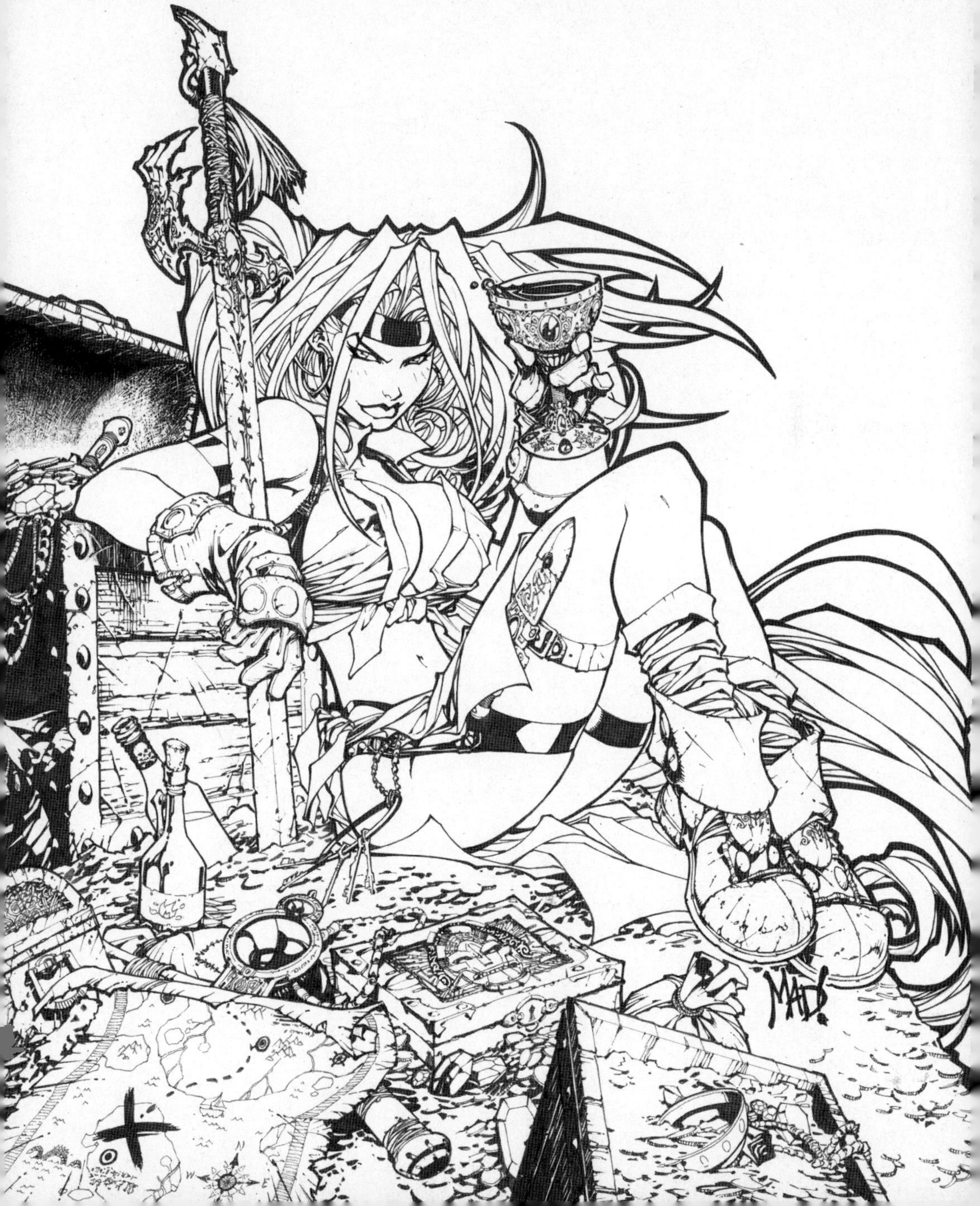
MAD

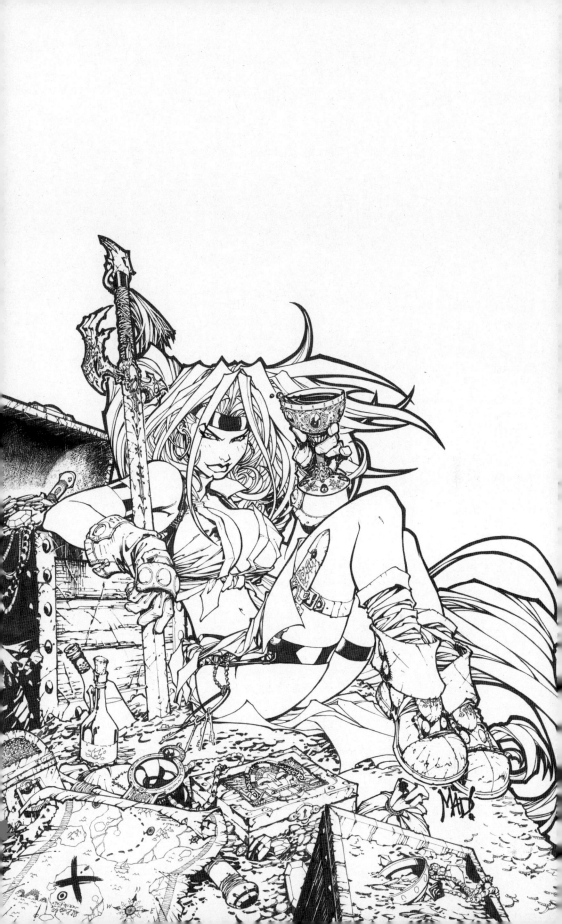

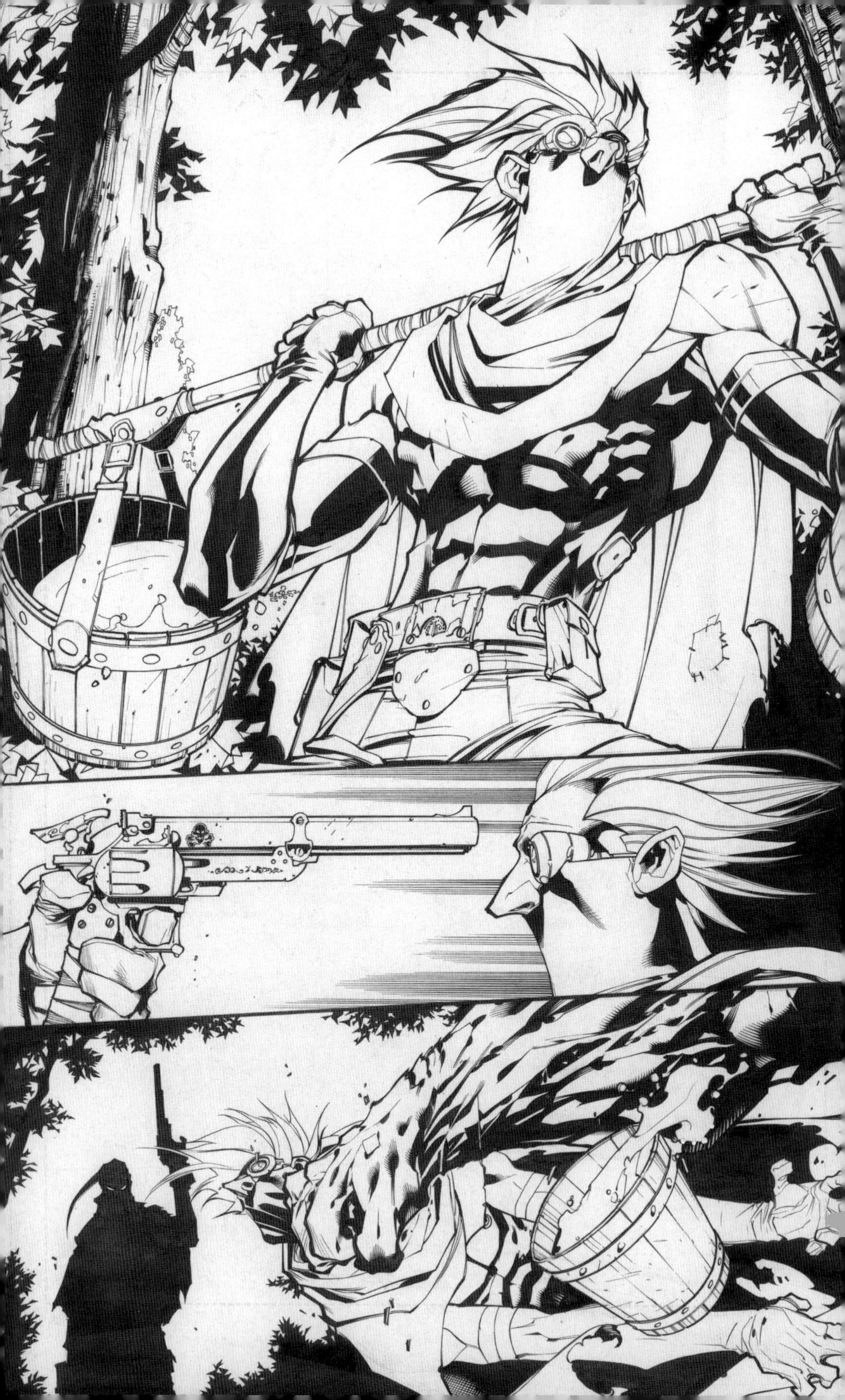

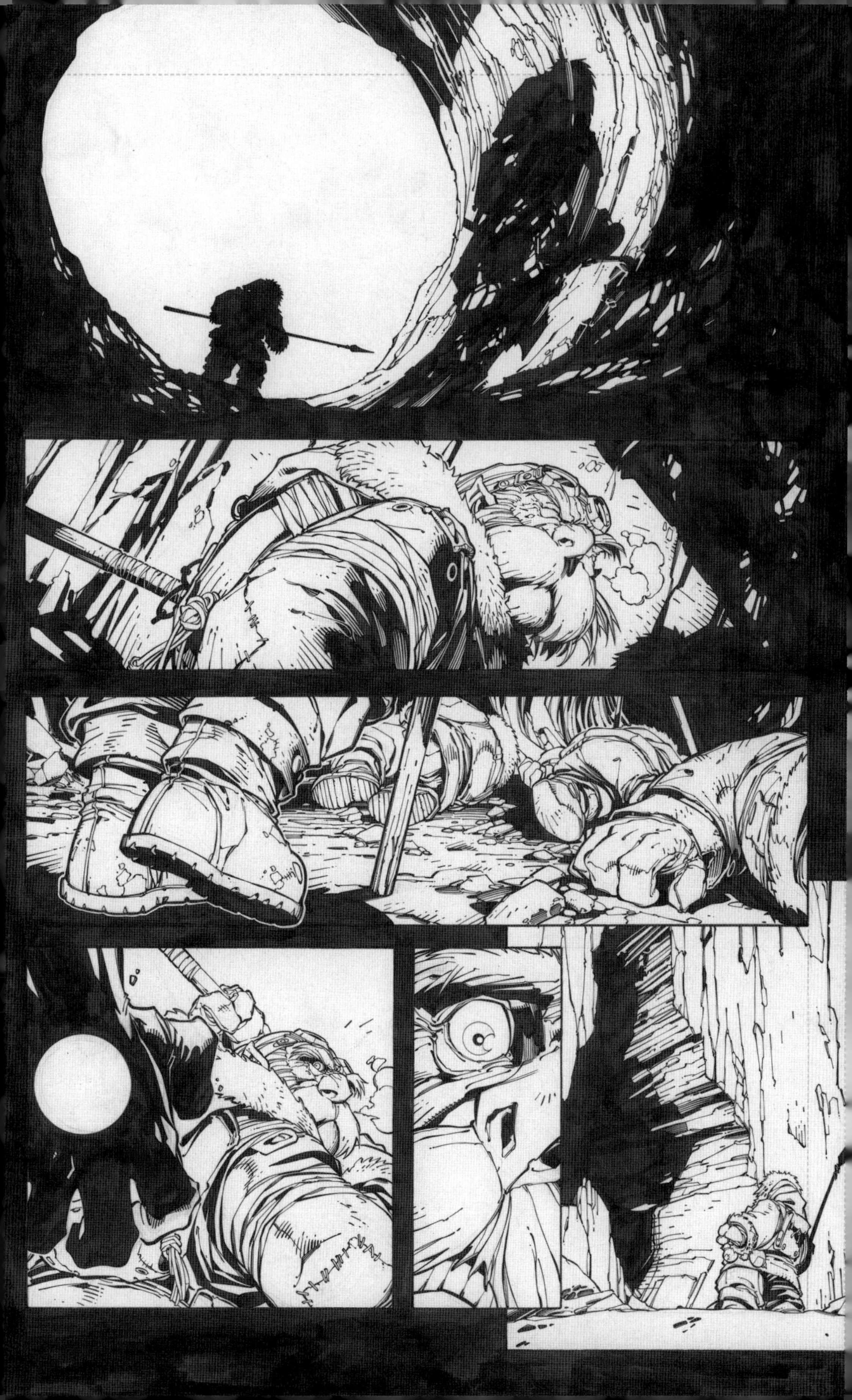

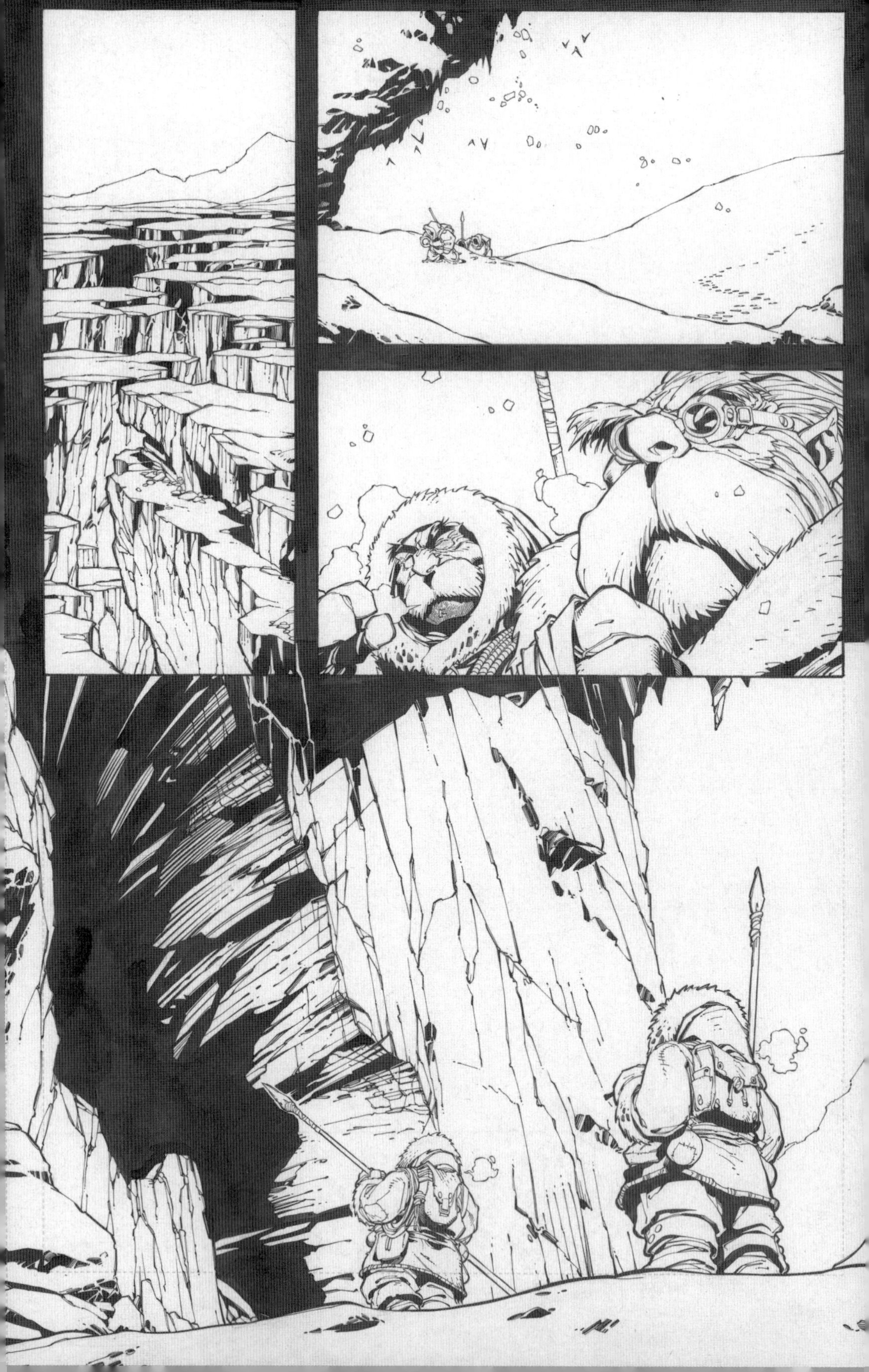

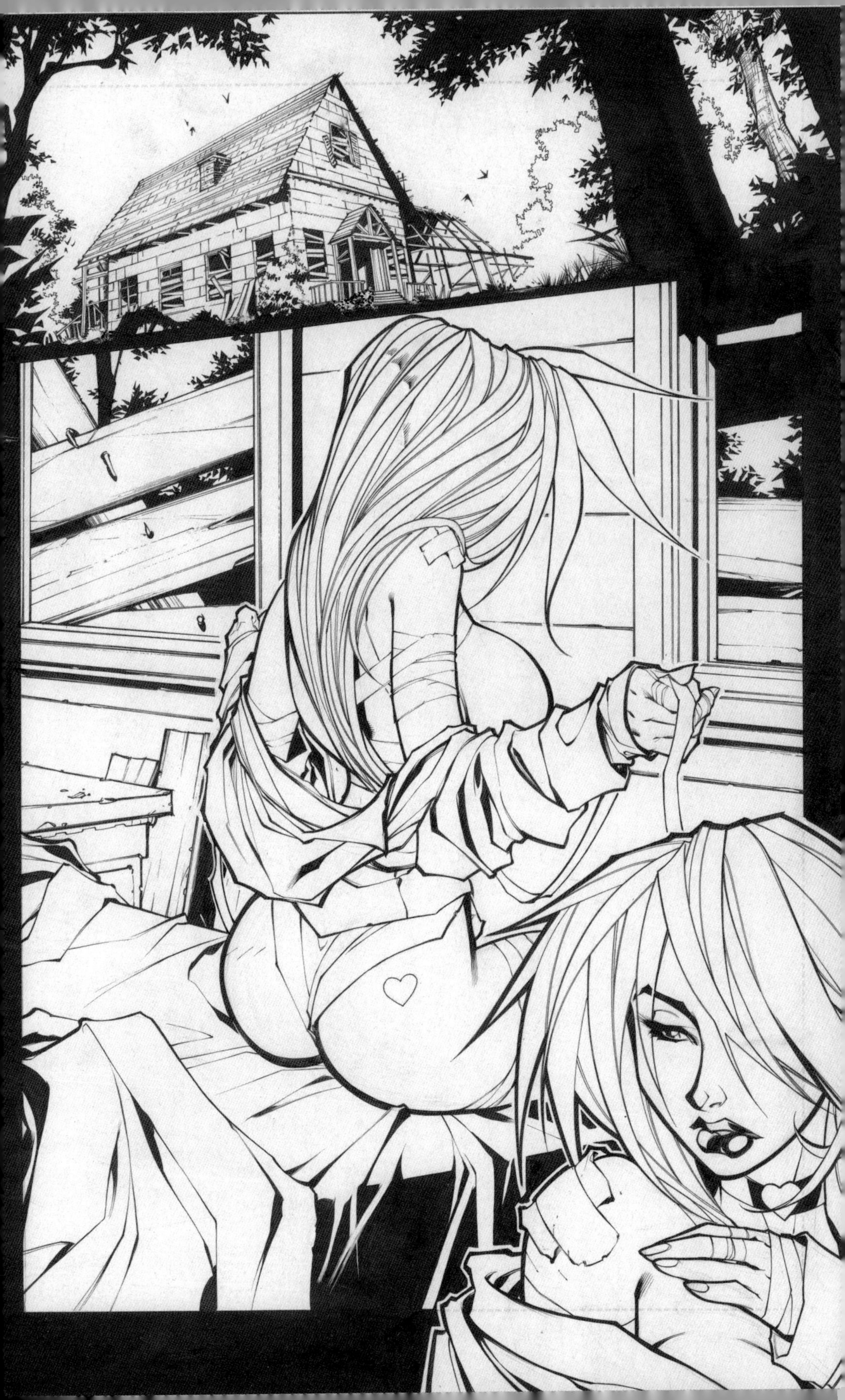

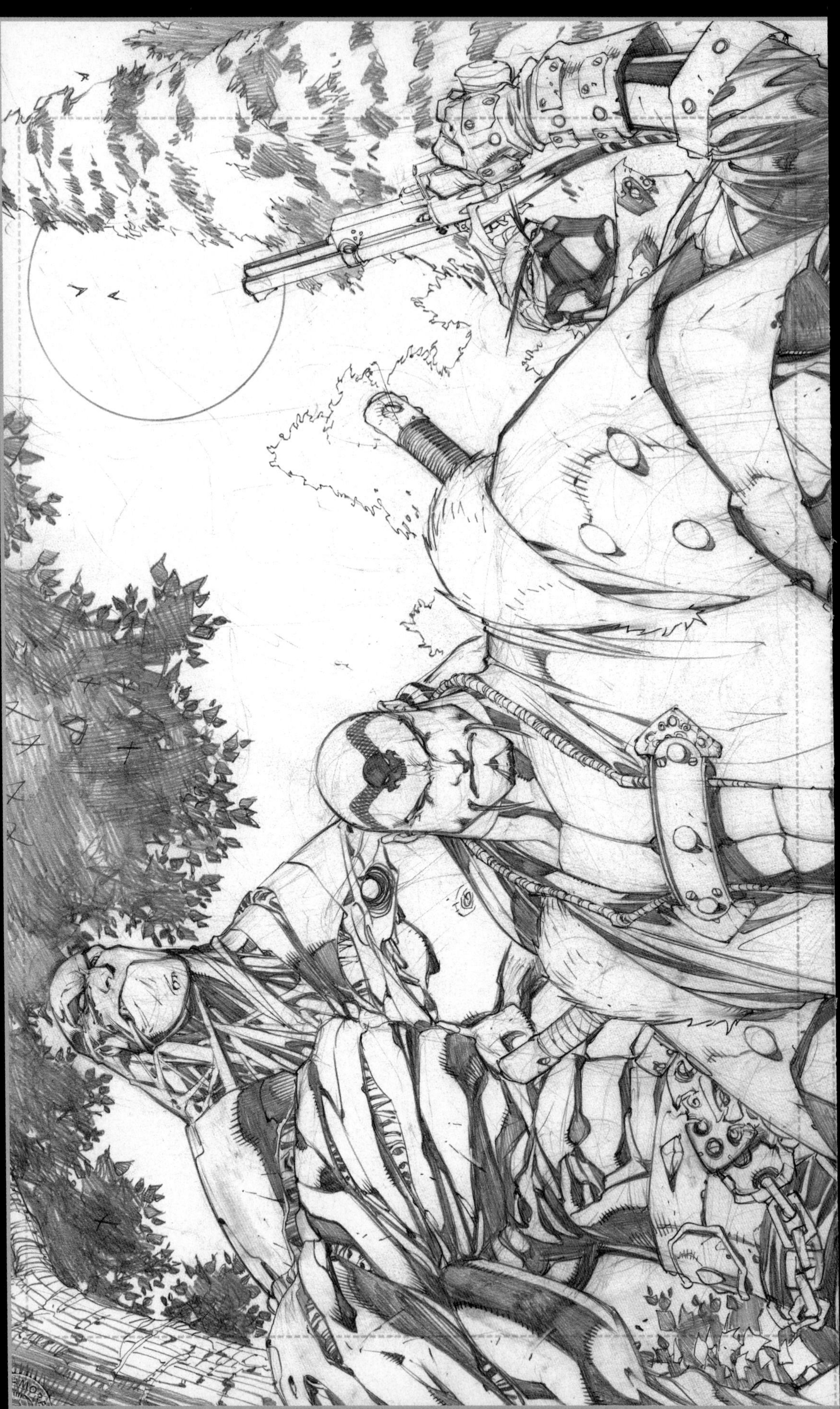

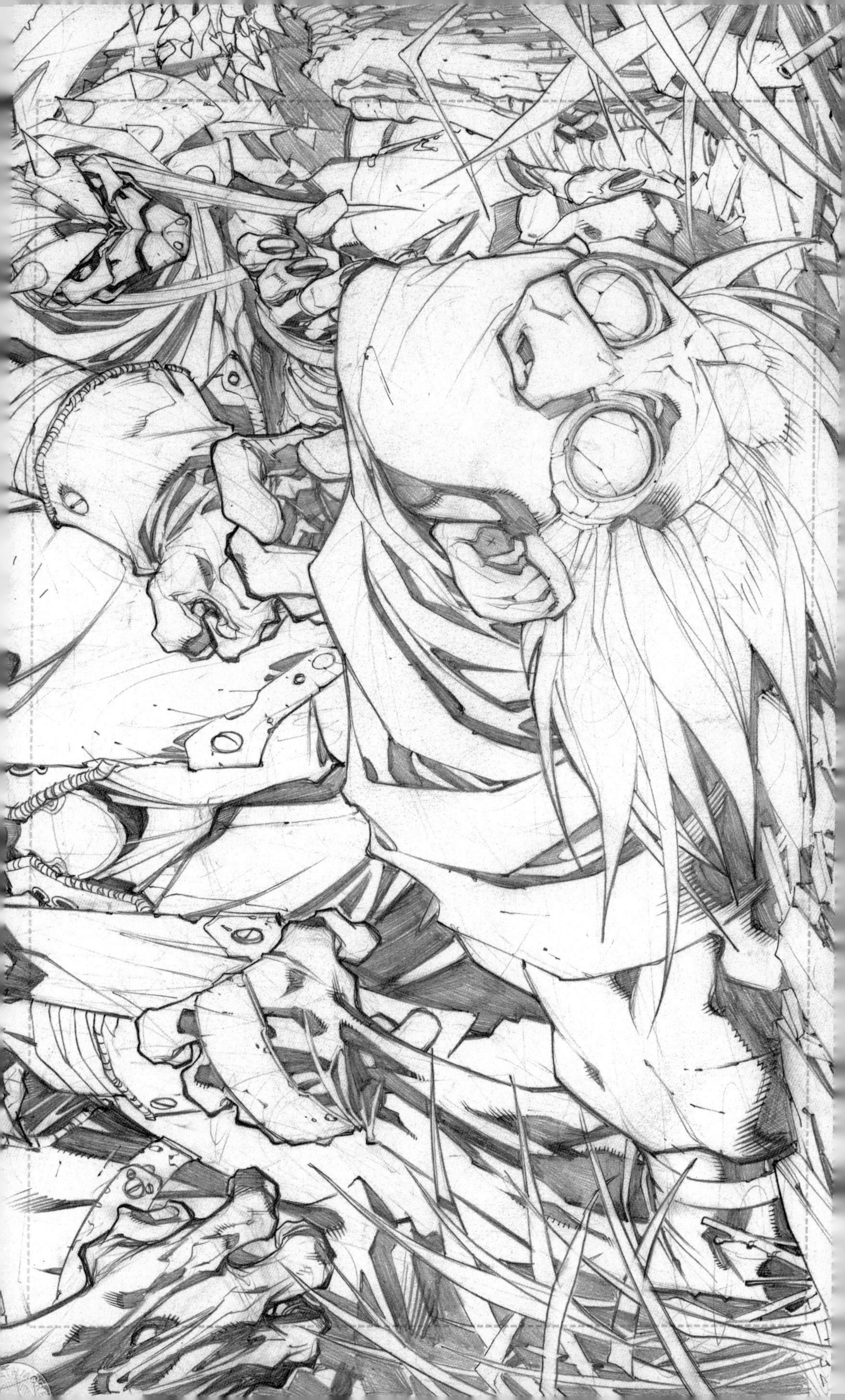

CONGRATULATIONS!

YOU'VE BATTLED YOUR WAY TO THE VERY BACK OF THE BOOK — AND THE SKETCH GALLERY! ON THE FOLLOWING PAGES YOU WILL FIND A SLEW OF BATTLE CHASERS MATERIAL THAT I'VE GATHERED OVER THE YEARS, MUCH OF IT UNRELEASED. THESE SKETCHES RANGE FROM VERY EARLY EXPLORATIVE 'IDEAS' (SOME OF THEM TERRIBLE!) , TO CONVENTION SKETCHES, PERSONAL SKETCHES, PROMO ART ETC. IT WAS VERY IMPORTANT TO EVERYONE WHO WORKED ON THIS BOOK TO GIVE READERS A 'COMPLETE' COLLECTION, AND WE DUG DEEP FOR EVERY LITTLE SCRAP WE COULD FIND.

SPEAKING OF EVERYONE'S HARD WORK, I'D LIKE TO TAKE THIS OPPORTUNITY TO THANK EVERYONE INVOLVED IN PUTTING THIS MONSTER TOGETHER. THE OLD CREW — MUNIER, CHRIS AND ARON AT LIQUID!, RICHARD AND COMICRAFT, TOM MCWEENEY AND EVERYONE WHO STEPPED IN DURING CRUNCH TIME TO HELP GET THE BOOK OUT THE DOOR. THANKS TO IMAGE, FOR THEIR PERSISTENCE AND TIRELESS EFFORT. TRACKING ALL THIS STUFF DOWN AFTER SO MANY YEARS WAS NO EASY TASK, AND HONESTLY, THEY BEAT DOWN MY DOOR FOR YEARS UNTIL I FINALLY AGREED TO RELEASE THIS THING. THANKS TO DC AND WILDSTORM FOR BEING COOL ENOUGH TO COLLABORATE WITH EVERYONE TO TRACK DOWN THOSE LAST FEW MISSING FILES.

MOST IMPORTANTLY, I'D LIKE TO THANK YOU, THE READERS. YOUR OVERWHELMING SUPPORT HAS BEEN A CONSTANT SOURCE OF INSPIRATION THROUGHOUT THE YEARS. YOU, MORE THAN ANYONE MADE THIS COLLECTION POSSIBLE.

THANKS, AND ENJOY!

JOE MADUREIRA

SKETCH GALLERY

DESIGNS & SKETCHES FROM THE WORLD OF BATTLE CHASERS

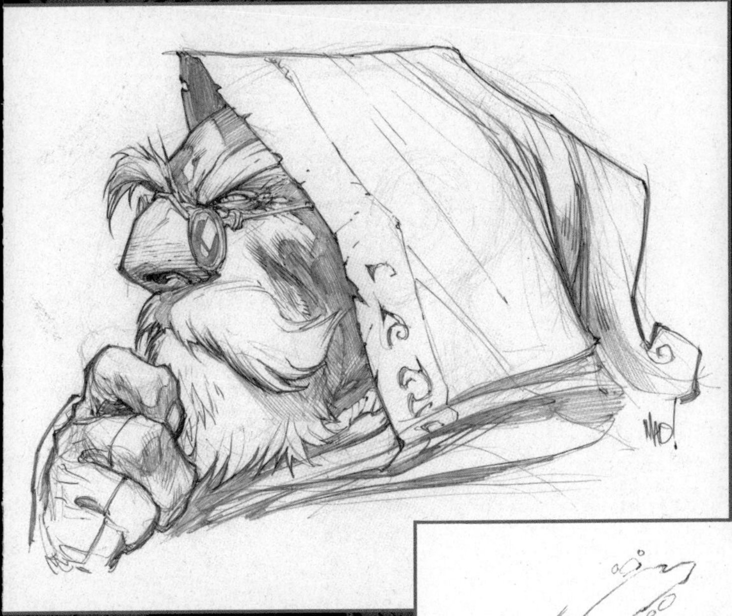

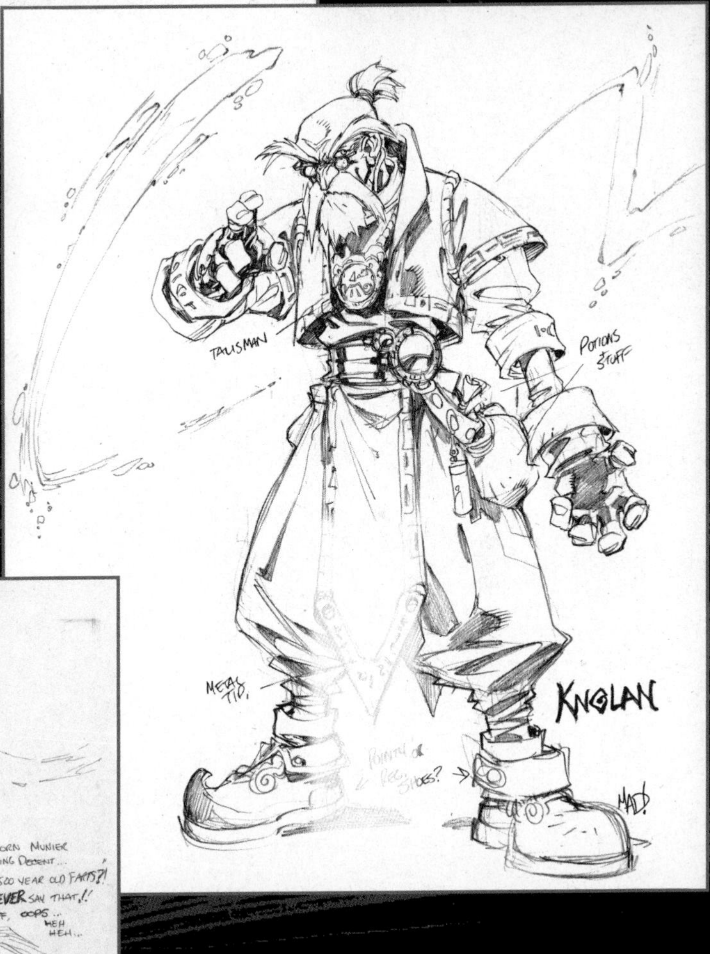
TALISMAN
POTIONS & STUFF
METAL TIP
KNOLAN
POINTY OR REG. SHOES?

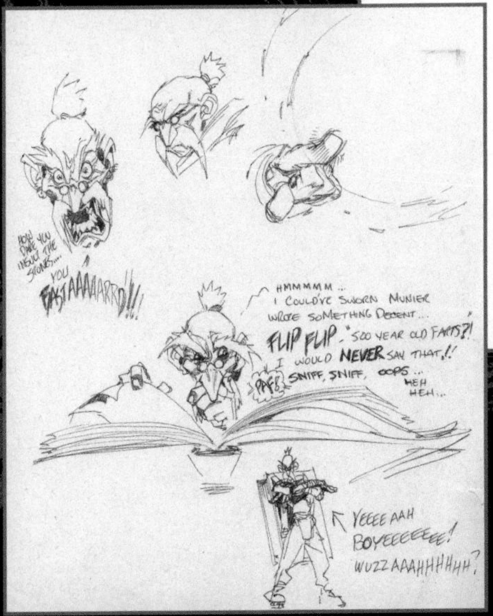
HOW DARE YOU INSULT THE STONES.... YOU BASTAAAAARRD!!!
HMMMMM... I COULD'VE SWORN MUNIER WROTE SOMETHING DECENT...
FLIP FLIP
"500 YEAR OLD FARTS?! I WOULD NEVER SAY THAT!!
PAF!
SNIFF, SNIFF, OOPS... HEH HEH...
YEEEE AAH BOYEEEEEEE! WUZZ AAAHHHHHH?

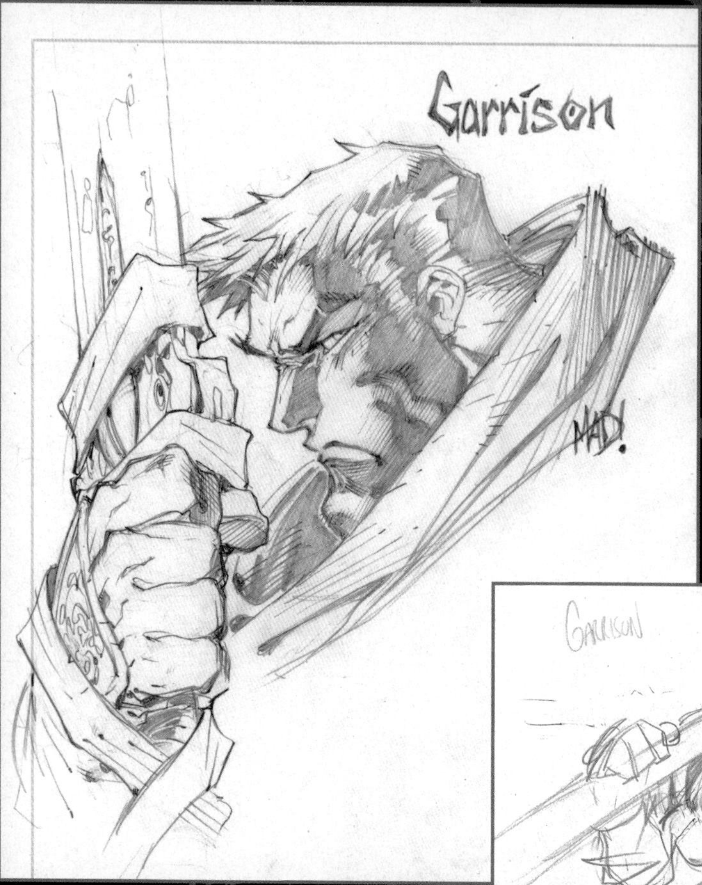
Garrison
MAD!

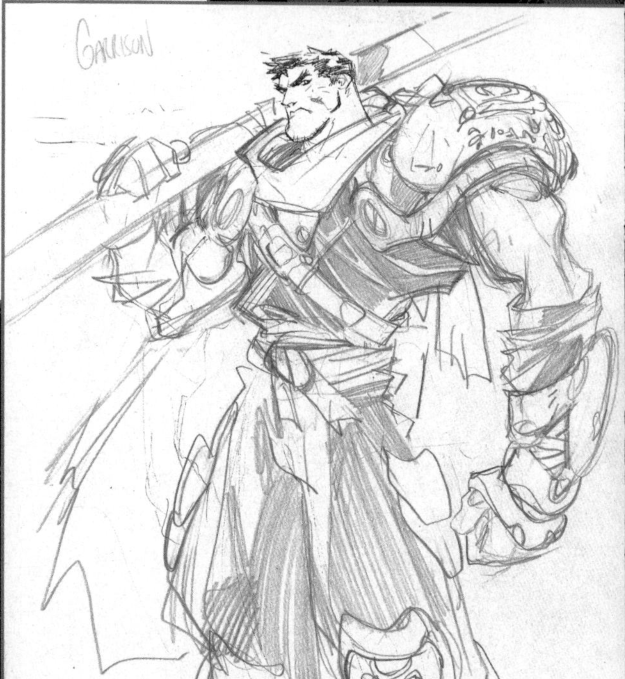
GARRISON

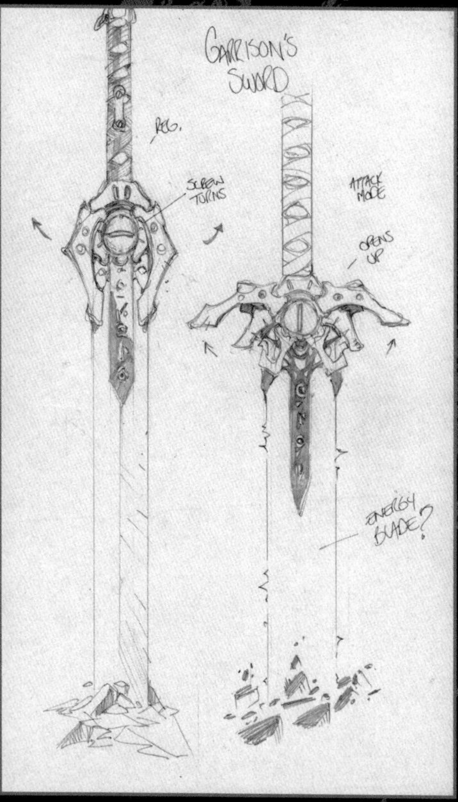
GARRISON'S SWORD
REG.
SCREW TURNS
ATTACK MODE
OPENS UP
ENERGY BLADE?

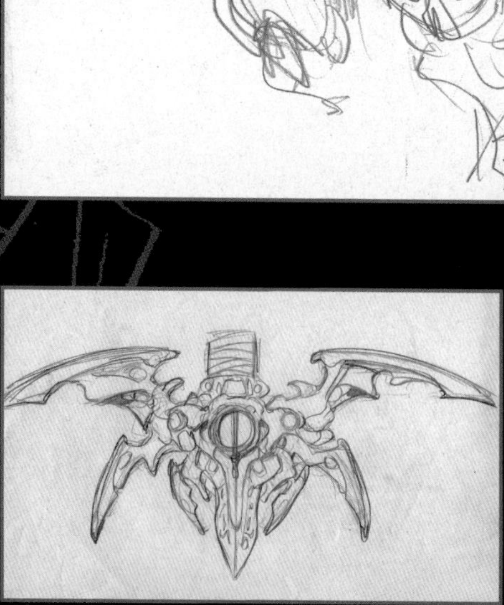

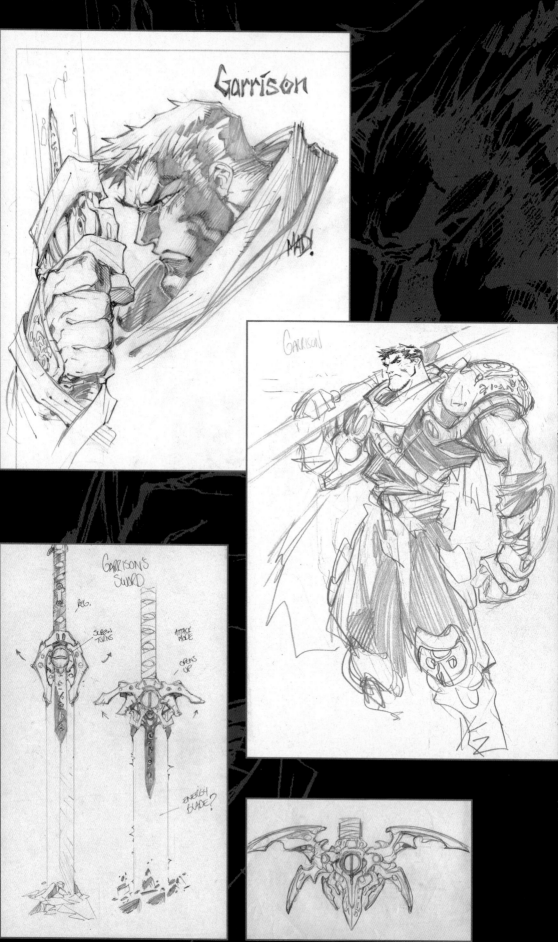

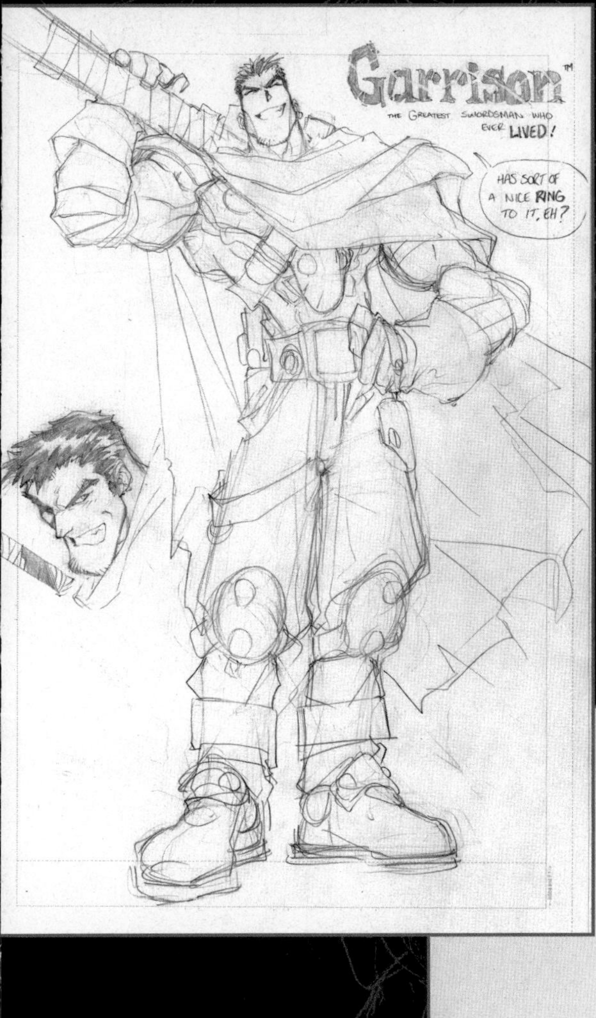
Garrison™
THE GREATEST SWORDSMAN WHO EVER LIVED!
HAS SORT OF A NICE RING TO IT, EH?

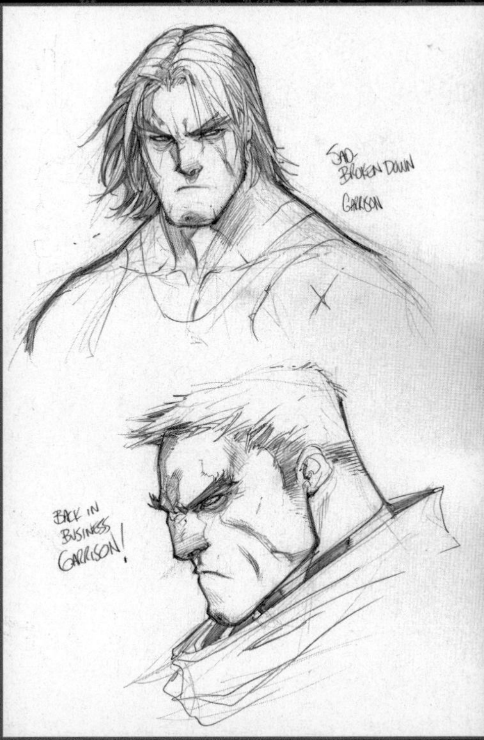
SAD BROKEN DOWN GARRISON
BACK IN BUSINESS GARRISON!

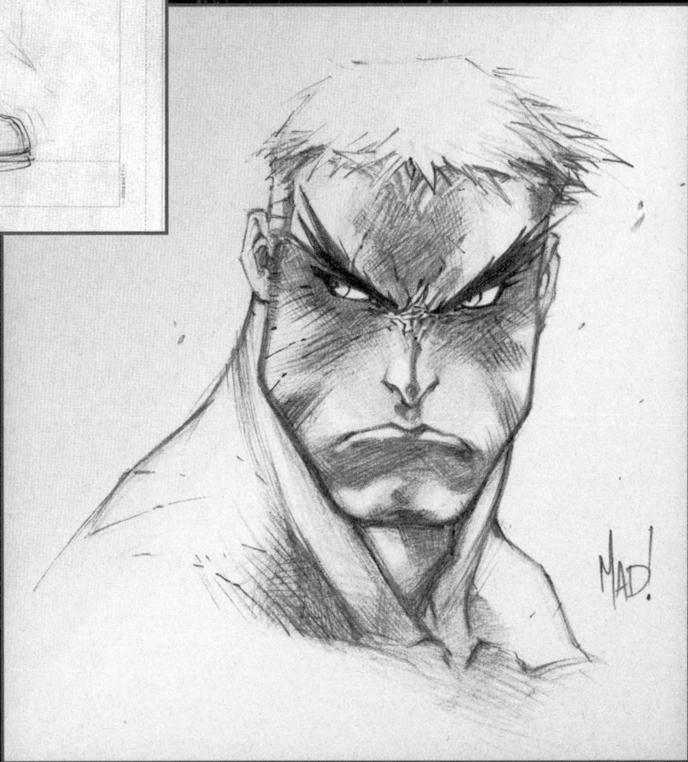

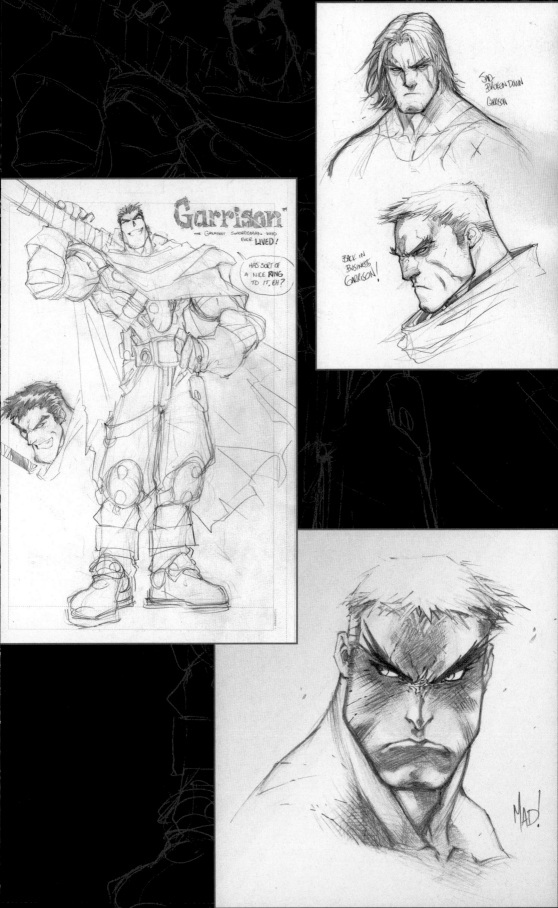

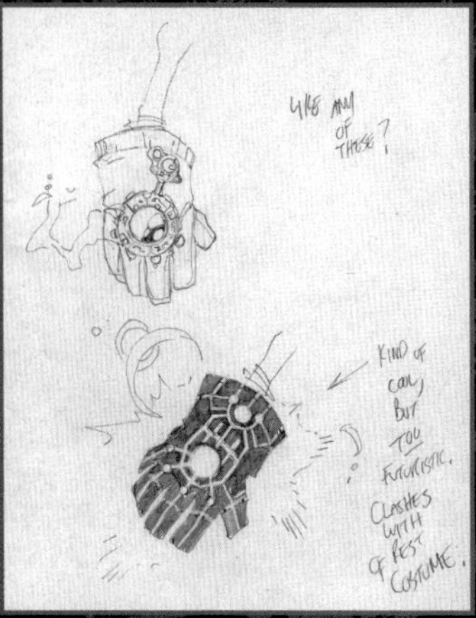
LIKE ANY OF THESE?
KIND OF COOL, BUT TOO FUTURISTIC.
CLASHES WITH REST OF COSTUME.

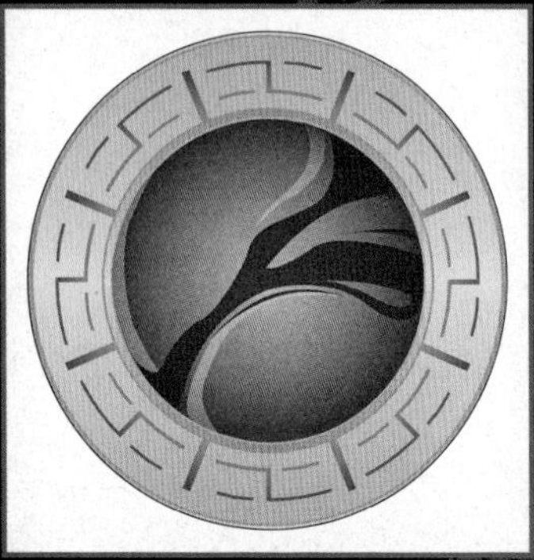

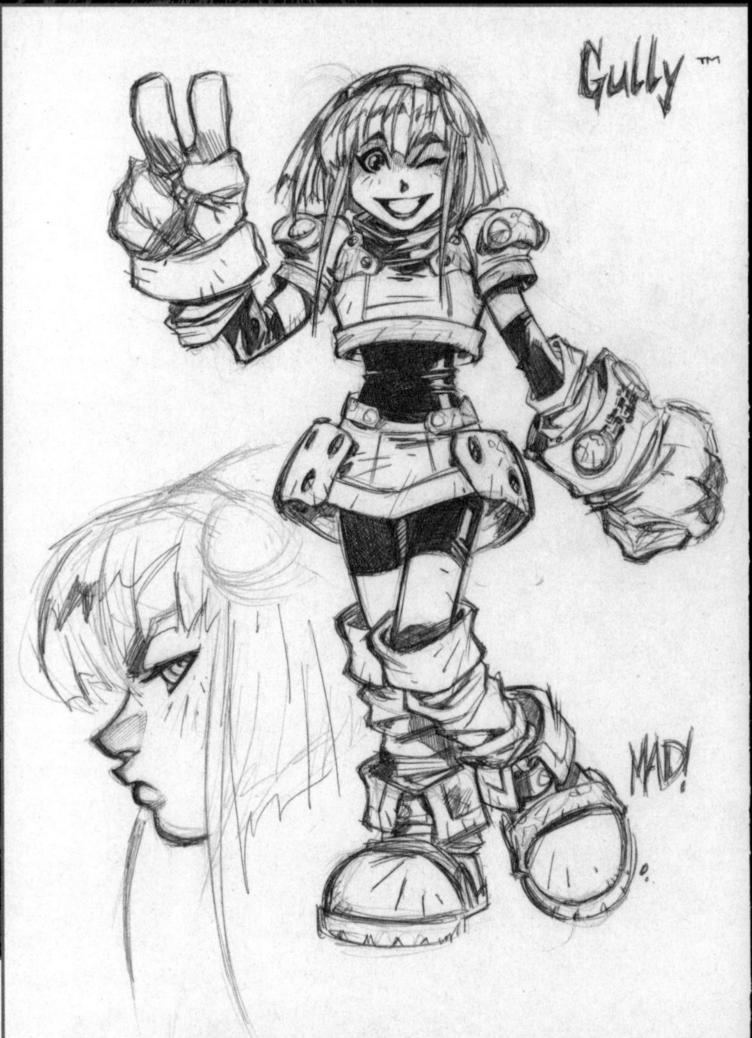
Gully™
MAD!

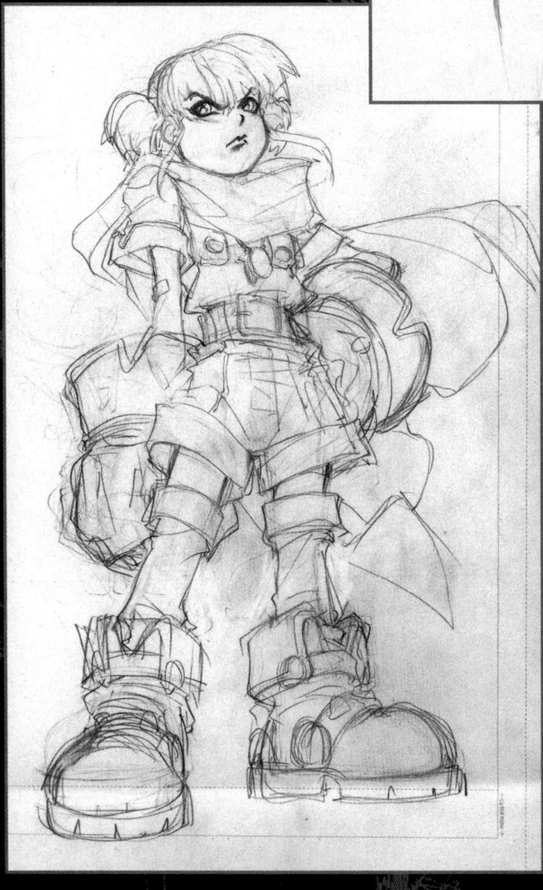

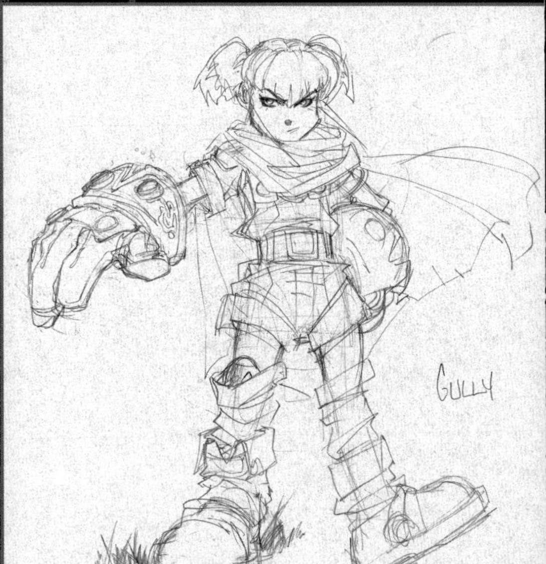
GULLY

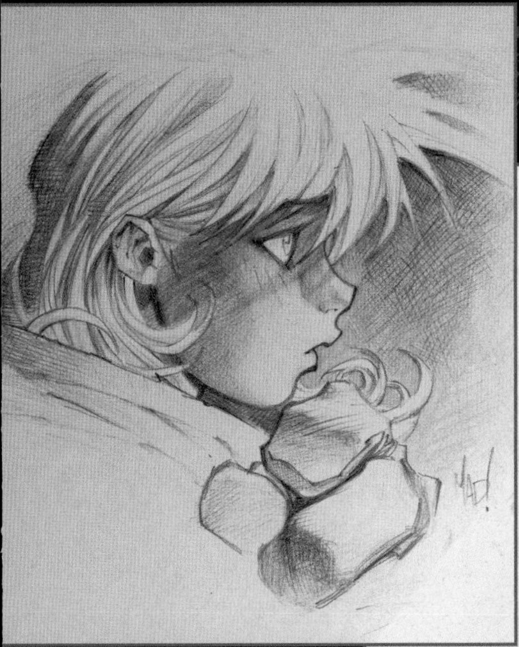

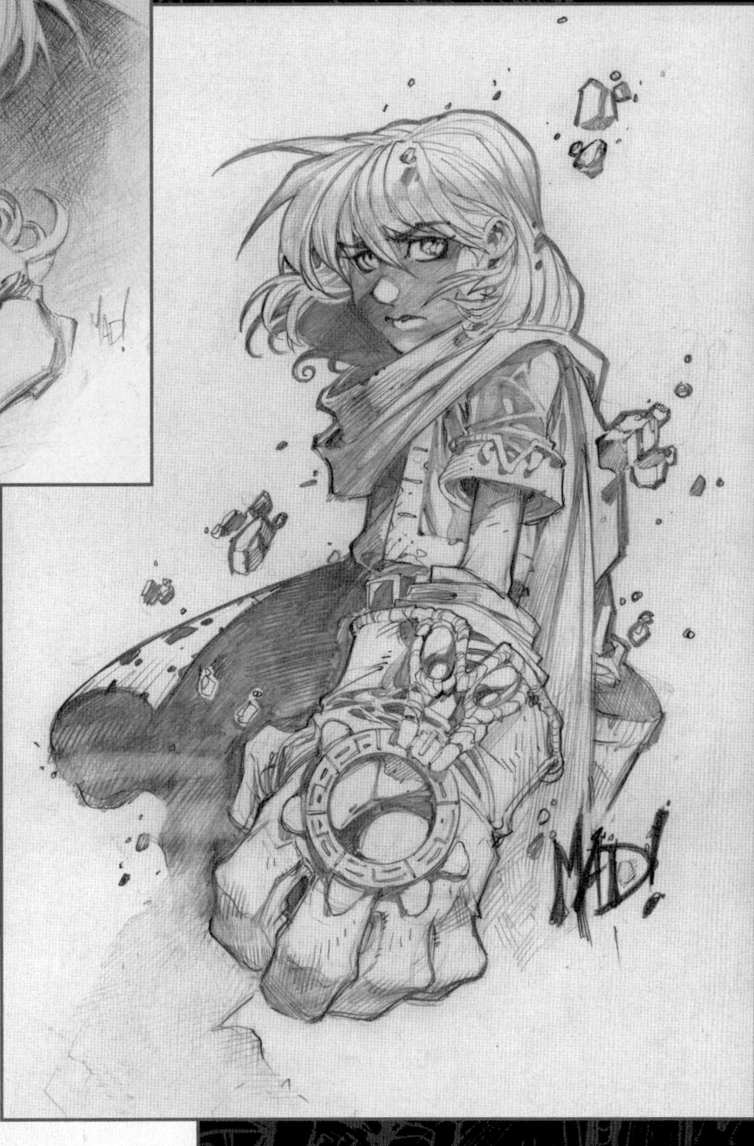

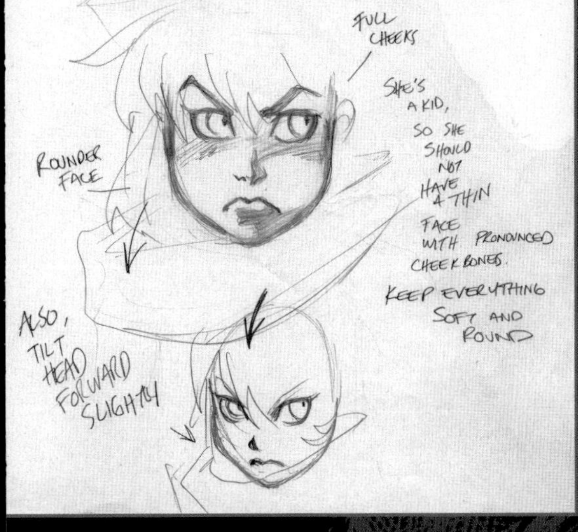
FULL CHEEKS
SHE'S A KID, SO SHE SHOULD NOT HAVE A THIN FACE WITH PRONOUNCED CHEEKBONES.
KEEP EVERYTHING SOFT AND ROUND
ROUNDER FACE
ALSO, TILT HEAD FORWARD SLIGHTLY

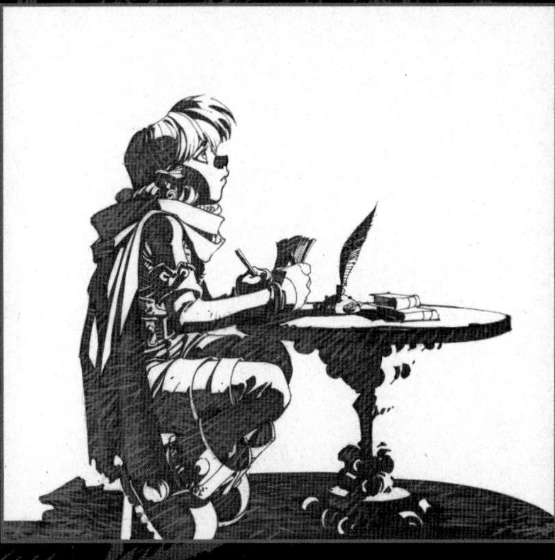

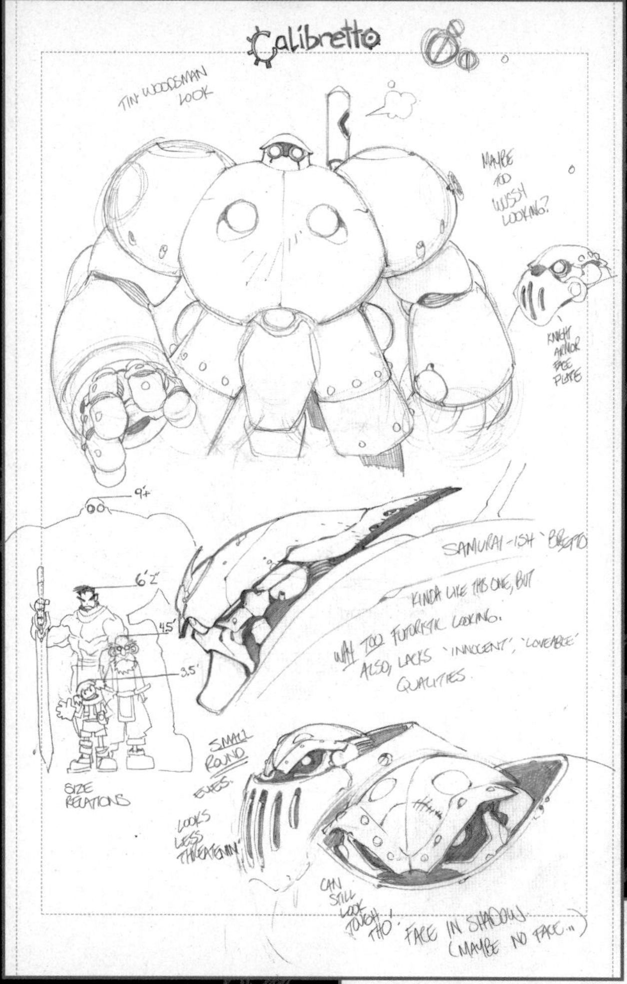
Calibretto
TIN WOODSMAN LOOK
MAYBE TOO WUSSY LOOKING?
KNIGHT ARMOR FACE PLATE
9'+
6'2"
4.5'
3.5'
SIZE RELATIONS
SAMURAI-ISH 'BRETTO
KINDA LIKE THIS ONE, BUT WAY TOO FUTURISTIC LOOKING. ALSO, LACKS 'INNOCENT', 'LOVEABLE' QUALITIES.
SMALL ROUND EYES.
LOOKS LESS THREATENIN'
CAN STILL LOOK TOUGH THO'!
FACE IN SHADOW (MAYBE NO FACE...)

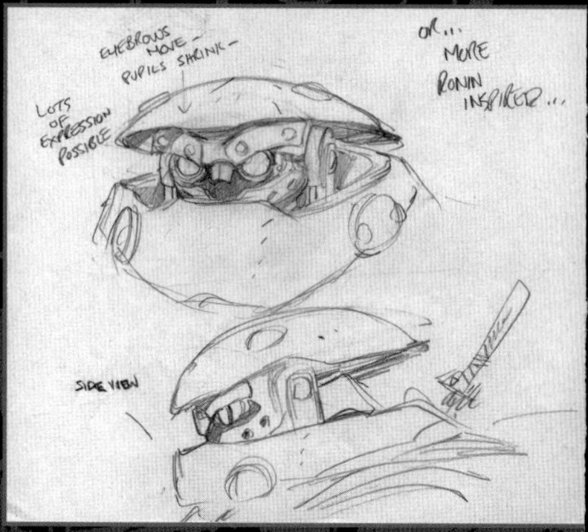
EYEBROWS MOVE - PUPILS SHRINK -
LOTS OF EXPRESSION POSSIBLE
OR... MORE RONIN INSPIRED...
SIDE VIEW

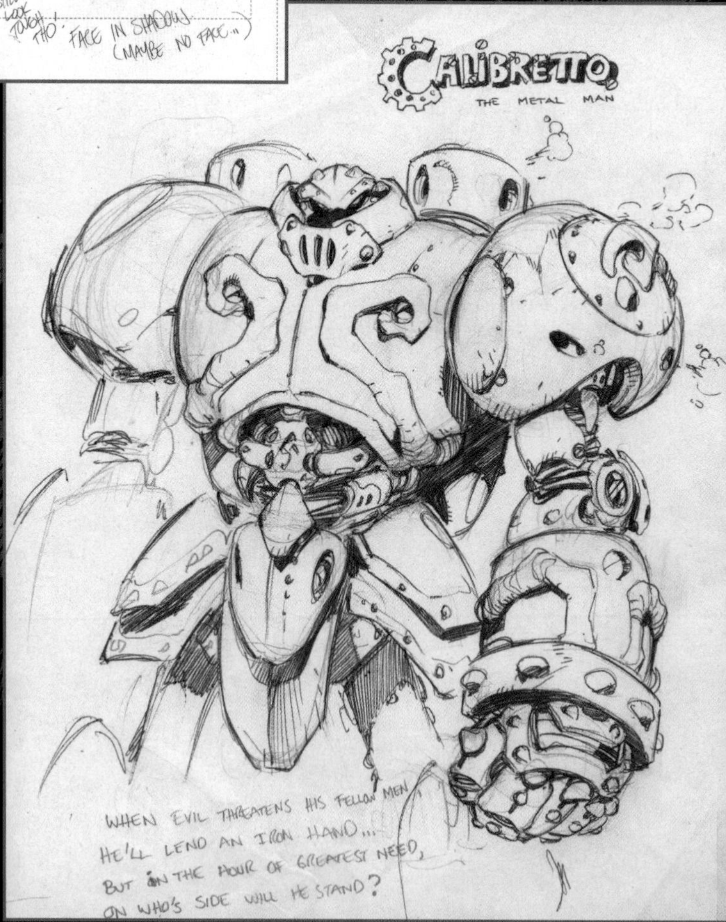
CALIBRETTO
THE METAL MAN
WHEN EVIL THREATENS HIS FELLOW MEN
HE'LL LEND AN IRON HAND...
BUT IN THE HOUR OF GREATEST NEED,
ON WHO'S SIDE WILL HE STAND?

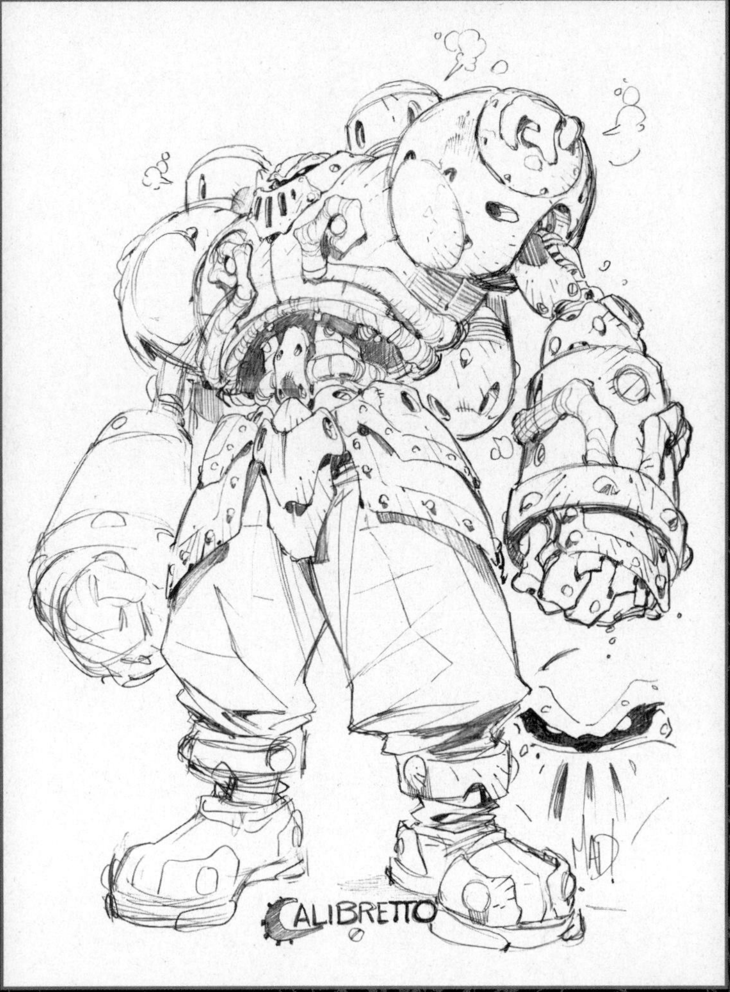
CALIBRETTO

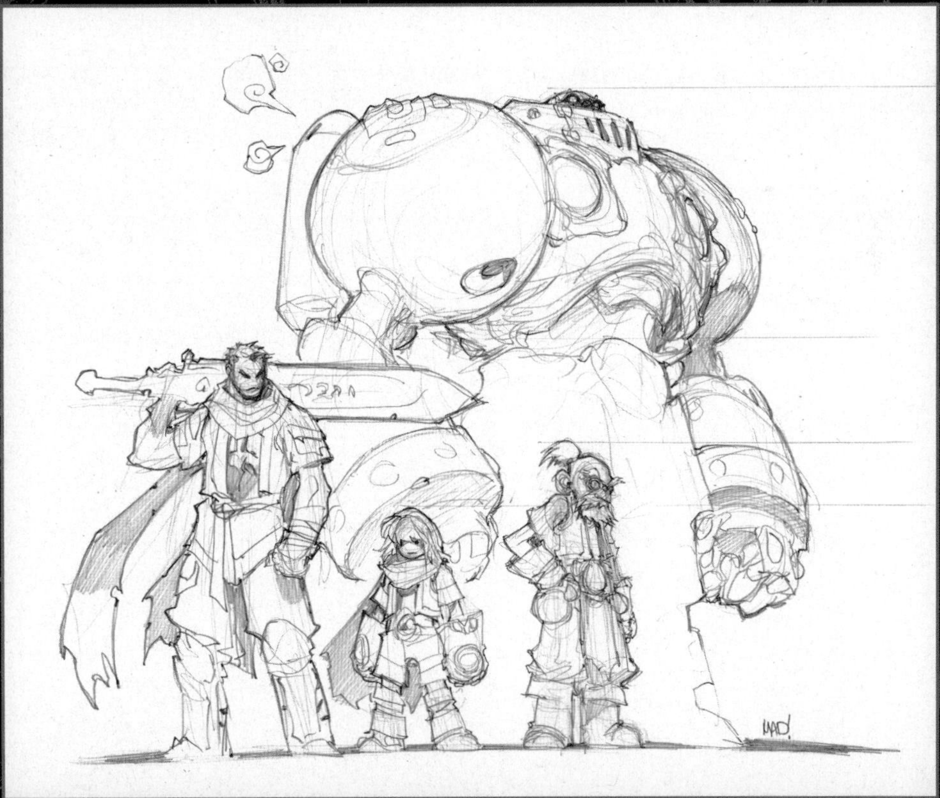

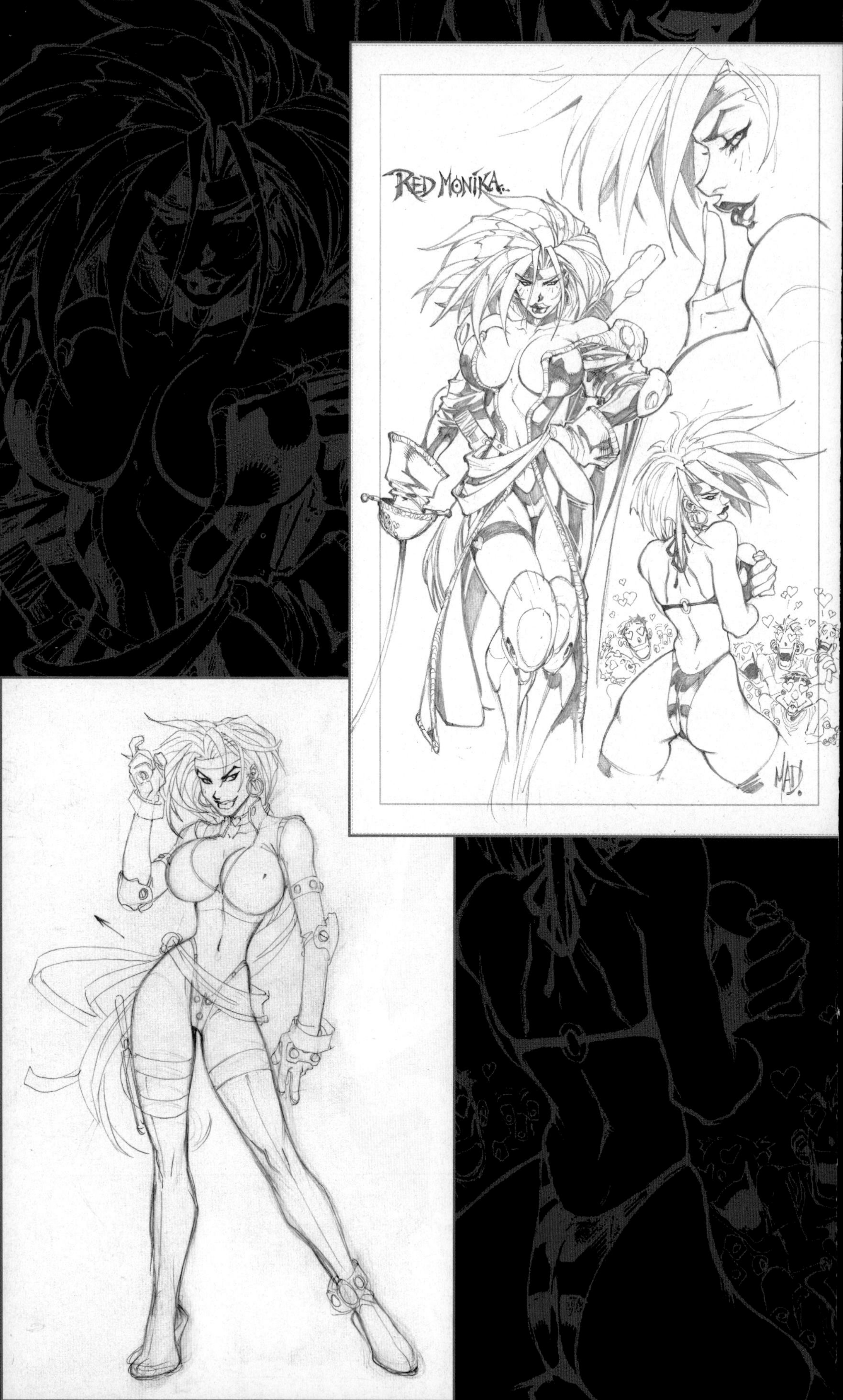
RED MONIKA...

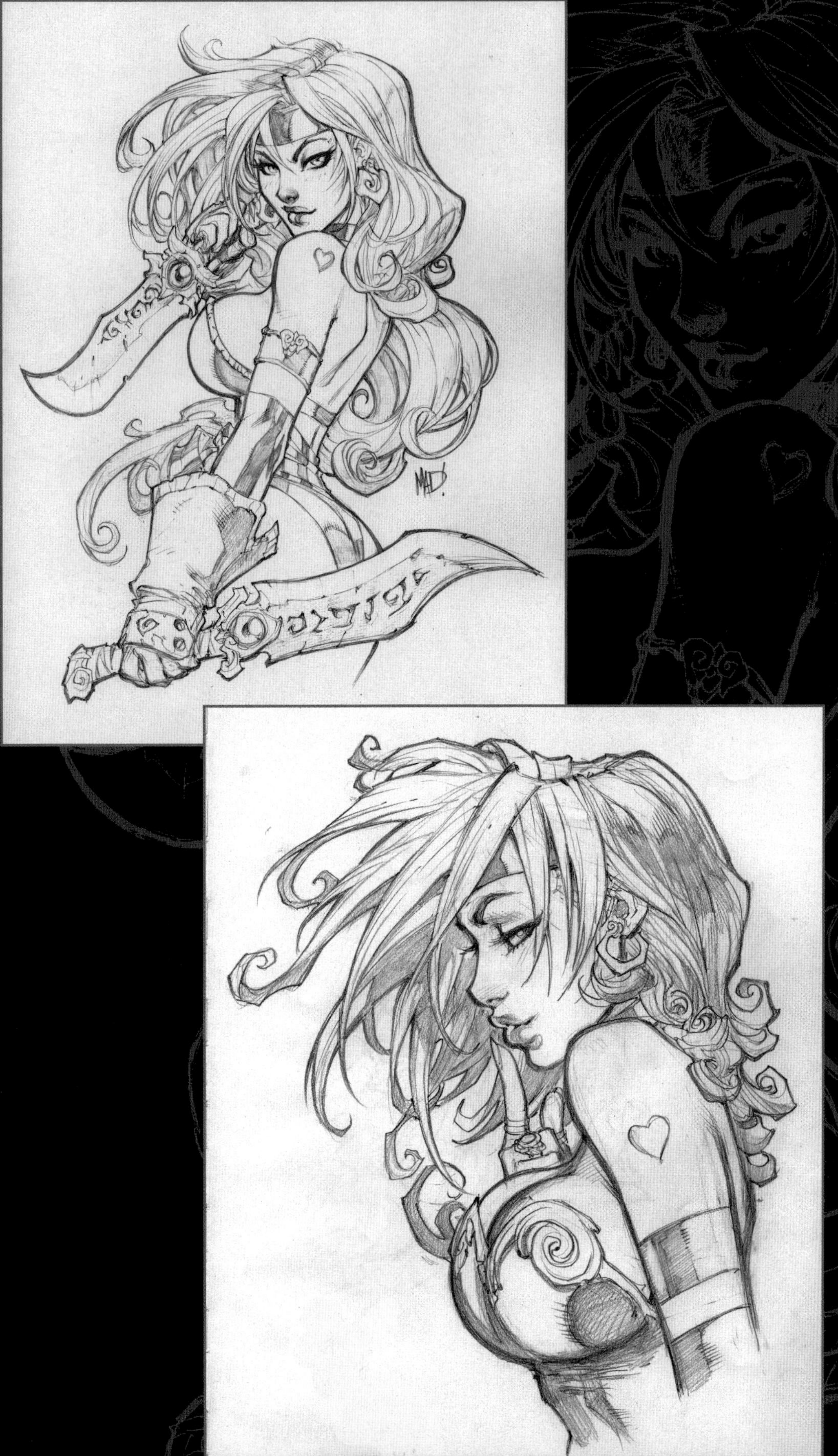

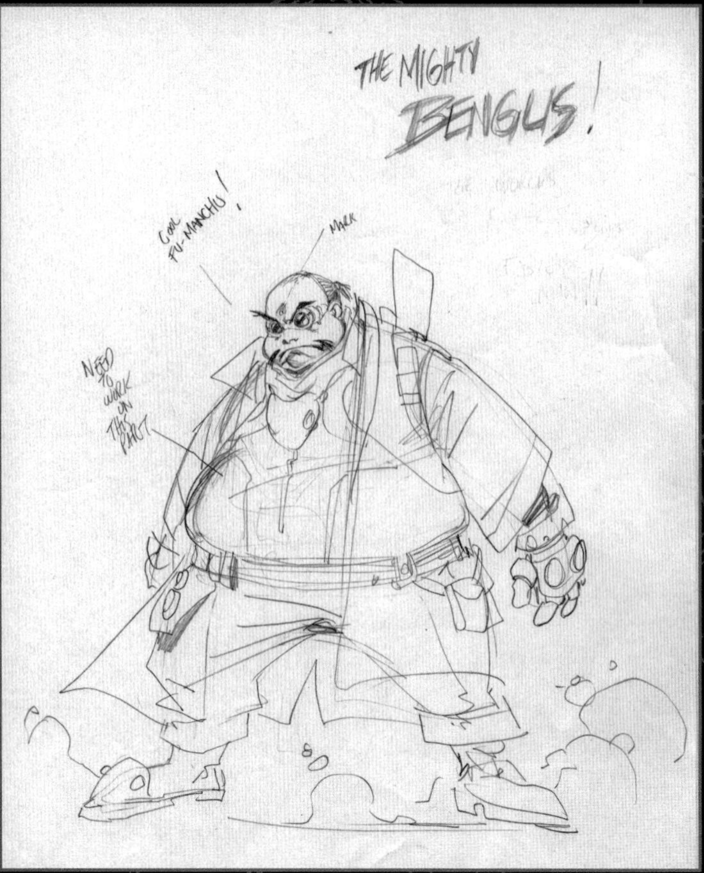
THE MIGHTY
BENGUS!
COOL FU-MANCHU!
MARK
NEED TO WORK ON THIS PART

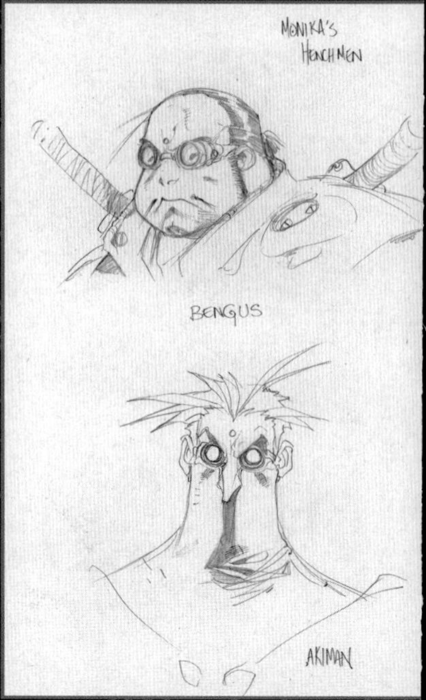
MONIKA'S HENCHMEN
BENGUS
AKIMAN

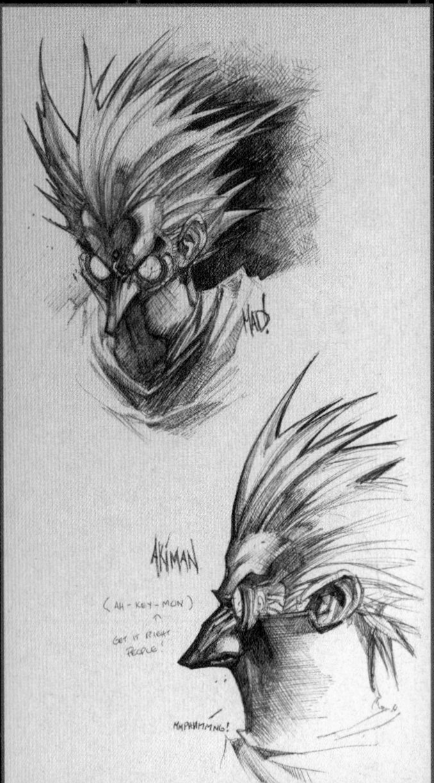
MAD!
AKIMAN
(AH-KEY-MON)
GET IT RIGHT PEOPLE!
MMPHHMMNG!

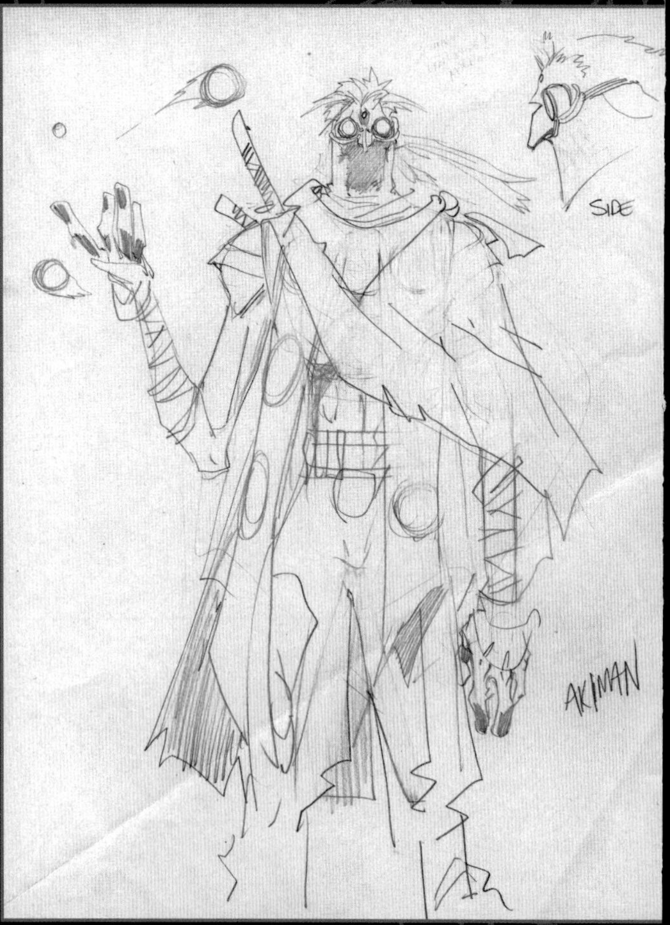
SIDE
AKIMAN

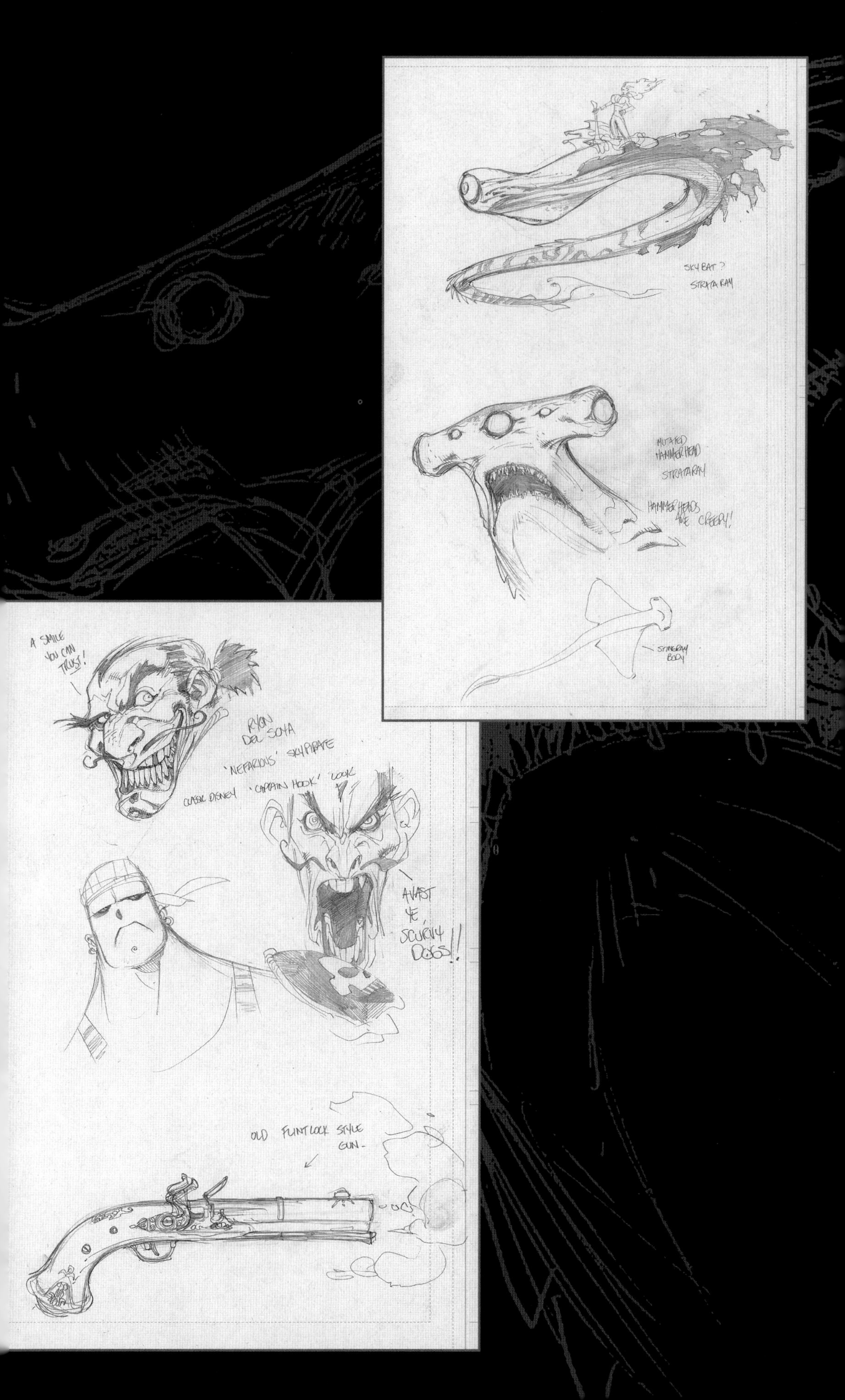
SKY BAT ?
STRATA RAM
MUTATED HAMMERHEAD
STRATARAY
HAMMERHEADS ARE CREEPY!
STINGRAY BODY
A SMILE YOU CAN TRUST!
RYON DEL SOYA
'NEFARIOUS' SKY PIRATE
CLASSIC DISNEY 'CAPTAIN HOOK' LOOK
AVAST YE, SCURVY DOGS!!
OLD FLINTLOCK STYLE GUN.

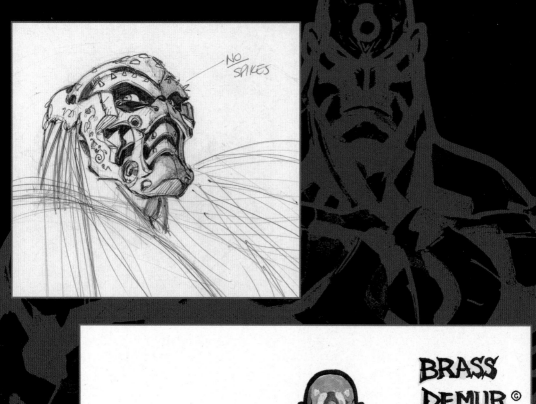

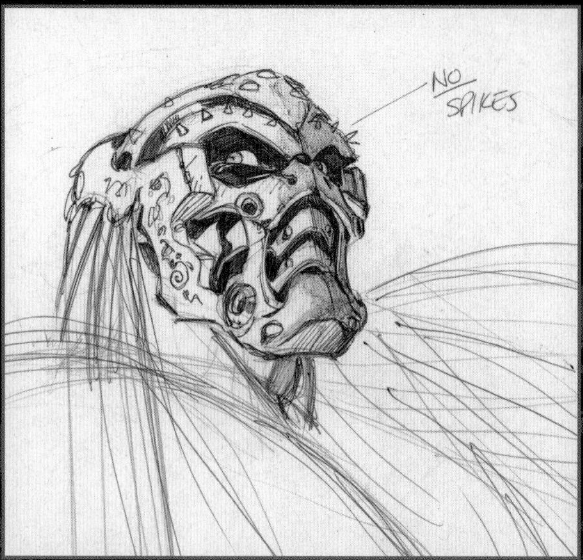
NO SPIKES

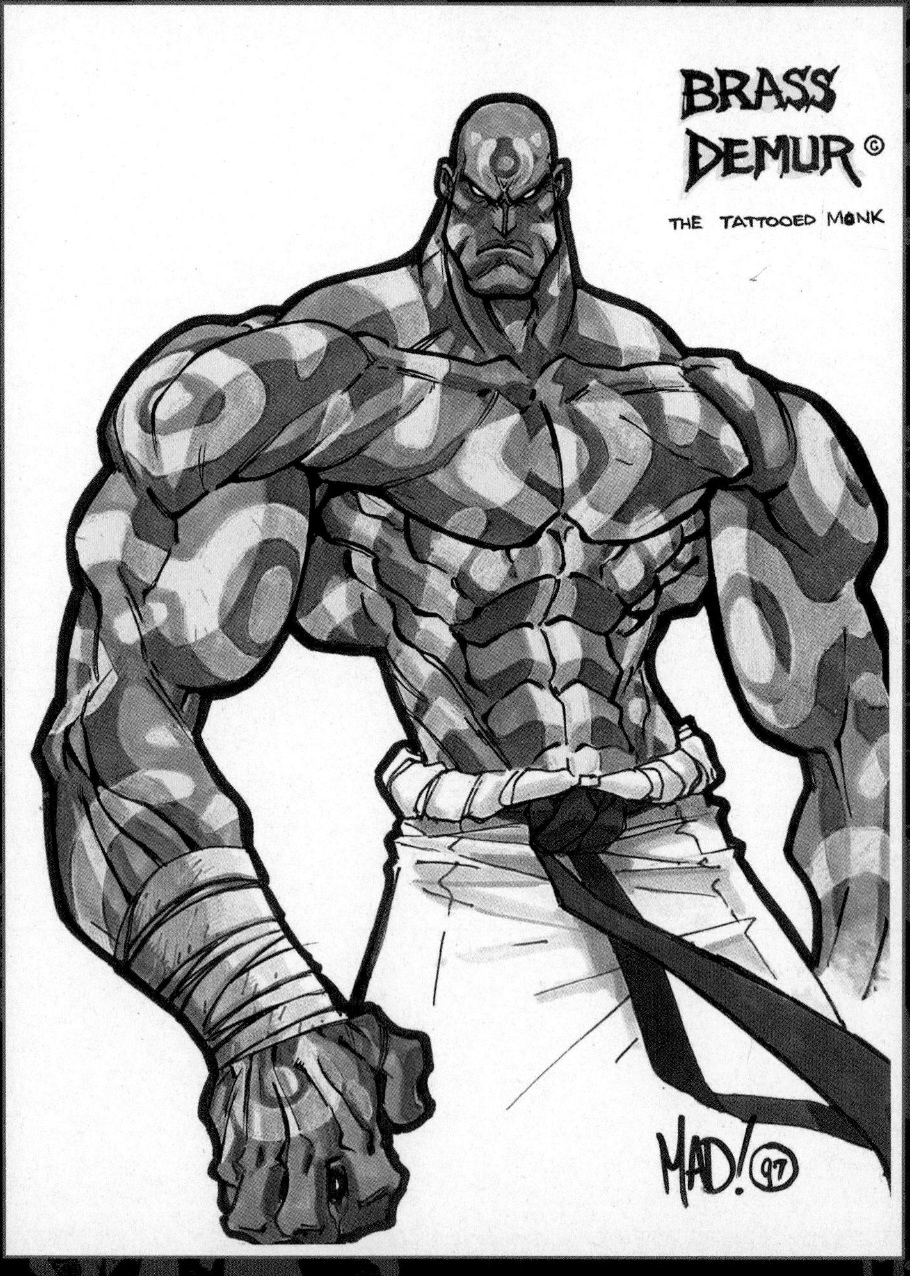
BRASS DEMUR ©
THE TATTOOED MONK
MAD! 97

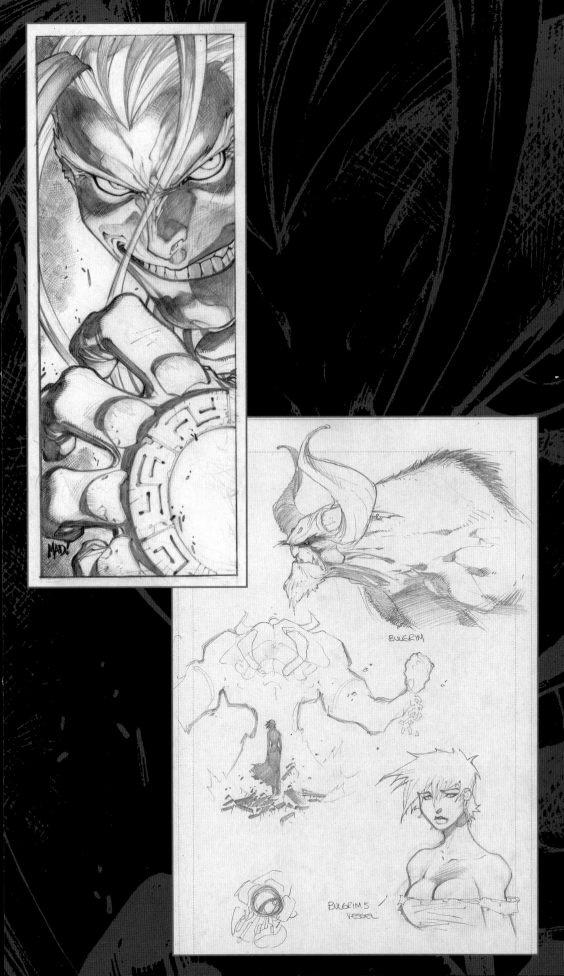

BULGRIM

BULGRIM'S
VESSEL

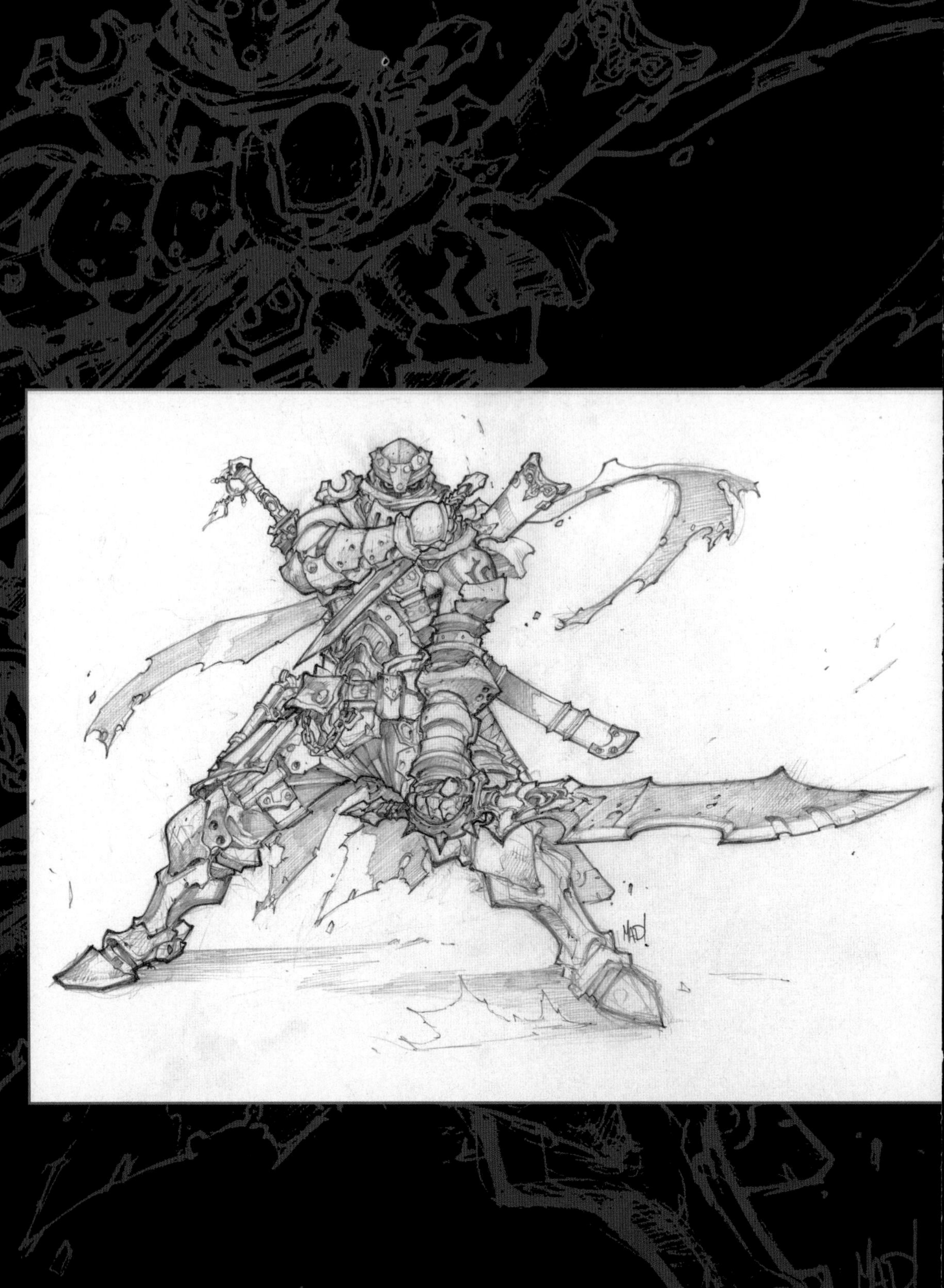

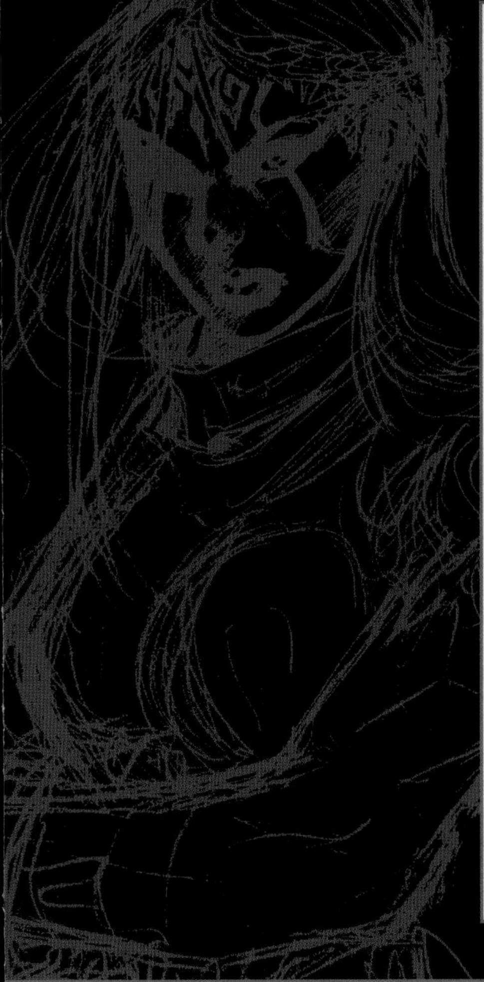

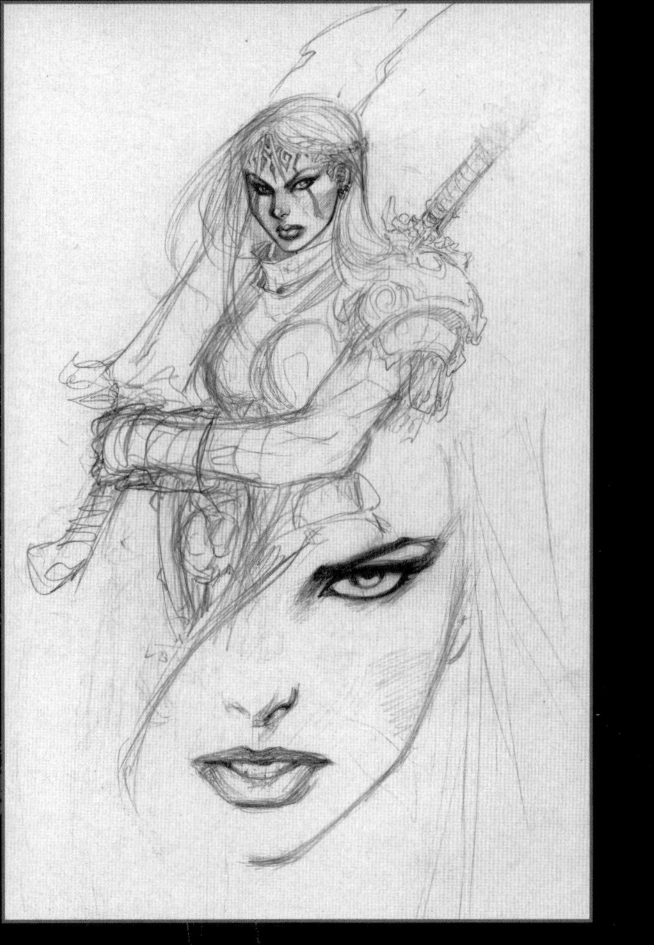

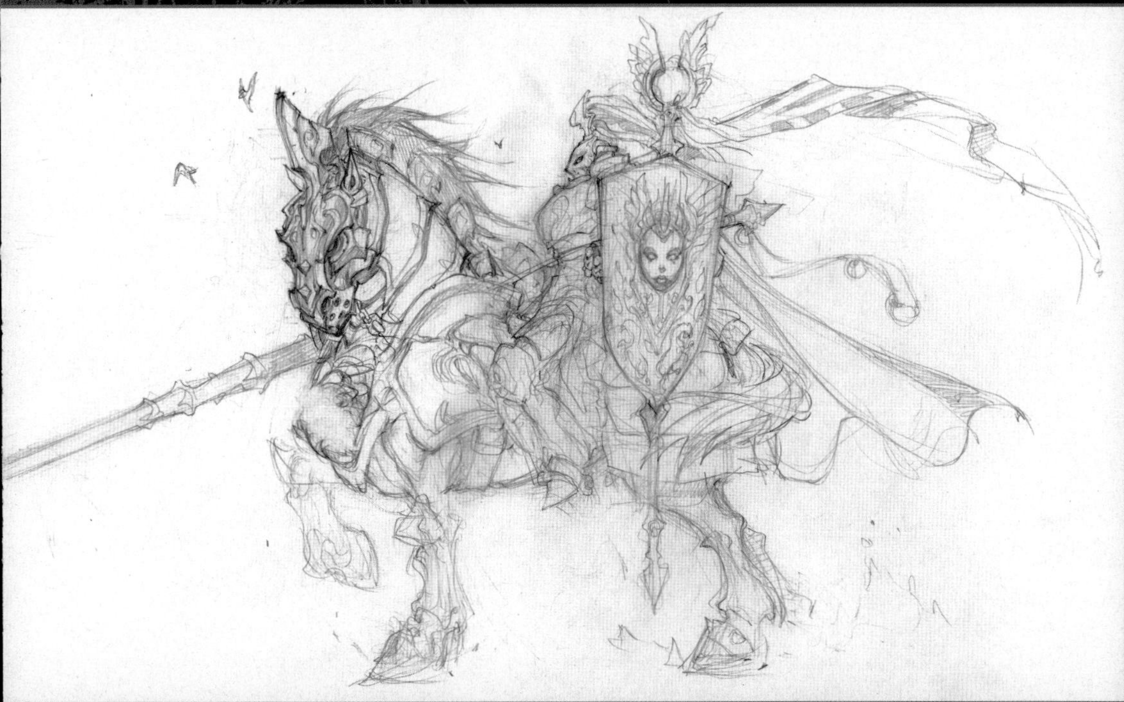

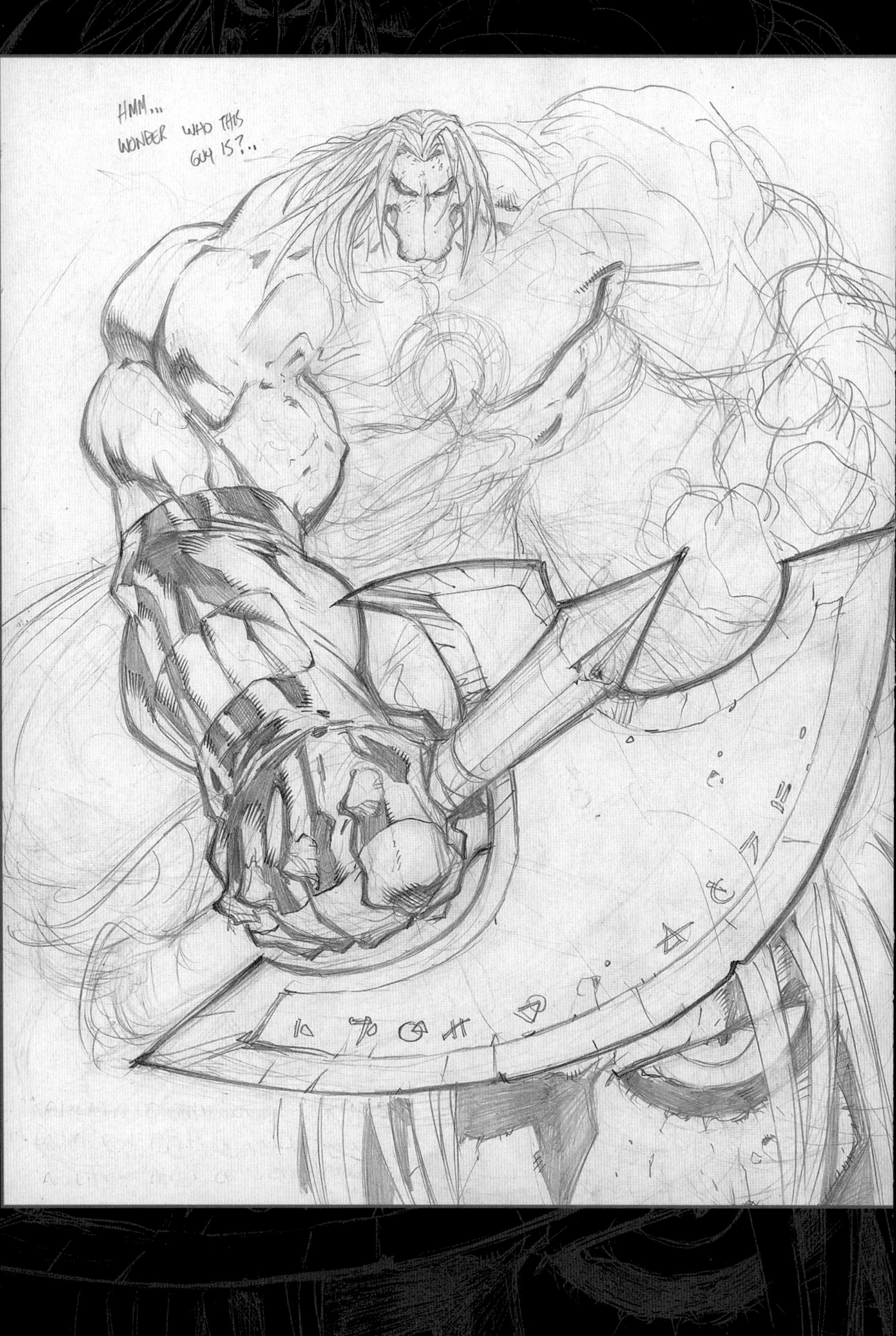
HMM...
WONDER WHO THIS
GUY IS?..

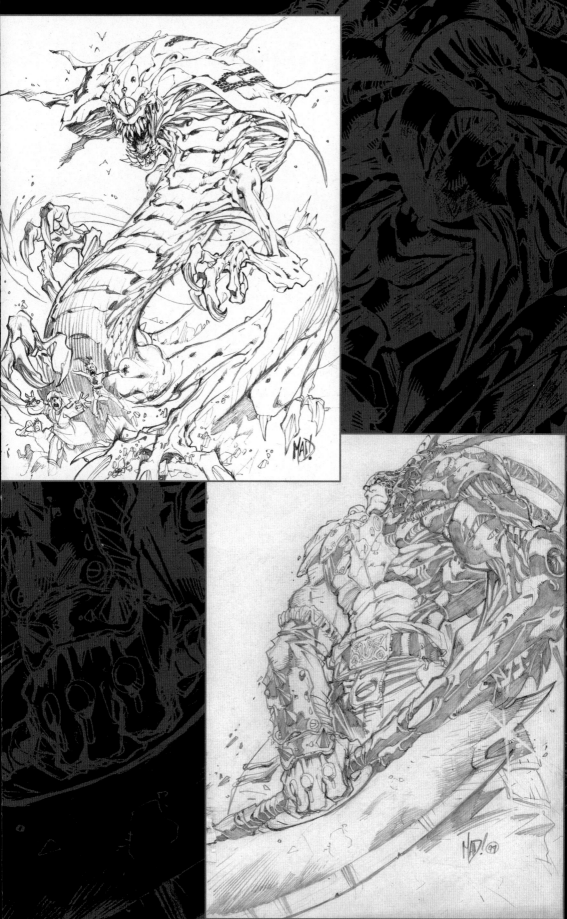

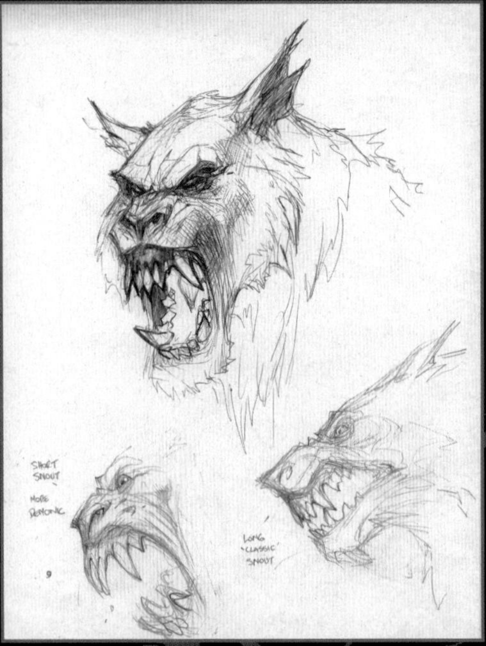
SHORT SNOUT
MORE DEMONIC
LONG 'CLASSIC' SNOUT
9

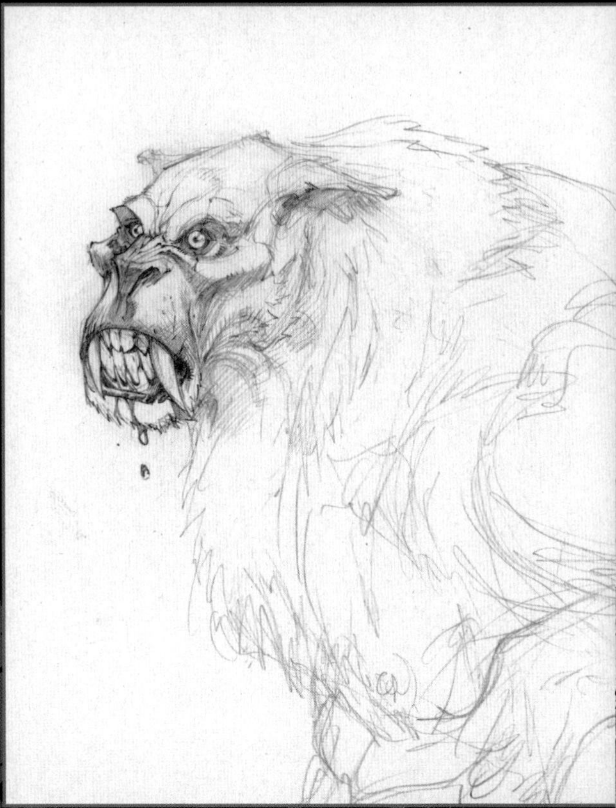

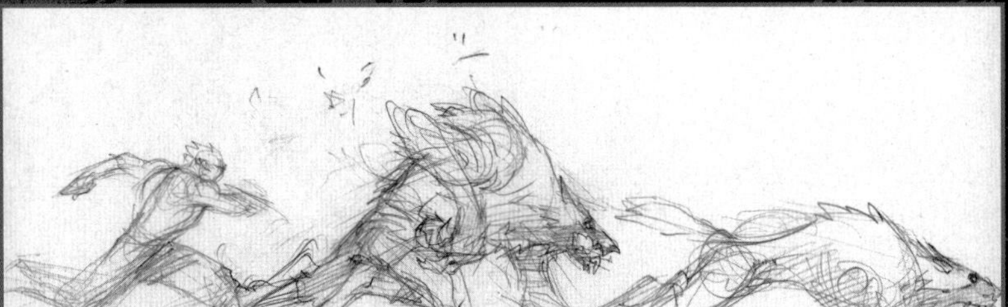
HUMAN MODE
BATTLE MODE
SPEED/RUN MODE

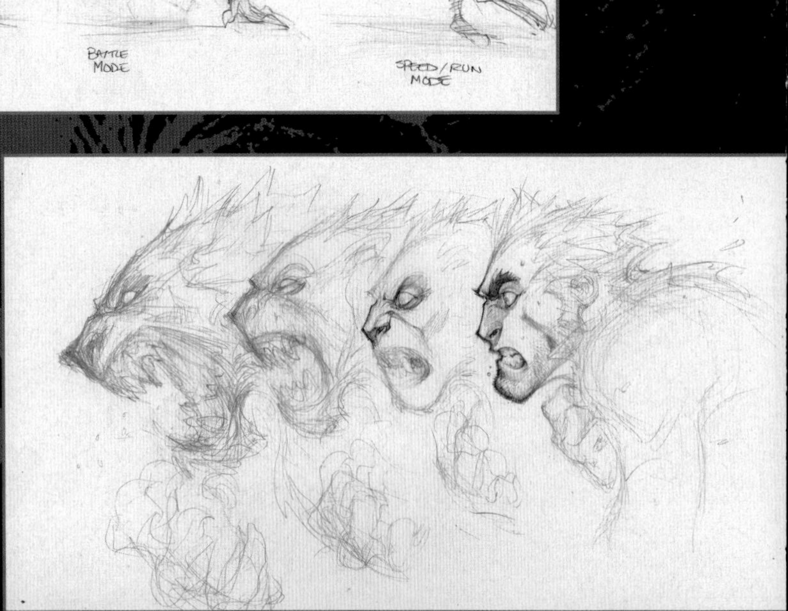

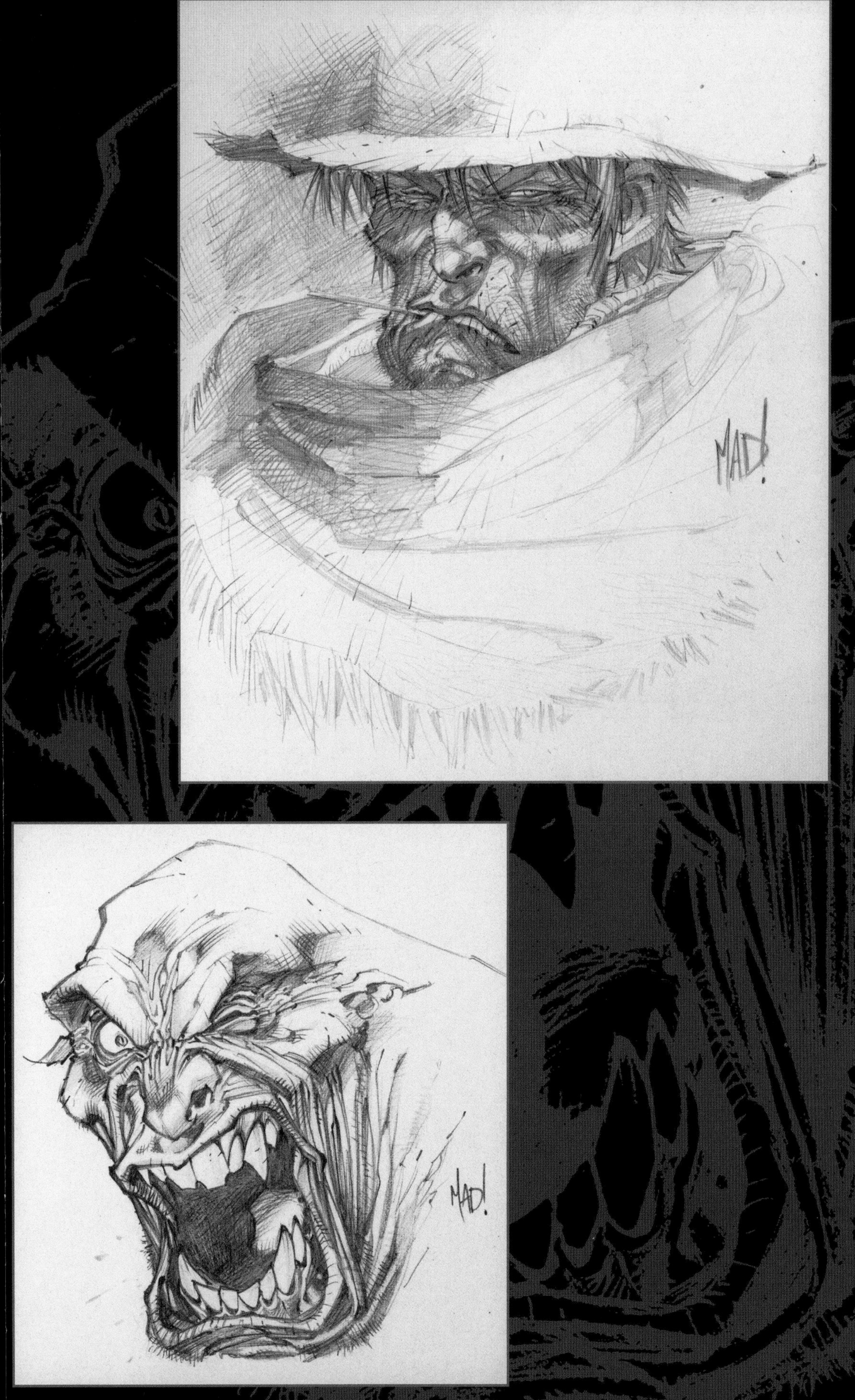
MAD!
MAD!

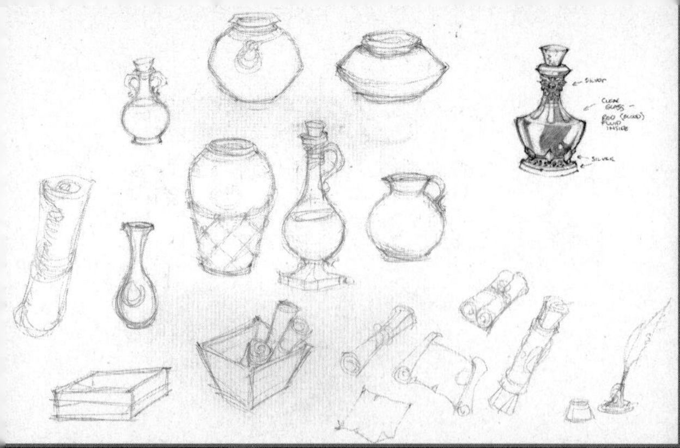
SILVER
CLEAR GLASS
RED (BLOOD) FLUID INSIDE
SILVER

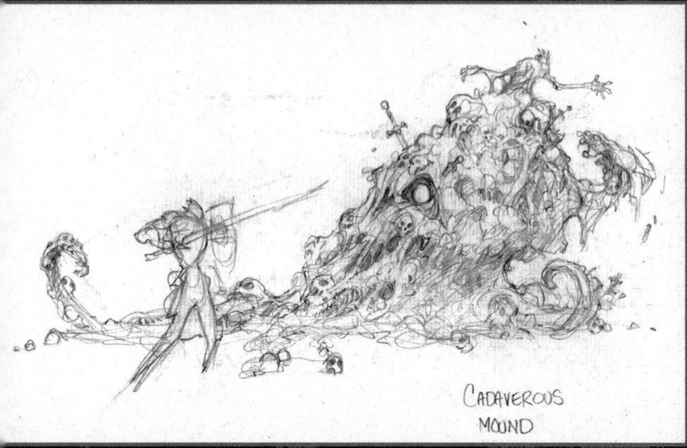
CADAVEROUS MOUND

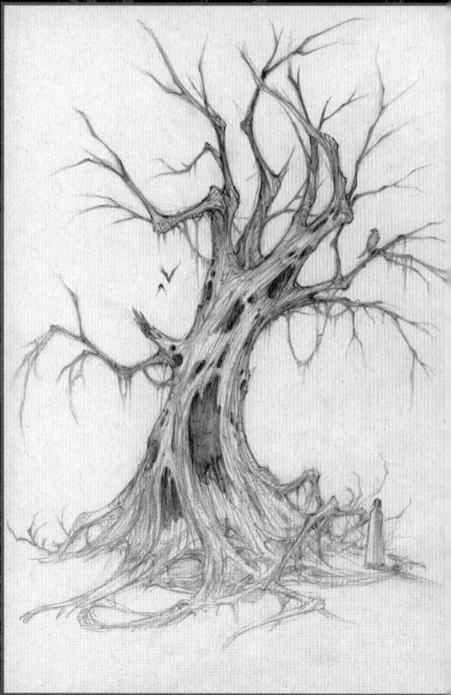

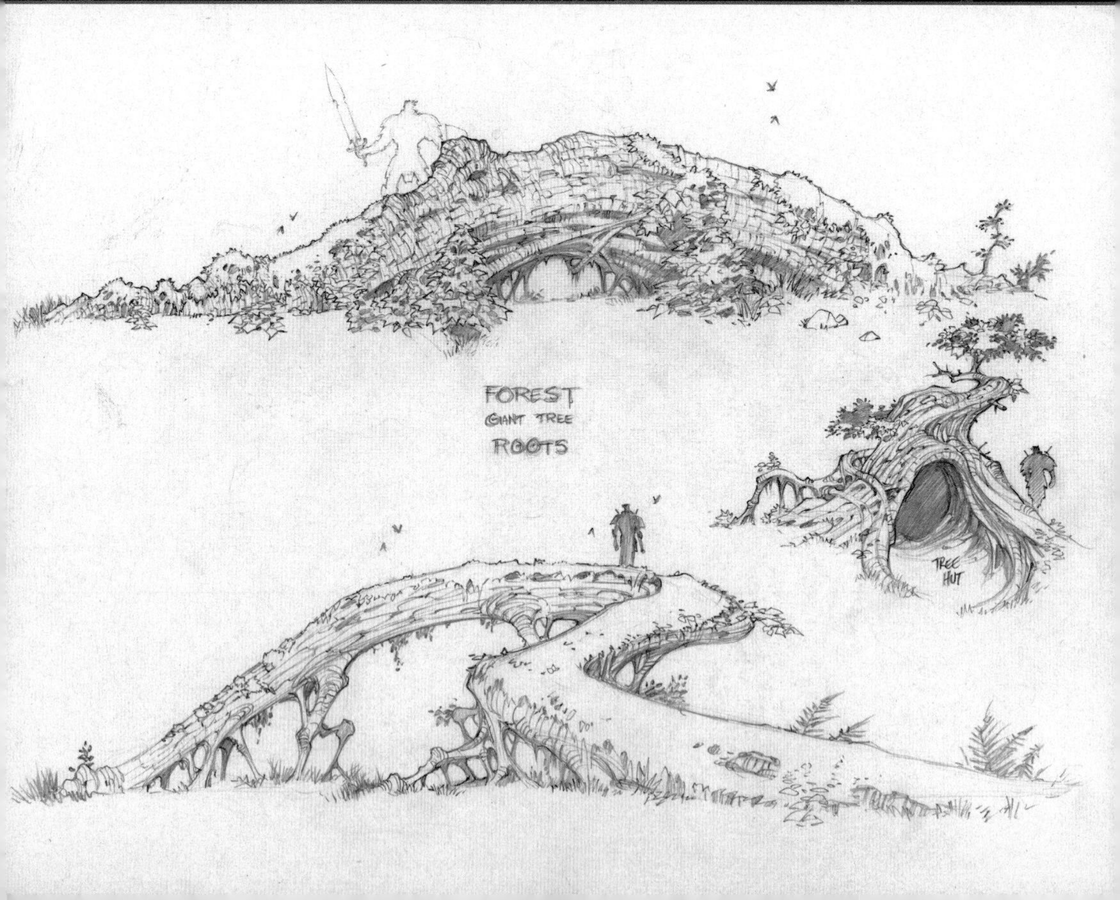
FOREST
GIANT TREE
ROOTS
TREE HUT

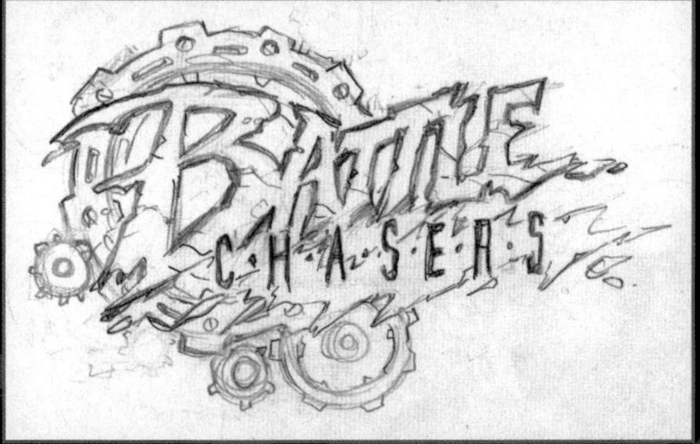
BATTLE
CHASERS

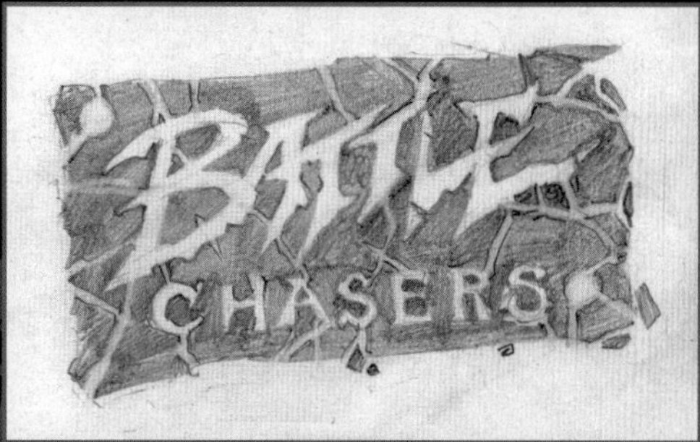
BATTLE
CHASERS

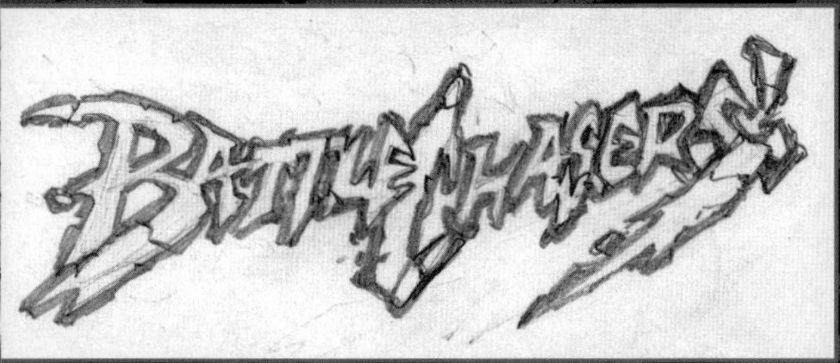
BATTLE CHASERS!

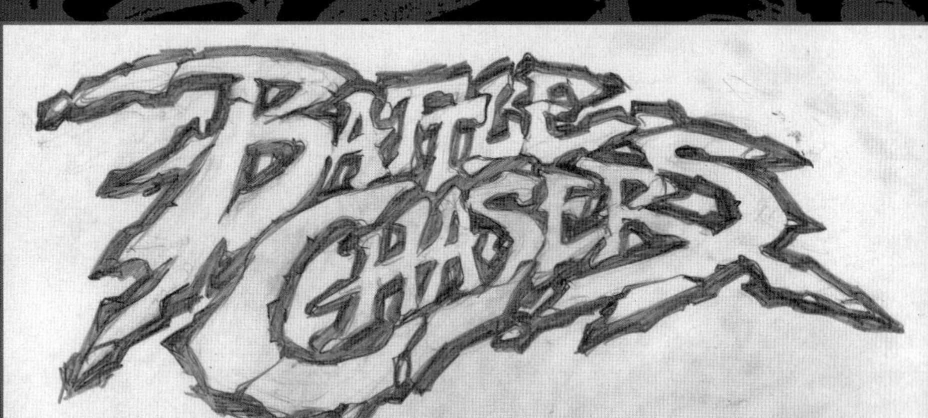
BATTLE
CHASERS

BATTLE CHASERS

FINAL LOGO DESIGN
BY JOE MADUREIRA
& RICHARD STARKINGS

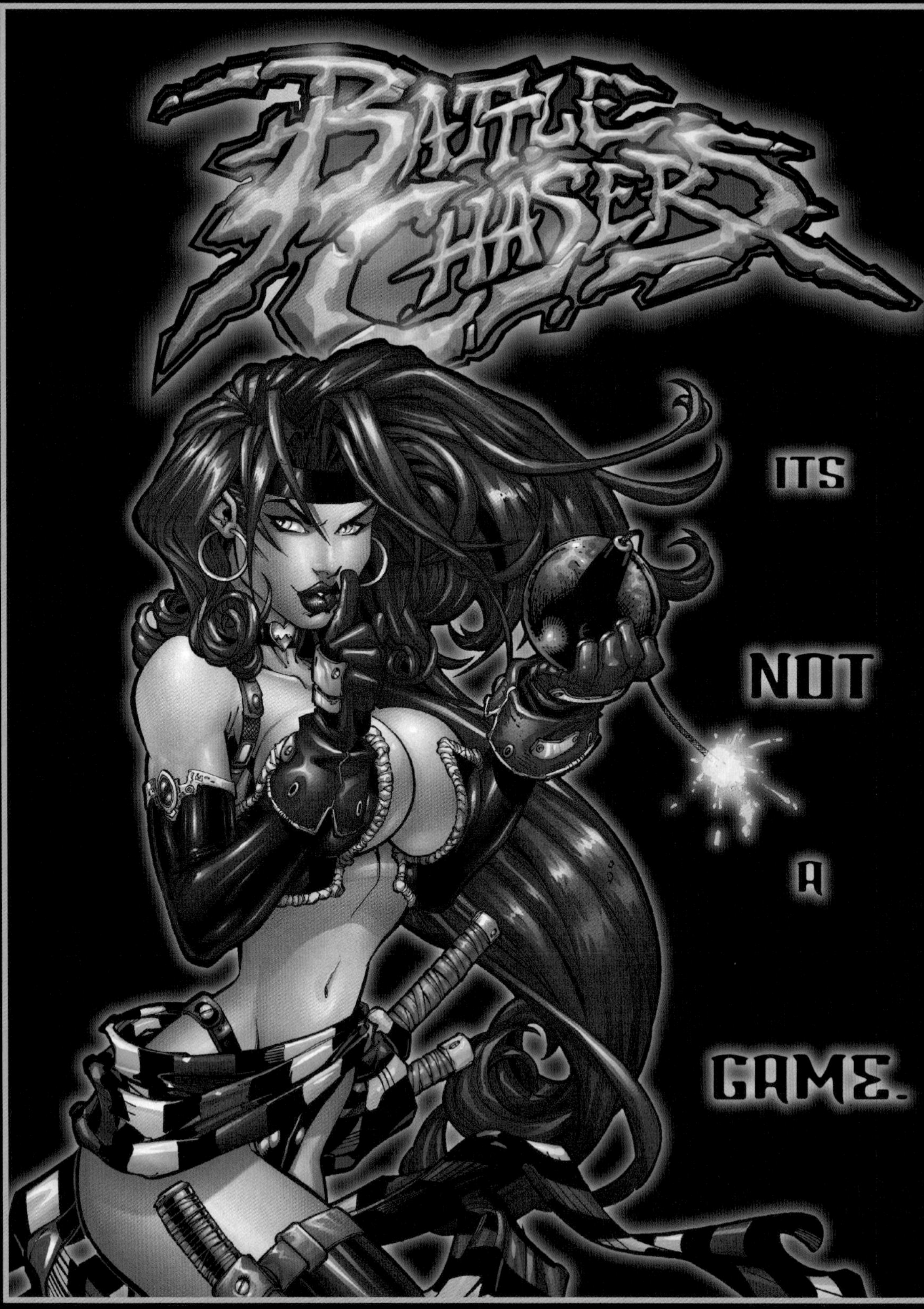
BATTLE CHASERS
ITS
NOT
A
GAME.

BATTLE CHASERS ADVERTISEMENT FOR PSM MAGAZINE

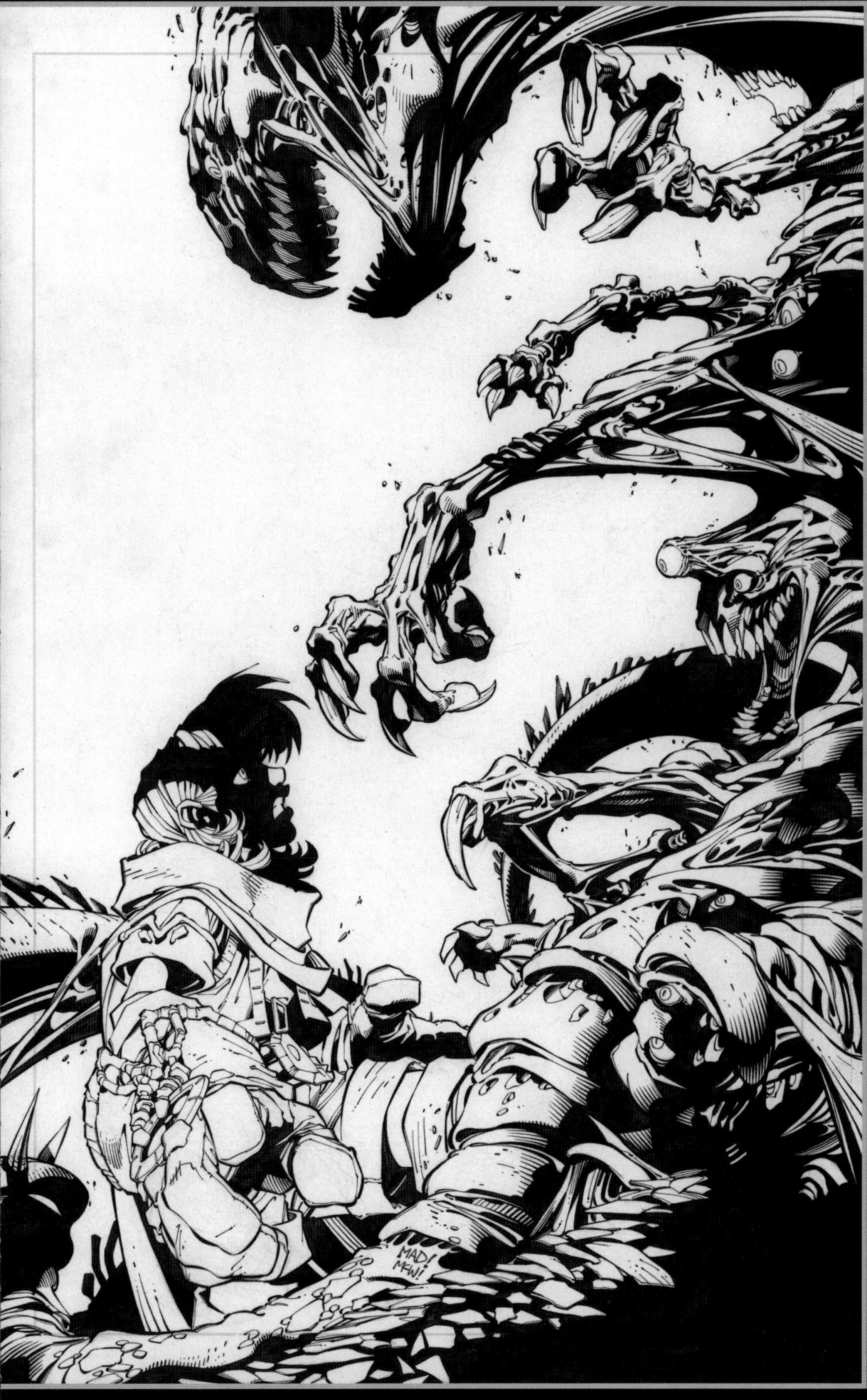
MAD!
MCW!

BATTLE CHASERS ADVERTISEMENT
BY JOE MADUREIRA & TOM MCWEENEY

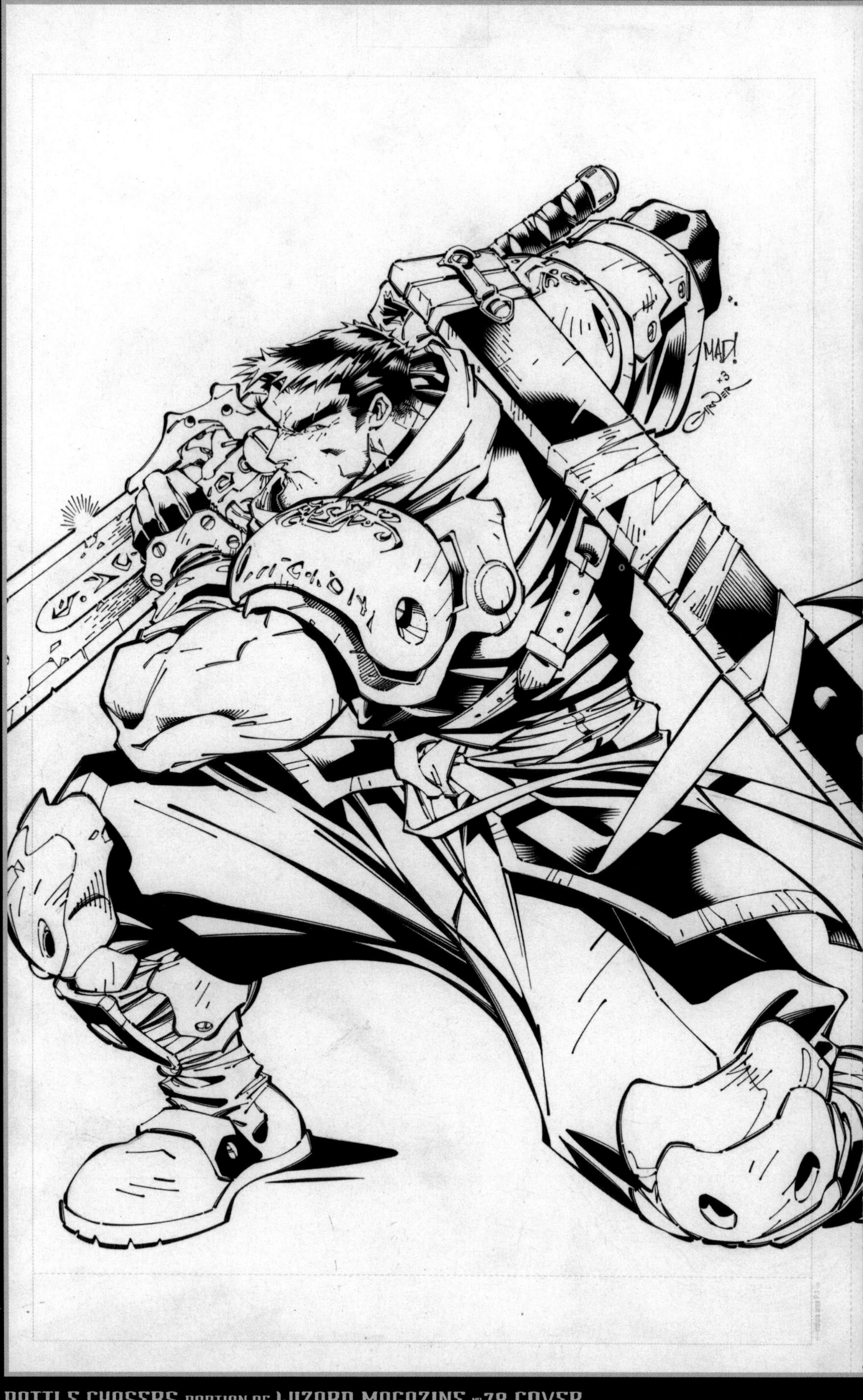
MAD!

BATTLE CHASERS PORTION OF WIZARD MAGAZINE No. 78 COVER
BY JOE MADUREIRA & ALEX GARNER

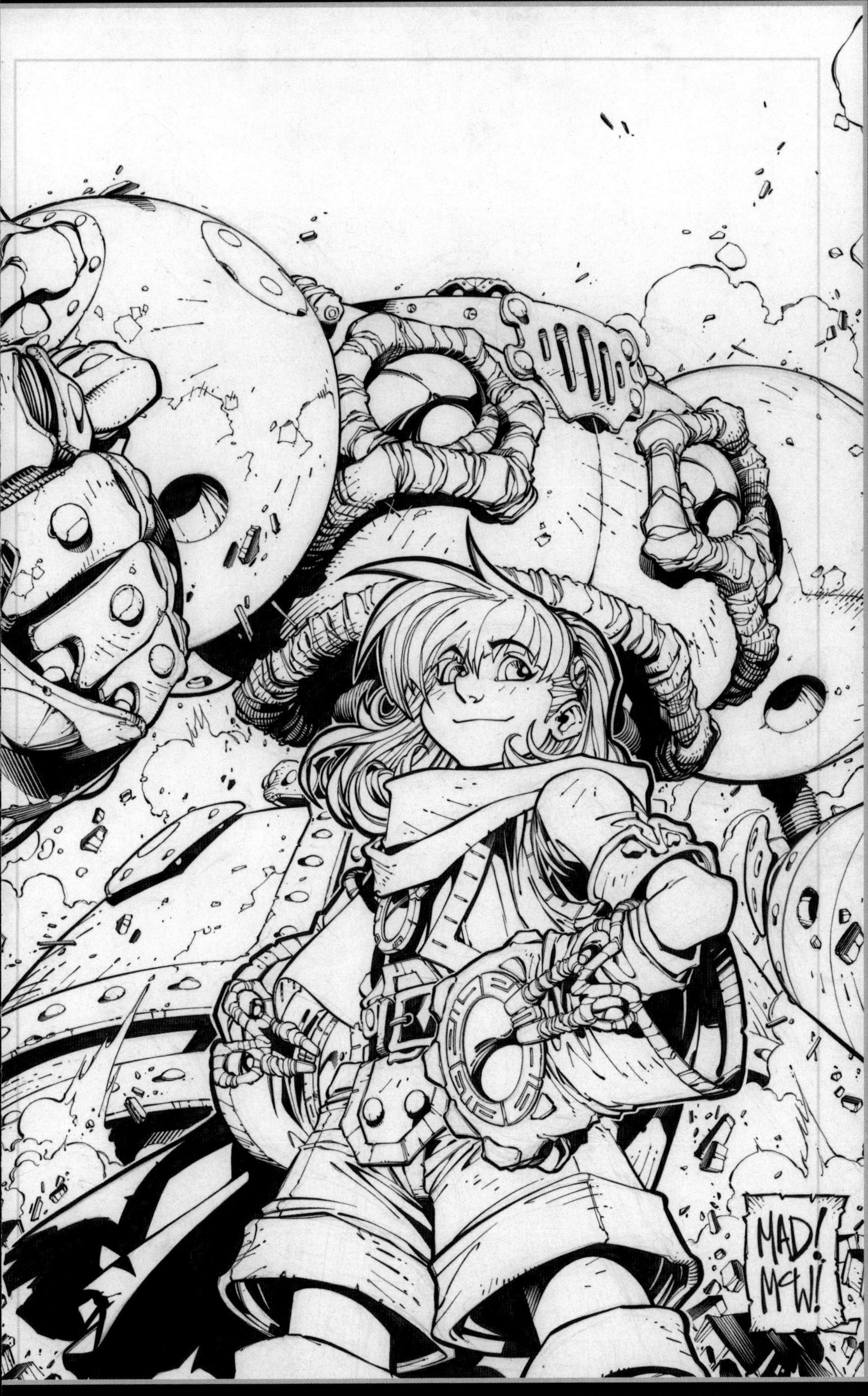
MAD!
McW!

WIZARD MAGAZINE No. 88 COVER
BY JOE MADUREIRA & TOM MCWEENEY

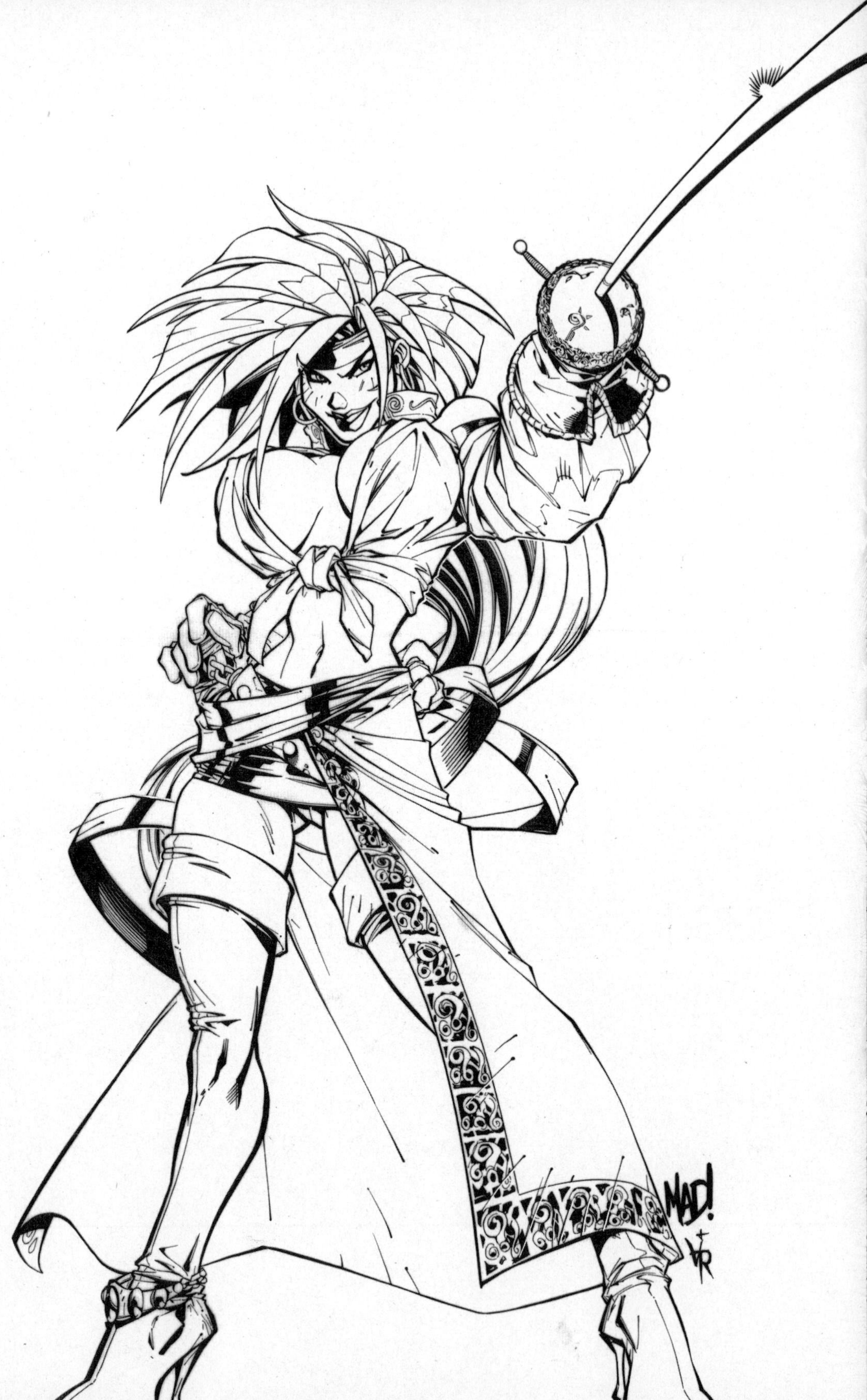
MAD!
+
VR

BATTLE CHASERS PORTION OF WIZARD MAGAZINE CLIFFHANGER! SKETCHBOOK
BY JOE MADUREIRA & VINCE RUSSELL

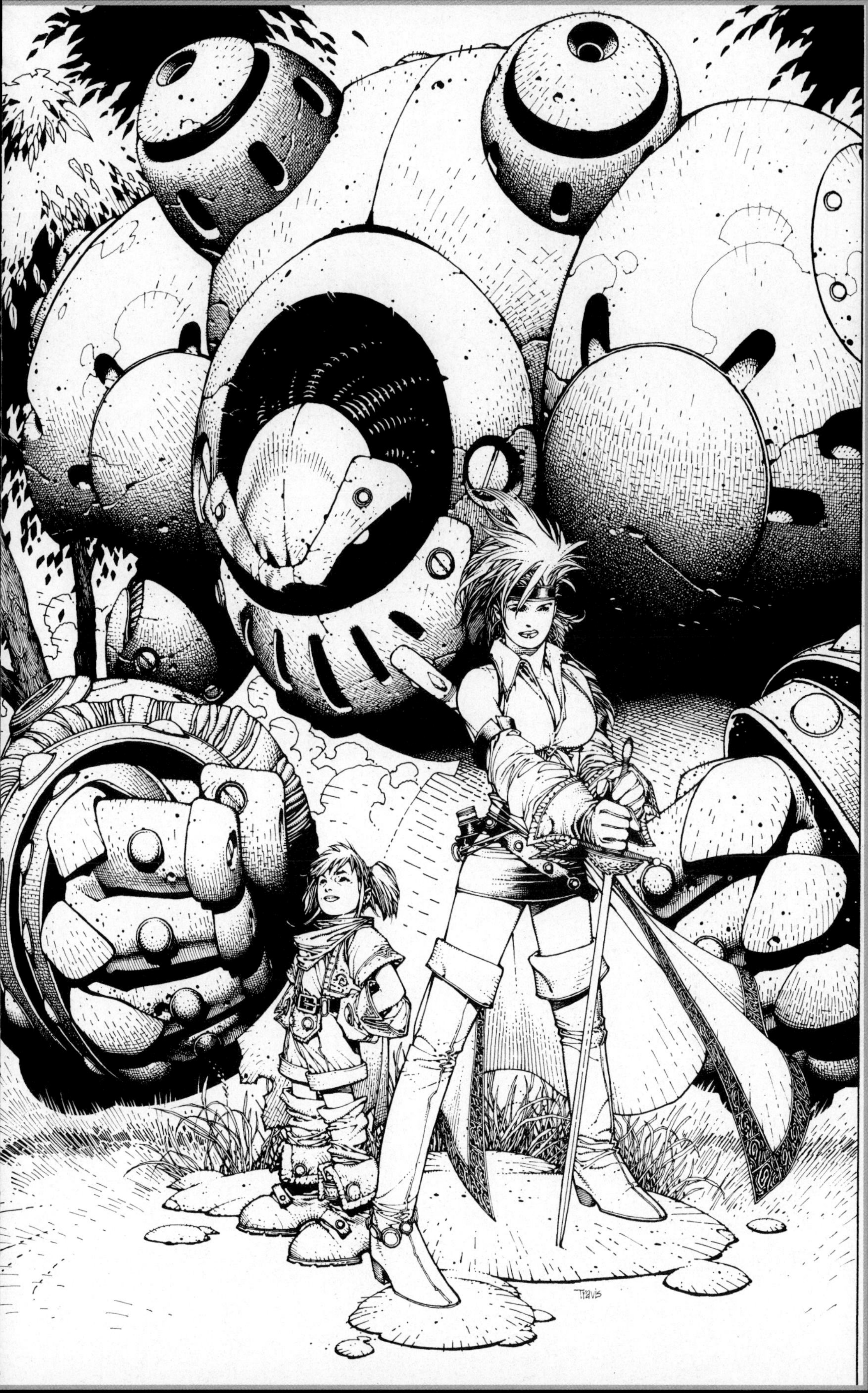

BATTLE CHASERS NO.1 VARIANT COVER
BY TRAVIS CHAREST & RICHARD FRIEND

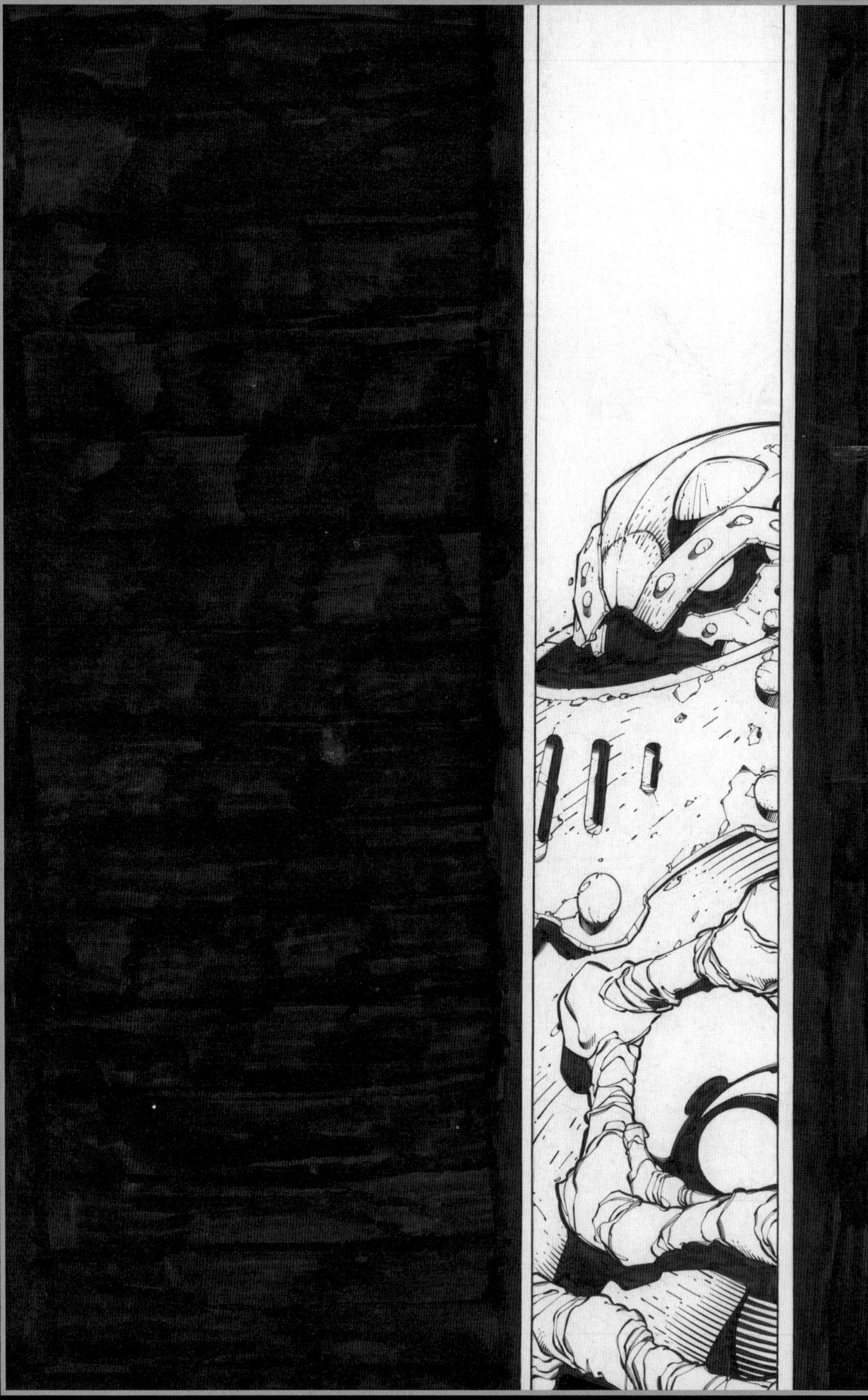

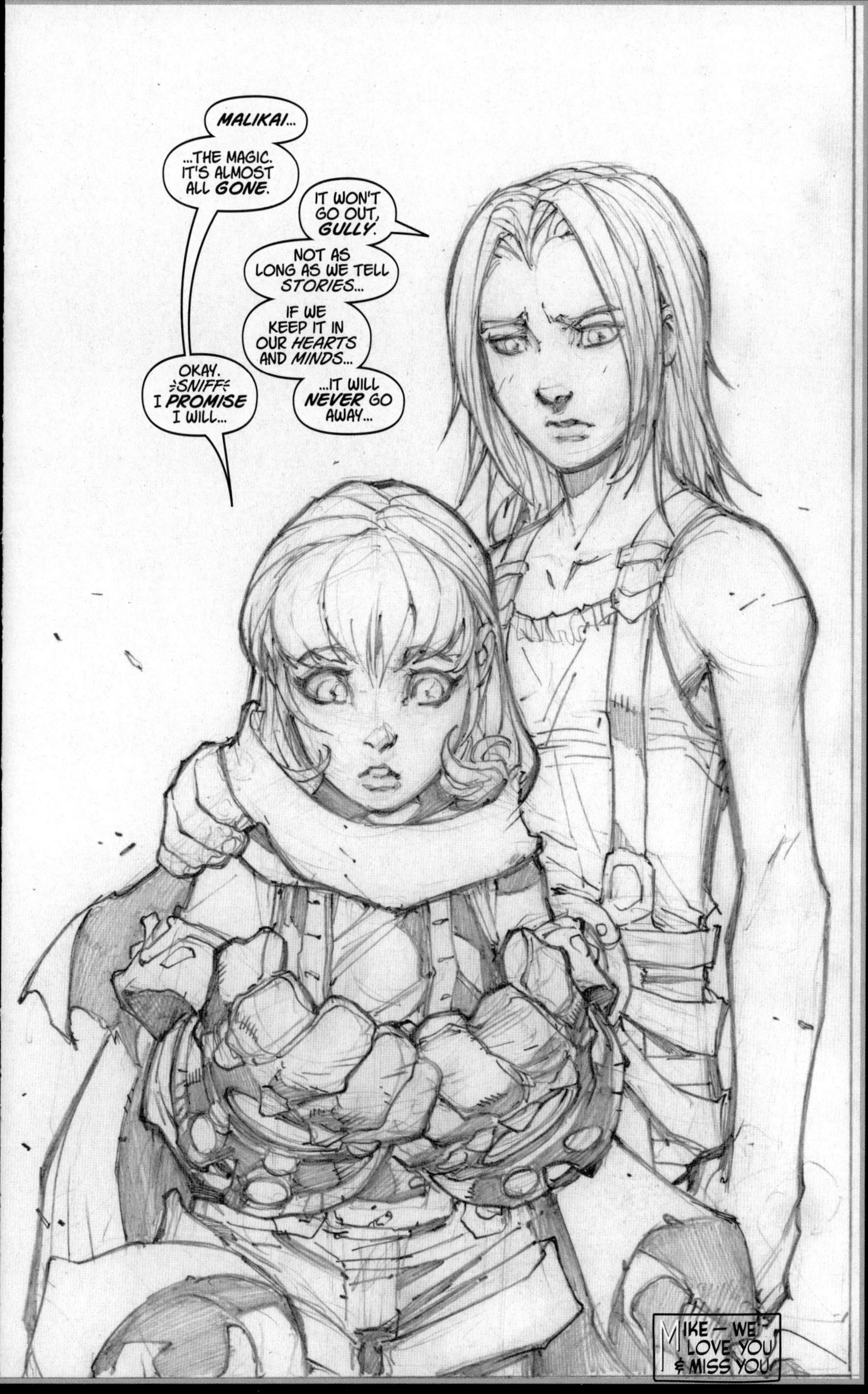
MALIKAI...
...THE MAGIC. IT'S ALMOST ALL GONE.
IT WON'T GO OUT, GULLY.
NOT AS LONG AS WE TELL STORIES...
IF WE KEEP IT IN OUR HEARTS AND MINDS...
...IT WILL NEVER GO AWAY...
OKAY. *SNIFF* I PROMISE I WILL...
MIKE — WE LOVE YOU & MISS YOU

MICHAEL TURNER TRIBUTE ILLUSTRATION

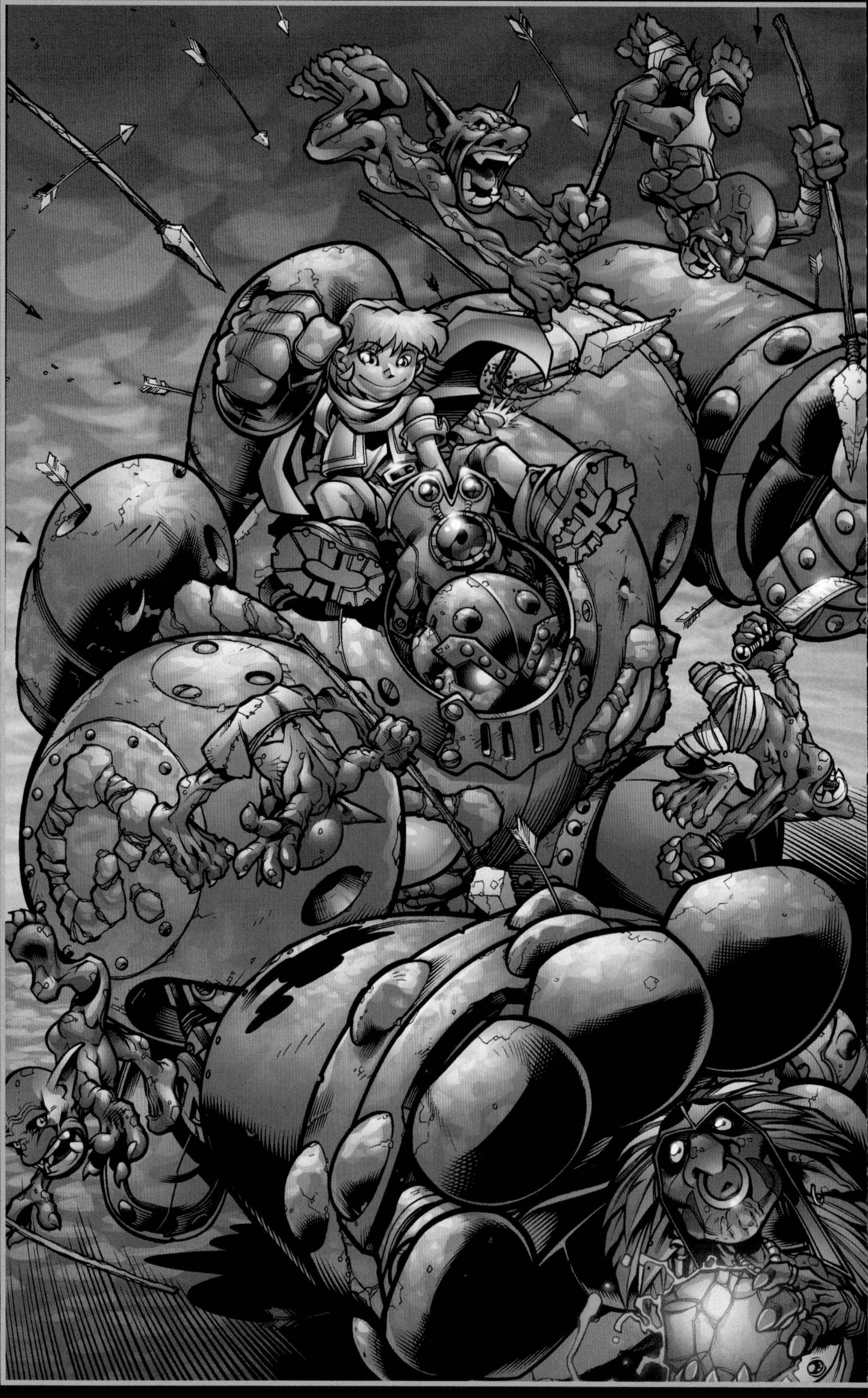

CALIBRETTO & GULLY PIN-UP FROM BATTLE CHASERS №4
BY ED MCGUINESS & LIQUID!

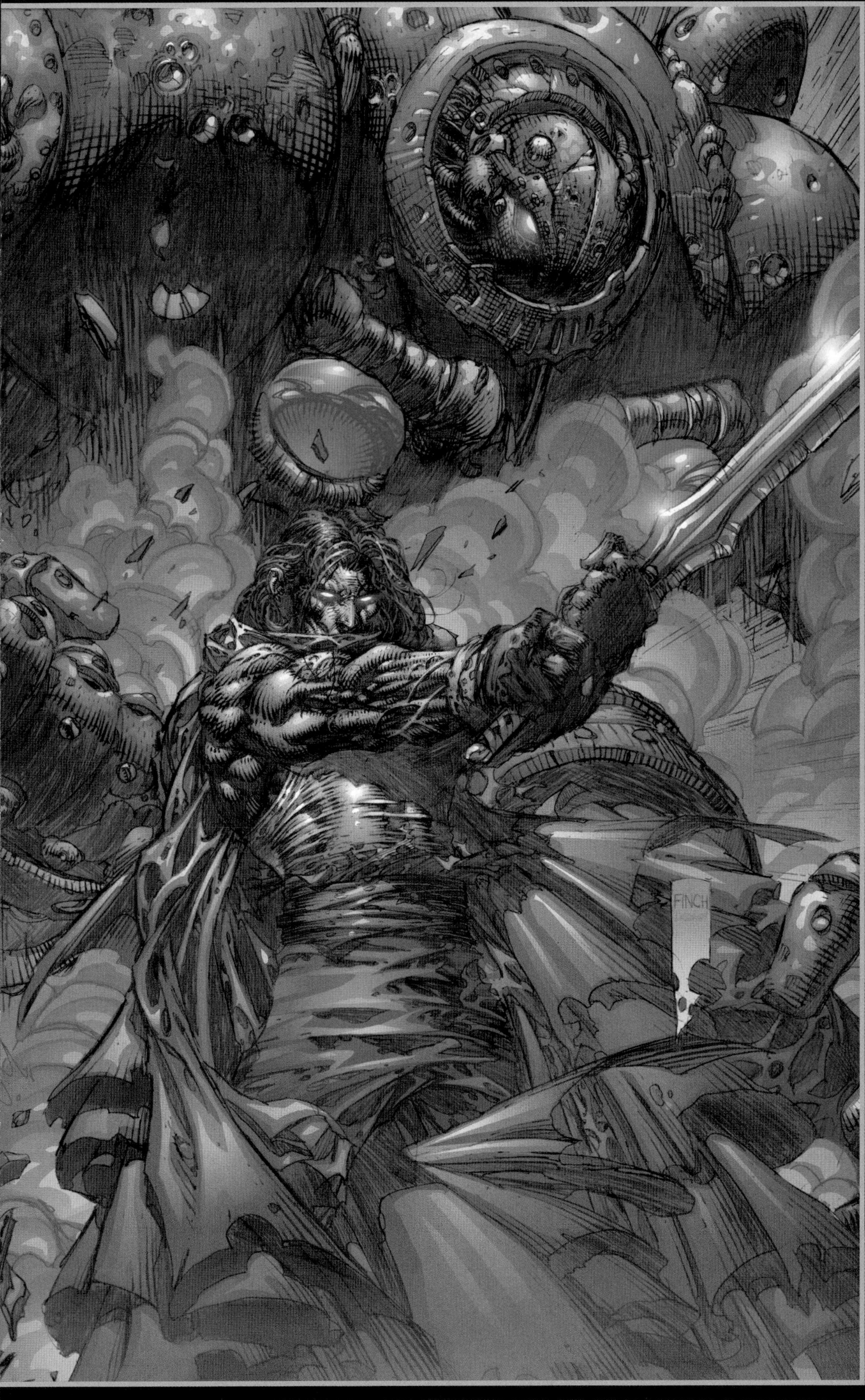
FINCH

GARRISON & CALIBRETTO PIN-UP FROM BATTLE CHASERS No.4

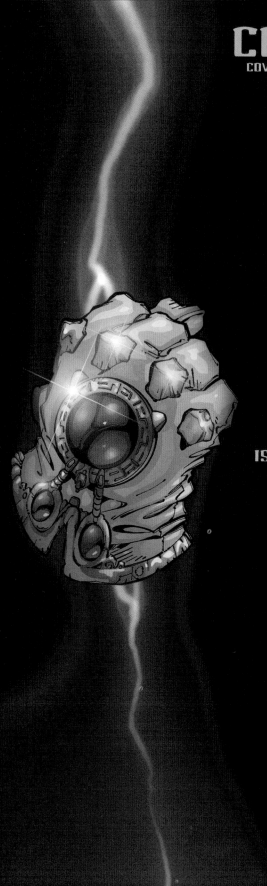

COVER GALLERY

COVERS BY JOE MADUREIRA • TOM MCWEENEY • LIQUI

PRELUD
(ANOTHERUNIVERSE.COM EXCLUSIVE
BY JOE MADUREIRA & VINCE RUSSELL & LIQUI

ISSUE No.

ISSUE No.1 VARIAN
BY TRAVIS CHAREST & RICHARD FRIEND & LIQUI

ISSUE No.1 VARIAN

ISSUE No.

ISSUE No.2 VARIAN

ISSUE No.

ISSUE No.

ISSUE No.4 CALIBRETTO COVE

ISSUE No.4 GARRISON COVE

ISSUE No.4 GULLY COVE

ISSUE No.4 KNOLAN COVE

ISSUE No.4 BACK COVER PUZZLE PAINTIN
BY JOE CHIOD

ISSUE No.

ISSUE No.

ISSUE No.6 VARIANT COVE
(ANOTHERUNIVERSE.COM EXCLUSIVE
BY ADAM WARREN & LIQUI

ISSUE No.

ISSUE No.7 VARIANT COVE
BY HUMBERTO RAMOS & LIQUI

ISSUE No.7 VARIANT COVE
BY J. SCOTT CAMPBELL & LIQUI

ISSUE No.

ISSUE No.

ISSUE No.1

COLLECTED EDITION No.

COLLECTED EDITION No.

No.1 SPECIAL EDITIO

BATTLE CHASERS PORTION O
CLIFFHANGER! WIZARD SKETCHBOO

HARDCOVER DUSTJACKE

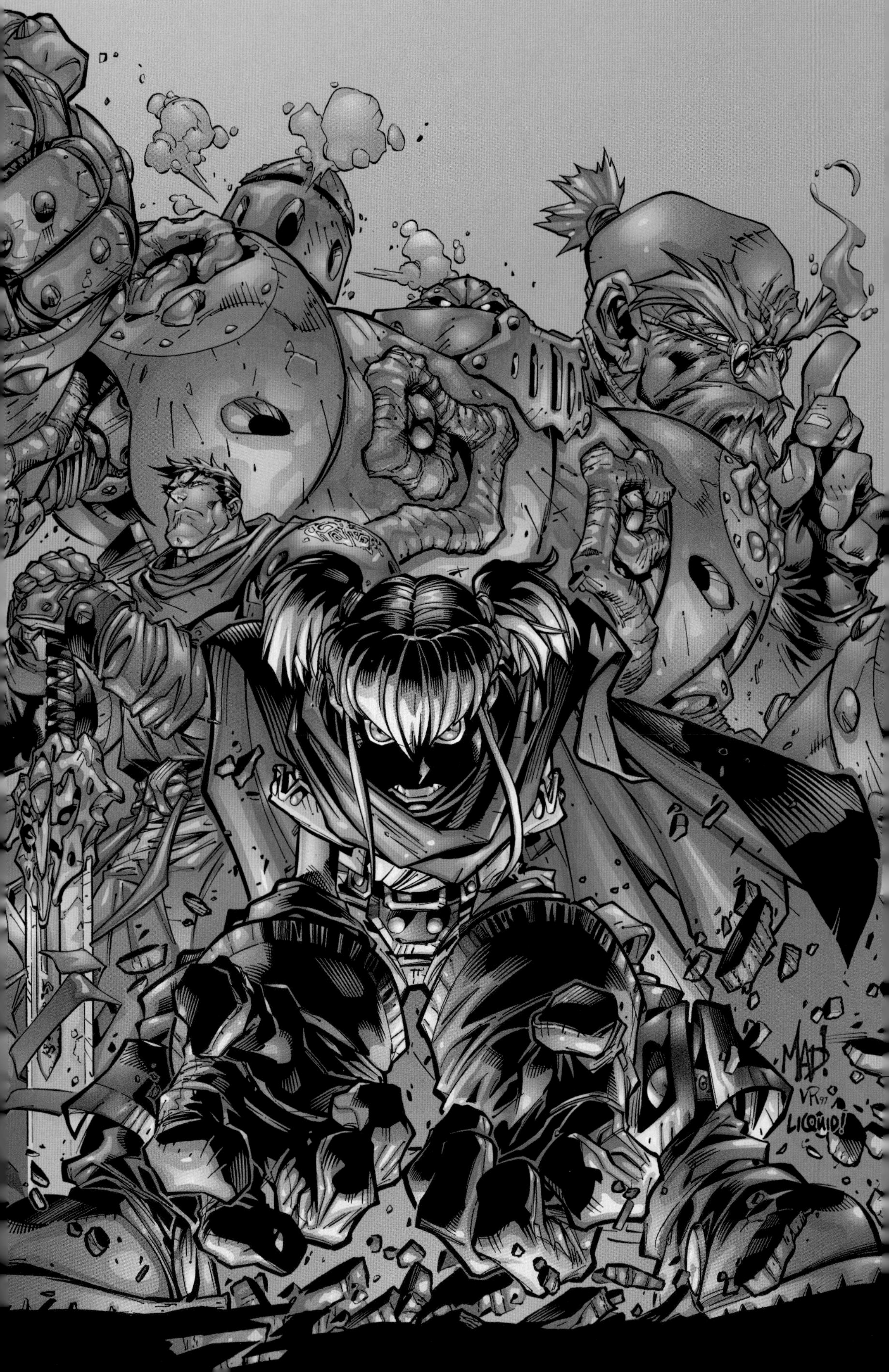
MAD!
VR97
LIQUID!

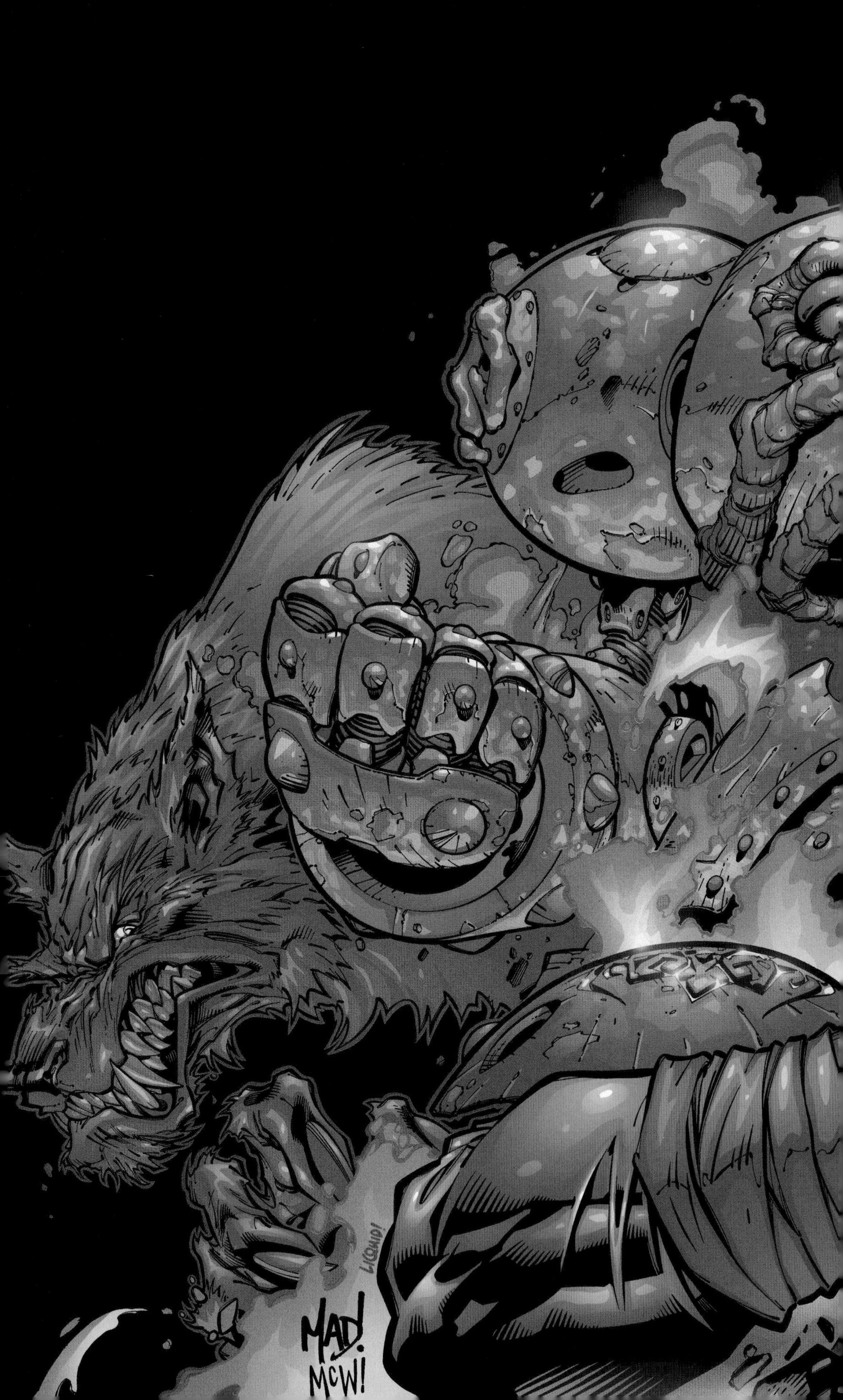
LIQUID!
MAD!
McW!

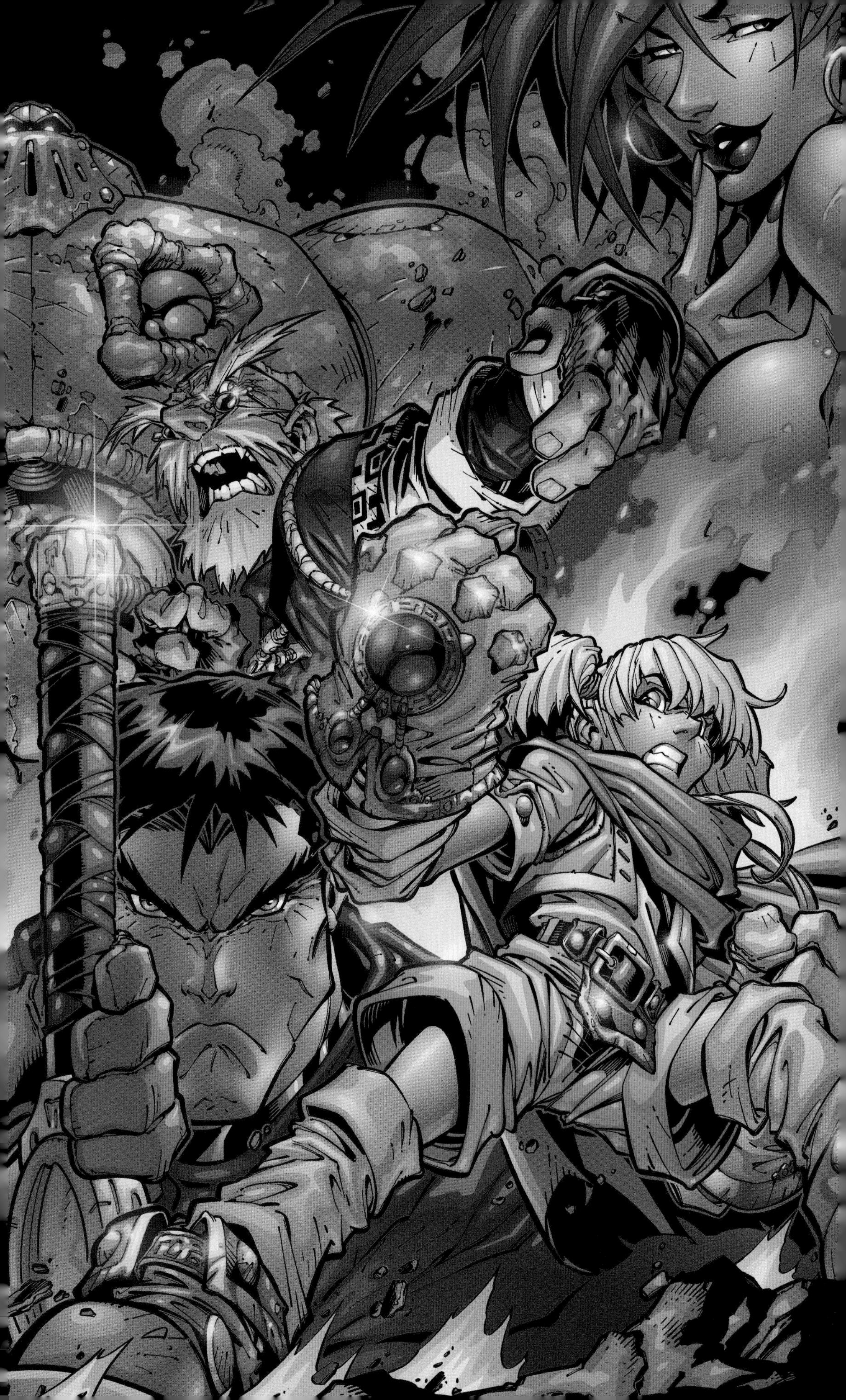

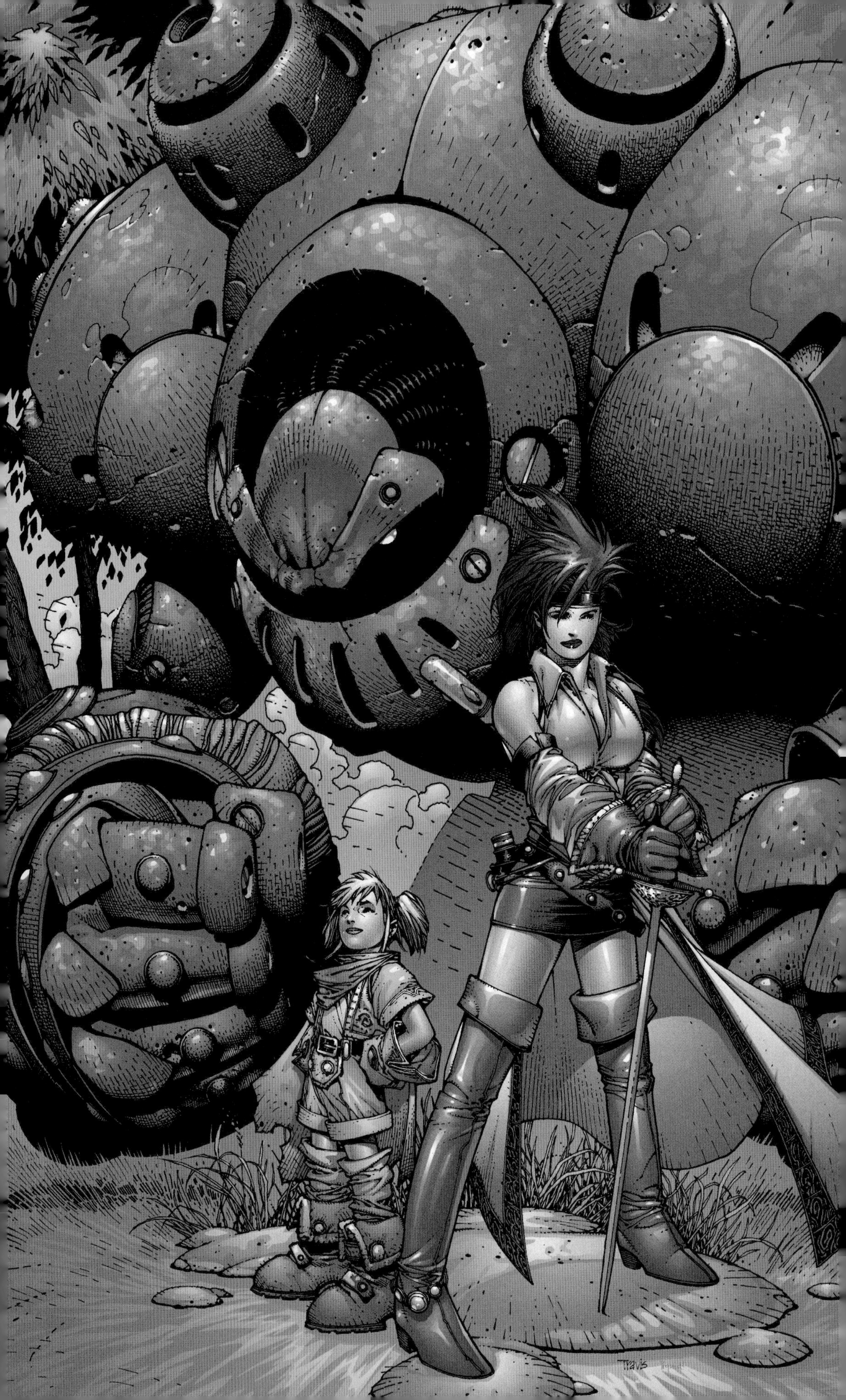
TRAVIS

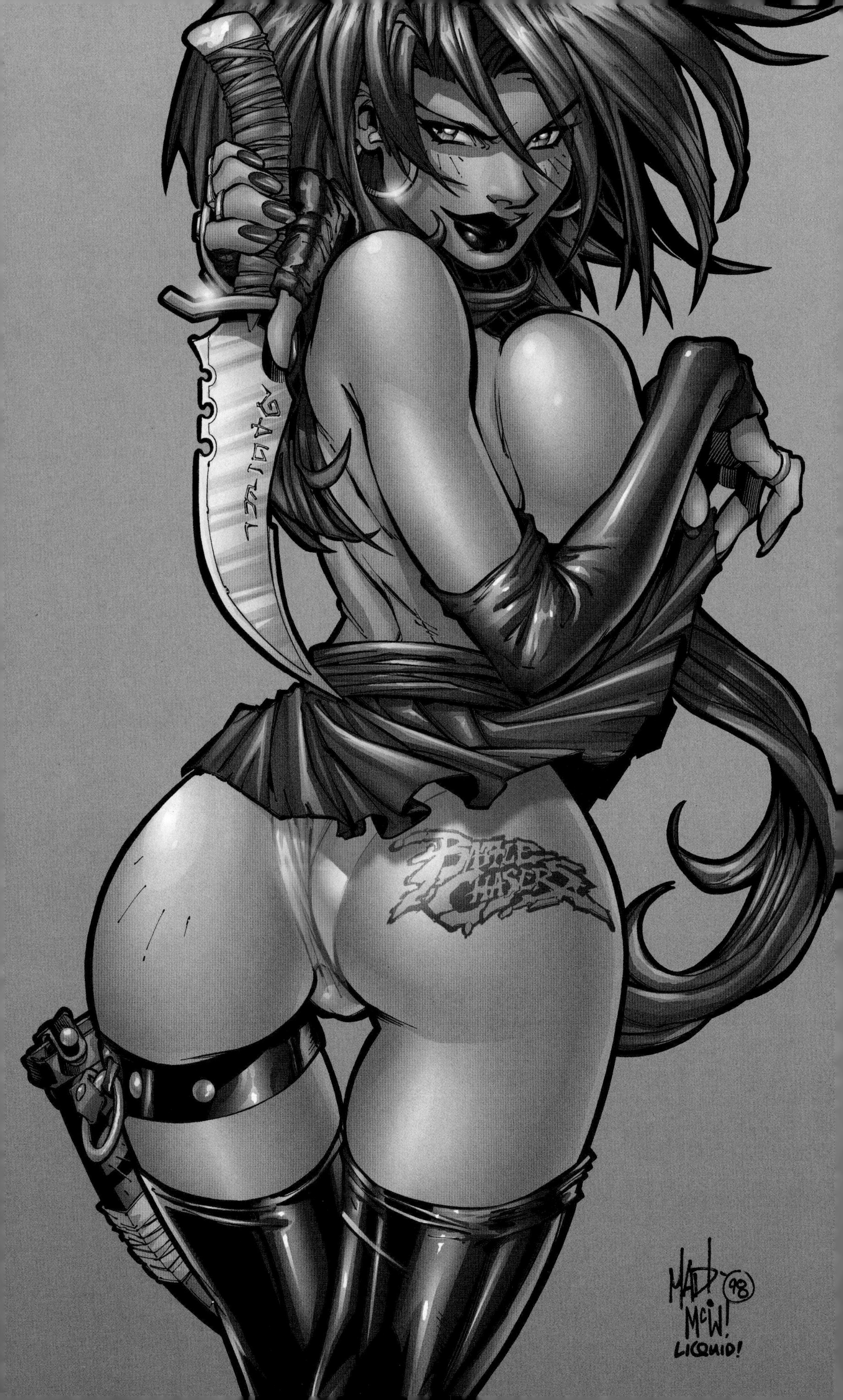
BATTLE CHASERS
MAD! 98
McW!
LICQUID!

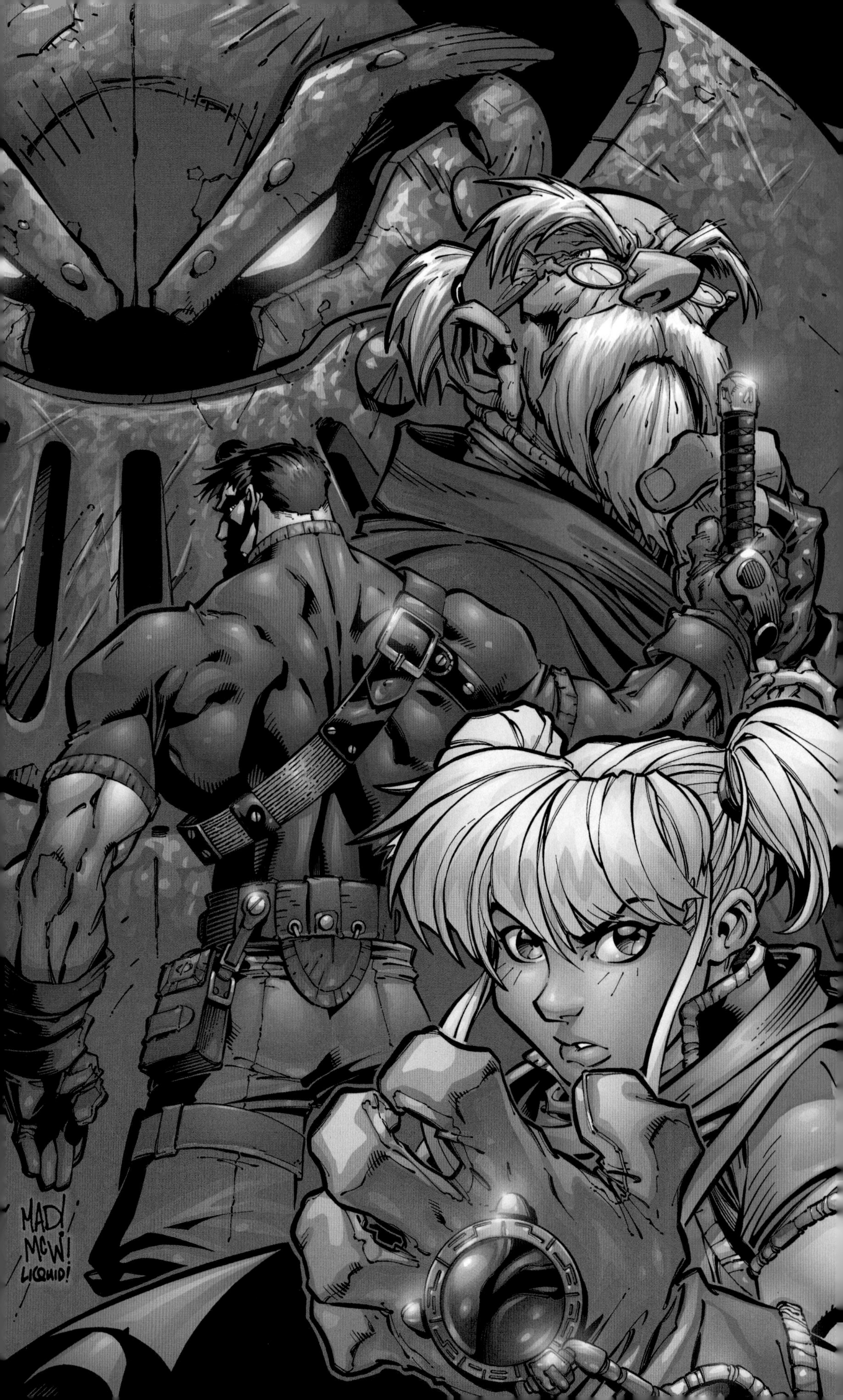
MAD!
McW!
LIQUID!

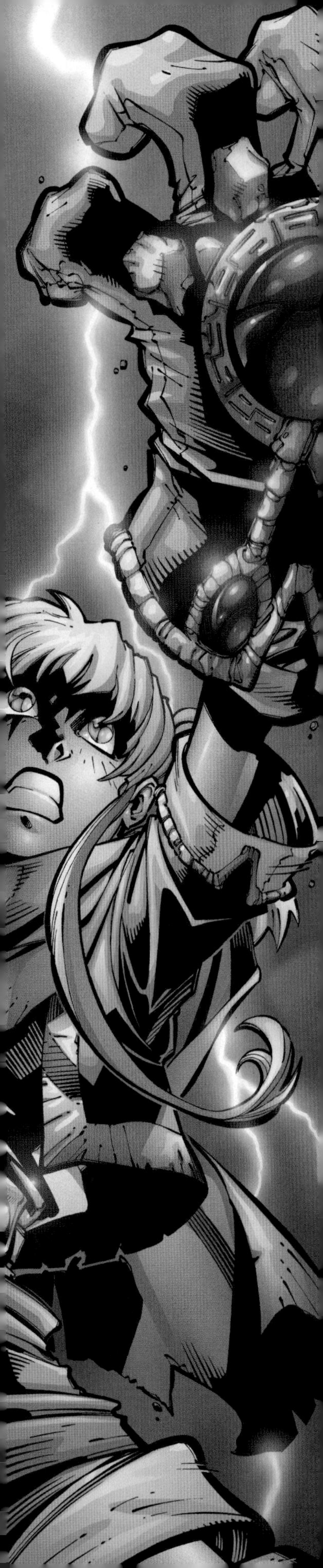

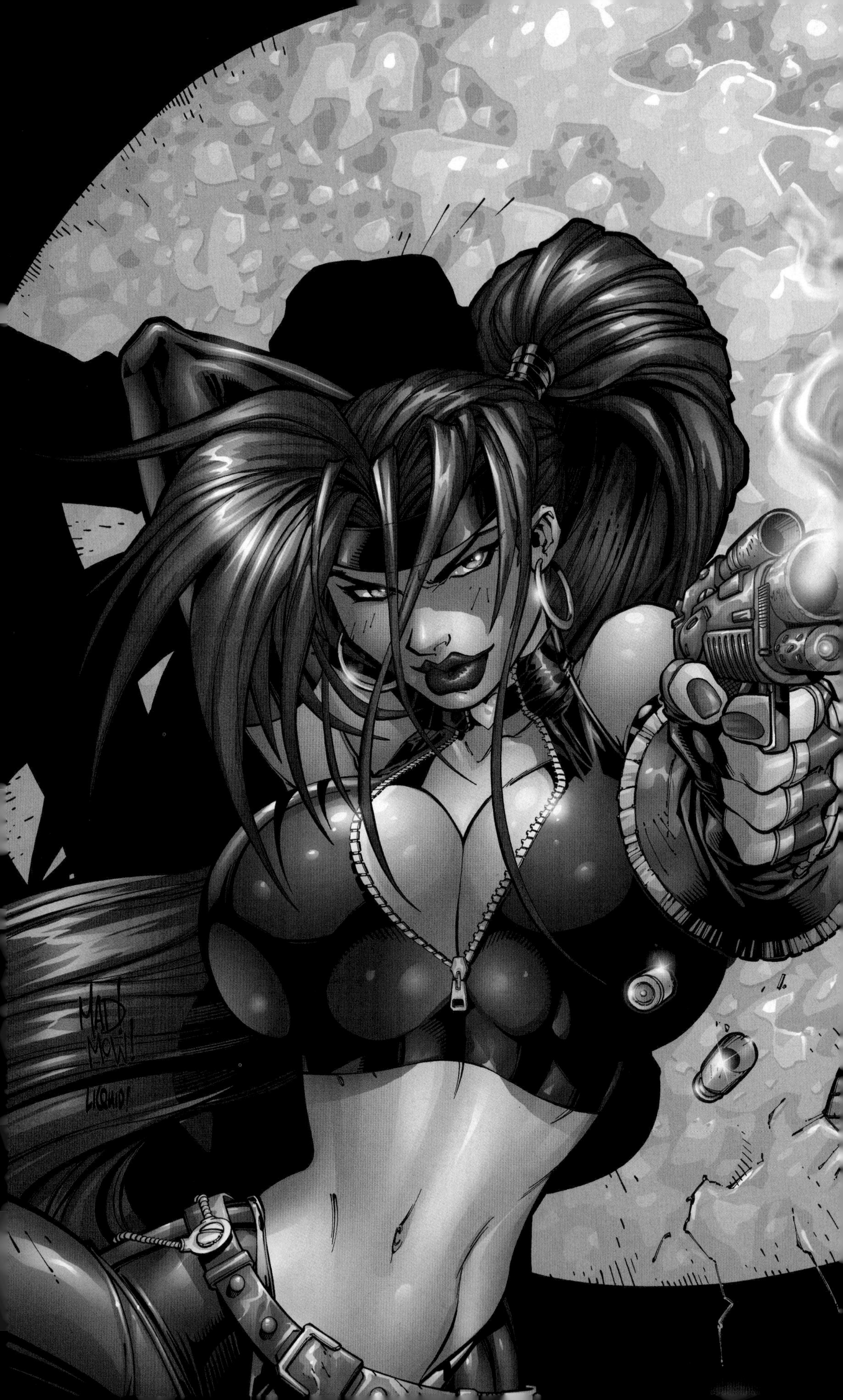
MAD MOW!
LIQUID!

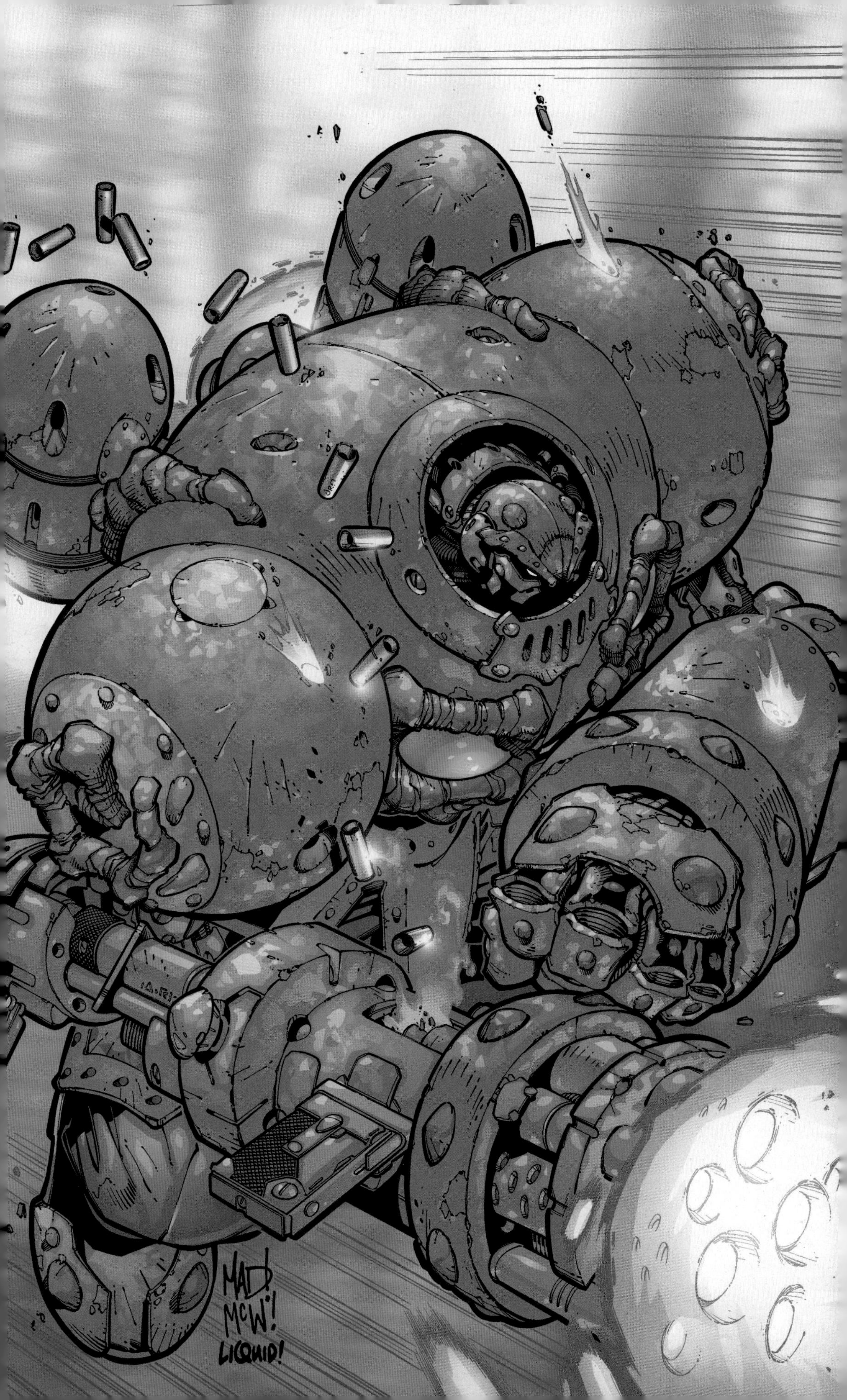
MAD!
McW!
LICQUID!

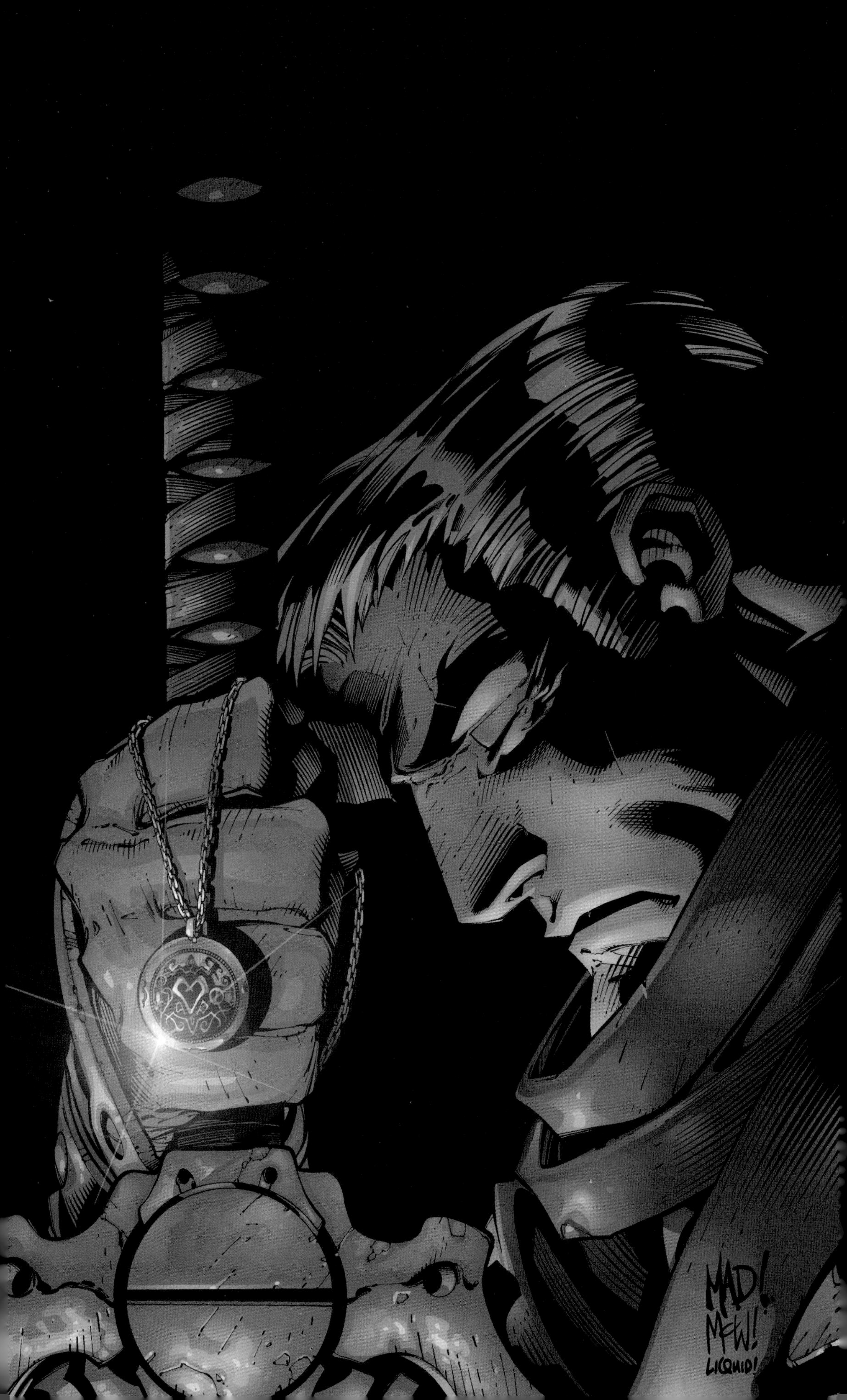
MAD!
MFW!
LICQUID!

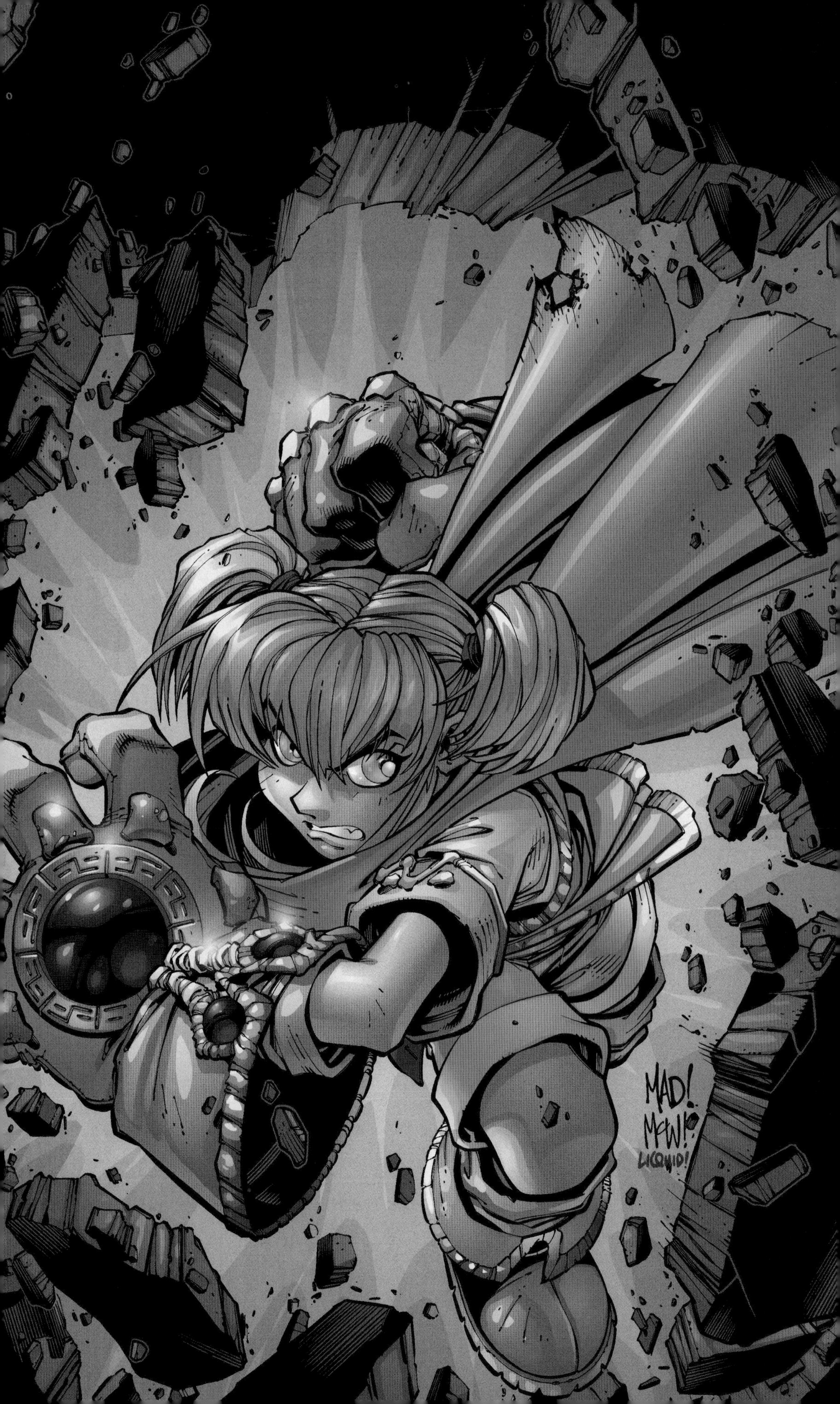
MAD!
McW!
LICQUID!

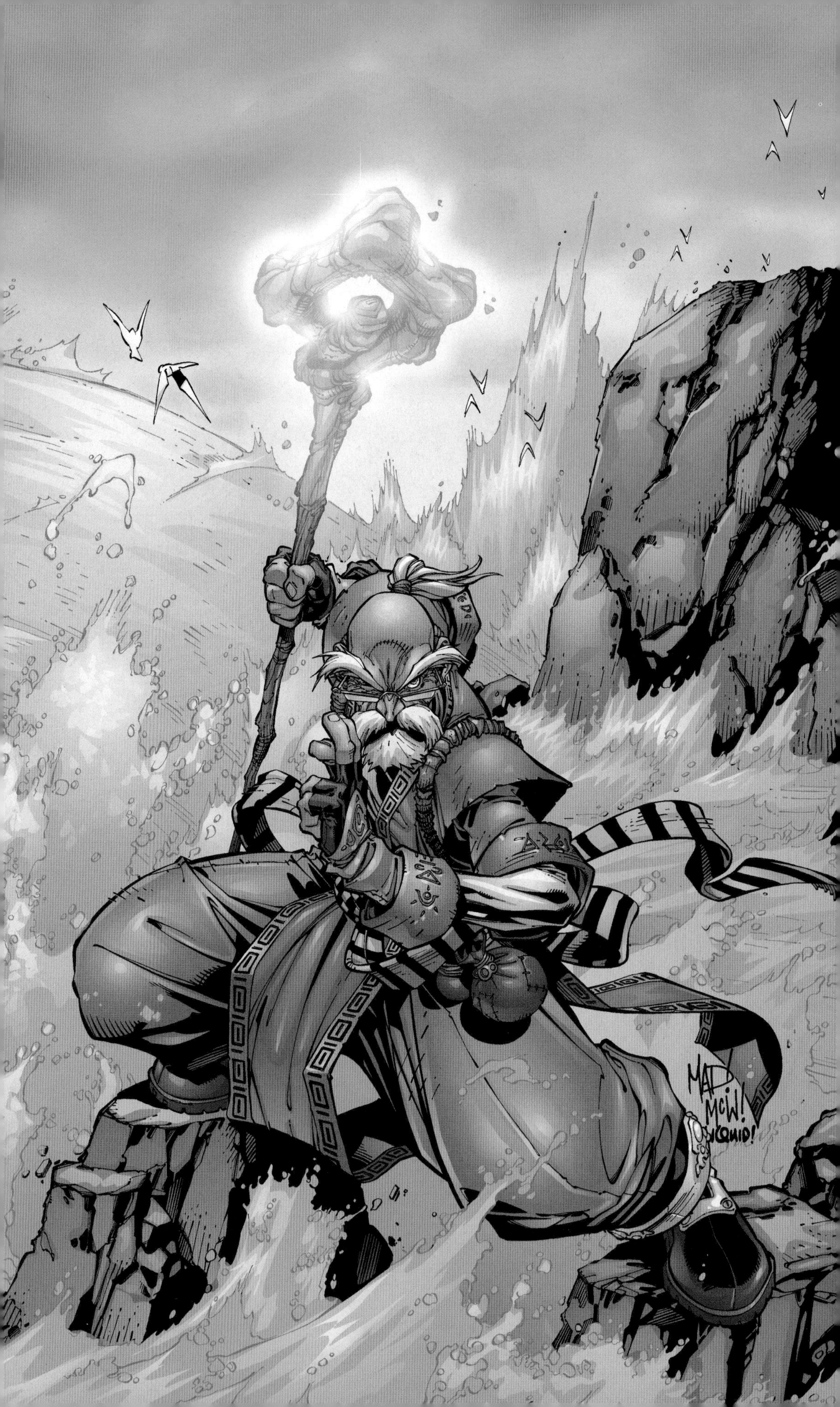
MAD
McW!
LIQUID!

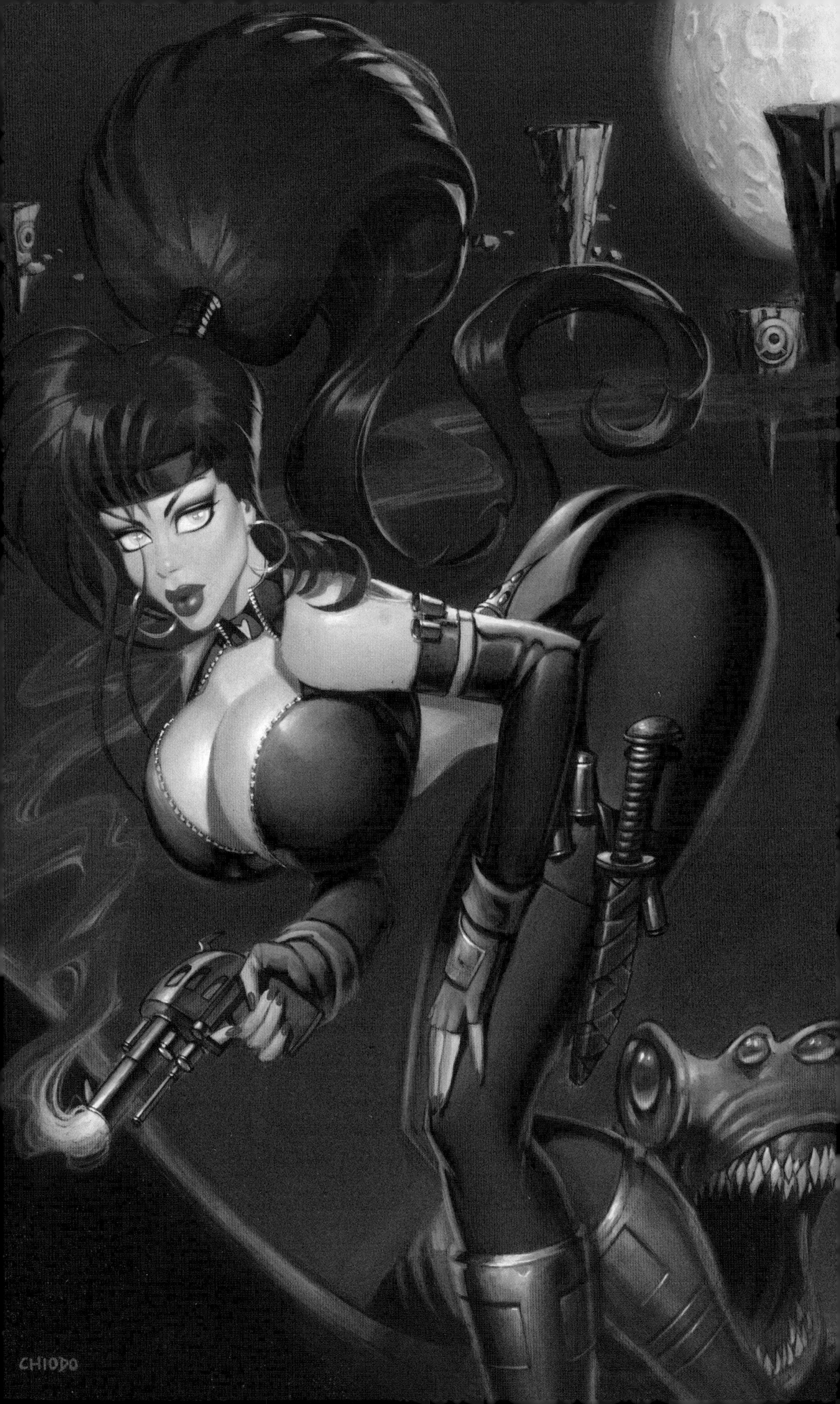
CHIODO

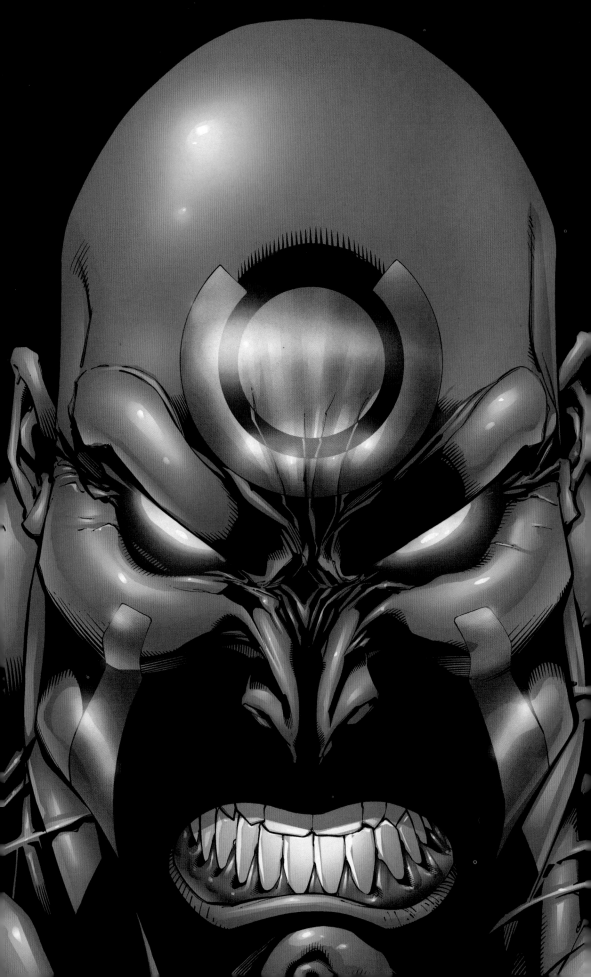

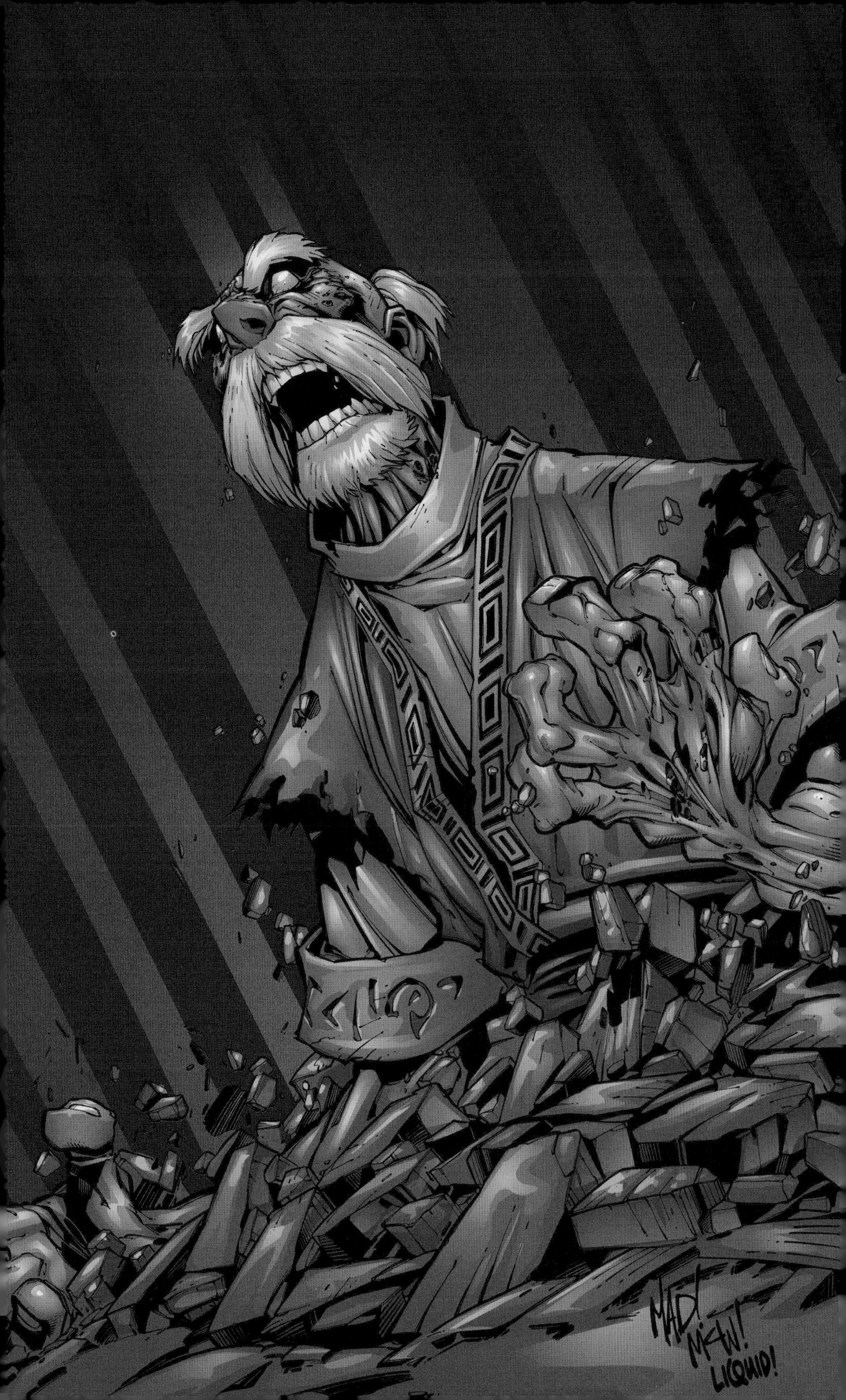
MAD!
McW!
LIQUID!

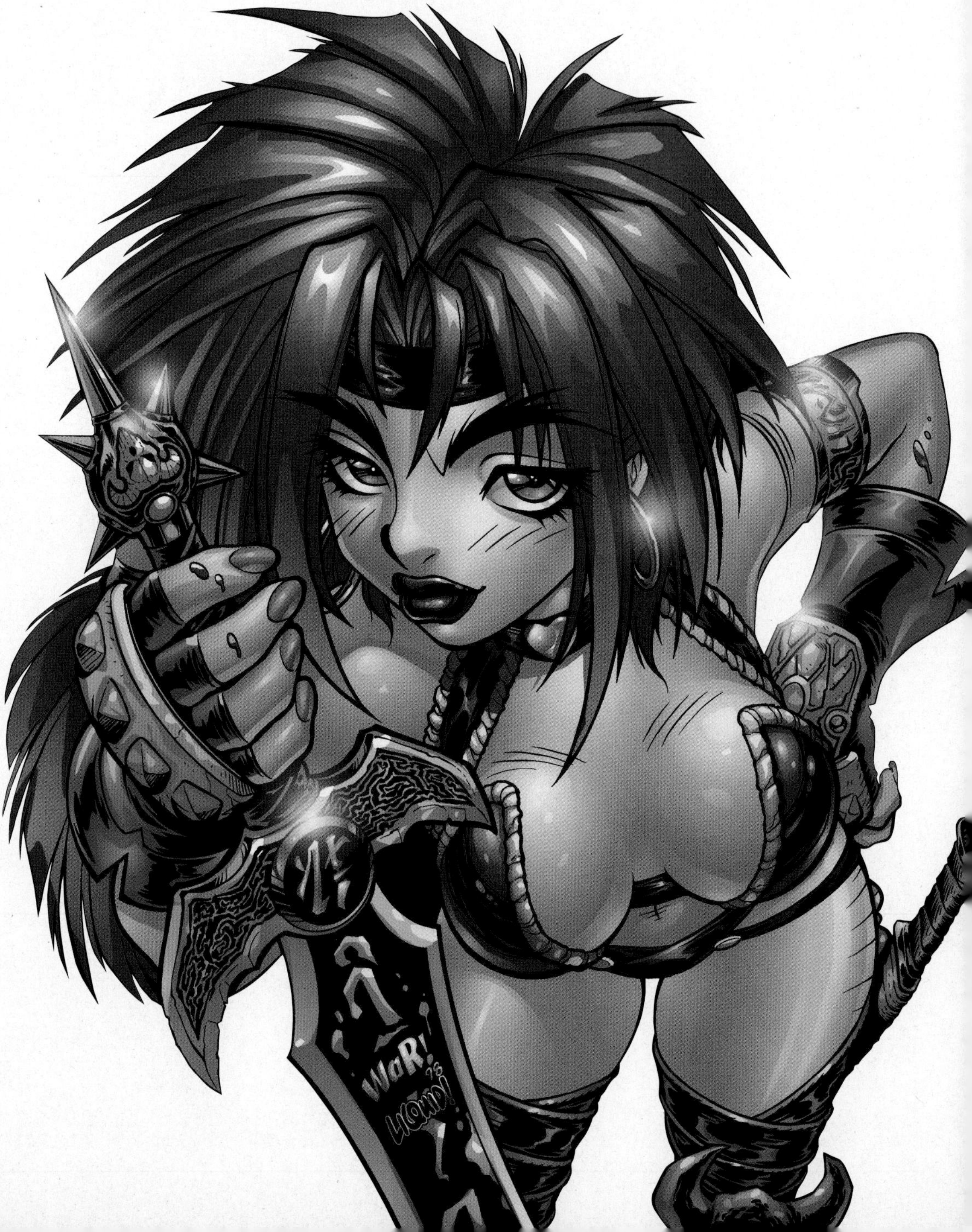
WaR! '98
LIQUID!

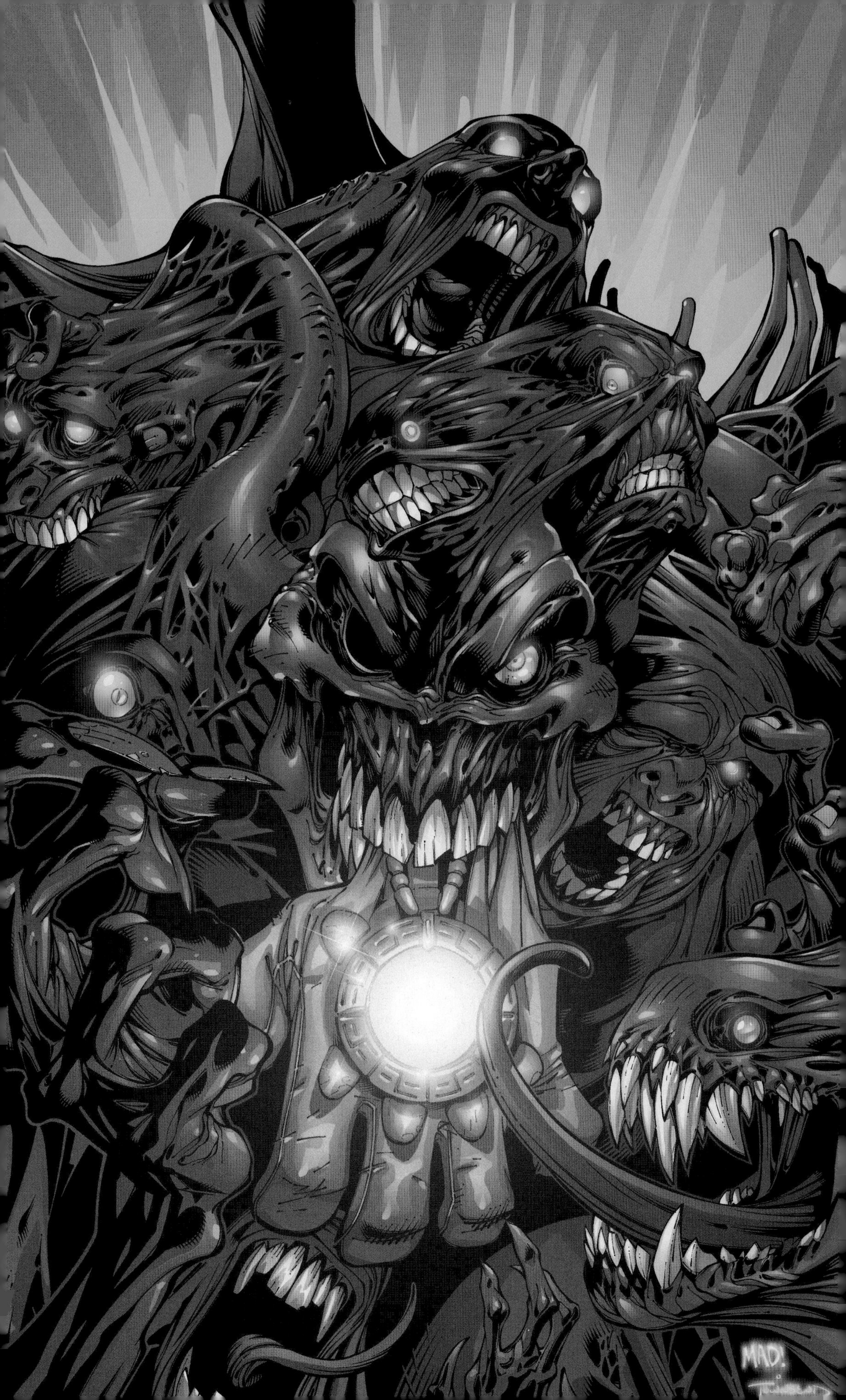
MAD!

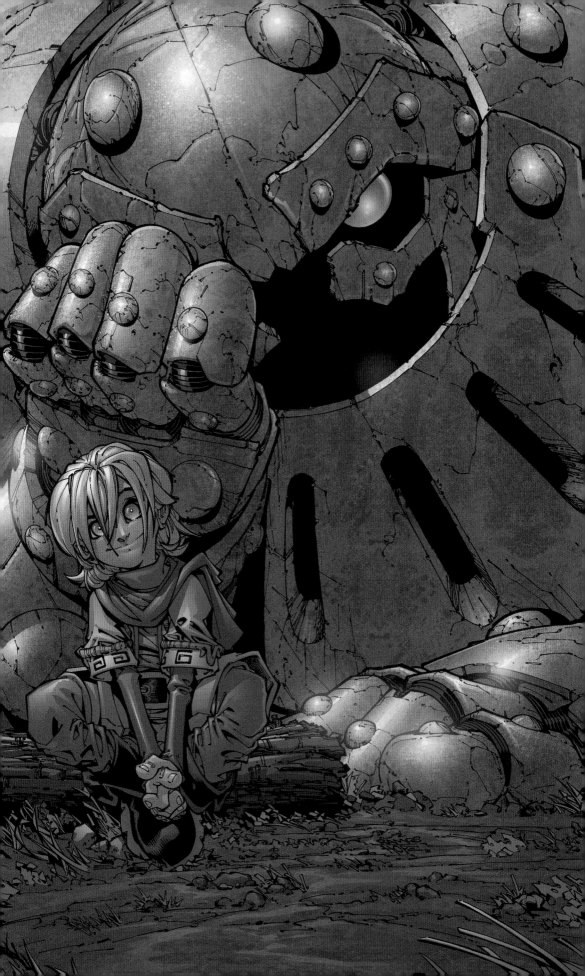

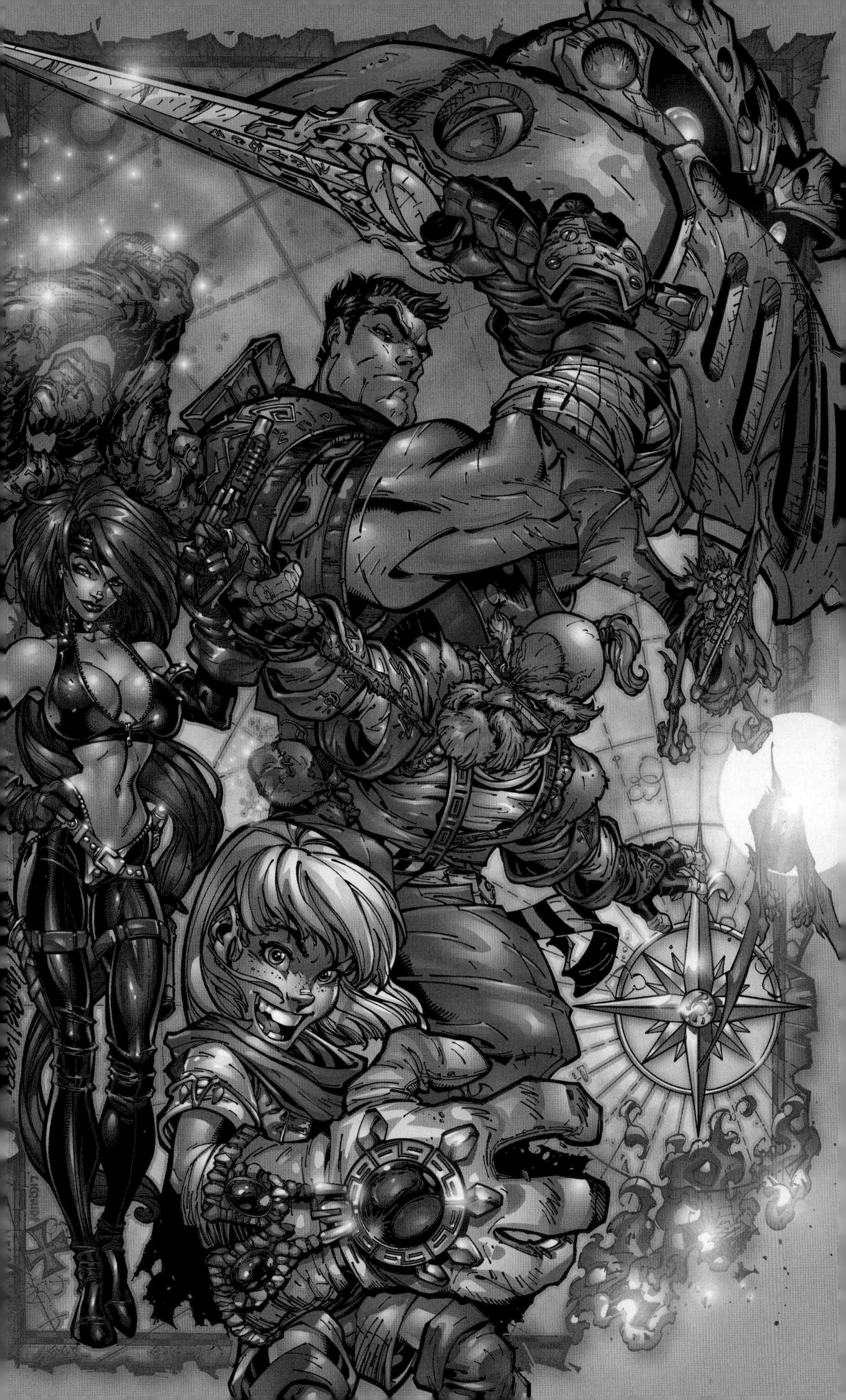

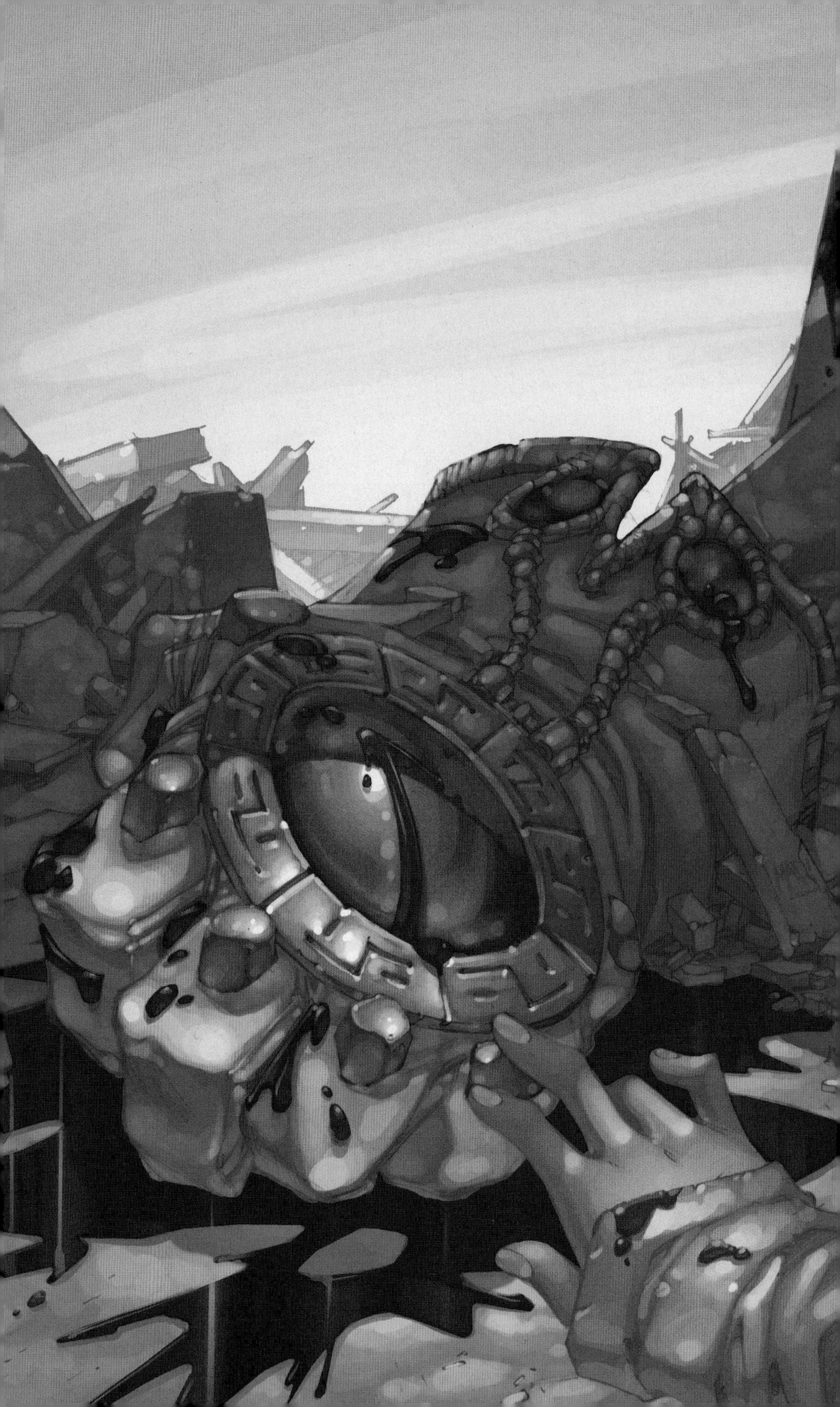

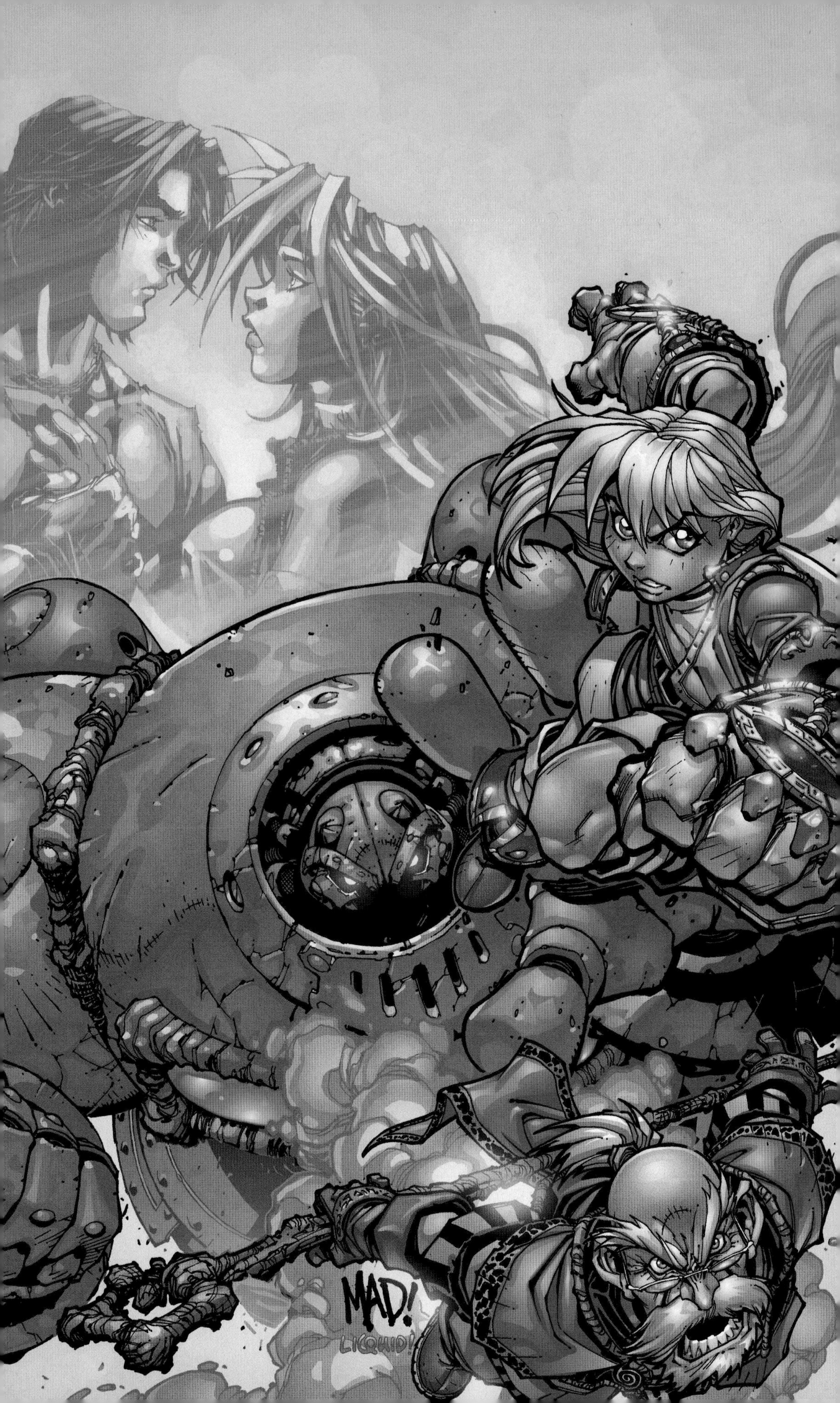
MAD!
LICQUID!

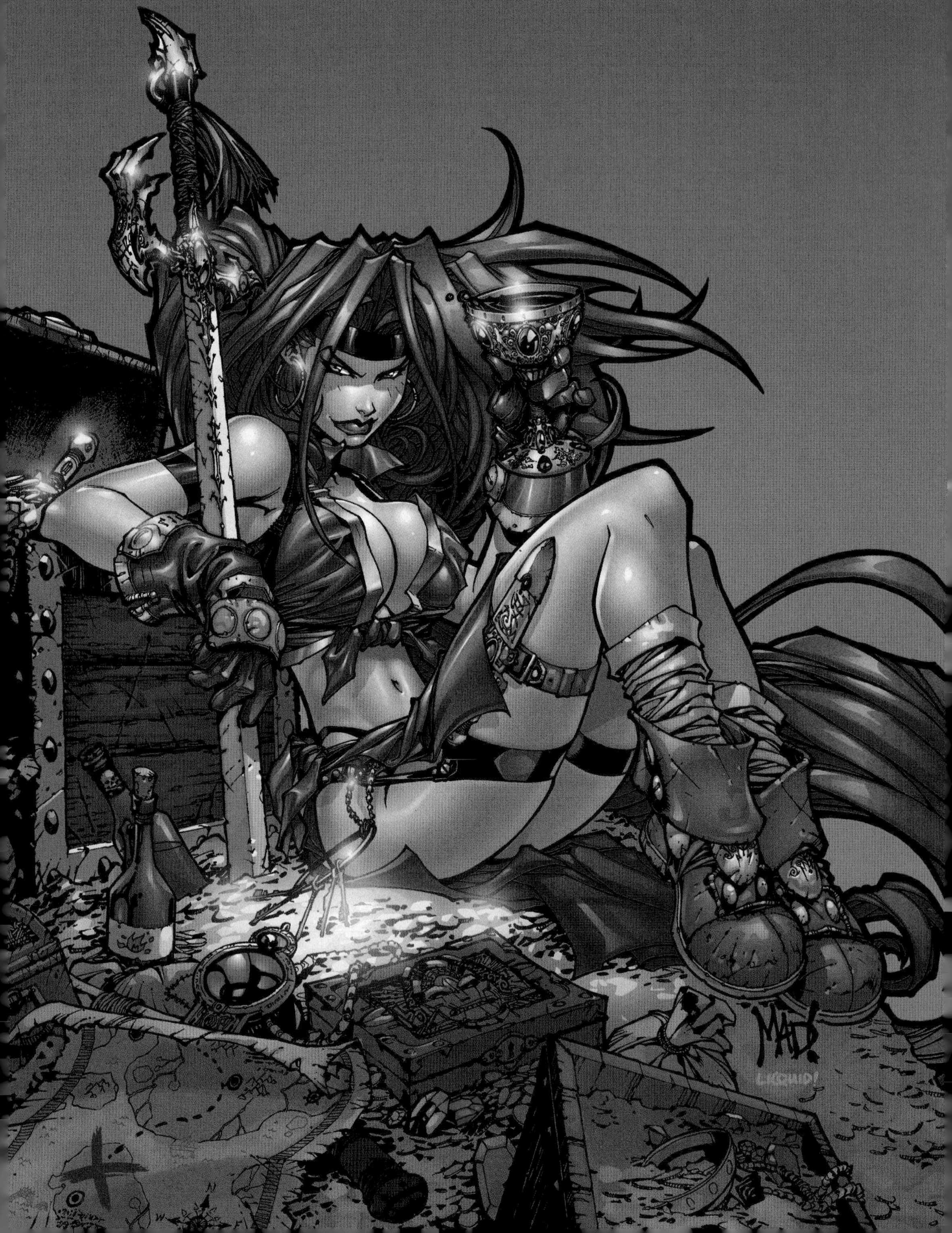

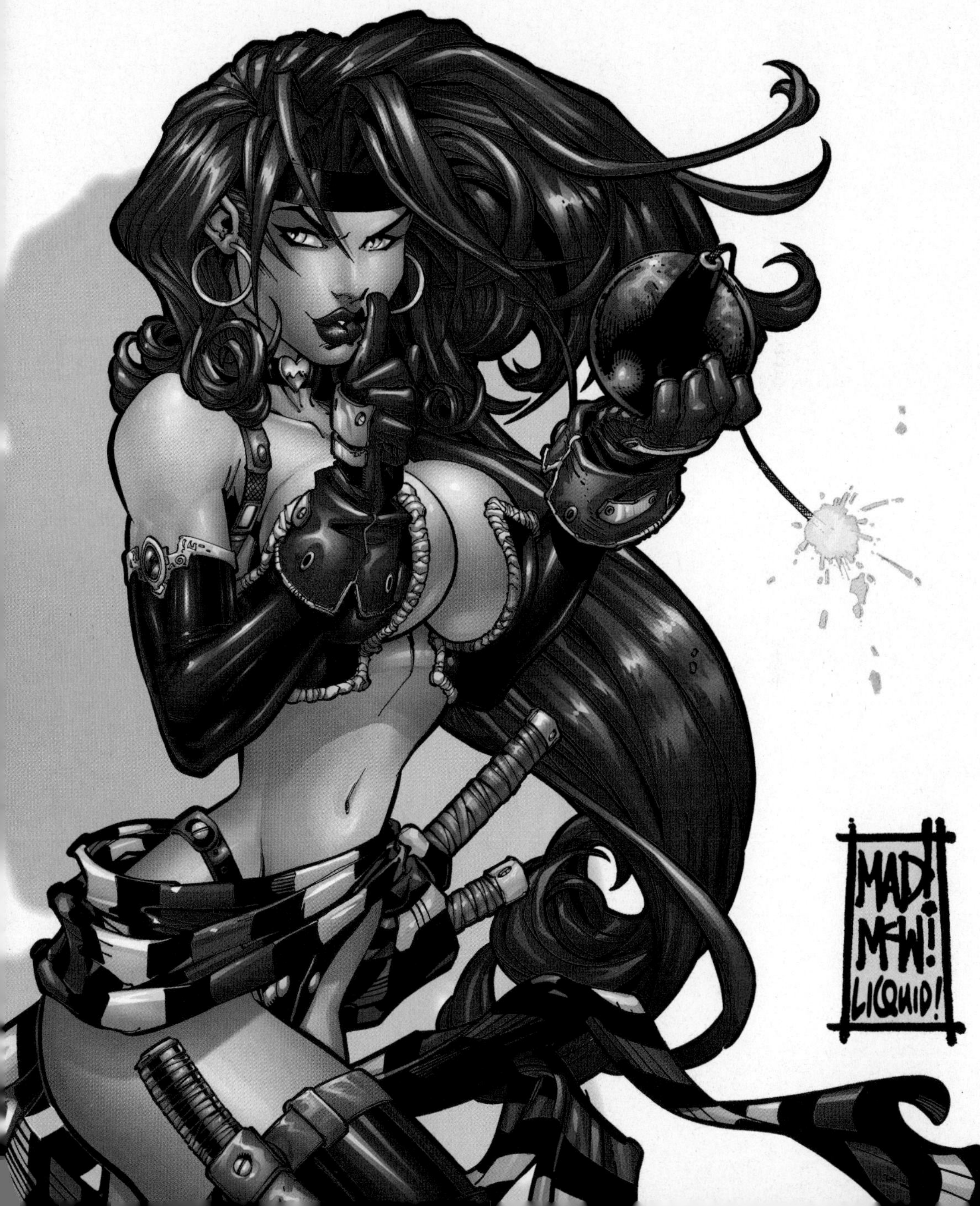
MAD!
McW!
LIQUID!

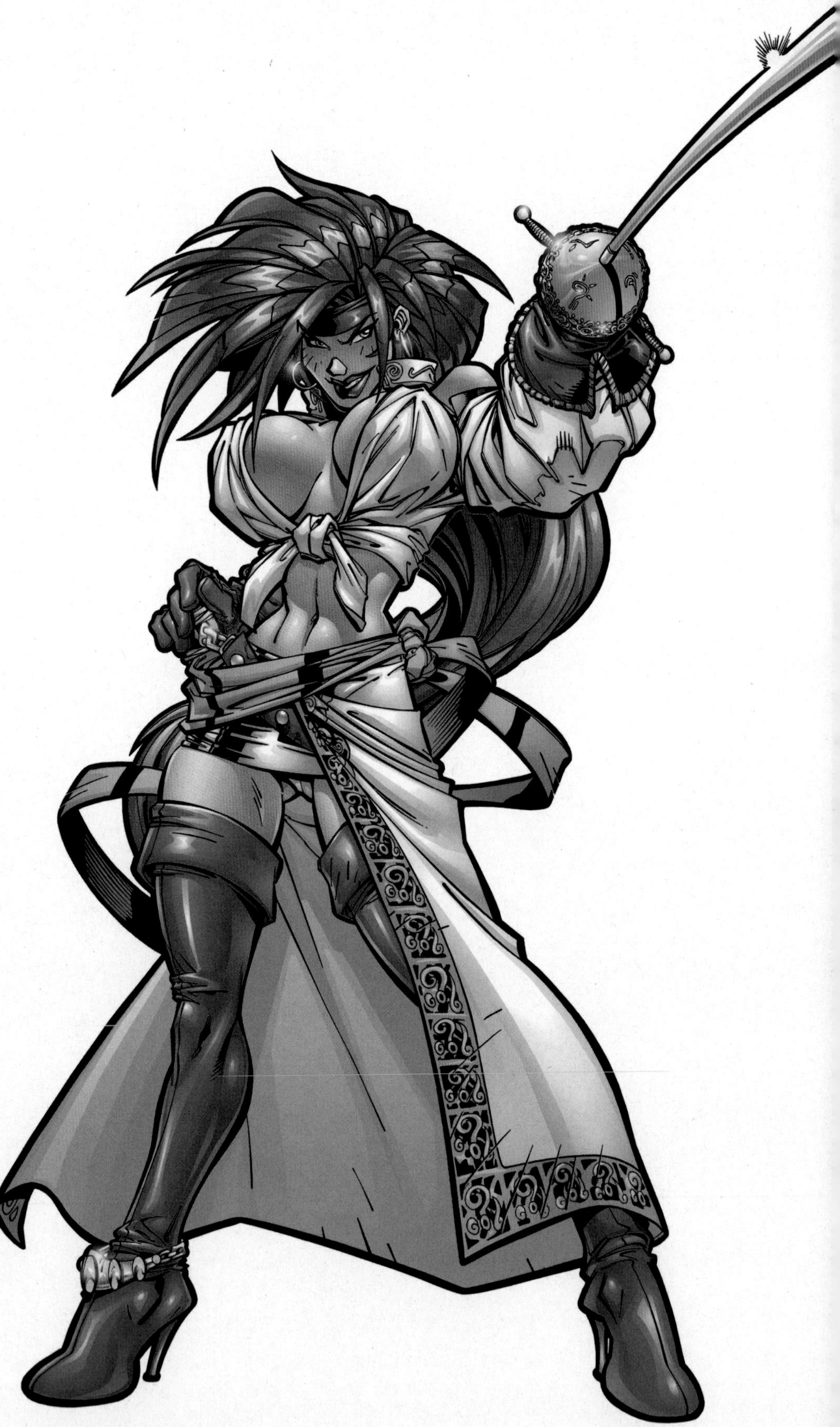

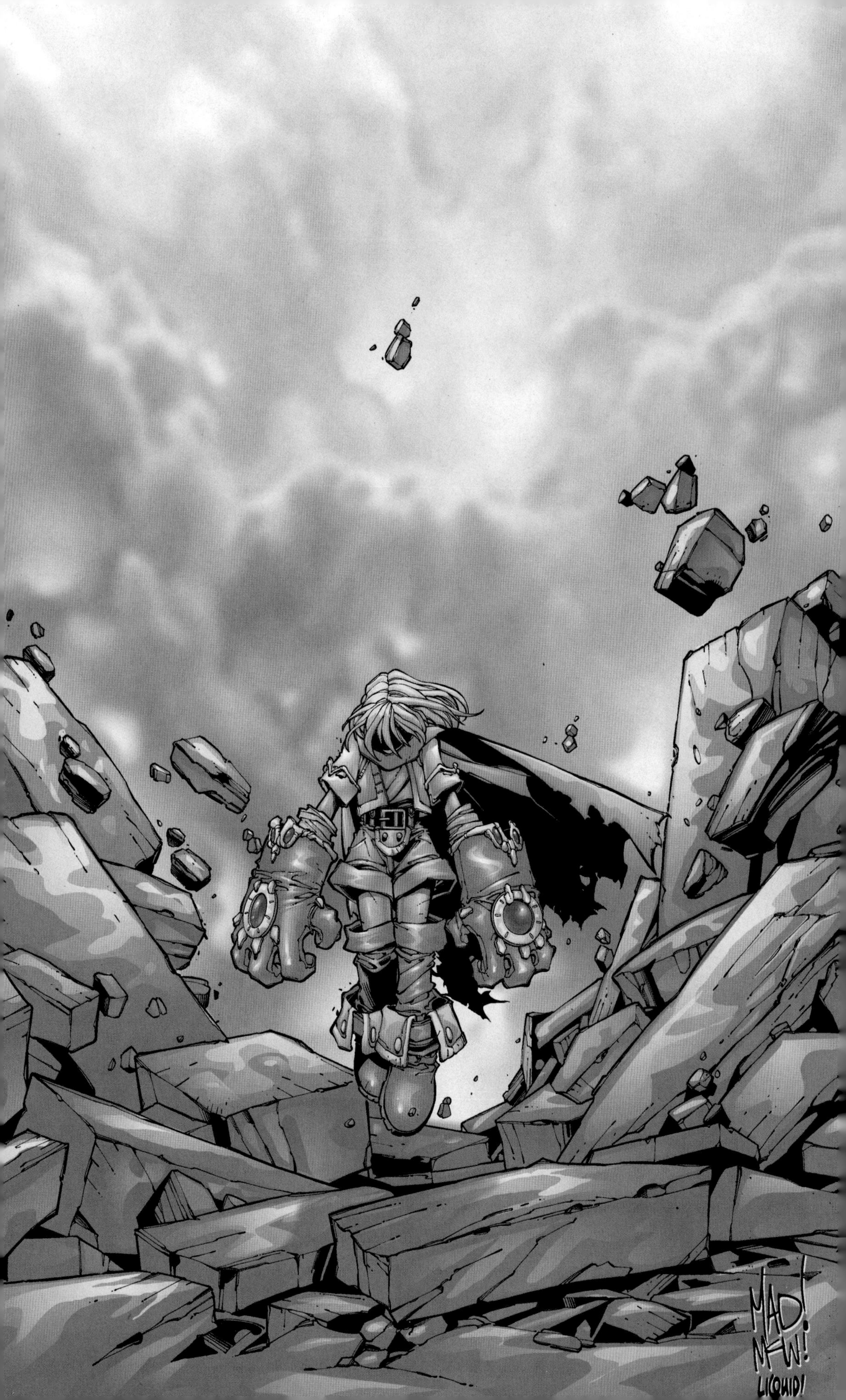

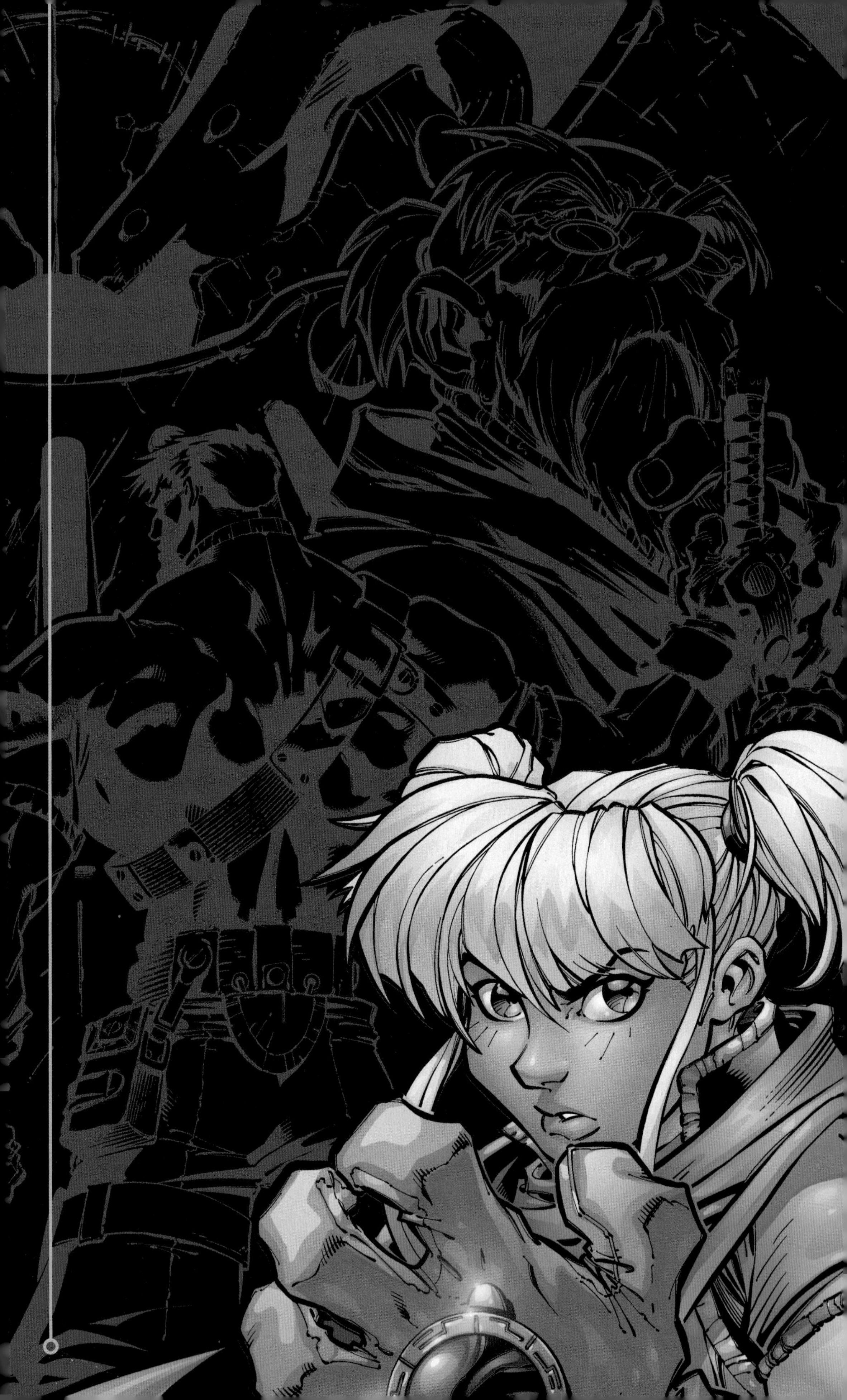